I, Dragon

I, Dragon

A Journey of the Spirit

Robert Joseph Ahola

I, DRAGON

Chronicles of the
Last Dragon on Earth

The Unicorn are all laid low.
The Gryphon is done in.
Chimera and the Mantilough
Are whispers on the wind.
Of all the Mystics bold and proud,
Only the Dragon still flies
Riding clouds
In far forbidden skies.

All you have read about dragons in the past is a myth. Here at last is the true story of the decline, fall and ultimate extinction of all the Mystic Beasts told by the 3,000 year-old dragon who lived it.

Contents

Prelude..ix

Canto 1 – Dager 3

Canto 2 – Magpie...15

Canto 3 – The Shadow Council 45

Canto 4 – The MasterSinger...53

Canto 5 – The Great Orf 76

Canto 6 – Gembox Baptismal 99

Canto 7 – Mother of Tongues 123

Canto 8 – The Diamond "I" 143

Canto 9 – The Skymaster 169

Canto 10 – Pod.. 186

Canto 11 – The Crater of Nebul 205

Canto 12 – The Gift of Resolve 233

Canto 13 – The Slavern 247

Canto 14 – The God Tree 269

Canto 15 – Gudae 289

Canto 16 – Shala...303

Canto 17 – The Ether of Dor 325

Canto 18 – RuSiva..339

Canto 19 – Nativity 359

Canto 20 – Shimbagh...373

Canto 21 – Preparation 381

Canto 22 – The Captain 391

Canto 23 – Severance 401

Canto 24 – The Time...405

Canto 25 – Sabotage 413

Canto 26 – The North 426

Canto 27 – The Gathering 441

Canto 28 – The BeastMaker 453

Canto 29 – Crimson Skies 467

Canto 30 – Sleep Eagle 485

Canto 31 – Answered Prayers 503

Canto 32 – Dark Angels 511

Canto 33 – Judgment 525

Canto 34 – Tibbuk 537

Canto 35 – Candle 561

Glossary of Terms 569

Acknowledgments 579

Author's Note

The Author/Poet/Artist William Blake once
prophetically observed that any writer must, "Create your own
mythology or else become slave to another man's." Not surprisingly, it
is one of the least heeded and most important admonitions in literary
history. It is carries with it a Warning Label, not to be ignored…and
yet so many writers do.

I will not be one of them. This work, *I, Dragon*, is my homage to
that core belief; my mythology, if you will, and constructed for that
purpose—to open the mind, to awaken the spirit, to tap into the
chakras and reveal a whole new universe—an inner-verse—where
entirely new realms of awareness await those with the courage and
the vision to pursue them. (The question is Dear Reader: "Do you
possess the courage, or the patience, or the will?")

As such, *I Dragon* is not just another "dragon book" (God forbid,
they seem to number in the thousands by now!) They lay before you a
sweet, soft, escapist carpet of clichés for all to trod upon and dare to
go no further.

This book, by contrast, has teeth. It summons in a kind of pain, and with it an unexpected new sensation. It is, as the subtitle tells us, *A Journey of the Spirit*. It is also, from page one to the final footnote, a Metaphor and a metaphysical satire. It tears into the mythologies of ancient Greece, Rome, Sumeria and Egypt. It breaks off pieces of Hindu lore, the Buddha, the Tao Te Ching, the Talmud and finally the Judeo-Christian legends of the Old Testament, and weaves them into a coat of many colors. And once sewn, it challenges one with the defiant notion that all religion is invariably steeped in its own mythology—one that helps it survive, and even thrive, to very this day. All these form the fabric of who we are and how we have gotten to this place and time.

By revealing them, by reforming them into a new level of awareness, *I, Dragon* makes no attempt to disabuse you the reader of your faith, but to help you understand it, and by that understanding to reinforce it. And along the way, we assure you that you'll have a very good time...with new awakenings, with original characters and unexpected twists and turns to uncover that "buried treasure" that all true legends promise to provide.

To help guide you on your path, *I, Dragon* also offers a "Glossary of Terms," at the end of the book—something to refer to so you can remember what is what, who is who, and who is doing what to whom...and why. ☺

Of course, *I, Dragon* is technically a Fantasy in that all things in it are phantasmagorical, allegorical and (God willing) original enough to be awarded with the term: compelling. But that much, Dear Reader, we leave to you. *Namaste!*

~ Robert Joseph Ahola

Prelude

The Last Dragon's Song

You who read this are in danger, as am I for sharing these hidden secrets. As my scribe and my witness be warned but take great pride as well. The journey ahead is fraught with peril, and yet the treasure that awaits you may save your soul and your sanity in the bargain.

As for me, my days are numbered. If they even knew that I existed, they would hunt me down. They would marvel at the fact that I lived at all and then kill me for what I know. Such is the curse of modern times. They're threatened by naked Truth. The lords of this earth are intent to butcher all buried magic — to lay dirty hands on the fabric of the mist of imagination.

So, I hide.

Outside the slit in this mountain's open mouth, this cave I have called my home for the last thirty years, the wind tears at the tired earth's face. It is my face too, for I am at last becoming one with the earth from which I sprang and the mother who bore me from her dragon's belly so long ago that her face, in a sea of time, has all but washed from my memory. But faces and forms are tools of vanity and are not important here, not in this place. It is energies that surround me now, the energies of those I have loved that will reside joyously inside me until the sky again claims me as its own.

I no longer mind the wind. Her carping seldom fazes me. Mountain winds dig-in their heels, do their mocking dances, and go their way. But in the Nepalese Himalayas, winters know a special bite. And though I hold no awe for this season (I've survived three thousand, give or take a few), even I, warmed by the power of my body's fires, can feel it here.

The mountain that lets me sit inside its heart is called *Pachi*. It rests somewhere between Everest and K-2 (the exact latitudes elude me at the moment). Pachi is a cruel mountain to man but kind to me. It recalls my father and his fathers before him. It carries in its cells the remembrance of grander times when this world was young, when dragons filled the skies, and angels forged the land with thunderous hammers that rang out the songs of God.

Those were the days before the rise of the pygmie who chained the world in tiny thoughts, who made a slave of Nature, and who brought us finally to the struggle in the wars of men. My father lived in that time of struggle, and it was to that struggle that I was born. Now, the fires of true magic have cooled. The Mystic Beasts have vanished and the lies persist. And only I, Dragon remain.

Yet, before I shed this final skin and fly to meet the loving master of this sphere, I'll have one last dragon's song to sing.

It is a song of truth. It is a canticle to man, a hymn to the nature of angels, a mantra from the dragon's throat of secrets past and futures that can neither be left untold nor abandoned to legend.

It is not my choice that it is sung. Ours have always been the ways of silence. Although we have been blessed with the many tongues of earth since the pygmie rendered Babel into chaos, we have never spoken out before this. Even when we were hunted down and killed, even though our names have been vilified throughout the mythologies of men, and our reputations have been brought to reside with the creatures of the Pit, we have kept our vows of secrecy.

If I had my way we'd keep them still. Man has yet to show me that he loves the light. But for some reason I've yet to determine, I've been elected by the Seven to tell this tale. So, as any soul must do, I yield to the wisdom of the collective will. This is not an easy chronicle to begin. I approach it with no small degree of skepticism for the impact it will have.

It is the beginning of the 21st century as the pygmie measures time. And yet practically nothing has changed. The grind of technology is loud and pretentious, but the spiritual seam beneath is even weaker than before. War is still man's most eloquent hour, predation his sole expression. And art and music and paths to heaven provide no more counterpoint than does a whisper when placed against a gale.

At the outset, I realize that I have sounded contemptuous of man, and I should not. As I have served all things in Nature, I am man's servant and not his enemy. Still, since I bear some wounds from my encounters with humankind, I cannot hide them, totally. The burnings and the whip cracks, the duplicity and betrayals, the cuts incurred by the whims of expedient morality, still smart in the scars on my tough old hide.

A dragon has a long memory for a wrong done him. He also never forgets a kindness shown. There were moments of kindness, love, and beauty spent with human beings that gleam like pearls of recollection. They uplift all the others and bring the taste of forgiveness to my breath. And since forgiveness is an essential quality of the dragon's nature, it is to the sweet charity of that Higher Mind that I attune my thoughts.

Forgiveness has become the dragon's credo. That is how we've survived — that and our longtime mastery of illusion. Those among us who remain can shrink to the size of a cockroach or swell to the size of a mountain. But Pachi feels that, in this time of man, nothing is entirely safe. So, I yield to his cellular wisdom and his active sense of concern.

Conversations with this wise old mountain are pleasant, to be sure, but my happiest times these days are passed in flight. There are no Shimbaghs left to fight. I'm far too mature to take any real pleasure in terrorizing a village. Dragons long ago decided not to procreate. So, flying is my last great joy.

On a rare morning when the still air calls me to the challenge, I emerge from my cave, spread my mangled thorny wings, and shoot like an arrow toward the sun. I climb and dive and swoop and soar at such great speeds I'm told that on three separate occasions I've been mistaken for a UFO. Despite my advancing years, I can still breach the speed of sound. Recently, in a lapse from prudence, I swept past a jetliner whose pilot — refusing to accept what his eyes had seen — reported me as an SST. In my younger days when the coals of passion burned hot inside me, I was known as Shartallion the Swift, and Shartallion "the Sound Stealer."

The Sherpa guides in these mountains call me *Dragon Star*, and say I come from *Shambalah*. They know I mean them no harm and in fact consider me a harbinger of good fortune. When they see me in flight, they wave. They sing songs to me and burn scented offerings in my honor. They tell outsiders of my presence but are not believed. Their tales of the "Dragon Star" are dismissed as mountain lore.

At this, I both rejoice and lament. Man's vision is blind to me. Here, astride these mountain shoulders, I shout to the wind and am not heard. I fly to the heavens and am not seen. It is here, unmolested at last, that I unfold all my secrets, so that I may go my way in peace, and you may pass The Word.

Pray that it remains so.

Book One

THE
LIGHTNING DRAGON

Canto 1

Dager

My forefathers were forged in the fire from the left eye of God. They were brought to this world from the constellation Draco to act as messengers and healers, and to be caretakers until the time of man had come to fruition. They were nobles among the dinosaurs and learned the secrets of survival that those ancient savage beasts were unable to comprehend. Dragons were helpmates to the Titans and wrought their steel and used their dragon wings to carry the rocks that knit the continents together. When the Fallen One drove the Titans from this sphere, the dragons—at great peril to themselves—stayed on as guardians to humankind, to terrify and teach them. The former, they did a little too well. The latter has been left to me.

(That's the myth we were told; and in that narrow context it was true. But our true beginnings, what we had been before there were measures to time, make up the fabric of this story, and the reason I've taken this task.)

I was born Shartallion XII, High Dragon of the Kiln, descendent of Shartallion I, the Firebringer, of Dager V (the Earth Dragon) and great grandson of Knot IV (initiator of the Shimbagh Wars, in whose last battle I would fight).

I was sired by Dager X out of Drilg, the Fair. Ours was a noble house formed of the grand alliance of the Dragons of the East and West. My mother, Drilg, was of the Kunlun Dragons of the plains above Tibet. She was radiant, sleek, beautiful, just and kind. She never lost sight of her mission here—to bless all she touched and to teach the secrets of the light. She died too young.

My father, in his early years, was known as Dager, the Mountain. Looking like a piece of the Carpathians from which he came, he was the most immensely powerful dragon of his time. To this day, I could never match his massive strength; nor did I ever try. Later, when the pain of remorse and a near fatal wound drained his mind of all reason, he became known as Dager the Scourge and Dager the Plague of Nations. He became a rogue and a butcher. He thirsted for vengeance-blood and grew obsessed with destroying the societies men had built. He died in his nine hundredth year, in his prime as dragons go. The masters of our clan said he lived too long and swore the scars he left on dragonkind would haunt us to the end. I, among them, understood his madness. In his place, I might have done the same.

There were three dragons born to Drilg that summer, 3,000 years ago. Our nest was high in the eastern Taurus Mountains above what was then known as Assyria in the south and not far from the Hittite nation to the North. The Taurans were a dry prohibitive range traveled little by the primitive dwellers of that place, yet far enough from the complicated societies of men to keep us out of danger.

High in a mountain cradle where only eagles dared to fly, we were hatched—the eggs of Drilg. I was the first. Two weeks later, my sister, Seti was born. After another week, came the third—my brother Karman, the poet.

Although conceived at the same time, dragons take three years to hatch and can be born as much as two months apart. Usually, there are three young. It is the number of divine geometry and is therefore ideal for the triangulation of energies.

At this point I must be candid and admit that, even among our own kind, dragon young are not the most comely of creatures. We are born in foul-smelling fluids from the eggs in which we were hatched (juices, were are told which carry the secrets of our long lives). Our bodies, only five feet long at birth, are covered in a "forming skin" that resembles a clustering kind of soup, unsavory to the touch. And no matter how our mothers lick and preen us, the skin stays foaming upon us for a month or two at least.

It is then with a perverse sense of irony that I remember that we dragon eggs, no handsome crew at best, were trussed luxuriantly. Nestled in down brought as gifts from the Cloud Geese and swaddled in silken webs spun by the Kohmm, the heliotrope spiders from the Sea of Thral, we were made to feel among the most prized among God's creatures.

Even in our earliest days, we knew our fair measure of affection. Seti was by nature testy and easily spooked, but she was loyal to her siblings and was maternally protective of Karman. Karman, with the nature of a fawn, was shy, withdrawn, and seemed to hear sky songs in the distance, holy choirs that played for no one else but him. I, from my moment of birth, felt myself to be an old soul in a protomorphic body. I detested our ugliness and our blind, prehensile groping about. But there was a higher voice inside me that counseled me in the ways of patience. 'Your time will come,' I heard it say. 'Your time will come.'

Although I was young, I realized we were the homeliest of creatures and would not have wanted to continue at all had I not seen Drilg—her sleek golden beauty, her soft amber eyes, her glorious melodic laugh that brought the winter roses into bloom. In Drilg I saw what we could be. She was aglow, an aura of glistening hues that lit the dark night and played the sun's mirror in the day. She guided us gently, regaled us with stories from constellations far away, and—when we needed—would admonish us with a brush from her twenty-foot tail. There was an element of might within her that one could feel, and yet from without there glowed an aura so resplendent in its clarity that eagles gathered, proclaiming her an angel come to earth.

At sixty feet, Drilg was not large, even for a female. But for the first two years of my life, she was all I saw of dragonkind, and I was certain she was the grandest creature in the universe.

Then, for the first time, I saw Dager.

We were nearly three by then. Dager, a warrior dragon from birth, had been fighting in the Shimbagh campaigns for more than a year when we were born. Drilg sang of him often, sang of his royal mien, of his courage, and of his generalship against the minions of the Fallen One. In the time before the forging of iron, Dager had led his fiery forces to the mouth of the Endless Void, had slain the giant Shimbagh, Toth, and had earned so formidable a name that even his mortal enemy the evil sorcerer, Rakushar had sought him for alliance. Rakushar, the Beastmaker, who could rape the sensibilities of the most virtuous warrior on earth and draw him into vortices of passion he'd never known, had pitched her tawdry woo at my father and had been turned down flat. Enraged, she had sworn her vengeance and prophesied the end—that someday she would take down the Mystic Clan, and the son of sons that Dager would hold most dear.

Dager scoffed at the prophecy.

"Corruption has no life where noble hearts are joined, and purpose is divine." He'd left their *parlez* in a gust of flame, the green of his contempt, and for that the lady swore she'd take us down some day. But Dager was the breath of saints. He was the warrior's warrior. A mountain in the heavens with the halo of truth as its crown.

So lofty had been Drilg's tales of Dager, I came to look upon him as a god; yet I wondered too if I would ever see him.

It won't be long, "Drilg assured me. "The word is out upon the winds, he has a brood...It won't be long."

That same day at dusk, upon an amethyst horizon, Dager appeared, one hundred feet of rippling armor plate and scale. His silhouette like an alien planet loomed above us. His eyes, comets in collusion, hurled their glare upon us, covering us in the heat of their scrutiny.

The sudden appearance of this ominous being shocked us to the bone. My brother Karman whimpered. My sister Seti hissed and feinted combat. I stood my ground and returned his stare. To this day, I cannot say what instinct led me to it, to hold stick still and match this thunderous creature gaze for gaze. Perhaps I was too frozen with fear to run, or perhaps I was too fascinated to reflect upon my actions. But when all is said and done in life, conduct is the bottom line: I stayed and stood to face my father and, by looking him in the eye, found my way into his heart.

For a moment, he deliberately tried to intimidate me, lowering his head as if he were about to swallow me whole. Detecting a note of mirth behind the menace, again I held my ground, and — because I did — Dager arched his head and roared into the coming night. The flames of his elation lit the mountainside. He looked from side to side to let the silent world know he approved, then turned back toward me joyously and, with his flanged wing, swept me up as if I were a gnat.

"This is the dragon's own!" he bellowed, holding me aloft. "This one has the wisdom to carry on our quest!" Even though I now stood more than eight feet high, I could have walked untouched through the arch of his eye. Yet he clutched me gently in his foretalons, lifted me to his face, and whispered, "Come my little dragon prince. Let's chase the sun awhile."

He set me in the break behind his neck and arched his wings. The updraft sucked the leaves from a nearby tree and sent rocks tumbling down the cliff side. In an instant, we took flight. At speeds that stripped away my senses, we chased the sun until the sky again grew light. For the first time since I was born, I saw the earth as few would ever see it. It was domes of light, lush green valleys, red dawns and golden deserts; seas of jade; lakes of crystal; mountain glaciers glistening, the yawning ivory teeth of the great Terran giant waiting to be fed the thunderheads of sky.

The skies belonged to the dragons then. The birds, our cousins, willingly granted us domain. The pygmie had not yet learned to fly. Even the Shimbaghs, who had to hover near the Pit, could not challenge us here in this open range of iods and ethers.

Here, from the view of the airbound soul, all elements in life were one. All sense of isolation was gone. The walls of my tiny mountain roost had been peeled away to reveal a universe in which to play my role (whatever that role might be). I was so young and full of questions. I asked many, but Dager did not answer. He merely flew and tipped his wings occasionally to let me see. The answers, the voice inside me said, would come in time.

It seemed only a few moments before we again swept back into the dancing light of the morning. Drilg, in wifely pose, was waiting up. And Dager, like any peccant husband would, landed softly on the nest.

"Is this the way you come home?" asked Drilg. "Terrify your brood, whisk your eldest son away, and disappear all night? What kind of greeting to your loves is that?"

"My thoughts never left you for a moment," Dager answered, knowing as only old souls know that flattery is the first line of defense.

"You *do* have other children," chided Drilg.

"And beautiful ones they are!" my father said. He swept Seti and Karman up to his face and tried to bounce them playfully, but Karman cringed and hid, and Seti hissed as if it were an enemy she faced. "Ah, we have a poet and a warrior in our midst. Too bad their genes were mixed. Seti, is it? The name of a great king, given to a female. And Karman, may your name be your destiny and may it be blessed."

"You scare them," Drilg scolded. "They're frightened half to death of you."

Dager roared again with laughter. "But not this one," he said, passing the soft side of his wing across my brow. "This one has the white dragon's soul. You mark my words."

Although I hadn't the vaguest idea of what he was saying, the rush of a new emotion charged through me, and I began to puff out my chest and strut about the nest. Certainly I must have looked ridiculous, because Dager howled with delight while Drilg admonished me to be mindful of the virtues of a quality called "humility."

"Let the dragonette enjoy the moment," Dager insisted. "He'll come to learn to be humble soon enough."

"You never did," snapped Drilg, scowling at him without the least betrayal of relenting. It was the first harsh expression I had ever seen cross her brow. She was, no doubt being censorious, but even in her censure her voice caroled like a wind chime. Dager, revealing an aspect of himself that few would ever see, was openly conciliatory. Pleading with her to forgive his seeming favoritism, he nudged her beneath her chin and love-bit her on the throat.

"I love them all," he let out a licentious growl. "And I love you above all else."

He was nearly twice her size. Furling his wings around her, he took her to the morning sun where they made love for all the world to see.

Subtlety is a substance lost upon the dragon's passion. For three days and three nights they locked in an embrace both violent and tender. For three days and three nights the mountains shook, boulders split and fell in avalanche, and the smaller creatures of the rocks below fled twittering to safer ground. On the morning of the third day, Dager let out a yell that tore the clouds in half. Drilg fainted. And the two, still locked in an embrace, floated like leaves to the canyons below.

Dager didn't stay long after that. He passed a few more weeks with us, until the brood came to know him and to feel the tender power of his caring. He took Karman under his wing and taught the little poet many songs. He tried to win the affection of Seti, but she—regarding him from time to time as if he were some hideous stranger—found cause to hiss and feint her nasty little combats. It was even then that I, for one, saw seeds of madness taking root in her.

Suddenly, one autumn day, the dusk that brought my father to us took him off again. His warrior instincts, always at a simmer, boiled anew inside him. He sniffed the air and joked that it carried the scent of Shimbagh blood.

"The Fallen One has brought more of his khados from the depths. I can taste them in the ethers."

Dager was a noble warrior in those days, the strongest the bravest of his kind. He was leader of the dragon generals, respected by all lesser creatures as a being who was strong and fair, and praised by the dragon masters as having carried well the standard of the clan. But this praise from others, this adulation, had always rung hollow to Drilg. From our earliest moments, she reminded us that heroes have short lives, but her attempts to remind Dager of that simple truth were drowned in his rising tide of anticipation to return.

"The Shimbaghs have grown more powerful," she said. "The more energy we expend to overcome them, the more their numbers increase. It's as if our violence nourishes them somehow."

"Nonsense," Dager scoffed, making light of her concern. "Each victory we win is more decisive than the last."

"But dragons can be killed, despite what you think."

"Nothing dies. It merely changes form."

"Whenever you're on shaky ground, you always wax philosophical."

Dager, trying to make light of Drilg's concern, was meeting only with moderate success, and I suspected they had undergone this strange ritual of debate before. On this occasion, however, Dager too turned solemn.

"It's not the Shimbaghs who concern me, now. It's the pygmie who grows to be the danger. He's made great progress in some ways, while in others he grows even more savage than before. In the past, his paltry weapons were little threat to us, but now he's found the secret of steel. He's always feared us out of all proportion. He continues, beyond all scope of reason, to be fascinated by our powers. Now that he has weapons aplenty to do us in and many to instruct him the ways of using them, I fear our days are numbered. It has been inscribed that these days would come upon us. Are they here? I wonder."

Dager erased all traces of concern from his visage, for our benefit I thought, and bade us all goodbye. With his searing comet eyes mounted on a ten-thousand toothed grin, he turned to each of us.

"Soon you'll go to Sagro's canyons and learn the Mastersinger's skills. So pay strict attention to your teacher, for he's the best there is. Except, perhaps for this one." With the tip of his plated nose, he nudged Drilg, and in a moment of silent understanding they caressed.

"Keep an eye out for the Sorcerer," Dager said. A rare acknowledgment of vulnerability for a dragon, I thought, not to mention a dragon in an aerie such as this. I was soon to learn it was a jest made out of sad experience.

In an instant, Dager had set himself in flight and soon became a glimmer on the violet face of night. In his wake, an entourage of clouds fell in behind, changing form, filling the air with a star song from the rhythm of his wings.

Seeing my father leave after so short a stay filled me with a sense of abandonment. I felt both love and anger toward him, and knew some injustice had just been done that I could not define. It was only later I was to learn that monogamy was not at all the dragon's way. It was not out of some savage animal indifference that the males behaved this way; there were reasons for it. The males were warriors and servers of magic. The females were educators and bringers of song. Most male dragons fought in the Shimbagh campaigns or served as secret counselors to the white magicians of the growing societies of man. For those reasons and many others, it was the rare male who took any time at all to tend the young. Dager was a rarity. Drilg made sure we

understood this, just as she made sure we understood the cause
of his obsessions with the Shimbaghs.

Originally, the marriage of Drilg and Dager had been one of
convenience, a union brought about through a pact between the
dragon empires of the East and West. It had been set forth by
the master dragons of those clans that they would match the
noblest male and female of their kind to unify their houses.
Dager X, Tiger Dragon of the Knot, had been the overwhelming
choice for male. Drilg, though not the most spirited or robust of
the Eastern females, was without question the most evolved soul
among them and therefore the perfect match for Dager's
boundless passion.

The pressures of tradition brought them together, initially,
but in the end it was their love that made them stay. At first,
Dager had been rebellious toward his forced pairing with this
lithe Kunlun princess. He succumbed to the pressures put upon
his house and agreed to mate, vowing all the while he'd be
quickly on his way. Never once did Drilg try to hold him in place
or remind him of his vow to reproduce his kind. She simply
loved him and let his comings and goings belong to him. She'd
adored him instantly, she told us, and knew the merging of their
earth and fire souls had sewn the seeds of great beings inside
her. Dager loved her too, she knew it, although it was never his
way to put such avocations into words.

Ours was not the first product of their mating, we came to
learn. There had been a brood before: a male and two females
several years earlier had been the first line of their seed. But
when the three had turned little more than a year they had been
slaughtered by an agent of the Fallen One, a priest of his inner
circle.

Dager, as was his chosen path, had been away on a campaign.
Drilg, who never left her young untended for long, had stayed
away past dark in search of food. Out of the night from which
Drilg had not yet returned, this sorcerer disguised himself as a
rainstorm and fell upon the dragon nest. Reforming on the cliffs

nearby, he brought a firestone from beneath his cloak, squeezed the blood from it and set the nest ablaze.[*]

The three dragonettes, barely out of their birthskins and vulnerable at best, turned instantly into ashes in the deadly firestone bath. Yet, before this sorcerer could complete his dirty work, Drilg descended on him with the fires of vengeance. Knowing he had no power to take her on, the sorcerer resumed his well-formed deluge and fled into the night. She gave pursuit and called upon the clouds to swallow his energies, but he was swift in his fear and escaped by route of the dark hole through which he had come.

Drilg recognized the sorcerer who'd slaughtered her brood and later named him to Dager as RuSiva the Firewind, a principal human lieutenant of the Fallen One. Dager knew him to be the highest order of Shimbagh and knew too that once he'd been a man who had let his Godsight fall and had traded his divine gifts for worldly power.

"This is the disease that festers in them," Dager lamented. "They must wear all the masks."

Dager hid his agonies from those around him. Although he grieved, he let his despair fuel his resolve to drive the Shimbaghs into the Pit for once and always.

In life-blending tribute, Dager and Drilg covered themselves in the ashes of their young and wore those numb, gray coats of sorrow until a healing spring shower washed them away. Together they vowed this would not happen again to a dragon

---

[*] *Firestone* is a transmutive mineral and — when poured upon them — is instantly deadly to dragon young. As is the case with all transmutive elements, there is a conundrum here. As firestone is deadly to the dragon young, it is food and resource for mature dragons and provides the framework for their being. When dragons are destroyed by certain mutable elements, the ashes of their remains will soon harden again to become firestone in even greater quantities. Since firestone is prized by alchemists as a key element in making gold, and since it is believed to hold in it the secrets of the prolongation of human life, the desire of men to obtain it soon becomes both obsessive and perverse.

brood of theirs. Later, when the wounds of their remorse had
healed, they mated once again, and in three years came this
second brood to which I was born.

In the healing hands of time, Drilg learned to bless this
enemy who had destroyed her young, to release the power that
hatred of him held over her and let it die upon the wind. What
Drilg had found in her consciousness to do, however, did not
meet its match in Dager's mind. He remembered all too well that
the murderer of his children had been both a Shimbagh and a
man. Since this Sorcerer, RuSiva, had once been in a high order
among men, Dager saw this as a sign that this pernicious hybrid
might cease to be a hideous affectation and might instead
become the rule. He tried to warn the other creatures of the
Mystic Clans but was admonished by the elders of each and told
that all his premonitions were premature.**

"Patience!" the elders counseled him. "All will be fulfilled in
time." He had been seduced by their admonitions before, he felt,
but would be no longer. Soon, he became even more obsessed
than ever with destroying the Shimbaghs before they could
complete their infestation of this planetary body. Drilg recalled
this time with heavy breath. "It's not the dragon's way to seek
revenge," she sighed. "In its own time, the universe takes care of
whatever justice needs to be dispensed. It's just that dragons
such as Dager are inclined to rush the process. It is his nature to
be this way. Do not make it yours."

In the months to come in the nest of Drilg, in the years to
follow in the MasterSinger's school, I was to learn of many
things: the ways of survival, the secrets of the dragon's power,
the many tongues of mother earth, and flight. Yet of all the
lessons I would embrace through their poignant, kind didactic,
the first—by far for me—would be the hardest.

** *The Mystic Clans.* These were the clans of the Chimera, the Unicorn,
the Gryphon, the Gamberol, the Rahntish and the Khomm. These are
creations once believed mythical, but as this chronicle will reveal, they
really existed.

Canto 2

Magpie

When the Magpie sings
Too pretty a song
Beware!
Take care!

Before the seasons changed in full, we outgrew the nest of Drilg. We three—clumsy, molting, and anxious for the gift of flight—grew disquiet in our aerie, a restlessness of spirit born of growing bodies and spreading wings. The autumn air nipped at us reproachfully to chide us for such notions and to remind us that soon another cold, mean season would be upon us. Soon we'd be taken underground and warmed in a dark moist cave by our mother's loving flames. But confinement would no longer be to my liking, I vowed, not since I'd begun to feel this passion for discovery rising in my chest.

Of course, our little dragon triad was still a forming lot. We grew in our waxy yellow skins and shortly began to fancy ourselves the noblest of creatures, a notion not the least diminished by Drilg who washed us daily with fresh waters from an opaline lake below, fed us blue melons left by the Kohmm, and told us of the many havens of planet Earth.

"Later, when the days grow long, and you've matured a bit, I'll take you to my homeland in the East where the days are kissed by the sun the whole year 'round, where creatures live as one, and antagonism is a distant stranger."

"Why are we not there, now?" I asked, a sensible query, I thought, but one she did not answer.

As the weather cooled, we held the dream of spring inside us and, nurtured by the harvest of the land, we grew. I was over half again my birth size: a rippling eighteen feet or so and larger than my siblings. Seti, estranged to me for reasons I would never understand, glared in ire at my prodigious length.

"So, you're bigger by a yard or two. So what?!" She snarled. "It's what's inside that counts. And that we've yet to see."

Drilg scolded her for her envy. "It's a disease that eats the soul, and not worthy of a dragon princess such as you."

Seti listened but didn't hear. Somewhere inside her another voice spoke, another master for whom she played a more willing disciple.

In a few days, Drilg told us she would have to leave us for a time. And though she felt we were well-developed enough to go it on our own a day or two, conscience and the pangs of her past calamity prompted a new set of rules.

"Engage no visitors in conversation," she warned us. "No creature of the earth below dares cross the dragon's bounds. Those who arrive unheralded are enemies or fools. In either case, they can do you no good."

The three of us promised obedience, of course, and—of course—lost sight of our promise. The world below was a thing to be touched, a thing to be tasted, relished and enjoyed. Warnings have little impact when sensation hovers near. And "sensation" was the only thing in view. We tried. We remained steadfastly in the nest a day or two, and then curiosity overcame us, sending us scrambling about the cloud strewn cliffs looking to see what we could see.

I told Karman and Seti of the many wonders I'd beheld, riding that night on Dager's back. My stories made them long to savor such sensations for themselves. But we were up to such a height and fixed in such a place that the clouds which passed below obscured our view.

Seti was intemperate. She popped her wings like whips at the sky, as if doing such things could chase the clouds away. "There's such a thing as being too elite, too far above it all. If we head for lower ground we'll see much more."

"We have to stay in sight of home," I cautioned. "If we lose that point of reference, we're in hard luck."

"Mark the way!" she barked, a sensible suggestion I had to admit.

So, mark the way we did, with pyramids and rocks to notch each turn along the path, an avenue that suddenly widened as we ambled toward a tree line set a few pheasant flights farther below. Valleys visible beneath the cliffs gave signs of teeming life, movements of creatures other than ourselves. Diminutive beings we'd been told, though we'd seen precious few 'til now— cattle grazing, geese in gaggles flocks and flurries, mountain-climbing sheep now came into place as little more than miniatures in eyeshot. Unable yet to gauge proportion, we could only imagine how these tiny docile creatures looked up close. Would they be larger than we, we wondered, or little more than ticks upon our wings?

"Larger than you think," came the certain answer. "But not so great as the mighty dragon. None so great as that. Not in this world, anyway." The creature who spoke read our innermost thoughts. That was enough to impress anyone and certainly startled us. Seti hissed and flared her wings. Karman darted behind a boulder. I turned quickly toward the sound to see, on a rock bound branch above us, a bird pecking on the bark. He was a gaily painted creature, well-groomed, sleek and natty to his toes —wings of onyx, chest of snow, ebony crested head that nodded with a sense of wit at everything he saw, dotted by a piercing set of cogent black-pearl eyes able to peer into worlds beyond our own. He said he was a magpie; his word was good enough. (He was the first I had ever seen and the last I would ever care to.)

"Out for an evening stroll?" he warbled.

"Sort of," I replied, without thinking. I realized to my chagrin I was disobeying Drilg's first caveat. But we were so far from the nest, I reasoned, this creature had not sought us out. After a fashion, it was we who'd come looking for him.

"Don't trust him," Seti sensed at once. "He's far too familiar with us."

"Not wise at all for the dragon young to be strolling about like this," the magpie countered. "The dragon's hide brings quite a prize for humans who hunt their fortunes."

"Good advice," young Karman whispered. "We've come a bit too far. And darkness is no friend of ours. Let's turn back while the sky is light and we can still find our way."

I read my brother's canny instincts to be a dose of fear and had quickly come to disregard my sister's fulminations. After all, I was the eldest here, more mature than my siblings by at least what seemed an epoch. Without question I was the wisest, (or so my father had said); so I had to hold my own counsel in this quest. One shouldn't negotiate the world in fear, I calmly reasoned. After all, this charming fellow had no stock in store with us. He stood his branch, did a dance and preened his feathers smartly. We were articles of passing interest for him; nothing more.

"Of course, I shouldn't concern myself," he cawed. "You dragon young can fly, I'm sure. In fact on an evening clear as this, it comes as some surprise to me that you're not already out threading the clouds together."

I fell silent to weigh those words, but Karman took the query, feeling free to answer in my place. "Oh, we can't fly just yet," he said. "We won't do for some time. Sometimes I think we'll never fly at all."

"You don't say?" puzzled the magpie, flapping. "This is the first I've heard of that. It's always been my understanding that a dragon beyond the age of two can fly circles around any other creature in the sky. And you must be at least, why…three, anyway."

"About that," I answered assertively, but cautiously this time. Karman started to speak again but I felt the sudden need to silence him with a passing of my wing. He caught the gesture and kept his place. If we were meant to fly by now, I was certain we would have been the first to know.

"Well then, sure you can do a few darting dives, ins and outs, barrel rolls…things like that," he trilled, tucking a tail feather into place. "Standard fare for a dragonette of three. Or so I'm told."

"Lies! He lies!" snarled Seti, beneath her acrid breath. Yet I could feel her supple mind-sands shifting. What if the bird were singing true? her squinting eyes did query. "Or does he?" she added, in voice, forgetting that even the dragon's whisper is a trumpet for lesser creatures of this world. My dear sibling's paranoia knew no bounds, it seemed. She even mistrusted her mother's motives and might well have been swiftly moved to any other convenient alliance.

"Of course, we fly," I answered. "But perhaps not as well as you might think. We're still young and have much to learn. But we get around well enough."

Bluffs did not prevail against so wise a bird as this. The magpie took my best and yawned, his inner mouth a bloody red. "Well…I'm only repeating the things I've heard…and seen upon occasion. But as you say—and I take your word—your skills are good enough."

He paused. Pauses are holes where plots are hatched, I once heard someone say. We'd taken ourselves up to this ridge but still had yet to learn how to define the fine art of elusion.

"If you'd like to sharpen your talents a bit, I could show you a trick or two. A dip, a dive, an arabesque, whatever you'd like to do. Just hop up to cliff side, set out your wings, and whisk through the canyons below. Just so you three can warm up a bit. Work out the kinks, don't you know."

Glancing around for a safe plateau from which to test our mettle, I noted a flat place just above our slope. Try and fail there and no injury would befall us; little more, that is, than the pains of embarrassment.

"Well, we'll just fly up to that flat place, there. Looks good enough to me."

At that, the magpie sized me up and down. His air was more direct with me, though charm still oozed from his every feather.

"Hardly think so. But, as you well know, the dragon young can't just flap into flight over so short a distance. He's a lot like a condor, the carrion kind. Only large winds can lift him." Then he closed one eye, cocked his head, and looked at me askance. "But surely you can brave the wind. The wind's a friend to us all. You're large of frame and light of bone. You're sure to sail rather than fall." His voice in pentameter, humming hypnotically, drew us unwittingly out to the cliffs. An energy droning with a force and a pull we could neither resist nor diminish.

Knowing from a higher mind the folly of trying untried skills, the three of us grew suddenly bold and ready for a ride. Heady with the glory we could sniff upon the air, drugged by the sudden sense of our unlimited potential, we followed along to danger's edge, ready—at the magpie's signal—to lift our wings in flight. All at once we were willing disciples to this strangely compelling bird whose idle cawing had become a bell tone, calling his faithful to the sweet suicide of the canyons below.

Somewhere on this road to ruin, a hook of logic caught me. Stopping short at the very edge, I hiked my wing to hold my siblings away. But by now they were both hell-bent upon making their dive. Brushing by and over the top, they'd already taken the plunge. Not daring to look, I reconciled myself to the simple realization that there was nothing I could do for them except do my best to survive.

"I think I'll pass, this time," I said, but the magpie called me on, chanting his chant and flapping his wings with an updraft that sucked small bushes from their roots. "We've been instructed not to practice without our elders to help us. And I think it's good advice..." I said, or tried to say, when several dust devils swirled up their grit to coax me on my way.

Determined to make my stand, I drew back my chest and dug in my hind-talons, but this force of sound was more than mesmerizing. It had become a physical presence, a living energy field that swept me off the cliff side and into the waiting canyon's mouth.

To my everlasting surprise, I flew. The wind, like a long lost friend, filled my flanged wings and held me in perfect balance. I soared. I swept. I swooped. I sailed. Flaring out in ever widening circles, gaining confidence with each passing of the spiral, trailing downward with ever-increasing ease, I followed the course made by my siblings, gaining on them all the while and feeling my own speed thunder against the cliffs. My head was light with a sudden rush of fantasies fulfilled. I was giddy with elation. We'd not been betrayed but had been brought to this moment by this elegant stranger, this feathered angel unaware.

While we glided, the magpie darted above and below us, shouting with joy at our newfound skills as if they were his own.

"Isn't this grand?!" he crowed, with delight. "What a miracle, this dragon flight! A christening to behold! I know what you thought, but now you know. My word's as good as gold!"

There was no arguing that anymore than it could be argued that this, our first adventure, was turning out to be a banquet for the senses.

To give substance to my budding trust, the magpie came alongside me and motioned toward some mountain shoulders which opened in a kind of yawn. In their midst there sat a crater of glistening glowing rocks, a crimson red far brighter than any I'd seen before; and yet no heat came from it. The day grew cold as we moved toward those shoulders, chilling and foreboding in a way, but bright and beautiful and clear. And crested in its midst—a clear red, crystal crater lake.

"A lake of brimbrod shards!" cackled the magpie, in proud announcement to the world.

I didn't know to be impressed. I was told this was a rare find, a treasure and a feast shown only a privileged few. All I knew when I came to land was that its energies were mixed: a lacerating cold, jagged bed of rocks from which seeped a steaming carmine smoke in mutable hues of what I'd suspected to be a tainted promise of paradise.

We landed successively—one, two, three—but exchanged no glances. The compulsion we felt for this crater of shards drained our will to resist. In just the proper passage of time, the magpie came to light, choosing that moment to hop atop a crest of crystals.

"If you think they're a feast for the eyes," he said, "just wait until you sample them. Go ahead, enjoy," he coaxed us, passing his wing before them in invitation. "Most dragons go through a millennium without partaking of such delicacies as these. But for you my little royal dragonettes, nothing but the best. Savor the brimbrods! Know your fire! Realize an ecstasy that few will ever share!

"It's a feast finer than the sweet blue melons of the Thral or the cloud cakes of the Eastern skies! Partake, my little dragonettes! Enjoy!"

By instinct I was brought to stop and weigh our progress to this point. This offer seemed to come without condition. But what sort of price would we have to pay? My gut asked a question my mind could not answer. And yet, I held my tongue.

Had I counseled my peers to weigh the ease of all this, I would have been opposed in any case. My brother, having been imbued with powers he'd never known before, was too totally enthralled to pay heed to any counsel. Seti was already fulminating at our absent mother for having held our rites of flight so long in check.

"They hide our own potentials from us!" she hissed. "Why?!
By what authority are we denied the right to decide for
ourselves?!"

Following the magpie's careful instructions about how to
partake of these morsels, both were digging in with obvious
relish, using their foretalons to break the crystal shards off and
popping the steaming scarlet into their mouths. The taste must
have enchanted them, because they lost control, hurling
themselves into a feeding frenzy that almost sent me reeling.
They stuffed their mouths with shards, pounding their tails upon
the ground to drum their pleasure to the world.

Watching them gorge in such a way moved me even further
toward caution's side: I merely nibbled and, even in supping
lightly, noticed the almost narcotizing effect these brimbrod
shards were starting to have on me. Even so I chewed them
slowly, spat out what I could and hoped no one was monitoring
too closely. Someone was, of course, for nothing that we did
escaped the magpie's notice.

"Cautious little dragon, aren't we. T'would make his mummy
proud," he sniped, then caught himself in mid-rebuke. "Don't
get me wrong, young sky-lord. I've nothing but respect for
anyone who knows his mind, especially someone of your young
years…Still, you can't blame your siblings for their passionate
fancies. These are tasty morsels, you'll admit."

"No question," I conceded. I accepted an offering he made to
me, one he'd plucked clean with his beak. Ostensibly, it was too
large for him to lift, but he passed his wing over it as if to offer
consecration.

"Now, there's a winner," he said. And I had to admit, this
shard, gleaming before my eyes like the mother of all rubies, did
seduce my appetite. Had I discovered it on my own, I'd probably
have eaten it anyway; it was that enticing. At the magpie's
insistence, I tore it from the crystal floor and took a bite.

"Ah, life, what delicious mysteries await us on thy path," the
magpie cooed, pleased to see that I too had succumbed to this
orgy of eating. Seemingly satisfied that I had become more

"sociable" as he put it, this jayebird turned his attentions back to my kin who were now so caught up in the moment they were doing thumping jigs while they ate.

I too found the gaiety contagious and, like the others, began to thump my tail and pound my talons on the ground. But something stopped me. For reasons I could not for years explain, the slivers inside my mouth began to burn. They seared the linings of my guts with such a force I had to spew them out. I turned my head and—like a geyser—blew the brods into the air, a fiery flow that seemed to bake the mountain shoulders that flanked us.

Karman and Seti didn't notice. The magpie had engaged them in a frenzied dance that stole their will and shook the floor beneath. They were high and merry, and for a dash I envied them that sense of abandon that seemed to be so much a part of their elation and part of my pain. All the more reason I hated to rob the moment of its joy, but rob it I would and rob it I did.

"We have to go," I said. My words struck the air like a reprimand. The others stopped for a moment, regarded me, then continued with their eating and dancing. "Soon it will be night," I added. "Then it'll be too dark to see. And we're farther from home than you might think."

"Bullocks!" barked Seti. "I'm tired of conforming to someone else's rules. We'll set a course when we're good and ready, and not a moment sooner. The skies are ours now—day or night! We're dragons in the full, and no antiquated prohibitions can deny us our birthright and what we're meant to be!"

"No, your brother's right," the magpie corrected, marking the path of the setting sun. "Soon it will be too dark to find our way. Finish your snacking and then be off. There'll be another time. I'll do what I can to guide you back. It shouldn't take long at that."

He was not an easy read, this curious black and white bird. At every turn, he sidled up to my suspicions and embraced them, putting them to rest. How nonchalant he was; how reassuring!

After all, he'd done nothing to harm us. In fact, he'd made our safety his principal concern.

I sensed in him the making of a friend, one whose amity might soon be tested, for now I wasn't altogether sure we'd be able to get back home. Even what little of the brimbrods I had eaten, now seemed to set an anchor inside me, one with a density a dozen dragons could not have lifted. What's more, I was growing giddy and could not help but notice that my siblings—in movements far less dexterous than my own—were weaving about like any drunkards at a bar. And when they tried to launch into flight, they stayed pinned to the ground, flapping and fluttering like hatchlings.

"My, my, my," the magpie squawked, a portrait of concern. "Oh dear, oh dear, oh dear!" With an involuntary shudder, he ruffled his feathers—black and white—then preened them back in place. "Well, this sort of thing *does* happen from time to time. Get a little too much of the brimbrod in you and you just can't get off ground. I've even seen it happen in adult dragons too from time to time…from time to time."

"You have?" Karman strained to ask. He now maintained his words and his balance with the same degree of difficulty.

"Oh, indeed. Indeed!" the magpie insisted, looking around him warily as if to study the terrain. "Looks as though you'll have to spend the night. But not to worry. You're still upon high ground. Well above the reach of lower creatures. Besides, I'm the cause of your over-indulgence, so let me make amends. I'll circle above your little roost and warn you of any danger."

Before he could say another word, my sister had snatched him up in her foretalon and had brought him beak to snout.

"You'd better be telling the truth, little jaybird! Or we'll make a snack of you!" she said, laying to rest the notion that diplomacy would be her forte.

"Oh, rest assured, sweet Dragon Princess, your life is as my own! And I hold mine quite dearly, I can tell you." Quite composed, despite the peril, the magpie softened my sister's spite at least to the degree that she did not have him for dessert.

Snorting her inebriate contempt, she tossed him with such velocity only his desperate flapping could brake his crash against a tree. Resilient if nothing else, the magpie kept his humor. He righted himself, brushed off his feathers and, in a show of good faith, guided us to a place on higher ground. Considering our bumbling state of mind, we made good time and arrived at last, breathless and looking down at a broad flat plain of earth.

Quite accessible, I thought, for anyone with less than pure intentions. But the magpie seemed intense in his desire to help.

"You'll be safe from visitation, here," the magpie said, himself a little breathless. "And I will be your sentry for the night. After all, it's the least I can do. I got you into this mess." He was contrite and, I must say, more than a little kind. He fretted over us at length and reassured us that "everything will be all right," before he flew away.

I watched him depart, circling as he promised, as if to keep an eye out for intruders, gliding higher in ever widening circles, his black wings spread, his white breast iridescent like a beacon in the sea of night. I couldn't help but be struck by his sudden, shifting pattern of flight. More than a simple barnyard thief, clever and adroit, this jayebird took on the aspect of a hawk, a bird of prey whose proportions seemed to swell as he rose higher, gliding with the sinister grace of wizardry in his wings.

I for one hadn't tried my wings to fly home. Since my brother and sister had not managed to get themselves airborne I thought I'd spare us further chagrin and pick another time. For now, I couldn't leave alone, although I'd wish I had. Now, dizzied by the myriad sensations this day had fed me, I too grew heavy headed and began to doze. Above us in the sky, the magpie continued his hypnotic vigil, soaring around in ever broadening arcs. For a moment, I could have sworn I even saw a wake of red light stream out from behind him like the tail of a kite. But I was no longer seeing with my own eyes. Instead, another force directed my vision down that solitary path that led to sleep.

From tormented dreams too filled with demons to belong to an innocent youth, I awoke with a start to find the night covered by a canopy of stars. The magpie had quit his airborne vigil and was now nowhere to be seen; I'd quite expected that. No one, not even the mighty dragon, can hope to fly forever. So, I surmised, the bird had probably sought to perch on a nearby cliff. Yet, when I called out to him, I got no answer for my trouble save the darting retreat of a wolf on the rocks below.

As a rule, there is a celestial harmony about this time of night. But from everything that I could see the rules had been abandoned. Just below us in the Lake of Shards, its garnet crystals glistened red like teeth laid bare in the maw of a wounded god.

There was no magpie. But above us I could see that, though this bird had flown, he had indeed left a trail of light, a swirling coil of scarlet that signaled our haven in the rocks for all the world to see.

I wondered if Drilg would see such a light, if she'd returned to find us gone. What agonies would it have put her through, thinking she had lost another set of offspring? Would she have been able to find us even if she looked? Certainly she'd be able to see this cone of light pointing the way to us, I reasoned, but then I reasoned too: so could anyone else.

It was in that dash of sobering logic that I was suddenly seized by a sense of urgency. I rushed to where my brother and sister lay and tried to wake them—a study in bathos, I might have known since Seti only hissed and returned to her narcotized slumber and rancorous dreams, and Karman lay quite catatonic (only his snoring like an off-key oboe put my mind at ease). I bellowed at them to awaken, batted them with my foretalons, and even lashed at them with my tail.* I was desperate and would have tried anything short of immolation, but my kinsmen lay there and would not, by any force at my disposal, be moved.

To accommodate my premonitions, I sought a place on higher ground. If we'd lost our magpie sentry then, I reasoned, I'd be the watchtower for our brood. Drilg would have no more

---

* A taboo among dragons, since tail-lashing is a call to combat and elicits an instinctively hostile response.

27

chicks to mourn, I vowed. This was something I would see to personally. Staying posted for the rest of the night, I cocked my head, watched and listened for every noise, for every flicker of movement foreign to this place. Nothing would catch me by surprise, I swore. But when I saw the violet dawn that marked the plain below, I realized it was not just any slip in decorum of which I should be wary. From all that I could hear and see the danger, when it came, would come in spades.

Karman was still in a torpor, and Seti, though she stirred, would respond to nothing, not even the hurling of rocks upon her body.

While I waited for them to come to their senses, I thought to test my wings, to fly around a bit. The morning would be still and, in that stillness, no one would witness my folly if I fell. But before I could summon the attitude to see it through I looked on the broad apron of land below and saw the sun open on the day like an oven door and unleash a fury on this place. Out of that furnace of light came a creature, a whorl of dust and limbs with single purpose toward making its way to this lake. This creature was made of men, the first of their kind I'd ever seen. Their chariots glistened. Their wheels were scythes, slashing all life that blocked their way, their horses lathered and bleeding from the bits that laced their mouths — these men came scrambling toward us with a desperation born of fear. Men with grapples, hooks and spears, in armor from head to toe — three hundred by the slightest count — were thundering toward this maw of scarlet with a lust for the dragon's heart.

This was the pygmie I had heard of, a furtive uncertain species whose morals our elders held in question. By himself, he might have been a mite of a thing and little for the dragon to fear, but in his mass he was a madding carnivorous beast, knotted together by malicious cause yet without a head to sever or a heart to spear and kill. The beast in his collective form was *Army*. If well directed, as this one was, it knew no equal on the Earth. And this one had directed itself straight for this throat of shards.

Though it was still a league away, seeing this ravening beast moved me to awaken my brethren at any cost. At no loss to make my presence known, I hurled missile after missile—rocks, shrubs, trees, anything I could uproot and toss—at Seti and at Karman. In fact, I threw so much I might have injured a lesser creature and might have even put a hickey or two on their still forming dragon hides. But better an irritation than certain mayhem, I reasoned (and I reasoned well), for the hydra-headed monster was making its advance with a speed that I had underestimated.

Hurling everything I could grab from rocks to tiny trees, I finally managed to wake my sister and direct her attention to the advent of her demolition. Still groggy, she lifted her head just in time to see this welter of frothing creatures vying with one another to make their way toward her.

Why I didn't fly to her aid that moment, I'll never entirely know. But if I dare to be truthful (and in the end we must all dare the truth), it was fear that morning which froze me in my place. Hidden from the sight of this rabid mass of armor, horse, and steel, I prayed that I'd not be brought to its attention. My sister, I thought would rise and flee, that she'd seize my sleeping brother by his scruff and take flight just in the nick of time. But retreat was not a corner cut in this one's orb. She was a warrior to her core and, like a warrior, held her ground and fought. By instinct of bloodlust she stood astride her brother, caught a wave of lance and arrow and flattened a score of screaming warriors. These madmen fulminating fear fell back and then attacked again, a mistake to try upon this dragon princess.

Though she stood no more than six meters tip to tail Seti welcomed the second wave. With swiping motions both deft and deadly, she caught a pair of attackers squarely with her foretalons and snapped their backs like poppies. It was an act so fraught with force it sent the rest withdrawing for a time to reappraise their resolve.

"This wasn't what the master told us!" I heard more than one voice cry. "They'd all be sleeping, he said."

"And there'd be three," another shouted. "The third is not among them. And if it's left to warn its elders, we're all toast in the dragon's mouth before this day is done!"

"Silence!" roared a voice above the others. It was a bold if not endearing tone, one that came from a creature used to leading others of his kind.

From this hurly burly came a man. He was larger than the rest, a bearded man the soldiers called "Captain" who carried a trident tipped in silver that he twirled about with ease. "Dragons or not," he reminded the others, "these are yearlings and far too young to fear." Courageous words, yet I couldn't help notice he approached my sister with respect. Circling her warily, he cast before him a net of such immensity it could have snared the giant Naanworm that dwelled beneath the Sea of India.**

Back and forth, he popped this net, bringing its silvery threads to glisten in the morning sun, whirling until it fused to form the shining face of a giant mirror that shot the daylight into my sister's eyes. Seti was blinded for a time. Had she been a more seasoned warrior, she would have known to avert her gaze or to turn her back on this pervader. The dragon's tail is a terrible tool, so she might have picked his bones, but my sister was still in her forming skin; all her weapons were not intact. She could only rely on her instincts, and rely on them she did.

Charging toward her adversaries she worked a furious front to make her seem the most fearsome of dragon warriors. Such masks no matter how well worn paled before an army such as this. This Gorgon lurching at my sister had too many heads, too

---

** ***The Naanworm.*** A brackish-brown giant sea worm three miles long, the Naanworm sleeps beneath the Sea of India and only awakens when ships sailing west to east cross over his domain. If of a mood, he can offer sailors a safe harbor for the night, and considers himself after a fashion the Chief of Police of the Sea. When aroused or made angry, the Naanworm breathes ocean refuse from his bowels that turn into schools of vicious sea snakes at the surface. He has also been known to suck down a pirate ship, slaver or other unsavory craft, deep into the belly of the Ocean.

many hands, too many weapons for one so young to hope to penetrate. Seti did the best she could, but she lacked a sense of tactics.

The soldiers at the heart of the phalanx braced themselves. They made no attempt to run, but panic was a signature etched upon their faces. Many took cover behind their shields, many behind their horses.

The Captain was entirely another kind of creature. This dragon fighter had faced the worst. By comparison, my sister was small game. Taking her measure and finding her inexperience to his liking, he stood his ground and waited for her youthful zeal to bring her into his snare.

Indignant at the arrogance of this fraction of a being, Seti roared, broke blindly at him and clearly missed her mark. Sidestepping her assault the Captain thrust his trident, catching her with a blow that bit her squarely in the flank. Wounded, blindly thrashing with tooth and tail and talon, she released a scream so shrill it split the shields of a nearby column of soldiers. The warriors, even the Captain himself, crouched and held their ears, for the roar of a dragon, even a young one, could cause their ears to burst.

However gravely injured, Seti made a show of it, flailed and fought and tried to fly away, but her struggles soon made it apparent she could not. Bleeding from the trident still imbedded in her side, weakened and confused, she flapped her wings like a fledgling dropped from the nest. Bearing witness to this circumfusion of flailing dragonkind brought the soldiers once more to their feet. Led by their Captain, they began to converge on my sister, sword, spear and arrow at the ready. But Seti was a dragon. She gave as good as she got. She clutched her brother with one talon and fended them off with the other, whipping her tail like a reaper against the troupe. With a strength surpassing all limitation she tried to take to the sky, but she was vitiated now and fell back down to earth.

So that was this magpie's legacy to the dragon young—that we could fly down but not back up, that we'd been taught only half the trick—to glide but not to climb, part of our powers but certainly not the whole. Half-learned lessons are fatal fare, and we'd been led by that sweet piper to this sour deception all according to plan. Whoever that misbegotten bird was, he had our curses in his ears, and Seti's would always fall upon his soul.

Heartened by my sister's loss of force, the warriors re-encircled her, jeering now and then with uneasy courage. Taunting, they jabbed at her with sword and spear while on a ledge behind them three rows of archers loaded silver-tipped arrows into their bows, straining them string and sinew to the max. Before they took their prize, however, the Captain held them at bay.

"Give the vanquished their rightful due," he commanded. "There is a ritual to all this. And we must be mindful of it." In an unexpected show of reverence, he doffed his helmet, and bowed in the direction of my kinsmen. Uttering some mantra or other, he shouted out the word, "*Atohh!*" and from the throng emerged a manacled old man who handed the warrior a blazing heat-fired sword. Taking the weapon in hand (a "holy" one, I reckoned) the Captain carved a cross into the air.

Somehow, there was truly magic in this, for its fiery lines seared in a way that cut even through the strident light of day. Again the Captain chanted, carving a kind of cross.

"*Atoh!*" his voice broke into the hot light. The song that rang from it was almost sweet, and had it not been the prelude to an act of butchery, one easily might have taken it for a prayer.

This ritual might have persuaded a creature more supplicant and refined to be accepting of her fate; not Seti. Spurred to combat, she called upon a harsher more sinister force, vomiting forth a fusillade of angry fang and fire. From whatever Power it came, it sent the Captain tumbling and scattered his soldiers to the rear, some of them burned from her flames that cut through their armor and tore into their skin. Only the archers held their steady vigil and awaited the command.

Regaining his feet, the Captain shook his head.

"There's more to this one that meets the eye," he muttered, then turned his attentions to his rows of bowmen, ready for a strike.

Who can ever say where courage finds its wings? Filled with a rage at many things—at my sibling's mortification, at the magpie's well laid trap, at my own vacillation—I set myself in motion. I was high enough to swoop, that much I knew. Getting down would be a snap. The rest, I calculated would have to come from a higher source, one higher than my own. The dragon's rage, the dragon's fire, the dragon's blinding light, an angel of retribution, waited to answer my commands *if* I could summon the words—the Word, the elusive, magic mantra. I asked. I prayed for it all in a flickering instant (for time was not on my side). Let it come through me, I prayed, and in that moment all that could pass upon my trembling lips were those of the Captain's strangely righteous prayer, this holy ritual whose crown word he had shouted to the sky—that would be my word now, and I used it to the fullest of my power.

"*Atohhh!*"

The cry I set loose didn't come from my mouth but surged through me instead like a thunderclap that shattered the day and brought it darkly down upon the army rimming the crystal pit. In their clamor and confusion, these soldiers could not tell what mountainous apparition had beset them. But it had caught their fears enough to set them into flight; all but the intrepid and their leader.

The Captain stayed; the archers too. Steadfast in their duties, they poised to launch their arrows straight at my throat. Yet there was a pause before the Captain dropped his hand, a still-caught moment while he gauged the wind which swirled around them. That was the instant for me to strike. This gale-force ally, this surging Kamikaze hurled me from my shelf and set me down upon them like a torrent. I arched my wings, spitting my fire, as certain as could be that I was a mystic beast three times my size.

My arrival didn't go unnoticed. In the instant I had come upon them, these bowmen had turned, pulling taught their shafts to burn on me. But it was just a tad too late. By then I'd made my play. Driven by warrior instincts seeded deep inside my cells, I swept them aside like reeds beneath a storm. Before retreating, out of reflex, some of the bowmen fired. Their arrows left their strings and pierced my wings. But these were merely pinpricks for the warrior I'd become. Scathing them with mordant fire I didn't know I had, I set some into living torches and others in pursuit to the flames that I, Dragon had set. As I made my second pass, even the Captain gave me ground. His honor guard, it seemed, had lost control.

Even then I had to admit this titillated me. Some sinister sense of pleasure rose from embers in my loins and made me all the thirstier for more. And well I would have stayed to indulge that darker notion had I not been pressed by another hidden counsel. Some inner voices warned me that I'd surely not survive it, that I would fail and my mission would die in the trying.

As it was, I had just enough time to rescue my brother and sister before the Captain and his soldiers could regroup. I reasoned my third and final pass would have to be a short one, or else I'd be a target too ripe to miss. I worked my way to the side of my sister, grabbed her by the scruff behind her neck and tried to lift her. Yet, despite this heaven-sent surge of power running through me, it was all I could do to get her airborne. Her thrashing about and cursing did little to sweeten the moment. I was doing my damnedest to get us to safer ground, but rather than help in this, she saw this as a fitting time to vent her spleen on me.

"A little late, you craven coward!" she spat, spewing blood from her tongue. "Bastard offspring of Shimbagh lust!"

I thought her rebuff ill-timed at best. While she poured ire from every pore, she also writhed and twisted, causing our flight from harm to take some unusual patterns that proved to be a blessing in disguise. The spears and arrows headed our way either missed their marks or dealt us such glancing blows even my underdeveloped armor could protect me. Lifting us finally out of range and taking roost on the cliffs, I tried with little luck to tend Seti's wounds.

She ordered me never to touch her again, then for a little while slashed at specters and cursed in tongues I'd never heard before. With her tail she seized the trident still sticking in her flank, tore it out and dashed it into bits on the rocks below. The fishhook flanges from its tips had ripped chunks from her hide and would have caused a lesser being to cry out from reflex if nothing else, but Seti bore it without so much as a whimper. Courage born of rage prompts admiration (not from me). Seti's fits for now would have to belong to her alone. I had to focus my attentions on my third and final pass, the one to take me down to save my brother.

Reviving from his stupor, Karman knew from moment one that all hell had broken loose. He tried to bring himself to his feet at least to flee his captors, but he was too feeble to undertake even that simple task. He rose and stumbled back to earth, an act that cost him his resolve and heartened those about to do him in.

Those minions might have finished him then had I not risen again from the rocks and let out another deafening roar (something louder than a sparrow, but far from the voice of God. Anyway, it did the job at the time). Whatever it was the show still worked—my beating of my breast, my flashing flaming tongue made them pause just long enough to redirect their aim. This would be no easy raid; I wasn't about to surprise them. Already they had enough weapons cocked to make a steak of me.

Staring into the teeth of this, gave me second thoughts. But whatever fate awaited me below would seem easy game compared to the challenges about to come. Just as I'd mustered the courage to assault a convoluting energy—a blinding orb of light—whirled into their midst and came to rest. It was enough to set them back, and this force of hardened soldiers gave this astral entity the widest possible berth. Any hopes I might have had of having found an ally were instantly dashed (and never raised again). Once it ceased its iridescence, this orb formed into a man unlike any other I had seen. This one was even more imposing than the Captain—a priest/high-priest, a shattering power before whom others knelt, a wizard dressed in raiments ribbed in black and white. A black skullcap pointed at its furl adorned his down curled brow where eyes as cold as lapis could work their will. Covering his angular face jointed by a deeply cleft chin, there was a black jackdaw of a beard streaked with a white shock-line; the kind that hides a scar, some mark of Cain to bar him from redemption.

When he raised his arms to rebuke his troupe, his robe unfurled from his soul black and flowing, baring his snow-white chest where some arcane medallion seemed to hypnotize the sun. Yet as he spoke, his meanest words danced through the air like a song. It was then I recognized that it was the Magpie!

This was the engaging little jaye, the betrayer who'd led us to this calamity! How smoothly he had set us for sacrifice! How roughly now he'd pay! If I had my way (and I swore I would) he'd rue the day he'd done this.

Abandoning caution or strategies that might have served me well, I fired myself at this muezzin of the Pit. Launching from my perch I heard my beating wings cry out like the song of a spear as I streaked toward my holy mission—my rendezvous to slay this evil thing.

It was an ill-timed gesture.

Despite the swiftness of my swoop, I took too long to get from A to B. The High Priest now stood placidly, a silvery mace in his hand, waited until I was close then hurled it with unerring force straight to the bone of my heart. The thunderous power with which it struck seared into my sternum, making it feel as though it had split in half. Stunned, I rolled and tumbled almost crashing below into the warriors waiting to snare me. But just before I did, some inner song carried me swiftly beyond the point of peril. Wounded to my heart, I nonetheless banked and swept toward the sky managing somehow to get back to the roost from which I'd dived.

Seti awaited my return, not angrily as I might have expected, but cast in resigned and faded hues. Rather than revile me for my failure, she laid her head down on a rock and sighed. "You did the best you could, big brother...did the best you could."

The ultimate temperance of her reply told me she wasn't well, and yet there was relief to know there dwelled a heart in her. For once, we shared a common bond far deeper than our blood—one from which we would never come entirely correct.

The hot-ribbed silver shaft of the mace that seared into my hide had fallen out as if to seek retreat. Already the wound that steamed from my chest had shattered my grip on awareness and made me lose the caring for this sorry incarnation. So quickly were my passions slipping from this dreary drama it didn't even matter when I saw the Magpie perch.

"My, my, my! You don't look well!" he said, scandalized, it seemed. "Well, these little moments of travail are set to try us. Just goes to show you never can tell just where our little ventures will take us...Then, again let's try to look on the positive side of things. I never dreamt you'd be so splendid in the learning. So precocious! So evolved! T'would have made your daddy proud, if he could have seen you (which he won't)."

To this day, I've never understood the dubious art of gloating. Such ironies, then as now, have always eluded me. Wounded, seared and branded as I was, I was much too wracked with pain to see where this visitation could be heading. I could only note with dazed perplexity that, as the Magpie spoke, a vapor of clouds poured lively from his mouth, enveloping us like a shroud. Fading as I was from care for this hot and vicious world, I could only be aware that my eyes were growing dim and losing the desire to see what lay ahead.

§§§§§§§

It was not long before I reawakened to the dark purpose of their mission. Beside me, my sister, delirious to any awareness of this world, now held on only by raw instinct to her life. It was best that it were so, because had she been awake she would have borne witness to an event that might have driven her mad.

Below, in the barren cradle of rocks, the Magpie had slit my brother opening him like a shellfish from collar to groin. With kneeling warriors gathered around him, he stood astride sweet Karman and held up a chalice filled with blood; dragon blood. Making some grave and igneous sign, this Wizard raised the hideous grail, making supplicant gestures toward a jagged, darkening sky.

His *faithful* called his title aloud. "RuSiva! RuSiva! RuSiva!" As if it were a rosary of praise.

The name of this ape of perfidy struck me with a slap of recognition, reminding me that this had been the assassin of my brothers born before me. Yet recollection took on new meaning as I was forced to see the rape of a soul now being performed before my very eyes.

My brother, Karman, though vivisected, was still very much alive! His wings pinned, his talons fore and hind tied and tacked down on the rocks, he was permitted to watch his own bloodletting. Aware that he'd been turned into a living offal, he lay there entreating, while warrior after warrior made procession to receive this bloody Eucharist: a cup of dragon's blood to slake their thirst, to steal their minds, to compromise their souls.

Although savaged by the blow I'd received and barely able to move, I rose to fly back to attack, to lay down what remained of my young life to end this travesty. It was only upon attempting to bolt, that I realized we were now enveloped in a cocoon of mist as hard as crystal and meant to encase us there. Whatever ritual was taking place by the Brimbrod Lake below let me know that we'd be next—dragon under glass!

"The dragon's blood brings courage," I heard RuSiva say. "The dragon's blood brings long life, good fortune, and freedom from disease."

Like some barker in a sideshow scam he hawked his auguries, careful to delete the important part: the hitch.

I hadn't known 'til then how generous were the dragon's veins. While my brother lay there dying, his blood flowed like a river—enough to quench an army's thirst! Still drugged, his wits now at their end, dear Karman had become no longer the frail young creature I had known and loved. Although laid out for sacrifice, he neither wept nor moaned, neither bewailed his condition nor mourned his fate. While those poor human beings dipped into his cavernous chest and feasted on his blood of hosts, he forgave them. He cried out to them with love, compassion, and forgiveness, preaching to them of the brotherhood of all creatures under God's eyes. "When one dies, all die," were the harshest words that left his lips.

Karman was still too young a being, and from his day of birth too awed by the things of this earth to show such infinite wisdom at this moment of his doom. It was as if his oversoul had risen out of him, giving higher meaning to this hideous ritual, invoking the miracle of transformation right before our eyes.

There is never a moment so bleak that it cannot be redeemed. Soon my brother was silenced. RuSiva saw to that, ordering his tongue to be split, his jaws sewn shut with threads of ancient gold. No question, this wizard feared the truths Karman spoke and would have killed him there and then were it not for their belief in the myth that the blood of the living dragon flows endlessly.

Although Karman's lips were sealed, his words had done their work. Many warriors fell sick with shame. Others vomited up the host that filled them.

"I am defiled!" one warrior shouted, weeping. He soon was led away.

"I feel unclean!" another shuddered and spasmed by his shield.

Finally came the Captain's turn.

Up to now, he had chosen to stay outside the line, withholding any intention to partake in the ritual he saw. When it came time to drink, he pushed the goblet aside and very swiftly drew the Wizard's ire.

"This was not in my contract," the Captain declared, refusing the chalice again. Squarely standing before RuSiva, he met him gaze for gaze. He was a warrior taller than most and hovered over the mage, a body language this wizard simply couldn't abide.

"You refuse the sacrament!?" the High Priest asked.

"You have undertaken the sacrament without the Asking Prayer," the Captain challenged. "Without that sacred ritual, the bond of protection is broken, and the dragon's blood becomes a poison for the soul. It robs a man of will and rapes his logic. The dragon takes his vengeance in more ways than one, and I hold my own more precious than that! What's more you take a sentient creature and drink its living blood. This is the work of demons not of God!"

"The sacrament is holy!"

"Only if it is given holy intent."

"And you do not?"

"I do not judge another's motives. My faith is mine to share. And no one else's, priest! I am a dragonhunter, nothing more! I've done a hunter's work this day. My contract is fulfilled. But be apprised of this, my liege: The eldest answered the Prayer. Now we've received benediction from his brother."

Although the meaning confused the soldiers (and eluded me at the time), RuSiva knew entirely what the Captain had implied.

"And you did nothing to change them?!" he murmured. "Or slaughter the Answerer right there?! What kind of leader are you? Has your courage left with your brain? We must end him now, or now begins the Game!"

"I set my contract for slaying dragons, not for stealing souls. And as for the Game, I realize now that you serve another master. I can no longer be part of this. My soul and my lance are free. What you do from this point on, you do in spite of me."

The Sorcerer paused and slyly smiled. The Captain cautiously took his leave and would have made his way unscathed, for RuSiva—by all appearances—was giving ground. With a gesture of conciliation, he bowed ironically, expansively thanking the soldier for services rendered.

The truce was a ruse, and the Captain knew it. Glancing from side to side, holding his shield on high, this wary warrior backed away to mount his chariot. His stallions pranced uncertainly, fearful of the glaring light that danced off RuSiva's mace, a fiery missile thrust above them and into the Captain's chest, sending them to whirl in a madding circle. The Magpie had fired a deadly blow; the mace like a white-hot missile melted the Captain's armor plate and sank into his chest, knocked him from his chariot to be tangled in his reins.

My brother Karman had died by then. As if this last act of treachery had sapped his vital force, he finally breathed his last— a single sigh that struck the air, transmutive yet unheard. My brother's notes, if nothing else, sang their way home to me, for he had given all and did not judge the takers. The blood let so sweetly from his heart had so confounded these men that one among them had found the will to rebel.

For that the Captain had paid a price that nearly cost his life. Half dead, he was now being dragged by his own blinded horses who raged at the insanity of the moment. Torn by loyalties recently lost, staggered and confused, the warriors tried to rein them in but were hapless at their work. Blood-drugged by their unholy host, they vacantly cast their nets, tossing them in the air and snaring nothing. The horses, sightless and confused, were the better-guided beasts. They held their own, eluded capture and sent the soldiers running. Another force of men came at them specially armed for slaughter, but before they could carry out their act a miracle transpired.

While his horses stood off the horde, the Captain had revived, struggled to the back of his chariot and took hold of the reins. Heartened to feel their master's touch these stallions pierced the line, slashing through a phalanx of archers poised to gun them down. Somehow sanctified by their courage, the horses regained their vision and pulled the chariot at full gallop to its liberation. Half slumped against the brake-piece of the wheel, the Captain held with fading strength to what remained of his life.

Written off as good as dead, the Captain made his escape, forgotten in this infamy as if he'd been a whim. Once again RuSiva had summoned the devotions of his soldiers, calling upon them to focus upon the crematorium before them—the immolation of my dear brother. In the wake of Karman's expiration, the High Priest set about preparing an alchemical pyre and ordered two soldiers to bring forth an urn filled with deadly firestone. Taking from it a bluish powder—nectar of its essence—he cast it upon that once sweet dragonette's remains. The rocks resounded with canticles that poured from the Sorcerer's throat sifting like smoke to fill an empty sky.

> *"Fire of fire!*
> *Stone of stone!*
> *Fire of Stone*
> *Of Fire*
> *Of Stone*
> *To come!"*

RuSiva repeated his mantrum again as he scattered the firestone powder on the body. Instantly it burst into transmuted tongues of flame, giving new light to a day grown dark with age. Brilliant bright vermilion to blue-jade-emerald hues—those tantalizing vapors—danced like harlot specters stealing the soul of the day. As the flame screamed out, I looked to the Pit in horror as the last vestige of my brother disappeared, while in his place a new harvest of firestone ash was poured into oversized golden casks. In keeping with the pact between the creatures of the fire and this transmuted stone, my dragon brother had become what had consumed him, had given form to new energy, matter without a mind.

I was not aware of its powers, nor did I understand how this High Priest of low intent could hold such sway over others. I could only vow that, if I survived this day at all, I would bring the Magpie down, even if ending his life would end my own.

As it was, the end of my life might very well be at hand, for once the firestone was set into its place, this darkly driven Magpie had commanded his army of tainted souls to complete its quest. With a gesture toward our crystalline cocoon RuSiva marked us well, ordering a company of soldiers to climb and seize us.

"The others!" he motioned with his dagger held high, a large obsidian carapace for cutting into chests.

Half-dead, held captive in this dome of dark crystal, all my sister and I could do was wait while this squalid, slavering irrational band clambered up the rocks. These pygmies were such minions of this Wizard! Had they no wills of their own? Could any creature conceived by God be quite as dull as these? Could any be so self-directively cruel?

There was no escaping for me. I had lost my resolve to do it. Enfeebled by my wounds this day, I saw an end to my life. Yet, as the day dimmed with our fading hopes, as darkness came upon us, the dome of sky above grew raging hot, and from behind me there came a roar so rapacious and mean it was as if the mountain itself had risen in reprisal.

The soldiers climbing toward us froze in place. Awestruck by the sudden scorching light, they couldn't move. They couldn't turn to flee. Petrified by his secret stare, they fell into a frieze, monuments to their own demise, ridiculous in their fear.

Below by the sacrificial pyre, the army took to flight. Warriors scurried, took to their chariots and fled—none so swiftly cunning as the Magpie.

The moment he had seen this terror, he turned into a dust storm and blew himself away, leaving little reinforcement for the warriors in his wake. The rest were ossified in their tracks and hurled down the mountainside like so many pebbles loosed from an avalanche. The few who tried to move were cindered by a blast of flame or ripped by talons that could have etched a glyphic on the moon. Although my fading eyes could not see, it was then that my heart could feel the howling hot, sweet breath of my father the Mountain.

In the last violent act of a brutal day Dager whipped his wing across the cocoon, shattering the crystal into beads of acid that scarred the ground as they struck. Tucking us softly beneath his wings, he carried us aloft, mindful of the fragile cargo that we had now become. Sky borne again I felt secure, safe from worldly harm as if my father's sweat were a sacred tonic. Although losing the waking need, I somehow felt more whole, touched by the loving surety from his surely aching heart. As we flew toward some hidden place where great souls seek their rest, I prayed my thanks to a distant star that called me by my name.

We had survived, that much I knew. Yet something in us had died, an innocence whose sweet soft cradle would never hold us again.

Canto 3

The Shadow Council

A poison from RuSiva's mace had nearly brought me down, had nearly taken my life before it had started. In the next few units of measured time, my fate remained in peril. My body scraped the edge of death, while my vital force went wandering through astral planes where doomed souls and Shimbaghs frolicked in a void and beckoned to me to join their naked force. They all came cloaked in contradiction, luculent and horrid, a saucy nectar of corruption that had to be tasted once. I was drawn to them yet held my center and, in that reluctance, drew a power that cleansed me in a light. Not from above but from within this light inside me glowed with a sense of love I'd never felt on Earth. It washed away that astral mural and left my vision clear to catch the prism of my full potential. Though my eyes could not yet see a world familiar to my senses, I still could feel the light. I still could know the touch of presences both holy and serene. They enveloped me, yet I could not awaken to them.

I emerged from my travels through the passage by Coma to hear a convening of voices in my ears. Somewhere in the brightening midst of this realm of towering shadows, my sister and I lay on beds of herbs freshly strewn to salve our wounded souls. Comfrey, coriander, foxglove, aloes—leaves and petals from these loving plants offered themselves to comfort us while a shower of crimson light cleansed our open wounds.

On the threshold of transition, neither waking nor asleep, half-dead to this dimension, half-alive to another, I could feel but not behold the entities around us. Through the cloudy heights from which they watched us, I could sense their dark grandeur; I could feel their divine love. They were cathedrals with wings, Seraphim of cosmic tribes, blood of my own blood, mystic soul mates and yet somehow strangers to my purpose.

While they healed my sister and me, they scanned us in somber study, noting our peril as if it were their own. As if our recent memories were freshly ripened fruit, they plucked them from our wounded thoughts examining each in turn. Some they culled. Others they studied in the rapture of intent. One, that special One, brought them simultaneous sadness and a sense of culmination.

They forgave our disobedience and the tragedy that it spawned. In wandering from the nest we dragon young had only followed natural laws, the innate desire of the seeking mind to see its world anew. We had wandered far and in that wandering had been deceived by the Magpie; 'twas true. But it was at that turn where our course and the one the Magpie had planned for us had parted ways. We were not supposed to have succeeded quite so well. It was not in the dragon's master plan for its young to fly or even to glide at so early an age as we. Nor were the Magpie's displays of delight quite the sham I'd suspected. RuSiva, it seemed, loved the challenge of drawing out the bait. And since, on rare occasion, some dragonettes had shown prodigious talents, he'd had a plan for the second phase already set in place.

By report, the Lake of Brimbrod Shards was a seed of debauchery, a table of corruption even for adults. The brimbrod itself was drug enough to melt the underpinnings of a mountain. The red crystal shards were forbidden fruit for all the sons of Draco, and most had learned to steel their wills against it. It brought the high dragon low, turned its females into wantons and its males into hopeless eunuchs. It rendered all the Mystic Beasts as inert as stone. It marbled their perceptions so they could not tell right from wrong. It froze the ruby firesource, the secret of dragon-flight, while it prepped them for sacrifice, flooding their veins with warm black blood that flowed on endlessly.

As the scheme had been set by RuSiva, he would have had us coming or going—either by our deaths and sacrifice or by the taking of our souls to the Shimbagh side. Yet from the moment of our despoiling at the teeming Lake of Shards, we three had failed to play by the High Priest's rules. First, I'd been saved from certain ruin by my aversions to the hot dross of them and had been able enough not only to avert capture but also to warn my siblings. Despite being drugged, my sister Seti had fought with the courage of a full-grown dragon queen, had used her energies to nearly upheave a force of 300 men. In my return and rescue, I too had summoned some Seraphic source far greater than my own. Into the face of danger I'd flown with the facility of a wind god, borne my burden and battled that beast called *Army*. My conduct, though I thought it only instinct at the time, had been right action to the last. At last and most transcendently, my brother in dying to this world had allowed his angels to come through him, and through that collected angelic mind had forgiven his defilers to the end.

I was aware when I had done what I did that I'd had some help from on high, but I hadn't the foresight to know that these instinctive cries of combat would have brought down the wrath of angels.

"These are the ones who were prophesied," a deep voice raised above the murmur.

"The first of the translators," voiced a second, in tranquil confirmation.

"These three had all evolved to this, and this presents The Time," agreed a third in lilting female tones. "The signs are there. The signs are there. Others will follow soon. The path is set, and we'll need them all if it's true. When comes The Time, we'll need them all and more."

Even then I had my doubts that we were destiny's children, and the mention of "the Time of times" is unsettling to anyone. Since my soul's body drifted in suspension at this point, I knew neither how to move nor ask; nor would have I dared had I been able.

I was also aware of dissenting voices that gave the moment perspective—the spear of debate hurled from the ego's throat.

"Three dragonettes bestowed with prodigy do not fulfill a prophecy. Not to this cleric's eyes," I heard a voice somewhat stridently declare.

"They still must be schooled in the Ancient Ways. It is the order of things," a deep voice added, verging on the brittle edge of ire.

"It is the way," another, softer voice concurred. "The way must be followed."

The matter of our training brought no contention. All agreed that, whatever the cost, it had to be undertaken according to tradition in the Mastersinger's school. Only there could our souls be read in their entirety—not only our souls, but also the destinies that drove them.

This matter of "the prophecy" seemed to lock this counsel in dispute. And even though its significance eluded me, for time past measuring this conference of high souls raged at one another until one sage voice settled the issue for good.

"The Asking Prayer was answered!" he noted, stinging the air of debate with the singular undeniable truth.

What I had done by the answering the Asking Prayer had never been so much as broached by a dragon before. Shimbaghs and rogue dragons were denied the power of summoning and could not answer the ritual. Only those enlightened in the Mastersinger's school knew how to summon the power to answer, and they would not have called it into being, for it would have marked The Time, the Ending of the Days. I, in my need, had called the source and it had come into my being; its name had fallen upon my lips. God had answered my prayers, but for a price, it seemed. In my struggle to survive, I had become the unwitting agent of destiny.

The Asking Payer, I was to learn, had a tradition as old as the pygmie's time on earth. In any confrontation between the two, The Asking Prayer was always made by the man but never answered by the dragon, According to the legend, if the dragon were to repeat the prayer, it would turn upon him like a sword. From that point on, the Asking Prayer would turn into a Ritual of Banishing. Rather than define the dragon as they had done in all times past the pentagram and the cross could expel him from this realm of Earth. Not only the dragon but all the mystical beasts as well could now be lost forever. The door to our demolition was before us, and I had picked the lock.

By sense of cosmic reason, the power could not be given to all men — only to the man that the dragon had answered. This had been the pact between the Mystic Beasts and the pygmie for ten thousand pygmie years. One hundred score times before had the Asking Prayer been offered. Never once, until now, had there been a reply.

There were some avenues for escape. Since the power of banishment only belonged to the man who'd asked, the Captain could now be among the most powerful of his kind, could wield great influence and could devastate all magic — *if* the Captain were still alive, and *if* he were not struck dumb. If the Captain were not dead, and if he could be found, he could be killed or silenced. That would end his power and save the dragon race.

But he could only be killed, so the prophecy foretold, by the dragon who had answered him. I was that dragon.

It was not until later that I was to learn all the ramifications. Yet I had learned this much: I had become the Chosen One, the Answerer, a creature destined to hunt this dragonhunter down and finish my business with him. For that, this Shadow Council ruled, I would be kept under special scrutiny, subjected to the most rigid tests the MasterSinger's School could devise. Then I would be readied to undertake this monumental quest. I would have to be ready by the age of 22—a master year by any measurement.

Yet even then there was no guarantee that he'd be found. Where was he now, this Captain who brought morality to the immoral act hunting of dragons? Even with their powers of scanning to secret realms unknown, even with their telepathic gifts of silent wisdom, these elite of the Shadow Council touched upon his scent.

"His aura must be deathly low. He's come to that dark door. We're going to lose our single chance at reconciliation."

"If he is, that's the end of it. So we're the better for it." a pair of warrior dragon lords continued to debate.

"Don't bet your crystals," said an older, wiser Master voice. "The prophecy has come to pass intact. And lest you doubt its verity, I suggest you cast your eyes on this one here."

As he spoke, I could feel the energies of all the Shadow Council turn their heated gazes back on me. "A streak of lightning scars his chest put there by an evil hand. He is, as was foretold, the Lightning Dragon."

This drew the last measure of doubt from the Council that I—charred on my heart for all my life with this livid mark of Cain—was the one they would call the Lightning Dragon, a deliverer of sorts. Of this the Master Voice would say no more, except to note that free will would mark my future path and my destiny was my own to make and choose.

"In the meantime, what of this Captain?" the old sage voice inquired.

"A well untapped is water yet untasted," the feminine voice spoke out. "He shows the promise of a human being who can reason out his powers, who doesn't heed the counsel to abuse them. He doesn't walk with other men blinded by ambition or sell his soul for subsidy by wizards. In all of this there's cause for hope. We behold a higher conscience in him. And anytime there are minds such as this, there dwell for us the friendly spectres of fortune.

"If he is alive, we'll feel his energies return," the Master Voice replied. "We'll monitor his recovery but give him a very wide berth. He is a source of harm to us—until The Time. Until The Time."

"But how will the others know him?" a serene young voice inquired. "Mere energies on this plane of life can be a bit confusing."

"He bears the mark of evil on his chest," the Great Voice answered. "The brand of RuSiva, the Lightning shard. The same as young Shartallion."

Even though adrift in limbo, the mention of my name by one so clearly exalted sent a surge of strength through me that revived my spirit more surely than any medication could have done. Destiny of destinies, I was born to the task. Just a notch out of the nest, and I was already charged with purpose, a mission to be fulfilled. Thrice blessed is the soul who from the beginning can know the course his life, who can set his sail and catch the wind of Fortune.

I had a brother of the brand. I had a twin by Evil's hand. A valiant dancer among men to make my start, to mark his end! My path was his. His fate was mine. What could we do? Until the Time, so it had been. So it would be, until The Time would set us free.

Canto 4

The MasterSinger

It Might
Be the Light
 in an Angel's tear

Or it may
Bring the Way
 to the Bringer.

It Could
Sing the Truth
 to all who will hear

But the Song
Still belongs
 to the Singer.

 – The MasterSinger
 Lesson 12

We had aged before our time, my baby sister and I. Looking through the veil of years it seems a trifle now, but it was devastation for us then. Through salves of winter's recompense in a mountain sanctuary, our bodies healed from all the wounds these men had wealed upon us. Our hearts and minds still bore the scars and always would, it seemed; forgiveness is a language only angels know to speak.

Eventually we learned to play as dragonettes again. Yet we carried the weight of three and always would. At times we sensed a wicked purpose in the subtle movements of day and shuddered when we saw the shadows of night. Our fragile shell of innocence had been shattered for all time; it was a most deformed initiation to this world. We needed so desperately to be shown the shape of our purpose here. And to that task our mother, Drilg, addressed herself entirely.

Dager had made a mince of the army, had driven RuSiva from our midst. After that he brought us to a mystical aerie where our lives hung in the balance, and The Shadow Council had put us in its Surgery of Lights. The rest was up to Drilg, our mother and teacher. To protect us from the frozen nights of winter, she forged a crystalline tower where we could feel safe from that world that had shown its darker face to us.

There, in the warmth of its stone and jewels, Drilg fed us the harvest grains of autumn, the herbs of the honeyander tree, and the eggs of the generous Géle Ostrich. My mother lit the loving fires of winter with her tongue and shielded us from the icy Northern Wind.

"Korlig has a bite," she'd say.* "But he has a sense of justice. He'll soften the sting of his breath against my wing."

---

* *Korlig.* The blustering, obstreperous wind god of the North, he is said to have been born in the North Star. Although foul of temper and rapaciously candid, he is also said to be fair, occasionally sensible, and certainly better balanced than the rest of his mad clan, the Tarewinds.

She sang to us of Edens past and poetized the present. She was our only harbor of calm in this stormy sea of souls.

"I'll speak to you only of beauty. It's all that really matters. There are generations of others to teach you all about the rest." She reminded us of our brothers the birds, of our sisters the seasons, of our children the clouds, and our cousins the other beasts forged from the same sword as we—the unicorn, the gryphon, the Chimera, and the Gamberol, the Rahntish, and the Kohmm; and the mystic Mantilough who vanished with the morning dew.

"These are the creatures who carry your light. Look to them when you're in trouble. Give them refuge when they come to you for help. You can rely on them always. They will not deceive you. And though some of them may not bear you love, they will always honor their word.

"With others, you must summon your instincts. There are good and bad among all beings. Use your powers of discernment; they're the dragon's unfailing friend."

She told us that the secrets of the dragon's strength lay in the understanding that there was life in all things, and in that life a soul, and in that soul a oneness. And it was only when one life form perceived itself as absolute and dominant over the rest that evil could ever come into the picture.

"Power is the issue here," she said. "It is the grand illusion, and lust for it is the greatest flaw of all." A tinge of bitterness swept across her face; then she would speak no more of it.

These lessons were not new to us. By then, we'd heard them all. Drilg's sweet entreaties had filled our ears so often that in some small way we'd grown indifferent to them. Aphorisms lead a fragile life, and many had been lost on us. Circumstances had scarred our psyches more than words could heal.

Despite our mother's good intent, we had seen too much in three days to ever accept a homily offered as innocently as that. Take birds, for instance (and you could take them). The Magpie was the first we'd met who'd dared to broach our lines with what he disguised as social intercourse. If this were a brother to our kind, then spare me the incest of his seedy conversation. And as for power!? Why, power on this plane of life was apparently all that mattered. That alone was the bone of contention between the dragon and this pygmie, and were it not for our ominous size and mystical force of flame we'd be meat on someone's table right now. Such were the ways of this wicked world. Such were the gods they divined. Such had been the fate of my brother in it.

Rather than pain my mother by giving tone to these rustic thoughts, I simply blurted out, "Nothing's quite as simple as it seems." In any case, she read my meaning and answered it with care. "It's true," she said, and then would say no more.

In the spring Drilg led us eastward across three mountain ranges and four shoals of water to a broad, lush, valley where creatures shared their venue and harmony ruled supreme. There, in this well-concealed apron of land hidden by a cathedral of trees was a forest filled with magic and a human village carved from the land by skillful, caring hands. High upon a mossy cliff where no one feared the dragon, we sat with Drilg and watched the season pass.

Here in this Valley of Harmonies, I reveled in what may have been my happiest season on Earth. No longer threatened, safe at last, my mother at my side, I slept beneath the stars at night and in the daytime watched the unicorns bring the fleeting rainbow as their train. Unicorns in grazing herds sipped nectar from the fruit trees and called to us as soul mates in survival. Our cousins, the chimeras flew in thunderous flocks, landed on the rocks around our mother and told her saucy secrets that made her laugh.**

** *The Chimera* was a beast who had the head of a lion, the body of a goat, and the wings and tail of a dragon. Though not prodigious in terms of size, the chimera was believed to be a fierce fighter and, when provoked, one who could vomit flames and whose howls brought thunderstorms down upon the tribes of man. Some of this is true. Chimeras could be pretty nasty when brought to the test but were, by nature, docile. In the early days, they were garrulous fun-loving

They flew away and, in their noisy barking conversation, brought a trace of lightning and the showers of spring.

Day-in, day-out, the children from the nearby village brought us harvest wheat and great green melons. Old sages of the human clans came and sat with us and talked to Drilg in tongues that we had yet to understand. And when they left, waves of peacocks, pheasants, sassy blue-tits and finches, wrens and robins flew in flocks to peck the leavings of our feasts.

At times we'd watch the other Mystic Beasts where they found comfort—the ever-roaming rahntish, and the dazzling unicorn. We even found traces of the ephemeral Mantilough.

The unicorns were arrogant and swift, with a pride that mocked the wind, and a sense of remoteness that only the loving Mantilough could soften. They carried the host of man's most wanton secrets. They were the creatures of high romance, and in their single uni-horn held the essence of human potency. In the lore of human beings the common myth persisted that merely to touch a unicorn would bring them love on wings. Entirely devoid of subtlety, the pygmie thought it smart to strike these mystical horses down and bring their hides to their cities where they could sell a stroke of them for a hefty price indeed. But pygmies have never understood that death has no magic in it; by slaughtering their mystic friends they had begun the dreadful process of slaying their own dreams.

So now the unicorn herds were forced to sift through silent forests, hiding in the shadows of a chilly afternoon and whispering the secrets of the night. But their whiteness carried purity, and their equine beauty could haunt even the most indifferent of voyageurs. I marveled at their strength and grace, at their legendary courage. To be in their presence made me feel the ugliest creature on earth.

---

creatures who only wished to serve all creatures and be left free to roam the lands of the East. It was only later, after the Last Shimbagh Wars, that they were made to turn hostile, hunted down and destroyed to the last one.

They let us come to a clearing and hold counsel with their herd. They were cordial but o' so very cool. It was a distance kept more out of caution; that I understood. Somewhere in their evolution trust had fallen victim. The noblest one among them, a beast of iridescent white, danced in circles of protocol at the trine we'd set on the ground. He was a rippling specimen, a prince among his kind, and held himself more proudly than anyone I had ever seen.

"You gawk, dear Dragon, at your friends," the Unicorn Prince cried out. "You feign some sense of empathy for what we call discretion. You think us weak that we hide from man, but we haven't the dragon's tenure. And you'll learn soon enough that too much attention can be the darkest curse. You may intimidate them now, but the pygmie is resourceful. You'll pay the price for your pride if you haven't already."

"You're wise, dear Prince," my mother answered. "And yes, the human grows, often in ways that terrify and depress me. But the Mystic Clan is strong, my brother. And if we keep our bonds, nothing can destroy us in the long run."

"Is it kindness or naïveté that makes you seem so gentle? My queen, you've always had my respect, but now, you've my pity as well. Bask in the world as we see it now. For we stand in the sights of the Ender. The days of the mystics are flesh, and man is the arrow."

The Unicorn Prince tipped his horn politely and led his herd away softly, as if they were carried on clouds. And though there were scores, they vanished behind a wall of willow trees without so much as the sound of a single hoofbeat.

The Rahntish were a different clan—herds of exquisite deer with multi-colored wings of eagles that flared like rainbow sails in the drafts of summer, carrying them aloft in the sky whenever they came of a mood or needed to evade a confrontation. They were equally fleet of foot or wing, both genders carried antlers, and they spent their days in frolicking as if they hadn't a care. They never fought or strived for power in tests of territory, as was the custom of other creatures. They only fed on fruit that had already dropped down from the tree, and they wouldn't even trod on fallen flowers. So docile and so beautiful were these wondrous flying deer that I couldn't help but wonder how they hoped to defend themselves. (In later days I was to learn that they were a match for any. That their antlers were tipped in arsenic, and their tongues turned into adders' venom whenever a force of evil would appear. Then they bonded together in herds to form a fist of spikes and a phalanx of deadly tongues that could fend off any army of assailants.)

"We greet you, dragon brothers and sisters," the Rahntish Lords cried out. Some flew up to join us during our swifting driftings through the sky. They flipped and rolled and cried in laughter at the freedom that they felt.

"There's a noble strain of humankind in these latitudes, dear friends. There's hope for them after all, if there are other nations like this. We've been here for a generation without so much as a frown; they only applaud our speed and grace and bring us fruits to eat. Their children pet us and ride our young (and we're careful not to harm them), and we carry them home before the sun goes down. We know we take great risk in this, but these humans are worth the gamble. It is the soul that matters here; their hearts are pure, we know."

The Rahntish were our constant companions, and it seemed such an odd mélange to see the beasts of fire and flame with such gentle creatures as these. It was the magic of this place, the best of all possible worlds, and I couldn't help but wonder whether I'd see its like again.

During our entire stay in this Valley of Harmonies, Drilg never once condescended to us or tried to ply us with philosophies of life. She simply let the light of these moments leave the salve of their healing, and carry a message of hope into our hearts.

I was in my element, here. I glowed in the richness of it. In tribute to my brother Karman, I sang ballads to the colours of morning, and though I could not yet speak all the tongues of Mother Earth, I played each day with the human young and carried them on my thorny back. Had I known then what I know now, it would have been much better had I stayed and never tried to find the night.

Seti knew. Alone among all the beasts of magic only Seti, distant Seti, stayed back and would not be persuaded by the poetry of the moment. As if she were a guardian over us, she tested every gnat that flew our way, watched the horizon for the invaders she was certain would finally come, and kept her paranoia to a finely sharpened edge.

"There's a price to pay for all this dancing," she growled, in admonition. "Don't say I didn't warn you. This place is Aberration, an island of illusion in a sea of holocaust." That was the extent of her pleasantry and may have marked the height of her caring, either for me or anyone else on this plane of life.

There was a moment when I thought her right. One shiny brilliant afternoon, the sunlight glistened on a column of soldiers mounted on horseback and wearing pleated armor—not the gleaming armor breastplates that had adorned RuSiva's men, but crude, disfigured pelts of skins and hide. They seemed to make their way for us but stopped. Catching sight of dragons hovering over the valley, they gave their venture second thought and turned their caissons to the south. We were to find out later, they were a warrior horde seeking tax and plunder from the villages of the east. But upon sighting our formidable triad, they knew this valley was protected by magic. So they took their nasty business further up the road.

A village elder passed this on to us, and the story seemed quite logical. Still, the motions of it haunted us; Seti most of all. From that point on, she watched the horizons and would not close her eyes. I closed mine, and it seemed that each time I did another week had drifted by.

By the end of summer the weather grew hot, and the land dried to the hue of golden wheat. The people from the village, dressed in gaily colored raiment, held a festival in our honor, formed parades and groups all gathered in the happy chaos of civic ceremony. Line after line of merrymakers danced around in silken centipede dragons, blowing powdered smoke from their clown-faced cartoon heads. It was sport and frolic, and their jollity lit the day. Yet all this celebration was orchestrated to a plaintive tune. After the villagers snaked in column to our roost, some leaders from their ranks gingerly trod to speak to their Queen of Dragons. They knelt before our aerie and, in oaths of supplication, held out their hands to ask that they be heard.

"Great Dragon Queen of our homeland," they called up to our ledge, "bring us a summer rain to save our crops."

It was an easy wish to grant. The dragon was a brother to the skies, and the clouds in these climes were allies to our quest. Gracious guest that she could be, Drilg granted the village masters their requests, set herself in flight and changed the day.

It didn't take her long to do her work. In graceful circles, she weaved her way through patches of sky and, cocking her jaw, called with thunder from her voice. It was a power to summon even the chimeras would have envied, for in the shifting of a shadow's moods in early afternoon a bellicose flock of thunderheads lumbered in from the mountains to the west.

Drilg returned to resounding cheers of the human throng below. Accepting their adulation with aplomb, she landed at our cliff-top perch and gathered us to her side. The coming rain would signal the end of our tenure in the Valley. It had been the Kunlun Dragon's legacy in decades past to bring this parting gift, and now for another season the dragon queen had fulfilled her role.

Drilg did not regard us for awhile. Taking measure of some distant realm where another consciousness reigned, she waited until the energies were right before she spoke.

"Old Sagro's ready. I know his call. It steams from the stones beneath us. It's time to take you to the MasterSinger's School."

The inclination was strong to ask all about the School and this great instructor whose name had crossed the lips of others with such awe. But some queries are best if left unmade, and this was one.

We took our leave at night. Torches of the villagers lit the roads over which we flew, while they—like living votive candles—waved adieu in adulation. Their songs of praise for the "Dragon Angel" came from their hearts and lifted us into the sky as surely as the breezes beneath our wings.

The journey to Old Sagro's school was a scarred-sky passage south, then west to a majestic mountain range. Though my sister's skills at flying were no more up to mine than mine were to my mother's, we all were tested sorely on this voyage. For days we flew through hard gray tempests that barred us from the sight of land, a test it seemed to the limits of our strength.

Drilg never opposed the forces of Nature directly. She charmed them instead, won them over, made them want to be her allies. She slipped along the thunderheads, avoided their wrath, and used the power of their raging breath to aid her in her flight. Although stronger now than ever before, I had not yet learned my mother's sense of the ebbs and flows of time and air. I was losing sight of Drilg and, through the rain behind me, could no longer see my sister's struggles to catch up.

Suddenly, when all seemed lost, those same burly thunderheads changed to cirrus slips of white that seemed to guide us home to the open throat of a volcano. Not a dormant hole greeting us with slight warmth and casual frothing, this mother mountain growled. Between its popping brimstone rocks, a narrow cavern shelf pointed the way below to the MasterSinger's realm.[***]

Breathless, dodging living stones that lashed out as if to reproach us for daring to enter, Seti and I trailed behind our mother. Obeying to the letter her admonitions to follow her closely, we glued to the hot ground beneath us while an ocean of

---

[***] There is a mention here of *brimstone*. In anticipation to certain questions: yes, brimbrod shards do come from brimstone. Before brimstone can be formed into brimbrod shards it must be cooled, crystallized and aged thousands of years. Then, and only then does it retain its corruptive magical powers. Otherwise, brimstone is just a hot foul-smelling rock with a deservedly lousy reputation.

pitch lay just ahead. With fires from her mouth Drilg did her best to light the way, but in this dark immensity her arcs of flame were little more than candles in the wind.

Terror is never so terrible when one can behold its source. But this was different. Inside my mouth I tasted the metallic bite of fear, and the emptiness a soul must feel when coming to rest in a void. It intensified with each step we took, each beating of the wing.

Finally, from a source I could never quite define, the pathway ahead grew light. And in time the stifling blackness had transformed into a second sky glistening with a hundred thousand multi-colored crystalline stalactites, celestial spears pointing downward to prohibit our entrance to heaven. Below, along a winding pathway that heated beneath our feet, there yawned a canyon of shining gems: diamonds, rubies, amethysts and bloodstones; emeralds, sapphires, tourmaline and jade; each reflecting colors with an aura of its own.

Through this shower of reflections we followed Drilg until we came to a point exactly halfway to the bottom. There we stopped at an escarpment and dared to look below. A thousand feet farther down surrounded by a million teeth of diamond-ice and crystal, flamed a lake of pure white fire. It beckoned to me with a force my instincts nudged me to obey; obey, I would.

"Don't be afraid," Drilg told us, "Fire is the dragon's birthright. Whenever it calls, answer it."

Without further study or so much as a parting kiss, she bade us well. "We'll all be changed when next we meet," she said, and with a hiking of her wing swiftly sailed from sight without a goodbye. As she departed, the dark path behind her closed like a distant door, as if it had never existed at all and could never be found again.

Deprived of options, we took the plunge into this lake of white fire. Before we knew it, we were diving at speeds far beyond our control, plummeting toward the silent flames below. With a soul's desire to soar, I somehow caught control and instinctively brought my wings out to brake my fall. Slipping through fire, which burned like ice upon my body, I felt reborn to an unbreachable silence, a sepulcher of quietude from which there was no exit. Surrounded there in the cold white flame, I could neither hear nor see a trace of anything, except the silent heat of my own thoughts.

Finding no measure to the moment, I waited and wondered and worried that this might be an end to me, that I had been abandoned, left to be punished for my sins, to be exhumed in flame. I wondered and I thought and feared and wept and screamed until there was no matter to any of it—no dread, no joy, no highs nor lows nor vapid inbetweens. At last I knew an emptiness—that and nothing more.

It was then, and only then, that the MasterSinger came.

Spires of crystal, curtains of ice, veils of steam communed to mask a looming faceless silhouette whose eyes I could not see. Instead, I could feel them cleansing me with total understanding. At the time, I could not tell if he were Seraphim or dragon, but from the outline of his back there arched a set of wings in rainbow-patterned plumes, and from his being there glowed an aura so radiant and pure it numbed my earthly senses, filling me with a levity so high that it brought me to leave my body.

I couldn't hear this being's voice or make him out at all but felt instead a presence filling me like a gourd with the sweet wine of serenity. I lost all track of time, all sense of place, all need to be. I simply was a soul at peace, comforted and whole.

§§§§§§§

Never go to sleep when you're in heaven. You may wake up to find things somewhat less than they had been. After a doze of some duration, I opened my eyes to see that my etheric haven had taken on a stench and density for which I had no reference. Where once there had glistened a brilliant realm of diamonds, lights, and fire, there sat in its place a dank Triassic cavern around whose dripping pock-marked ceiling swam voleries of bats who darted back and forth from wall to wall,

from rock to ridge to dodge the jaws of hissing *cavern crogz.*
Immense amphibians with sucker pods where normally feet
would be, with mouths like toads and teeth like crocodiles, these
crogz looked more like rocks and rills than creatures with a
heartbeat; until they struck. And when they struck, their hot
pink tongues shot out to snare their prey and suck them down
their gasping vacuum throats.

Below, what had been a lake of holy light where we'd spent
heaven in a night, had now become a bog thickened with mud
and muck and mire. If indeed there were a Hell, it had a rival
here in this swamp too filled with scandals to record.

As if to strain the limits of our toleration, this lower realm
was filled with roaches, mantises, flies and arthropods of every
genus ever known, all with hungry eyes and appetites to match.
They slid about the oily waters that slipped up through the filth,
and might have abounded had it not been for *skinjie fish.* These
raunchy creatures, partly fur and fins, had chewing teeth at head
and tail and ate anything that could be swallowed. I counted my
blessings that these skinjies only measured a foot or two and
gazed up at me with worship in their eyes. Since they apparently
adulated dragons as close to gods, it created an irony that they
would soon become our pets.

Little more could be said of this place except to note its
essence could be caught entirely in our host. No angel of light
cloaked in crystal columns sat before us now. Instead, entangled
in a mass of webs and moss, a doddering old dragon sat snoring
like a tremor winding down. Streaked with grime, pocked with
wounds of ages on his tired old skin, this decadragon scarcely
had a tooth to call his own. Yet even as he slept he chewed
incessantly, while on his head a graying, spotted, shriveled rat sat
having his supper, furtively plucking lice from the decadragon's
brow.[†]

[†] **Decadragon.** A dragon that has lived more than 10,000 years. An
extreme rarity even among dragonkind. Decadragons are also called
dragones, another name for a very old dragon.

He paused long enough from his parasitic vigil to alert his master to awaken. That would prove no easy task, and the gray rat seemed to know it. He stomped. He sang. He danced. He prodded; then he poked and jabbed. He even called the decadragon's name a time or two.

"Sagro. Sagro! Wake up. Your umpteenth class is here! Wake up!" Just as happened with all before this went to no avail. Old Sagro, like a tatterdemalion at a crossing station, yawned and snored right on. In a gesture of futility, the gray rat shrugged his shoulders. Then, watching as if to fix us in our place, the little vermin cleared his throat and let out a whistle so shrill it could have made a banshee pale.

I used my wings to cover my ears, but there was still a ringing in them. My sister, rousted awake by the whistling, recoiled in horror at the same discovery of this new world that earlier gave me pause to think.

"What the hell is this?" she roared.

"Lesson One," the decadragon answered, cocking one eye open as if it were Seti and not the gray rat's antics that had brought him back to consciousness. "And Lesson One is: Illusion. Everything is illusion. Unless, of course, you choose to make your reality. Then everything is reality. The choice is up to you. You may choose your realities. And you may choose your illusions. So, what'll it be?"

He cocked his open eye at us, expectantly, then closed it down again.

"So this is who we came halfway around the world to see?!" Seti snapped, aside to me. "A lot we're going to learn from this old fart!"

Although she'd said it in a whisper, her words sent up a maelstrom, a force of foul hot wind that stirred up the bog in which we sat and blew Seti half a hectare away into a cranny of rocks. She landed with a jarring thud that knocked her halfway silly.

"Lesson Two," the decadragon said, half-cocking his eye like a bloodshot sun that had never seen a clear day. "Each thought has a life of its own and every single word you say is a prophesy fulfilled."

With that remark he cocked a brow and waited for my reaction. Since at that point I hadn't a clue about what to say or do, he took his four-horned tail and scooped a mound of mulch into his mouth.

"Well," he said, chewing while he spoke, "that's enough schooling for one day. We'll talk again tomorrow." At that, he finished chewing and went to sleep.

§§§§§§§

While Sagro slept and Seti recovered from her costly indiscretion, I thought of what the lessons for us had been. If I gauged this old dragon correctly, he wouldn't be wasting his words. So it paid to take everything he said to heart.

If everything was illusion, this was illusion. If everything had the potential to become reality, then I would transform this illusion into a reality. If my thoughts and words had life, and if that life would be fulfilled, I would command it to be perfection that I beheld. For days on end I beheld a world of utterly flawless beauty, of radiant lights and endless gem-filled bounty. I beheld and concentrated and spoke of it in conversations to myself. I repeated affirmations and all the prayers I'd heard. I strained and tried and worked, until the energies ran from my body like a creature bled to death—until, at last, I gave up.

My abject failure, so it seemed, again awakened Sagro. Absently scratching the rat off his head (and knocking him into the bog), he bent down to whet his whistle, took a gulp of brown swamp water, spat out a skinjie fish or two, and drank it down.

"You have the right idea," he said, "but your timing's a little off. Energy creates reality. The greater the energy. The greater force it imposes on its world. Right now, you're in my world. My energies prevail here. These are my rules by which you play. And I choose this reality for your to learn in."

"Why this?" I asked.

"Why not?" he answered.

"Why not the other? Why not the lake of fire and ice, of diamonds, sapphires, and serenity? Why not learn in that?"

"Too many distractions," came the answer. "Besides, all souls must go low before they can rise high. That's the law of incarnation."

"Can't get much lower than this," I thought, remembering not to say it, but I had only remembered part of the rule. The simple energy of thought had pulled me into the mire, sucking me into a vortex through hot tars and groping hands. Through all this suffocation, abandonment and dread came wails and shrieks and astral cries of pain that set my soul to tremble. But before I'd sunk too far below, a mighty talon seized me, plucking me out of the steaming muck like a canapé from a tray. Sputtering and gasping, I was hauled up to Sagro's face, with a quick and kindly answer on his tongue. "Oh, yes it can." Like a monkey with a banana skin, he tossed me back into the bog.

Typically, Seti wouldn't miss a chance at ridicule and let me know the absurdity of my state. "You look like shit. You silly git!" But her laughter was cut short, for no sooner had she loosed her fusillade of ridicule than she too was sucked below. Plucking her sputtering from he bog, Sagro lifted his eyes up skyward as if he were calling some higher source for help.

"A hard case," he said. "I'll do the best I can." With that, he tossed her back. She landed with a splatter next to me.

Off to one corner, ridiculing our humiliation, the gray rat chattered away, scrambling back atop old Sagro's head to pose in sycophantic splendor.

I didn't like that little vermin anymore than I cared to endure this caustic hole into which we'd fallen. What's more, neither this sniveling rodent nor his toothless doddering mentor represented anything that I would emulate. Suddenly it occurred to me, there were so many inequities in this place I decided to speak against them; and damn the consequences!

"This isn't fair!" I shouted up to Sagro.

"Who said life was fair?" the old sage answered.

"But you said we could create our own realities. Lesson One! Lesson Two: Words and thoughts have lives of their own! That's what you said! But only negative thoughts have lives in this place, it seems to me! I've been thinking positive thoughts and saying positive things for days. And nothing works!"

Sagro kept a quiet mien. Passion, I came to learn, was not a wheel on which he ground his axe. He waited for me to cool, then scooped a plug of mulch into his mouth.

"Lesson Three," he said, chewing at length. "Negative is easy. Positive is hard. This one isn't easy to accept, I must admit, but consider where we are. First, this form, this carnal matter where we *all* are in the flesh, is "negative" or we would not be in it. All mass is formed by charges of negative energy, which in turn solidify; basic physical law. So on this material plane negative manifestations come much more easily. If you are to overcome them, you must do more than think positive thoughts or to speak positive words. You must *be* them.

"If you fear you cannot be. If you love you can be anything and anywhere. Fear is the negative matrix. Love is the positive matrix. In matter you are the former. You must learn how to evolve to become the other. That's why you're here in this crock of dross right now. To cook out the impurities, as it were."

Taking the gamble on further repercussion for her actions, Seti turned to me in disbelief and sneered, "I don't understand a word of it."

Seeming to anticipate, Old Sagro swept a mossy morsel to his mouth. "Lesson Four," he retorted, oozing moss to the tip of his chin, "Any rule that can't be understood isn't worth remembering." With that, the decadragon nonchalantly finished his snack and vanished on the spot. As he did so, it appeared as if he'd forgotten about the rat, for he had left the little fellow in disarray dangling from a dead tree branch.

"Well," I thought, quite vocally this time. "If we keep getting our lessons at this rate, we'll be out of here in no time."

Hearing that, the little rodent pulled himself up to balance on the branch. "Lesson Five," he snipped, almost pompously. "Nothing's ever as easy as it seems." With that proud proclamation he slipped and landed with a splash into the mire and vanished as Old Sagro had before him.

§§§§§§§

One can never quite prepare for what comes next. Here in this subterranean swamp bathed in light from sources unkown, we waited for Old Sagro to return. It might have been a day or week that he was gone from us; there was no telling. There was no point of reference in this place. There were no planetary movements, no subtle shifts of day or night to give us mark, to let us know our hours on earth had measurement at all.

I couldn't help but wonder what the old dragone was up to, but if I'd learned a thing in our brief encounters it was this: Old Sagro wasted no action. There was purpose in every single move he made. He'd come back soon enough all right; of that I had no doubt.

We fretted for a time, of course; that was only natural. But having at least some intelligence, it hadn't taken us long to learn that worrying would only buy us a pot of woe in this bog. So we worked at keeping our noses clean. I thought high thoughts and held pure fantasies, though they did not come easily in those surroundings. Seti, in her turn, astounded me with good behavior. She neither ranted nor raved, and when she spoke she would only make the most positive allusions to her well-determined destiny.

"I'll be a warrior empress," she'd sing. "The greatest there has been! I'll spawn a horde of dragons like the world has never seen!"

She continued her war song, verse after verse. And though it had a sinister ring, I had to admire her sense of purpose. She knew what she was to be: the Warrior Dragon Queen. She was born to it, and everyone could see it.

I was a study in dissonance. I had been empowered by the Shadow Council to wear the "Mantle of Destiny" and carry some uncertain quest of holy retribution against a human who, by every measure I had of making, was not all bad. Beyond this ordination that I bore reluctantly, I had no sense of what was in store for me.

Even in the silences, I had no revelation. There were only dark images of futures I could not see. Some were awesome. Some were fierce. Most were simple and eloquent. (Those I conjured for second looks and heard my angels singing. I could not tell what song it was, I only knew for certain, it was something that I'd longed to hear.)

Those times alone in our circumstances brought my sister and I to share this world around us. I grew accustomed to its dankness—even its stench. Eventually, I found amusement in watching the mortal games of tag between the cavern crogz and bats go on above us. In the muck and mire below, we learned to play with the skinjie fish who, when they were not devouring every other thing of lesser size in sight, would lock their head teeth with their tail teeth and make themselves into furry hoops for Seti and me to toss in games of catch. We even acquired a taste for the salty mosses and mulch that grew like mold along the dead trees of the bog. They didn't offer the passionate delights of the great Thral melons of the Khomm or the eggs of the two-headed Géle Ostrich, but there was a savory flavor to them reminiscent of berries, nuts and leafy grasses.

One day, in our foragings we came upon a cave inside the cavern. Even though it was hidden from our common eyes and even though we happened upon it by a seeming stroke of chance, its sweet breath bade us enter. Its air was clear and cool like the breath of autumn, a crispness about it that offered sanctuary from the dross of the cavern swamp.

To our surprise, its mouth was ample for dragons of some size to gain easy passage. And once inside, we came upon a rare and delicate find—mushrooms the size of lions' heads, of deepest violet and radiating such an aura they cried out to be plucked.

Drawn to them as if they were a sacred feast, I reached to pluck one up and savor it while Seti, looking on, recoiled in horror.

"Awful to the touch, I feel. Deadly to the taste, I know. Don't say I didn't warn you."

So she warned, and so I chose to ignore. Yet as I did, as I reached to pluck these luminescent living things from off the cave floor, I saw Old Sagro loom before us.

"Lesson Six," he said. "Follow your inner truths."

"And if they contradict those of another?" I asked, as if I'd known he'd been there all along.

"Your truths are *your* truths only. They belong to no one else. What is poison for one may be heavenly host to another. Each soul is different. Each vibration is unique. Each vulnerability is individual. You can only know by listening inside yourself. In this case, you have fared well. These radiant violet mushrooms you see here are the potent leaves of the *vulpa*. They are planted by the OrfBears and are placed here just to test you.[††] For the male of the dragon kind, they are a feast of revelation. They fill the soul and open the gateways to new senses of perception. For the female of the dragon, they keep a fatal pact. They are her death of flowers, the perfume of her pathway to

---

[††] ***The OrfBear*** was also known as the "Gem-watcher." A giant blue bear nearly ten meters high, the OrfBear was very gentle, almost completely blind, except in caves with very dim light. Though by a hex deprived of normal eyesight, OrfBears could sniff out all kinds of rare exotic plants, herbs, and fungi such as the violet vulpa mushrooms which only bloom for three hours on moonless nights under cloudless skies. The vulpa mushrooms cannot be seen by the naked eyes of men or other creatures of the earth's surface. They're only visible to bats, lizards, and the subterranean OrfBear.

another life. When the draga decides her work on this mortal plane is done, they show her the way to the next."

"They poison her," Seti answered in a show of common sense.

"If you care to put it that way…"

"What other way is there to put it?"

"It's all a matter of timing. What may seem poison to you now, may be a transitional preference at some later date."

"Don't bet your smoke," my sister snorted.

"I do not choose the truths of others," came the decadragon's answer. He stood studying us both, pausing as he did to gauge more clearly, and as he did, the small gray rat reappeared atop his head, nattering in his ear as if to answer some silent call for counsel.

"You petition no truths of us," I challenged. "But you petition truths *for* us. You hold us captive in this filthy bog and lecture us at your pleasure. And you do so without ever having asked our names or ever having told us yours. We live on faith and assumption of things that may not be right at all. Then you nearly poison my sister to prove some point that may have no point at all. What kinds of truths are these, I ask you?!"

Dangerous ground, I had to admit. Thoughts and words have lives of their own, especially when they went against this dragon master. But we'd taken all we would. Someone had to bring this old codger to account and damn the consequences. And when all was said and done, it might as well be I.

"Lesson Seven," Old Sagro answered without batting so much as an eye. "Question everything…"

"We have," my sister interrupted, "for all the good it's done."

"And once you've learned the answer," Old Sagro continued, "then learn the value of faith." He graciously awaited our reply, but we had none to offer. The gray rat too paused, standing astride his master's head and crossing his arms solicitously.

"You've already learned some lessons well, I see," the dragon sage continued. "You question well enough. But do you believe? No harm was done with the vulpas. I appeared in time. But what of the other things you've learned. What do your inner truths tell you now—about me? About yourselves? Have you figured it out?"

He waited again but not for long, for in my heart I already knew he was the Sagro, the dragon sage of ages, the MasterSinger come to teach us well. And we were exactly where we'd put ourselves, cavern, dross and all.

"It's good," he nodded, reading me clearly. "Your truths are well intact. I am Old Sagro. I only say what you know because words give comfort to thoughts that burn. And to give you further salve, my little dragon prince, you are Shartallion XII, the Lightning Dragon, scarred by the sorcerer's mace. 'Dragon of Destiny,' they say. And *they* are usually right."

He turned his attentions to my sister. "And you are Seti IX, the fires have told me. Forged with a warrior's steely mien and cursed with a warrior's pride. You'll get your wishes, little one. You'll be all you want to be; that much I guarantee.

"Of course," Old Sagro, as ever, took the counterpoint. "I tell you what I see. I stake no claims to prophecy, which brings me to Lesson Eight: Prophecy is a fool's pursuit. No one knows the future. Time does not exist for God. So the rest of us entrapped in this illusion look on to far horizons claiming futures as our own. We seek to know the time ahead by looking into mirrors that only reflect our energies for now.

"Mirrors are the thieves of life. Yet it's the mirrors we perceive. There's only one reflection of the self that counts; the inner self. Yet we spend our lifetimes obsessed with images. I've been guilty of it, in my time. And in your time, so will you be. That much prophecy I know."

Some thoughts strike chords inside the soul. They sing a song so perfectly attuned that every cell of the living being answers in celebration of their truth. So it was when the MasterSinger spoke like this. And yet some lower part of me, a balanced part I felt, couldn't help but ask: Wasn't this too rich a serenade? How long would it take to take it in? Or were we being taken in right now?

Old Sagro cocked an eye at this. Reading thoughts as deftly as he did, he knew I was taking a perilous route. Yet I felt the question had merit, and he gave it the respect it deserved.

Clearly having noted my silent query, he replied aloud, "Receiving lessons are one thing. Learning them is another. And you'll be given time to learn. Have no fear."

"How long?" my sister asked aloud.

"Only as long as it takes."

Sagro's answer, made in a way that barred retort, ran with echoes along the walls of the cave. He speared a vulpa mushroom and popped it into his mouth. He followed it with another and bit off a morsel for the rat who perched on his nose, begging a share. The rodent caught these potent crumbs but paid the price for doing so. He tripped, tumbling in somersaults and headed for a crash until the dragone caught him with the back of his wing and guided him to ground. There at his feet, the rat crouched, shivering, his eyes dancing peevishly from place to place about the cave—first to the vulpas, then to the walls, and finally to us, glaring down his nose at us with a kind of peevish admiration.

There was more to this little vermin's comings and goings than I had first surmised. His fleeting bouts of clumsiness now struck me as a pose. There was too much intelligence behind that frightened gaze to dismiss him as merely a denizen of this subterranean swamp. And I couldn't help but notice too that Old Sagro and this scrounger were never far apart for very long. It was then I came to understand that, whatever I may have thought of this tiny satellite, he could not be overlooked. Overlooking little at present, I could not help but notice that neither Sagro nor the rat were nearly as attentive as they had been before. Having partaken of the vulpa both seemed to have been simultaneously thrust into dimensions that overlapped our own. Soon, they were awash in fantasies, wholly immersed in worlds to which we'd not yet been granted invitation.

"It seems that lessons may be traduced as soon as they are learned," I ventured to Old Sagro.

"Oh?" he rhetorically ripped his reply, scowling through one eye barely open.

"Like Lesson Nine," I said. I don't know why I knew what Lesson Nine would be, but somehow I'd just learned it. I hoped that merely by giving it mention I might at least pull some enthusiasm from Sagro. But, as I might have guessed by now, my hopes went unfulfilled. Sagro grunted, burped, and smacked his lips.

Receiving no response from this stoned old fossil, I dared the answer, anyway. I cleared my throat and said aloud, "Lesson Nine: Nothing ever happens by chance."

"Nothing?"

"Nothing," I answered.

As if it were a gong to mark the moment of my folly, "Wrong," tolled the sound from deep inside Sagro's throat.

"Then what is Lesson Nine?" I asked, somewhat out of frustration.

"Lesson Nine..." came the blithe, insouciant answer. "Never Deal in Absolutes." With that the dragone closed his eyes, his chin dropped to his chest, and he didn't awaken again for what seemed like a month.

Canto 5

The Great Orf

Thank heaven for the gift of chance. Without it the universe would become so perfectly ordered even God would die of boredom. Without these little nymphs of whimsy to tear away our expectations, we would freeze in all our icy fine perfection, and expire.

I didn't know the truth of it down inside that school. I know it now. Old Sagro knew. He knew I'd have chance to learn firsthand, for while he danced with the rat in some hidden ether where souls such as those collected their fantasies, my sister and I grew restless.

I tried to reexamine the lessons we'd learned thus far and came at once to Lesson One.

"Perhaps this is illusion," I thought aloud, watching Old Sagro snoring. "Perhaps he's testing us."

"Looks real enough to me," said Seti, drumming her tail on the ground as if she were announcing a call to arms. "But

whether it is or not, I've had enough of this reality for a while."
Carelessly she slipped away, probing the pathways beyond the
throat of our cavern, sniffing as she did so. Although a dragon's
not a hound, such actions aren't all together out of character for
us. We have an excellent sense of smell but never sniff
compulsively, unless we catch the scent of treasure or
Shimbaghs on the wind. For that reason I soon became aware
that Seti's aspirations had taken a compulsive turn, punctuated
by deep-throated sighs that crossed the bounds of ecstasy. By
now, she had to have penetrated deep into the cave, and though
I called her time and again, she didn't come back to answer.

The essences that poured out from that cave spelled peril, yet
there was a drawing force from within that I could not deny. And
yet I did. Out of some filial sense of concern, I had to look for
my sister (at least that was my rationale for snooping).

As I made my way deeper into this place, I felt the cave
become a labyrinth, a course of twists and turns that led to
nothing but dark ends. My only reference through this trek was a
faintly floral odor, drawing me toward the left-hand bends along
the way until before too long I'd come to be enraptured by such
feelings of sheer elation that I too felt giddy and inclined to
laugh. The dark walls all around me illuminated, and with that
luminescent hue, there poured forth an aroma so sweetly
exhilarating it made me dizzy when I breathed.

This alien bouquet was a narcotic to my senses while the
source of its light soon grew so bright it nearly blinded me. Still,
I couldn't resist the urge to press on. Lured there by the sweet
perfume, propelled by an urgent need to reach the epicenter
before I lost this glimpse of paradise, I banged the sides of the
caves like a rampant randy boulder and surely would have
knocked down any obstacle in my way. Just as I found my
desperate passion reaching its crescendo, the walls about me
widened, leading me to a divinely sculptured chamber whose
crystalline vapors radiated in a way that bedazzled me—a sacred
gemstone gallery, a mosaic of precious stones more bountiful
than I could ever hope to count.

Was this reality? I wondered. Or another fantasy? And while I wondered, I heard my sister whisper-shout to me.

"Shhhh!" she hissed, beneath her breath. "You've the subtlety of a earthquake! You'd wake the dead if given half the chance!"

Above her, atop a mound of gems that seemed to tower to heaven, there lay a giant blue-black OrfBear, dozing. I had never been in the presence of one but had heard it described so often I'd already seen it a hundred times in my dreams. Even so, this massive creature beggared all description. A burly monster with deep blue fur, he was no less than thirty feet from nose to toe. And even though deprived of eyes (as the world has come to know them) he was a rippling hulk — more than a match for anything that walked.

It was spoken of in legend that the OrfBear race were blinded for all time, because the Prime Bear of their clan had made a pact with a Shimbagh Witch: all the gems the OrfBear kin could gather for all time in return for an article of theirs of value that the Shimbagh witch desired. It's said that no contracts made with Shimbaghs ever bring a bargain to the taker, and this was no exception. This witch demanded the OrfBear's eyes as payment, and eyes it would have to be. For generations, at the birth of every OrfBear cub, the Shimbagh witches came, plucked the eyes from their small sockets and left these orfcubs sightless, whimpering and without hope.

But the Orfs were not without allies. To their aid the dragons came. And though the dragons could not give them their eyes they even went one better. They gave them the gemstone from their own third eye — the holy sapphire. These sentient stones helped the Orfbears learn a keener sight, a cool deep sense of every single creature large or small. Now, though blind and without a sense of vision as we see it, all OrfBears could smell a warrior horde a hundred leagues away, could hear a poem whispered through a maelstrom, and could taste honey in the dewdrops of a flower stem. And with their single gemstone eye

they had a second sight; the foresight to see into other realms
and places far into time.

All this might have served as a gift for a being in its rightful
mind. But the OrfBear had become a creature cursed with his
obsessions. By compulsion, he would cultivate the violet vulpas,
deadly to every creature save the mighty male of dragons, and
would plant them at night for unwary travelers to feast upon.
This was not an evil act, for the OrfBear too could eat them, and
in fact derived its power from the partaking. As for other living
creatures, well...*caveat emptor.*

The vulpas were not the problem here. The "stones" were
another matter. For their worship the OrfBear had lost its eyes,
imprisoned by its desires. Now, from generations of obsession,
the Orf had grown into a violent custodian of treasure. Once it
found its mount of gems, it slept atop them, bathed in them, and
even ate them on occasion. It could feel their heavenly energy
but never behold their beauty or see the colors that reflected
healing. Materially, this creature had desired them. In material
terms had it been paid; and until a key unlocked this curse the
OrfBear would be blind, tied to treasure by the chains of its
desire.

There was another aspect to this creature, both ethereal and
fatal: that was its breath. The OrfBear meant no creature harm,
preyed on nothing, and ate nothing more than vulpas, gems, and
gold coins dipped in honey. When it slept or when it sang its
soundless winter songs, it breathed a scent as floral as a garden
of delights. But when aroused, when driven to defend its cubs or
treasure, it could belch a gas to drop a mammoth in its tracks.

The mighty dragon, with quite an oral arsenal of his own,
could stand the great blue bear at stalemate, could neutralize its
vapors for a time, until one or the other ran out of breath.
Usually, if it came to that, the dragon would prevail; not always.
Nor did the apprentice dragon ever stand a chance. Even if the
OrfBear were to keep its breath in check, it possessed a godly
strength and foot-long onyx claws that could tear the hide from
any living thing.

Knowing this (for we'd been told of all creatures in our time) Seti stood tantalized and unable to resist his sweet intoxicating breath and the precious stones all dancing in lights before her. It is the dragon's weakness too, this wanton love of treasure; there's no secret about that. But there are degrees of desire that vary from one dragon to the next. Seti's longing for this crystal cache now bordered on obsession. She wanted this prize for her possession—toys to bring her pleasure, a throne of gems to make her sparkle as if she were one herself (a common malady among females of all species I have found).

Was all this materialism her reality manifested? If so, it came with one slight hitch—an OrfBear added just for spice to flavor-up the feast. True to his well-earned reputation, the Orf was a notorious dozer. Lost in the latitudes of his dreams he could spend a year in slumber. Noise could not awaken him, nor could a bump or jolt from some benighted interloper bring him to a stir. The OrfBear was such a mighty beast he felt little threat to his person. His treasure was altogether another matter. Move a single topaz from its mother-lode of gems, and he would rise up and strike with the speed of an earth shear.

Seti knew this going in but had more greed than fear, plunged in her foretalon and scooped out a cluster of gems. Then as if to defy all reason she held those jewels aloft, letting them shower upon her, taunting me all the while for my circumspection.

"Some spend their days just watching life, while others know to seize it."

I dashed to restrain her from this folly, but she had already taken a scoop, this time plucking a single stone—the OrfBear's sapphire eye.

Waking to her gemdance, this great blue bear had burrowed deep into the stones and, biding his time, had waited in angry silence; then, he surfaced. A clear corundum geyser spewing forth his wrath of gems, he leapt into the air then crashed back down on her, seizing my sister by the scruff of the neck and staring her face to face. Instinctively Seti tried to torch him, but the OrfBear shook her as if she were a naughty cub, then gassed her with a breath so vile that she vomited instantly. Drooling in a death-like torpor, she hopelessly hung suspended while the great blue bear—in howls of outrage—hurled her into the ice-white wall some several yards away.

I mentioned that he howled. This was astonishing to me at least, because in all the tales I'd ever heard the OrfBear was allowed no voice for his pain. This was something I'd not expected, for it flashed upon me in the urgent revelation of the moment that this poor ursine monster was tied by bonds of gut and heartstring to the very gemstones that he guarded. Anytime he found a treasure, he became a part of it and was bound by chains of inner self to stay. This had been the hidden key to the OrfBear's struggle for its peace. This then was the answer to the riddle of his curse.

In his frenzy this particular Orf had neither heard nor sniffed me, and had made straightaway to finish off my sister. Waiting until he'd lumbered by, I slipped over to the treasure. Taking pains to verify my newly formed suspicions, I tore some of the gemstones from their housing—just a glittering rock or two, then a sizable scoop. And when I did, it was as if I'd ripped the hide from off his back. He reared straight up and shrieked, a burly ball of fulmination, and made a dash for me to tear me limb from limb.

By now I'd grown two meters in size and felt myself a power, but this OrfBear in his mass and malice dwarfed me like a twig. All the while I didn't move, for at once I'd realized that I could control this day. If I wished to bring this tortured creature to his knees I needed merely to rip more treasure from its roots, and he'd be writhing on the ground. I knew this just as I knew that if I didn't act or move to step aside in just a moment, he could bury his claws in my chest and tear out my very heart. I didn't move, and in that instant, in that microspan of time, I came to feel myself at one with the Orf. I knew his pain, his noble heart, a heart imprisoned from birth, held captive by a pact made long before his time. I alone knew the OrfBear's secrets, and I alone could bring him out of the dark and into the light again—if only I could meld with him, if only I could show him the pathway out of his material prison. His mind was my mind now. His pain was mine. His soul and mine had melded, if only his lower self could comprehend. Bolting at me with mad volition, it seemed that he did not. But in the midst of his final stride he stopped. He rose up on his haunches and came to meet me face to face, his nostrils smoking anthracite flaring with noxious fumes. He sniffed. He growled. He sniffed again. Furious with confusion, he hiked his claw to tear my face but stopped himself instead. Then he breathed a deep and gentle sigh.

It was a high perfume that filled me then, a fragrance so loving and pure it would have made archangels tipsy with delight. In that slight moment I knew an ecstasy more transcendent than the pungent pure aroma of his breath. It was the boundless joy of knowing: He'd felt my oneness with him. He had embraced me as a liberator for his kind. He probed me gently and touched my scaly skin, and as he began to feel, the facets of his sapphire eye glistened with tears of thanksgiving.

It was then I heard a voice behind us say, without inflection, "Lesson Ten: Become One with all things, and you will have no adversaries.

"But then, I see you've learned that lesson well. At least you're off to a good start..."

Old Sagro with the rat perched on his shoulder found my sister hammered into the wall, stuck by her wings like a gargoyle sconce and squawking like a chick. She hadn't died, nor was she injured, but her pride had taken a blow. Without malice of judgment, Old Sagro pried her down, letting her drift without comment to the cold white floor below.

I'd never seen her so contrite, nor would I ever again. And yet at this moment she struck a penitent's pose, spread her wings to cover her body, trying to hide her shame, while Sagro gently raised his admonition: "Lesson Ten has a caveat, and the second part is this: Be mindful of your heart's desires. You are bound to them in fact. You will become whatever obsesses you." Point well taken but not belabored. Seti had all the example she could handle. Still feeble, she nodded her pallid recognition. The MasterSinger wouldn't have to sing this song again.

Held fast in my cosmic dance with the OrfBear, I felt the strain of music rushing through him by a transcendent light. A peace now crossed this ursine monster that, to this very moment, I'd never sensed from any mortal thing. Though at one with him in time and place, I could not quite discern what had transpired, and yet I knew: in a very sacred way this tortured soul had been granted absolution. Sensing Sagro in our midst, the great Orf turned to him, his gem-eye glistening, his mouth agape, a sounding of sweet airs.

Standing before the MasterSinger, the OrfBear genuflected. Old Sagro helped him to his feet, and though the two said nothing, a whorl of white light descended and drew out their oversouls. Above their bodies these resplendent forms converged to some decision I could not hear but could somehow apprehend. In time the light ascended, these higher selves returned to their lower forms in ways that left these beings changed: Before my eyes the great OrfBear began his transformation into a flower, bright and brilliant, standing taller by far than any on the earth. Where it had been forced in life to breathe perfumes both beautiful and vile, it bore no scent this time. And where the Orf had been cursed to see no light and hide inside the earth he now would bask unbridled in the daylight, covetous of nothing save the sun that blessed us all. In fact he even named himself: *the Sunflower.* And to this day in parts of earth, I'm told it brightly blooms.

Ever after, I was to learn, this would be the fate of all the OrfBears—a fate I'd helped bring forth. I, a magician in spite of myself, had done this! The unwitting midwife of this blissful transformation, I was able at last to behold the product of my labor. By now, this Orfbear breathed its last sweet scent and stood alone and tall, a bloom so bright and golden yellow it brought us joy to behold.

From its center the sapphire, the jeweled eye it no longer needed dropped to the floor of the room like a fallen icon. In an instant, Sagro scooped the gemstone up and swallowed it with a gulp. Then he lumbered from the Sunflower and paced back and forth before me, shaking his great head as if he were dismayed.

"Well you've done it now," he said.

"I have?" I answered, not quite sure of his meaning.

"Quite an impact you make, young one," he observed. "First, you answer the Asking Prayer. Now, you free the OrfBears from their curse, leaving us dragons to take their place. To be guardians of treasure."

"I did?" I answered. Had I betrayed a sacred trust? I wondered.

"Of course!" Old Sagro railed. "Who do you think will guard these treasures now? Somebody's got to do it! The OrfBears were our allies in this bond. Now they're gone. So thanks to you the dragon must take their places, suffer temptations, and risk assaults from the greedy ranks of men. Before, the dragon and the OrfBear were partners. We balanced one another. They guarded the treasure. We protected them. But now with the OrfBear gone, we have another job to do; as if we didn't have enough already!"

Was I hearing this correctly? Could it be that the great MasterSinger, knower of all things, was carping like a fishwife, denouncing this right action as some untoward stroke of folly? I felt the need to challenge, and challenge this, I would. Damn the consequences!

"Is this evolvement I am hearing?" I countered. "Is this the nature of the mighty dragon to regret a noble act, to free another creature from its chains?"

"No it is not. You did the proper thing. The only thing you could." Old Sagro answered, and then he smiled, a mischief-making, self-confessing grin that bared his rotting teeth along with his wisdom.

"Then what is all of this?!" I asked, growing short of patience, for I detested games and always would.

"Call it a test to see if you had learned your Lesson Seven. And so you have, at least in part. You challenged me in my consciousness, and you were right to do so..."

"Games!" I shouted, interrupting. "I'm tired of these games!" The pressures of our tenure here had left their marks on me. As far as I had been concerned, we'd suffered through them long enough. Now was a time for action.

The decadragon read my thoughts, yet placidly spoke on, without so much as a wrinkle in his brow. "Of course, we've planned these lessons carefully so that you may learn them best..."

"What lessons?!" I demanded. "You hurl them at us like a bag of wind, leaving us to pick up the debris. Then you run and hide. We have no one to show us how to use them, and nothing in this wretched place on which to practice!"

To that the old dragone smiled, "You've had everything you need in these chance places you have found. You needed only to recognize it. And recognize you did, despite your mind having told you otherwise. Besides, I've taught classes in legion just like yours. They're all the same. No matter how they learn their lessons here, they forget them in the end; and so will you. They'll wash off your back and out of our mind, and you'll have to relearn them out there. That's the way it is. That's the way of the world. Application is the lesson of this life.

"Then, why haven't we had the chance to apply them, here?!"

"You never asked."

"I'm asking now!"

"And high time too."

"Games! I'm tired of playing games!"

"Good! Then school is ready to begin."

§§§§§§§

Some creatures carry fate in their hands as if it were the child of their own design. It's not that they do so consciously; not on this plane of existence. Sometime before we put life in these physical shells, our souls agree to the task. The rest is left on destiny's waves and the way we choose to ride them. By what I'd done at the Lake of Shards and by my actions here, I had altered the course of things to come and would again, I knew.

By freeing the OrfBear as I had done, I'd fulfilled yet another prophecy—of coming transmutation, of the changing of the guard. Now the tale would soon be spread that the lightning-scarred dragon had helped a brother creature break the chains that bound its soul. I hadn't at all, the truth be told. Old Sagro had granted that grace and did so without another witness to glorify the act. That was just the matter with this. I would be the one for whom the myth-songs would be sung—the mighty Lightning Dragon marked by wizards for all time. Witches would curse me. Men would fear my name. Shimbaghs everywhere would gird their loins for those dark and terrible days when I would come. The world outside would spread outlandish tales of my adventures. And here I was, a dragonette as yet without a clue.

Old Sagro told me of these things before he brought my sister up to join us.

"I tell you this that you may understand a little better, so that the world will not offer you any more surprises than it has in store already, and so you might learn right here and now the most important lesson of all: not to take yourself too seriously. Others will do that for you. That's their cross to bear; don't make it yours. Just remember, whether you transform everything you touch or whether you die tomorrow, it's no big deal and neither are you. The sun will rise, the earth will turn, and another player will play. The universe will be what it is no matter what we do."

In a while he went to nurse my sister, passing his wing across her, gently seeing to it that she revived. As if a divine wind had whisked across her, she came back to herself. Rambunctious, feisty, and alert she barked for retribution, looked sideways for the OrfBear and was only satisfied when told him that we'd helped him make his transition.

Noting how things had gone with her, Old Sagro gave me a wink. "Lesson Eleven. The Double One. The Master Number. Learn this and you will need no other rules.

"The dragon is a treasure trove. A strand of gems marks his essence from head to tail enriching him beyond the scope of physical means to measure. This treasure cannot be taken from him except by deep betrayal. And it cannot be owned by another, for in stealing the dragon's treasure the thief's own consciousness pollutes him, and he soon too will perish. I tell you these treasure secrets now, so you may see in them the destiny that you may carve from these rough cuts. But understand in the beginning what only the highest of beings know in the end. All spiritual creatures stand in reach of these mystic crystals. Few have captured their secrets. Learn them, and you have mastered the game. Each dragon must take his journey alone, and only when it is completed, only when all the jewels are found—and all their facets learned—will you gain the mastery of this Lesson.

"It was no accident that you found the OrfBear's cavern. Finding treasure is in your nature. But finding treasure is one thing. Being one is another."

Old Sagro paused to let us weigh the impact of his words, but his pause gave only time for prompt reaction.

"Humpph," Seti grumbled. "If this is really the only lesson worth learning, then why bother with all the rest?"

"Because, little warrior princess, I can count the souls by the hairs on my nose who've stayed to the end of this one. Rare is the dragon who wears five gems. The dragon who wears six sits among the most high. And Seven! Not a dragon in a millennium can take that diamond crown.

"So hold to those other lessons, Seti. Learn them well. They may come in handy when this eleventh one eludes you."

"Why does it have to 'elude' us?" I asked.

"It doesn't," Old Sagro agreed. "Everyone learns the lesson in part. They get what they want, but not always what they need."

"Then why not learn it all?" I asked, knowing fully that I would.

"Why not, indeed?" the decadragon said, with a sad, indulgent smile.

§§§§§§§

Lesson Eleven, the double one, the jewels of our potentials, the secrets of the powers to which we all aspire. No longer would we spend our waking hours in this subterranean swamp. We stood ready now to play The Game! This was the reality we had hit upon—the OrfBear's gift for us: His precious cache of gems would be the gate to our gembox baptismal, the unlocking of the door to our inner self.

The gray rat was careful to remind us that we'd been lucky to have made it here. "Your collective consciousness brought you here." He whispered aside to us, casting a furtive glance about, lest the master dragone should hear. "You could have done much worse, you know. There are classes I've seen—believe me!—that have spent a score or more of years down in this bog.

"You've come quite far quite soon. You've started very well, but where you end up is altogether another matter." The gray rat had never waxed prophetic up to now; nor had he ever entered conversation with us two. Yet he picked this occasion to go on talking, running up and down both his discourse and his master's leg as if they were newfound fancies for his busy little mind. An odd diversion for the runt, I thought, his running to and fro, until I saw what prompted his saunter. For while the rodent dazzled us with footwork, the decadragon changed, transformed himself into a younger bolder being.

He was still no masterwork of physique, mind you; there was yet Old Sagro in that body shell. But his visage had softened, markedly. Neither toothless, decrepit, nor sad of eye, he was a stronger creature now, more fully formed, imbued as though his once elusive life force had returned to him again.

Through a gaze that sparkled with azure light, he roared with sheer unbridled joy that challenged our resolve. "So you think you're ready for the Double One...We'll see. We'll see." Taking our measure, one on one, he read our thoughts aloud and laughed. "Well some of you are and some are not. But that's what this is all about...Isn't it?"

In the months that followed (in fact they were years) the MasterSinger sang. In his songs we learned more lessons in the one than we ever could conceive. And those lessons were hard and hardly come by. By rhythms we could come to count Old Sagro would isolate us days on end and have us sit in silence, silences through which our busy minds would run until they grew exhausted. It was only then the truth would come; I could taste the honey of it. Truth, when tasted, leaves a precious flavor on the tongue.

It was in those times, those lonely journeys into self that I could feel the MasterSinger sing his songs most clearly. With eyes like fired antimony and a tongue that poured ingots of amber flame, he locked me in his third-eye sights and poured into my open vessel of a mind the arcane secrets that were his to share.

"The stones are seven that line the dragon's body to his soul," he said. "Master each and you have climbed another step toward your enlightenment. Master all and you have reached your highest destiny. But heed a word of caution here. Each step along the way is both perilous and tricky, and each gem can seduce you with temptations of its own."

"*The ruby* fuels the scarlet flame that lies in the dragon's loin. It is the power of his passion, the well source of his personal force. It is his blessing and his curse, for in its higher use it burns away the clutter of the world. It warms the hearth of loving homes and forges the ploughshares of our friends, the innocents, the men. In its lower aspect it is a blaze of retribution, a Nemesis we summon to punish the pervader, the Shimbagh and the drone, a furnace for the greedy pygmie who would slay us for our secrets. In combat this fire rages to a searing heat the sun would claim as brother. And God help the adversary—be it Titan, lord or man—who tries to stand before it. When cooled, the ruby fire unlocks the secret of the dragon's speed in flight, a secret only few are meant to know.

"But be forewarned. If worshipped as an end unto itself, this scarlet messenger of purity can kill, can consume its holder with compulsions to destroy, can fill him with a fire of rage only death can bring to a merciful completion. Such are the burdens of its power. Handle the fire with care.

"*The amethyst* is the stone that forms the dragon's shield. From its facets come his rock ridged hide, his armor that covers him head to heel, the power that protects his throat with an orb of gem light no weapon made can pierce. Bronze cannot harm the dragon. Iron has no will. Gold will not strike home to wound him, for gold is the dragon's spirit. Steel can cut him and drive him down, but it cannot finish the job. Of all the metals found on Earth only silver can find the weakness, for silver is the Earth Mother chalice of our clan. It can both bind and free, can kill and resurrect its dragon kin. When put in the hands of the knowers, the wizards, it holds the dragon's fate in check, and only high knowledge of the purple stone can set it free.

"*Liquid onyx* is the dragon's blood. It is the hot volcanic earth of early times that courses through his veins and unifies him with all creatures of this world. It is his insight and his foresight, his own gut contact to the great Sol in the sky. The high dragon's blood, like the water of the holy sea, is pure. Carried in that purity is a prescient understanding of all things yet to come and a power for self-healing that cannot be matched on earth.

"Yet, it's a shallow dream of men to think that simply by drinking the dragon's blood they can make his powers their own. At best this lust avails them nothing. At worst the blood can drive them mad and make them slave to those who sell such illusions of mastery. Your brother paid the price for this, and so, very nearly, did you.

"From the dragon's heart comes *the crimson garnet,* the very core of his courage, and from that core is born his gift of flight. His power is fueled by the fire of his loin, but his heart is what masters the skies. The bolder his heart, the stronger his wings, the quicker his speed, the broader his range. It is universal law. It's what sets the dragon apart.

"Beneath the Sons of Draco's tongues, *the gleaming emerald* sits. It's the shard of a crystal wave of light that rises from the throat. From its radiant atoms flow the strands of all the cosmic network. Not just languages of men, not only the cries of beasts, but also the breaths of flower and stone can find the master's tongue. It comes through the Node of Empathy, the sacred gland of the throat that connects the light of each soul directly to the other. Once that fluency is found, the simple gift of speech comes just as the tail obeys the kite, following in its flight yet guiding it to its purpose. The dragon who wears this radiant jewel may speak with equal fluency to king and cockroach, to river and sky; all tongues are one, and all are his.

"But pay equal heed to this: the dragon who has come to know the tongues of Mother Earth cannot use them in a lie, for if he betrays the truth a single time, he will lose his ear to the Powers who give it.

"From the dragon's eye comes an azure glow. It is *the sapphire* that lines the path to his soul, the power of the lapis and its once eternal single sight that lets the seer see through cloud and veil. When thieves in guises, invaders in mail, and wizards with agendas try to work their will, the Sapphire Dragon foresees their corruption and warns his magical brothers of their intent. Baked in the oven of their own fears, these miscreants turn to stone, desiccate and blow into the night. Truth seekers need fear nothing from the dragon's cool corundum glare. He will see them too for what they are. The pure of heart may ask anything, and the true blue dragon will answer. Yet there is a lesson in all of this. Only a master can master this stone. On its own the mind is the Deceiver, and arrogance of mind is his fatal foe.

"At last we come to the ultimate gem, the crown for the dragon's head, the crypto-crystallis of clear white light, the Venus hairstone that iridesces from the oversoul. This is the transformer, the radiant *Diamond I.* The Diamond brings time and space into one while never losing the essence of itself. Knowing this essence makes the high dragon the master of illusion. He can become one with the microbe or one with the sea. He can wear their form and make them become his own. Yet the peril in this is dire.

"The Diamond is a maze of facets whose mirrors face one another, catching themselves in infinite airs can trap the *poseur* forever. Whoever steps into the Diamond's realm must know himself in truth. Or else he may enter and never again be free from his disguise."

Abruptly, the Sage fell into a silence that caught us like a slap, its quiet gravity drawing me into my physical self again. By now, I had become a war-zone of inertias. My brain was teeming with a plethora of questions that my higher self assured me were *de trop*, and yet my thoughts steamed onward, forcing their way through a body that rebelled, a mouth that would not speak, and a tongue that had surrendered its forte.

Whatever I desired to know at any level would, it seemed, not be mine for the asking. Yet, although I sat before this master dragon dumbstruck with understanding, all my questions came alive in the queries of my sister. She spat out questions in so rapid a fire even Sagro was hard pressed to answer; in fact, he did not.

"It appears each gemstone has a power complete unto itself, does it not? And each of the powers overlap to some greater or lesser degree? Then if each power is complete and if each overlaps into the other, the dragon who learns but a few can master almost anything that dragon might encounter. True or not?"

The answer wasn't given right away but came, when it came, slowly as if it were cut from a reluctant host.

"True," Old Sagro slowly acknowledged. That and nothing more.

"Then even three or four stones whose secrets are mastered could render the dragon invulnerable to anything upon this plane. Correct? Or do I err?"

No pause preceded his reply this time. It came like a slow roll of thunder across the decadragon's lips.

"No creature that takes its house in flesh is invulnerable. To be born in this skin is to die to this skin. Those are the rules, and the dragon is no exception. The dangers to us are many, and it is wise to note them all.

"Steel can lay the dragon low if thrust in just the right place. Silver can slay him and bind him to the earth. Water in too great a quantity can dampen his ardor. Torrents and monsoons that seasons bring will stupefy the dragon, plunging him into lengthy hibernation. And the sleeping dragon, as we've learned, is as vulnerable as a babe.

"Brimbrod shards, sham garnets that they are, will put an end to the dragon's flight, will drug him, ground him, and turn his wings to lead.

"Shimbaghs with their teeth and claws are weapons poisoned in the cauldrons of the pit. And even when they merely strike the dragon's hide they can leave wounds that can fester on his body and can drive him quite insane.

"The Firestone is an element not of this world. It came in a meteor from Draco, our constellation home. It is the stone in which we were formed, and if it is ground to powder and tossed upon the uninitiated dragon's body it can turn him into a cinder on the spot.

"You have seen this done; you know. But you don't yet know the rest: the dragon's ashes in themselves contain the secrets of long life. They're the food of transmutation of all metals. Alchemists have been known to sell their souls to get it. (There's a reason.) Gold can be made from our bitter dust; the witches and sorcerers know. And whenever the rest of the world finds out, the dragon will be hunted down until the end of time.

"Then, just so that I don't forget, there's necromancy, magic, and the conjuring of demons, not to mention poisons, potions, charms, enchantments and spells. A baker's dozen, I would say, can put the dragon under. So, before we take our intimations of Godlike powers to extremes, let's all grab hold of a little perspective here. To give our modesty an added touch, let's all remember this: the Asking Prayer's been answered. Now there lives on earth a man who, by passing his sword in a certain way can make us disappear, vanish from this plane of life as if we never had skins at all."

"If he lives," I heard my own dry voice cry out. I'd come into myself again, drawn down and earthed at last.

"He lives," Sagro answered, "though not yet back in 'the thick of things,' as it were. Like you he goes through guided preparations of his own. It should be quite a match when you two get together; and you will, I'm sure."

"Prophecy is a fool's pursuit," I said, reciting Lesson Eight.

"One does not have to prophesy the truth. It simply is. This truth you always know. It's in your bones."

Food for thought tossed my way by Sagro while Seti pressed her issues, firing the final missiles of her queries.

"Of all these 'dangers' you describe, most are made by man. More than the Shimbaghs, I do detect, the pygmie seems to be the one who threatens us, *n'est-ce pas?*"

"So it seems," came the answer, in a matter of fact.

"Then why do we even coexist? Why waste our time? From what I've seen in this short life of mine, the dragon can have his way upon this Earth. So why not have it? Why not rule? If this pygmie sets his sights on us, let's turn our fires on him and have done with it? We have powers to immolate the world, and it's time they knew it. So why not this pesky hybrid first of all? Seems logical to me. He's the very reflection of Evil as I see it.

"And every image of angels, I've ever dreamt of seeing. Something doesn't fit here in the least." I added the last of these observations, though it didn't come from me. It was as if a second self now spoke for me.

The MasterSinger didn't answer, though the rat did in his place, stomping his feet and dancing a ditty of protest. "No, no, no! No, no, no!" He repeated like a mantra, collapsing at last into a breathless heap against the horn of Sagro's wing. Sagro sighed and looked away sighting some faraway answer. "There are some vile creations among this entity called man. And, even though touched by angels, he's slow to wisdom and ever quick to folly. The light of heaven still terrifies him, so now for now it eases his pain to seek sanctuary in the familiar caves of his consciousness. He sees evil and exploitation in all things save himself. What's more, he's the only one with the power to put an end to us."

"All the more reason to put him out of his misery and have done with it!" Seti snapped.

"I've heard that argument countless times."

"It's the only one that makes sense!"

"By all logic of survival, I suppose."

"What other logic is there?!"

The dragone looked upon my sister with the sadness one reserves for one whose soul is lost and always will be. "There *is* a higher logic," he answered. "But console yourself with this: Our fate is tied to his. It's our debt to pay."

It was here I again inserted myself. "What debt?" I asked, and asked again, for truly I wanted to know.

"When you're ready to hear the answer, rest assured you'll be told." He didn't want to dramatize, but it called for nothing less. He paused as if to weigh his words, a gesture in which he'd seldom indulged before. "Now you start your journey of gems. But before you begin, remember, a creature who's learning is a vessel into which a host is poured. For good or evil, once the host has risen above the rim, there's very little room left for other things. But hardly any cups run over, so pouring is a tricky game. Just fill it as best you can and be prepared for what comes after."

There was nothing left to say. He'd said it all for now. He led us away from the dome of light toward a pair of dark holes on the other side, cold black passages heading downward into limbo, toward a place I could never hope to fathom.

As usual, the situation never fazed my sister. Seti, without blinking, made a bee-line for the left, her cold-cut linear voice calling out from behind.

"What the hell, it's six of one. It's all bullshit, anyway. Catch you at the bottom, broh, whatever the hell that means."

While she dropped out of sight, I froze in place, ever the cautious warrior, until I heard the MasterSinger say, "This is one path you do not choose. It chooses you. What is beyond is everything you ever dreamt of, everything you ever feared. It's everything you want to be, but not unless you enter. It is your christening. Have the courage to go forward or go backward forevermore."

The voice behind me was not Sagro's, nor could I hazard to guess, for when I turned to face him he had gone. The gem crown crystal dome had vanished, and in its place sat a chamber without dimension. Faced with that alternative, I headed for the hole, its dark drafty passages calling out as if I were a friend. I left knowing all the while I'd lose my self in there. Another dragon would emerge, the same and yet transformed. That was the greatest fear—sensing that this creature I was about to become might be someone I wouldn't like at all.

Canto 6

Gembox Baptismal

*"Is the treasure worth the fire
that fronts it?
That is the test of desire."*
— *The Chthonic Chronicles*

This was the finding time. Here in the blackness, in the stillness of Nil, left with no other resource but my self, I had to probe. Along cold smooth passages, pulled by some lurid gravity I could not see, I traveled downward. The journey must have taken months, though in this timeless darkness with only silence and my soul there were no hours or days or weeks to measure. In and out of chambers stripped of light whose dimensions were only measured by the resounding of my breath, I pressed on, trudging downward as if I knew that soon I'd touch the very core of earth, fearing when I did I'd find it void of hope and marked by no way out.

Fear clutched me. Many times it seized me by the throat as if to choke me to death and leave me without so much as a breath of flame to carry on. Here in this nothingness I'd remain— forever condemned, untouched by love or hate or any living thing. This was the greatest fear I'd known or would ever know again. Abandonment! Anonymity! were the final expressions of Hell. What could one dare to look for after that?

After time I changed. So familiar did this desolate emotion come to be, I grew to understand it—not to hate it but instead to wear it like a shield I carried on before me in the darkness. I came to treat this master taunter Fear just like a friend, loved its coldness, and recognized it was a seedling overgrown and overburdened by the weight of an entire universe whose worship of it had raised it to a god. When I came to comprehend it and give this demon love, it could not stay. It fled me like a whore right after payment.

Finally, the cold dark way was broken by a light, a glimmer of ruby red radiating an energy that reeked of pheromone and put out a heat so searing that it broke a sweat on me.

The closer I came, the brighter the light and the greater the heat did burn, until I came to stand directly over it and saw a brilliant ruby stare me in the face. There was an eye that glared upon me more terrifying than any I had ever seen. Even the gaze of Dager was the glimmer of a nix compared to this.

All the while I stared deep into its depths I could see all the Shimbaghs of the Pit spit their caustic gases up at me: all the drujes, demons, khados, kingus, witches, bitches, stragas, specters; all mavens of the Fallen One challenged me to take them on.

It was a horror, this ruby stone, wrathful yet compelling. It had no voice to make its feelings known, and yet I knew its intentions. Either I would find the courage to seize it from its sinister setting and drink its scintillating essence, or it would suck me down into the maelstrom of lost souls, into the eye of the Demiurge to become one of them myself.

Dancing in the midst of them singing with such splendor it might have formed a web of angels breath to line the path of heaven, was the Magpie. With arachnaic skills, he spun his pretty paradise, weaving all around him such a world of sweet serenity where a creature could lose his soul and never miss the taking. This was a ruse of which RuSiva was a master, and masters know the limits of their skills. But patience will forever be the victim of ambition, and soon enough this wizard flew his colours. With a blast of anger he had torched that false Nirvana and now revealed for my young eyes the hellishness beneath.

"I am the master of your fate," he said, with eyes that drew me in, with gazes that could rival any mystic beasts for their impassioned stares. "I hold the core of your successes in my hand. You will be mine and you will thank me for it. I will abjure, disgrace, torture, kill and maim all whom you hold dear, and you will bless me for having done so. You'll be my captive, my dog's body, and you'll *love* it. It's written in the folds of time, and you cannot erase it. You cannot burn it away or change the course."

All the time he spoke, a claque of Shimbaghs cloaked as dragons clapped and drummed their tails along the walls. Not just any dragons—these were females, dragas, wantons, breathing hot perfume and ululating lewd remarks that I cannot deny excited me.

Some passions go beyond resistance, and my glands were out of control. I wanted to fly toward all of them, crush and conquer them all, rape them, mate with them, enslave them, become their Beast of Hearts. I wanted to join them in their lust, to dive through the ruby's facets. And yet a breath of clarity gave me pause. It was not the time for this. For me to have answered this beckoning would have meant the loss of my soul. Yet it was so sweet in its decadence, every bit of it stoked my passions, touched me with temptations that I'd never known before.

I nearly did it anyway. What the hell, there'd be other lifetimes. If I were to bypass this little test, I could find another life. One a little less demanding, I surmised. This heavy mantle of destiny was all too self-important. No wonder we were trapped in this pact. We'd done it to ourselves. Life was simple, it seemed to me: Take the pleasure and run. The rest was little more than cosmic bluster.

The alternative was pain. Merely picking this ruby up brought the sting of a thousand suns; too much even for a Son of the Flame. I did this at least a dozen times. Yet every time I did the ruby caused me to shrink back, to withdraw in agonizing pain. The thought of the bite of the Sun on my tongue, tasting my own mouth ignited, feeling its wicked flavors fill my throat, caused me to blanch. But Flame is the Dragon's brother. We were fired in the kilns of Draco. Our souls were one with this element. It was the passion and the power, and the very source of life. Could it be so soon that I feared again? Didn't fear arrest me? Wasn't that the only pain that could have punished me now?

I picked up the crimson stone this time and popped it like a candy. And though it ate my tongue, I drank it down. Though every facet cut into my gullet, gnawed at my stomach, sheared its way along my groin, I felt the uncertain elation of an angel gone to Heaven. Then for a moment I thought I'd die, that I'd be driven mad, that I was a vessel far too fragile to contain such a violent force. In a time that seemed interminable, I saw the energies transmuted. I felt an implosion of power slowly rumble deep inside of me, filling me with a cool crimson well-source of control. It grew inside me with such a searing heat that soon I felt as if a sun stood like an archer in my throat, waiting there with white hot arrows to launch at my command. It was then that I realized I'd earned my dragonfires for sure, for when I drew breath to let my happy airs of celebration out, a hot vermilion flame blew forth that could have turned a day for half the world.

No darkness now would shadow me. From this point on, I was the source. I was the light to guide my self on this journey through the gems. I'd become a torch in the darkness to cut the throat of night. Whenever the demon Obscurity threatened, I knew I'd been forged in the flame. I was ready now for whatever came.

§§§§§§§

In time the path ahead grew blue and cold as a
somber light drew near. The light, a lambent violet, brightened
with each step as if my feet had trodden on a Titan's drum.
"Kohmm! Kohmm! Kohmm!," the sounds echoed resounding
rhythms in cadence to my ever quickening steps. I moved with a
certain cautious ambition toward the searing purple ray. No
sneaking up on this one. No suzerain's arrival could have drawn
more fanfare than my own. Even louder than before, my anxious
marching thundered like a cosmic calling card. "Kohmm!
Kohmm! Kohmm!"

As I came into a larger room, a chamber glowing in hues of
white and heliotrope, I stopped. There were many passages on
the other side and yet to reach any of them I knew I'd have to
make my way across a web of milk-white silk so finely woven it
could have snared the breath from a neutrino.

It was enough to give me pause. From the moment I beheld it
I knew it was the chamber of a Kohmm. I had recognized when I
approached that sacred web that the Kohmm played a terminal
game. Only fools dared play it, and surely they would lose. But
damn the peril! I had thought. The Kohmm were the dragon's
allies. These spiders of the Thral had made our swaddling
clothes, had spun the silk that lined our nest. And though I'd
never seen one I had always heard they respected our clan, paid
us homage, and brought us special gifts.

I'd never had to face a Kohmm, though tales of this
arachnid's sinister beauty had long since grown into legend.
With bodies of clear crystal that glistened in the sun they'd lived
high up on mountain cliffs that overlooked the sea. They were
etheric violet in color and their legs were amethyst shards said to
span five meters. They worshipped the sun. They basked in the
light of day where they weaved their silken threads for the
creature young of all the world to take and spin into a million

garments if they chose. They gave of everything they had and asked for nothing in return.

Although a deadly foe (as anyone could see) the Kohmm were by their very natures timid. They gathered their food from the air plants of the mountainsides and drank only sprays of sea mist as it blew upon their webs. Occasionally, they would trap a passing hummingbird in flight and milk the nectar from its throat before they set it free again. But that had been the extent of their exploitation.

Yet the Kohmm carried inside their bodies the deadliest of venom for which there was no antidote on earth. It was a weapon they used seldom and only to protect their own. Often that necessity arose, for it was widely known that the female of the Kohmm laid eggs of amethyst crystal, each one housing a spider young. Not only were these amethyst eggs jewels of such chromic intensity that they could hypnotize the passerby, they had also spawned a tale among the pygmie: If a human warrior were to seize one of these eggs and freeze it before the spider young could hatch, he could forge it into a silver shield and remain invincible for the rest of his natural days.

This was myth and nothing more, and yet like so many it had made its mark. And what it marked was the end of the Kohmm's life in the open ocean air. Hard pressed to defend themselves day and night from greedy pygmies in search of their young, the Kohmm were driven into caves. At first they found open caves near the seas they loved so much. But even when protected by webs of thickest silk, not even that deadly lacework was enough to hold these pillagers at bay. Some of the Kohmm chose to stay and die while fighting for the life they loved. All the rest went deeply under ground into the core of earth; those that did went slowly quite insane.

When in the sky near sun and mist and prana, the Kohmm could be a sister to all creatures, but now in this subterranean world their thoughts, now irrevocably turned dark, made them hate the surface and all the creatures who dwelled upon it.

In spite of that there was some pact the Kohmm had with the dragon, a pact whose nature had yet to be worded in song. I knew the few sky spiders who remained by the sea were still stalwarts among the mystics. Their chthonic sisters, in their mourning, had turned to madness as a refuge, killing all who came their way and leaving the husks behind.

As I looked at the web so finely spun I saw the grim confirmation. Where once there had been warriors charged with life, there now hung a score of empty skins twisting before my eyes like doll-shells dancing in angel hair. Some were Shimbaghs. Some were men. Some were cave bears caught in ventures too near to this arachnid's lair. Some were even dragonettes, dangling by their wings, rattling above me in reminder that "school" was getting rough.

The pattern lay before me now, a deadly veil of sticky silk that lined the way to a crystalline egg with a life source all its own. It lay like a solitaire on an altar, a ceremonial throne, a gift from an arachnid queen seemingly set out just for me. This was the second test for me: the amethyst—my shield of honor—was to the precious egg of the dark and deadly Kohmm. Not a very noble quest to my way of thinking and contrary to the nature of the higher soul pledged to honor life. Or was it a riddle I'd have to solve before I made my move?

I began to pick my way through the web but felt it clinging to my skin like a slattern to a streetlamp. All the while, my predecessors played their empty tunes, their body shells all rattling to remind me of the fate of the rash. But since my instincts told me that this course was carefully staged, I knew somehow that the power I had acquired was just the one to pull me through this day.

From the fire of my ruby crystal, I breathed my first true flame and torched the web with the heat of the Holy Fire. The bodies above me fell to the floor and pulverized in an instant, so that all that stood before me now were the altar and the orb.

It was a prize, this egg, this violet chrysalis. No amethyst could more have graced a sultan's throne than this. What made

it glitter with a light that shined from every facet was the
movement of the fetal Kohmm clawing from inside, gnawing at
its gem-shell to draw the air of life. Not a natural thing, this
hatchling's goings-on, it was an act of desperation as if the air
from within its shell had recently all voided. More intent upon
this struggle than on any precautions I approached to give it
study, and when I did I heard its mother Kohmm. Her strident
voice was a symphony in chaos as she screamed toward me in
challenge. Ready for the throes and poised to strike she raised
back on her crystal legs, her pincers dripping venom, purple
almost black.

"Who defilesss my houssse and covetsss my young shall taste
the kiss of death," she hissed. And she took pains to back it up.
A full five meters by the spread of her legs, she certainly gave me
pause. Yet as I circled her I could see she would not come
forward to attack but moved instead at angles to best defend her
egg.

I was moved by reflex to try my fires once again, to blast away
this sad mad wretch and have done with it. But this was a time
for learning one's powers: when to use them; when to hold back.
And force of logic told me that, as the amethyst was the dragon's
shield, so it was this spider's heart. Were I to conquer her with
my flames, I'd corrupt the crystal's integrity and lose the best of
it.

I also saw another thing: this spider's child was suffocating.
Trapped inside its amethyst shell, its light was dimming. Its
clawing to be free had come to nothing, and soon quite soon it
would breath its last, passing on to something else the life it
might have owned. Its mother knew this too, for her movements
were distracted. Darting first to threaten me then to tend her
dying young, she shifted her attentions. Trying to do both things
at once, she did neither very well.

Negotiation is the child of need. She had something I must
have. If I could offer to save her young, we could form a kind of
pact. Suddenly a thought surged through me, an etheric clarity—
one that could save us all and make the day.

"Spider Queen," I urged her politely. "I mean your offspring no harm. The Kohmm has suffered enough in its time, and I will not add to that indignity. You know the dragon and the heliotrope spiders are Kinsmen of the Kiln. Then you know too, I'm on a quest that begs to be fulfilled. I only ask your help."

The mad possess a quality to supersense the truth. It rings to them in tones to which all others have grown deaf. This Kohmm queen cocked her thorax, lowered her eyes and studied me for flaws. Finding none she paused, still wary, yet ready to hear me out.

I continued. "I cannot help but notice that your hatchling's life's in peril. It needs to be freed, but its amethyst shell has turned into its prison. Since you cannot crack it without killing your young, then let me offer my skills. I need the amethyst for my shield. It's true. But I sense with a gem so rich as this, part is as good as whole. Let me break the shell between my jaws. It will free your young and leave a little piece for me. Enough, I think, to let us keep our bond intact."

"The Kohmm now bondsss with no one," the spider queen said. "We lost that futile luxury a generation ago. Now, anyone who invadesss our realmsss—pygmie, Orf, or dragon—will be killed." The heliotrope spider spoke her piece but spoke it like a mantra prattled by rote rather than driven by conviction. Her body language did the talking now. She relaxed her striking stance and stood, "all eights" on the ground.

Now was the time to seal the bargain, to make the offer she'd accept. "To show you I will keep my word, I offer all I have," I said, "While I have the egg inside my mouth, I'll bear my throat to you. If I bite too hard and your young should die, you may take my life as well."

She paused for quite sometime to sense my energies in full. "Ssso be it! Ssso it is!" she said, finally. Reluctantly rising back on her legs, she granted me permission to caress the egg.

This next bite was to be the most carefully measured mouthful I would ever take. Lying back, my throat exposed to this addled arachnid queen, I took the egg into my mouth. I hoped it might dissolve and let my hot saliva do the trick, but the more I waited, the more agitated the Kohmm became, until I realized that like it or not I'd have to chew my prize. I squeezed my jaws together carefully as if I had a flower on my tongue, and it was done! The crystal cracked. The egg was halved. The pieces floated down my throat. The spider young was free and feisty in my mouth.

I tasted pure exhilaration as the amethyst became my self, but such revelries were not to last for long. No sooner had I felt the surge of such elation than the baby Kohmm had stung my tongue, causing it to swell three times its size.

I wondered if this was my end, if the baby's bite was fatal as well, if this had been the trick I hadn't watched for. My inclination was to bite the little bastard right in half and hand it over to mama *al fornaio.* But since this was a testing time, and even though the image of this place began to blacken right before my eyes I let the little creature slip from the side of my lip and into its mother's waiting arms.

The Kohmm clasped her baby fast to her breast, making elaborate gestures to release me from my pledge. "I cannot harm you now," she said. "The shield iss up. The amethyssst is yoursss to keep, and there'sss a gift besidess: The bite of my young will nourish you. It fillsss you with stores of forethought, some you'll need to get you through the deep black belly of the *Griivre.*

"You've kept your word, young dragon prince. And I've kept mine. Now go! Before we lose the blesssing of thisss truce."

I meant to ask her of the *Griivre* and what mysteries awaited, but I could not. Her offspring's venom still had left me groggy and slow to move. Nevertheless I was aware that my personal perceptions had suddenly sharpened, able to cut through an edge to my senses that I'd never known was there.

I thanked the queen and took my leave, exiting through the only door still opened up to me, a hole through which a light shined leading up, it seemed. Yet, as I approached, I couldn't help but notice this gaping hole was barred in places by stalactites curving inward. They were pillars of ancient ivory, and as I made my way between them I took a fall straight down, sliding out of control along walls so cold and smooth they felt like chalcedony to the touch.

Even my fires, bright as they'd become, availed me nothing, here. Black does not reflect; black swallows. And it was as if I were being sucked down the gullet of some denizen of Brobdingnag, a morsel for a Titan's tongue swallowed live and whole. Dark, rank, putrid oils lubricated my slide, a kind of mucous to digest me once I reached the end.

§§§§§§§

It was the Griivre I was in. Like a fool I'd

strolled into his mouth and even took pains to squeeze between his teeth. I'd tumbled down his throat and now sat in his belly — all because I hadn't used the forethought the Kohmm had awarded me. I hadn't even asked the question: what were these gifts to bring? And yet somehow I knew. I knew the coming of all things. Just as I knew that I'd plummet into this!

The Griivre was a wily creature: part Shimbagh, part dragon, part evil and part good. It was the offspring of a dragon lord seduced by a serpent queen. To be sure not all dragons are good, but be sure as well all Shimbaghs are bad, and *all* serpents are Shimbaghs. Such syllogisms lead us to conclude this at the least: that this was at best a creature in conflict. To the *griivre's* endless confusion and to his eternal torment, the dragon's element is fire; the serpent's is water. And though these elements don't mix well at all, in the Griivre, they blended into hot black oils that hardened to purest onyx.

The Griivre was a serpent with the head of a dragon. It flourished in water but mainly in waters scalding hot. The Griivre could sprawl to the length of a mountain range or shrink to the size of a worm. But always it remained a griivre trapped inside a Griivre — two creatures caught in unholy conflict in one.

As I sat inside this dragon-snake's stomach, I felt its steaming onyx oils baste into my skin, either baptizing or corrupting me, I wasn't really sure. What I could foresee in all this darkness was a double set of eyes observing me. The griivre, the inner being, dark and perversely polite, wouldn't come forward until I spoke his name.

It is not the dragon's way to call out the name of another, for that shows weakness and a lack of understanding. The dragon knows; the dragon senses; the dragon remains silent. The gifted dragon anticipates the name of every living thing; this is the gift of premonition. Since calling out is always a question begging an answer, we leave that badge of insecurity to others.

The griivre, I had to keep in mind, was very much part snake. Snakes are insecure and strike at everything in time. So this serpent, in good time, made his move toward me.

Neither affrontive nor hostile, the griivre was a creature of crafty charm. He never overpowered his guests or ravaged his quarry wholly. Despite his rapacious low intent, he relied upon subtlety to do his visitor in. Knowing his abilities lay in striking at just the right moment, this sly dragon-snake took his sweet time sizing up his victim: he could sense their coming; he could read their fears; he could dowse their frailties before they knew their own.

Being a creature inside himself, the inner griivre stewed in the juices of all beings who passed through, drew from those the images of all things past and knew them first to last. He knew the "nows" of every living thing that came his way but, to his chagrin, knew nothing of the future. He was a soul in darkness and, in that bleak sanctuary, clung to all things near and dear. He feared all things from this moment on. That fear alone had kept him inside this place, inside his darkest self. It was that very fear that made him call me out and put an anxious edge into his voice.

He knew my name. "Shartallion XII," enunciating each syllable as if it were a truffle upon his tongue. "Son of Dager and Drilg the Fair. Royal Dragon of the Kiln, welcome!" He feigned cordiality. His voice was as cheery as a gnome's hearth in winter.

I couldn't see but could feel and hear him slither toward me to stand before my face, his red eyes glaring even in the dark.

One's eyes adjust. I could make out his silhouette, his head and body bobbing before me, a taunting partner for a deadly dance. And though I felt like summoning my ruby seed and turning my breath upon him, the heavy oils that soaked my skin warned me: this was not the thing to do. We'd both go up in flames with that, and even dragons can take just so much of a good thing. Nonetheless, I breathed a little sigh (just enough to throw some light upon the subject, you understand). In fact, I wished I hadn't.

He was a fierce one, this dragon-snake. His head was twice the size of mine, and he looked me squarely in the eye. Putting his muzzle up to mine, he pressed me nose to nose and, parting his red lips to reveal large fangs and forked tongue, drooled with anticipation.

The hot oils soaking on my skin fairly crackled when he smiled, and somehow I felt as though I were being basted. At once it was as if my skin could see, could penetrate this abyss of despair and know the entity beneath the mask.

This griivre, horrendous though he first appeared, was still no match for me. Otherwise, he would have been picking my bones this very minute. Even with the meager powers I had acquired to now, I could take him if I chose and win the moment. But what about the days, the weeks or months to follow?

I could hear this greasy serpent smiling. I could feel his mind-flow fluids coat my skin, penetrating deep into my veins and stirring me with images profane. I could hear the griivre's thoughts; and he could know mine.

"That's right my dragon prince," he said. "I'll not take you head to head. I don't claim to be a powerhouse to match the dragon's fang. But I have one advantage here. I can wait. You can't.

"I'm at home here inside my seamy self. I'll outlast you. It is just that simple. So while you wait some days or weeks to die, may I suggest we engage each other in lively badinage? It helps to pass the time, before you pass the time."

"I thought swallowing me once would be enough," I said, noting the irony of being where we were.

"That's just the trick," the griivre answered. "I get to devour you perpetually." He leered. And even in the darkness I could see his red lips part. It was his mindspeak; not his heart. This blackened, dismal creature, it occurred to me, was a rank impostor, a grinning, mocking surrogate sent forth to fake me out.

The true heart of this miserable creature was that of a dragon, and it was the denial of the dragon's need to fly that kept him self-divided.

It was then I realized that if I were to win the griivre I must feel this creature and not think him, moving from cell to cell until I touched the heart his thoughts disguised. If only I could evade the mind, salvation would be the reward—for me and for the griivre as well, I suspected.

Remembering that the griivre could read my mind as easily as I could read his, I dared not put this into thought. I had to feel it in my own heart and find where his was hiding. Meanwhile, keeping his mind diverted was the issue; and true diversion is task enough.

"Could it be this is a deception?" I queried.

There was a pause. "Is this a trap you're setting?" he asked. "Trying to trick me into freeing you?"

"I'm only asking for proof," I answered. Indeed I was. "Let's face the issue squarely. I speak my mind in this place. And you speak yours. So what my mind is asking yours is this: Where are we now?"

"In the belly of my Self," the dragon-snake answered.

"You couldn't prove it by me," I said. "I see neither beginning nor end to this, only blackness and a sea of oils. Now, if I could see the light of day from an open mouth above—just a crack—I might believe."

"It's not allowed," the griivre answered. "And it wouldn't make a difference. Even if my outer self were to open wide his jaws he'd simply close them tight again before we could break free."

"Was that a *we* I heard?" I queried. So he was a prisoner as well.

"A slip of the lip," he quickly snapped, as his tongue licked the air to sense it, to probe for any exudations of fear that might help him gain advantage.

"A slip of the mind," I thought, aloud. Now there was a weakness to exploit.

The griivre denied the truth again another time or two but it availed him little. For a quite awhile, he quite grew angry and arched his back at me.

"Don't play mind games with me, young dragon. I cannot eat you just yet. But I can make this stay a pretty nasty one for you. When it comes to passing time, why, lad, I am time's tutor. And time will sweat you out as it does all things."

"Then time it will be," I answered. Two could play that game. Thanks to Sagro I'd spent a year just sitting inside my mind. I could wait and think of other things, of bountiful futures I would find and great lords I would be. I could think of all those days of perennial sunshine, all those fantasies of winter lights, aurora borealic nights the griivre could not conceive. And those, I ventured, were fantasies this worm could not endure.

It didn't take long, a month or two. (Who knows in perpetual darkness?) In time he broke and started crying until the oil from his tears filled the void.

"It's no use," he moaned. "I've tried to come out of myself before, to no avail. I've tried a thousand times in the past. Each time the door has closed on me."

This was not the mind I heard, but a different voice—his heart, a kind and long tormented thing with a will to fly and a truth to sing.

"Then let us open that door," I answered. "The mouth must be opened and kept open. That's the trick."

"Easier said than done," the griivre's mind-voice answered, a skeptic to the last.

Challenges are energies asking for response. Challenge made and challenge answered, I found my way to the stomach wall and held it fast in my foretalons. Surely the outer Griivre could feel it and react.

"We'll make it howl," I said. "Surely it feels pain."

Before the griivre could make his protest, I'd dug my talons in, and like a cancer raging, kept on digging until the greater Griivre screamed.

It worked. The giant yawned and bellowed. His leviathan stomach spasmed, its huge walls in convulsion. The downdraft from the Griivre's gasping sent me tumbling to the bottom of its stomach, to the onyx oils now cold and hardening on my skin. It was a torrent wind of cold, wet downpourings. Yet the light shined in, and in that shining shined the light on me, and on the griivre. This glow of day blessed me and blinded him, but in that blinding made him weep with joy to glimpse its beauty.

I needed more of this. I dug my talons in again and prompted the same reaction from the greater Griivre—the violent spasms, the gasping and a screaming sound without, the taking-in of torrents of light and air. But when the light shined down again it did more than transform us both with hope, for as it lit this sordid place I saw my cell mate screaming his agonies in tandem with the self same greater Griivre who held him captive.

It was then that it occurred to me. They were inseparable, these two: as without, so within; as within, so without. Every action the Griivre made, the inner self would have to ape; and conversely. The outer Griivre would be a mere expression of the inner griivre's moves. And if I were right in my suspicions it was the inner being who was the stronger of the two; if only he could learn it.

"You're wrong!" he cried, still in convulsions. "He has me prisoner here, and what is left of me can only pick at his leavings."

He begged me not to torture him again, but I prevailed upon him.

"You are the dragon. He is the serpent. The dragon rules the snake, if only he will choose to do so, if only he will seize his destiny. All you have to do is open your mouth. Keep it open. Let the light shine in, and I can lift us out of this.

"No! It cannot work. I'm a prisoner here, forever," the griivre said.

"Have you ever tried this way?" I asked.

"No," he answered, numbly.

"Then how do you know?"

"This is just another trick from the dragon's clever mind," the griivre closed himself down. "There've been others before you. Some have fooled me. Most have failed. There's more than one way out of here. So why not try another?"

"I offer you your freedom too. Have others dealt so fairly?"

"They all betray me in the end and so will you," the dragon-snake replied. "I'm here to stay, I can assure you. I suppose it could be worse."

"I will not betray you! My word on it as a dragon prince," I said. (I wasn't sure I could do this, but at this point I'd try anything to leave this gruesome place.)

The griivre paused and breathed a sigh. And as he did the great Griivre's mouth did open, sucking in a downdraft.

"The force of air from above is awesome, and my mass will weigh you down," he lamented.

"But you are the griivre," I told him. "You can assume what you wish to be."

"Not true," he corrected. "Or else I would have swelled to twice my size and devoured you by now. Only once can the Griivre change his form. And that master lives outside."

"We'll do it anyway!" I said.

The griivre eyed me incredulously. "Even if we pull this off, what makes you think you can trust me? I may attack you when we get free. Or wait until you've weakened from your flight and drag you back inside."

"Who knows, when you come out of yourself, just what you'll be," I answered. "I'm betting you'll be changed. Besides, a dragon never forgets a kindness paid. And it's to that dragon heart, I now appeal."

The griivre did not confront me further. He came to my side instead and whispered his collusion. "Let's go." As I lifted myself into the air, he coiled himself around my legs, and we flew.

Living in this pit of dross for epochs had made the griivre heavy. He tried to make the cargo light, but his serpent's body wrapped around me were manacles of lead. He tried to compensate by balancing his energies with mine, but his fear was more a burden than a help.

Ready at last, he opened his mouth into a yawn and held it open. As he did the mouth of the greater Griivre yawned widely, revealing patches of clearest blue above, the ridges on its throat lining our pathway upward like a ladder to infinity, like a staircase to the sun.

For a few beats of my wings I felt as if we'd be outside in no time. As if shot from below, I streaked toward our goal just beyond the Griivre's bleating lips, toward the apex of potential into the sun's anointing light. The monster breathed, and when he did a furious force of wind confronted me, knocking me back into the pit of him nearly crashing back into his stomach.

I held my stance. I would not stay down. Each time there was a pause in the Griivre's breathing, I made another mad dash toward the sky. I seemed to do this in infinite variation, on each occasion growing weaker than before, each time watching the griivre watching me, his visage diminishing from one of hope to one of anguish, gasping as if his own identity were fading in the light. And as he did the force of his winds from high above overwhelmed me. I was weakening. My wings grew pained like leaden pallets pinioned at my side, held in place, and we were going nowhere.

We began to fall headlong. I looked up for one last time to behold the crack of sky between the Griivre's closing jaws when I saw it: a ray of crimson light beckoning to me. It was minuscule

at first, but then it swelled to the size of a rising red moon, filling
the whole horizon. It was a godsend to me, an anvil on which the
fires of my inner strength were forged. My heart filled with its
power, and I rose again to face the torrent. There would never be
a loss of flight as long as the flyer's heart was pure. I could stay
airborne forever. My wings had been baptized.

The griivre did not share my vision. Trapped in his own
sense of limitation, he lamented.

"Were I not a bastard son of dragonkind and had no wings to
fly, it could be different," he wailed. "But this mind that soars is
cursed with a lowly serpent's form."

"A dragon does what a dragon does, because he knows the
potential. A snake does not!" I called out. "Make the choice,
cousin. Make the choice, and act! Breathe out! Hold your mouth
open and breathe out!"

The dragon-snake grimaced but obeyed. He let his jaws yawn
widely, continuing to force the rush of air out of his lungs until
he had collapsed.

It was enough. Between his breathing and my beating wings
the two of us flew free, shot out of the great Griivre's mouth like
a pair of unwanted seeds. Tossed high into the air, I brought us
coasting to the place where the crimson light had shone.

Half a hectare away an arbor grew, a haven for the weary flyer
where bloodstone leaves danced on trees whose branches were
dusted in kaolin and hardened to porcelain against the morning
sky. From one tree in the center, cradled in the bow, there lay a
single piece of fruit—the garnet, the crimson lightsource that
had guided me to it. Radiating from its facets all the force of
inner will, it had been my beacon, and I'd responded. Just how it
had grown or who had left it there, I didn't know. But this much
I knew: that prize was mine, for I had earned this day.

Lest this vision become illusion and fade from my sight, I
sped right to it. With a passing of my wing I swept that sweet
pome garnet to my mouth. Touching its facets to my lips, I drank
its essence, and I was transformed. Serenity became my heart—a
need to sing, a need to soar. Filled with this new host, my body

bolted, shuddered, hovering above the earth and tree as if these elements were foreign to me, as if I belonged now only to the sky. The gift of flight, the true flight of the inner soul, was mine. I had not only passed the third test but seized the fourth in the bargain.

The issue for the griivre still lay in doubt. The inner being, having flung free, now faced the outer Griivre, a giant creature who—now that he'd spat out his prisoners—had shrunk quite nearly down to size. The Griivre was still a larger beast by far, fierce, malicious, and more than just a little disarrayed.

Steaming in a river of sulfur, he made his call to combat, a deep-pitched battle horn that groaned up from his throat and let loose a jet of hot black bile and reeking waters from his mouth. His eyes glared in shades of deepest orange, and his body coiled around itself in a manner set to strike.

The inner griivre simply waited. At first he did so out of a need to grasp the beauty of a world so long denied him. But when he saw his sense of wonder work on his behalf, he tarried even longer. While the adversary outer Griivre fulminated and fumed the inner griivre basked in his assimilation and, in that basking, took an even longer measure of time. This pausing drove the Griivre to distraction, causing him to threaten with every move he made.

"Come and meet your master, you bifurcated bastard! Come give us a hug and we'll digest you once again."

Silence was the answer; stillness the response. The griivre had waited too long inside himself to lose the value of the moment, or to let his passion push him out of his element. Instead, he waited patiently, and let the Griivre undo himself. In what surely was his finest moment, he had brought the contest home.

The Griivre could not endure the wait. Exploding in a cannon of fangs, he flew to attack, slashing, spitting, lunging out then back, letting venom, fang, and rancor shoot forth from his mouth. He dared not leave his steaming waters, yet his tantrum brought him to land; that was when the griivre made his move.

Waiting until the outer Griivre had spent his fusillade, the inner griivre snared him in the air and brought him hard to ground. Locked like lovers in an embrace, they bound themselves together, one griivre indiscernible from the Other. In their mortal combat they had merged to become one monster with two heads each trying to devour the other. The Griivre still was larger and more powerful by half and seemed to have gained some indistinct advantage. Yet I knew he could not win. Though by far the more ferocious of the two, his spit and venom, his roars and writhing, netted him a legacy of fatigue. In a short time, he'd shot his wad and left the griivre to take advantage of their entanglement.

No foe is more determined than a slave who's been set free. Venting wrath born of an epoch's worth of obscurity, the smaller blacker dragon-snake began to squeeze his adversary senseless, bit and strafed him with a black bile of his own. Then—to the amazement of every creature looking on—just as victory seemed certainly assured him the griivre surrendered himself and suddenly went limp. This untoward act of resignation utterly confounded the Griivre (and every creature watching, I'll admit).

It didn't take the Griivre long to seize the moment, and in that moment, clutched the griivre by the head and commenced the act of swallowing him whole.

I thought to intervene. But when a creature engages himself in mortal combat, rescue is the last thing on his mind. The garnet had given me new heart to fight, new strength to perform great wonders. I could have turned the tide of this; and yet I didn't dare.

In due course, the Griivre swallowed his better half and held him once again inside his dark recesses. A wicked smile of victory streaked across his face, and he returned to the boiling river to bathe his gushing wounds. But no sooner had he resubmerged than his body blew apart, burst into a billion particles of light. What remained of him—a shell of skin—fell into the sulfur stream, dissolving there and dying it black for all time. From its onyx ripples there emerged the inner griivre freed at last, renewed in celebration of himself.

He called me in to join him, to wash my wounds and bathe my hide. I followed him there and took some pains to cleanse my aching body. And yet as I emerged it struck me that my color did not change. Where I'd once been the color of flax, I was now a midnight black.

Observing me, the griivre grinned, a smile of hard sardonyx. "This river cleanses one to his true color, cousin. It seems that black is yours. Except, of course, the mark."

He motioned to the gash upon my chest, the living scar, the jagged nail, that lightning streak of torment. Neither transformation nor holy christening would rid my hide of that. That little gift was as deep as my soul; it was a part of me. And despite the garnet heart beneath, it stayed a livid white.

We said farewell, the unified griivre and I. Without indulging in effusions of gratitude, he thanked me simply but with heart.

"You've made a friend here, cousin. The dragon within the snake is free and thanks you for all time. And though I haven't wings to fly, I'll learn to like the water. Rest assured, it's a River Lord I'm meant to be, and rest assured I'll be the best. I'll baptize all who seek the truth, and give drink to all who ask permission. I'll honor all creatures in this delicate ecology and make sure each being gives another its due. But God help the takers; those who would plunder. If they come upon this gentle place with arrogant force of will, they'll deal with me. For I'm the two-in-one: I am the Griivre."

He took time from his pride of self to look upon me with concern. He bade me rest. And by that time I must admit, I was careworn. My energies had run their course, and a sense of completion at all this had left me with an overwhelming need to lie down. This River Lord had seen it, even though I had not.

"Sleep awhile, cousin," he admonished. "You've done much in a short time. Sleep awhile. I'll stand your guard for the duration."

"I have to continue on my course." My insistences were weak; my eyes grew heavy; I had lost all resolution.

"Wise is the dragon who knows when to rest," the griivre admonished. "Trust me. And trust this truth as well: Challenges will endure. When you're ready to meet them, they will stay their place.

The griivre stood beside me, a different creature now. Where once he'd been a hungry serpent who might have picked my bones, he was as good as his word: a River Lord. Above all else, even above my own prize garnet, I took heart in that transformation.

As for mine, this crow-hued onyx hide unsettled me. I'd dreamt of other grander of armor—of white and platinum, halloid crystal eyes, a diamond crown and silver pecs and shield. The white dragon's banner was my soul's desire, not these fierce black bones. Was that my reward for all I'd done—to present a front so fearsome that I'd frighten half the world?

My thoughts had voices; the griivre heard them. With a grin that reflected sunlight, he confidently stood his watch and merely let me be. By the bank, I found a field of dahlias lolling in sunlight, a place whose sweet petals would make my bed for a year.

Canto 7

The Mother of Tongues

In my dragon's sleep I'd been immersed in four
seasons of dreams. A year had passed and I had missed the party.
Flowers and sun, leaves and frost had covered my monstrous
form, burying me in a terrene blanket until the flower time had
come again, a year to the very day.

Dandling voices brought me to my body on that hour.
Merriment from creatures small in stature, artless in their mirth,
were polyphonies of wind chimes, love upon the air. I could feel
one of them dance on my eyelid, squealing with delight when I
lifted it and sent him tumbling akimbo. I raised my head and
heard more twitters, shrieks of sheer elation as I saw a host of
human children taunting me with laughter.

This time I had my bearings. I'd returned to the Land of the
East, my mother's homeland where humans looked upon the
dragon as their friends. Fear had found no haven in these
almond-colored children. They looked upon me with sloe-lipped

smiles, with eyes that danced in wonder, with calls for this young "dragonflower" to awaken and teach them to fly.

Why did they call me dragonflower? I wondered, until I raised up further and came to realize I'd been buried in white petals to my nose, flowers grown from sod that also covered me. I wondered at what protector had buried me in this blanket of compost; then in an instant I remembered.

I looked off toward the onyx river and saw the wake of the griivre curling eastward toward the rising Sun. I caught only a glimpse of him but even in that shade, realized just what that snake had done. He hadn't stopped to say goodbye, but he'd had his little fun. He'd seen me through this hibernation, had guarded me as he vowed. Meanwhile, he'd made a garden of my face. More important, he'd kept his word. No longer a creature of guile, he'd released it like a molting skin. I didn't know when if ever I would see this River Lord. Yet I knew this much: Of all the gems I'd earned thus far, this Onyx One had changed me to the core.

Whatever I had become was lost on these innocent young who regarded me as if I were some scaly Gulliver for their Lilliputian sport. They'd strewn me with a bank of flowers, tied ribbons to my tail, and turned my many tailhorns into a maze of slides and ladders. They shouted "Dragon Prince" at me and took turns shooting down my wings, and some of the more venturesome among them came and stood upon my nose, engaging me in languages I soon would come to know.

All this they did utterly unblemished by a single trace of fear or curse of judgment. As children, they were in that natural state of trust that left them knowing what energies to mix and which to shun. My fierce, dark visage, even when I eyed them onerously a time or two, served only to make them giggle. They perceived the intent behind the mask; they perceived no harm in me. Would that all the pygmies saw so well or used such uncanny gifts.

I wondered at these little ones. Were these conceived from the Seed—the same as those minions we'd met at the Lake of

Shards? Were these from the selfsame savage strain who
counseled with Shimbaghs, sorcerers and witches? If they were,
at what rite of passage did they come to their corruption? Were
they all alike? I wondered. Or were these islands of purity in a
rank ungodly sea? There was no consistency with these
creatures. They were devil and angel in one; and they never
seemed to know which role to play.

I wished for a sage to ask these things; I wished but could not
have. Discernment was the Lesson of this school.

In a few moments these selfsame children who had taken me
as I was, shrank back from a feral form in flight now speeding
toward this place—a shroud of rage, a flying furnace ominous
and grand, a towering dragon fresh from the Chthonic Schools. I
tried to coax them to remain, promising I'd protect them, but
their fears had made them suddenly deaf to me. Suddenly, I was
an enemy too; they beheld me with different eyes. They took
their wonderment with them, and they fled.

I lifted my head to greet the source of this discord face to
face but knew by the swagger and the fearsome force of flight
that this creature was my sister.

Having won her gift of flight at some private testing grounds,
Seti had taken her garnet crystal close to heart. She reached her
apex in the sky then zoomed to land before me. (I was touched
that she truly cared what I thought at all.) Passions bright, red
marrow fairly oozing from her pores, she was a larger dragon
now, a sinuous saucy lady, a creature quite resplendent for her
kind. Seeing her in such a light surprised me in a way. Not so
much her beauty struck me (I'd quite expected that), as the way it
had apparently come to pass.

Seti was red enough, 'twas true; Scarlet was her color of
choice. Yet it seemed she'd come to it by the hard way. This
carmine/auburn hue that coated her was made of myriad cuts,
lacerations from others far less diligent than she—enemies
who'd lost the day, lovers who'd failed the night, others who'd
been scorched by their indecision. Proudly festooned in her

blood and bruises, she perched on a rock above me, looking with disdain at the creature she perceived me now to be.

"Well, aren't we cute?!" she jeered. "A flower dragon! Or is it a flower bed? Whatever it is, it isn't much—a giant pansy with a tail. My gawd! You look so goody good, I think I'm going to puke!"

One does not run to the dragon's ground to take the dragon on; if Seti hadn't learned that much, I had. I didn't answer as she might have liked but chose instead to rise and let my bearing make my statement for me. I had partially submerged the mass of myself beneath the soil. (I'd done it so as not to scare the children.) But this unexpected instance of my sibling's crass arrival prompted me to respond in sibling fashion. Sensing I'd make a sizable impression, I stood up, arched my wings and shook the sod from my back, Yet even I hadn't known what I'd become. The remnants of my earthly blanket fell away to reveal a tower of sinew, muscle, and armor plate. If Seti were fifty feet from tip to tip, I was on to seventy and growing—Onyx black as the core of night down to the cut of the bone.

Even Seti (as much as Seti ever could) was forced to grant me my due. "Well, big broh," she said." You've made it. And a jet-black flying machine at that! A warrior's armor. How masculine! How butch! You sure there isn't some mistake?"

She challenged me to tests of flight, a circus of aerial dexterity, a challenge pregnant with pride and milked of logic. It might have been a sport for me to put my sister down, but restraint is evolution's dearest friend. Besides, this was not a wholesome being that stood before me now. She was racked with pain and virtually on the rocks. The occasion required some tact, so I suggested she take a rest. She rebuked me for the thought of it, but her body had a wisdom of its own. Steeped in the brine of her own lather she staggered, nearly fell, but caught herself and blurted her challenge again.

"I can take your measure anytime. I'm more than a match for you. I can take the measure of any bull in town."

"I'm sure you can," I chose to agree, then took her to the river where we bathed in the Onyx waters that had altered my soul. They salved her wounds, cleansed her hide, and turned me blacker still, for I'd been anointed in this holy oil.

We dried in the sun. We watched the clouds sift down to kiss their Mother. I beheld the peace. Seti saw it as an act of war: the sky and mountain ridges in conflict. She could not relax. Although she had not rested one moment on her journey to the gems, there was a rage that fueled her, a pot brought to the boil, and she could not cap it. We'd both come to the same place. We'd both garnered the same gems, but that was where the similarity ended.

"I suppose you made a host of friends all along the way."

"After a fashion," I replied.

"No doubt!" she said, spitting disdain from the side of her mouth, along with a clot of blood. Until that moment I'd believed all courses in this college were the same: same challenges; same tests; same outcome; you either pass or fail according to whether or not you unlock the secret. I was wrong. Seti showed me that. Without the least bit of encouragement from me, she recounted—blow by blow—her bloody ride through the halls of the Chthonic college.

She'd attained the first level without either trouble or challenge. She'd taken the ruby from its cradle and swallowed that gemstone whole; no agony, no burning, no Shimbagh apparitions to tempt or torture her. The stone had been hers, naturally; her birthright.

This revelation taunted me. I even felt a twinge of envy, until she told me of the other levels she'd achieved, each one emblazoned with her personal brand of pluck. How had she achieved the amethyst? I asked her. How had she met the Kohmm?

"I killed the mother and ate the egg," she told me. "I swallowed that sucker down. The little one bit, but what the hell. I got what I came for; I survived."

And what of the griivre? I asked about the journey I'd just been on.

"I did the rascal in, fried his face with my built-in stove, and ate the entrails for dinner. As soon as I did, the Griivre excreted me, coughed me out like a poison plum. It was as simple as that."

Seti belittled the experiences, called them "cosmic plumbing," but her ravaged visage told another tale. None of the goals that she had reached had come without expense. Some of the wounds she bore were old and seemingly had healed; others were fresh as an angry mountain rain. Behind her mask of nonchalance she was clearly haunted. Her inner voice cried out and pain was the only song it sang. But grant her this: She'd done it. She'd reached the very same level I had to this point. Taking her objectives with Prussian strategies—a terrible swift sword, an instinct for the kill, an obedience to the warrior's code without the so much as a token gesture toward taking the higher path—she'd made her way through all of this, and done so without a gesture of regret.

That revelation jolted me. There were many paths to the finish, as many as there were travelers to take them. And yet the ends were reached. Whether high path or low, when taken with intent, the selfsame powers were granted in the end. So, sin and virtue nourished themselves at the very same fountain of light without either running the risk of evaluation.

Where was the justice in that? I asked. Was all my straining to play by the rules a fool's game? Had Seti been right all along? I wondered. Was this plane of life so dross that only the bold and savage among us could make it theirs to hold? I wondered, and in that wondering felt cheapened by my doubts, for no sooner had I asked the question than it had been answered.

After some cold reflection in the light of a purple sunset, Seti told me of how she'd achieved the gift of flight—the crimson garnet—and how it had been given.

When she'd freed herself from the Griivre, she found its tail had ended at a mountain top, and that she'd been let loose at a falcon's aerie high upon a ridge of cliffs.

"There, gleaming before me in the nest, in the midst of some peregrine eggs, a master garnet sat, a prize for the taking." Seti, her carmine eyes aglow, her hard face subtly softened, spoke with a gentler voice than I had ever heard from her. "There it was, a crimson ray aglow with holy light to fulfill my deepest soul's desire—to have my speed in flight. It beckoned to me like a lover, yet when I moved to take it, a blood-headed falcon swooped before me and snatched it from my midst. A winged wizard in the sky, he circled me three times, taunting me to come and get it, the arrogant little cock! Never one to shrink from a challenge, I chased that bird for weeks, but this was a falcon of the peregrine clan, the fastest bird on earth. A dragon with the gift of flight might run it down in time; a novice dragon is never a match; and neither, dear brother, was I."

Pursuing her deepest soul's desire with a warrior goddess's zeal, my sister never gave a thought to relenting. She chased that doughty bird another month until, at last, she cornered him in a ravine. Knowing at last the prize was hers she reached to take it from the hawk and devour him too, if he were so foolish as to resist, when this bird blossomed into a full grown gryphon male ready to have his say.

Gryphons were brothers in the mystic clan and allied to dragons by ancient bonds. But the bonds were loosely tied, and the gryphon was a proud, defiant hybrid. With head and eye of an eagle, with the body and heart of a lion, the gryphon grew to the height of a willow with wings that could shear a minaret in two. It was the product of the off chance pairing of two of Nature's noblest creatures, and its beauty knew few equals. So vanity and willful pride were its downfall. In this eagle-lion's sense of self, it held the dragon grotesque. We, the Children of Fire were also objects of contempt. Yet there was in that loathing a fatal attraction—to the one creature born to the most hideous strength of all.

The Gryphon offered liege to no other creature on the earth—neither dragon nor Shimbagh nor man. It took its place in the thunderheads of heaven and coveted the garnet as its own heart. For any dragon to fly with the speed of God's breath it had to take a gryphon's heart, or else receive the garnet as the gryphon's willing gift. Seti had not been born to that right. So if she were to have it at all, she would have had to earn it against the gryphon. But earn it she would, for this lady was willing to go all the way to end of her self—to surrender her vital force for that singular gem. Reeling from her earlier combats, from her weeks of giving chase, she was nonetheless ready to stand her ground against a being who might easily do her in. The gryphon was a fearless fighter, in some ways much keener than we, and skilled in the means of bringing a dragon down.

"'To the death,'" my ruby red sister had screeched. To the death it would have been, had the gryphon not relented. As if in a moment's caprice he praised her audacity, called her name and dropped the red rock at his feet.

"'Take it. You've earned it,'" the eagle-lion called. "'I've another in my cache. Otherwise you'd fly until you surely lost your soul. You would never get this gem from me. But true passion has its rewards. You may be a dragon, lady, but you have a lion's heart. Take it, and go! It's the only gift the gryphon ever gives. And only does he give it once." With that, and with no other explanation, the gryphon flew away, slipping between the veils of clouds, and into Heaven's mouth.

Seti didn't think to question her good fortune, until now.

"Imagine that," she said. "All that time we'd spent in chase, all those wasted months. Then he gave it up with a cavalier gesture. I'd have fought and died for that crimson heart, and this cat-bird tosses it over nonchalantly like so much pocket change. It wasn't for lack of courage, as you know; a gryphon will fight under any pretext just to keep himself in tune. Then why, may I ask, would he put me through all that?

"The gryphon knows the soul's desires of every other creature. That is his secret strength. Why could he not have read my heart and just *known?* I ask you. The questions I ask are rhetorical, of course. I know the answer, now! These are games the masters play with us!"

"I don't know that they are games," I said. "None of us can be sure."

"Don't be naive!" my sister railed. With that, and with some devastating secret lying in wait beneath her tongue, she turned to face me. Making certain she had my rapt attention, she let it loose like a gas to poison the air of the arbor where we sat. "You know those children, those human young, you cozied with when I arrived? They were the reason for my coming. They were about to make a meal of you, about to pluck your eyes out of your head and grind them into sausage. They're not children at all but Shimbagh warriors in disguise. All you had to do was make yourself a bit more vulnerable, and they'd've had you *en crotte.* It was a trap.

"I saw this little vignette from the sky. I didn't know it was you at the time. I thought, of all creatures on Earth, you would have known better. You of the all-knowing soul! Surely your prescient onyx cells had warned you of this happening, had they not? Surely you've acquired more awareness than that!"

Had I not been as black as obsidian I would have I would have turned beet red. I hadn't an inkling those human babes would pose a threat to me. Had my senses gone so obtuse? Had my ablution in that onyx stream been such a hoax that I lacked all premonition of foul intent? I wondered. In my mind's eye, I reviewed the events of the day, my awakening, my utter vulnerability for a year. The dragon is most vulnerable when it sleeps. Why not slay me then? After all they'd had enough time to do so.

"To have their games!" My sister barked, answering my tortured thoughts. To add substance to her charges, she saved her worst for last and told me all: While I had slept my full year through, Seti in her time had pressed hard on, rushing toward the next gem—the Mother of Tongues, the emerald. Intent upon completing her quest, she too had come upon a school of children, human flowers wafting in the sun, beckoning her to play with them, an invitation she perceived as wanton, a temptation to avoid or overcome. And overcome, she did; so she'd believed. With a swat from the back of her wing she knocked the little ones aside and made her way toward a path lined with an emerald light, a light that was soon obscured.

The moment my sister had made for the path the children had risen up, not as children anymore but as warriors in full regalia. In silver-tipped spears and silver breastplates, they made their way for her. Where there had been seven children who bade her play, there were seven warriors to test her mettle. Proficient at the art of dragon combat, skilled in keeping their spear tips pointed toward her throat, they spread before her in echelon, spanning a breadth from wing to wing, careful to keep their distance from one another and from her.

Seti, never shy to act on instinct, slew them on the spot, cut them down and laid them low. And yet from their corpses more warriors grew — seven times seven strong and ready for combat, and from each of those slain seven times that number came, until an army took to march on her.

She should have flown. She should have known to take flight, to use her garnet heart to set her free. Still she stayed on and in that staying fought with frenzy to survive. Overcome by bloodlust and her warrior's need to strike a blow for each blow struck against her, she at last was overcome, overwhelmed, and wounded; mortally, she felt.

"But I did not die, brother! I felt the spears go in! I felt the axes, the hatchets, the swords sheathed in silver cut through my hide, yet I survived! Even when I resigned myself that this was it, I still survived! I had been wounded enough to be slain a dozen times, and yet I did not die! Instead, I flew out of harm's way and watched while they regrouped below, a phantom army with no other purpose than to give me test. Now, I haven't been around this tiny globe a lot, just yet. But this much I can say: Either I'm one tough lady, or this is just a dirty game they play with us. And just in case you have a doubt there's more.

"The green-lit path that gleamed its emerald promise disappeared. But so did the Shimbagh warriors. Rather than pursue me they slipped away, vanished as if they'd never cared to fight at all. Even the trees and grass, the flowers—even a nearby brook—everything before me was erased as if wiped clean. I was stripped naked and alone, and a voice inside me told me I had failed to catch the 'hallowed' green. So what?!"

I didn't try to tell her that, from where I stood, her wounds looked real enough to me. Perspectives have a way of daunting one's ability to judge, and little I could say or do would change my sister's point of view.

As it was, she didn't waste much time crying out against this apprenticeship of ours. She had held suspicions going in and would leave with them intact. She had evolved in many ways, and even acknowledged it. Still she resented this school and all that it represented.

"I've gone as far as I care to go. I have my warrior fires intact. I have my healing shield, my speed in flight. And I have something else you don't! I know it's just a game!

"We possess these powers already, you and I. We've merely let the dictums of these 'masters' lure us on. They try to sell us qualities we own from birth. They're ours to be, not theirs to give! We have the ability to grow these on our own, and in time, I assure you my black brother, I will do just that! I'll get the rest, these other jewels for my crown, in *my* good time; not theirs. All they sell are games—human toys of mind and Shimbagh lies!"

"If these are so easy to obtain, why did you lose? "I asked. "Why did you not use the power within—your natural gift of tongues? It was your challenge to find it in yourself. Could you not look for it?" I didn't try to control these thoughts. They rolled off my tongue as reflex.

Just as reflexively Seti answered to justify her actions. "I may have lost the quest of gems, but I never lost myself. I have kept my own counsel and my self-respect! Will you be able to say the same when this charade has ended?

"Stay to play then brother dear. I choose to find the real game—not this pallid hypocritical useless dress rehearsal! There's a world that needs my visitation, continents for the taking. And they're fodder for the dragon with the will to make it her own.

"There's only one way that I can see to run this course of life. Kick ass and make the rules; the rest will follow. That's what's real. That's what works on this ungodly level of existence. I'll catch the edge of that blunt truth, I know. I've heard they play for keeps up North. And North is where I'll be. If you ever need to look me up, you need merely ask around. I'll let them know that I've arrived; you can bet on that."

By morning, we'd said our last goodbyes. Seti didn't tarry long. Sentiment was never her long suit.

"Later in life, perhaps," she said. And later it would be. She set flight path toward the hostile glaciers of the North—the land where the rogue dragons ruled. The place where they plagued their world with dark caprice and random acts of mischief. Neither evil nor good, neither Shimbaghs nor High Dragons of the Kiln, those robber clans were made for her, were sauce for her ambitions, were meat for the stew she'd already stirred to set her course in life. She would become their queen for sure. She would seize the skull-crossed throne and rule that cold gray kingdom with an iron will. She would torch the land with her passions, beget a clutch of dragon young, and learn some hard, dark lessons along the way. Watching her speeding her flight away, beating her wings like drums, I doubted that I would see my sister again. I doubted less, she'd make her mark; she'd made her mark on me—in all the wise and dreadful ways such driven creatures do.

§§§§§§§

Returning was no easy thing to do. A cage of inexperience already rife with doubt, I had three gemstones left to gather, and hidden in one of them awaited the dark angel of denial.

No sooner had my sister disappeared into the clouds, than a shining path stretched out before me one that luminesced beyond the natural colors of the morning, a trail all wet with prisms made with of pixie tears and sunbeams, leading to an arbor of trees whose branches had leaves of lace wafting like the wings of cherubim.

I paused, for this was all too pretty, and I was too filled with doubt to accept this mural of tranquility as anything but a trap. Where was the game, this time? I mused. What was the riddle going to be? Why should I bother to solve it? Why should I go at all? Perhaps my sister had been right; this was a ruse after all, a plot laid out by some mad galactic gamesman having sport with us. Perhaps winning was simply an act of learning when not to play. Seti had seen things more clearly than I. These gifts were not given; they were ours to own. I knew it to the core of my being yet doubted all the same. Just as surely as I doubted, a voice inside me said this game was meant to be won. Having gifts, after all, was one thing; knowing how to use them was another. If this were a game, and surely it was, then so was everything else.

I dashed toward the arbor, toward the green light and the forest set like porcelain against the morning sky. Suddenly, it seemed a fortress ready for assault. The treetops at once became minarets crowded with warriors poised to strike. I made for it with abandon. Amethyst armor set in place, fire gouts flowing from my mouth, I followed the path through the trees whose darkening branches held malachite apples dropping like bombs around me, sending forth hissing jade vapors with fingers of poison mist. As I sped toward an emerald light, the flora around me darkened, growing to a forest filled with black oaks two hundred feet high.

The emerald light brightened until I could see it fully. Sitting in the bow of the largest tree, cradled in an arc, there it sat—a gem of greenest green so pellucidly brilliant that it stung my eyes to behold it. And from each of its facets roared the cries of a thousand battles in a pitch so harsh it deafened me to hear. I blanched. I started. I covered my ears. Then all the lights went out.

I came to land, and as I did, the war-zone orchestrations fell dead silent. All at once it was still and dark as night with the only light a trace of sunshine dancing on the tree-tops. I trod the ground lightly. At least, I could have sworn I did. Yet each step I took prompted a chorus of voices breaking the air: outcries of protest and pain from the grass beneath my feet, anguish from the bark that clung to the trees. Whispers of warning came from the flowers and stones. Boulders like bailiffs, stern and deep-throated, cautioned me to beware. The malachite crystal hanging in fruit forms, each holding a soul in check, sang new songs in contrapuntal solos striving to be heard.

This was the world so many would deny—the world of tongues, the world in which every particle possessed a consciousness of its own. A legion of them spoke to me this morning. I could hear them all at once. Yet by hearing everything, I was listening to nothing. This was how the greater creatures of Earth had lost the gift of language. This was how I too would lose if I were not on purpose.

Recalling those sacred silent times at Sagro's side when my higher will took hold, I stilled this mad cacophony and brought the light to bear. Light was the higher vibration, so I let it rip the moment. My angels feeling my silent pleas would soon send me a sign.

Once my thoughts were stilled, my eyes found the clarity of light, and with that light an answer: "Look for an island of silence. Find the stone that does not speak; there will be your helpmate; heed only its counsel; listen to no other voice but this, and to your own."

Scarcely moving, scanning with ears attuned in ways they'd never heard before, I waded through myriad madding voices knowing my faith would bring me to that stalwart *consolateur*.

In a crosscurrent of tranquility, a slip of quietude, I found it—a round smooth rock from which there came no voice. I put my ear to the ground to confirm that this indeed was that source of silence, then took my foretalon and scooped it up. Instinctively, I knew this cold hard lump of stone was meant to be my guide. I placed it beneath my tongue, and the instant I did, the disharmonies were put to rest. The forest stilled. The verdant light returned.

In front of me, half a hectare away, the bow of a tall dark oak split asunder, revealing beneath its ancient bark a core of hematite from which an emerald ray now hurled its light down at my feet. Down a giant tree-lined path, it called me to approach it, a sole seductive siren voice that whispered "Shartallion" on the wind. It was then I knew without a doubt, this was the Mother of all Tongues, the green jeweled source—the Emerald.

Drawn as I was toward the light, I found my path blocked by warriors who stepped from behind each tree, seven warriors armed to the teeth and leveling spears at me. They were huge (as humans go). And even though they menaced me with cries of "Halt!" and threats against my person, they were not a force for which a dragon of any stature would give much pause.

Unless I slew them.

I remembered well my sister's tale and vowed I would not fall victim to that same unreflected act of folly. Yet I knew that these warriors were guardians of this gem. They would resist me by all means at their disposal and to whatever lengths were necessary. I had also to assume that this was not an echelon of ordinary men. This was where illusion was bred, and these were its creations.

At once, the rock grew hot and turgid on my tongue. It was alive and teemed with voices counseling me. "Do not kill but bind them up, "it said. "Then your test can be met."

"With what?" I asked, but asked too much, for in an instant the rock went silent.

Slowly and with cautious intent, the warriors formed a nexus and, raised their shields, leveled their spears and made a march on me.

I scanned this forest for some twine. I was running out of options; it was either kill or find a quick retreat. Since destruction is a last resort and forever wounds the soul, diversion was the wiser move to make. I took a side step, when just above me I saw my helpmates: Vines! Hundreds of them interwoven in branches dangling high enough to bundle these warriors up.

In an instant, I soared to grab these tendrils from their trunks and dived back into the midst of the warriors waiting below. With a single swipe of my wing I knocked them down, swept them up into a pile, bound them (shields and all), and wrapped around the split oak tree. Above them, in the bow the emerald ray intensified, calling again to promise me that the stone was within my grasp. Yet as I reached, the rock I'd taken burned white hot on my tongue, singeing me into sensibility.

"Lesson Five," it reminded me. "Nothing is as easy at it seems." It said no more, but by the time that soft gray stone had cooled, I realized the cause for that reminder.

Around the trunk of the great split oak where I had bound up the warriors, a violent metamorphosis had taken place. The tree had formed seven new branches, and from each branch there was a Brobdingnagian human head crying out from a mouth with tongues all blackened and spitting poisons. Each head had five rows of teeth. Yet when those mouths closed and acted in repose they were creatures of great beauty, female faces with rose petal hair that shined suns of serenity from their citron eyes.

None of the heads remained serene for more than a moment, and it wasn't long before I came to realize that only one head at a time could rest, while the other six would snap and spit at every move I made. The heads bobbed and darted, extending to their fullest, with voices like a chorus of sirens taunting me to dance with them in deadly combat.

This was unlike any challenge I had faced before, if for no other reason than this: this was a Shimbagh, a Tree Fury, a monstrosity from whom there would be no quarter. There would be no truce with this one, no mystic bond to swing open the gate once the secret was unlocked. This was one creature I'd have to defeat or be slain in the attempt.

It was said, the Tree Fury was made of a beautiful maid's love for seven different men. She could not be all things to each—for each man loved her sincerely—so she sought to tap a potion called *Ubiquity* from the tree divas in hopes that she might love all seven men at once. But in order to receive her potion, she had to answer the tree-divas' riddle or become one of them herself.

She failed, and in the irony of that failure was granted part of her wish. She could share herself with her seven lovers in any way she chose, as long as she stayed at one with the tree that held her captive. But this fair maid was not the loving kind and swore that if she could not have these men, no one would. She courted the Shimbaghs for the gift of song, a gift which was granted at the cost of her soul. Singing with a voice no human could resist, she willed her lovers to embrace her one by one. As each lover came to this enchanted tree, this fury slew him. And for each lover this maiden slew, she gained another head. Finally, as the last lover succumbed to her fatal charms, she had seen her vile wishes granted. She had enfolded her lovers into her hollow heart, into this one seven-headed beast—the Tree Fury. Now, though the faces resembled hers, the souls were all in conflict, their voices sang in dissonant choir, and their teeth carried the poison of their eternal futility.

I took the time to make this study because I also ascertained that my movements sent this monster into frenzy. Even as I glanced at the bow from where the emerald ray gleamed, the Tree Fury's heads would lift and move to block it off. All the while, these faces came snapping, lurching out at me—all except for the one that remained serene through all the chaos.

I didn't need a further push; my Heart told me the rest. If movement drove this creature to distraction, swift movement might drive her to ruin. The garnet heart, the speed of flight, was mine to make the most of; I'd show my stuff and find a way to run circles round the bitch.

The very of gesture of flapping my wings set the Tree Fury into frenzy. Every movement I made with my wings caused her heads to snap in tandem. Trapped as she was, it occurred to me that she was fixated with movement. Movement, the first illusion of life, was her obsession and her rage.

Feeling the power of blinding speed, I began to circle the tree, pressing on, moving to break all physical limits to myself. I flew faster in circles around the trunk while the fury's heads whipped round and round to follow my dizzying path. Like a carousel gone mad it spun together as one, its heads tied into a knot, the emerald light fused into one unholy blur; until all definition and color became one luminescence; until all sound reached a high-pitched screech a thundergod would covet.

The repercussions cracked the face of the forest and came right back on me. The force of sound had knocked me flat into a giant oak, which could not withstand the thrust of my velocity and broke in two. My wings were now plicated, pressed in and doubled under in a way that made me wonder whether or not they were broken. I arose and rearranged myself. My head was spinning, and as I cleared it, I looked across the way to see the fruit of my revolutions.

The Tree Fury, by my force of flight, had melded into the emerald ray. Now they had become fused together, body and light as one. Six of the Tree Fury's seven heads were stilled and dangled down like fur bells on a bonnet. But a single head remained ensconced. Jutting out from the tree's split bow, the fury's final face awaited—a woman's head with raven-feathered hair, white gardenia skin, and sloe mouth full with passion. Knowing her power to enchant, she taunted me with lust. Her eyes were closed. Her lips were sealed. And though her neck was a serpent on patrol, she hummed a saintly song.

As I made my move this fury came alive. Her mask was off in a flash. Her eyelids snapped back unleashing laser lights of hard chartreuse that bored into my core. My amethyst shield could block those embers, but the last surprise was hers.

That she'd been vanquished, she admitted; surrender, she would not. Her gaze had cooled to a mint green truce, but her mouth had another message. As she opened wide, her jaws revealed the emerald, the Mother of Tongues herself. The siren sounds of seven voices sang aloud the triumph of their vengeance:

"You think you have the prize my love.
Quite possibly you do.
If you unmask the guise, my love,
if you can find the clue.

"Because you see, whatever you do
to seize will take too long;
to grasp is only to lose your grip;
to wrest is deadliest wrong.

"Move on me and I swallow the stone.
You'll lose it
once and for all.
Slay me; my numbers multiply,
And you are the one
who will
fall.

"Steal the gem and go stone deaf;
that's the curse upon it!
So pick a card, love,
any card!
And regret it
once you've done it!"

Having trilled her little ballad, the remaining maiden head gave me an ironic bow then raised her face to let me see through her wicked smile—the gem.

Curses! I wasn't ready for curses! I'd had trouble enough as it was. And riddles were the liar's way to the prize. That was the catch, of course! The Mother of Tongues was held captive by the Mother of Lies herself! Yet, as lies are deadly, they are only so if there's a truth among them.

Picking the puzzle line for line, I found no point of attack. In fact, if her riddle were to be believed, to make any move whatsoever on the witch meant I'd lose the stone. Unless she'd never had it in the first place; that was the ruse. "You think you have the prize, my love. Quite possibly you do." Those were the first words to come from her mouth, and it was upon those phrases I would now focus my attack.

The instant I embraced this thought, the stone beneath my tongue steamed its sublime corroboration: That celestial crystal was home in my mouth already. And since no force of flesh on earth, not even the dragon's anvil jaws, could crush the glowing emerald, all I needed do to make this hardy confirmation was bite down. Before I bit, this dark forest came alive again with voices from a thousand houses of thought—each with its own truth to tell me, its own sides to choose. Each sound had powers of its own and had all joined ranks, working like a sonic wedge trying to lock me out. But a dragon, if he's to come of age, must use his wits as well. If sound could hurt, then sound could heal. And I had a furnace raging in me one that could burn out any negativity. From my scarlet light within I became the flame in my mouth, freeing my jaws to make their move, to bite down on the stone.

Bite down I did. And when I did, I ended the Tree Fury's reign. Emptied of pretext, she fulminated a thousand emerald shards that seemed to grow like flowers. It was a malicious energy I saw trying to renew itself, and I knew in an instant this lady would have to be torched. Throughout its long reign this Shimbagh had seduced so many souls and in those cloudy seductions had become so corrupt that every cell, every quark and atom, would have destroyed itself and given life anew. Summoning my whitest flames, I blew that Bitch to cinders.

The moment the flame struck, the kunzite crystals on the ground burst open, liberating a soul from each like silver sylphs of light. Reuniting in the skies, they joined in etheric choir, singing joyous hymns of celebration. Raining light upon this forest, they called my name in praise, causing the oak that housed the fury to brutally break in half. The oak, freed from its bonds, split asunder, causing the ground to tremble and open a livid crack of Mother Earth right at my feet.

Beneath me, in an indigo cavern, an icy vortex waited with a gravity so compelling I had no power against its pull. I was sucked down against my will but with the taste of Glory. The Emerald, the Mother of Tongues, was mine.

Canto 8

The Diamond "I"

The Mantilough feeds on mists of night
on primrose and on prana
and never lets the harsher light
of Morning
Cross her breast.

The Mantilough lives in
No World
where the edge of time has curled
to form the roof of a sepulcher
where souls in flight
may rest.

— The Legend of the Mantilough

In a free-fall between night and day, between darkness and my dreams, I floated to a meadow where there flourished a nether realm — a confabulation of fabulous forms of life beyond my ken gathered to create a perfect haven. Butterfly flowers, *lapidrops,* danced along shadeworn shadows, yielding up their honey with every flutter of the wing. Bowing to caress their petals were trees with crystalline branches bearing fruit made out of gemstones that glistened with inner light. In the midst of this, knee deep in lace from moltings of angels' wings stood gathering flocks of deer-birds who added Sol to the night. With the faces of fawns, with doe eyes, with ivory wings of doves, with tongues from the favorite fabric of the hummingbird's secret song, they nourished themselves without a sound by grazing on mists and air that licked the dew from the petals of flowers around them.

Whatever I was witnessing here was something above and beyond, another plane of reality closed even to the Clan. Here, creatures poised at Heaven's Gate went about their lives without threat, without toil or any burdens of expectation. Their only joy was to be and do and live in the light of God's love.

What a counterpoint to the strivings we had put upon ourselves; the Mystic Clan in all its hidebound glory. In our overblown sense of destiny we'd made such work of it all, made labor out of every breath we took, while these beings in this sacred place were simply out of the loop — beyond the cares and woes that came with "duty." These fawn-birds who gracefully grazed in this shelter were no doubt the Mantilough. I'd heard them described by my mother in the most reverent of tones.

"They reveal themselves to no one except by general consent, and only then to pass on ethereal wisdom. They live but a Dominion's breath from this harrowing plane of life. Yet no one who lives in flesh has ever touched them. Only the Mystics can see them at all, and none of low vibration, for they vanish with the slightest hint of the Sun on the morning dew. Yet these are creatures of such magnificent power that few can measure. They bring the Spring, they end the Summer, yet do so with such ease that only they are keepers of the schedule. They work their influence on all of us without ever harming a soul. They feed on prana and fresh fallen showers before they kiss the earth, yet never ask a single thing from another.

"To Shimbaghs they're invisible. The beasts of Earth cannot hear them. Yet when called to duty they can turn a battle's tide. For when they sing their silent song, the Mantilough breathe a mist that clouds all reason and veils the way to intent. It is the Mother of Illusion, the Eye in the Mirror of Hope. It is the sonnet that dances the eagle to sleep."

So heartfelt were my mother's words when she spoke of their glory, her voice quite naturally broke out into song. Hearing her sing of these magical beings nearly made me weep. But I was much younger then, and my emotions were swift in their honesty. Now, in my deepest dream state in the midst of my longest journey when fatigue had flung me into a corner of Morpheus' darkest room, I beheld them and once again my apprehension was a garden, and I knew from that moment I was in a healing.

No doubt, these were angels of a sort sent to guide me through. No doubt they had answers before I'd thought to ask. I started to pose a question but remembered as well the truth— that calling out to the Mantilough might cause them to fade away. As it was I felt their essence shimmer like diamonds in water, for one never knew when they would simply slip from view. All I knew was that the sky had grown light, that morning would mean goodbye, and I could never let such a moment pass.

The legend of the Mantilough was that Sun never creased their brow, and that they merged back into the morning dew. I felt if they left before I could catch them, I might never see them again, for the Mantilough rarely came twice to grace one's life. It was also said that if their queen liked you, she might bestow a wish that could be granted by putting the words on the wind. And though beholding them in this moment would be gift enough for most, my soul was hungry for everything these magical beings could share. One was never supposed to confront these fawn-doves. They were such independent souls. But it's not what we attempt in life but what we let pass that haunts us. As yet, I wasn't even certain what dimension I'd found, but being among them made me feel grotesque. I was, after all, a dragon, the heavy handed handiwork of some tasteless cosmic blacksmith, while these were crystal, love and moonlight, the breath of a child's first prayer.

Even though I hadn't yet spoken, the sound of my desires resounded like a whiplash that shattered the docile silence. And even though fear was something these creatures gave no harbor, the jolt of my desires sent shock waves through the flock. They started, nearly bolted when their princess calmed them down, reminding them that nothing on earth could harm them.

"It's nothing more than the thought waves of a very young soul in quest, and though he wears the body of a monstrous, fiery being, his heart is pure and his mind is growing clear."

She turned to me. I wasn't sure that she could even see me. Yet her posture and position left me little doubt that she could see through the nimbus clouds that masked the darkest day. Hovering like a hummingbird, she flew into my midst, infusing me with a kind of compassion that flows from a higher soul. She was larger than the others and so exquisite in her aura that I could see an archangel shining from within. She scanned me for a moment, her eyes glinted with delight, and she let me know by a brush of the wing that I needn't utter a word.

"Your journey takes you through the gems. It is an arduous path. But every step of the way you grow much stronger. And even though you near the end, the final path is the steepest because it takes you to the loss of self. Listen to your inner-soul and remember, though it seems the end of your world, the real adventure is waiting just beyond.

"The hardest part in all of this is discerning your own bodies and learning the ones in which you really dwell. Most creatures get lost in their desires and come to believe them to be their destiny. That's what leaves them pinioned to this earth. And though I see that very soon you'll fall victim to that delusion, the course for you is clear and its yours to choose. Just remember, wherever you go, your angels are at your side. Call to them, and they will enter your heart.

"Now, I have a wish to grant, a gift of your own choosing. But it's how you choose it that will surely take your measure from now on. You can wish for yourself or your nation, or wish it for your clan, for if it's within my power to do I'll grant it."

I wondered if I could be released, and come to the end of this test, be granted all the rest of my gems and go on. My inner self told me that I could, but told me that if I did that I'd regret that easy path to knowledge. I didn't know enough to desire the other things of this world; and I knew revenge was a petty pursuit in any incarnation. So, I let my future guide me and asked the Mantilough Princess to see into my stars and tell me the best that I could want.

She looked and in an instant beheld the moment that I'd need her, and almost sternly nodded her commitment.

"If the moon is masked and the risk is high and the winds are devoid of direction, danger threatens your life, and only we can match the game. Call for us, and we'll even the odds then quickly go our way. For we're not of this earth, or your illusions of right and wrong. Still they're important to you, and you've set your course in time, to clear evil from the path of civilization. It is a hopeless task, I see, but part of your learning process. So, we will help you with your studies and buy you a moment's reprieve.

"If you put the prayer upon the wind, just name it *Equinox*. And we'll be there to work our little magic.

"I pray for your clarity. I rejoice in your strength. I respect the path you have chosen. Glory will mark your days to come, and Honor will come with it. You'll know your share of pain as well, and mourning will cross your countenance. You'll uncover secrets unknown before, and you'll find the treasures of man. Eventually you'll even find your self...I wish you peace."

With her final phrases the Mantilough Princess had thinned to a pink wisp of air and risen into the light of the dawning day. But her blessing had surely made its way to my heart. As the sunlight came I realized my soul had been adrift in all this, and this Chthonic School was still a part of my path.

§§§§§§§

The Mantilough Princess had predicted it well.

The last path was the steepest. And destination's end was a complete surprise to me.

I felt as if I'd seen it all by then. Neither Heaven nor Earth nor all the ethers inbetween could catch me unaware, could hold a secret I hadn't shared, for I was certain I'd seen it all before. But arrogance is a catapult to folly, and no sooner was I able to claim those feelings as my personal law than they were rendered useless. After the mad cacophonies of the dark forest, after the furious twists of language hurled at me by the Tree Fury, there was nothing here—not a noise, not a sound, not a breath from my body nor the wild churn of my thoughts could be heard in this ether of solitude.

There was no place to hide in here, no dimensions around which to slip and feel clever. I was emptied of presence, allowed no form at all. For time beyond caring, I neither saw nor heard a measurable thing. I was weightless, a nonentity who found treasure in the distinction.

But there is always a void to be filled. Slowly, as if the dawning of a dark blue sun had bled onto this weightless world, there glowed a dazzling azure light, reflecting crystal powers of the ancient sapphire making its presence felt.

It was a presence—high and holy, unblemished and utterly pure. There was no hydra guarding this one, neither monstrous apparition nor tricky mage. It was clear, evolved from base vibration, a blue beacon, a commingling of deepest indigo and starlit hues. It was the most sublime of all the stones that I had yet beheld, and by every faculty of that perception it was there for the plucking, this sapphire, this crystal sky fruit to feed my middle eye.

I sensed all this about the stone, yet I felt compelled to forsake it. I rejected its simple eloquence. I was explicitly suspicious. I "knew" there'd be a catch. It was then I realized the toll that the Tree Fury had finally extracted. Gone were my wit, my guile, my taste for mental intrigue, my physical strength, my emotional resolve. I was drained, emptied and detached, no longer a cadet in this bizarre initiation. If this were another trial for me I decided this time they could have it; there was only so much that one could be put to the test.

It was then I was reminded that this fear came from my mind, a mind scarred with experiences of combat, angst and pain. I stopped. I looked for a place to retreat, but there was nothing; nothing was there to fear. "The mind is the slayer," I heard my own voice say. "Let the mind go, and listen to the heart."

I heard my heart. I went behind it to the garnet gem and found my soul's desire—the love that transcends all. And in that love I found the oneness, the sense of unifying with all things I had come to know would be my greatest source of strength. Re-approaching the sapphire, standing in its light, I unified with this gem. I became one with it and in that oneness found an answer: it was mine to have *sans façon.*

I took the sapphire and, as I took it, a body of purest vapors loomed up from its essence: an apparition of the OrfBear, the Great Orf Oversoul, appeared. It was a blessing vision, a guiding spirit that stood me in a light of indigo and kept me in the silence where only deepest thoughts reside.

This sapphire, the Great Orf let me know, was a gift to me for ending the curse upon them, for liberating its clan to the Sol of us all. For every energy put forth there is an equal payment. For what I'd done to free the OrfBear, the Sapphire would be mine.

Learning to accept a grace may be the most difficult lesson of all. For I, Dragon, born to the Struggle, this was beyond my abililty to accept. But I had learned some other lessons too. And every cell on my body told me truly; this was real. There was love behind these thoughts that I would not resist. If this were deception then I had learned nothing and deserved to go no further.

I placed the stone between my eyes and felt its true blue essence cool my vision, helping me to see things that I had never seen before. This serene corundum light of high angelic vision fused into my forebrain, flowed into my amber eyes and turned them azurite. Now with this true blue sight, I could see all dimensions merge at once. I could summon masters from planes that no one else could see. That single sight, that understanding of oneness, had been my own cosmic calling card from the day I arrived on this Earth. The Great Orf spirit helped to let me see that every creature on the earth, by divine right, possessed his personal gem—his birthstone, as it were. Mine was the sapphire. With that single eye, I could see all planes of life and, if the host were willing, merge with anything on this planet.

I was elated! If this were true, then by receiving the sapphire, I was home already. The Diamond would be just an angel's flight away. All seven jewels in the gembox would be mine. I'd be aligned, complete and whole, a master dragon at such an early age!

"Knowing the tune does not make one a player," I heard a voice say. Like a slap across my face, it awakened me from my flirtations with euphoria. There was no mistaking it. After all this time, I could have picked that voice in the largest choir in heaven. Unless I was wrong, and I wasn't wrong, it belonged to the MasterSinger, and I realized that another test still awaited me. Just as the lonely truth of it struck me, the OrfBear spirit vanished, leaving a trail of cleansing mist as its lasting gratitude. It stepped through that gentle shower of truth, and the moment that I felt it, I was dropped from that ether to another level far below—a bed of slate marked by neither moisture nor light. I was a solitary creature once again, surrounded on all sides by stark stone walls from which there seemed no exit. Only one surface at that, the wall directly facing me, showed the slightest trace of flaw —a crack, no wider than a serpent's smile through which some lower form of life might gain passage.

At first glance, this partition seemed impregnable to me. Had it been a mountain or a sea, had there been pygmie soldiers in legion, I could have taken the measure of it. But there was no measuring this; this was monolith. It surrounded me on all sides, offering neither ceiling nor sky nor ground for me to grip.

Since oneness was my challenge, here, I tried to unify with the walls. If oneness were the only issue, I would unify with this monolith, absorb its vibration, and find the passage out.

I tried to merge, but no sooner did I try then my own energies reflected upon me as if some mocking adversary had just returned a volley. I was blocked. Obstructed by the shock of my well-intended, failure, I stood at wits' end when a speck appeared on the floor before me. I'd had little eye for such things in past and, all other things being equal, would probably not have noticed it in the least. But necessity makes explorers of us all.

Lowering my head to study this minuscule being more closely, I tracked its moves, its pauses, its subtle shifts of direction. It was an insect and, other than the oversized arthropods that skated on the waters of Sagro's bog, the first I'd ever seen. How tiny it appeared to me, yet how adept in its movements. Following this insect's every step, I found myself admiring its singularity of purpose — to make its way to the wall in front of it. Since I had mastered the Mother of Tongues I could speak its ancient language. But seemingly heedless of me the insect wouldn't respond.

Calling out, I strained to make it heed me and even thought of more forceful measures such as sweeping it off its feet and bringing it right to my face. But there was such disparity of size, I was quickly made aware that I was so great an obstacle, so huge to this small being, I must have seemed a continent at least. Unless he understood me fully and was actually playing dumb, I now stood at an impasse in the game. Yet as I felt this, my skin began to crawl with newly honed perceptions. And what it told me was that this tiny master bug was blocking me on purpose. He was more than a little aware of all that I wished and was simply putting me through his own examination. Yet in order for me to employ his guidance, I would first have to find my way to him: reach his mind, strike his senses, crack his sly resistance. Summoning my inner powers, I unified with this creature, becoming one with his inner self and in so doing I was humbled.

This insect was a cockroach, a noble among its kind, the ancient multi-cellular conqueror of this earth. He had been here first, and promised to be here when we'd all gone.

"You think your force of presence makes you rulers of all...Be warned. Your prodigious size renders you extinct from the beginning. Long ago, before the mighty dragon had come to Earth, before this tiny plane of life had bought and sold its universal destiny, *we* were here. We might have dominated too. We might have grown to the proportions of a pygmie or even a dragon. But having pioneered in other worlds like this we kept our perspective and learned the truth that in the end the small devours the large.

"No creation can permit another larger than itself to thrive. And in the end the microbe wins the battle of physique. So if you wish to last awhile then learn to be less grand. Meanwhile there might be thing or two I can teach you."

I began to see this insect's point, to empathize completely. As I took that empath to him, he began to merge with me, drawing me down to his tiny world until I had released the need to be the dragon and joined him in his body. I had released myself; that was the trick. I had caught the roach's mind. Now I strolled around in its shell, in its tiny master's skin.

The world was largely different now and, in its new immensity, a more terrifying place than it had ever been before. The floor on which I lately stood, smooth as a glass in moonlight, had become a course of dunes over which we traversed on our way toward the single sheaf of rock whose facings from this upcast perspective seemed like friezes carved with codes of gods. The crack in the wall (which I had almost forgotten), had now taken a plausible perspective, becoming the walls of some timeless canyon, a route through which I could crawl until I found the sanctuary of some other side of space.

Expecting see to some black hulking dragon skin I'd invariably left behind, I gave a backward glance, and saw instead not a single trace of what I'd been. Instead I'd become a one inch "roach," a mere fleck of a life form scurrying through hostile canyons to an uncharted land.

For a time, I enjoyed in this strange duality—two souls housed in one, the roach edifying me in all the ways of getting through his tiny world. We conversed for a while, quite candidly I felt, until I realized this essence of the other soul—the roach soul was subsiding. From all I could tell, it was departing this body to let me take its place.

"I'm fading from myself, as is agreed," the cockroach admitted. "You may stay as long as you will; for eternity if need be. You may resummon me when the time is right, if that comes to pass. And if it does...well, of course, you know the holy mantra that gets us back into ourselves again. You have the Diamond in your grasp, of course."

"Of course," I answered. Of course, I didn't. But what was I to say? To tell him otherwise was to lose the moment and would have defeated us both. After all, what choice had I? Getting out of this *cul de sac* was the only issue at the moment. And one must live in the moment. (My sister would have understood.)

The cockroach left me, slipped away to some astral rendezvous where souls in suspension dance in indeterminate cycle. I let him sense my gratitude before he went away but didn't tell him all that would face me now.

Not at all sure I was able to assume the full responsibility for this uncharted transmigration of souls, I sped through the canyon crack in the wall, a lonely little insect scurrying pell mell toward a destination of undetermined virtues. All along the way I encountered creatures seldom perceived before, single-celled pernicious beings with pseudopod sucker feet. Fungi and ground mites I had never dreamt were here, took on an aspect of importance in my life, furrowing up from the stone, clinging with sticky residues that my body cleansed by rote. On the way a gang of fleas, each one-hundredth my size, threatened me with reprisals should I tarry.

I wasted no in time getting on my way. A dragon in uncertain skin is just another soul in conflict, and I had no way of knowing the things of which this roach was capable. I made a vain attempt to fly and, though I flew, was quickly made to learn the limitations of this narrow place through which I passed. I smacked into this canyon corridor, came crashing down and for a moment lay upon my back. Fully expecting some damage to be done, I righted myself and to my surprise had avoided either deformity or pain. (Sensory deprivation was a key no doubt to their longevity.)

From time to time negotiation in this strange little body was difficult. But I had to remember I was a cockroach now, a creature gifted with some wit and a decent measure of intelligence but with a body utterly alien to me, one without a manual to tell me how to use it. Cells have an intelligence of their own, I seemed to recall. Having merged my cells with his, I finally came to realize that all I had to do was let this roach's bank of muscle-memory proceed and simply go along for the ride.

Flying was out; fair enough. I carried on as best as shank's mare and my (six) spindly legs could carry me. Exhausted, I emerged from that hostile canyon and felt a beam of taupish light, a time-torn stairway undulating upward toward the source — an ancient doorway whose passage was in part at least obstructed by a sombrous, smelly, hirsute mound of mold whose single sign of animation was the grinding of its teeth that somehow glowed with yellow iridescence in the dark.

Seeing only shadows from where I stood, I might have had some cause to start at such a noxious thing, had I not glimpsed its murky aura many times before. And though my feelings were somewhat mixed I had to laugh to see, on the landing leering down at me, old Sagro's friend, the rat.

§§§§§§

"**Well, well, well!** Look who's 'arrived'!" the gray rat sassily yawned. He never once looked up from his preening and even took some extra time to lick his fur, using his razor-blade front teeth to snip a hangnail from his toe. Finally, peering over the ledge, he cocked an eye at me and, as if he were calling from a cliff by ocean's roar, shouted loudly: "And just what rock did you crawl out from under?"

Despite my demi-insect guise, the rat was never fooled. He knew me in my essence and made no pretense of affection. He called me by my dragon name and at the same time let me know just where I stood with him.

Sneering quite perniciously, he leered at me and said, "I know you've never liked me. And your snobbery frankly bores me. But since I've long ascribed to the politics of survival, I accept your shallow disdain. I've chosen to rise above it. I've endured your elitist ways, your patronizing stares and your condescending airs. But now things are a little different. Now, you're a cockroach. At this very moment, I could crush you beneath my feet like the loathsome bug you are, or maybe catch you up and hold you between my teeth while you squirm and squeal for freedom. Then, I could bite down a time or two and grind you into mush. And you could do nothing, because *you* don't know the mantra to get you out of this one. Do you?"

He had me there, this little runt, though not so little now. Our roles had been reversed and how he gloated. Where I'd been dragon to this vermin, he was now monstrous to me. That I had changed, there was no doubt. But somehow so had he. He'd dropped his sly conspiracies, the helpful little asides he'd used like coupons to ingratiate himself to us. He was lord of the moment now and made sure to let me know it. He held the power of life over me and might well have exercised it had he not been acting on strictest orders to bring me home.

I bit my lip (such as it was) and took his pompous prating in good spirit. He strutted and pranced his way about the steps for a time but, growing quickly bored of that, ordered me to follow.

"Well come on, 'roach," he barked aloud, making a motion to leave. Without waiting another moment, he dashed up the stairs, stopping only long enough to remember that I was not the creature I used to be and to reproach me for what I'd become. "Don't think you're going to get out of this one so easily. You may have passed the first six levels with flying colors, but you tried to take the short cut here. Dumb. Dumb. Double dumb. Shows you've learned nothing, to *my* way of thinking."

I scrambled to catch up. Using my nimble insect legs to scale the jagged steps, I moved (I thought) with considerable dexterity. A step or two ahead of me each time, the gray rat kept running, pausing only to scratch himself and pile on the ridicule.

"So this is the Lightning Dragon of such legendary potentials. Has reached six levels up to now, has he? But tut tut tut, it looks as though he's going to come up short. I don't know how the MasterSinger will like it, but I don't think he'll like it much. Maybe he'll send you back for remedial training. I've seen him do it before. You never know, he just might do it again."

On the threshold of completion always sits the Imp of Doubt. Listening to this rodent's prattle, I felt a rush of fear. I wondered what would happen if I had to face it all again? I blanched at the expectation of it, yet knew inside my cells that this path was not to be walked a second time.

Suddenly, it occurred to me. This pathetic little rodent in his impotent contempt had let me know at last just where I stood. I had come far, quite far indeed, and was exactly where I was supposed to be.

This was not the grandiose return I'd hoped for, I admit. But it was the right one. By following this "lowly" insect path I had taken the final step toward my destination. I had become the roach: the roach had endured for all time and, in the end, would outlast even the industrious rat. The roach, perhaps, and not the dragon was the master of physique.

Willing to take whatever fell upon my insect's path, I
followed the rat through a crack of light and out into the dim
gray open space where once again we had returned to familiar
ground. It was a homecoming of sorts, for this last leg of the
journey had led me to the dying branch of some tired starving
tree overlooking a bog. Not just any swamp, this was *the bog* in
the Cavern of Living Thoughts; Sagro's home and mine for so
long a time.

All memories intact, I gazed above and saw the cavern scrogz,
below the skinjie fish enmired in their foraging—the muck, the
mist, and in their midst Old Sagro gnawing mulch. He barely
raised his head to check me out, and even when the rat took
mocking pains to herald me, the dragone cocked an eye and kept
on chewing. No signs of elation came from him, no uttering of
"job well done." He wasn't one to stroke the ego, this old dragon
sage. And yet my voices told me he was pleased.

"Not bad," he nodded, finally. "Of course you're not there
yet. And part of the danger of seeking the Diamond is getting
trapped in the wrong facet of your consciousness. You tend to
forget just who you are and why you started in the first place.

"That's the danger of oneness. You become so much a part
your subject that you forget entirely who you were. You've tasted
that deadly sample already. You've started to become the roach.
And tomorrow you'll be more so, I assure you. There have been
many highborn souls who got lost in their new skins. They
became absorbed in their earthbound roles and scotched their
holy mission. That's how we all got into this mess in the first
place."

He was studying me, expecting an answer, and wouldn't
indulge my reticence. "Well, don't just sit there," he said. "You
got yourself into this. Get yourself out. And I suggest you do so
before a skinjie singles you out for a snack."

I'd expected further revelations, but those were not to come.
Faced with this dilemma Sagro had challenged me to solve, I
now would have to answer in some demonstrable way. It was as
simple as that.

"Oh, by the way..." he added, quite offhandedly. "Regaining your former self in no way awards you the Diamond. It only grants you license to pursue it."

Nothing ever ends, I've learned; there's always *something* else. I'd rather expected this might come to pass, and yet I'd hoped somehow that better would come of it. It didn't.

"Only one more," the MasterSinger answered, hearing every whisper of my mind. "Ah, but what a beauty! And don't be so disparaging, my young friend. Life outside's just a continuum of this. One challenge will just lead you to the next...until all tests are taken, all puzzles solved, all prayers answered, every issue complete. That's the fun of it."

If that was his idea of fun, he could have it all. I'd take another plane of existence in another kind of world. But what the hell, I was in for the finish, so finish it I would. And the first step was to get out of this little roach's skin. I breathed deeply, and as I did I saw the gray rat break away. Darting down from the branch on which we sat, he ran for the dragone's wing, skipping with his scrawny legs across the muck where a pair of hungry skinjie fish made a lunge to catch him in their jaws. The skinjies missed but made the miss quite close enough to put a nick on the little runt's rear just before he bounded to the top of Sagro's head and sat there breathing heavily with quivering relief.

Another time, another incarnation, and I might have enjoyed the sport, but such as I was I came to realize and quickly that I was fair game as well. Before I'd had time to catch my breath, a double-headed skinjie fish had arched out of the muck and mire and made a leap at me.

Reminders come from hungry jaws that we are only mortal. I quickly had to come into my dragon self again. What I didn't know for certain was just what dragon I would become. Would I become The Lightning Dragon once more? Or would I be something new? There was no longer time to ponder. By now, I'd drawn a crowd.

Remembering that I was a dragon after all, I merged with old Sagro himself and found a feast of knowledge more bountiful than I'd ever dreamt could be. Rather than block me the MasterSinger had let me know him in his entirety, a being to be seen as soon as I unlocked the door to his mind.

I was close, closer than I had realized, for in my roach's body I felt the power of all my gems fire me with sensations. From base of thorax to third eye, I was alight, a flame of purpose. I saw inside the MasterSinger, heard his prayers, knew the nature of his higher and his lower selves. His lower self—the rat—as I'd suspected was this mini-miscreation held in check by divine resource.

"Most beings are their lower natures," his inner voices said. "To eliminate the lower self entirely is to ascend, and I'm not yet ready for that Leap. So I keep this little fellow here to remind me of what we've become. Besides, having a lower nature is a joy, and I've learned so much from him. We have become great friends and love one another dearly."

There was more. He could only show me the being of his higher nature, it seemed, if I were able to pluck from him a release into my self. That seemed a plausible task in the beginning; not in the end.

I probed. I dug. Yet I found nothing. And from that nothingness, there finally came an answer. His higher self (the dragon) and his lower self (the rat) were one. And if his higher self and lower self were one, then his higher self and angelic-self were one. Finally, of course, his angelic-self was one with the God-self. Such was the order of things.

We were all cells on God's body; perfect or blemished we were all one. This was the order of our understanding; this was the truth that gave ultimate peace to the long tormented mind. At once the truth of those thoughts surged through me in a charge of electricity that fired out of my mouth in a torch of revelation.

"All selves are but selves of God," I said. "And in that self Thou choosest for me, Thy Higher Will be done."

I don't know from where the words had come. One does not conjure that kind of lofty imagery *de novo*. Rather than try to force my self to come to be, I had released it. I had let go of the need to control my destiny. It was that letting go that blew the cap for me.

In a rush that came more quickly than a quark could sift through a nanosecond, the roach had re-entered his body and I'd exploded upward, shooting forth in plumes of light, a full grown dragon eighty feet or more of fire-forged onyx marked with a livid lightning bolt rampant upon my chest. I felt supreme. I was the dragon prince I'd always hoped to be, without course, without cost! And yet I felt a sense of loss.

I looked back down to see what I had been and realized the sacrifice that had been made. This roach, this tiny friend, had lasted only long enough to be a chrysalis for me. He had given me his body to use as my cocoon, my lowly pupa held in check before I came back home. Now that I had emerged, he lay an empty shell, his own soul only then vacated and on its journey to another place.

Even though I'd only been with him awhile, I felt a rush of sadness at the sacrifice he'd made. Where once I might have taken such a life for granted—where I once might have crushed this brother creature beneath my feet and never even noticed—I had learned: all that breathes its life upon this plane is worth respecting. Nothing that we touch is ever left undone.

"Don't mourn the soul that's raised to greater heights, my Dragon Prince! Celebrate!" I heard Old Sagro say. I heard him say and didn't believe. For once, his admonition stuck inside my craw. For the first time, filled with the fires of righteous indignation, I felt superior; right in my opinions. A full-grown dragon with a cache of gems to claim as my escutcheon, I gazed down at this old codger and challenged his detachment.

"How can one rejoice at the destruction of another?" I raged. "What kind of respect for life is that?"

"'Twas by consent," Old Sagro countered. "It was the only way to free you from your pose. The roach was in accord. No pain came from it. He was ready to transform, and so were you."

"But I had answered the mantra. I thought that would set me free."

"Not without repercussion of some kind. Not unless you've won your *Diamond I.* There's the rub, my young Shartallion. Nothing comes without a price. And the price you pay for the Diamond can be very dear indeed. Until you've mastered that rare crystal, you never know the havoc you reap.

"Even when you get it, or think you've got it, it can fool you. For the *Diamond I* forever is the teacher. Until you grasp every one of its facets you'll learn some very tough lessons. And don't be overly encouraged by this sense of oneness divinely given in your nature. Gifts are lessons too, my friend. Of that, you can be sure.

"It's quite the same with all the gems, you know. That you've attained the six thus far is a master stroke, a rare one to be sure. But they're not as much a blessing as you think. You'll be admired by some. You'll be envied by many. You'll even be hated by a few; a few more than you'd like. And most of all you get to spend the rest of your life relearning what you've learned."

"Never!" I shouted. It was a reflex; I knew better than to say it. Yet like a whale sounding salt for breath, I blew the words out of my mouth. Flames spat forth in high panache spelled out my frustration. "I've worked hard to find the way here! I've come by my gems honestly from the toil upon my brow. And no one, neither man nor Shimbagh, neither god nor master teacher can deny me that."

"And no one will," came Sagro's gentle answer. "What I've told you is the truth; it simply is."

"Then what use for the cream of dragonkind, anyway?" I thought, aloud. "We strive to seek the right, yet most beings fear us. We're likened unto Shimbaghs and mongrels of the Pit. We're loathed and feared by the pygmie who swears to do us in. We're fearsome, (some think) loathsome; and even though we're awesome, we're no great things of beauty, to my mind. And no matter what we do, it seems, the tides of time flow in against us. The Titans are gone, the gods of Olympus have fallen from their thrones. What hope have we of the Mystic Clan in this world of tiny things?"

"No one said it was going to be easy," Old Sagro answered. "This planet's too small for us, that's for sure. And perhaps we're 'peaking out.' But this much I can tell you, we've a job to do before we go. Whether we are able to do it or not, I haven't a clue. We can only try." He answered offhandedly, yet it smacked of presentiment, a deep disturbing hidden truth that caused me to rebel.

"Then why pretend we're something we're not? Why bother with it at all? Why serve a world that hates us so, when we could run it ourselves? There are force and numbers in dragonkind to quite devour this earth. Why not take it and make it ours to keep? Burn away the dross! Turn this sphere into a crucible of holy higher purpose! We have the eyes of God to serve; we and we alone! The pygmie's far too blind to see and lost in his own obsessions! We, the dragons of this earth, could make better custodians of its future than the pygmie. Why should we be condemned to abdicate this power?"

Other thoughts flowed out of me: some scattering of anger; others less profound; I said too much; I regretted parts; but Sagro was past regretting. Nonetheless, he answered me with some difficulty.

"We have a debt to pay," he intoned.

"What debt can be so grave that we must surrender all to pay it off? What measure of iniquity is that upon our kind?"

For the first time that I'd known this dragon his visage crossed to sorrow. He bowed his head. His eyes closed. His lips trembled as if he were uttering some rosary of contrition. Slowly from his mouth, the words slipped out in a whisper greater in its volume than any cry I'd ever heard.

"We are the Fallen Angels," he said. "We were the chosen to bring this world into the light of redemption, to uplift it, to raise its vibration to the consciousness of the All-being Universal Mind. But we were seduced by the Fallen One—the Angel who sat at his Father's hand—to take this garden as our colony, our playground in the flesh.

"We sought the realm of the sensuous existence and in that seeking paid the price. We followed the Fallen One in his rebellion, and we were driven down with him. We, the Sons of Draco, forged in the fire of God's left eye—glorious angels, beings of lambent beauty such as mortals had never seen—were turned to dragons, Shimbaghs, Creatures of the Pit, beings hideous and horrid whose visages the lesser creatures of this world were terrified to see. The Fallen One, the Angel of Night, reveled in this moment of abandonment, swore his vengeance and made a vow to reign over this tiny orb of light until the end of time. He swore to rule it with a Pride that only fear could foster, to make it his mistress, to waltz in the turmoil that mars it to this day.

"Most followed him. The Shimbaghs, the khados, the kingus, the serpents, sorcerers and witches dwelled with him in their corrupt uncertain power.

"But dark powers have their facets too, and from them sprang rebellion. The dragons among us, the members of the Mystic Clan who'd kept our Godsight clear, rebelled again; this time against the Fallen One. In opposing Him, we sought redemption. Through God's love we were redeemed. But that vindication came with a penance that was both dire and severe.

"Where we'd once been dazzling angels, fountains of resplendency no mortal mind could comprehend, we were condemned to wear these awful towers of fire and scale for all our days on earth. Tarnished with the Shimbagh brand, loathed by nations, feared by all, forced to bear the stigma of our former reputation, we have endured. We've forged our honor in the flame. We've kept the secrets of the gems. We've borne the burden of the Light to pass it on to man, and through this complicated being—so primitive and young—to all the other creatures of this world.

"That is the secret of the Diamond. That is the Oneness you must find in that endlessly complex, multi-faceted, famously self-possessed 'I.' And when you do, you will come to know that simple truth: All selves are but selves of God. All must be raised. The dove and the roach, the worm and the tree, even the Shimbaghs of the Pit—all will be raised. And this tiny creature, man, has been chosen to bear that final torch.

"It is our job to care for him, to protect him until he comes of age. No matter what violations he perpetrates against us, we must forbear. Despite his ignorance and folly, his avarice and lust, there will come among him master souls to show us all the way.

"Therefore my dear Shartallion, it is we who must guard the path. We must share our secrets with them. We must pass them the Light. We must treat them as our children and keep them in our care until the time; until The Time."

Hearing such a revelation made me want to weep. I cursed my fate. It filled me with despair to realize that we were merely transitional beings on this plane of life called Earth. Here in this workhouse for fallen souls, we would be permitted to stay just long enough pay our cosmic penance. I became downcast. I held my head low and shuddered from horn to talon to think that I, Dragon was little better than a Shimbagh of the Pit. And though my clan was working day and night to keep these mutants in check, ultimately we'd have to embrace them as our brethren too.

"All selves would be but selves of God! All must be raised!" I heard the prayer again and recognized it well, this time. Yet there was a power behind it such as I had never felt before.

By force of energy alone the words had lifted my head, bringing me to face the MasterSinger. The toothless decadragon shell I'd come to know and love had now been shed, and from its molter had sprung a tower of odic light crowned by plumes of blue-white flame that arched and tapered at the end to form seraphic wings. From a face more splendid than any mortal being could know, a loving pair of sapphire eyes had set their stars upon me.

Between us roared the lake of fire, the blue-white flame I remembered. The stones, the crystals—glistening quartz, sardonyx, whitest white—now laced the floor where earlier the stew of dross had brewed. The ceiling like a citadel, celestial in its height, now topped the place where miscreants had earlier done their dances. The long gray rat had transcended too, and in his place a dove of snow and silver circled above as if it were a motile part of this bright angel's crown.

Between us yet above, suspended in a cone of crystalline light, there sat the Diamond. The Diamond! The holy gem! The capstone to my quest! It rested there within my reach and yet so far away that I felt as if it were the birth-child of another galaxy.

Suddenly I understood that, through this pain of being brought so low, there was a way to find redemption and rediscover the angel who dwelled within. For proof I needed look no farther than this holy entity—the MasterSinger, a dragon who had transcended his world.

"Your perceptions are correct, my dragon prince," he said. "There is a path that master souls take to create their realities at will. But finding it takes a dragon's lifetime, and only through the Diamond is it found."

Through the Diamond before my brow, I faced the MasterSinger one last time.

"You've come far, my Lightning Dragon. Of that you can be proud. But you still have far to go." His angelic voice bore no judgment—only love and understanding—yet in his closing benediction were these words of admonition. "You don't choose the *Diamond I.* It chooses you.

"I'll stand in its light until the end of time!" I swore. "I'll wait forever, if need be."

"Give it that kind of energy, and you will," came the reply. Although this angel of my enlightenment was vaporizing into a holy nimbus before my eyes, even as he dematerialized, his thoughts left a trail of firewinds in his wake. "Don't overdo it," he whispered in warning. "This one's tough enough as it is. Don't press it. Just let it happen."

Above the lake, the dove remained as a sentry for the Diamond as if to aid me in this vigil of which I'd become a part.

Yet it seemed at least an eon before a single thing took place. The lake of blue-white flame burned on; the dove flew aimlessly; the Diamond glistened; I stayed awaiting my epiphany of light. Nothing.

My patience was being tested to the fullest. If that be the case, I felt, so be it. If I were going to stay here 'til it was a decadragon I became, then I would wait. Until oceans dried, until the earth turned to dust, until the sun died in the sky and hell froze over, I would wait until that Venutian tendril was in its home in me for once and always.

I spoke these things outloud. Though thoughts have long lives, it is words that give them force of physical intent. As if my resolutions had slammed against this core of inner earth, there came a violent shuddering that shook me where I stood. From underturnings deep within, this cavern crucible began to crumble. Rocks of brimstone, firestone, lodestone and sard were splitting, shattering about my head and flanks. Above me, boulders of marble came crashing all around, and everywhere jaws of quartz, carried on a tongue of white-hot lava, chewed their way toward the sky.

So this was to be my final test: courage in the face of death. Not just any death, this was cataclysm, the ending of a world as I had known it. Gotterdammerung!

In the midst of this upheaval, I felt another kind of jolt. A loss of reference, a sense of desolation, the destruction of this physical realm now overshadowed me. I was being buried alive in a cascade of falling stones, raging comets of this inner world each aimed smartly at my head. Yet that was not my peril. This was all a game of sorts. My body was a chess piece in a test-match. Were it to be knocked off the board, another would come in its place. It was this cycle of destruction that concerned me most. It seemed never to end. It set its course relentlessly through all points of measured time, and I was nothing more than a hanger-on, a feckless, helpless part of it. Even if I were to survive this cataclysmic trial, there would only be more of the same awaiting me outside, a sentence of three thousand years for a son of fallen angels.

In the end, the dove flew. It is written in the lore of ancient prophets that, when the dove flies North, the hope for peace is lost. This dove flew north, and my heart flew with him. I would have gone that very moment without the slightest hesitation had not a glistening from the Diamond caught my eye. I stayed, watching the fire white crystal glistening in the turning wheel of light. And in that reflection of divine love I saw my destiny. At last alone, I shuddered in surrender. With nowhere left to turn, with nothing else to be, I gave it up.

"Not my will but Thine be done," came tumbling from my lips.

I had surrendered, and as I did I saw the Diamond too begin to quaver violently from its place. It burst out of the cone of light and landed in my midst. Without a moment's hesitation I clutched it to my breast. I embraced it with my arms, my wings, my flame, my very self, and made it part of me. But before it reached the crown of my head it started to shatter — sending a billion particles of light throughout my being.

Propelled toward a light that shone above the chaos I streaked up toward the sky. As I felt my body fly free from the depths of this bleak training ground, I knew the kiss of spring upon my face. I felt the sunlight bless my brow, and I rejoiced. I had completed the quest. I had made the Seventh Level. I was the dragon of destiny to set this tortured world aright.

I had captured the Diamond. I could feel it crown my being. Yet even as I did, I heard a challenge from below that chilled me to my bones.

"But are you sure?" it trumpeted, mocking as I soared, echoing a voice I had yet to hear. Below me, through the smoky yawning mouth of Mother Earth, the crater I'd breached had now sealed shut, locked off to me forever. I had come full out this time; there was no turning back. The Chthonic School had closed, and the Sun was high.

Canto 9

The SkyMaster

Freedom filled me like a sacred self finally coming
to birth. I flew from that throat of dread and dreams and
streaked into the day. I soared, rootless, fearless, released from
gravity's tether, a meteor fueled by the joy of divine intention. I
had left limitation behind like a molting in my wake. The crystals
that crowned me — clearly visible now against the sun —
christened the land and the waters below with a wash of rainbow
colors. Throughout the morning and on to the dusk I chased the
light until the sun, I was almost certain, fled from my pursuit.

Into a night so dark the only lamp that lit its blackness
radiated from the lightning slash across my chest, I bounded for
the stars, knowing those celestial towers were but an angel's
breath beyond my reach. But I soon discovered God's house has
high ceilings, and not even a diamond-crested dragon could
reach them in a day.

Ceaselessly creasing along the patterns of clouds by day and night, I'd all but forgotten the barbs that had brought me such pain in that university of dark and terrifying truth. To my utter surprise and delight, I only recalled the pleasant times—the sense of fulfillment that I had actually gotten these Gems on my own.

I spent the second day as I had spent the first—in celebration, in celestial transportation and heavenly resort. I stayed in the clouds through currents of air and anointed my wings in the mists of the stratosphere. I paused to rest only once on that second morning of my new life, and then only long enough to bathe in a waterfall that covered me in prisms of liquid color. I basked within it for a while and through its watery veil observed a thousand forest creatures peeking from behind their leafy shields at me—deer and rabbits, birds and monkeys, great cats and timid marmosets all gawking back in wonder. What a sight I must have been! A half a mountain at the least, dark onyx hide and ice white fangs, and with a speed of flight that could be matched by no one that I knew.

Well, why not give them a show? I thought (but didn't think it out).

With a roar that sent these little beings running (just to let them know who was boss), I launched again into the air, singeing the treetops, skimming the hills and valleys until those aggregations of green became a whir, until the ground shook and my senses split at the crack of my velocity. At first I thought to slow myself, to ease these concussions with the ground, but then I decided to blow my cap, to unleash my powers in full. If I could not catch the sun by its tail, the very least I could do was to crack the veil of limitation.

As soon as I set my Heart on it, I released from my garnet flame a force of speed that nearly broke my bones, that sent my head splitting with the vibrations that my wings created until the trees bent, the rocks ricocheted their outrage and the earth propelled me outward like an arrow to the clouds with an explosion so shattering it put a chip in God's teeth.

Then, nothing…

Silence released me. I flew free from the forests and launched into the skies at speeds no mortal creature had dared before. Neither dragon nor gryphon, neither Vyngorch nor chimera had attained this velocity. Only the windgods of the North had ever pierced this dimension, for in that moment I would learn that I had shattered sound. A wondrous thing, I'd thought at first but was very soon made to know that this just wasn't done.

Dancing on air, coasting along the silent spheres of accord, I felt a sudden chill. Although it was summer in this world I had breached, a wall of hail slashed at me, icing my view and piercing my ears with an ultrasonic scream.

"Who summons me?!" Before I could even think, a high-pitched fury with a tongue of sleet stung my skin and sent me tumbling a thousand feet through the air. In a wink, a slashing gale-force hand flew into my face, seized me by my throat and tried to hold me fast. But I was too quick and dashed away to regain my composure. Yet as I did an angry cluster of jagged stratus clouds had formed a face that pressed against me with paralyzing breath. Its eyes could have frozen the fires of perdition, with a disposition to match. Whatever this furious entity was it was somewhat short on forbearance.

"Who summons me?!" he said again. "Who challenges the windgods of the North?!"

Although I now possessed the powers to perceive the face behind any mask, this was no mask that I beheld. This was a terror. This windgod tore the ice from the air to give visage to his rage. Otherwise he was a bolt of energy, neither good nor evil, doing only what the seasons and the shifts in time required. He could even be kind as winds can be. But my endeavor had rousted him out to duty before his time, and that unwitting rudeness had summoned the beast.

If a lesson remained for me to learn, it was never to piss off a god. Dodging as deftly as I could to avoid this one's attack, I knew I couldn't evade him for long. Although I was surviving his burly onslaught something was draining my strength, quickly sucking it out of me with vampiric efficiency. His drafts were too swift, his teeth too jagged, his icy pursuit too relentless for a creature of flesh and blood to resist. Wholly enveloped and nearly freeze-dried, I realized this called for conciliation on my part; not to mention a modicum of wit. Finally, once our tête-à-tête had tamed a bit, I cried:

"I summoned you, o' ancient gale, to ask about my sister, the Princess Seti! She was lost to me sometime ago, and I have grave concerns! I am her brother, Shartallion XII, Prince of the Dragon Kiln. The dragons and the winds are brothers, are they not? So I called you out. Shattering sound's barrier, I heard, might do the trick."

Intrigued, this windgod ceased bombarding me with missiles, swept up to my face and sized me up and down. The jagged nimbus of his brow arched high, unveiling scowling zirconium eyes that pierced through my intent. All the while a small Armada of sycophantic breezes goaded him into action.

"Slash him, Korlig! Dash him to the ground! Tear him limb from limb! Show him he must pay for his audacity."

Brushing them off (I'm glad he did!), he fell upon me fully, trying to decide if I were worth a single breath he'd spent.

"The Northwind gods align with no one!" He scowled. But then a bolt of revelation struck him, causing him to soften his resolve. "I know you. You're the one they spoke of; you're the Sound Stealer the prophets said would come. Usually, prophecy's a joke! But this time they called it right. Well...just when you disregard a prediction, it bites you in the ass!"

He was not one to stand on ceremony, this burly liege lord from the North. Noting my apparent loss of speed, he hurled me to a mountain top where I could catch my breath and, sweeping along with more sociable intent, joined me on a nearby peak. His name was Korlig, First Son of the Maelstrom. Born in the North of Seas, he was the eldest of twelve windgods of the northern latitudes of Earth, a vicious oligarchy known as the Tarewinds. It was rumored that the Tarewinds, were they ever to band as One, could turn the Earth into an orb of ice within a day. This had never come to pass; the Tarewinds held no love for one another, so never did more than three of them band together at a time. Among them, Korlig was known to all the others as 'the loner.' He was a sea wind and trusted none of the windgods of the land. Only the mountain gales that never slept and blew the whole year round were allies of this cagey zephyr, and even at that he could only count on them in emergencies such as this extraordinary energy that I'd just created.

I thank the Creator God of us all that Korlig didn't judge me. He just observed I'd cracked the ethers with my unexpected skills. It was a talent they hadn't allowed for; a false alarm, if you will. I tried to avert his attention from this, and pressed him about my sister, a gesture that caused him to pause if only to savor his reply.

With a cold, caustic whip of air he resounded, "What a prize we have in that one! It's been five years, a twitch of God's nose in sidereal time as it were, and already that scarlet princess has left her scars upon the land: Twelve combats in the sky—two with gryphons, ten with dragons—she's won them all; eight villages razed; four castles assaulted; one leveled to the ground; three armies decimated; one Northmen's naval fleet dashed upon the rocks. Oh yes! And a slew of Shimbaghs sought and slain (her good deed for the decade).

"At any rate, that's one bad lady, and she runs the show by now. Everyone who dwells in that bleak realm between the Fjords of the Finger Lands and the far seas of the West—be they dragon prince or human king—must pay her all the tribute she demands.

"She runs a band of robber dragons with an iron claw. And to spice the broth a bit further, it seems that now she's wearing her navel high. Heavy with a clutch, she is. Pregnant by the robber dragon, Urfuwl. He was the most fearsome North dragon of all before she came to roost. As chance would have it, they met in mid-sky and mated in the downdraft. He thought to stick around awhile. She slew him within a week. Not much of one for cuddling, your sister." Korlig made these observations without malice but not without a sense of irony.

"Truly, you should fly due North and pay your kin a visit. With equipment such as you possess, you'd not fare half the bad. You might even clean up the place, school them in the ways of virtue. But then your sibling simply wouldn't abide that point of view. If I know her (and I think I do), you'd get ridiculed for your efforts. She doesn't take much stock in goodness, has no patience for good works. Come to think of it, neither does anyone else in that wasteland of moors and mountains. They look upon virtue as weakness and treat it with contempt. They'd rather eat it that mete it any day.

"It's bitter in that desolate place. It's the afterbirth of perdition. Nothing lasts for long up there, and dragons are no exception. Your sister might as well have her fun, because her reign is doomed by the weight of time and the ebbs and flows of that collected evil. Urfuwl, her erstwhile spouse, enjoyed the longest reign on record, and he only clipped the top side of a century or two. Not much for longevity as dragons go, but at least his days weren't dull. It's the price one pays for diversion, I suppose. One *always* pays the price."

Korlig was right to one extent; the North would never be the place for me. My destiny lay on other paths. I knew that much, at least.

"To the West," he said. "The answers to your dreams begin there. Where they end is another matter."

He blew himself off of the mountain peak and whipped down in front of me. Just to remind me of who he was, he gathered his wind gust entourage who did a feral dance. Their whirling, swirling mocking airs chilled me to my bones, tore away the shrubs, and filled the crags with sleet and rains of hail. They finished in a frenzy, screaming out at me, then returned to cling to Korlig like the satellites they were. To respond to their seeming expectations, the windgod cautioned me.

"We'll let you dance, my Lightning friend, as long as you know the dancer. When you steal the Sound, you summon us.

And you'd better have an answer." With that, he paused. As if in afterthought, he reminded himself there was a means, a key of power, that would grant me license to carry on at will. For a moment or two, he seemed to convene with a host of invisible brethren. Then, as if having received approval from some absent quorum of souls, he proceeded to let me know.

"There is someone better than you, a more brilliant flyer than you have yet to dream of; this creature might have broken sound's barrier anytime it liked. But this one plays by the rules. That's why this one is Master of the Skies.

"If you want to fly as you desire and do as you damn well please, then first you have to outdo the SkyMaster, challenge this master to feats of skill—with all the windgods watching—and prevail. Then the prize will belong to you. And for all the days of your life, the skies will be yours to enjoy, to play with impunity as no other creature can. That is…if you win, for if you lose, you do so at the SkyMaster's whim. Not a position I'd like to be in, I assure you."

Korlig laced his stipulation with a dash of implication, the implication being that I wasn't in this aeronaut's league. I wondered who this creature might be, yet that seemed academic. It was a dragon, of course. Dragons ruled the stratospheres. Any fool knew that. So I asked the simple question:

"And what dragon would that be?"

I should have known better than to take anything for granted. As it turned out, my drift of thoughts set Korlig awhirl with gusts of ridicule.

"You dragons and your vanity. You think you're the only ones able to fly like gods. Well come to times, Shartallion XII. There are others that match you. There are some who will surpass you. And the SkyMaster's surely one." He didn't offer to tell me who or what the SkyMaster was and would not tell me when I sought to ask. "You'll find out soon enough," he said. "And rest assured, the SkyMaster knows you're around. The whole damned world caught your act!"

Without further ceremony, the windgod tore away the clouds that gave him form and became a chilling air-form once again.

"I don't stand on ceremony," he said, in parting. "I'm sure I'll see you again, if for no other reason than to preside at your comeuppance."

This windgod made no raucous exit; he simply was no more. His departure was detectable only by a return of warmth to the mountaintops. The sun burned through the cloud train he'd left, and it was second spring again. A warm breeze with a friendly face followed shortly thereafter, a holy white horizon crowned by swirling thunderheads and the scattered rays of morning.

It was through those towers of cumulous clouds that I climbed into the day and first saw a graceful flight form gliding in and out, soaring up through spokes of sunlight and indifferent to what I was. It was at least a league away. And it kept its distance from me. Yet, by its lissome vigil it appeared to have reached the apex of serenity.

It was the SkyMaster; it had to be. It seemed aware of me, and yet diffident to my poses. I couldn't help but wonder if it had come to await my challenge. Yet it seemed to know, as I did, that this wasn't the time for such things. After a while this lofty creature dissipated from view, flying higher into a light I wasn't yet ready to see.

§§§§§§§

One can become too much a creature of consequence. I was beginning to wonder if this were not the case with me. Already in my short life I had answered the Asking Prayer. I had been challenged to find the man who bore my mark (before he marked the end of the Mystic Clan) and had imposed upon myself the task of destroying The Magpie. As if that weren't a bout-card filled out to the edges, now I was on the SkyMaster's hit list. I'd shattered the limits of sound. Breaking that rule alone meant I'd be monitored by the winds, spied on by the breezes, all with the slavish expectation that I was going to challenge their "champion" for supremacy of the skies.

Give me the simple life! I thought, though by now I'd come to believe that life itself was one endless caveat.

I longed for home. I wasn't even sure where home would be, but I had felt a longing just the same. There are instincts that guide us all. No matter how long the absence or how far away the source, it rings in our hearts with holy chimes that call us to it: Home! I could hear the songs of dragons on the winds. I could feel their voices from the West bathing me in light, inviting me to spread my wings and join them.

The sun was now bloodstone Eucharist on a tongue of jasper sea whose rays in vermilion rivulets reached outward toward the mountains. Rising up from the sting of the waves the light sifted across my face, dousing me with a draft of hard salt air. The journey would be long, I sensed, much longer than I'd wished. All journeys were, it seemed. It was the way.

§§§§§§§

Under ordinary circumstances, my travels to the West might have taken no more than a day or so. Even had I tarried, taken in the sights, and caught a brief excursion on the side, two days would have been an ample span of time. But there were human beings along the way.

These curious little creatures, these inheritors-to-be of all that I held dear, had pocked the earth with signs of their communal gatherings. Villages and townships, nomadic huts and tents, congeries of cottages, fields of crops for cultivation, fellow creatures they kept enslaved in pens to use for milking, wool, and slaughter—I'd seen it all before when I was younger. But I saw it now with different senses—eyes attuned to auras, energies, and truths that hid beneath the physical illusion.

Even though I flew high above and looked to be no more to them than the outline of some graceful bird of flight, I could see them close enough to feel their breathing, to hear their inner voices. There was order in these places, but it was born of fear. Their buildings, their communes, their water sluices, the very ruts made by the sleds along their way to busy commerce were structures clawed out of the earth with little more in mind than the raw animal need to survive. They had structures like those of no other creature on this planet, but they had no freedom. There was laughter. There was joy, but it was tenuous and fleeting, while fear held sway and lingered like a vapor through the air.

These were not the serene societies I had first seen in the East. Merchants in their commerce, farmers in their fields, peacekeepers on patrol, each in their way reacted to the slightest sign of movement on the horizon. It was as if some rapacious force were riding on the wind. This was not a singular case as I might have imagined, but a numinosm of fear that festered and spread the further I flew West.

As the night of the first day began to fall, I came upon a final valley like so many others I had seen this day—flourishing, flowing, surrounded by mountains and a broad, green apron of land. In the middle was a city like so many others, larger perhaps than most but surrounded by a wall, oversized and seemingly built to withstand a god's wrath.

This community of human beings might have otherwise escaped my notice were it not for the mountain shoulders high above it, and were it not for the lights marking the parapets that stood above the wall. The lights were bright. They shined on men uneasy in the art of war, men in quilted skins of animals who took these torches to and fro, darting like fireflies in a frenzied dance, stopping only long enough to let one of their warriors take a post and strike a pose of valor. It seemed they were expecting company.

The night was a sheet of hematite. Its shadows hid me well. I flew above the valley to the top of a mountain shoulder whose ridges blended smartly with the hard lines of my wings. I posted in the dark and watched the villagers awhile, wondering if their frantic cries would last throughout the night, would carry as long as the dread they carried with them. I wondered less that they had reasons for fearing, for the stench of visitation was in the air. Army was already on its way. "Army," a creature whose hideous instincts I had learned to foresee, was always persistent in its intention to do efficient harm.

Night crept into early morning. The torchlights of the sentries began to fade like the fire of their expectation. This *ad hoc* garrison had grown weary, had lost the edge it held and saw its focus slip into fatigue. Whoever led this army was skilled in the masterful art of tactics, knew his opponent would fade with every moment that wore on. The commandant waited until the sharp edge of their apprehension dulled, until the cock called out the first notes of a new morning, until it seemed as if they might enjoy another day unaccosted.

It was still dark when I felt the force of them—armored men slipping quietly over the ridges to the right and left of me. Intent on the business at hand, they brushed by me as if I were a stone and made their tricky way into the valley. There were two lines of soldiers, both slithering and skulking with all the tawdry deftness of two serpents about to mate. One had to admire the skill with which they went about their business. One could scarcely hear a blade rattle, a man cough, or a horse trod on stone until the moment when these two deadly columns locked in their embrace.

Then there was hell to pay.

It was not until the final moments of this army's sly advance that the city garrison saw them fully. By that time it was too late. Battering rams at the throat of the wall, spears and swords at the ready, arrows drawn, the army struck and laid low everything in its way. A hail of missiles fell upon the outposts, dropping men like flowers in a storm. The garrison was lean at best. When one line of soldiers fell there was not another to take its place. This first line of defense was also its last. This was not a warrior cult that stood upon this wall; it was a union of tradesmen unaccustomed to the skills of cutting throats. Still they fought bravely. They gave a fierce accounting of themselves and, though their numbers fell by three to one, they held this horde of warriors off and withstood the first assault.

For no good reason, this invading army, standing on the threshold of its scabrous success, withdrew. It was as if this striking snake now coiled around its victim had released its grip to probe for any signs of life. Eventually, it struck me that this army was now toying with its prey. It hungered not for victory but total demoralization, breaking the will of this society behind the wall. There in the dark, this force of invaders paused to celebrate its ill-gained victory, the imminent reprisals and spoils awaiting them. Their leaders argued over turf. An emissary under a banner of truce marched up to the city door and offered terms of surrender no self-respecting vermin could accept.

"Lay down your arms, and we'll spare the children. The women must be given over to us. The leaders of your town must be turned over for trial and execution. All wealth and property is forfeit…" As if meant to wither their resolve, this list of outrageous demands poured *ad infinitum* into the brightening air.

The sun rose on the mountain ridges. I felt it on my back. And as it spilled into the valley, I saw a sight that touched me to my heart. Somewhere in the course of time that passed between the darkness and the dawn, the city's walls had filled up with defenders once again. Although most of this township's soldiers now lay slain or wounded, their places had been taken—by the women and the children—some old and feeble, some so young and small their hands could scarcely fit around the weapons that they held. Yet they were determined to defend their own with their last vestige of resolve.

There is power in a gallant gesture that always stills the heart. These citizens knew the cruelties awaiting them and, rather than embrace the kind of degradation offered, had chosen instead to taste the bitter rice of death. Such willpower even gave this attacking army pause. Some, already drunk with the wine of celebration, laughed to see the enemy that now confronted them. Those were the few. Their ridicule, like their breath, polluted the air and brought the contempt even of their fellows. The other soldiers went grimly to their business, girded their loins once more, and grumbled at the prospect of having to slaughter children.

Suddenly, I found myself not caring for the odds. As if a fever had overcome me, I began to see this rout of virtue as an offense to all the universe. I was moved by my very nature to counterbalance the weight. The mountain on which I stood made known its ire as well. Its every, boulder, rock and pebble seethed at the injustice of it and made my talons hot to leave their perch.

In the valley below, the battle was being rejoined. The attacking army resumed its formations and started advancing again. The villagers who remained to fight stood rigidly at the wall, a line of dignified resistance only courage can inspire. Outside, a raiding party had now clustered at the city gates putting a battering ram to the task that was nearly as large as I. It was only a matter of time now, a tap or two at the door, and another civilization would come tumbling down.

Enough was enough! No more blood of innocents today, thank you very much! I stood to let the sun at my back throw my shadow onto the valley below, a shadow that crept over them like the scowl of an angry god. It caused a few to jerk their heads. Then, like a wave of wheat, each warrior in his turn looked back and gaped in horror at the monster in his midst.

Just to give the moment added drama and strike a little fear into their hearts, I roared my consternation to the sky. Plumes of my fire clawed the clouds, put a haze on the face of morning and even caused the ground beneath to shake.

I glanced back down to note the effect and was somewhat surprised to see that my very presence had sent this army into a wild mazurka of retreat. The foot soldiers in the rear were first to flee, the ones that were nearest to me felt the angry heat of my breath from a thousand yards away, they broke and ran. Ignoring the commands of their commanders to stand their ground and fight, they turned to rout and collapsed the beam that held this force together. The chariots and charioteers were next, and then the front line soldiers. Everyone at last, even the commanders, dropped their rams and ladders, tossed away their shields and spears and fled in disarray. Never one to let the issue go unaided, I descended on them with a passion, scorching many with my flames, catching others who dared to look me in the eye and turning them to stone where they stood.

I left a score dead and dying. (I could have left a legion). And though I had certainly wrought my share of retribution, I'd been mild in my punishment compared to what this army had done. There is no debate about the fact that I scared them half to death. And terror after all has its rewards. But those are minor as I'd soon discover and have their drawbacks too.

Rather than see me as a friend these stalwarts of the city misperceived my rescue. They couldn't distinguish, as I had done, that there were shades of conduct easily read by all the sentient creatures of this world. Some sinister source had clouded their minds so that they'd been blocked from comprehending the equality of things. I could see it in their faces. I could hear their cries of loathing and realized to my chagrin that they perceived me as monster—little more than a huge, mean, hungry bird of prey, a mindless agent borne of the Corruption. But I was young, and ego drove me across the boundaries of discretion into a world where I was convinced that all was mine to win.

After having driven the invaders far away from this place, I thought it only fitting that I land at the City gate and receive my roses and accolades for all the good I'd done. How naïve I must have been not to have recognized that I'd be perceived as a force far worse than the one they had driven away.

Utterly ingenuous, I dropped down in their midst, trying to give a nod and a wink to put them at their ease. But this beleaguered band of remainders gaped at my casual air, then rallied only long enough to plunge into panic, rewarding me with a rain of hostile fire that included every weapon they had. Since the missiles they hurled were mostly of iron and bronze, they bounced off my skin like toys. Still it hurt (a matter of pride, you see), and flung me into depression, spiced with a minor case of umbrage. Rather than move to flee or to rebuke, I merely cocked my head and asked the question: "Why?"

Somewhere along the way I'd become a cosmic baritone. My voice echoed with an overwhelming timber. Even though I asked the question as gently as I could, my query did fairly throttle the City gate, splitting the oak and iron door in two, sending it crashing down—an act that a regiment of soldiers couldn't achieve. The villagers weren't able to hear the simple question I'd asked or even note that I'd spoken in their language. The sound of my voice was simply too much; they shuddered at the impact. Style, it seemed, had utterly smothered substance.

In the clamor that ensued, a woman among them peered through the refracted rays of sunlight and, finally able to discern me fully, pointed at my chest and screamed, "The Lightning Dragon!" This oath, as if it had marked the End of Days, plunged this City into the throes of pandemonium. To the last, they deserted the wall, trampling one another, scrambling clawing through the streets to get away from me.

Strange creatures, these human beings. They spent generations building civilizations and yet tore them apart in a day. They could lock arms and, in a show of courage, stand against all odds, yet in the next moment stampede one another into dust—all to flee an energy they couldn't comprehend.

I thought to put that demon to its rest by showing these pygmies that I only wished them well. I leapt atop a parapet and called out after them. I was fluent in the languages of men and made my purpose clear.

"Why do you run from me?" I cried. "I want to be your friend. Haven't my actions on your behalf shown you my intent?" Unfortunately my voice was like a war drum in their ears. It echoed throughout the vacant streets, loosened tile upon the roofs, sending it crashing to the cobbles below. I tried to be affiliative. I flew to the City square, crouched down to make myself appear as small as I possibly could. I even lowered my voice to a whisper. Although I was three times the size of any house to which I came, I stood outside them and made my civilized pleas.

Irony will have its say. As it had come to pass, my physical presence was the obstacle to this ever happening. In my bravura dragon's form, I was too terrible a thing for these human beings to hope to comprehend. Never mind that with a breath or two I could have burnt their city to a cinder, the mere murmur of my voice alone had thrown them into such hysteria that they'd put an early ending to their day.

There was only one solution, I could see: Unification, the perfect blending of body and soul, mergence of the metaphysical kind. If I could merge with one of these beings, could take the Empath into one of them, I could become the teacher. I could share with humankind the secrets of the Mystic Clan.

Just as I beheld this thought, a little human creature ran onto the path before me. It was a female of their kind, lithe and swift and, even in her flight, blessed with a grace of movement that I found alluring. Without so much as a whimper, she glanced back at me and even (I was certain) slowed her pace a bit. It was as if she were altogether too fascinated by me to continue her fleeing. I took advantage of the moment. Before she could change her course, I swept her up with the furl of my wing and brought her to my face.

Trembling as a woman would, yet nonetheless serene, she stared at me and to her everlasting credit did not scream. This was contrary to all human behavior I had ever witnessed, (especially among the female of their species). And yet it struck me instantly that this woman was exceptional. That she was beautiful was something even I could see. Cold and shaking though she was, she took on the aspect of an alabaster icon, with a tranquility of spirit that no physical force could repress. Even though I might have devoured her on the spot, she gave me blessings with her thoughts. She calmed herself and let her blue eyes sparkle in acknowledgment of the Christ that dwelled in me. She let her aura open up and merge itself with mine.

I was transfixed. I would have offered words of love right then. I would have let her know how much her silent passages conveyed, when at last I was brought to realize the futility of my cause. By the disparity in our sizes, by the timber of my voice, by the holy heat that sat on my tongue I might have done her harm. There was nothing left to do but simply set her down.

Gently as I could, I let her slip from my wing to the ground, brushing her softly as she came back to her feet. We regarded one another for a moment. She didn't try to run but stood instead and watched as I launched into the sky. As I flew above the city, spinning coils around the clouds, I looked below and saw this female gazing up at me. Although she told me nothing, her message was implicit: her world and mine would have to be as one. If I were to make my mission in this life truly into something of value, I would have to reach these pygmies and teach them at their level. I would have to merge with a human male, become one with his spirit, and walk among his kind as one of his own. Were I able to do so, I could return here. I could find this woman once again and bond with her as a man. I would love her. We would meld our lives. She would share her secrets with me, and I would take her to those sacred spaces in the hidden corners of time.

> *Our mistress of the ancient wind,*
> *Our priestess of*
> *the High*
> *Upon that day did drive*
> *the Lightning Dragon from*
> *the Sky.*
> —*The Song of Shala*

Canto 10

Pod

The Lightning Dragon came that day
to save the father of our clan,
to rain his ire
upon the land
and mark our heraldry of fire.

—The Vyngorch Sagas
Book I

Synchronicity is the key that turns the Lock. It didn't take long to learn that truth, and if I thought to doubt it, all I needed to do was remember the places I'd just been. A sudden alteration in my flight plan, a whimsical air-dance and a contretemps with a windgod had prompted me to take respite on a mountain top—all of this had led me to the city, to the battle, to the human female, and to no small part of my fate.

I wondered at my feelings for this woman, at those wild vines of desire that intertwined my heart the moment I saw her. No thought of any dragon queen had ever made me quite so drunk with passion. This fascination had already broken the laws of Nature, had crossed the interspecial lines and brought me to taste the bittersweet nectar of desire. Yet I could not deny it or her any more than I could deny the other events that had befallen me to that moment.

I'd been flying quite some time by then. The day was drawing near an end. Dusk had once again become a red reality. And I could taste the high, rare Taurus air of home. I had set my steady course due West, and even though I'd come so close to destination I could hear the songs of dragons drumming through the clouds.

I felt myself begin to drift downward toward the South, caught in some pull of energy that drew me like a lodestone, seeming to suck the metal from my gut. A brother of the Mystic Clan was somewhere near in peril. I didn't know who or what this creature might have been; I only knew I had to be there when the time came for accounting.

Scanning the horizon, I couldn't detect the cause of this premonition, and yet here I was already awash in its naked validity. I could taste it in the air, that too familiar loathing—the stench of ritual, the fetid husk of sacrifice, the rancid cocktail of sorcery that surely soiled the soul.

It was the selfsame ceremony; I could feel its evil echo off the cliffs that lined the Tourmaline Sea. It was coming from the southern coast. I could hear the waves strike angrily on a shore obscured by the vector of my flight. I landed on a precipice and looked below to see a broad expanse of beach. Just beyond the breakers, white sands shifted in the wind. A savage storm was coming, another way that Nature marks her frequent protests to the things we creatures do.

Carved into the cliffsides as if it were the frieze of a passion play, was a scene so deeply etched into my darkest recollection that I could never quite erase it from my thoughts. Just as it had been at the Lake of Shards, so it would be again here on this desolate loam.

A dragon, not a High Dragon of the Kiln but a corrupted kind of hybrid dragon—a Vyngorch—had been pinioned to the rocks below. Still struggling, still thrashing with one wing not yet tied down, still spitting hot green streams of fire from a mouth sewn shut with silver chords, he was not ready to submit to his complete undoing. The lesions on his hide from lance and arrow had left him weak. Soldiers in their busy fright ran up and down beside him, aware (if he were not) that they had gained the hour.

This Vyngorch like all Vyngorchim was a hybrid, the bastard offspring of an interspecial miscegenation—the mating of a gryphon with a dragon.* I had never seen one up to now. I'd only heard them mentioned many years before, and not in the most glowing of terms. Rather than inherit the better qualities of both the beasts, it commingled what seemed to be the worst—a dragon head and wings with the feathery body of a bird, two eagle legs that tapered into clumsy lion's paws and a scrawny feline tail disproportionate to all the rest. For both predation and defense the Vyngorch belched meager blue green flames from its mouth, emitting a kind of nauseous gas which could stun some smaller prey such as pygmies, horses and cattle, but which scarcely rendered it a match for what it now had to face. It had teeth enough to cut and tear yet, apparently out of need, seemed to grow a row each week, because no sooner did it bite than it would lose a score, leaving them sticking in the objects of its desire, creatures who would often break free and escape with half a bridge of Vyngorch molars imbedded in their butts. But

---

* *Interspecial Miscegenation* among the members of the Mystic Clan was always frowned upon, since these violent acts of sexual passion more often than not produced demented or genetically inferior offspring. Some of these offspring were easily corrupted and converted into Shimbaghs. This was more than occasionally the event of the mating of dragons and gryphons, the most powerful members of the Mystic Clan who were capable of engendering the most unruly and inconsistent of all progeny—the Vyngorch and the Slavern.

Nature has her compensations, and the Vyngorch enjoyed redeeming virtues of a sort. He was, by divine genetics, surprisingly graceful in flight. As a singer he was nonpareil. His throat was lined with silver harp-strings so that when he sang he also formed his own sublime accompaniment, the sound of which gave perfect pitch to both instrument and voice. Above all, the Vyngorch was glib. Whatever he might have lacked in physical prowess, he more than made up for in guile. A Vyngorch could be clever, articulate, and more: unfailingly convincing. His tongue was made of purest silver. So when he spoke his words—no matter what he said—rang true. He could spin illusions and could convince even the most hardened adversary that the sun only shined at night, that seawater tasted as sweet as nectar and elephants lived in combs. All illusions and more could this cosmic drummer make seem real if given half the chance, which was precisely why he was at this moment bound tightly at the mouth. It was not his fangs and claws that these men feared. It was his dreams.

Yet they wanted him for the same reasons they wanted us all: to flay our skins; to dig deep; to pry our secrets from us; to turn us into rubble-dust and fodder for their magic. Even more than the dragon, this odd bird of the arcane was an object of the pygmie's quest, not only because his bones like ours could be turned into the firestone but also because of its silver tongue. Excised from the Vyngorch and melted down, it was believed it could be reformed into the hidden chapters of the *Book of Enoch.* It was apocryphal to be sure. But it was upon such false beliefs that the pygmie had fabricated his universe.

For reasons not yet explained to me, the Vyngorch was not acknowledged as a brother of the Mystic Clan; yet surely he was one. Granted he was not the most nearly perfect of beasts. But it didn't matter to me. Had it been the Devil himself stuck in this farrago, I would have done what it took to get him out.

Even in a world replete with the blackest of black arts, this was a calling card from one so perverse that it had to be the Magpie.

My recognition conjured him. Having bridled a great white shark this wizard rode the brine, taking the sand without ever breaking stride. A ninth wave carried him to shore, black waters mauling white sands, leaving a carpet of corruption for him to trod upon. So he came, this scourge, this wholly unholy mage with a stare so carcinogenic even his commanders averted their eyes.

Silver chords wrapped his raiment, marbled black and white—he wore them with a vile *éclat* whirling like some hideous *cuisiniére* toward the oven door.

The mouth of the Vyngorch was now sewn shut and squirting flame that fell to sputters of smoke on either side. Standing astride this ersatz dragon, his sacrifice made ready, RuSiva unsheathed a scimitar and held up to the sun. Waving it about hypnotically, he chanted lyrics that chilled my blood and sent it to my feet. At the same time his incantation lit my lightning gash, causing it to crackle to the bone.

I should have dropped him there and then; without a second thought. I could have swooped down from my perch before he'd made a move, and that simple act would have more than ended his days. But I was young and given to swagger, to making my presence known. Determined to make a show of it, I launched into the sky, set myself in the mouth of the sun and screamed back down toward earth. Fueled by rage, I released my song—an emerald laser from my throat that struck the Wizard's well-honed blade and shattered it to bits. I must have seemed an avenging angel, incandescing invective, carving a smoldering rip that melted the sands upon the beach.

Caught in the glare, frozen in their awe, the warriors waited long enough to mark me with their cries. "Mataam, Mataam!"** They groaned the words and instantly fled, stampeding one another in their frenzy to escape. In their frenzied flight, they did

---

** *Mataam!* was the arcane term used in some ancient societies to describe the dragon. The term specifically referred to its oft perceived role as the Mataam or Bringer of Death. Another vile canard foisted on dragonkind by pygmie storytellers and weavers of myth.

more harm to one another than I ever could have, but the stories would grow of the damage that I had done this day.

As for RuSiva, the Fallen One's own...a terror crossed his brow. For one indelible gash of an instant he was truly afraid. It was not the sudden surprise of a dragon in his midst; he'd seen thousands by this time. It was not what I was but *who* I was that caused him to come undone. Unfurling his cloak he twirled it until he became a black spout of water whose white caps dashed behind him into the sea.

Now that was mergence! I had to approve! While I in my vainglorious dive had looked about for some way I could catch him, he had simply eluded me by taking another form. He had become one with the water and departed from the shore, leaving me to gaze at the brine and gawk at the ease of his exit.

Had I tried, I doubt I could have unified with anything so quickly as this dark mage had done. Perhaps he'd had more chance to practice; I could only guess. But he had the edge on me now, and always had.

"What kind of God," I wondered aloud, "would grant this kind of power to someone so low intended as this? How could a power such as the Diamond Light be given to one so base?" It was as if the Source, once found, were like a fountain that gave every living thing its lot to drink. Yet this was not a gulp of water but the power to transform.

I circled the beach a time or two, not bothering to give chase to the soldiers who scurried like sand crabs scattered across the dunes. I landed in a quiet triumph. The beach was deserted. The ocean breezes strafed along the shore, toppling swords and shields and armor abandoned in the rout. The Vyngorch still lay bound and gagged like a turkey trussed-up for trimming. This dragon-bird was a male. I could tell by the plumage of his lower half—feathers of brightest royal blue crested with crimson tips.[***] With a foretalon, I unloosed his bonds and snapped the silver

---

[***] In fact, all the *Vyngorchim* on record to that time were male.

chord that bound his mouth, the legendary mouth from which duplicity, like honey, was said to pour.

"You are the greatest dragon of all time," were the first words that crossed his lips. Bloodily he hummed them as he went to loosen his bonds, tossing aside this indignity with an engaging sense of style. He didn't once bemoan his fate, but concentrated on me. "I mean, don't take my word for it," he went on. "The legend of the Lightning Dragon's been passed around for years. The savior of the Mystic Clans, the terminator of Shimbaghs, the harbinger of better days for all the creatures of magic. Ask the trees, the birds, the brook. Ask anyone. It's on the winds; it's in the air. You're quintessence itself, my handsome young friend. It's an ominous creature you are." He winked. I felt as if I'd had a pocket, he surely would have picked it.

Unabashed and apparently unembarrassed at having spieled off such obsequious patter, he continued. "Frankly, I didn't believe a word of that story 'til now. But *here* you are. And *there* you have it—the Lightning Dragon in the flesh!

"Thank God! You saved my bacon! But I guess that's daily fare for you. Or soon will be. From what I can surmise you're a recent graduate of Sagro's 'Academy of Attrition.' So you're just starting out."

I didn't answer him. I wanted to let him play his hand. I scanned him closely and, to my surprise, found him free of deception. His aura, though erubescent with pain, was amazing in its clarity. He hadn't lied or even tried to, yet how had he known all this?

"Oh, don't be surprised that I know what I do," he said, sensing the cause of my reticence. "There are few secrets left in this universe, and those won't be secret for long. Nothing is sacred anymore. No one respects the arcane. If you live on this earth you're 'under the glass,' so to speak.

"Of course, let's not sell my savvy short. I'm a pretty perceptive fellow. But then as you've quite rightly observed, I really have to be. When one is given the body I have, one learns to hone *other* skills; especially one's powers of observation. I could even tell you more about yourself than you ever might imagine…For example, you're an onyx dragon (very rare indeed) which means you'll sense the coming of everything and be very hard to fool. No Shimbagh ambush is going to get you; unless they catch you napping. *And* you're twenty-two in linear years. I can tell by the rings on your tail. One ring for each year. Young dragons have rings on their tails that are deep and wide. Says something about the degree of their energy, I guess. Old dragons, dragones, have myriad rings to count, more like wrinkles, really."

There was much of this I hadn't heard. I wasn't even certain of my age or how much time I'd spent below, though everyone else in the known world seemed aware of it. Twenty two, I was all right; right on schedule with my "destiny." It was all getting a little too pat; even this clever creature's attendance to me now.

I wanted to doubt his veracity, and yet for some reason I couldn't. Every time I scanned him, his thoughts were clear, his aura was uncluttered. And his words, though turgid with flattery, rang true. Either he was quite sincere, I fathomed, or I'd lost my skills of insight.

He was perceptive, as well. Ostensibly, he lacked the clairaudience to hear my innermost thoughts, he answered anyway. "Don't trouble yourself to think I'd lie. I couldn't lie to you, not if my life depended on it. No one lies to a blue-eyed dragon. The blue-eyed dragon sees *everything*. *Everyone* knows that."

"I hadn't ever thought to look," I said, mostly to myself. It was an expression of doubt the Vyngorch immediately seized upon. Ushering me to a nearby tidepool, he bade me look into its sparkling light that, like a mirror, reflected upon my face. Even in the muted hues of dusk, I could see clearly. My eyes were iridescent blue.

"The road to self-awareness comes with valuing who you are. You wear your level of achievement like a badge. Nowhere to hide your excellence. Lucky for you, there's really no need to try. It's an honor to be a blue-eyed dragon. And a power. And a

glory!. You're the best. The *crème de la crème.* No one can top
you now!"

He did tend to lay it on a bit thickly, but he was sincere
enough. And though he was an outlaw of sorts, he held himself
erect and strutted about as if he were a cock. He couldn't have
been one-half my size but considered himself an equal. It was his
way, I came to learn, of coping with his shortcomings.

"Pod's the name," he said. "Vyngorch! Bastard son of Darna
(gryphon Mother of our clutch) and a Master Dragon of the Kiln.
Born to royalty, I'm told. Though I've never known my father,
seen his face, or heard his name. They say I was the product of a
seduction—a red-hot one-night stand!

"And you…" He examined me fully, sizing me up and down.
He strained to remember my name but couldn't quite bring
himself to do it.

"Shartallion XII," I answered. "I'm surprised you didn't
know. You seem to know everything else."

Vyngorchim blush, and when they do their entire body goes
yellow. Embarrassed beyond words, Pod turned the color of a
summer squash and spewed green gas out the sides of his
mouth. "Shartallion XII, of course! I should have known!" he
groaned. He stamped his foot in the sand as if to punish himself
for this inexcusable *faux pas.* "It's just that Vyngorchim, facile
fellows thought we are, have lapses of memory. That's one way
even the unenlightened can catch us in a lie. You see, oftentimes
we can't remember what we're saying from one minute to the
next. So if you listen, you can learn what is truth and what is
fable.

"I suppose I shouldn't be telling you this. It's a secret we
keep among our own. But then, the Vyngorchim can't keep
secrets either. So, there's no use in trying to hide it."

Patronization can almost be as much an offense as a lie. I was
beginning to understand that this Vyngorch, Pod, was for some
reason making a fetish of his honesty, was laying bare his inner
thoughts as if he were relieved to know that I'd see through them
anyway. He was so ingratiating I couldn't help but suspect it. Yet

as he spoke, I saw another kind of face—an interface—become as much a part of him as his own. It was almost that of a needful pup pleading for affection. He was alone somehow. Since the Vyngorchim were not a trustworthy lot, they were especially not able to trust one of their own kind. One Vyngorch could not face another and taste the lies that were fed him; the fruit of one's own mendacity was too bitter to swallow twice.

Now that I saw his inner self, he became more acceptable to me. Although the Vyngorchim were never thought to be dependable allies, in Pod I sensed an exception. We passed the night in conversation, and though I asked my share of questions, it was Pod who did most of the talking. As such, he proved to be a boundless source of information. With a few deft strokes of the lingual brush, he brought me up to date, providing me with a purview of this world I'd left behind. As if I hadn't seen enough already, it seemed as if this were a trying place to be. Violence was its cycle of expression—a brutal urge in earlier times now refined into an art.

"It was bad enough before, but now the pygmie makes it sport. He murders his own kind in droves and calls it 'holy war.' He slaughters every other creature that he can get his hands on. Those he can cook and eat, those who can clothe his naked little hide, he calls fair game. Those he cannot (like you and me) he decries as 'monsters,' and hunts us down for trophies and the 'magic' that we bring. And as if that weren't enough, he enlists scribes to write false chronicles that justify his actions. They twist the strands of hearsay into something they call 'history.' They justify their slaughters of their fellow creatures through the myth of interpretation, calling them 'legends of valor,' and 'the Will of God.' That of course leads to their attributing every mad act they commit to visitations of God. Of course they put so many faces on that concept, it's a scramble. To compound that outrage, some scribe has written in some recent apocryphon that man 'has dominion over all the beasts of the fields and all the fish that swim in the sea.' In other words, he can do what he damn well pleases and hang the consequences.

"Of course, since it sanctifies their vice, men have bought the mythology, and they follow suit by sacrificing everything they do to their gods, giving every maledict deity a 'slice of the pie' so to speak. And lie?! The Vyngorch at his equivocal worst can't begin to match the pygmie when the pygmie's on a roll. They lie to everyone *en masse* and call it 'propaganda.' They threaten everyone *en masse* and call it 'law.' They bridle everyone *en masse* and call it 'education.' They enslave everything else *en masse* and call it 'civilization.'

"They're a strange breed, these little fellows, and I'll never understand why the dragon's chosen to let them last this long. Of course, I'm not an expert in these matters, and there must be some cryptic logic that commands us to forbear in such a way. But to my way of thinking, we're best rid of them."

"It's not as easy as you think. There's more to this than meets the eye," I was sorry to say.

"'Nothing is ever as easy as it seems,'" the Vyngorch quoted to me, to let me know he knew of the lessons we learned in the Chthonic Schools. Because the Vyngorchim were barred by tradition from higher schools of learning, Pod had never attended the classes but learned them all the same.

There's something noble in the self-taught soul; a superiority of sorts. He learns from love and not from obligation. The reward is not the "mark of achievement" but knowledge unto itself. So Pod, a scant few decades older than I, had taken on this life and sought his awareness on his own. That endeared him to me. I wanted to teach him the rest of what I knew to share with him my secrets. But as it would come to pass there was more to be learned from him.

"As far as concerns this creature, man, I'm not in total disagreement with you." I said, finally. "But I've seen things in my time that give me cause for hope. There's a beauty about them, a striving for poetry no other creatures seem to hold as dear. There was a village in the East..." My speech followed my thoughts, trailing away to that time that now seemed very long ago. I wondered if it had been reality or just a remembered illusion, a world created by my mother's wish upon the wind.

Pod's answer snapped me back like a whip. "The East is a long way away. This is the West we bear. There are Rogues to the North and Shimbaghs to the South. In the middle, amid the kingdoms of power and magic we stand alone to inherit the turmoil that wants to devour us all. Not that I regret it for a moment, mind you. This is where the action is—Rakushar! RuSiva! The Dragons of the Kiln! I want to be here when the crunch comes! When the Shimbaghs get their butts kicked, when the Lightning Dragon makes his play! And the righteous will prevail!"

I was amazed at his *joy d' vivre*; I suppose I shouldn't have been. As with any bastard breed, there was a kind of cruel naiveté about the Vyngorch, one that fed their addictions to corruption and sport. They loved to watch a war or a fight or witness a copulation, anything that titillated their lower natures, so long as they did not have to participate. They were voyeurs and held aversions to anything resembling commitment. Why then was this Vyngorch, Pod, so solicitous of me?

"You surprise me," I told him, finally. "You get yourself practically ground into firestone, and yet you're ready for more. You meet RuSiva, you have his sword at your throat, and yet you talk of seeing him again."

"There's a knowingness I have," he said. "Not like others of my kind. I *know* when something is about to happen. Not the perceptive onyx blood that runs through the high dragon's veins, but nonetheless effective in its way. Don't ask me how I come by this; I couldn't begin to tell you. I just *know*.

"Just as I knew I'd get out of the jam I was in, I knew a dragon would save me. Just as I knew a dragon would be my deliverer, I knew it would be you. Beyond that, I'm not ready to say. But I know a thing or two that you're not ready to hear."

"If you know so much my Vyngorch friend, then tell me about RuSiva. How can one so very evil have a power as great as his?"

He was perceptive, this demi-dragon. He knew I hungered for the answer, yet gave it as casually as he'd perceived I'd asked it. "His vanishing act, you mean?" he replied. "Pretty good, you must admit. Can merge with any element in a trice. Phenomenal! Truly phenomenal!" For the first time since I'd encountered him, Pod felt a sense of power. He knew something I wanted to know and thought he'd make the most of it. He even milked it for a moment, though sensed as well it was not wise to push me too far. "Surely one as worldly-wise as you knows the story behind all that. But then, you've been in your own little world, so to speak. It's simple, really...I'm sure. It's no secret that RuSiva was a white wizard once, the very best among his kind, a healer, a servant of the light. But then (and this is no secret either) he sold his soul, became a Shimbagh, a lieutenant of the Fallen One, second only to Rakushar, the Beastmaker.

"Well, what else would turn a white wizard black, turn a hero to a snake, twist the finest mind into the basest blackguard of our time? Power! The ultimate power—the *Diamond I!* He had mastered all the levels save that one, and though he strived through all his life to get it, he could not. And, since he wasn't getting any younger, he took the shortcut; he summoned the Fallen One.

"He got the Diamond, sure enough, and a considerable life extension. But what a price?! Oh, don't look so shocked. You can get just about any power you want if you don't care how you go about it. That's why the Shimbaghs number in legion, and the Mystic Clans number in small. And as for those of us caught inbetween, well...it's not very good at all."

"Then commit," I said. "Join one side or the other."

"It's not that easy," Pod said, offhandedly. "You see one club doesn't want us, and the other we won't have. At least, that's the way it stands, for now." He tried to be nonchalant, but there was no hiding his intensity.

Every creature in the universe is out to make a sale. That lesson wasn't written anywhere in Sagro's book of wisdom, but it should have been. So that had been it. That was the reason for

both his candor and his patronage. All the while this clever
Vyngorch was getting me up to speed, he was making his case: a
petition for acceptance to a prince of the dragon clan, a tactic to
find these mystic misfits some measure of respectability. That
put me at ease. Once the hidden card is played, one can either
yield to it or trump it. In this case, I might just respond in kind,
take it to the master dragons and gauge them for reactions. Why
not plead his case and see, just see, where it might take us?
Chances were we'd all learn something in the process.

He might have asked. That would have been the dragon's
way; direct and to the point. But Pod was a Vyngorch and, in his
essence, could not walk a straight line if a sidestep would get him
to the mark. I began to understand that, yet still could not find it
in my heart to reward his cunning with ready response. I
changed the subject.

"And what about the one they call 'the Captain?'" I asked.
"Or does such a man still live?"

"Oh, he lives to be sure," Pod answered. "And everyone
knows *his* name. At least they'd better."

"And where does he stand?"

"I don't know," Pod replied, at last. "He doesn't traffic much
with us. The Vyngorchim don't merit his attention. And frankly,
that's one snub we don't mind at all. But God help you, please, if
'dragon' is your name. Or 'Shimbagh' for that matter. A wave or
two of his mighty sword, a few choice words that only he
commands, and you are gone—vapor, history, a mist. A few have
bought eternity that way by now, and many more will follow, so
they say. He's been going on that way for a decade, and is a law
unto himself. But he's a strange one, this Captain. With his
power and his secrets of the banishing, he could have been a
suzerain, an emperor; at the very least, a prince. Yet he's like an
ascetic and only comes when summoned. He's a hired gun, but
only charges those who can afford it. He arrives, confronts the
adversary, goes through his magic motions, and poof! The beast
is gone! Sometimes he's done this in the face of grave danger
and has nearly been 'aced' once or twice. But never has he failed.

The dragons have diminished due to him, but so have the lists of the Shimbaghs.

"And there's the enigma. He's inconsistent. He's been known to let a dragon go—unharmed, unchecked, unchallenged. And he's done so without explanation to anyone, not even to his kinsmen. He'll work to banish other members of the Mystic Clan —a gamberol, a gryphon, or a troublesome Kohmm—but he'll do so quite reluctantly and only for a hefty fee, a commission so outrageous that it nearly breaks the coffers of the community enlisting him.

What's more, he keeps a company of soldiers always around him. Not the standard kind, these men are zealots such as he, armed to the teeth, skilled without equal, and devoid of humor or greed (and otherwise just don't seem like human beings at all). They're small in number yet go throughout the countryside unchallenged. No city will resist them or even think to try. Not even the legions of RuSiva have dared to take them on.

"RuSiva, for his part, hunts the Captain with a passion. He has offered rewards large enough to ransom a suzerain for anyone who'll turn this soldier over. Recently, he ordered the executions of an entire battalion of men who'd encountered the Captain but had somehow neglected to catch him. Once he even razed a city to the ground for merely having given this holy warrior a safe night's lodging. I call him *holy* solely because no other word will do. He keeps his own counsel, fears nothing, and talks daily with his God. He has what few men of his time can claim: a sense of higher purpose. And in this world of savages that's sanctity indeed.

"Strangely enough, the Captain has never avoided RuSiva anymore than he has sought confrontation with him. He has simply not been there. He calls no place his home and goes where trouble beckons—even to the North, even to the South where Shimbaghs hold their court. Yet RuSiva, with all his powers of darkness, cannot get a grip on him or even catch him in his sight. Figure that one out?"

"I can and will," I said. "The answer's more basic than you think. RuSiva is a Shimbagh now, a man who's sold his soul. If what you say is true, and the Captain can banish Shimbagh and Mystic Clan alike, then the Captain can banish RuSiva. And that's a power that dark magician won't dare to face directly."

"Not so easily, it seems," the Vyngorch softly counseled. "Sometimes the Captain's powers fail him, and he must resort to force. For that he has a company of spearmen, archers and mount with weapons dipped in silver that will strike down even the heartiest of dragons. To add to the peril, they're all adept at averting their gazes whenever they confront a Mystic Beast whose powers can't be denied."

"That may be why the Magpie stalks his prey with deliberate caution. The sorcerer, RuSiva, is the most cunning of miscreations. He has ways to sidestep any confrontation he desires. He'll come for the Captain, and soon," I insisted. Yet he hadn't done so yet. And what had it been now? Nearly twenty years? Why hadn't this dark sorcerer sought to draw the Captain out? With his powers of both mergence and corruption, he could have easily formed himself into a deadly snake or spider and stung the man to death while he slept, or simply become one with another human being, an assassin who could have easily infiltrated the Captain's ranks. That would have seemed the ticket. These creatures were so susceptible to bribery and stealth, it had to have been considered or least to have been tried; yet it had not been. There had to be something else at play of which I was yet unaware.

Night turned into a sheet of black. The stars were choked from the sky, and only a few white clouds like timid waifs danced across the darkness. Pod and I passed the hours until morning on the cliffs above that sea, watching the lascivious waves lick the shoreline.

Pod was always afraid of the dark; he made no bones about it. Yet he felt safe with me. "A Vyngorch under a dragon's aegis is a lucky bird for sure," he said. To keep me amused, and to keep me awake (lest he face the night alone), he regaled me with more tales of Vyngorch lore and valor. They were amusing and, for the most part, untrue; but they helped to pass the time. It was a pleasant way enough to get through the night until the sun shone and blessed my journey home; that is, until he sang.

There are no masks for singers. When one lifts the heart in song, the force of one's true inner self breaks free. That was his Vyngorchim message to the night—that from the harp strings in his throat and the silver tones from his tongue, the story of his soul's desire could finally be told. He longed to be a soldier of the light, to be respected for his courage, to be a thing admired and know the face of God. Such a song could not be falsely sung. It came from the angel within and rang so truly that even the rocks would weep at its majesty.

I could not deny it either. When the sun broke upon the open sea, and I was ready to depart, I turned to Pod.

"Come with me," I said. "Come to the dragon's world and be one of us." I said this as sincerely as I could and hoped that he could accept but realized my invitation had driven a wedge between us. More often than not, a wish fulfilled can be a frightful thing. The hope that shined in his eyes at first dimmed with the awareness that I was promising something forbidden. He bowed his head and acknowledged me, sadly.

"My Lightning friend," he answered. "I could think of nothing I'd rather do, but I must decline not for my sake as much as I do for yours. The Vyngorch is pariah to the dragon. We're treated like the Plague itself and kept outside your bounds.

"For you to attempt to introduce me would bring shame to you and punishment to me. Don't get me wrong. It's not the punishment I fear; it's the rejection. One can not be turned away at the very gate of one's dreams and somehow not die inside. That would be too much for me to take."

I understood but pretended not to. That was hard to do, for clearly this demi-dragon perceived as much at inner levels as I, with all my training, ever did. So now it was I who wore the mask. I feigned indifference to his fears and hoped he could draw up some courage.

"You want respectability, then you must fly to reach it. Take the sky with me and have it. Or squander the rest of your days in doubt for what you might have been. The choice is yours. So seize it now! It won't come this way again."

I didn't wait for him to answer. I launched and headed West. Hoping the Vyngorch would pursue me, I flew slowly for awhile, sensing by the fires of my solar plexus that he'd be joining me. But the day grew cold, clouded over and chilled my expectation. Alone, and somehow saddened by this strange little friend I'd found, I wished him well and wept for all the victims of desire. I released my attachments at the mountain crests and wove through the clouds toward home, when suddenly there ripped a winged intruder spewing fog and spitting mist. Circling up and outward then gracefully back toward me, he came to greet me fully. It was Pod.

"What the hell. Let's do it!" he shouted.

"What the hell. Why not?!"

A creature in sight of his destiny has reached the steps of heaven.

Canto 11

The Crater of Nebul

Fires of their celebration lit the skies. Roars of their reveling and bawdy conversation crackled along the highlands, making it seem as if the mountain crests had birthed a young volcano, spitting flame and brimstone and the voice of inner Earth. It was a gathering of dragons, righteous in its intent, to let the intrepid guest behold the staggering synergy of that place.

This mountain's jaw was the crux of power for the dragons of the West. Its stones were metamorphic teeth that had chewed their way out of time and formed into a throne room high among the clouds, amid the songs of sunbirds and above the minds of men. It was called the Crater of Nebul, so named after the husk of a meteor hurled here by the Lords of Draco exclusively for the Mystic Clan's conventions.

By structure, it was a sanctuary that was meant to have been shared. The dragons, the gryphons, the chimeras, the unicorns, the gamberol, the rahntish, and the Kohmm—the ones who kept the secrets of magic—were meant to hold their councils in this place, to apportion them equally, to plan their strategies and keep their peace with one another. That had been the plan. Plans, as we have learned, can go awry.

When the Crater of Nebul had manifested, it was lined with ruby crystals entrusted to the dragons' care with the implicit understanding that they keep its doors open to all creatures of magic. The dragons held that seat of power and came to covet it. And though they offered refuge to any of the Mystic Clan who came in need, they also let it be known that only God could help those who entered without knocking. This may have been acceptable to the easy-going Chimera, but the proud unicorn and the gryphon could never accept such terms.

Whatever its intent in the beginning the Crater of Nebul had, in the end, become an exclusive forum for the gathering of dragons. And, except for the chimeras who were impossible to offend, none of the other Mystic Beasts ever stayed to pass the time. A unicorn might sup there. A gamberol might fly in from the sea to plead his case. A white wizard from the East might even come to strike a deal or bargain with the Council for the secrets of the Kiln. And yet even these infrequent guests were distinguished by both the rarity of their appearance and the brevity of their stay.

It wasn't that the dragons weren't good hosts. They were terrible, in fact. They weren't adept at socializing, had never learned the meaning of hospitality, and unless their mystic guests were willing to understand that these dragon claques were social stews in which anything might cook, they would have found these gatherings to be raucous, bilious bores full of fiery laughter and foul report.

We'd taken our time, this Vyngorch and I, before our pointed arrival. A nasty storm sent up from the South delayed us even further, but Pod was given to procrastination, which did not surprise me at all. He even had us pause on the way for lunch by a silvery lake. He claimed he wanted to "catch his breath," that flying long distances tired him, but I knew his hyperventilation came from the will to flee.

"We do it now," I came to insist. "And that's my final word." We'd made good time since that event, but the day grew dark again. The sun sank into the floor of earth, and poor Pod's evanescent grit went right down with it. Even though we sped along in our flight, his wings began to flutter like those of a timid butterfly. Just as we were ready to fly up to the mountaintop, he took his leave on a nearby ridge. A strand of sweat broke his brow, his green face flushed to yellow, and he rattled like a shudder in a storm. He tried to make light of it, said it was fatigue, but I could tell that his will had turned to water.

"You go ahead," he said. "I'll catch up to you presently. It's cooler here, and I feel overheated. Besides, I might do better with some sort of introduction, don't you think? A bit of fanfare from one of Draco's favorite sons—to give me credibility, so to speak."

He might have been right. I didn't really stop to think of that because it was a moot point anyway. Pod was no more prepared to face this dragon outing than I was to know the state of affairs into which I was bringing him.

§§§§§§§

Dragons pounding dragon tails, signs of animation. Dragons expounding, dragon tales, reflected heroics, flames of remembrance, roars of celebration; hot tears for friends lost in the Shimbagh wars; the spicy wine of prophecy, the forged fires of alliance; master dragons sitting in the middle, seven chairs in a semi-circle, seven stone thrones. One was empty. Dager was gone, Dager the Mountain himself; even in his absence, he was the warrior's warrior. Around the perimeters younger dragons, ferocious fighting machines waited to strut their stuff and boast of their deeds. Wily females sinuous and sexy, dropped pheromones and gossip, licked the air with taunting laughter, the heat of invitation teeming from the flames that lined their lips. Around the ridges rocks and rills, like gargoyles grinning, perched an army of chimeras hideous and cheerful, happy to be there, delighted just to be; grinning gloating lion-dogs who lined the path to purgatory, danced to songs the wizards played, and took delight in terror.

I landed with panache, I thought. Wings furling like black sails in a sea of opportunity, I posted on a barren rock on the highest crest I could find. Cool downdrafts marked my coming, sending a chill across the floor, a tricky way to make my presence known. All heads snapped to the rear of the crater, all regarding me. Ancient faces of council dragons, younger bulls eyeing me with wonder and a will to banter written in their eyes; chimeras, kites, and even the *munzels* jerked to attention for a moment, then resumed their business. Only my mother, the golden Drilg, instantly recognized me, saw the sardonyx warrior presence I had become.

She swept away from her seat of honor and flew up to my side, wordlessly caressed me, and looked with pride upon my face. "You've done so much since you flew the nest. And we have learned of it all. Most of us are proud beyond all words. But take heed of this: Without your knowing it, you've made a rival or two. I won't have to tell you, you'll know when you meet them. Just take them as they come, and don't take issue with them. They sit in seats of power. So, they're best met with good humor and a little bit of tact."

"And what has brought this on?" I asked, as if I hadn't known.

"A few broken rules," she answered. "A few toes trod upon. Just chalk it off to the quest for high achievement. We've all done it. It's nothing new. It's just that once in a while they make an example of one who's waxed too bold."

I learned a secret long ago about the meaning of *rules*. There are only two kinds: those of God and those of flesh. Learn the first and forget about the second. God's rules come from the gut. Obey them and stand in the truth. Disobey them, feel your stomach turn, and live in pain until you learn. Any other rules—

rules of pygmie or wizard, lord or lizard—only work if they follow those of God. Otherwise they're just games for our busy minds to play, means by which the deceivers among us keep us under sway.

Drilg knew this truth. I looked into her soft cerulean eyes and I saw it. Although she tried to simulate concern, there glimmered the hint of sweet amusement like gemstones beneath the water.

She embraced me again, took her leave, and said she'd be back, presently. "You have to be formally introduced," she said, "by one of your own blood kin. I'd hoped your father would be here to present you, but I guess I'll have to do."

Back to center stage she moved, whisking by her kindred dragons. Graciously greeting the curious chimeras preening at the back, pausing to regard even the lowly *munzels,* the less-than-human beings, she didn't miss a soul. She honored everything she touched and was honored in return. And as I watched her go back to her throne, I couldn't help but notice; she was the only golden creature in all this place. Yet even if it were anomaly for a dragon to wear that color, she wore it like a crown, a hallowed light that covered her from her master angel's gown. In her seat of stone she was, in her gentle aura, a contrast to the garrulous council around her. Docile yet direct, she was a guiding force and the favorite of the younger dragon females.

To my surprise but not to my delight, this was more than I'd expected. But more of what? That it had exceeded my expectations, there was no doubt. But exceeded them to what degree and into which direction? The air was heavy in this place. This Crater was turgid with the hot wind of ego. There were clear eyes and unsullied auras to be sure; but there were others with earthbound gazes that rendered them unable to see beyond the brittle boundaries of this dimension. Many young dragons were disposed in such a ways, but I perceived this was the case with some older ones too, a pair of whom sat upon the Council of Seven, the circle of the elite marked by scars of an epoch of doing battle, of knowing only the pain of rejection, the loss of their ideals. There were no more springtimes in their hearts; winter had come to rule.

Each member of the Council of Seven wore his destiny's colors. My mother was gold. Another was green. The only other council female, one with deep kind, yellow eyes, was a garnet red. There were no black dragons in the circle of stone except one who might have been—a slumbering, decadragon in a soft bituminous grey. There were no white dragons I could see. Only the MasterSinger in his final angelic form had revealed that seraphic summary of colors.

My father, I vividly recalled, had a hide of deepest violet. Like the amethyst stones on the empty chair that marked his royal mien, he was the warrior through and through, the wearer of the shield of the Kohmm. He was the leader. He could bring order to this council meeting pocked by conflict and energies run amok. He was the one they were waiting for, and yet he was the one who was missing.

Where was Dager, after all? He was not so devoid of prevision that he failed to know what others had heard from the winds. Was he in danger? Was he at war? Was he so far away that he couldn't get back to greet me here? It was clear, my father sat on the Council. The seat, the vacant seat marked by the violet tresses and amethyst gems, was clearly his. Clearly, he was the power with which to be reckoned, yet he'd delayed his return. Why?

Time passed quickly while I waited; still I waited, watching others who dared not look at me. I was untouchable for some reason yet unrecognized, high above and isolated, left alone to feast my eyes on dragons in convention: the perimeters where younger dragons loitered males on one side females on the other —separated by tradition, until the time.

Until that time the young males, bulls, indulged in contraband, chewing shards of brimbrod brought from a lake not far away, doing so defiantly beneath stares of watchful dragon-guards patrolling everywhere.

At the epicenter, in the council semi-circle, the dragon sages —oblivious to all else in the world—gorged, eating giant azure melons brought in by Kohmm, melons grown from spider webs and sea-mist ripened in the sun. Skewered, roasted tamboar and antelope were fed from hand to mouth, fed to them by trembling *munzels,* the less-than-human beings.

One did not see munzels outside this place, for the Crater was their cross, their penance, and the source of their absolution. These ugly two-faced dwarfs cursed by fate and cowardice to serve in the Nebul were once human warriors bold and strong—soldiers in the armies of men—who had betrayed their strength and valor by selling out, turning traitor, or simply turning tail. Those who were not caught and executed, those who could escape and find their way to the hidden grounds beneath the earth, might happen upon an Urwitch dame who would offer them a Hobson's choice. Since they were marked as turncoats by societies of men, they could either squander the rest of their lives marked for execution, or they could opt for a perilous path to redemption and be transformed into munzels. Munzels were uniforms for the soul. And the visages that they wore were hideous mole-dwarfs with livid white limbs, scarlet caps and clothes made out of straw—pallid creatures bereft of hair but doomed to wear two faces front and back. Mole eyes and a lifeless smile, a mask of servitude, was fixed on the face in front, while on the rear they wore their emotional currency of the moment.

Most of the munzel's moments were spent in the fen of deep despair. Tied by the Urwitch's contract to serve as slaves at the Nebul, they swept the Crater floor, cleaned the dragons' bilge, and waited for the first night of the waxing moon when they would have to serve the dragons at their tables, dodge between their twitching tails, duck their bombastic farts, and hold up tridents to feed them morsels of melons and meats that dragons liked to pluck from the air with a talon dipped in spice. Fortunately for the munzels, the dragon's aim was good and the fresh meats (and an occasional trident) were all he'd take inside.

But every once in a while, a bull would take a careless bite and munch down munzel, morsel, and the batch; that was the hell of it.

By and large, dragons treated the munzels with deference, never abused them, but seldom pampered them either. They realized after all that this was no country club. The munzels had a debt to pay, and dragons were demanding creditors.

There were brief periods of reprieve for the munzels; those came when they were forced to defend the Crater against invaders. Dragons only convened at the Nebul once on the first eve of each waxing moon. By morning the dragons would all depart, leaving their holy ground untended except for the sentinel munzels, who were bound both by honor and by loss of alternative to guard it with their lives. Although slight of build and hideously misshapen, munzels had been endowed with powerful arms, stretching the length of their bodies. They'd also been permitted trident-spear and shield to use in defense of this, their conscripted home; and defend they did, with valor they had never shown as warriors in their handsome human hides. As men, these creatures had been incontinent cowards. As munzels their death in combat defending the secrets of the Mystic Clans meant they had cleared their karmic debts. That, for them, was the "death of roses," the shortcut to their paradise, the end of their misery in this life and a clean slate for the next.

Otherwise the munzel's tenure might be long and arbitrary. Forced to labor in servitude, a munzel might languish for decades. A dragon, as arbiter of the munzel fate, could set a munzel free, declare his debt paid in full, and break the spell upon him. But since all munzels looked the same, a dragon not blessed with "the Eye" might easily mistake one for the other and let the wrong one go. So a virtuous munzel might labor for years, ignored, unsung, and unredeemed, while a neophyte or a scurrilous wretch might go free at a moment's notice. Such was the perilous path of the munzel; such was the wheel of fate. (Life is not always fair but often surprising.)

Since blue-eyed dragons possessed the insight into a creature's soul—munzels favored them highly and devoted more time to them. But if blue-eyed dragons were the munzel's hope, the Kohmm was its despair. The Kohmm, driven by men from their ocean havens, hated humankind. And because munzels were once miscreant humans, the heliotrope spiders detested these mole-dwarfs most of all. It was they who brought the melons for the dragons that the munzels would have to gather. And it never failed that, once outside its silken nests, a Kohmm was most inclined to snare a munzel or two and drag them away to feed upon. These spider ladies would visit whenever the dragons held court, and even though dragons would not allow such breaches of etiquette as killing to take place in their Crater, the Kohmm would often bring gifts of healing rainbow melons to barter for an ill-behaved munzel or two. Now here was a rub if there ever was one. Since most dragons could not tell one munzel from the other, who was there to ascertain who was ill-behaved and who was not?

I belabor the issue of the munzels and the Kohmm to make a self-evident point: all was not perfect in this dragon world of ours. The Mystic Clans were at best at an uneasy peace with one another. Dragons, despite their intimations of holy ordination, were susceptible to improbities, not the least of which was looking upon other creatures as something less than themselves. That was pygmie thinking and did not become us in the least. And yet we seemed to have more in common with man than either would admit. It seemed to me we were unrepentantly elitist to the core and prisoners of convention, a suspicion confirmed the moment the Kohmm arrived.

Arrive, they did. Being polite, if nothing else, they knocked upon the Nebul's door, a pellucid gate of amethyst that they themselves had sculpted. Permission granted by the dragon council, the Kohmm came tripping in like bandy-legged ballerinas nimbly maneuvering the huge blue melons along the crater's floor—the Thral melons, ripe and pungent, with a bouquet as sweet as an orchid's. Trundled in by these crystalline sisters in the light of the dragon hearth, these melons glistened with a rainbow hue that caused our mouths to water.

"We bring the fruit, the holy fruit that givess the dragon ssstrength, that givesss him immortality, vitality, and power. We bring it out of no sssmall inconvenience to ourselvess, through mountain passes filled with perils, to nourish our dragon friendsss.

"We make no claimss but those of gratitude. To thank the dragonsss for guarding our homesss, for driving away the pygmie invaderss, and for sssaving uss from the wrath of the Shimbagh. Partake and please enjoy these sssymbols of our undying devotion."

Altruism has its limits, and the Kohmm had long passed theirs. They had come for more, and everybody knew it. It was munzels these arachnids wanted, and munzels they would get—a victim or two as a thank you note for the strange fruit that they brought—a bloody bit of barter that had somehow become tradition.

It was tradition at its most wretched. All the Mystic Clan knew the Kohmm were more than a little insane (and, as such, not the most dependable of allies). Pygmie excursions to pilfer their eggs and the sorcery of Shimbaghs to steal their secrets had driven them to such distraction that they now attacked everyone, except the dauntless dragon.

When human lust for the amethyst caused them to slaughter the Kohmm, it was the dragon alone whose very presence kept the pygmie hordes at bay. They did so for nearly a generation until what remained of the Kohmm could reproduce, regenerate and flourish. Now, although their numbers were by no means what they had been before, at least their special survival was no longer at issue. But survive at what cost? The gentler spiders, the pure of heart, had died in the beginning. The mass of the Kohmm had gone into hiding beneath the earth, had lost their sun and sanity in what seemed the selfsame day. That left the survivors, the killers and the outlaws, to carry on the line. With a consciousness sent from parent to egg, these Kohmm had passed their quantum madness on to their young. Where once they had fed on pomegranate, ocean mist and honey, it was now understood that these spiders lusted for munzel blood. They honored their alliances in every respect; there was something to be said for that. Nevertheless, there was the unmistakable air of the predator about them.

The Crystal Spider Queen, their leader, made deceptively sweet entreaties. Having seen to it that melons were laid at the council's feet, she came to the fore, made her bows and cooed, "A sssweet munzel or two for our efforts, a couple is all we ask. You have ssso many. More than you can count. And they've become of sssome use to usss. Just one or two, or a handful, will do. And we'll be on our way."

These were not the heliotrope spiders I'd expected. I'd had my own uneasy traffic with them and had found among the subterranean Kohmm, if nothing else, a purity of pain. True madness carries a kind of integrity that one can sense is there. The Kohmm in the caverns had it; these did not. These arachnids wove their agenda with silken cunning.

There was a pact between dragon and Kohmm. I'd heard of it many times—of its arcane nature and untold depths, of the impact it made upon the Mystic Clan, the dragons most of all. Its nature had never been revealed and wouldn't be tonight. And yet I knew. The Kohmm, though oozing supplication, held some trump card over us. I suspected the rainbow melons from the Thral. Luscious, blue, changing to a neon spectrum hue, the fruits these spider ladies had vinted left this crater salivating. Every dragon, young and old, was drawn to them as if they contained the elixir of life. The Council, lost in gourmand fantasies, drooled their *pro forma* permission to bring the munzels forth and let the games begin.

"Bring out the munzels!" The command, from the semi-circle where the Seven sat, was bellowed by a scarlet dragon seated on the ruby throne. This dragon lord was a hardy fellow, short of temper, loud of voice, exuding power from his loin that commanded begrudged respect. It was he, in my father's

absence, who seemed to hold the council's sway, a living
testimony to the maxim that, in lieu of genuine force of strength,
bluff is the first resort. His name was Rueg; his epithet, the
Wroth. He roared his order once again. "The munzels! Bring
them forth!"

Out came munzels trembling with dread, struggling to carry a
leaden cage in which more munzels sat—those who through
some misfeasant acts had brought the dragon's wrath. Then
again, I wondered: if all munzels looked alike, how could their
judges tell just who'd done what? Even I, scanning with my
single eye, could see that some inside the cage were being
punished unjustly. Surely other blue-eyed dragons could have
scanned them and seen the truth of this as well. Yet they did
nothing; they let the moment pass. Even my mother who
perceived things clearly, had let this injustice proceed.

There was a sense of sport about this munzel-baiting. The
entire Crater fell silent. The Kohmm, in their hungerlust, were
kept at bay while the cage was brought before them, a cage
whose leaden bars had blocked all rays of light. After Rueg, as
self-appointed spokesman for the Council, passed some words of
condemnation, the prisoners were set free.

The munzels who had brought the cage threw back the door
then flushed, disappeared from sight, as had suddenly all the
mole-dwarfs in the Nebul. They'd 'gone to home,' slipped down
holes, like those of moles, which they had burrowed deep into
the Crater floor, covering them with self-sealing lids so *no one*
could follow them. That left the condemned alone to face the
Kohmm who now stood poised, wantonly dripping venom like
honey from a hive.

No killing was permitted in the Crater of Nebul; house rules.
But the Kohmm were free to hunt and capture, and the munzels
free to flee. (Just where they would run was another matter since
the Crater walls were cathedrals, since no other place would have
them, since this was their last best hope.)

The prisoners remaining, a handful at most, broke and ran
from the Kohmm. The Kohmm—the selfsame spiders that

minutes before had danced so nimbly on the melons they'd trundled in—now stumbled after their quarry, clanking about with all the grace of clumsy chandeliers. Accustomed to gliding along their ocean webs of sky and silk, they were out of their element here. Their delicate amethyst crystal legs were jolted by the schist of the hard Crater floor. Chagrined, but driven by addiction, they stumbled after their prey who either ran or hid in corners, hoping to be overlooked. Those hopes were dashed by the dragon mob who roared its fires of delight while it pointed out the munzels to their pursuers.

Forced to play this degrading game of hide-and-seek, the Thral spiders resorted to the guile for which they were renowned, set snares into which the munzels were invariably to run. Outnumbering the mole-dwarfs four to one, the Kohmm now worked in teams. Laying out their webs then giving chase until the munzels in their panic ran back through these traps, got stuck, then tripped and fell, rolling around in sticky silk and struggling in a panic. Quickly, the Kohmm cast covering nets of silk snaring them head to toe, and bundling them up like cabbages for market.

But courage finds its way through any skin. And there was a pair of mole-dwarfs different from the rest. These two had the soul of wit to find their way to other corners of the place where the Kohmm could not surround them. There they held their ground, kept their composure and used their weapons with such remarkable skill that their thrusts and parries drew cheers from the Crater throng, from younger bulls and lion-dogs alike to "let them go."

All other things being equal, they might have gotten out. All other things were not. A four-foot dwarf is no match for a ten-foot spider. Although this pair kept the Kohmm at bay far longer than any human warriors would have done, they still were flesh and bone. Eventually, their massive arms grew heavy. Their human hearts grew sore. And their hope for freedom waned. Soon, they too were forced to make the fatal choice—conciliate or flee and flee they did. One was caught and bundled immediately. The other broke and ran, showing insight as he darted up the crater wall toward the teeth on which I stood.

Even on a dead run, even through his dead mole face and hollow soulless eyes, this creature's soul-light shined straight through to me. He'd been little more than a lad of twelve when pressed into a battle, when made to hold a warrior's sword and look on the face of death. He'd simply been too young and when, facing a superior force, his fellows broke and ran, so then did he. Forced to wear a warrior's armor and a coward's shame, he opted for the Urwitch caves and sought to save his soul. But at what price? For ten years he had served here in the Crater and, to add injustice to his ignominy, had been falsely tapped for having been a thief. Now, in this hapless mole-dwarf shell, he struggled up toward me, seeing something in my sapphire stare that told him I might help.

I'd seen enough. A pair of Kohmm, who were much better climbers than runners, had come in hot pursuit up the Nebul wall and surely have snared this boy-soul had I not intervened. With a swipe of my wing I blocked their path and carried the munzel aloft.

"You are absolved. Be free," I said and, with a touch of my wing, transformed this poor accursed soul back into the warrior he had been before. A boy of twelve no longer, he was a full-grown man of twenty-two, a handsome human being now armed with trident, released from stigma, and soon to be extricated from danger. Once absolved, the warrior youth was freed from service in the Crater and out of danger from the Kohmm; so it was written. But one does not often reason with madness. Obsessed with snaring their prize, these spider ladies had clambered over the horn of my wing and now sat poised to rain upon their victim who, having returned to his human form, was more of a prize than ever. Frenzied, dripping venom, and ready to poison anyone opposing them, they shrieked and made their move to pounce, a move I quickly altered with a gentle tip of my right wing that sent them sliding back to the Crater floor, dazed but quite intact. With a sweeping motion from my left I set the warrior onto the ridge and down a path that would lead him away from here.

Human nature is a curious thing. Where any other creature would have darted down the mountain slope and never once looked back, this young warrior stood regarding me, trying in his noble little way to let me know his gratitude.

"I'll not forget you, Dragon Prince," he shouted back to me. "The Lightning Dragon is what they say. A beast of majesty." He said this with a rhapsody that bordered on ode, and capped it with a series of oaths that no one could bring to bear. Finally, the sugar of such patronage was a bit too much for me, and I blew plume of flame up his butt to send him down the path.

There had obviously been some breach of etiquette here. No sooner had I turned my focus back toward the Crater hearth than I heard a roar from center-stage where the Dragon Council sat. The Kohmm had turned black and clanked away, hissing as they went. My fellow dragon bulls gave me a hike of the wing (a sign of their approval). That was interrupted by a blast of rage from the Scarlet Dragon's throne.

"Who violates the pact?! Bring him forward!" The great Red Rueg shouted, as if he hadn't known.

Before I could blink, two dragon guards — brackish brown and nondescript — appeared in my midst and offered me an escort. They were strapping fellows, seventy feet or more with scars of combat on their hides only lately healed. But they were deferential to me, and seemed to make this escort as something out of routine, a tempered introduction to the fiery wrath of Rueg.

"So this is the Lightning Dragon, honor graduate of late, prize pupil of the MasterSinger's caves! I, for one, don't see it! Out three days, and already he has trod on every caveat we have. Interferes with the petty goings on of man, wrecks an army, terrifies a city, all of which serves to add more notoriety to his already overblown reputation!"

"I didn't know I'd..."

"A dragon never interposes in the intercourse of men. It just isn't done. It disturbs their fragile equilibrium and makes them even more afraid of us than they already are."

Two Council dragons, acting as grand inquisitors, put me through my paces to make certain I'd tow the line. Rueg was one. Vituperate in his ardor, he fired the first barrage trying to make me feel as if I were a mountain of transgressions utterly befouled with ego scarcely fit to be here. The second—a green dragon— though less abusive, was still quite critical of me. He was a stinging nettle, pretty to behold but not to touch; at least, that's what I scanned. He was older, sight of build, subtle of carriage. He called himself Claarik. Although he wore the emerald mantle of abundance, he gave it something of a citron tinge that bordered on ill-will.

"Of course, you can't be expected to know *everything*," he was moved to emphasize. "But there is a modest set of rules which surely you have learned. Cardinal among them is never to traffic with humankind unless absolutely necessary. Leave them to their petty wars, their little follies, their civic mutilations. It is not our role to police their daily lives. They do not appreciate it one iota, I can assure you."

"And *never* befriend a Vyngorch!" roared the haughty Rueg. "Much less bring one here, to our sacred home! The Vyngorchim are a plague to magic and a danger to us all! And most of all, never violate a pact with another member of the Mystic Clan, which you in your self-styled gesture of largesse have done tonight! By freeing that little miscreant, that less-than-human scum, you've put our spider sisters in a snit!"

Credit Rueg with this: You always knew where he stood. With a sweep of his hot jasper wing he postured toward the Kohmm now clustered at a boulder where they wore a deep purple hue. That they were pissed, there was no doubt. They hissed like angry snakes and hovered over their tightly bundled munzel cache as if to guard them from the whims of dragons such as I.

Chastenings should be endured only when one is wrong. When one is right and knows that rectitude down to his core, he must speak his mind or let compromise enshroud him evermore. I had tried, through the avenues of silence, to forbear and show respect. Now, I felt, was the time to show some respect for myself.

"I acted as I did, your grace, because I saw an injustice done. Scanning that poor little wretch who ran to me for help, I could detect he was an innocent. Not only had he long since paid his penance, he was being punished for crimes he did not commit. It only seemed just to set him free. Any dragon with the gift of sapphire sight could have seen it and would have done the same as I, if only they'd taken the time."

I took the measure of Claarik, glared into his mawkish amber eyes, and stared him down. Rueg, though defiant to the last, had no recourse to confront me, for his eyes hard and golden though they were—were not of the sapphire forged. Having been diminished before the Crater throng, they both withdrew from me, dropped their gazes to the floor, and bit into the silence of reflection.

As I look back now, I realize that I'd done a shoddy thing. One should not lord one's spiritual rankings over others. It is the weakest show of strength a creature can ever make. But I was young and hadn't learned the codes of charity. Puffed up and seeing only through the windows of my pride, I added outrage to my sense of vindication.

"But what I cannot see," I said, rising up with waves of indignation, "is why we've become such prisoners of convention. As ritual is the beginning of folly, so are we buried in it to our necks. The Kohmm feed us strange fruits which we repay by awarding them victims to further feed their loss of reason, one addiction carrying the other like cripples on a backslide into hell! Those are the ways of men and Shimbaghs, not of dragonkind!"

Arrogance is a knife turned inward. I had gone too far, had said too much, and had breached another boundary. But just how deeply I'd transgressed, I had yet to know. Claarik, who had held his gaze downcast for quite sometime, now lifted it again and leered. "Out in the world five days and sees it all so clearly. My, my, my. We've a master dragon in our midst!"

"Master disaster!" Rueg irradiated his reply. "His every word, his every deed, violates the creeds we've set before us. Looks to me as if this one should go back for remedial training."

"Not a bad suggestion," I replied, "for some members of this Council."

Silence was the last report. Perhaps I'd gone too far, but Rueg's incessant badgering had done its work on me. If this were the chosen of dragonkind, then we were all in trouble. I looked past Rueg's teeming rage and Claarik's wry twists of phrase to the others on the Council—those silent ones who said the most. My mother, in her modest downfixed gaze, would not regard me with her eyes. The ash-grey dragone, doddering on the precipice of paradise, dozed on, seeming to have heard little beyond his own seraphic dreams. The other dragon female, the Crimson Rhonda, had yellow eyes that gazed with sorrow on our altercation and the heavy air of acrimony that had spilled onto the convention. The Kohmm fidgeted. The chimeras on the ridge crests stilled their barking prattle and listened most intently (a feat for them since they couldn't focus for more than a moment in time). The dragon bulls, with smoky rumblings, gave hushed voice to their amazement: never had there been a Council challenge such as this.

There was another from whom no one had yet heard—a dragon, cobalt blue and so serenely silent he seemed, until now, invisible. When he chose to make his presence known, make it known he did. Simply by lifting the lids that had veiled his cool cerulean eyes and, letting their pure crystal glow shine forth, he brought a peace to the moment. He showed no preemptive flaunts of personality; he beheld us all and, in that beholdance, revealed himself. His name, to all who uttered it, was Skye.

"Let us unify," he said.

"Unify!" the erubescent Rueg agreed. And so, in echo, did all the others on the Council. In an instant, they had joined together in the ritual of silence, a deeply throated *aum* whose loving notes encompassed me as well.

Unification. Scanning time. Supersensory introductions—six on one—the elder dragons sensing me sensing them, phasing back and forth and back again. Oversouls are blocked from speech when words get in the way. Egos parody true intent and blunt the truths at hand. It is only in the blessed silence—in the inner levels that high intentions could have their meanings felt.

Still the mind, and the symphony begins. Here, in the silences where thoughts might channel unauditioned, I was helped to see (again) that things were not as simple as they seemed.

As I had suspected, the rainbow melons brought in by the Kohmm were opiates in fact, but opiates whose addictions found root in life and death. For each bite of these neon beauties contained a mystic salve, the only kind that could heal wounds inflicted by the Shimbaghs. Shimbagh wounds as we'd been told could drive a dragon mad, could turn him to an evil being almost overnight—a rabid, fulminating beast, bereft of wit or reason. Death, if it were merciful enough to come at all, came long and late in months or years, and not before a kind friend's talons might slit his comrade's throat. Even the slightest scratch or nick from a Shimbagh claw might bring this madness on, and more: turn a dragon to a Shimbagh, a slave to the Fallen One.

The rainbow melons of the Thral served both as shield and antidote. Dragons returning from Shimbagh campaigns could, upon partaking of these melons, see their wounds heal in a normal course of time, and could do so without fear of relapse. Melons taken prior to an excursion would help guard against the barbs and claws of the Shimbagh clan and could neutralize their poison, to a point.

Only the Kohmm could cultivate them; only the Kohmm possessed the secrets of their powers. Although grown in silken webs and sea mist like any other melons of the Thral, it had been said that these multi-colored fruits were sanctified by the spider's kiss, that they'd been lightly laced with a hint of venom to gird the dragon's loin.

In return for this rainbow benediction, the munzels were a paltry price to pay. Reciprocity is the fundament of custom, and these were trying times in which to live. After all, there was a higher goal for which we strived against which lesser things had to be put into perspective. All this was said on higher planes but lost on higher thought. Rationalization, at any level, is self-deceit in a mask. There was a violation here, a betrayal of principal. And every soul who sat in this circle knew it.

I challenged them. In my heart of hearts, I drew them to the issue: If offending munzels were to be adjudged and hand-bundled to the Kohmm, then we as dragons would have to be more mindful of who they were. Was this the dragons way, I asked, to be so disrespectful of other forms of life? Soon we'd be thinking we were the only creatures on this earth with souls, and this planet was our playground to keep. My God! We were getting more like pygmies every day!

If we were ever to overcome those easy inclinations, the time was now. The place was here. And these poor pariahs of the world were here to test our wisdom. If we were to be as we purported, we would have to begin with them—to understand them and discern, to see the inner selves beyond the mole-dwarf masks and find who was clear. That, in unison, these master dragons assured me would be done. With one mind and one heart, they thanked me for my insights.

Having made my point with the Council, I was able to see clearly that, beyond the hulls of personality, these beings were high souls indeed, capable of perceiving the things that could be known. Why then, I was moved to ask, could they not give passage to the Vyngorch? In the silence I again made my petitions to be heard. In the silence, in the unified vibration of the Council I was told: there was little hope for it. The pressures of the times were bringing this to bear; 'twas true. But the Vyngorch was too unstable, too inclined to corruption, and worse. Even had every other Vyngorch vice been easily redeemed, each Vyngorch still held inside itself a horrible dark secret that no one—not even these high dragons—would dare to put to breath.

Even the most prescient soul cannot penetrate a closed mind. I didn't know what the dark secret of the Vyngorch might have been, nor had I ever been told. I only knew the Council—even my enlightened mother—wanted nothing more than to bury it. But as there comes a time for all knowledge to hatch out, the time for this arcane child of misfortune was at hand. No sooner had the Council called the issue to a close than from the crater shelves rang out the cries.

"Dager! Dager! Dager!" barked in bellows from the rear—younger dragons fanning flames of warrior adulation, cried out their allegiance to their mentor in the sky. The shadow of my father's wings, like a thunder on the Moon, cracked across the Crater floor and tore into the night. He circled once above us and then landed with a flurry, stirring up the expectations of the hall. It didn't seem to matter that he'd shattered the sanctity of the inner circle's silence, that he'd sent the Nebul into an uproar no phalanx of Shimbaghs could have matched. He was Dager. He was the Mountain. He was home.

Not the cheers of the younger dragon bulls, not the flirtation of the queens, not the righteous ire of some Council dragons, not even my mother—had brought this dragon general here. He'd come for me.

He swept to his seat on the Council stoop and held me in his stare. That I was in size and stature nearly a match for him and more than a match for any other dragon I had met pleased him endlessly. He stared me fully in the face, scanning every millimeter of my being, and finally let out a roar of approbation.

"It's a blue-eyed dragon that we have! A blue-eyed dragon in my son!" He said it proudly, tossed the issue of his pride out on the floor, a challenge for which he knew there'd be no answer. "We've heard of the feats of the Lightning Dragon from the core of the Chthonic Schools. Already, they ring out in legend to sound the last days of the Shimbaghs! Or do I boast?!"

Of course, he boasted. Of course, no one moved to challenge him, it would seem, save me.

"Prophecy is a fool's pursuit," I said, though I kept my words tucked closely to my breast.

He eyed me, taking full measure to see if this would be my move to challenge him. But scanning me with blue eyes of his own, he sensed the truth and stood corrected. "And wise, he is, I see," he added. "Wise beyond his years."

I questioned my own wisdom, but I didn't question this: beneath my father's wild bravado, there distilled a reservoir of pain. If my coming out had brought him, it had brought him to the line, a line that he had come to and was now prepared to cross.

"I call for cloture, "he said, suddenly. It was an appurtenance that surely sealed the night, for no sooner had the motion left his lips than the council members nodded their compliance.

"Cloture!" Rueg announced. And as he did, so did the dragon guards to all the mystic creatures there assembled. Chimeras flocked and flew away, unaffected by the sudden call to leave. The Kohmm, somewhat acquitted by the judgments late at hand, carted off their bundles, scaled the Crater walls and strung their silk across the ridges, using it to skate from peak to peak. The younger dragon bulls and queens, nonplused by this untimely cancellation of their festivities, took to flight, filling the rouge of morning sky with their sullen mute departure.

It was nearly dawn. Since the first crack of daylight after the new moon would have brought this mensal convention to adjournment, the call to close a little early did not seem so rude a thing; yet it was. The fires of expectation had still burned hotly in the eyes of all, and quite obviously Dager's arrival coupled with my own had prompted a larger gathering of the clan than usual. Many were disappointed. There was no doubt of that. Yet for Dager to have come (and come to close the night), it seemed in order. Rightful order as it turned out, since a matter of some enormity was about to come to light.

Dager, to his everlasting credit, was direct. Bring the issue out and, good or bad, have done with it.

"I call to vote the matter of the Vyngorch," he announced. He said it rather dryly, yet not without a glance in the direction of his wife, my mother, and myself.

"Discussion," demanded Claarik, and all those on the council quite agreed, but as they did they turned not to my father nor to Rueg the Wroth for their accordance. Rather, it was to Skye that they all looked. Skye—with his admirable composure, with his serenity intact at every moment—nodded his permission. It was then, and only then, that the discussion proceeded in fact.

Contradictory to his own nature, Dager was more deliberate in his speech. His searing cobalt eyes settled to soft smoke, and tact became the mantle that he wore. "There are two points," he said. "One is practical. The other, strictly mine. First, we need the Vyngorchim as our allies. The conflict with the Shimbaghs grows intense. It's not the skirmishes against them that weigh against us. Those are perennial. They will occur as long as there are Shimbaghs. What concerns me most is that their numbers multiply. Like the serpent of Aetes, the more heads we destroy the more that grow again anew. The chimera are a help. The unicorns are bold and brave. But the Kohmm are decimated. The gamberol can only fight beneath the crystal sea. And the gryphons in their nests of gold remain as remote as ever.

"But the gryphons, as you know, are solitary. They seldom join in more than pairs. And though they fight with the ferocity of twenty times their number, they only link up with others when forced to do so. They will not join with us..."

"Except to mate," shot forth a caustic interruption from Claarik, with an eye cocked and a mouth set for altercation.

"Except to mate, indeed," Dager added. "And from that mating comes a private ally."

"And a public curse!" Rueg countered.

"We need the Vyngorch. We need their talents. They can help to turn the tide."

"With what?! They're toneless, feckless freaks, ambiguous of courage, and given to vertiginous morality! They're uncoordinated, uninspired, and unreliable at best! And worst of all, they are the better half. Need I mention all the virtues which their lovely siblings own?"

"You need not!"

Rueg and Dager, snout to snout, had brought the issue home. The secret of the Vyngorch then, was his paternal twin, though still no one would bring to mention who this "sibling" was. I tried to scan the Council once again but found *again* the thoughts of each were closed to that vile subject. It was as if they could not or would not give it energy of thought.

Skye quietly called the Council to recall. "Dager has the floor," he intoned. "We'll all have our chance to speak."

Dager continued. His rancor cooled but not his ardor, he pressed more fully on the issue at hand. "We play the Vyngorchim down, because it covers our guilt to do so. They are among the swiftest fliers in the skies. And their songs are like celestial calls to jaded Shimbagh ears. They can seduce them into anything, including self-destruction. This we know. This we have seen. This we can put to use. If we could but embrace the Vyngorchim, accept them as our own, I'm certain, we could win the gryphon too, find the way to stronger alliance with them, and enlist them for the dire campaign to come. And it will come, I assure you. Much sooner than we think."

For all his verbal *savoir faire,* my father was striking hard ground. The others had steeled against him; one could feel it. Only Drilg and Skye seemed willing to abstain. But it was not for nothing that Dager was the dragon general. He had one tactic left, and though it was to cost him dearly to deploy it, deploy it he would.

"Confession is our final lot," he said. "And I must now confess to you. There was a sobering reason I was late to my council seat."

Words that come slowly pull a weight, and the weight they pulled was this: Dager had sired a Vyngorch.

"'Twas in summer of my second hundredth year," he recalled. "A score before I paired with Drilg. I'd been wounded by a Shimbagh, a *sprachus versatilus,* the deadliest of all.[****] That I had dispatched it was a miracle. I was the first dragon ever to have done so, the first ever to have seen inside The Door Where Evil Dwelled. And it was that, I think—as much as the wound itself—that left me devastated. That I'd escaped at all was another miracle. But now, seeing what has come to pass with my mate and with my Lightning son, I understand the reason. I was meant to survive. I know that certainly. Just as I now know I was meant to meet the gryphon.

"Gryphons, we know, are anchoritic. They wisely guard their secrets. They do not interact with us except before the Devil's mouth.

"How this eagle-lion knew just what to do, I'll never know. I only know that, by pilfering some melons from a web of ocean Kohmm, she had the wherewithal to bring me back. From the nectar of the rainbow fruit, she cleansed my infection, washed away my madness, and won my mind. Somewhere along the way, her wings had brushed against my heart, so much so that no sooner had I recovered than we mated on the spot.

"I know what tales you've heard of dragon-gryphon love— that it is fire of loin, heat of semen and little more than that. That there are ecstasies from this forbidden pairing, there can be little doubt. But in my case at least, there was much more: a helix formed; a completion of a soul's desire; her secrets locked with mine, secrets which were meant for all the Mystic Clan to share.

[****] *Sprachus versatilus:* Also known as *the Branga,* this awesome creature was a convocation of vipers formed into a lily whose twelve anthers bore the tongues of twelve separate poisons, each one deadlier than the last. It was spoken of in legend that these giant flowers adorned the Gate of Hell and guarded all the evils kept inside. Since my father was the only one who'd ever come that close to the Devil's living room, his was the only verifiable accounting from one who'd met the branga and lived to tell the tale.

"As fate does have its way with us, the progeny of our long embrace were soon to come to breath. And we all know what such a birth can bring—the pair whose blemish stains the very fabric of our clan. And as is the sad misguided custom in such things, we both abandoned them. The gryphon took her secrets far away. I took mine as well and somehow, through all of this, took heart.

"The gryphon princess and I had shared our time in the sun and, having done so, knew that sweet intensity had departed as soon as our corrupted offspring had arrived. Desertion of this odious issue has always been the way—the hasty exit before attachments override the fragile threads of logic, the quick escape before paternal instincts pull us back. It is fatal for a gryphon to look back upon her daughter, but it's holy that the dragon looks behind to see his son. I looked back and, though I saw an ugly Vyngorch in the nest, I saw much more. Blessed-cursed with the single eye, I saw inside his shell. And what I saw was a creature to the dragon born, with dragon heart and dragon mind, and dragon seventh sense. And *Yes!* to answer the unanswered question, he could become as well evolved as we.

"I shuddered at the sight, not because I felt that I had spawned the seed of evil (as so many of these pairings have); quite the contrary. There was a harbinger of hope born there that day. And though his sister may have been as sinister as all the rest, it was this creature's soul-song that I heard. It prophesied a deliverance. I hear it again this morning, the song of my son outside the Crater door.

"It was news of him that carried on the hot winds of the South, winds that brought me to the omen that I now pass on to you. He was summoned here at this moment, not by forethought but by fate. He was brought here by my other son, the Dragon Prince, Shartallion."

Let me be the first to grant the waves of chance their place in our cosmic sea. But this was no accident—that I, of all the dragons in the world, would rescue this particular Vyngorch from the throes of demolition and bring him to the Nebul was something that had been ordained on High.

I wasn't surprised. I was amazed. In my most sensitive moments my prescient onyx cells had let me down. I had anticipated nothing of this (or perhaps I hadn't listened), and yet it was as it should have been. I had come to realize: there was another mouth to feed, a brother, to replace the ones I'd lost. And yet this was a different kind of creature: one with an unstable constitution, one with a secret twin of whom no one would dare to speak. What kind of kindred soul was this? I certainly had my doubts. Yet, in doubting, I looked upon my mother and, not to my surprise, I found her composed, at peace, in sight of horizons I hadn't the eyes to see. Without judgment of emotion or a furrow on her brow, she closed her eyes, said a prayer, and sanctified the moment.

"Let us unify," she said.

With wings spread out and touching tips, unify we did.

Canto 12

The Gift of Resolve

It was a morning for the baring of souls. Through the Nebul's teeth of stone, the Sun spread its welcome, splaying light like a warning shot across the crater floor, a radiant refraction of higher thought designed to transform the moment, and open the doors to all the hidden rooms.

In this light of unification it came to be revealed that Dager was not the only one who'd sown forbidden seed. Rueg too had tasted the wine, had sired a Vyngorch, and had seen its paternal twin freed to work her wretched ways upon the night. But unlike Dager, Rueg had been mortified by his inquilinity into lust. He saw no source of redemption in it and felt he could only atone for his sins through a proper act of contrition, an act which meant the cleansing of the clan from all corruption of the sort— no rapprochement with the gryphon, no acknowledgment of seed, only the continuum of denial and the disavowal of compassion.

"It would be better for us all if both the Vyngorch and his twin were destroyed in the nest, rather than let the 'bitch' escape and set her ugly brother loose to sing his scheming serenades." So said Rueg, and so he meant, though much more out of sorrow than of wrath.

Where these two dragon bulls had shared a common indiscretion, their common choice of penance was far from one accord. Dager wanted to bring the Vyngorch to the fold. Rueg would not hear of it. The vote was cast, and the influence of the Wroth was felt—four to three. My mother voted with her mate as, surprisingly, did the ash gray dragone who'd awakened from his doddering slumbers long enough bring the issue to a close. So Dager's plea to embrace the Vyngorchim as members of the Mystic Clan was defeated, and perhaps rightly so.

Yet from this opposition a resolution was born: First, the Vyngorch would not be taken to the Mystic Clan, as such. Nevertheless a test case would be permitted. My brother Pod, since he'd already been acknowledged by his father, would be taken into the dragon family, but not without a hitch: Conditionally, he would be accepted by the Kiln Dragons as a member of the family of the dragon lord who'd sired him. He would be permitted entrance to the Nebul only as far as its outer perimeters and would otherwise be marked as a "probationer," the first of his kind.

The resolution was a fair one. Even I had to admit that— despite my fondness for Pod, despite the fact I now had a brother waiting at the Crater door—I was not yet ready to welcome all of the Vyngorchim into the fold. There was a dark side to these malformed beasts that exceeded their awkwardness. The mention of their more sinister half was quite enough to chill my blood; so terrible was her presence that no one would mention her name. Yet Dager had been resolute about bringing the Vyngorch into the Mystic Clan and had been equally insistent about doing so now. For him, the community of mystics would be coming under siege, and soon.

Well, "soon," in terms of dragon time is a relative thing indeed. Our lives occur in waves of unexpected fluctuation. Sometimes a day's an eternity, and the wink of an eye ends a decade. So it's always best to hold the moment fast. My father had sharpened his perceptions on the honing stone of combat. So his sense of timing, it seemed to me, was more critical than ours.

We broke the news to Pod. The Council then selected me to find him with instructions not to overstate the case. I was simply to inform him that for a time, with some condition and considerable reservation, he'd been temporarily reluctantly accepted.

As for Pod when he was told, to say he was elated would be to cheapen the emotion. To have been recognized even tentatively was more than he'd expected. But to find that he'd not only gained acceptance but a family in the bargain was more than his poor misbegotten heart could bear. When he came to face my father and was told, he burst out into song. As if the soul imprisoned in his odious physique had just flown free, a melody poured forth upon the mountain sky that brought in doves and thrushes from a hundred miles around.

This was his day of transformation, an elemental change, a resurrection of his spirit self, a brightening of the light. He was to be a finer creature from that moment on, changed in essence and in color to a glowing golden hue, a value of both skin and aura nearly matched by his new mother, Drilg.

Drilg, to the surprise of no one, embraced him on the spot. She saw in this new charge the heart of my father and was stirred to show a kindness for him that he had never known. It was as if he'd helped to take the place of Karman and somehow assuaged the pain of losing Seti to the North. Pod, for his part, was moved beyond either action or response. He could, in his ungainly way, do little more than glow, and accept the love that had come to him at last.

Make no mistake about it; Vyngorchim were not dragons yet. These discards of the Mystic Clan, despite their pretty songs, were slick and glib and given to whims like weathervanes in gales. And yet I had a brother here. Somehow I had known, just known, that Pod was one of us and would always be. He might not have been the comeliest of creatures, but there was a vein of loyalty that flowed from his heart into his eyes. I had seen it from the beginning, even through all his patronage of me. He was, through all his mottled hide and rumpled fur, quite pure. I told him that in a weaker moment and finally watched him break. He tried to hold composure, but his loneliness betrayed him. And finally, letting go, he began to weep.

Never make a Vyngorch cry. Their tears come down in torrents that could irrigate the Rahn of Kutch. Pod, as I was soon to learn, would never be a bastion of restraint. He was particularly susceptible to acts of kindness shown him. In alternating currents, he laughed and wept and wailed, and in a matter of moments drew flocks of birds to hear him sing, only to have them nearly drown in the lacryma of his joy.

Of course, he swore his loyalty embellished with effect. "I'll be the best brother a dragon ever had," he vowed. Trying to wipe his teardrops with his wings, he sent a spray of tears enough to cause a salty shower. "I'll make you proud of me, you'll see. I'll be bold, brave, and courageous, and fired with a dragon's will."

"Then be so bold as to stop your sniveling," I answered, wiping dry. "The first lesson that a *dragon* learns is dragons never cry.*

The Vyngorch could be stoical or utterly effusive, and no one ever knew which swings of mood were ever quite sincere. Emotionally, the Vyngorchim were the summary of inconsistency and very much like pygmies in their way.

Those creatures known as human beings were mysteries to us. Those angels-in-waiting were pygmies in practice as far as we were concerned. Forget the claims we dragons made to know

---

* Dragons do cry, of course, when sighting the Aurora Borealis, when mourning loved one's lost in battle, and when seeing angels face to face. At those times, they pour hot ingots from their faces which form the slag for steel in warrior's sacred swords.

them; we did not. They were such a mass of contradictions, of scattered dreams and ever-present fears that we saw only dim reflections of what they hoped to be. How could we know them, after all, these numinous tin angels? How could we hope to know them when they didn't know themselves?

As I had an answer for all things in those days, I had an answer for this. I, with the mergent gift, would put my plan into action. I would become one with a human being, learn his ways, come to assimilate his minuscule complexities, and probe his inner self. From the experience I had undergone inside that village wall, I could bring this all to bear. I could bridge the gap between these elementally different species, between these creatures so remote from us in body yet so closely tied to us in soul.

§§§§§§§

On day two, we resumed our visitation at the Nebul. I was again permitted to sit-in with the Council while the probationer Pod tap-danced atop the teeth of the Crater and drew a horde of munzels to his side. While they took respite from their toils around the floor, my brother sang them ballads filled with hope and love and joy. Although I was engaged in other things, I couldn't help but notice, that while the songs were sung—the color of these mole-dwarfs changed. Their auras rose from a sickly yellow phlegma to a vibrant green. It was as if a Vyngorchim song could wash clean their iniquity, baptizing them in the energy of sound. The songs my brother sang could carry quite a way and reach the Seven sitting there as readily as I. The Council was already unified and melded into one vibration, so upliftment would have been a matter of degrees. Yet I couldn't help but notice that they felt the transmutation—that Pod's sweet music had stirred them as if they'd heard the songs of angels for the very first time.

The Council seldom overstayed its time. That it remained here after the first night of the waxing moon was exceptional. I was the exception. In the holy time allotted us to meld our souls and become of one vibration, the Council of the Seven Dragons held me in their bond. The circle was now complete. With my father in attendance, the masterminds—all Seven—could focus on the context of our quest. That our mission was a high one I no longer had a doubt, for this was, to be sure, the Shadow Council —the same convocation of higher souls who had healed my sister and me.

In my crisis when I lay dying and my life had hung in the balance, I could feel their energies commingling with mine, lifting me up, bathing me in a shower of purifying light. Now, in this hour that they had predicted would someday be at hand, I had come to fulfill the quest that fate had set before us.

Once again enfolded and allowed to feel their love, I was granted a mentor, another member of the Council who would act as my guide. After briefly scanning, they came to a consensus that my counselor would be the clear blue Skye.

Skye the sapphire dragon was respected by all who knew him, for clearly he could see through the veil of material things. It was said of him that, when he was still in the nest, his mother baptized him in a morning dew, and that even now he could, like the Mantilough, evaporate late in the day and materialize again only at night when the world with its hot brews had gone to sleep.

It was Skye, in his clarity, who let me know that all the dragons in the Nebul, young and old alike, had awaited my arrival, had looked upon the Lightning Dragon as the harbinger of change. "But change to what?" he asked. He asked and did not answer. There was a fork in his silence, the peril of free choice, the spectre of a divided legacy that danced before us all.

Apparently, the Captain now posed a greater danger to the dragon than even Pod had led me to believe. He had, of late been on something of a rampage, had been hunting dragons with abandon, Shimbaghs with a passion, and had even shot and killed a unicorn or two. What had prompted this crusade had been the rumor that the Lightning Dragon had emerged. My little sortie at the City walls had gotten his attention, and in the three days just since I had been there, the Captain had already paid a visit, had combed the City, grilling the citizens on every last detail of what they'd seen: my dimensions, my wingspan, my depth and scope of being, my behavior before the face of them, the vector of my flight when I departed. He hadn't missed a trick.

The City doges, predictably, had been scandalous in their lies. By underplaying my courage and overplaying my size, they had diminished my role in saving them and had blown my ferocity out of all proportion. My attempts to get to know them were made to sound more like an attack. And, of course, they made it seem as if they'd won, as if they'd driven me back into the thunderheads from which they'd said I'd come.

Apparently, the Captain was no fool. He caught the subtext beneath the words. He knew the ways of Mystic Beasts and had even come to know the ways of men. With his coterie of stalwarts, he vowed he would return, and offered a prize of treasure to anyone who brought him word of me.

What had not been told was that the Captain was obsessed with me. Like Ahab with the Whale, he was setting his soul's course for mine to finish our unfinished business. What he would do when next we met would be quite another matter. What I was to do with him was clearly before me now: Kill him quickly or win him to our side. He was too dangerous to dragonkind to leave the way he was, and the way he was made him the only man on earth with such a power.

"Of course, there is a darker side to this scenario: RuSiva. He wants the Captain quite as much as we. If he were able to engulf him and destroy him, the job for us would be done. The sorcerer's magic is powerful, but he cannot destroy us as such, not with the Asking Prayer, not the way the Captain can. Only the Captain can cut us short. Only the Captain can banish. But RuSiva can deal with him. And once RuSiva has dealt with the Captain, we can deal with RuSiva. The Dark Sorcerer can flee from us, disguise himself and hide, but he cannot confront us, not a proper dragon fully armed in crystalline regalia. If we could in our subtle ways let the Sorcerer know the Captain's whereabouts, we could have the ends we seek, have done with the Captain, and later have our dealings with the sorcerer."

Shielding his inner thoughts from me, Skye looked me in the eye, keeping his energies so focused upon me that I couldn't penetrate their business. But the Mother of Tongues has many facets, and my emerald locked on his. Since language is the agent of confusion, I listened to little of what Skye said, and felt through waves of empathy that he was testing me. He no more meant to traffic with Shimbaghs than he would become a worm. This was to be my koan—the test of my mettle. His twinkling blue eyes told me that beneath this mask of piety was a jester full of pranks, but one who never jested without cause.

Sometimes out of mischief there are great ideas born. Whether he had intended it or not, Skye had given me an insight that might benefit us all, a point so obvious we each had overlooked it. With the power of the Asking Prayer the Captain could banish any of the mystic clan. A passing of his sword in pentagrams and crosses, some words of intonation—we were gone. But so were Shimbaghs. He could wipe away the Shimbaghs in a trice, while dragons had to battle them, get slashed and cut and risk life and limb in the bargain.

I had come to this conclusion when I'd heard the tale from Pod. But now it came to strike me that RuSiva knew this too. That was why he'd sought the Captain so desperately yet had, at the same time, approached him with such caution. For RuSiva was a man who had become a Shimbagh too. And since Shimbaghs were beasts of magic just as we, this wizard could be banished just as easily as I. So, as the perversity of fate would have it, this evil magician and I shared a common bond: with the Asking Prayer and a few quick strokes, the Captain could put us away. We knew it, yet I felt quite certain the Captain didn't yet.

Somewhere along the way it struck me that we'd overlooked the obvious: The Captain, being human (therefore fallible and blocked), looked upon the Mystic Clan without benefit of discernment. It wasn't that he didn't try. He seemed to have some system whereby he adjudged a dragon bad or good and snuffed him on the spot or let him go. But his judgments were irregular and not altogether clear. He lacked the seven magic gems that opened the doors to the cosmos, that gave him the eyes to see the pathway to God. If he had them, they were lying dormant like some buried treasure. That was it, of course. That was the task we leaders of the Mystic Clan had set before us: apprise the pygmie of the gifts that were already his, the gifts that he had only begun to probe. That was to be my task with the Captain. He was a leader among his kind—a man of justice, feared and respected. If I could teach him the laws of natural insight and help him learn to see, we could fly together to the Gates of Hell and slam the door forever.

Then again, "reaching him" was RuSiva's plan as well. He too was obsessed with the Captain, for RuSiva had also realized that the Captain was the only man who could put him down forever.

I could be the first to find him but only by the way I'd chosen: merge with a man, mate with a woman—that very special woman —and seek the Captain on human terms as an equal and a peer. If I could reach him in that way, I could help him gain perspective and a clarity of sight.

I revealed my plan to Skye and found his reactions to be mixed. For my insights into the Captain, he had praise. "We dragons have been fighting the Shimbaghs for so long, we've lost all perspective of them. Of course that's it! We assume, because these pygmies have the same basic gifts as we, that they can differentiate. They can't. They need translation, the Captain most of all. Well done! As for the other..." he paused. He was patient, but when scanning him I saw his past rise up in patterns before me, patterns which revealed to me that they nearly fit my own. "Of course, you believe you have the gift of mergence, that you wear the Diamond Gemstone in your crown."

"I believe I do."

"But are you sure?" he asked, mocking me with the admonition he had also shared.

"Does anyone ever know for certain?" I found myself asking, in return.

"Only in the doing," Skye placidly replied. "And the doing... and the doing," he repeated. "The *Diamond I* is not a high-stake prize one wins at a gaming table. It is forged in the white fires of experience."

"But the mergent gift...I know I have it," I insisted. "I can become one with many things. And I can join with man." Methinks I did protest too much. But then a single ounce of grit weighs more than all the talent in the world. It was a matter of attitude, and my attitude was this: I had done it once before. I could do it again.

Skye was kind. "I've done it once or twice myself," he said, quite modestly at that. "But be apprised: mergence with a rock or roach is one thing. Mergence with the complex little mind of pygmie man is another altogether."

"What you propose, of course, is nothing new," I heard another voice say. Although he did not face me at the time, the high pitched voice and scholarly tones were the calling cards of Claarik. "Others before you sought to merge into the world of men, to learn their ways and do their masterworks from inside out. Like you, they thought they'd been crowned with the *I*, that they could merge without recourse. Many have gone, but *none* have ever returned.

"More than a dozen in my day have played the 'sapient' game. They were blue-eyed dragons like yourself who thought to make that terrible transition, to be the rainbow bridge between the mind and spirit. They took a man's body and a homo sapiens heart. They lived a man's or a woman's life and died. Now they're travelers trapped in time, caught on the Wheel of Life. They lived and died, lived and died, and lost the meaning of their mission.

"Many were close to this old dragon's heart, but none would listen to the warnings I tried to give them. I miss them. I will miss them 'til the other side of time. I don't want to have to say the same for you. You see, despite our little differences, my onyx dragon prince, you are one of our own blood. We need you here, in these days most of all."

I was touched. Of all the creatures I had yet encountered I'd perceived that Claarik was antithesis to everything I felt; I had been wrong. Where were my supersenses, after all? Did all our talents honed below so quickly lose their edge up here? I felt equipped to take on this mission. My force of will was there. And yet these master dragons expressed their grave concern for me. I might have expected such admonitions from Claarik or even Skye. Yet I couldn't help but notice that, when I looked my father's way (perhaps for corroboration) he too responded gravely.

"It's your choice, my son," he said with sadness, and quickly looked away.

"For God's sake let him go!" From the center of the semi-circle, from the ash-gray dragone's chair, there came a rumble like gentle thunder that caused all heads to turn and all souls to heed. "We stand so long on precedent, we forget what must be done. Past failures have no place in future plans. The task has been set before us, and we have a volunteer. Rejoice! He's young, courageous and, from what I can see, given to invention. Trade all the gemstones in your bag for that rare combination, and you'll do well on any plane you choose!"

As he spoke his eyes drew wide. Closed at first like ancient doors that hid some Arcana of dreams, they opened slowly letting shine a blue-white light that penetrated deeply into me. Not since my times in Sagro's cave had I seen a light like that.

"Who sponsors him?" he quickly queried.

"I do," Skye evenly assured him.

"Then you alone remain with us. All others, give us leave."

When this one spoke, the Nebul cleared. Even Rueg—even Dager—left in silence, flew off to adjoining mountain peaks where they waited still in view for the summons to return. The munzels slipped into their holes. Even my brother, the Vyngorch, knew his place to depart. He darted from the peak on

243

which he sat and took a position by Dager's side, sitting there erectly with no small amount of pride.

This dragone who held me in regard, now took a stance upon his onyx throne and gazed fixedly at me. There was so much of Sagro in him: a presence of divinity, yet with a fundament of clay that only ancient sages possessed. There was also in his demeanor an uncommon sense of pride, a pleasure in having beheld me, as if I had been his seed.

"I was so much like you, you know. A rebel filled with ideas that I was certain would resurrect the world. There was a fire that burned inside me then. My passions shook the ground. I screamed the truth so loudly and often that I could light the night and turn it into day. I fought until I nearly bled to death. The scars of Shimbaghs festered on my hide and nearly drove me mad a thousand times, and every time I came back at them, giving every fray my best, giving every day of life my earnest energy.

"Then one day some mystic creature said: 'Put things in perspective.' And I did. And from that time I learned to heed the gentle calls of reason. I took some time to love and wait and let some other force make impact on the world. I became passive, objective, universal in my love, and distinct in my indifference. Convinced that my sublimity was the ticket to Nirvana, I gave up the struggle. I waited for my angels to come. I waited. And I waited. I was a fool.

"*Never* give up the struggle. We are here to fight the good fight. That is our role on this Earth. That is our destiny. There are those among us who are gifted with a gentler soul. They balance us. But you! Like me! You wear the onyx armor! You will inherit this throne on which I sit when my passing time is done. You have been brought into this place to make things happen. Do it! Your angels will come to get you soon enough.

"You've sharpened your lessons well below. Don't let false perceptions here dull them to you now. The fears that others hold for you are theirs to own, not yours. Listen to them, to be sure. Let them moderate you. But don't let them dissuade you from what you must do. Listen to your heart, for it is pure. Other eyes have their own perceptions of truth."

Having had his say, he passed his wing before me in a gesture of approval, nodded back toward Skye and back again to sleep. Now, for me, his slumbers had a deeper meaning. By now I'd come to understand that, as Sagro had done, this old dragone spent his dream state convening with Powers from other planes of life.

I was grateful to him, touched and moved and very much in debt, and yet I hadn't even come to know his name.

"He is the great one," Skye said, feeling all my thoughts. "He is the Initiator, the one who began the Holy Wars in which we all now struggle. He began the Shimbagh Wars, and he cannot leave this plane until they're done and the issue is brought to a close. That is his choice *and* his curse. He is Knot V, your father's father, and you are the seed of his seed."

Canto 13

The Slavern

Knot V had not spoken in a century. He hadn't deemed it worth his while...until that morning. Until that morning he had spent an epoch in the Silence, dreaming decadragon dreams, wandering ethers only master souls could chart, dipping his auric rings to this dimension merely long enough to make his presence felt, to hike a wing, to cast a vote, to state his aye or nay on some referendum he felt merited his attention (but not his voice). It had been said of Knot on the day he took a vow of silence, that he would not again trivialize his thoughts by giving energy of voice to any but the most august of moments. The moment to which he had referred, was to be the time that marked the coming of final Shimbagh War. That he had given voice at all was his cachet to me, to let me know that The Time was drawing near.

Whether my mission was conjoined with his decision to give voice, or whether it was merely the happy child of chance, I had no way of knowing; nor did any of the Council. That he had spoken at all was enough. That gesture on my behalf removed any further opposition to my journey into man. It also supported Dager's long held insistence that the most consequential battle in mystic history was soon to come to pass.

That was Dager's opinion, of course, and the course of perspectives change. Wars come and go in every age. And partisans of every age will think theirs best and last when they're nothing of the sort. But this was, after all, the Shimbagh War; no mere bagatelle. And we would make our terminal embraces soon enough.

What puzzled me to some extent was why Knot stayed at all? Why did he cling so tenaciously to his desiccating hide when, by virtue of his wisdom and his spiritual evolution, he seemed ready to ascend whenever he chose?

Hearing my thoughts, Skye answered. "Few if any ascend at will. It is the dragon's curse—this love of battle and strife. Since Knot was the Initiator, it is his plight to remain until the very last Shimbagh battle is fought and won. Until that time, he travels through the ethers to convene with other souls such as he who've risen above the rights and wrongs of this lonely little place."

"But he himself said that we're in this world to do business. Why does he not do it? Why does he not live in the moment, let his spirit manifest in flesh, and be an exemplar of physique? If this is the board we all play upon, then why not win the game and do it with style?"

"Oh, mighty ball of fire," Skye sighed, expanding his ice-blue aura, surrounding me in healing glacial light. "Because this is not the only board and not the only game."

"Then again, I may be right," I insisted.

"Then again, you may," Skye agreed. He closed his eyes in silent prayer for guidance and thanksgiving. I, for my part, pledged another course. Find those ethers, learn those secrets, and put them to use here and now. Surely, they could be found through the *Diamond I.* And once I'd mastered mergence, the other aspects of it would be mine to know; of this, I was certain.

I was prepared for my journey into man. My mentor, Skye, no stranger to excursions into other forms of life, shared with me the lessons he had learned—some happy memories of his mergings, some others more obscure and even perilous to recall.

"Mergence with the forest flora is the purest path to take. Flowers, plants, herbs and trees are pieces of God's heart. They live to serve. They give to all who pass and touch, asking nothing of the taker in return. So infused are they with the Holy Spirit of the High that unifying with them is a wondrous thing to know. Once you share that consciousness, that Christ become the self, you're never quite perceived the same again. Merging with so innocent a life will set you free, yet in that freedom hold you fast, for there is nothing more compelling than an open door—the knowledge that you may come and go unburdened by expectation, unfettered by condition or demand.

"But there are other life forms that will cling to you, that will covet the power you put inside them, that will try to draw you down so that you lose yourself in them forever. This, I fear, is the case with humankind. The dragon's power inside a man must be a heady wine indeed, so much so that the host will often self-destruct and become a derelict—forever a slave to pleasure."

The word "forever" sent a chill through me. I knew one never dealt in absolutes, but this one seemed to have the cold, hard run of truth to it. I wondered, if Skye had actually merged with a man, if he'd been corrupted by the wiles of human nature. Perhaps this was why he tried to put me off taking such a course.

"Has this ever been the case with you?" I asked, hoping secretly it had. "Have you ever found your way into human shell?"

"Take me for a coward, not a fool," Skye answered, pointedly. "I never had either the madness or the courage to go into that endless canyon of pride and vanity. But I have had my flings. I went into the Gnostic maze of fairy lives for quite a time, became an elf, a gnome who mined the secrets of the Sard. Yet with fairies, as with creatures of whimsy who circle the rims of night, there was neither substance nor intent. I felt weightless, shiftless, without fundament, a soul who's supped on cosmic candy when raw bone was the fete I sought. My vital forces craved the fires of passion and the roots of heavy power. I came back. Although my hostess (on that occasion a luscious fairy queen) coaxed me with every seduction known to mortal mind to stay, I bade my leave, begged her pardon, and nearly didn't emerge.

"There's the rub, dear boy. Finding a willing host is difficult enough. Finding the way back—even from a flower or a pebble—is a task.

"No...mist is my best trick, I'm afraid. Evaporation, that's the secret. Find a willing particle of air and you can disappear at will. I've done that much and have often thought that anyone could do the same, and yet I'm told they can't. It's not a conscious effort that makes it come to pass. It's a gift I have, they say, just as speed of flight and keen obsidian intuitions are the gifts innate to you. We all are given sacred tools with which to work. Maybe mergence, as we would like to have it, isn't one of them. I don't claim to have all the answers. No one does..."

Such intimations of limitation were not a part of Skye's nature. Why, I wondered, was he suddenly playing coy with this? Why was he, the very model of serenity, suddenly playing the neophyte with me? Since he was not a prevaricator in any sense of the word, why did he strike this ruse to throw me off? Was I delving into areas for which I was unprepared? And what if I were? It was my hide not his. I knew in every onyx cell of my being, he'd taken the gift of Mergence on to its limits and beyond. Why then was he so abstruse in his handling of this? Didn't he know I knew he knew I'd know?

I recalled my single episode of mergence in the MasterSinger's school. The roach, even though I hadn't filled him long, had gained a hold on me, had made me feel the responsibility of taking life. Yet, even in that early test, I had emerged, and I could emerge another time from anyone or anything; I simply knew it. So had my cousin. He smiled as I thought it, and an azure flame of amazement escaped from the side of his mouth. Skye, blue-eyed, sapient and kind, withheld all judgment but held me fast in his gaze.

"Let us unify a final time," he said. And standing in the Sun of Fire, unify we did.

§§§§§§§

Late in the day of my departure, rods of wind pried the Nebul, vied with rancorous summer heat to fly into our faces. By now, the Crater had become a family affair. The other council dragons had departed, had gone to those hidden tabernacles only high dragons can find.

Immediately after our unification Skye, true to tales about him, had evaporated, turned into a mist that swam up through the hot white light of day. Knot, powdered gray like the silica on which he stood, blended so explicitly into the Crater wall that one could fail to tell he was there at all.

My mother rejoined me. We said our goodbyes as if it would be an even longer time before we met again.

"Remember. Merely put my name upon the winds, and I'll be there," Drilg said. Lovingly, she brushed her wings across my face as if in sorrow to stroke my brow for some images she saw through the maze of time. No one could ever fathom the depth of this amber angel's soul. Yet I knew then as now that she saw more than anyone else. She never spoke of it. It would have changed nothing, but then she knew that too. True wisdom learns to leave the best unsaid.

Drilg whipped away in an updraft of wind late in the evening light even before my father came to sit beside me. And when he'd come (as when she'd gone) the energies above the Crater shifted, stirred as from a gentle breeze into a storm. Dager, I had come to realize, drew gusts wherever he stood. And where he flew the downdrafts of wind sucked up small trees from the earth, blew them to another place and planted them again.

"So you want to merge?" he roared. "Well…if you must. It's the path of clever souls. I've never been much for subtleties, as you know.

"I did merge once, though, in the MasterSinger's school. I became the mountain in which we dwelled, shook that pit of pedantry right to its core. That got that old buggar Sagro's rapt attention, I assure you. It was only once though. Haven't done it since. Haven't wanted to. I Suppose I could if I tried. But frankly I never found another creature I ever cared to be—except a dragon! Break the flimsy bonds of circumstance! That's my creed.

I had learned by now that when Dager waxed magniloquent he had grave concerns to hide. His concern quite obviously was spent on me and on my coming venture into humankind.

"Do me the favor, son, before you go. Spend a day or two with me in flight. Let's circle the world, scar the sky with our fire, and set the land below aglow with traces of our brilliance!"

How could one turn down an offer such as that?

"Done!" I said, before I'd even had the time to think.

In an instant we had spread our wings to fly, yet as we did a horde of munzels poured out from their holes—all the munzels in the Crater, so it seemed—to run and gather at our feet, sending glimmers of hope through their once-made soulless eyes and gazing fixedly at me. I wondered at this for a moment. Seeing all these mole-dwarfs clutching at my legs like gypsy children pleading coins from some kind stranger's purse, I wondered why they'd come to me. I felt that there was nothing I could give them; but there was.

"You're something of a hero, so it seems," Dager reminded me. "You freed one earlier, I recall."

"Now that you mention it, I did."

"Then, they gather round you hoping for a chance to be the next."

"Then, let's oblige them. Free a munzel. Make a friend." A nearby mole-dwarf, a lucky child of fate, caught the brush of my wing. I uttered the words, said the mantra that set him free.

Dager, too, apparently grasped the charm of such an act, for in a gesture that was both casual and grand, he gently swiped his wing across a pair of anxious mole-dwarfs, elocuted the proper codes of absolution and unbound their fettered human souls.

"Free a munzel. Make a friend," he mimicked. "What the hell. Maybe we'll start a tradition."

"Bound to be good luck, don't you think?" I queried, quite rhetorically.

"Bound to be good luck," Dager was quick to agree.

In a moment we had set our wings to fly, had caught a mountain gust and launched into the night.

It's always nice to leave in the midst of cheers, if one could call them that. Munzels had a way of making all forms of emotion sound exactly the same. Rage or laughter, tears or rejoicing, they were able only to respond with a monotonous kind of croaking reminiscent of a frog. Yet, as we took to the air, I couldn't help but take pride in that. Even in their repressed celebration they had let us know, we had become their champions and their friends.

§§§§§§§

My brother had been waiting for us. Darting back and forth in the sky like a string-cut paper kite, he wandered, quite uncertain of his fate. Pod had spent his days waiting for this moment when we three, father and two sons, could flaunt our talents in the sky, rip the clouds and make the weather change with our bedazzling flights of fancy. Now the time had come.

It was a contest of a sorts. Dager with his awesome power, Pod with his articulate twists and turns, and I with my star-blessed gifts of speed were more than all the elements could bear. We were rumbling storm clouds, whirling dust devils, raging tsunamis that tore the open the stomach of the sea, spanked the land, and sent the water back again. Although we harmed no living thing, we let no creature pass the night altogether undisturbed. So outrageous were our revelries that even the giant Naanworm from beneath the Sea of India reared his ugly head, spat a host of seaweed children from his mouth and bellowed out his wrath. Green and bilious when made angry, ten thousand eyes peppered along his three-mile body all brought red with ire—he let us know in no uncertain terms that we were breaking cosmic law. Crying out with a voice that boomed like a community of whales, he hurled his objurgation.

"You the dragons, of all creatures!" He shouted. "You should know, there is no cause without effect! Your primal size and power can jar the earth down to its core, *and has!* Just keep it up, and you will shake all remaining Shimbaghs awake. And when you do, all hell breaks loose! Soon the war begins. Soon the creatures of the Pit will come to call. How could you not have known this, Dager? You of all the dragons in the world? Could you not have realized this?! Or perhaps you did."

Arching his neck into the clouds, the Naanworm widened his eyes and poured them on my father, railing all while. There we were, hovering and humbled in the midst of an angry morning sky, feeling the censure of this very ancient soul whose stare was both compassionate and mad. We, the mightiest beings on this earth, were made to feel small and shamed; at least, I was. And yet instantly I came to realize that when Dager did at last reply, he did so without sense of either consequence or chagrin.

"It was an accident, oh Ancient One," he answered. "The offshoot of a youthful celebration. Nothing more. Then again, you shouldn't fill your holy mind with thoughts of the profane. The final Shimbagh War is in the ethers. It *is* imminent."

"Then let it come in its own time, Dager. Not in yours," the Naanworm grumbled, "lest we all pay the price of your impatience. Remember, I take all the negativity that spills into the sea. And right now I am stuffed up to the gills. Do not feed me more than I can stomach!"

Without a gesture of salute, the Naanworm went back to his ocean, leaving a warning bed of dead fish in his wake.

We trimmed our jubilation after that. Tamely, we flew back inland, engaged in a bout of aerobatics that gave a facelift to a canyon. Dager buzzed a forest filled with human hunters. Pod, in artful twists and turns, bundled up a flock of clouds and bounced them off a waterfall, while I, with all my speed of flight, made laser trails that carved dragon frescos in a canyon wall. When we had finished, we perched on a mountainside, breathless and reflective. And though we basked in the pleasure of one another's company, there was a sour note to the end of our revelry. The Naanworm's warning had left us in doubt. At least I had felt the sting of his rebuke and so, I sensed, had Pod. Dager, unruffled and with his wild bravado utterly intact, moved soon enough to put us at our ease.

"Don't let the Naanworm's auguries upset you," Dager said. "That old sea-bred garbage pail eats fear for a living. He swallows so much worldly bilge his thoughts become as polluted as his diet. He speaks of past as prophecy and only knows the refuse of history. He's lost most of his abilities to discern. And he was more than wrong, I can assure you. All the Shimbaghs in the Pit are wide awake by now and have been for an epoch. So, whether or not we do our little adagios in the sky, the course is set. The dance will soon be joined by other dancers."

Although Dager was thorough in his explanations about the Naanworm, I had my hunches it was only prelude. He was setting markers and in his way was making silent apology for having used us as a kind of bait, for now he took certain measure to weigh what he had to say.

"The Naanworm was right about one thing," he admitted. "I knew what I was doing. And I must confess to you, my sons, what one of you has come to think already. There was a reason for all this, for the aerial acrobatics and the strutting of our stuff. It was at least in part to put on a show for the greatest flyer of them all—the SkyMaster."

The name, for some reason I could not explain, brought fire to my thighs. Not in all the time I was at the Nebul had there been mention made of the SkyMaster. It was as if there were some cryptic code of silence surrounding him. Now, it was my father who had invoked the creature's name, and it was now that I could make known my challenge to his primacy.

First, I had to sate my curiosity. Up to now, no one had deigned to tell me who this dragon was and why his identity had been so well kept a secret. I knew my father wouldn't hold this information in such precious high regard, and I was right. "The Sky Master," I said, repeating the name with savor. "Who is he? What dragon is this? And why does he fly so out of range?"

"He," my father answered, "is a *she.* She is a gryphon and the most eloquent flier since the angels first grew wings. By bringing us three together, the best in our respective fields, I hoped we might draw her out; but I fell short of that. And yes we're all aware, Sharto, of how you've broken sound. But, shattering sound is only one part of the mastery of flight. And though you may someday be the greatest in the sky, you can rest assured that you're not there yet."

"I can beat her," I heard my own voice say. I don't know why I'd chosen this of all times to cut loose with such a display of unabated conceit; but I had to the degree that I was embarrassed at myself. Yet somehow, as I knew that I could merge with man, I knew that I could do this too. I could take the SkyMaster on and win! "Gryphon or dragon," I continued, "I'll challenge this SkyMaster to a stage of combat in the sky, and I will prevail. I know I will. I'll wager her, her ultimate wish against mine. And when I've cut her down a notch or two I'll demand as payment whatever it is you seek."

More than a little bit amused, my father grinned. "Ah, the arrogance of innocence," he said. "And yes, while you're out there jousting mirrors of your self-esteem, ask the SkyMaster if she might ally with us."

"Ally with us?" I queried, sounding like an echo as I did.

"Yes. That's the reason for this bait in the first place," Dager said; his voice intensified like the trill of a battle drum. "Forget who wins or loses the contest. If we could gain the Sky Master's support, woo her to an alliance, then others of her kind would follow—male and female, gryphons from all corners of the globe.

Gryphons are solitary creatures, this is true. But up to now, they've never had a paragon, a queen around whom they could unify their innately rebellious natures."

And if I defeated her, she would no longer be the Master of the Skies. She would just be another gryphon who could fly with skill. Dager didn't say it, but the words sat behind his tongue. So, it was an exhibition and not a challenge that he wanted. Then I could accommodate him on that score as well.

"You waste your breath, both of you." Pod interrupted. My brother, Pod, ingratiating at the worst of times and always solicitous of me, had suddenly grown a voice deep in its authority. I turned to regard him and saw, beneath his easy Vyngorch charm, that he wore a mask of gravity. He cleared his throat and spoke haltingly, yet made no attempt to equivocate.

"The SkyMaster won't be paying a call today," he continued, "for a pair of reasons at the least. First, she isn't in the sky these days. She's gone on an hejira to some place only of her knowing.

"Second (and you can forget the rest), she wouldn't come in any case. Not with me here. You see, the very presence of the Vyngorch constitutes a danger to her. Not that I would harm the gryphon in any way; even if I were inclined. But, dear blood of mine, there is the matter of my other half, my sister, my lovely evil twin. And it's time we talked of it."

That the secret of the Vyngorch was an awful truth to tell was best told by the evident haunting of my father. Dager, though he feared no living thing in heaven or in hell, found this topic so distasteful that he clenched his iron jaws until they cracked with strain. As if to find a fantasy on which to fix his mind, he scanned the horizon below and beyond us, blocking as he did all mention of the secret Pod would share.

That the gryphon-dragon pairings produced bizarre offspring, there was no doubt; the Vyngorch was fair evidence of that. But even though they were riddled with vices, the Vyngorchim were tame and loving alter egos to their dark sisters. Invariably, whenever an ill-fated dragon would meet and mate with a gryphon, the two would give birth to twins. The

Vyngorch, quite nearly always a male, would be the first. The second would inevitably be female—beautiful and deadly—who, upon the moment of her birth, would try to kill her sibling and rip the heart from her own mother. That was why the gryphon, after having birthed this misbegotten pair, would fly the nest and never once look back.

This daughter of perfidy was seldom mentioned by any of the Mystic Clan, and her name was never spoken at night, for even to put the breath of it upon the air might summon her and bring the sayer to the very edge of doom. She was called the *Slavern*. And as her paternal twin, the Vyngorch, was a callow, homely lot, she was the very lethal illusion of beauty. With the face of an angel in transition, with the wings of a swan in flight, she could enthrall the most incorruptible souls and draw them in to the deepest waters of her charms. Those who beheld her would see her always as a lovely lady caught in peril in a lake, a frail Ondine who promised sweet delights to whoever rescued her. Few mortals would resist this kind of temptation; few ever even tried, for once any guileless human being came at last within her reach, the Slavern would draw him in, would will him toward her body of waters and tow him under. On the surface at a distance, she put forth a lovely light, but when brought up eye to eye, she was a hellion. Behind her sweet, angelic face there was a dragon's fire. Beneath her flowing angel's gown hid talons dipped in venom. Her voice was that of a chorus of banshees. And when she sang in concert, she could split the eardrums of any man on earth.

She flourished only from dusk to dawn, and she was chained to bodies of water—to rivers and streams, to lakes and falls, swamps and marshes, to places where innocents might come to drink. In daylight she slept like a buried stone. At night, she was a marauder. She loved to seize runaway children, random travelers, and lovers who watched the double moon that glimmers on a pond. But more than any other thing, she lived to steal the soul of her own brother.

As by the grace of universal balance the Slavern was restricted to work her evil only near bodies of water, there was one thing that could release her: the mention of her name. For anyone to call a Slavern out was to invite worst imaginable fate, for she would know his voice and stalk him through the night until she found him, and until she found him she was freed from her watery prison to hunt him down.

As the Prince of Irony would have it, the Vyngorch did not fear this, for when awake, this dexterous little dragonette could hypnotize the Slavern with his songs, freeze her into half a torpor, and then bundle her up. Binding her in silver strands that he pulled from the harp inside his throat, he'd leave her for the morning and the Sun to do their work. Once caught in deadly daylight, the Slavern would melt into a mire, and form the bed where it was said that poison mushrooms grew.

The dragon, too, was more than a match for this crass bitch, for one blast from a dragon fire, and she'd disintegrate, splash upon the face of time and never be seen again. So, at all costs, the Slavern stayed away from the masters of the kiln as long as they were awake. But sleep comes to all of us, and in the course of weeks and months even dragons can get drowsy. When they do, as we have learned, they'll sleep a cricket's life away. A year was not uncommon, and it was during the dragon's dozing times that the Slavern came to call. She could hear the dragon's snore ten leagues away, could slit his throat before he blinked, drink his blood, and sell his hide for firestone to a wizard of the Shimbagh clan.

The Vyngorchim had problems of their own. They were nearly narcoleptic. As corruptible as the Vyngorch was, he was more susceptible to sleep, and his strongest soporific was to say his sister's name. To mention it at all not only summoned her but also made him drowsy. Any Vyngorch who fell asleep was more in peril to this wraith than any creature who gave breath. For, while the Vyngorch slept, the Slavern could come to steal his soul. The Slavern, being a Shimbagh, had forsaken her soul and had no life beyond the guarding of her murky little waters.

But if she could steal the soul from her brother while he slept, she could keep it and use it as a bargaining chip to buy a second life from the Fallen One.

Pod, even in the telling of it, lost sight of his monition and boldly called the creature from her lair.

"Slavern! Slavern! Slavern! Let the witch come on!" he shouted, barking his rejoinders like a drunk inviting a brawl. With garrulous good nature, he called her name again, shouting it in levity against the fading sun. Yet even in the fullness of day, my brother began to yawn. His eyelids grew heavy and his head began to nod.

"For God's sake, son, shut up!" Dager commanded. I'd never seen him worried before, but he was worried now.

"Don't concern yourself, father dear. If this bitch comes calling, I'll bind her up in silver, then baptize her with Vyngorch piss to hasten her demise."

"And if you can't stay awake?" Dager replied.

"Then I'll have you to protect me." There was an impudence about my brother that was never there before. It was as if the telling of the Slavern tale released some drug in him, some endocrinic trigger that shot him full of self-importance.

"It's the mention of her name," Dager whispered to me. "Once he begins to use it, he can't stop. He'll sing that wretched lady's tune until she comes to call. In no time, he'll be sound asleep, and that's when fun begins."

"It doesn't sound like fun to me," I said.

"It's not!" the Mountain answered.

In moments, Dager's point was made. Pod had nodded off. It was still daylight, so there was no danger, yet. But when Mother Night had pulled her shade, there'd be all hell to pay.

"Thank God, we're here," I said.

"Not even God could help him if we weren't," Dager answered. By now, all traces of bravado had departed from his visage, and it was because of this that he chose to sew together the remainder of this unwholesome tapestry.

There was the matter of the gryphon. Gryphons never slept; they never needed to. Since they, like dragons, were born of fire, they merely needed to sit in the molten lava of a volcano, and they were revived, and could return again to the world outside. In that regard, the Slavern with her nocturnal half-life was no danger to them. But the Slavern, of all the Shimbaghs the gryphons faced, had venom on her talons that was deadly to the female. As if it were the Slavern's rite of retribution, she could merely take a swipe and break the skin, and a gryphon queen would fall.

"Surely that would not dissuade a creature so highly evolved as the SkyMaster," I said.

"Part of high evolution is knowing when the earthly energies are in tune and when they're not. And they're not now that Pod has put his toxic challenge to the wind."

"And the SkyMaster, to be sure, could have foreseen this," I thought aloud.

"Her perceptions are honed as acutely as any Dragon of the Kiln could be, and maybe more, for there is so much time this gryphon spends in solitude she crosses streams of consciousness in just a single day."

No one could be that admirable, I thought. Yet I could not help observing that my father rhapsodized at length about this regal lion-bird and also spoke further of her elusiveness, for that rare quality and not the codes of violence was her *passe montagne.* It was both bizarre and quite unsettling to hear one such as Dager spend so much time in paean of someone not betaken of his ways. Only when he spoke of Drilg did he do so with such evident admiration, as if she were a consciousness a touch beyond his ken.

Those revelations made the time go by, perhaps a little too quickly, and brought the curtain down on day. The sun bled into the earth and brought a waning half a moon out in the summer sky, a dark marmoreal covering, turbulent with cirrus slips of clouds that passed like trains on some mad, feral lady's gown. Seeming to take a will of its own, one of those clouds tore away and started slipping toward a mountain summit directly facing ours.

I could not see it clearly, for it kept its numinous shape, but it was shaping-up to be a woman on wings.

She took her time. Forming into clouds again, a breath of fatal fog, she slipped slowly toward our roost. She was insidiously eloquent and so subtle in her disguise that I might have missed her movements had I not felt her black eyes dancing in the night. She couldn't hide them; they stabbed the darkness. They screamed with their own voice like that of some strident harpy out to steal a soul.

She was no fool. Having known I'd sniffed her out, she took her poison mists back across the mountains and slipped again from sight, emerging as something else: an image of the beauty Dager had described. More than a beauty, her likeness was the quintessence of the woman from the City, that vision of frail beauty I had held upon my wing and vowed again that I'd return to see. She had filled my thoughts and had never left them since. Now of all times she appeared before me, calling me from across this chasm to fly to the other side. It would have been an easy shot, and I just might have taken her up had my father not seen the illusion and broken the silence.

"That's the other trick she has: to pluck your wishes like fruit and become the image of your desires. If you chase your lust and I chase mine, she can split us far enough apart to slip in and slaughter your brother. Never sell short her speed in flight or her willingness to strike anymore than you could deny her talent for shifting shapes." It was then that the realization struck him: the fantasy that had taken form was mine.

His eyes were azure with disdain as he arched a brow and groaned. "So that's the reason for your journey into the human shell: to mate with a beautiful woman. If that's the case, dear boy, God help you. The rest of us cannot."

There wasn't much point in denying it. This Shimbagh witch had taken from my mind the one desire I had managed to keep hidden from everyone, even from myself. Now my father, love me though he did, regarded me as if I'd lost all reason. He said no more about it, for he saw fully that this course had been set for me.

Having seen we would not follow, she came back to herself—a lovely woman, to be sure, with hair of raven feathers, crested wings of white, and a gown from which there flowed a universe of diamonds. Yet when she screamed, the rock on which she stood was ripped in two and bled as if its heart had just been broken. But just before she launched I sent a gout of flame at her that caught the hem of her gown and scorched it black. She turned to rivet her stare on me, to watch my every move, then mockingly tripped away on tongues of moonlight.

Dawn came mercifully early, cutting the silence that now sat like a visitor among us. Pod woke up with a yawn and, oblivious to all that had transpired, thought he had just dozed for a moment.

"Just a little kipper," he noted, and wiped his tongue beneath his overbite when he finally took notice that the sun was sitting on his left shoulder, yellow, bright, and full of fight as only morning suns can be. "Did she come?" he asked, suddenly quite shaken.

"She did, indeed," Dager answered. "And she had her eye on you."

"I would have kicked her butt!" Pod, puffed up into a combat stance that somehow made his mottled little hide seem almost formidable.

"I'm sure," the Mountain answered, and then looked askance at me and winked. "Well, you'll have a chance to test your 'dragon' mettle soon enough, Pod."

The challenge was a wish fulfilled, my father's word to his hybrid son that he was being granted permission to join the dragon flight in the upcoming Shimbagh campaign, leaving this very day. I was not mentioned. Pod had learned enough discretion at this point not to inquire. Dager simply passed the matter off.

"He has another job to do," he said, with some solemnity, as if my task were the more formidable of the two.

By midday, the sky was black with shadows—dragon bulls in disciplined formations, flapping wings in unison, singing mystic songs whose lyrics soon would haunt the coming days. I looked into that sky so filled with vigor and resolve, and for the first time in my life I knew what envy was.

"Dager! Dager! Dager!" came the greetings from above, anthems of salute to their leader, their field marshal. And I was the son he'd hoped to have beside him. Instead he'd have this freshly molted substitute, a creature risible to look at but with a lion-heart and a will to show his courage no matter what the cost. He'd do his daddy proud; that I could feel, and so could Dager.

At last my father came to me and held me fast in his gaze. "I won't pretend we'll be seeing each other soon, not by the way that mortals measure time. All I know is this: as far as I can see you'll make it through; you'll be the first to do so. And you'll be beside me when the Battle comes and our fate decides the world."

Words spoken with conviction are spears that angels hurl at denial. My father and I slapped wings and set off sparks that marked our rapport. The air crackled as he exploded away charged with determination. His bastard son my brother, Pod, tried to wait behind, to say good-bye, to show his utter gratitude to me. Such gestures were *de trop;* and words could not define the moment. We unified before he joined his circus in the sky, taking his probationer's post in the "Vyngorch notch" at the rear.

In a while, the dragons had all gone South, their wingbeats and their war-songs drumming echoes across the day. Once they'd left, the mountaintops grew lifeless in their wake, like battle-weary wives all bowed in waiting. Now I sat alone and watched a solitary kestrel dive into a crevice from which he never did emerge. At once I was overshadowed with doubt. Should I have gone with my kin? Should I have tasted the temper of combat and returned a bolder creature? The answer came quite clearly: I should have, but I didn't, and I could no longer afford to mourn or tarry. I had cast my lot, not as warrior but as spy. At last I had come to my fantasy. But at what cost to me? I, Dragon would become a man and might never return again.

Book Two

———————

THE SKYMASTER

Canto 14

The God Tree

A cleansing cloth of clear blue sky washed clean my trepidation, crystallizing my warrior's resolve as I flew throughout the day. Without a moment's hesitation I found myself rushing toward my destination as if that tiny valley held my soul's own natal flame. I don't know altogether why this feeling overcame me, but it stayed there pulling at my gut. At last, circling high above this same community of men I'd chosen for my bourn, I paused.

I hadn't seen this city fortress since I'd rescued it from Army. I hadn't scanned its energies since I had stood before its gates and felt the tide of loathing from its people. Yet despite that moment's ignominy suffered at their hands, I felt a fondness for this place I couldn't define.

I didn't dive straightaway into the valley. Instead, like a cautious bird of prey, I circled at a distance, recalling only too well how the very sight of me had once plunged this community into chaos. I could only imagine what would have happened had I decided to be so rash as to have dropped into their midst a second time. Only disguise would serve my entry. Only stealth would do. Mergence would be my *passe partout,* were I fortunate enough to find a subject who had abandoned all sense of self.

I waited for night and, as before, took to the mountain's shoulders, deciding how and where I could enter this microcosm.

Even in my brief exposure I had felt to the depths of me that there was a higher purpose for this City, a destiny, a place wherein the truth could be inscribed.

Yet, from what I could scan, new forces were at work here. As if their recent siege had laid waste all reason in them, this city had embraced a bodyguard of mercenaries dredged up from purgatory itself. It was as if the decent people had all been driven underground like spikelets of wheat planted in a kinder season, while a bumper crop of bullies now rambled about the streets, blustering their drunken revelries and extorting tithes from everyone they could. I watched this in amazement, wondering all the while exactly why these militias had been allowed to take over. This seemed the more perverse nature of the natural selection that virtue held no credit in the currency of survival.

Hadn't these pygmies supposedly been initiated as mystics? Did they not possess a piece of universal mind? Why then did their societies embrace such a cruel design and exhibit more anxiety than hyenas on a scavenge? It seemed the siege and the threat of me had robbed them of their reason. So what could I do to help them find their courage once again?

Yet despite this civic paranoia, despite the "mercenaries," there was a locus of virtue that managed to endure. Virtually taken for granted, it was numinosm, connecting each native to his roots in Mother Earth. I could sense its source thrived somewhere just outside the walls. It flowed from a meandering stream that ran beneath an immense tree. The tree, ancient, gnarled and twisted still had branches giving flower, flowers whose healing petals stroked the ground.

Even watching from my vertex in the sky, I could sense it was this loving Tree that fed this place. It was its pillar to the heavens. The citizens felt it too; felt it and yet did not understand. More out of custom than meditation, the faithful came around to seek small comfort at the bower—to lay their young and wounded at the base of it to be healed. Betrothed came to plight their troth, and what few wise men there were, brought their revelations to the river as it passed. This was the closest thing these people had to sanctuary. They had their temples, to be sure, paid homage to their gods; but these were idols carved in stone and certainly not their hope.

Well, why belabor the obvious? If one must take different form to reach another plane of life, why not find the clearest source of energy? For me, it was this splendid tree—this singular lucent bower whose aura, like the angels of highest Dominion, poured out in fine array. This, I vowed, would be the perfect place for me to bide my time.

At night on these plains, the sky turned blacker as if to blot the stars. Eventually, the torchlights of this city feebly flickered out, and the veil of darkness cloaked me once again. I swept down beside the tree, stood in its midst and found it possessed a stature that virtually matched my own. Though night breezes passed through it freely, it was full of its own abiding strength. The moment I touched ground its flowing branches met me, rose against the laws of gravity and touched my brow. Blood hyacinths were its flowers, and in the eye of each a dewdrop mirror reflected hidden pathways to its Self.

I'd known my share of trees before, and did not hold them all dear. More than any, the Tree Fury had taught me the lesson of shadows. Yet that experience also taught me that in every being good or bad there dwells a shadow-dancer to keep its energy in balance—light for its darkness, kindness for its corruption. Yet, instead of facing a hideous force in this angelic bine, I had discovered its other side of doing the work of angels, giving grace and healing whatever it touched.

There were no words to pass between this holy tree and me. Yet through the Empath everything was said. It was my destiny to be here, it was agreed, but I had not so much as chosen it as it had chosen me. All I knew was, when it came time to merge with this magnificent creation, it was done with little more effort than my breathing. Whether it ascended to me or I had risen to it no longer mattered in the least. The matter of the mergence was that it was done. It was all so easy, I was left dumbfounded. My inner voices called to me to spread my wings, enfold the tree and think of it as mine—as part of me.

I obeyed.

And it became me.

In a voice from a higher sphere, its inner soul sang through me, sang like the breezes in the cloud-peaks near the moon, places where only angels lighter than air took refuge, and where the mystic beasts could fly but could not stay. What was this arbor, after all? And who was I to take its place? I asked these questions yet received no answer, for before I realized, it was done: I was a tree. Not just any tree, I soon would be the master tree of the City, of the valley, and of all the thorps and villages around—an ancient talisman to everyone, one I soon learned was believed to house a god.

What I had yet to learn was that I had absented my body for sake of this. My dragon's body—full of power, flame, fury, single-eye and all—had disappeared from sight. I felt my mighty flanged wings meld into flowered branches and, turning back to see what had become of me, saw only a shadow lose itself in starlight.

Of course, we'd always been taught that this house of flesh was illusion. Still, I had to admit, it was an illusion that I had been quick to miss. Whatever bargain I had made with my vital force, I was suddenly lost in this mergence and bewildered by the choices I had taken on. No longer powerful or beautiful or free to do as I pleased, I was a prisoner anchored by my roots to do a service. I had blended with this most angelic soul, and had lost all that I was. The former bold Shartallion XII, High Dragon of the Kiln and heir apparent to the onyx throne, was now a tree.

And though I must admit I was the finest tree I'd ever seen, I nonetheless would now be forced to stand denuded, fair game for any dog with a full bladder or any country lad with a cold knife and a creative urge. I was a tree—a servant to all without the power of Will. No one would ever fear me now. Few would pay me notice. I was a whisper of awareness, a cosmic second thought. What had I done? My God! What had I done?!

§§§§§§§

One learns to adjust. I consoled myself with that small truth and came to realize quite quickly that, while I was a mystic, I was something else again. My toes were roots, and I was filled with such pacific thoughts I felt a comfort I had never known. I bowed with the wind, gave shelter to anyone who sought it and felt the rain as if God's own tears had fallen to wash me clean. No combat, no ego, no demands of performance against the darker forces—I simply was permitted to be, to let the birds play love songs through my branches, and let the warm day beam upon my face.

As a bower, I was never in danger of being rent apart or hacked to pieces for the wood I might provide. And my trunk was hard, so hard the sharpest blade was blunted, bounding off as if it had struck stone. From time to time someone would try—some woodsman with an axe or a soldier trying to test his mettle would pull his sword and have a whack at me. (Not much respect for a tree believed to house a deity, I must observe, but that was it: these little men were testing me, striking out against the legend.) They'd take their best shot only to see their own blades would recoil, occasionally shatter or break off at the hilt. The more I seemed able to repel these blows, the more men came to take them, until at last there was a virtual parade of muscle men ego-driven just to cut me down. They all failed, I'm glad to say, and to their credit not a one complained.

It seemed this was a testament, a kind of confirmation, for every time this kind of thing was tried, the tales of the "God

Tree" spread until more people came around with offerings than swords. It wasn't until sometime later that I came to realize that, when I had merged with this holy tree we had blended our qualities in fact. If I had absorbed certain aspects of its gentility, it had gotten my tough dragon's skin with armor enough to break the strongest blade.

After a time, most of these pygmies left me alone. Some sought my shade or climbed my branches, plucking flowers, while others came to talk to me. They regarded me as a deity, prayed to me with wishes not quite in my power to grant. And many, more than I'd expected returned with gifts of gold and silver that they laid at my base because (they claimed) I'd granted all they'd asked.

Soon enough, I came to be a sanctuary of sorts, a role I soon grew quickly to fulfill. Whatever instincts were harbored in my dragon's soul, they were soon diminished, for with every passing day I was more and more The Tree—an arbor with an angel's mind standing in awe of heaven for the grace of my simplicity.

I wasn't altogether sure why all the fuss was being made over me. After all, I was a tree and not the voice of God. Yet soon I came to realize that I was the best thing these people had to give them glimpses of serenity. Now that I'd been tested by the blade, it was all that was needed to confirm that I was matter above matter and something to be enshrined.

Some elders from the city came and burned incense at my base, chanted arcane absurdities, and talked of "guarding" me, discussed the possibility of building a wall around me and barring it with gate and lock and key. So fearful were they that some magician might come and steal me away that they even talked of uprooting me and replanting me in one of their temples. That was when clearer heads prevailed, and a pretty head at that, for a beautiful priestess shamed them for their superstitious schemes.

"It is never to be touched in such a way," she said. "I'm appalled to think that you would possibly endanger such a blessed entity as this with transplantation. It is there in its place and time for a reason: to fulfill its divine purpose, to give example, and to heal. Yet you would wish to mummify it, put it in a temple, deprive it of all rain and light and all that makes it holy!"

Although she was standing at some distance when she spoke, the elders in this gathering offered no attempt to countermand what she had said. Instead, they bowed their heads and backed away as if to make a path for her advance.

"Shala," the eldest among them murmured.

"Shala," the others intoned, as if they'd said a kind of prayer.

Sound, of course, has its own its own field of force, and I knew that, when carried to a pitch, my dragon's voice could crack a boulder in two. But we were dragons of the kiln, high born and masters of our fate. These were but humans, and yet from this genteel human voice there came a tone as pure as wind chimes in a field of flowers.

I'd seen auras on these little creatures too as varied as the flowers in the field: the young ones, the children and the babes in arms, clear and giving forth a radiant bloom; the older ones, dismal shriveled things, enshrouded in the faded graying values of their futility. There were exceptions, to be sure, and this was certainly one. This one, this woman, Shala, was a sylvan slip of light. Even though I could not see her, I could feel her clarity, sense the pulsations of her etheric body, and know that this was the life force for whom I'd come. This was the woman I had enfolded, had gazed upon and loved. This was the power that had drawn me to this tiny world of men.

Surprisingly, she wouldn't come near me; that is to say, The Tree.

Guided by some premonition she kept a cautious distance, while the elders now encircled me as if to ward her off. They feared her, and yet they respected the power that flowed from her fingertips and covered me in light. I doubted they could see this, though some at least could feel, and all of them in unison held their amulets to the moon. She laughed at their severity, sent them a cascade of light, silvery to fill them with the Chalice of Toleration. Surprisingly, as soon as she turned away, her energy turned with her, leaving in her wake a wisp of amethyst faerie dust.

"The tree will not be touched," the elders reassured her.

"I know," she called back to them, as she disappeared in the shadows.

Terrorized they felt impelled to keep their word to her, yet began belittling her the moment she'd slipped away. Some denounced her as sorceress; others called her a fake. One remained self-actualized enough to give her praise.

"She *is* a holy woman, after all," one in a violet robe observed.

"She drove the dragon from our midst," a myrtle robed elder added.

"She was nothing before that," another among them said, "a peasant maid, pretty enough but with no mark of greatness that I could see. What if her expulsion of the dragon had been an accident—that and nothing more, a freak of whimsy? It wouldn't have been the first time that prophets were born of chance. And certainly it wouldn't be the last."

A fourth fat man in a henna robe, who held sway over the majority it seemed, stood fast and listened, and then picked just the proper time to speak his mind.

"That she was inconsequential before, I can agree. But think back gentle men, and remember well: even as the dragon came, she changed. It wasn't just the act itself that made her exceptional. It was the contact with the beast. I recall even the morning of the siege, this woman began some sort of transfiguration. It was as if some unseen force prepared her for that liaison; and not just with any dragon, may I remind you. It was the Lightning Dragon who stroked her breast.

"I thought at the time, it was the heat of turmoil that caused her to emanate in such a way. But from that day to this she has not been the same woman. I feel her vibration and I shudder. It's a power that sickens me. I know it well by now; it is an evil, dangerous thing."

"She's a sorceress!" a blue-robed elder swore. "We must do away with her. We are the City leaders. We will have her executed—exiled at the very least! That's it!"

The elder in the henna robe demurred. "That she has become a sorceress, I agree. But to kill her at this point would bring ruin down upon our heads. She is beloved of the people and now held to be holy. However…if she were to meet with an accident, what would come of it?"

"To be perfectly frank," an elder in a robe of grey, averred. "None of us knows. Power as we perceive it in her, overawes our feeble senses and confuses us. And none of us—I'm sorry to say, not even I—can see her clearly. That she is possessed in some way, is something upon which I think we all concur. Yet whether it is by a good or evil power is quite beyond my ability to determine. She's certainly done no one harm. In fact, she does good works. She heals and blesses others in the City, and might well have saved us from a folly where the God Tree is concerned."

"Is he saying we should lionize her even further?" the henna-robed elder asked aside to someone else but loud enough it seemed for the mountains above to hear.

"I'm *saying* we lack the talent to tell just what she is," the elden elder quietly replied. "But there is one who can tell white magic from the black in the flicker of the moment, the only man I know of who can do this—the Captain."

"That sad, determined, impassioned soldier?!" the henna elder barked. "I'd rather deal with what we have than him. With her, we have a solitaire, a weak and lonely woman and no test for our authority. The Captain brings his retinue, his own perspective of virtue and force of arms enough to give backbone to his demands."

"He's apt to charge a hefty fee besides," the blue-robed elder added.

"And worse…" the elder in the myrtle robe observed, pausing to let all present feel the impact of what he was about to say. "Wherever the Captain makes his appearance, RuSiva is soon to follow, asking questions, spreading his infections of the soul and taking retribution upon those who deny him satisfaction."

"Must we always live in such fear?" the grey robed elder asked the sky. To the others he turned as if he'd copped the moment. "I think the Captain is a wise and noble man. So does any man with a mind. What you fear is his truth—that he might find her clear and holy, and not find us half so well. As far as RuSiva is concerned...he has powers to find a grain of sand in a skyhawk's tail. All his pretext of finding the Captain, I think, is nothing more than that: pretext. He misses the Captain at every turn because he fails at times to gauge the degree of his enemy's energies."

"That is your opinion," the henna elder challenged.

"That is *my* truth." the grey elder said, and as he did so scanned the others as if to bring a resolution to the moment. "Then, since summoning the Captain doesn't seem to sit well with this quorum, I propose an alternative: Observe the priestess, Shala, for a year. Watch her closely—her every word and deed. If, at the end of that time, we have sufficient evidence of her sorcery, we may take steps to deal with her, including the possibility of summoning the Captain. If not, then let us come to accept her as one who cares for and loves this community of souls. In either case let us, in the meantime, leave her alone."

Postponement is the offspring born of meetings. And so, as the grey sage had planned all along, it would be the child of this. He formally proposed that the judgment of Shala be suspended and left to passage of time. The other elders readily agreed, and agreed with equal haste that the God Tree would be left as is—in place.

The elden sage was named Horam, by the way. I remember his name and his only, for he was a human being. The others were pygmies who worshipped fear and clog my recollection. The elder called Horam was wise for a man; even for a dragon. It was he, I thought at first, who'd be a worthy soul with whom to merge. But I thought better of it. Horam, wise and bold though he had shown himself to be, had edged too far toward the ripening of his man-skin. If I were to assume his form (assuming he would have consented), I might not have lasted long enough to complete the task at hand. Besides, if I'd noticed anything in my brief encounters with men, it was that they were vain and worshipped youth. If I were to take this aging form in which to house my soul, I would possibly risk a fate much worse than death: rejection. Horam was a being whose vibration held rapport with mine, but he was man fulfilled and complete in his cycle in that flesh. Although in this earliest of my eras I was not well given to patience, I decided to defer before I tried to merge again. The time would come, I knew, when just the perfect vessel would emerge—a younger man vacant in his heart who felt the need to be whole. I would pray on it. I would put my soul's desires upon the ethers and await my guardian angel's high response. After all, this home in which I now lived was well venerated. I was a tree, revered by all, and more: I was a god. Gods could afford to wait if dragons could not.

§§§§§§§

Even the gods cannot see around time's corners. I remained a tree for another year, honored to be sure, paid homage by custom, yet all but avoided by all the City populace whom (I was later to learn) had been forbidden by decree to cross the boundaries of stones now set around me.

Oh, what distances these men put between their idols and themselves! Not to intimate I was a god in fact (any more or any less than they), I still was quite amazed that these poor people had now enshrined me and made me something more yet something less than what I was.

Eventually, thank God, there came the chance for epiphany. One steamy summer's eve, just as the face of night pulled taught with starlight, I saw a young man scrambling toward me. Across the rocks and dusty earth outside the city wall, up to the river where I stood, he ran. He fled. He stumbled. Pitching, rolling, clambering across the rocks, he made his way toward me.

Terrified, his tunic torn, his arms and legs bruised as if many people had laid hard hands upon him, he dived across a rock partition built to set me apart. Like a monkey given chase by a pack of hyenas, he climbed up inside my bow, cradled himself beneath my leaves and hid. He was little more than a boy, a young man not entirely in command of his own body. He was awkward, to be sure. Yet one could see there was a talent, latent in him, for agility. He was strong, but somehow could not come to grips with it. Instead of standing and confronting his pursuers, he sought instead to hide like the whimpering child he somehow still had chosen to be. Not just a child (that might have been some reasonable cause for what he did, for a child can be both bold and quick), it was some semblance of a little girl who had its hold on him. It was as if he didn't know quite what he was; or else he never had been taught.

"Gudi! Little Gudi! Pretty, pretty, pretty, pretty, pretty!"

"Where are you my little pet?"

"Gudi, Gudi, Gudi. Little sweet cheeks. We need you!"

The words mocking sweetness came from veterans of combat, soldiers upon whom tenderness was lost. These were hard men, creatures of outrage, men to whom life had small meaning. Oozing wine from their pores and blood from their fingertips, they cooed their overtures. Clad in kaunakes made from hides of slaughtered cattle, they kept their blades sheathed in their scabbards but waved their hands about as if they still held weapons. These were burly men. Beauty had no value to them, and yet it was in search of a twisted beauty that they stalked the night. Soft flesh was more their heart's desire, the kind this poor lad might provide.

There were five of them. Calling, cooing, they combed about a while longer, eventually growing surly in the chase.

"Where is the little bastard?" crowed the largest of the group. He seemed in rank and swagger to be quite in command. He was a Master of Spears (or someone called him so).

"Can't have gone far. He didn't have legs for it," snapped a wraith of a fellow with razors for teeth and slits for eyes and a voice like broken glass.

"Aye. And lovely legs they are," the leader drooled.

"Probably up in that tree," burped a drunken hog-faced man, barely able to hold his stance, yet constantly fondling himself.

"The God Tree?! Doubt it!" the Wraith snarled, sharply. "He wouldn't have the balls."

"And soon he'll have no balls at all. If I have anything to say about it," the Master of Spears, growing surly, announced to one and all. "Where in the hell is he, anyway?!"

"The mountainside," another soldier pointed. "I saw a shadow move along the rocks up there. He must have made it farther than we thought."

"A rabbit running to save his hide," the Hog Face laughed. "Well, let him run. We'll find him out again."

"And when we do…" another said, with a lascivious smirk. And all agreed. They'd wait another night to have their way.

The soldiers stumbled back into the City to fall into their drunken dreams. After they'd left, even though this was a gentle cap of night, this lad stayed frozen in the tree, shuddering, trembling with a heavy dose of dread. He wrapped himself around my thickest branch and cringed, grasping at it, clinging to it as if it were an anvil of lost power. Finally, releasing me, he lay back again against my bow and sobbed.

He cried himself to sleep. I wasn't aware at the time of the exact nature of the brutality from which this lad had fled. I only knew he seemed to fear it more than death itself and might soon find the latter preferable were something not done to change it. I was too young, then, to understand this longing humans had for death. Although I was older and more well-schooled in the formal arts of higher awareness, I couldn't help but feel that this lad cradled in my bow had seen much more of life's raw, wretched face than I. I wondered at him. And I wondered too if his frail young human body was to be the vessel into which I would pour my self. Or, as life was full of many tests for one's discernment, was he just another? Would there be a more complete, all-knowing soul with whom to merge—one who understood my mission and could embrace me fully?

As the night grew deep, I fanned him with the breezes that blew down from the mountains, gentle winds that helped to bring him comfort in his slumber, while they kept me awake with their lyric admonitions.

"Beware of the house of human flesh," they sang. "Its honey will ensnare you. It is a death. It is a death! You'll never be the same."

Their voices, whispered through the night, taunted me with pangs of dissonance. Disguised as airs from mountaintops, as kisses of mist in the evening, they wore the breath of dragons that singed me with reflections of what I had left behind.

§§§§§§§

Before the morning broke, the lad had gone. The night that hid him in the shadows of my leaves would not grant him such asylum in the sun. With the instincts of a hunted cat, he dropped from my branches, looked about furtively, and ran up the stream that flowed behind me, darting from rock to rock, from water to bank as if to cover his tracks. He was trying to leave the City and the valley that surrounded it yet seemed to lack the resolve to go. Despite the fact that he was both strong and nimble, there was something about him not quite whole; he was a creature not yet in command of himself. After a time, and when he was almost out of sight, he bowed his head and turned back in. With a slow gait almost like a limp, he made his way back through the City walls.

Why, I wondered, would anyone return to such as that?

I did not see the lad for a time, and yet I knew I would. Fugitives mark their havens well, and I was now this kind of place for him.

Others came to me meanwhile. Careful not to cross the low stone wall that marked my boundaries, they laid flowers, gifts,

and food before me, singing praises to my name, composing
poems no one else could sing save they, anthems to the "God
Tree." Asking me to answer prayers that were not mine to grant,
drowning me in platitudes and gratitude for miracles they said
I'd performed, they left me offerings day to day, their auras
somehow lifted by their interchanges with me.

Had I been one of them in their world, I might have tried to
warn them not to look in hidden corners for their gods. But who
was I, without a voice to call my own, to deny them the illusion
of my ubiquity? Besides, I was growing rather fond of these little
Glorianas being sung in my name. They gave me comfort on
those days when I longed to be in my dragon skin again.

It was a week or so until the lad returned, and by that time he
was even more besieged than he'd been before. Torn, tattered,
mauled and battered with the marks of many hands, he sped
across the apron of ground that lay before my shrine. He was in a
rage of fear, yet carried in his cells all the resignation of one
about to quit this life. This young lad, it now seemed to me, had
been pushed beyond the pale. He still possessed the will to fight
and flee, yet he lacked the physique to carry either out with any
measure of success. Even if he had (and even though he fought
as best he could), he was sure to be overwhelmed by the horde
that had come in hot pursuit.

He'd already made his way to me, had leapt the wall, and
come to hug my trunk when first they spied him. Among them
were the same soldiers who had sought him earlier, the Master of
Spears and the others who'd tormented him with their lurid
serenades. But this time there were even more, a gang of louts
from the City: Some wore kaunakes and the armor of the
soldiers; others were clad in the tattered robes and shawls of
vagrants. There was even a young noble or two among them,
coming in search of thrills.

All were drunk and impassioned with the sport of it, that
they called out his name in chorus. "Gudae! Gudae!" they
yodeled, laughing, bumping, jabbing one another. Then, as they

came upon him clinging onto me, their collective took a nasty turn.

"The Shrine!" one among them shrieked. "He desecrates the Shrine!"

For a moment the minions of this mob fell mute. So fraught were they with disbelief that none of them thought to speak out. Instead, they stood and watched as if to wait for some sign of divine intervention—some clap of thunder or some rod of fire to sear down from the sky to punish this blasphemer. But this desire to feed their superstitions was not to be justified by any powers in the force of Nature. So when these men saw nothing was going to come about, they stirred. At first, they stirred uncertainly, a hesitation bordering on confusion. But this was not to last for long. Within a matter of moments their cause was given force of voice by the perverse among them, the burly Master of Spears. Dripping wine from his hairy chin and sweat from his pitted face, he called out to the others.

"Well, it seems the gods are sound asleep, tonight. And since they are not quick about their duties, we must give them prompt assistance! We all know the punishment for such an act!"

"Death!" screeched the Wraith, his razor teeth sliced beneath his narrow lips. It was an exclamation met swiftly with the flat side of a sword blade to his crown. Dazed half-silly, he sat down mute, while the leader of this pack of mongrels, placing a foot on his throat to make sure his sidekick had no more to say, engaged the others.

"No, no, no," the Spearmaster corrected. "Death for such an act as this, only befits a noble. Petty creatures commit petty crimes and, therefore, merit petty punishment. Flogging is the answer for this little one of ours! Flogging and a few other punishments to let him know the curse of what he's done! After all, such measures are the Law! And we're here to see that the law is carried to the letter. Are we not?!"

With an appetite made harsh by drink, this snarling, drunken mob growled its agreement and looked on with unrestricted glee while the big, burly sergeant and his soldiers hurdled the wall surrounding me and dragged the lad out before them. Although he struggled to be free, the boy was all but lost. Overpowered by the men who had fallen on him like ravening dogs, he could do nothing to save himself. For him to have done so, would have frenzied them even more. Pummeled senseless, this Gudae suddenly went limp. He could no longer move even if he'd wanted to. Still it was not enough. Because of the sordid pleasure that bondage brings to some, the lad he was bound and gagged. Two knives stuck into the ground. His wrists were lashed to the handles, while everyone looked on in perverse anticipation while the Master of Spears ceremoniously uncoiled a whip.

Arching it above him, he made it dance high in the air, whir and hum, hiss and crack with the flicking of his fingers. Relentlessly, this burly soldier brought his whip tongue down, stripping bare the poor lad's back while he lifted up the hem of his kaunake. There, with his male member proud beyond its holding, he displayed himself to one and all, and—like a seed-bull to a cow—took to this boy and penetrated him. While the others in this leering hydra joked and called his name, this master spearman gave a taurine moan and, having spent himself, fell back in drunken glee, while others in his squad prepared themselves to take his place.

The Wraith was next. Then the Hog face. And by that time it looked to me as if the entire world of men (such as they were) stood ready to stab this boy to death. It was a death for which he pleaded now. Through a face bloodied and half-buried in the dirt. He begged someone to kill him, to put a blade up to his throat and slit it.

I had heard tell of these kinds of violations perpetrated by this animal called man. Rape, it was called. And nowhere in any universe this old soul would inhabit was there any act so vicious or so base. Not any being I had ever seen, not even the meanest serpent or maddest cur—not even a Shimbagh —would debase another of its kind in such a way. More than an act of vicious desire, this was a kind of murder, a killing of the soul while leaving the body shell intact.

My God! What were these creatures known as men supposed to be? They were not Shimbaghs, and yet they seemed in every word and deed to be worse than the Devil himself. And we were supposed to abdicate this place called earth to these?!

I was in rancor! Oh, how I prayed that night for my dragon form just for an hour. I would have shown them all the wrath they could endure, yet that alone would not have been compensation enough. I would have torn them limb from limb and hair from bone had I been able to move at all, but I could not. I was a tree — inert, immobile, chained to this curse of reticence by the very nature of my being, a passive being created to serve, unable to do anything but watch and weep and turn in my anguish to the winds to blow my branches and let them shield me from the sight of this!

But angels cannot hide from truth. If there was a way to bring this nasty issue to a close, I would manifest it. I prayed to all the Seraphims in heaven to bring about a change before another moment could be brought to pass. And so my prayers were answered with a roar. A crack of thunder in the sky snapped sharply across my face, and with it came the answer: "It is in you!"

The fires of the Kiln still simmered in my loin, and when I pressed them into service they let my branches take the form of wings. And while this mob took pause from their debauchery and watched their God Tree grow a mask of ire, they felt the ground beneath them quake as if it were about to hatch an awful creature. In deed I would, for far beneath the surface my roots grew strength and force of talons, dragon's claws that tore up through the sod and pried the ground above, cracking it, ripping it open the way an earth demon would when in search of a human meal.

Feeling the rage of Nature roar into its pygmie ears, this mob of randy scum plunged into pandemonium.

"We've roused the God Tree's anger!" one man among them cried. A young noble, gesturing pointedly toward my trunk, at once aroused the others. "Its bow now wears a vicious scowl! Its fingers climb out of the ground to seize my feet! Oh God, great God, forgive me!"

Howling like a beaten dog he scurried back toward the town, not waiting for the others who, like the curs they were, quickly followed suit yapping out their frightened cries with every step they took. Even the meanest men among them, even the Master of Spears, stayed only long enough to stand aghast at the fury. They broke and ran, trampling one another and quite forgetting the lad they'd brutalized and now had left to die.

I could do no more, for now. Despite my Herculean efforts, I was still to arbor bound and now quite utterly exhausted by the act of my upheaval, I now stood, all my roots torn from their home, naked, thirsty, and exposed. I felt as if I'd been in combat, and perhaps it was all in vain, for now before me lay a boy half-dead and no longer possessed of any will to recover.

With the strength I still had left, I dropped my branches down to soothe this Gudae in his pain, and in a lesser while than most men would have done, he slowly rose and stumbled to his feet. With a force of inner will that came from the self of his soul, he climbed into my bow. Bleeding, abused, his thin resolve utterly left undone, he lay there muttering some faint prayer that he be allowed to die.

"Dear God, please let me become anything but what I am, for I am dead unto myself. Take me from this weakling's shell into another life. I cannot bear this one I have a moment longer; not as I was, not as I am, not when I see the hideous face my future wears this night."

He soon collapsed into a coma. I brought forth my saps and salved his bleeding back. As I did I felt his ego release its hold upon his will. It was ready to take flight, to permit this dragon of the kiln to walk into its little human body and renew its purpose on this Earth. It asked for me by name, not as God Tree but as dragon. Seeing fully with its angel eyes the force of my intent, it embraced me. His soul's desire to merge with me poured into the ethers. And yet I was no longer sure I was ready to make matter of this offer. Now that it was laid before me, I gave pause, and for none of the reasons for which I had been warned. The rapture, the allure, the narcotizing essence of assuming human form—not one of these presented a danger to me, now.

It was not a fascination but revulsion that I felt. From all that I had seen of their conduct, by their every thought and deed, the pygmies were the most despicable creations that God had ever set to plague an orb of life. If we were fallen angels as it seemed that we had been, then these were risen demons, cosmic fungi come a crop and bred to do a Shimbagh's work in a thousand wretched ways.

No matter what I had been told to now, no matter what the rules, I for one could not accept the preparation of this planet for these miscreations. No doubt this was my lesson, one requiring great discernment. And what I had discerned to now was that this entity known as man was unworthy to inherit anything. To be sure, he had his moments. And there were those handpicked few whom I could say had worn the angel's kiss.

On that basis, alone, I suppose I'd have to follow through. After all, I had to remember I had chosen this assignment. No one made me do it; others had warned me of its pitfalls. Yet, those very pitfalls were not the ones I saw. What I saw before was a task, and clearly one of judgment. If I became a man, this man, and found all men as I had found these others, I would strongly recommend that we end their wicked tenure with a stroke—destroy them, before they choked this lovely garden world to death. For the time being, I would have no option but to follow my soul's assignment, become a man, learn their ways, and somehow try to discover what twisted set of springs and coils made these little devils tick.

I thought of what I had to do, had to face, had to be and— remembering all the cautions I'd received—began to laugh. "Beware of the life in human flesh," I had been told. "It will ensnare you. It is a death."

Ensnare me, indeed! That was the one aspect of this journey of which I had no fear at all.

Canto 15

Gudae

There is a hole in the head of every living creature through which the soul enters and exits. This is neither illusion nor metaphor. It is fact.

In most animals it is the left eye through which this *grand passage* is made. In man, it is the soft spot in the forebrain—the infant's eye to God. It is a window through which the young child sees life clearly. The full adult unlearns that subtle power. Time and fear and the blight of worldly ways can cloud it over until the older being can see only warped reflections of this world. Those who close that celestial skylight lose their view of Heaven. Those who keep it clear can see worlds other than our own, for this is the window to the third eye and the Diamond in the Crown.

I bring that up here, because this was the way I became him. Despite all that had befallen Gudae—despite the mockery and abuse, despite his constant cowering on the edge of ultimate

dread—this young man had somehow kept his God-sight open
and now stood to be redeemed. (It was my chance at redemption
too, though I was little aware at the time of just how far I'd
fallen.)

Through that painful night when he had all but died, when
he'd come within a hare's breath of giving up his body shell, I
answered all his prayers and came right through him. He had,
after all, prayed to be anything but what he was, and now he
would be what he was and something else again. The moment
he'd relinquished his conscious thought, his oversoul bade me to
merge. Yet before I did, it challenged me to walk the emerald
empath to see into his past—to redeem his future and to know
the perils ahead. But before I did, I had to know his present, to
feel the armor and the pain of every cell upon his body. I had to
taste the sting of his humiliation, to look into the loss of self he
had to suffer every day he breathed, and breathe the jagged air of
fear that sawed right through his throat. For that I had to
become as nothing, a whisper of morning air, yet in that whisper
catch his grasp on life.

Up to that point, I'd still enjoyed the option of turning back.
Now I had lost it. Now I was in transition from being a master of
the skies to becoming less than a man. What an urge I had to fly
away! Yet all the while I was being drawn down through this
window of minutia. I was a microbe on a drop of mist, a traveler
in space made to fill the heart of this meek human being so lost
even to himself.

I looked back at what I had left behind and became more
humbly aware that, even as I passed out of it, that tree perceived
as deity grew fuller in the flower, more graceful in its branches
and the way it touched the sky. The angel had returned into it.
Now it was the "God Tree" once again. Even the roots I'd torn
from the earth had gracefully submerged.

It was more graceful, more giving of itself, and more perfect
in its blending than I with all my armored power had ever dared
to be. I was chastened, for I had come to learn at last that no
matter what form the shell assumes, the shell is still a shell and

nothing more. It is the soul that gives the creature personality. And no matter what soft floral petals ever adorned this iron hide of mine, I was the spiritual warrior through and through.

That much was a good thing for this young Gudae. God only knew, he needed all the help he could get. And now I had the challenge to make this sorry sample into a man again. As I did, I recognized the fates had dealt an irony to me.

Wizards, harlots, masters of alchemy, charlatans with a bent for arcane power, voyageurs, drunkards, the wanton of heart, the abandoned of God, the necromancers, witches and priests of the Kabbalah—these were the hosts to the dragon's vital force, these were the vessels who invited us in. In the beginning, it was a truth I hadn't learned; I would learn it in the end. Wholesome humans filled with higher mind did not require entities to assume them.

I had apparently picked a git. At least it felt to me to be, for in the very moment that I filled this Gudae's frame, I marveled at how weak it was. Granted, the poor boy had experienced his share of vilification. Granted he was nearly dead when I chose to take him on. But let's speak frankly, shall we? I had been shortchanged. Considering all the showers of easy fortune I had basked in up to now, I suppose the laws of compensation owed me one like this. But it seemed to me there was some perversity in genetics, here: this was a woman trapped in the febrile body of a man.

Part of the pain of the empath's journey lies in carrying another's burdens. His every cell contains a memory, a knowledge of joy or pain, and into that memory there comes a season. To this boy, this Gudae, there had been too many seasons of confusion, and I was being given precious little time to set them straight.

He had been an orphan, so it seemed. His father was a soldier killed in battle. His mother died at birth. And he, without benefit of so much as the shadow of a family, was left to ride the currents of his own small river of life. After a passing stranger had given him the name of Gudae (a word in the language of these peoples for a "child of God,"), this abandoned infant was brought into a community of women and brought up as one of them. Taught to sew and bake, to wash and wear the soft things that always made a girl so like a flower, he was the very sweetness of a girl. It wasn't until his eleventh year that he found out in fact there was a difference: that he was not a woman but a man. Not a man as such, he was a boy—a disadvantaged boy at that, ill-prepared to meet the harsh face that the world would show to one so delicately schooled as he. To make the matter worse, he was too pretty. He was too soft. And before he was ready, he was on his own.

When he'd reached the age of twelve, when his sexuality came to be known, he was expelled. The moment that his tunic formed a tent (and stayed that way perennially, it seemed), he was an object of some ridicule. He was ostracized. Little girls with whom he'd played and shared his innocent years, were kept from him, told to avoid him, and warned that he had now become pariah in their world. The society of women who throughout the years had nurtured him suddenly cast him out into the streets. Abandoned by the women who'd reared him and not knowing the ways of men, this poor boy was easy prey for the scum of the streets.

Forced to roam the alleyways of the city, the lad was soon captured by a slave trader and sold to a local suzerain, a hirsute pudding of a man named Izo the Fondler. True to his sobriquet, this master of molestation had a penchant for young boys and kept the densest stable of young consorts within a thousand miles. He was wealthy beyond measure, extravagant beyond restraint, and generous beyond words especially to those he chose to be his toys. This young Gudae, so it seemed, was groomed to be the Fondler's perennial favorite, and for a proper length of time, this handsome boy was bathed and dressed, prepared in ways of poetry and song and brought, well-oiled and oozing subjugation, to be at Izo the Fondler's beck and call.

This lad, had he submitted, might have been a power to this day, a counselor in a realm whose influence spanned a hundred leagues. But Gudae was an innocent, full of innocent ideals. And this sagging, porked-up pedophile so revulsed the lad that he could not be in Izo's company without being moved to vomit. Try though he might to mollify the boy, to make himself seem comely and correct, Izo could not change the laws of human nature. And the nature of the young Gudae was this: the old fart made him ill, physically ill, effusively ill, ill beyond the remedies offered by the physicians of that time, for this was not a rejection offered by a stubborn mind; it was a reflex of the soul.

For the Fondler, accustomed to having his will worked on everyone he encountered, this was in the beginning some cause for fascination. Ordinarily, execution would have been the fate reserved for anyone who dared to say him nay, but Izo, in a show of forbearance out of character for him, tried to wend his way into the young boy's heart. He wooed him, had him pampered, even wrote him lines of verse, but finally grew weary Gudae's spontaneous emetics. Rather than have him murdered or punished in a way that all could see, this suzerain (as suzerains are wont to do) found fancy with another. They were mere toys after all, and after all there were so many. So, rather than face his Nemesis from day to day, the Fondler simply had the young lad flogged and set loose in the streets, where it was roundly proclaimed he was to be the bride of all.

Free but fair game for misfortune, Gudae ran away. Hearing that the City was the lesser of two evils, he traveled some miles to reach it. And when he did he felt he'd found a home; at least at first. He sought refuge in its alleyways, begged for bread upon the streets, and hoped for better days. But pretty callow youths in places such as this were easy game. Since he was bright enough, he lived by his wits and by those wits survived. But he was neither cynical nor swift, nor was he strong in any of the ways a lad his age might be. He could neither lie nor steal nor compromise his visions of the world, and for this folly he was made to pay. Besides, he had been taught the ways of women, and it was those ways that came most readily to him. Such qualities did not escape the notice of the mob of soldiers, drunks, and wastrels who fed upon such prey, and it was their lusts that brought him now to this: this limbo inbetween his death and me.

Knowing all this made my mergence easier. Whatever his burdens prior to this, he would lay them down. And I, of Royal Dragon House would walk away in his skin and taste the bitter salt of humility. We were meant for one another, this whipped dog of a lad and I. It was our destiny to be so.

By the time the sun rose the next morning, my higher self had infused this wreckage and revived him. I was now a part of him—particle of his particle, cell of his cell, blood of his blood. His memories were still intact as were his perceptions of the present. But I was in his vital force, in mind and will and soul, and I could not begin to half imagine where these things in him had gone, but gone they had—to other dimensions, to cosmic holding pens whose whereabouts I didn't dare to contemplate for now.

I didn't wear his body well. It was a pretty shell but weak, not at all a home in which a dragon could feel welcome. The legs were healthy enough from all that running, I'd surmised, but his arms were atonal and hadn't known the strain of honest labor. Of course, I had to realize, he'd known his share of shame, and all the draining of the light that might go with it. Even a child of destiny does not recover from such things in a day, and since I was now imprisoned in his flesh I had to do the best I could with what I had. But God, what did I have?!

He had my eyes. They were corundum and saw with all the keen perception that sapphire had to give. Not my power, his; and that astonished me. In all my mystical arrogance I had never, for a moment, thought that creatures such as this might see with eyes like mine, might feel with all the garnet heart that dragons such as I possessed. There was still so much to learn, and time was ever the college.

I awakened on the banks of the stream. The waters were a healing salve that granted me ablution. My wounds, though hardly healed just yet, were nonetheless made whole. My back, while still a mass of whelps, had scabbed and done so quickly; the cuts that marked my lower legs were all but sealed; there was an aching in my anus, to be sure, but most of that abated before noon. Credit that to my dragonhood. Mystics are remarkably quick to mend, and apparently that facility had carried to this pygmie body as well. That was perhaps where the physical transition stopped. This lad I had become, this Gudae, lacked the character to press on. Every movement I made his body take was an exertion. His muscles did not move with the agility of mine. And the prowess? Well, let's not belabor the obvious. This was, after all, just a man.

I couldn't stay here, I knew that. There are marking posts in life where a creature is not welcome and never will be. This City, for Gudae, was such a place. Since I had assumed him and was now wholly in command of his physical essence, I decided to act upon the obvious. It was more than apparent to me that his body was in no shape to risk exposure to civilization. Nature in such cases was the more indulgent foe. The challenges were truly known, and death if it might come would at the very least be swift and clean.

I made my move. I pulled his physical shell out of its ruin and made it run away from the God Tree, away from the river, away from the City, from its walls and its corruptions. Over the countryside we ran. Over the rocks, across the dry grasses that strafed the mountain slopes, we strode and dashed and climbed. His legs were strong enough, and yet we pulled against his will. His mind and mine were one. My soul was in his body shell, yet it resisted me. It was his cells that fought me to the last. Accustomed to the bleak familiarity of pain, they wanted to go home — back to the street slums, the derision, the physical abuse. It had become the fare of life to which they had become accustomed, against which they were armored, and it was now a field of combat for which they constantly hungered. Every cell upon his wretched little body had a consciousness, an ego of its own, and each had to be made to obey.

I strained with all the power in me, climbed and slid and climbed again. Like Sisyphus against the stone of circumstance I climbed into the mountains, down the other side and to another range again. Away from this vicious world in which he had lived, I brought him to the nape of solitude. We ran and loped, and we grew stronger, climbing long at last to a lofty mountain peak and finally into a cave where we could take our rest. There we could drink the rain, eat the berries of the land and know the warmth of solitude, the path back to the self this body called home.

§§§§§§§

Isolation is the Teacher. I spent a year and a season living in the wilderness out of sight of man and the hum of human commerce. I knew it was the proper course, and yet it was a trial, more of one for me, I think, than the pygmie I'd assumed. I for one had grown appalled at the deviant nature of these creatures. They did such base and venal things yet took such pleasure in it. What was it about their way of flesh that blocked their other perceptions? Yet block them I would if I could make him forget what I so longed to know.

We spent our hours, our weeks, our months passing through The Silence. I taught his lower self to learn the ways of meditation, the terrifying truth that leads to the Path. I struggled with his every cell to feel the things that I had felt, to learn the things that I had learned in depths of the Chthonic School. I gave him benefit of counsel, showed him the twists and turns that every soul must learn to take on its own. I gave him all of this and more, and yet he resisted me.

My God! What stubborn creatures were these men?! It was the will of mind, the will of cells, the personality of self, opposing armies bonded in a wicked brain alliance. They colluded to bring me down to suck my will into his, to put me at the edge of the void—the hollow lack of self.

It took all the higher will I had to bring him even to my less-than-perfect level of consciousness, to meld my higher self and pray the rest would follow. Daily we were forced to shave his face and keep it smooth, to preen his skin with balms, and to find grasses to weave cloths (a skill he'd learned from women) to cover his delicate body.

What the hell. It was the way of the world. Vanity is *de rigueur.* But there was more to it than this. I found it quite bizarre in many ways that these entities, even at the level of their oversouls, clung so strongly to their physical *id*-entities. We often ate when I was hungry and drank when he was dry, and generally lived a life of mutual inconvenience. To say the least it was a drain on what might otherwise have been a splendid kind of spiritual synergy, but there was time, and patience is a lesson to us all. I clipped my inclination to have everything at once and let him grow accustomed to me, let him feel the will he worked was all his own, and took the measures only I could take to reconstruct his physique.

In time, he became less meek. While we worked upon his will, I made sure that he underwent a daily regimen of labor. He lifted rocks, climbed ridges and ran across the slopes until his skin crawled and his muscles ached and every cell screamed for rest; until he became raw sinew, bone, and gristle; until he knew the dragon's will forged with the heat of passion packed upon his flimsy human frame. And in that time we freed him from his prison of physique, assumed his role as it had been ordained to don the masculine armor. After several months, we had become an imposing presence, hurling boulders half our size down from the mountains crests and looking as if the lad could finally do business.

In the end it was I, not he, who longed to return to the City, to taste the fruits of humankind, to know a woman's touch. He had found the joys of sojourn and no longer needed anything except the self, the sky, and God. Even his meager, stubborn cells of skin had been uplifted to that sense. At last, he'd become a man and something more.

§§§§§§§

One day I awakened to find that I had finally

become him. I had prayed for this every night for as long as we
had shared his body. And as everything will come to him who
prays before he sleeps, it had come at last to me to be at one with
Gudae, a perfect blend in centropy—one mind, one house, one
consciousness. At last *we* had become the I. Now I would move
this vessel. Now I would take us through fear and into the fray
ahead. I didn't know just what had made it come to pass, but he
had let go of this. And though his recollections of the past were
still intact, mine was now the will that moved the flesh.

I moved it quickly. I gathered what few treasures we had
glommed from nature and made my swift descent down from the
mountains. Down through the clouds that covered the valley,
scarcely feeling my feet, tasting the pollens of sweet adventure
and the fires that burned in my chest, I all but flew to it. I
scarcely paused to wonder at my movements as I made them, so
at home was I now in this young lad's body.

I could lose myself in here, I remembered thinking, feeling
somehow cleaner than I had ever felt before. As I ran, even as I
paused—even as I slept—I now thought human thoughts, dreamt
human dreams, and felt my dragon's essence fading. Not that I'd
forgotten, not that I would be allowed to, for as I paused to
cleanse myself, I saw I had been scarred. The jagged lighting cut
that RuSiva's fire had burned into my dragon's hide now scarred
this human chest as well, a vestigial brand marking me as a ward
of fate. Whether this persistent blemish was blessing or betrayal,
I could not say, but I could say this much: I had to hide it. I had
to keep it covered for as long as I wore this flimsy skin, for this
was the mark by which the Captain was known—the Captain and
no other.

I bathed myself, then covered my chest with a tunic I had
woven during my *hejira*. It was a coarse cloth but well
constructed. I tied it at the waist with a strand of hemp and
continued on my way. And as I made my way I couldn't help but
notice that this scar it hid—whenever I would lose my sense of

298

purpose—would somehow scald me with a pain, a recollection that I was veering from my course.

For now, my course was the City. I ran for days and nights until at last, upon a sundown, I stood above it. From the mountain ridge I straddled, I saw it teeming just beyond the red of the setting sun, still denying me the haven that rested behind its walls. I stayed the night on the mountainside. The moon with half its face and all the stars in heaven had convened to light the skies. The cool blue grasses of the early spring feathered over me. During the night, I dreamt such hopeful dreams—that I would conquer this time of men, that Shala would share my life, that I could end the conflict now before it came The Time.

§§§§§§§

Morning wore a rancid breath. I awoke from
all my fantasies to feel the presence of a scabrous churl, a monstrous man well known to me yet (to my dragon self) quite foreign.

"My little Gudi has come back to me. My little Gudi good," he hissed, in whispers loud enough for all the valley to hear.

I didn't have to turn to see. The massive arms that pinned me to the ground were those of the Master of Spears. But turn I would, and turn I did to catch him eye to eye, this ugly leering lout with a face upon whose skin a hundred battles had left their salutations. While he hugged me to him like a bear embracing a honey pot his eyes, alight with mockery, met mine.

Although I'd worn this human skin for the fullness of a year, my instincts first to combat were those of a dragon. I roared at him, hissed a plume of flame which turned to spit and hit him in the face. A mass of sputum running down his cheek, he blanched, leaned back and hiked me in the air as if I were a javelin he might hurl for distance. Then he roared with laughter.

"Well, well, well! "he shouted twirling me around and around to show me to his cohorts one and all. "Our little Gudae's brought a temper back with him. Hisses like a pussycat, he does! Nasty little pussy spits at his friends!" As I dangled above in this soldier's deadly grip, I saw the Wraith, the Hogface, and the claque of other toadies underneath this massive Spearmaster's sway—the hills and the village down below while I spun like a carousel gone rampant and felt it all come crashing to a halt as he slammed me back to ground, dizzy, panting, and crushed beneath this sergeant's heavy weight.

"So you want to resist, my little meat. Well I just *love* resistance."

He marked me well this time. He kept his sense of ridicule. He tried not to betray it, but there was a fear in him. I saw it in his eyes while he saw something else in mine, the specter of a sacred beast he didn't want to set free. Quickly, he turned me over and pulled me by the hair, tried to lift edge of my kaunake and ride me as a stallion would a mare.

"I like cat who scratches" he said, moving to finish this ugly job by doing what he'd done so many times before.

Well...I may have leased a weakling's body, but I owned a dragon's heart. This nonsense had gone quite far enough. So, with every scarlet fire I could summon from my warrior self, I turned and grabbed him by the throat and hurled him down the hill. He tumbled, slid and slammed into a rock but bounced back up and made his way toward me.

"So the strumpet grew some muscle," he snarled to a chorus of disconcerted laughter from the others. He bounded back toward me, circled warily to higher ground then set himself again to make attack. He lunged, both arms extended, but as he did I ducked and buried half a foot into his groin, a blow which sent him gasping to the earth. He lay there writhing, coughing, and too easily dispatched for any of the others to believe.

Shocked to silence *ex tempore,* they flew quickly into action once again. While some repaired the Spearmaster, the remainder fell on me. Now no longer the object of fun, a brutish game of rape and run, I was marked by these soldier-thugs who had drawn their weapons for business. The Wraith came at me first. His short sword at the ready, he lunged and plunged it into the

shield of amethyst I'd lifted up before me. Without reflecting for
the moment that I wore this human skin, I'd brought my
dragon's armor to the fray. Although it was a shield apparent
only to my self, it served its purpose well. The blow glanced off
me, and as I tossed the Wraith aside another weapon grazed my
skin, this time a knife thrust taken by the Hogface at my arm.
Since it was a misdirected blow, I lowered my guard long enough
to let the blood be drawn and in that timely gesture allay the
suspicion that I was anything but a man. Yet my power was
undeniable. I tossed the Hogface aside as a lion would a peccary
and roared at them while the others retreated to regroup.

The Master of Spears had recovered by now but by now he
was in terror, took his leave and quickly shrank from me. He left,
not in haste but in caution, and as he did turned to regard me
more than once. His coterie of minions followed like a train of
puppies yapping at their master's heels, a fearful frantic cry,
shrieking their bewilderment and awe. When they reached the
base, the Spearmaster hurled a spear at the heights that cut
through the air like a serpent's tongue and headed toward my
throat.

It seemed to me then (and always has) that the most violent
moments in one's life take place in captive motion, so that one
has an infinity to respond. Almost as an afterthought I ducked
and grabbed the shaft, then brought it to my knee and bent it
double. I hurled it upward toward the sky and watched it change
direction, landing at the Spearmaster's feet and scattering the
men.

That cinched it. All of them broke and ran. Each one
stumbling over the other to get as far away from whatever I had
become, they stampeded, ducking through an eye of a needle
torn out of the city wall. They took their rout so hastily they left a
trail of dust, abandoning not a shoe or two but a score of articles
in their wake—a sword, a knife with a jeweled hilt, a pouch of
coins, a pan pipe—all the things that I would need to start my
bachelor days.

They didn't come back to claim them, not while I stood on that hillside, arms crossed, a colossus among men. Whatever image I would project to others had been transformed this day — a force to be reckoned with, Gudae the wise, Gudae the brave, Gudae the magniloquent, a living Arcana in flesh and bone, *un homme de confiance.*

I reflected upon these potentials and quickly came to embrace them. I strode down the hill to gather their cowards' loot. I placed the jeweled knife and curved sword in my belt, hid the purse of coins next to my groin. As I did, I felt the Sun's warm carnelian arms embracing me above all creatures on this Earth. I felt its heat upon my back and recalled some subatomic detail when its light had been the flame that forged my soul. Then I strode triumphantly toward that maze of mind, toward that convoluted place they called the City.

Canto 16

Shala

It was the taming of the Night.
It was the rising of the Time,
the Mating of the Lady
and the Dragon.

—Song of Shala
Book 9

Contradiction prevailed in this society of humans. The gates of the City, closed to me as dragon, were opened to me now as a man. Dressed in the raiment of "citizen," and a warrior breed at that, I parted crowds as I came in. This entity that I had leased had grown a hand in height since we'd joined forces and had metamorphosed to such proportions of bone and sinew that people stood in awe of me. Yet I for one felt dwarfed by what I saw, and what I saw so filled my senses that the bounty of it haunts me to this day. Everywhere I looked, everywhere I turned, I beheld miniatures of creation, monuments of handiwork molded by these beings. These tiny vessels so filled with corruption, with paranoia and fear, so overburdened with self-contempt and outbreaks of futility could find no rivals when it came to molding beauty.

As if we had not been given everything on Earth to marvel at, these little ones had seen fit to improve upon it—to weave and bake and harvest and paint and carve and pour forth bounties as if they were in miniature the very hands of God. They recreated everything. Everywhere before me I saw masterpieces of sod and straw laid out upon display for the orgies of consumption that their gatherings seemed to spawn. One fruit, one meal, one house, one skin was not enough to fill their bellies, to cover their nakedness; they would have more. From their baskets poured their wares—cloths in colors, sandals, weapons, pottery and pewter—traded one and all for gold and silver coins whose mystic codes they sensed but did not fathom, set aside for "harder" times that they were certain would come. And when they didn't come, these brutal days, the citizens all praised the gods for their good fortune and set their prices higher.

One aspect of this world of men disturbed me most of all; that was their proclivity for slaughter. If ever a creature epitomized the stigma of predation, these pygmies were the masters of the lot. They wore animal skins, drank from animal gourds, used animal skulls to toast their own good health. As if they were ashamed of their bodies, they let other animals clothe them—in leather, feather, fur and tusk from every living thing. Beef and pork fat basted their foods, fish oils heated their lamps, and every animal that must have ever lived was forced into food or servitude or hunted down for trophies. They were the only creatures on Earth who murdered for sport. They alone did specialize in killing and eating their own.

Were all these creatures so innately perverse? Or were these just the exception? From everything I remembered, these were the rule. For now I only knew that their standards were not up to mine. Had any other animal manufactured death in such a way, there'd be carcasses piled to the skies and rivers gorged red, and they would be branded as "monsters" fit for extinction. And yet these bright and gentle beings had perfected their gift for killing into such an art that they kept it out of their conscience, leaving it to their abattoirs to do their dirty work. Meanwhile they were left to enjoy their spoils without ever reflecting the horrid effect that their wants and needs created. Convinced this was their right as ordained by the gods, they considered themselves the epitome of culture.

Where did this then leave the dragon or all the Mystic Clan, beings over whom the pygmie had no control? We could outstrip them. We could outthink them. Almost all were their spiritual rivals. What an appalling presence we must have represented! What fears they must have entertained that we might overcome them! We even dared to have angels of our own. To entities taught that theirs was the legacy to Heaven, we must have been the most frightening beings of all. If they were to inherit the Earth, they would have to annihilate us, unless some master soul among us would dare to intercede.

Somehow I had lost sight of the fact that this City was constantly under siege and fatalistic by force of circumstance. Its citizens were by custom unaccustomed to the stranger and guarded their wares with constant apprehension.

Despite the banter in the *agora,* a danger hung about it. Still, I couldn't help but see the beauty and the bounty, the sea of sunlit grains and rainbow wash of fruits pouring forth to rise in sculptured mountains to the sky. Everywhere I looked I saw a joy for me to share—a bauble, cloth, or fruit—and share I would. For coins, which held no magic of their own (I can vouch), I could buy these splendid things; and so I did.

Remember, this marketplace of human commerce was a new *mélange* for me, and I understood nothing of these elements of exchange. When I first went to take the objects of my desire I did so thinking all things were of God and therefore meant for all to share. Guileless, I plucked a melon from a basket and began to eat it with my hands when I heard a withered crone begin to scream, denouncing me as a lout and a thief and shouting for her money.

"Pay me!" she howled, without a trace of civility. "You soldiers think you can get by without paying for your pleasure. Well, you can't!" With her withered hands she motioned, rubbing her fingers together as if to wash them.

As I'd surveyed this esplanade of commerce quite enough by now, I was reminded I must give her something for her troubles. The trouble was I couldn't ascertain because, though I had come to share Gudae's thoughts, he'd left me in the lurch where social graces were concerned. Unenlightened in the ways of commercial intercourse, I had no way of knowing just how much this old hag needed, so I took a silver coin from my pouch, closed it in her hands and, hoping that would do the trick, began to walk away.

The woman let out a cry so shrill that everybody turned. Since it seemed to be directed at me, so (naturally) did I. And once I'd wheeled about I couldn't help but be astounded to find this old tare tugging tearfully at the hem of my kaunake, singing to the heavens of my "generosity." Etudes of tearful gratitude pouring from her eyes, she knelt and kissed the bottom of my sandal.

"Oh, great lord," she cried. "Generous is thy soul!" It seemed, she wished to strike a balance for the fee I'd paid, and so she showered me with melons, filling up my arms so that I hadn't room to carry one more piece.

"No, please!" I told her. "You owe me no more. Keep them yourself. Or give them to someone else you feel might need them."

"They are yours, Great Lord, to give or throw away," she replied. Bowing and throwing kisses, she retreated to her stand, leaving me to be swallowed by a river of hungry urchins suddenly tagging after me as if I were deliverance itself. They were ill clad, gaunt and starving waifs left to make their way as best they could, much in the way that Gudae had been before we had teamed up.

I gave them the melons; all of them. Making certain each would have a share, I even took my knife and cut them slices, divvied up the fruit and allocated one or two to each. I bought them other things as well: more food for them to eat; some garments for their backs; even sandals for the few whose feet were bare and blistered.

Need I say my entourage came to grow by droves? There were just a few to begin with, but soon their ranks swelled, until there came a cavalcade dancing in my wake. Boys and girls of every age tagged along behind me wherever I went, down every aisle and alleyway, through the marketplace, along the yawning shop displays, the open awnings torn by wind and shielded by the merchants who feared this rise of youthful energy, this outpouring of little ones streaming from the walls, coupling on as if to grab the tail of life itself.

So moved were they in joy and celebration that they began to chant my name in song.

"Gudae! Gudae! Gudae brings forth the flow of fortune! One of us has ridden at last against the tides of fate," they all sang out as if I still belonged to them when in fact I never had. All at once I was their hero, not merely for passing gifts but also for my vindication on the mountainside that morning. Although I didn't know them, they all seemed to remember me. I didn't know a one by name, yet each called out to me and formed my escort for the day (and for some time to come).

As it turned out, I was being honored not only by this entourage of children but also by the merchants, vendors, and laborers as well. Never mind that by now my purse was a bit of empty cloth, I felt as rich as any man could feel. What need had I for wealth when such impact as this could be made for so little effort? I'd bought the hearts and minds of a generation in the bargain, and so much more than I had ever bargained for.

I turned the corner to the esplanade, when a human wall confronted me—an echelon of elders, waiting to bring me down for disturbing the natural order of things. Not entirely the same group that I had seen in the God Tree's shadow, they were nevertheless led by one familiar tone of robe—the Henna One, the one who spoke his mind most vocally. Dour as he had been before, he was flanked by younger acolytes wearing robes of tan, and hanging like mynas on the wire of his didactic. They in turn were flanked by soldiers standing formally attired and set in disciplined stations (just to greet me, I'd surmised). What easy conquest this had been. This City rife with obliquity, riddled with suspicion, had been won over by a simple act of largesse.

Why not? I'd meant it well enough. What harm could there be in that? Apparently the little celebration held on my behalf upon the city streets had come to the attention of these wise men, and they'd now sought to honor me, or at least had sought to meet me and to seek my counsel for further solutions to their problems.

Yet, as I approached, this henna-robed elder came to the glower at me. The hood now fallen from his brow revealed a marble pate which crowned a discous neck and chins enough to mark the rings of Saturn. He held up his pork-link finger and pointed straight at me.

"This is the man, is it not?" he boomed, casting his comment behind him, waiting for someone in the rear to pick it up. His voice, like an adjudicating angel, tolled its righteousness. He waited for an answer, but receiving none repeated his interrogation. "Is this the man. Or not?!"

"It is," came the reply, at last. It came from a squad of soldiers. Voices without faces were all ones I'd heard before.

"Then, seize him!" the henna elder ordered.

For a moment, reticence reigned. Then the commandment fell again like a sword upon my shoulders.

"Seize him! I do not intend to ask another time! Seize him, or be seized yourselves!"

The soldiers paused uneasily. Then suddenly a squad of them surrounded me, holding me at swords' point. And from their middle came their boss, the Master of Spears.

"This is the man who fell upon us!" His voice was harsh and deep as ever, but in his eyes there glowed a fright so deeply seeded that it sprouted in sickly aura like a weed out of his head.

I could have made his life miserable. I could have picked him up and hurled him back into his ranks. Even the slightest thought of it caused my muscles to strain and in that straining sent the Spearman into madcap motions of defense; he jumped back half a meter and brought his spear up to my throat.

"Not one more move," he said. "Or it will be your last."

I bit the spear and snapped it in half, which caused the crowd to gasp. Then I spat the pieces out onto the ground. I hadn't realized at the time that the gesture was super human. But that was who I was and intended to be.

§§§§§§§

I was jailed. Marched ceremoniously to a holding cell, I was tossed-in and told I would be tried, the punishment to be doled out within a week. The charges were, to my surprise, those of assault and robbery against a soldier of the suzerain and worse: a blasphemy of a holy shrine, the defilement of the God Tree. Tossed into a mulch-strewn cell, I was left to recant untouched, told I would meet my inevitable ugly fate in time.

I was appalled at these human laws. They were made to serve power not the truth. False witness among the Mystic Beasts was easily detected, but this creature *homo sapiens* had refined mendacity to an art. Throughout my stay, I was never threatened once, but the grids of my small window provided clear view of the City square where justice of its kind was meted out. At the highest hour of every day, the hapless souls who shared my plight were brought out, tried and punished on the spot. The elders on the council, all somber-browed and sour, passed judgment while the accused were made to feel the sharp edge of justice.

None, I had the time to observe, escaped punition. One man, having stolen cloth, lost both his hands. Another for a robbery of kinsmen lost his nose. A third, for having stolen but a glimpse of a royal woman, lost his eyes. A treasoner, seditious and a spy to boot, was drawn and quartered and each quarter left upon the parapets that cornered the City's walls. Similar trials were carried out like daily fare that fed the masses great portions of fear as if it were food. Although at this distance my special senses might have let me down, from all I read that crossed the diadem of justice on those days, in every case but three the accusations had been false, the punishments extreme and off the mark.

After four days, just as the sun approached the crux of noon, I was led from cell to City Square and put upon a jagged malachite block. It was a slab with a single footpiece barely large enough to hold man. Bound like a lamb trussed-up for supper, I would stand and face my judges and pray to God to intercede in this mockery of justice.

I'd seen how procedures such as this had affected other men locked in bonds just long enough to let the sun desert their brow, to let the soil and soot of prison walls distort their faces so all semblance of their self-respect was stripped away. That's how it was done: Make a man into such a mongrel that any citizen would put him down without an inkling of remorse.

That's how it was to have been done with me; at least that was the plan. But for some reason, my skin was not like that of other men. Because of that year I'd spent in the wilderness it had grown tan and tough as a well-oiled saddle. This hair that crowned my human's head was golden in its color, flowed behind me like the mane of a stallion. What's more, it apparently never needed cutting. And as for what I wore: well my kaunake (made of strong white, hemp and interwoven from the grasses of the mountainside) was impervious to soil. Unlike others made of stinking animal skins, my white quilted one was radiant, resilient and pure, and even on this penitent's dais incandesced like gardenias in the moonlight.

The persona I represented seemed to unsettle the elders. As they took the platform just above me and read the accusations, all but one were ill at ease with me. The Henna Elder took the center seat and with a drab indifferent tone read charges at such length that it was made to seem as if I alone had raped the world and reaped the benefits.

"And how do you plead?" he bellowed from his chair; his eyebrows beneath his bald pate furled like asps in tandem set to strike.

"Not guilty!" I replied, more automatically than anything I think I'd ever done, and followed with an, "I claim the right to trial."

My answer, rather the way I answered, caught the elders off their guard. The elder in the robe of blue, the one in gold, another one in green, all gaped in horrified amazement, muttered to themselves in horror. Only the elder in the elden robe, the grey priest the others called Horam, took the time to study me without undue contortion.

I had remembered him from the day at the God Tree, recalling that he had permitted at least a modicum of wisdom to pass from his lips. He alone had counseled the others in the ways of temperance and since that time had seen his sanity held in question.

I also marked his behavior while I awaited my time for judgment. In those few days I had spent watching the trials, I noted that, of all the elders, Horam was outspoken and would often vote for acquittal. His spells of objectivity marked him as eccentric but seemed to serve as a tooth of justice in the aching mouth of their law. Since he was a majority of one, his acts of futile dissent were tolerated by the others and somehow served to appease the crowd.

Horam's opinion was ventured again this day and was, to the surprise of many, permitted to hold sway:

"He has claimed the right to trial and therefore gains the right to face *all* his accusers," he observed.

"So he does," the Henna Elder agreed, with a begrudging nod. "Call forth his accusers."

Together in a cluster all the soldiers who'd been a party to the persecution of Gudae came to the last rung of steps below the elders. Still at a level above that of the accused, they spread their lies like incense in the air. By the time they were through, I'd been made to sound as if I'd planned the damning of the world while they, "all decent family men"—soldiers whom the "tides of fate have carried here to protect this city from invaders"—had seen their savings stolen, had been fallen on and beaten, and far worse, had been forced to endure this from the same blasphemer they had seen the year before defile the God Tree right before their very eyes.

"...And to support this second charge," cried out my arch accuser the Spearmaster, "I call upon some of the City's most respected sons."

If honor were the linchpin of credibility, this machine of testimony would have broken in a trice. Following the Spearmaster's preamble, there proceeded the longest line of dissolutes the world had ever seen, each one with a story more elaborate than the last, each one making it to seem as if I'd been the seventh head on the Whore of Babylon. By the time they'd finished their perjuries, the elders were ready to condemn me, ready to end my human life that very afternoon. Yet when it came the time for judgment, the elden priest held fast. Arising slowly from this chair, he came to the edge of the platform. Raising an aged but steady hand, he pointed down at me.

"Before we take our final vote, have you any witnesses to bring to your defense?"

Of course, I didn't know a soul. But seeing that my fate had been sealed, I cried out, "Yes!" and prayed my deepest prayer for deliverance.

From the crowd came a bell in the wind, a single chime of the truth that cut through all this storm of lies. It was the voice of Shala.

"I am his witness," she cried out clearly so that all about could hear. "I will be his advocate, and more."

The singular act of her speaking out at once alerted the elders' verdict, caused the soldiers all to shrink back and the wastrels to scatter and run. However she spoke, wherever she moved, the citizens bowed before her as if she were a regal being, though utterly undeclared. As she walked up toward the platform, I could see her aura spread, filling the square with a radiant hue, crimson and violet like summer skies whenever the day is born. I had no way of knowing how others actually saw her, but the way they responded told me that they perceived her this way as well. Even the least among them could feel her presence as she ascended and stood in the dais directly across from my own.

For the first time since I'd seen her, I was now a human being, could feel a human's rapture, could taste the Eucharist of lust, and the sweet wine of desire. I felt all this while my bold new human life hung in the balance, and while it did I felt the need to cry out to her: "You're the only reason I came to take this fabricated guise; for want of you and nothing else."

Perhaps she knew and felt it too, but she never let on for an instant. Instead, she put forth the staunchest defense that I could have ever imagined.

Astride the steps, pacing the platform, leaning toward the judges, fist on hip, eyes defiant in their wisdom, she was more than a match for any man I had ever seen. Lithe yet strong, upon her frame a warrior goddess stood, calmly denouncing the hypocrisy and "the falsity of witness" put against me this day. Articulate as any sage, she brought a hush to the elders who suddenly sat chastened as if a Dominion were now regaling them.

Her voice came clearly, devoid of rage, yet pierced with the sting of insight. "You have taken deposition of the rabble of this City—perjurers whose lives in sum are tributes to deceit. You take as truth the testament of ne'erdowells and blackguards, while giving any decent defense the paltriest consideration...And this must stop!"

Well spoken, I was brought to feel and yet was quite amazed that this slight creature seemed to relish her role as the holy terror. The elders either met this priestess with their gazes quite averted or looked down at her with veiled resentment as if they'd like to do her in. But lacking the courage to confront one so venerated as she, they had to hear her out and reap the scrutiny of the crowd.

Only Horam among them spoke up and even dared to challenge her. He did so without fear or malice, something the Henna Elder and the others could not bring themselves to do.

"There is truth, perhaps, in what you say. And we will search our collective consciousness to ferret out the wrongs this system may have brought us. But this still leaves me quite confused as to your motive. What bearing does all this have on the fate of this young warrior we try, today?"

"Because he's innocent. And many of you know it."

"And have you proof?" the grey one asked, quite softly.

"I was there," Shala was quick to reply. "While going for my morning vespers atop a grassy knoll, I was somewhat repulsed to see a group of soldiers slithering up a hill toward this sleeping boy, creeping toward him as if he were some game to catch for dinner. The larger among them, The Master of Spears then attacked him from behind, trying to make a mount of him as if he were a pony. That's when the young man defended himself with the courage and strength of ten.

"It wasn't Gudae who attacked these men but they who fell on him, tried to beat him, tried to hold him down, tried to sodomize him, trying to take away his last vestiges of dignity. And when they failed, when he repelled them with a strength that outrage gives the wounded soul—they fled like hyenas before the lion's pride."

As she spoke, her gentle voice rang so clearly with the truth that all in the crowd bowed their heads as if they'd heard a prayer, the elders moved to the edges of their seats, and the Spearmaster and his henchmen tried to meld into the metal of their shields. Only I stood out at the moment, filled to my throat with admiration, my heart bursting with love, my loin a raging furnace of desire. Here I was, my life at peril, my fate on the trill of her voice, and all I could feel was my longing for this woman.

Emboldened, Shala took another step up toward the elders, her gown a flag in the wind, a tempest stirring, hurling now out of a darkening sky. Her legs, like flawless marble sculpture, moved in perfect rhythm while she turned her pose directly to the crowd. She made it seem so incidental, but my every onyx cell told me there was nothing this woman did that lacked intent. She tasted me; I knew it. Her nipples hoisted high, pointing toward the chill of her exposition.

The elders decided to confer. Although they huddled out of earshot, they radiated energies my very cells could sift from the air all bristling around us. Even though they had the power to do so, they didn't dare overrule this priestess, not since she'd so adamantly taken up my cause, not in view of the fact that she was a Holy One who had the eyes of an angel and had caught the Ear of God as well.

After taking an exceptionally long time in council, the elders ended their colloquy, came back to their chairs and studied their decision. Looking first toward Shala and at last toward me, they seemed to be waiting for the Henna One to give voice to their consensus. Leaning forward on his elbow, his head like mutton on a stake, he bellowed the judgment.

"That justly answers the lesser charge, but what about the greater? We've evidence of blasphemy, here, and many who have seen it. What have you to say of this, O Priestess? Or were you there as well? (As you are everywhere, it seems to me.)"

Looking skyward as if solely the sun were worthy of her counsel, she tossed her head and whispered her reply. "No, I was not." Her answer seemed to seal my fate and put a pall upon the crowd, when she recollected her intention. "But I have prayed about it. I have merged with angelic realms, have held converse in my meditations with the God Tree in itself, and this is what it told me…"

If there's anything I've learned in the many lives I've led, there is a single law that holds most true: When prophets talk to gods, all other games of men are lost. Shala knew that. So did I. So, did the elders' council. Yet they had no choice but to listen intently to every word she said and hear unfolded everything that happened to young Gudae on that night. It was as if this lady had either been there or stepped inside his heart and felt the hurt to mind and body, the agony of the soul, had witnessed what the God Tree saw, had known the God Tree's rage when I, Tree had uprooted everything and drove those cowards from my very sight.

She knew everything, this priestess. Yet if she knew so much, why had she never betrayed to me the depth of her awareness? She never paused a single time to gauge how I'd respond or watch me watching her with rapt attention. Instead, she pointed to me matter-of-factly as if I were Exhibits A through Z, the culmination of all calumnies worked against the have-nots of this world.

"...This lad," she said, in summary, "this poor beleaguered soul, went to that godhead to seek the very thing a holy place was meant to give—a sanctuary, a place where he'd be safe from persecution. He clung to it in prayer and for his troubles found this place of haven brutalized, as he was soon to be, by this coterie of curs who pose as our protectors!"

She brought her argument to a close, her finger pointed like an arrow cocked to shoot, and shoot it did—straight at the Master of Spears and all his cronies from "that night."

A well obscured rebuttal rattled from behind their ranks, a hissed and seething growl of "liar!" But no one came forth to own it. Instead, they stood there—impotent dangling dolls, suddenly disconnected from any power they might have once held. Their generals, having sensed that defending a rabble such as this was not in their best interest, withheld comment while the elders weighed their decision.

After they conferred again, the Henna elder came out of his seat, spread his massive arms as if he were performing benediction.

"The law is clear on this," he boomed. "When the testimony of a god is brought to bear, it is that deity who must speak out. We've had the testimony of the priestess, Shala; fair enough. But we accept it *only* as far as it goes. It must be corroborated by the sacred force in question. In this case we must take young Gudae to the God Tree, have him confront his accusers, and let the deity decide. We will have a trial by ordeal!"

§§§§§§§

It could have been worse. I could deal with deities any day. It was these damnably fickle pygmies I couldn't abide. As it came to pass, and quickly, we were led out to the God Tree. Rather, I was led there and was joined by my chief accuser. The Master of Spears as well as I would serve as their lightning rod, and would now come to know the whims of the gods and feel the bite of "justice."

According to custom we were chained side-by-side just out of reach of one another yet facing the bower where we would have our probity put to the test. There we were to remain without either food or water until one of us succumbed, until one or the other either died or confessed. Not a pretty prospect since, unless this Spearman was a fool and broke down somewhere on the way, the ordeal might well take several days, during which time we would receive the worst of sun and wind, assaults from predators like jackals, Urwolves, or hyenas or worse—Slaverns with a taste for genitalia.

There was an alternative. Some fatidic sign or other from the God Tree, or some omen from the sky could set the right man free.

When the pronouncement was first made, the crowd let out a gasp. This was to be a grueling test, long beyond the measure of endurance, barbarous by its very nature, and cruel even to the victor. Yet I couldn't help but visualize a flicker of some justice in it. After all, I was a damsite better off than I would have been before. And even though, in trials such as this, the innocent always suffer along with the guilty, I felt that I would somehow manage to prevail. My year in the wilderness had left this body fit, and this mind ingrained with disciplines to count the flights of angels.

Besides, it was a game of magic we now would have to play. And *Magic* was the name of the game for me. I was a birthling son of Draco, the hidden galaxy. I was the very breath of fire, the son of the Sun itself. I could only hope this procedure would not go on too long, for life in these human shells was but a trace of morning light.

§§§§§§§

We were led to the God Tree as the day began to wane. The sun was a ball of obsidian flame closing on the earth, blackened and made horrid by a horde of thundering clouds torn from the face of heaven and hurling toward us at a gallop.

The Master of Spears and I were under heavy guard, were followed by the elders and a gathering of citizens hell-bent on *gravitas.*

I was chained to one stake in the ground, one arm bound and one arm free; so was the Spearmaster. Both of us were bound at close quarters; both set close yet out of reach and forced to feel the heat of the other's breath. This all seemed to please the mob whose sole perverse attraction was the spectacle of it all, and what few thrills it might enjoy for a scattered moment or two. Such circuses of pain as this seemed to wet their whistle, and satisfied some primitive penchant for sacrifice of blood.

The elders presided. Arms crossed, faces etched with officious scowls, they observed us, watched our tensions mount as they remembered other trials of magic such as this, recalling how not one of the contestants had survived.

"The lack of water gets them in a day or two," the Blue Elder smirked.

"Then, of course, there is the Slavern," the Henna Elder chortled, dripping disdain from above the tiny slit on his mountain of chins. Both men sniggered at the prospect of that foul night witch coming to our stand and pointed to the irony that we were bound close to the river.

Only the Elden Elder made his way to us, to test the strength of our bonds and offer counsel.

"I wish there were an easier way, but custom binds us to this, and right or wrong, we must obey the rules as they are written."

There was kindness in his silver eyes; and a trace of sadness too. He was not of this time and not of this breed of "men." Even though his body walked among others his spirit soared above them. He had wings on his heart and eyes to heaven.

Shala had not joined the ceremony. Instead, she stood astride the mountain boulders to the west and lifted her arms to the darkening storm as if she commanded the sky, as if those western winds so tempestuous and vicious were energies awaiting her beck and call. In midst of those unfurling clouds, she was a darkening blur. Nevertheless, I could hear her voice. And hers was not a prayer but a command that this be done— that this Storm Force keep roaring in and shatter the moment with the cruel swift light of its revelation.

Thunder followed, sounding in the distance. At first, it ripped in with teeth of wind that brought a saw of hail to tear into the mob and put it on notice: Bearing witness to this revelation would carry a heavy price.

Soldiers, there to keep the peace, held up their shields to fend off the assault that, like a rain of darts, was cutting into their skin. The elders, there strictly out of duty, now sensed the breath of Intervention and ordered a tent erected on the spot. But no sooner had the soldiers labored to put it in place than it was torn to shreds, ripped by the jaws of wind that now barred all retreat to the city.

It all happened with such frenzy, none had time to react. In the midst of this dry scathing deluge, came clouds so burdensome and black it seemed as if the universe itself would puke its refuse down upon this place—swirls of faces spitting fury, splitting eardrums with their scalding wrath that came in blood-hail drawing wounds on those who had stayed for the sport. At the stake next to mine the Spearman was forced to bear the brattle of this hailstorm and was—as was I—dressed only in a tunic and a mass of lacerations. Cut and bleeding yet unheeding of his worldly pain, he gawked at me for reasons I was soon to realize, for as I looked down at my own skin I found it free of blemish. Though I was being assaulted by the same icy fusillade as he, there was not a mark on me. I neither bled nor hid my face. I did not cringe, nor did I wail but felt instead a vital current charging my heart, coursing through my veins, lifting my spirits toward the mountainside behind me.

It was there that Shala stood astride the peaks like an eagle in her aerie flapping her arms so furiously they seemed to metamorphose into wings, whipping all the clouds into a stagger and a storm. Finally my view of her at last was lost, was washed away to nothing by a curtain of black water which soon poured down relentlessly, engulfing everything and everyone but the Spearmaster, the God Tree, and me.

Alone and dry in the maelstrom's eye, we stood before the God Tree whose branches now poised in prayer up toward the jagged haggard heavens. We stood there for what seemed an hour, waiting for the silence to be broken. In a matter of moments, shards of lightning laced across the clouds, tearing through the sheets of water toward the bough of the Tree. First a crack came high above us, sky fire with a voice, as if to scream out the coming of a second deadly shaft. It ricocheted across a boulder, split the God Tree in two and made its fiery way straight for the Spearman's heart. Though all this happened in an instant, it seemed to take an hour, time enough for me to decide his fate—to let this utterly corrupted man be turned into a cinder or make a move to try and save his life.

The soul has reflex of its own and uses us at will. Although, my lower nature said forsake him to his fate, my higher self did not. It stirred me from my core and brought me to perform an act that would lift me into legend. With strength beyond the meager confines of my paltry pygmie shell, I ripped my tether from the ground and leapt.

A shaft of angstrom energy slashed out through the air, sped with deadly meaning toward the cringing Spearman's throat. In that stunning turbulent deadly flash of recognition, I had knocked the Spearmaster back, and had taken the shot for him! As I did, I felt a hot white shaft of light catch me squarely in the chest, splitting my cloak, searing my skin, and burning me to the bone.

For a moment, the orgone blinded me. But when it finally cleared, I realized that I had stood my ground, had kept my feet (and also kept my head). While all around me had been cut down, had hidden or simply fled, I had become a tower of intention. My kaunake had been torn apart and a jagged laceration etched into my skin, a livid brand of lightning carved by some seraphic sculptor who'd left me with his legacy and laughed his way back home.

The Master of Spears had been flattened. Torn from his tether like a joint from a chicken's back, he lay on the ground clutching a broken arm, yet less concerned with that than with the thing that I had done. I had saved his life, and although neither of us could explain it, I had committed the noblest act of all. I'd risked my life to save a fellow being and an enemy in the bargain. Such a gesture went beyond heroics. It canonized my behavior and in that moment turned me into a kind of holy man.

My chest, already scarred from lives I late had led, now took on more significance than I ever could have contrived. Out of this a paean would grow of how this "lightning warrior" came to taste the kiss of heaven. Now I'd be ordained to be the Champion of the City, to stand the holy ground against the monsters of the world, and fight "the wicked minions" of the sky. This put me in a category shared by just one other. (Need I say The Captain was mentioned in the very same breath as I?) For that reason tales of Gudae the Lightning Warrior soon would come to be spread. And in the damnedest irony of all, I would now be sent commissions to hunt my very own — the dragon.

That would be in future. For the moment, there was adulation pouring over me like syrup. From behind the City walls, from behind the shields and tents and chariots and horses set forth as barriers to the storm came citizens *en masse,* awestruck and confounded, clambering to touch me as if my skin were made of gold. The Spearman, Gudae's nemesis, now groveled at my feet, begging my forgiveness and tearing at his beard and face in fervent *mea culpa* gestures. The elders, their methods vindicated in this savage trial, burned their herbs and cast their voices high up to the heavens in a chant, proclaiming me the City's champion until the end of time.

> *"Fulfill the legends of the past*
> *Through the nether regions,*
> *Comes the warrior Lightning-cast*
> *To conquer Evil's legions."*

Their verse was as corrupt as their sense of justice, but one does not usually offer critiques at moments such as this. Nonetheless, it was not an easy banquet to digest, especially when I was brought to face those haughty cenobites who crossed their arms and joined their hands in some trumped-up chain of magic while the Henna Elder pronounced their judgment "clear, irrevocable, and *wise.*"

Since my extrication served their needs in many ways, I was vindicated on the spot.

"The City has its champion! Let us pray," the elders resonated and, while the others bent their bodies double to give homage to the Word, intoned a challenge just for me. "And for his first majestic quest, I hereby do decree that he pursue the enemy of all the skies, the evil being whom he this day was marked by destiny to slay: the bane of our brief history, the vicious and pernicious Lightning Dragon."

The crowd went barmy with applause, approval, and support while I, rather than spend my human life trying to accomplish a task that was anatomically impossible, went into a trance. I gestured quite dramatically, staggered once or twice, and audibly exclaimed, "I see the light! I see the light!" Instantly slipping into a daze, I fell on my knees to the ground, taking a moment or two to fabricate an utterly pious pose.

Contrivance precedes the magic show, and these creatures bought it all. Since they had little understanding of the spiritual corridors through which life truly takes its course, anyone who could claim them could work his way upon their wills. I'd witnessed the wonders Shala had achieved. I'd heard the Elders hint that they could always heed the chimes of heaven. And since I was never one to lose the merit of a lesson I tried my hand at visioning.

I awakened from my seizure, rubbed my eyes, and proceeded with no shortage of embellishment to tell the crowd that I'd beheld a force of angels who had told me that the city was in danger: that I must remain here as its living talisman who needed to be free from the daily business of such trivial pursuits as commerce and the demands of livelihood.

"I must stay here with the God Tree, be its guardian, and wait for the next sign," I said. "Meanwhile, I must see my needs attended." This small set of demands, I had observed, seemed to work for all men of religion. If it worked for them, why not for me? After all, who was there to argue? Had not I been anointed by the force of circumstance? Had not my scar now granted me an immunity of sorts?

The elders begrudged me this revelation but granted it nonetheless. The citizens who so recently had come out to see me die now bowed their heads at every phrase I spoke as if I had been canonized, a saint to be revered.

§§§§§§§

I found this lap of solitude a locus to be

cherished. I stayed out by the God Tree, watched its ruins
smolder, looked on as its branches charred and mangled by the
siege of lightning cooled to embers that glowed and died and, in
that dying, transformed into angel's wings spreading up to the
sky.

I'd traveled in some other worlds than this. I'd taken grander
houses in the flesh. By now I had begun to know my way around
this little sphere called Earth. And yet I knew that creations such
as this could dwarf me in my self. It had fulfilled its flight. With
all my knowledge of the ethers and dimensions of this planet, I
hadn't even broached a conversation. Perhaps I wasn't ready yet.
But when would I be so? Only time gives one the eyes of God.

The Tree was truly dead, now; I could feel its essence flown.
Still I jabbed at its cinders with my knife as if to prod it back to
life, as if to hope that some small pocket of its consciousness
remained and I would dig it out and capture it to keep as my own
treasure. I did this time and time again, mining for its energies as
if they were in short supply when I looked up to see Shala,
standing in its ashes, looking down at me.

I stood to meet her face to face. Not since I, Dragon had
furled her in my wing, had I beheld her closely. Even then I had
not looked into her eyes so dark beneath her golden hair that
they were the depth of life itself. Even with my deepest onyx
powers I could not probe them to their core, and yet even then I
knew that they were not altogether windows to this dimension.

Drawn by forces far beyond our frail human wills, we came to
one another, locked in an embrace that we both felt through to
our marrow. Still perched on higher ground as if she would hold
a power over me, she smiled as if to mock me yet invite me all
the while.

"I know who you are," she said, to me. "What you have come
to be, what you will be from this day forth, and what we will be
together."

To silence what I might have said, she kissed me on the
mouth, then kissed me on the mouth again and again.

Canto 17

The Ether of Dor

I had danced with this lady before. In a hundred different lifetimes on a thousand planes of consciousness, we had flowed into the soul of one another. And now upon this measure of life we'd done it once again. We'd touched and, instantly upon that touching, dissolved into inner Earth where roots of trees above hung like sconces to light the river of our passions. There we folded into corners of our selves —the other selves we'd never found before.

At last I knew the taste of a woman's touch, the cold sweet lust from her mouth, the moaning in my ear and the lather of a hot wet leg on my back. It was enough to steal the sanity of saner men than I, for in the madness of my ecstasy, I could hear her call my name aloud.

"Sharto!" she cried, while digging her fingers into me and calling out again, not to my human name but to the Dragon Prince I once had been. "Sharto!"

I didn't stop to question this; not at the time. I was so enraptured with her that I let the aberration pass. This union of the human body was beyond my expectation. So intoxicating was the scent of her, her yoni upon my tongue that I came to understand why these creatures thought themselves to hold the breath of God.

I hungered for her time and again, and time and again she fed me. Beyond all knowing in the flesh, our blending spirits took us to other havens I'd never seen yet knew, through faded symmetry, that once they had been my own.

Then, in a sigh of ecstasy, she abruptly abandoned me. disappeared before my eyes, leaving only a whisper behind her. "All this will be answered in time, my love, all you long for and more."

She was gone. She had fled from my embrace, and I was back out on the earth again. Standing in kaunake armor torn down to my pecs, I stood outside the City walls. I felt abandoned yet serene, an awkward stranger once again inside this human shell. For all the time I'd known the inner self of Shala I'd been set free from my body, loosed from pygmie limitations as if I held a comet in my heart. That we were equal I knew well, and knew as well that she'd been cut from the same taut mystic cloth as I. But who was she? I wondered. Where had this woman gone? When would I ever see her face again?

§§§§§§§

It was announced to my surprise that we would marry. Having entered the City walls I was given a hero's welcome with garlands of flowers strewn before my path. Lusty maidens, tactile in their desire, showered me in a fountain, lathering me with oils and admiration. Eventually, they dressed me in fresh raiments and told me that my kaunake, made of quilted hemp instead of animal skins, had given inspiration to the weavers far and near to seek a new ecology to make a more functional garb.

I hadn't taken time to rest, nor did I for a moment ever feel the numbness of fatigue. I didn't have time to reflect upon all that I'd been through or evaluate the admiration now pouring down on me. Now when I strode the City streets I found myself being followed yet again. Many of the same who'd come to see me half-devoured by animals and thirst, now bowed, all full of flummery and awe. How swiftly had this all transpired. How easily did these tides of human mood shift from scorn to fancy. What creatures of caprice, these pygmies. What perils lurked in the tangles of their moods.

Priestesses in parades soon became my willing consorts. Women dressed in gowns of white and scarlet descended from their mansions, swirling about me like water flowers dancing under a fall. Playfully, wantonly edging out the soldiers from my midst, they became my color guard, a coterie of beauties clearing everyone and everything before my path.

"You will be the groom of Shala," a crone in red called back to me — a woman who looked like more of a dragon than my mother had ever been.

The other females followed suit, singing sensuous serenades to our pending wedding day, each one casting longing as if she, not Shala, would have served me better as my bride.

As for marriage, I would have mated with Shala in a trice. I handed her my every truth when first our souls had touched, a mystic mating more than matrimony could ever be. But we were in these human shells, and men were bound by custom. So we had to ritualize our pledge, to grind it down with ceremony — that pygmie fixation with ritual that seemed to lend more import to their lives.

I was to be granted a dowry, a small fortune I was told, for simply being male. For taking this high priestess as my wife I was getting an endowment paid by the City, which apparently acted as her sponsor. It seemed I had little say in the matter; I could accept or walk away, and that was the extent of it. It was, I was to learn, the extent to which any human male had leverage in matters of this sort. So, I would yield to this odd practice and accept it.

To carry this farrago even further, for a time I couldn't see her. For some days, while we were both being trussed up like a pastry for a wazir's table, I was told it was the "custom" to deny the bride and groom the fruits of contact. All the while, those days and nights that separated us, I was beset by bawdy women who, in rituals that I could grasp, were brought in to indulge me in my rights of bachelorhood.

"This is your last temptation," one seductress told me. And in every instance I was presented, I succumbed. (I wasn't sure what was the custom of that time and place, but it seemed altogether impolite to have refused. So, what the hell?)

Although I found these women comely and their bodies soft and cool, they were but tepid imitations of the mistress of my heart. Where she scathed me, froze me, tore into my vital force and gently cradled the yoke of my soul in the soft warmth of her hands, these human women were quite overwhelmed by me. They giggled like small children, spoke to one another of my manly ways, and oft observed that I was a match for any one of them. Well, women in these pygmie lands were given to such praise. I came to learn this and learned as well that sexual patronage to their males formed one of the pillars upon which their societies were built. I also learned that reputation for wealth or power or physical gifts were illusions which titillated these the females more than any others—that, despite their spiritual intimations, they were still creatures of the pack.

Be that as it may, I was now apparently perceived as something of a paragon of manhood by this time—powerful and rich and something of a stud. Not surprisingly, word of my prowess was spread about this claque of maidens who sent gossip round the City like a breeze that blew through every door—and surely back to Shala where no doubt the issue stayed.

These were but drummers on the day. Most human rituals were, echoes blown away in time by the hard winds of the soul.

§§§§§§§

We were married. In a temple we said our vows. Shala, wrapped in gowns and aureole, intertwined in gold and silver, brought to me the diamond of her higher self for my inner eyes to see. Then she sent a fire through me that warmed my darkest corners. Her love and mine so lit the day that everyone around us glowed as we did, flowing with this energy of life.

In a ceremony watched by elders, priestesses, salariat and soldiers, we were joined by yet another element—suspicion. There was a dangerous union here; no one could to mistake the power. For even though we walked among them we were mysteries to their kind—somehow of their flesh and bone and yet dwellers in a brighter world, a pair of souls from secret places whose feats of magic frightened them.

Horam saw this too and warned me with a word of caution. I'd asked him, on this day of days, to give us benediction. He'd complied. He'd doffed his robes of somber grey and donned a priest's white gown denoting celebration. He read from ancient texts and gentle hints of admonition.

"Take care not to put your perfection on display. In this world so flawed with fear, your constant joy will come to be your enemy in the end. All master-teachers wear disguises. *It is the way, as you know.* So, wear them by all means. If you offer too much splendid countenance you'll overdo yourself. You'll remind these little creatures of their insidious corruptions, and the time will come when they will countervalue you."

He spoke beneath his breath not gravely, as one might have expected, but with such gestures of elation that all attending (out of earshot of his words) snapped their fingers loudly to celebrate the fortuity of the moment. As he walked us down the temple steps to present us to our guests he gave us one last parting gesture only those who knew to say the Asking Prayer would give.

He crossed himself and passed that cross before us.

"As above so below," he said, with kind adoring eyes. Even though he glowed, his motions sent a shudder through me. Although the words were different, although they were spoken in love, by every gesture that he gave—the star, the cross, the star—it was the Asking Prayer again. I knew it was a part of their culture. I understood that this was more a ritual than an actual work of magic. Still, I was too much a dragon for it not to leave me cold.

I wanted to ask about these gestures. I wanted to know much more about the way these beings thought. The way they spent their daily lives was still a mystery to me. Thus far I had only seen them at the worst of times, and occasionally at their best. Surely there were moments of some blissful inbetweens. I wanted to confide my concerns to Shala, but there was no time at all for such things. She who stood beside me now a part of me. She with her serene command of all these mundane things, somehow gave the moments meaning, clarity and joy. We were bonded. That was what mattered. The rest were a milieu best forgotten. Most who came to greet us now had only come to stand inside the montage of the moment, to bask inside these energies they couldn't understand. It was our "power" and position that drew them all to us. They would forget us soon enough, if time was as kind as I'd hoped.

There was one who came to bear his gifts, one whom I shall not forget if I live to be ten thousand: that was the Master of Spears. Waiting to the last much like a child with little to give, he ambled up to me, took me squarely by the shoulders and kissed me.[*]

A larger man by far than I, he stood before me, trembling on the verge of tears, struggling to recite a speech he'd carefully rehearsed.

"After all I've done to you," he said, "and all you've done for me, the only gift half worthy of this day should be my life; and so I give it...Such as I was, you chose to save me. Such as I am

---

[*] As was the custom of the men of that time and place.

today, I offer myself in service, in return. From this day on, I'll be your man; your soldier. Let any man alive know that from this day, the Lord Protector is my mentor. And I, until I've breathed my last, will be his sentinel."

He offered this in challenge in a voice so full of passion that it must have cracked the ethers that surrounded Heaven's Gate. In a stream of tears that fell to cleanse his pocked and ruddy face, he took a knee before me, lowering his head to plead for absolution. What better time for charity than this? And what kind of unforgiving brute would I have been had I refused him? This was a healing after all. Besides, an enemy converted is a loyal friend in deed. I granted his wish, and more: I gave him a silver dagger that had lately adorned my belt. It was a gesture that befit the moment and so moved the Spearman that he quite forgot it had one time been his own, that he'd dropped it when he'd flown from me in flight. Such was the auspice of this reconciliation that the Spearman crowed to me:

"I knew in all my time of dreams that we would come to this. I only never knew the how or where of it. But I knew, just as I know that at this moment, I will give my life in service to you and go happily at the time."

Such a premonition chilled me and confounded me as well. There was so much more to this tapestry of souls; I had merely begun to weave the pattern. Without a moment's hesitation I gave him blessing and allegiance. Yet, when I glanced away and caught the gaze of my new bride, I saw that tears were also falling from her eyes, glistening like crystals on her face. Was it out of joy that she wept? Or was it because she had dared to gaze through windows to a future only she could see?

§§§§§§§

According to custom, I was told, we were to spend the following weeks ensconced in solitude, attended by a flock of servants, and left alone to learn the inner soul of one another. I already knew her, so I thought. But soon I would find that no man ever knows a woman quite as well as he should.

Upon our wedding night, I was aquiver with expectation, remembering fully every scent and every touch of her, every word she spoke, every sound she uttered, remembering too those places where she took me where I'd never been before — beyond the ridge of our fantasies to the depth of our desires. Immersed in her as I had been, I prayed that once again I'd know an ecstasy ineffable as that had been; if only I could know it once again, I would part from this life happily.

At the darkening of the light, she came to me. A carmine cloth sculptured by the winds was all that covered her. A cool, dry sylvan waif was she, beckoning me to join her — not in bed as any maiden burdened by convention but far outside the City walls high upon a hilltop where a storm, it seemed, would quite soon come to fester. There, upon its apex where a bower of amaryllis was made into a bed, she pulled me to her midst.

"Lie down beside me," she whispered, breathily, "and we shall do our business."

Not atop her, not astride her, not beneath her to embrace her — but beside her, lying mutely like two godlings in repose.

"Let us close our eyes and meditate upon our former selves, the ones which we have chosen for this time upon the earth," she said, and drifted through her mind grids to a place she knew I'd follow. I lay there awash in her aura which, like a dew, drew down the evening light. Silvery white with streaks of blue and honeyed drifts of amber sifted from above this mound and kissed our flower-petal bed, lifting us — first her, then me — to higher planes of being.

Once again, she vanished from me. As if the night had dropped a curtain down between us, she slipped from sight, tearing suddenly away as if she'd been abducted. It tore my heart to see this happen. I felt urges to give chase but realized that if I did I'd violate the moment, lose the night and all the time I'd spent with her to now. So, despite my longing to know everything at once, I yielded to the mystery and waited.

In the time it takes a galaxy to blink, the light came back for me, pulled me through the veil of night into that other place—an ether where I'd heard that holy secrets dwelled. Still in my human form, I stood surrounded by a light that shined through towering crystalline pilasters where great souls found repose.

I was alone and yet with many. Hearing specters of my footsteps as I walked along the corridors, I saw the life forms, some of whom I knew. There was Sagro in his splendor—an angel, white with golden dragon's diadem upon his brow. And Knot, a younger Knot obsidian as the night, suspended in his chrysalis of crystal as if this ether were the only place his soul could find such peace. These decadragons and other great souls were here where their higher selves had taken them—to this crystalline chrysalis shielded from all the hardness of the world.

I sensed the love, heard the thoughts, yet wondered if I were the only being in this sepulcher of light who breathed in his own body. Or was this just a crucible for thought? Or had I (drawn here by my mortal desire) somehow misadventured? Well, if I had, then once again my pattern had held true.

I'd rather be lucky than wise. And wisdom, from what I'd seen, still remained the stepchild of good fortune. Then, as I turned the corner to another corridor, I spied the other end and saw in a patch of furious recognition of what this sidestep soon would come to mean: high above the nave of yet another row of crystal light there hovered, harrowing and haughty, the largest, most resplendent gryphon I had ever seen.

It was a female, to be sure. Her lion's body—golden, rippling with a fearsome power; her claws extended taconite razors now spread and flanged to tear obedience from the skies—beckoned to me. Her head and neck, a soaring eagle's, she spread her radiant wings in hues of azurite that arched behind and dared me to engage.

It was my first sighting of such a Mystic Beast. And from all the things I'd ever heard of gryphons it was true: the females were the glory of their race. Furious, raging, yet with a mocking edge, she called to me, and when she did there was a voice so gentle that it might have been dove's were it not human and clearly Shala's.

"You've come to know me as a woman. Then recognize as well, that there lives another side—the self you've truly longed-for. So, here I am. Come taste the wine only if you dare. And prepare to reap the holy harvest."

She soared. She climbed up to the pinnacle of cloudless air and in a Seraphim's breath had dived back to the place were she'd first hovered with such ease, with such style and swiftness that she'd done it all before my eyes could even catch the flow.

"Well...?" she said, just waiting like a woman to be wooed. And woo I would or lose her, for though she had never announced herself in this fabulous form, one glimpse of her in flight was all it took.

"The SkyMaster," I was awed, but not absenting logic realized the challenge that had been offered me. I had to remember quite as well that I had asked for this. In my arrogance as Supersonic Dragon Lord I'd named the game, to fly against the Master of the Skies, without reflecting consequence our outcome. I'd gotten everything I'd asked for, and now I'd arrived at the waltz but hadn't realized 'til now just who my partner would be.

Well, this was one hell of a way to spend a honeymoon, I can tell you, a feral kind of Bolero. Without a doubt the SkyMaster's choice—Shala, the Gryphon Queen.

Well, at least the venue was decent—*ethereal*, after all—and I was purely energy in essence.

"I'm waiting," she called out again. Her voice, despite her stare, lilted like a maiden's, mocking my human form. The irony of such a gesture slapped me in the face and, even in this sanctuary, filled me with a rage that brought the amethyst up from my back and set its rays aglow. Its virility coursed through my veins and with it came a power I hadn't felt since taking on this paltry pygmie shell. From my garnet heart there rose a shaft of radiant force so irrepressible it burst my mansuit like an eggshell, leaving it shattered in pieces on the ground. Where moments ago my arms had meekly railed against the sky there flared a pair of dragon wings fifty meters from tip to tip. And like the pitch that bathed me when I first was born to conscious thought, my obsidian armor brought me to my dragon form again.

From the ruby in my groin, I breathed the holy fire to free me from this vestuary and launch me toward the sky. I bellowed in my dragon voice, "I'm here, my love," and for my efforts found response I hadn't bargained for.

"And *I* am here." The emphatic reply ripped across the sunless sky. No soft or taunting human singing greeted me this time, but laughter like *bkati marga,* a sultry goddess from whom Shala somehow found her power. Above, below, behind, above again, this gryphon queen had flown with movements so ephemeral it seemed as if a hummingbird had taken soul in her. "It's not ferocity, you know, that makes you fly your best. It's love. It is the utter joy of being."

Joy indeed! I vowed I soon would show her how the flame and bridled passion could be channeled into speeds unmatched on the physical plane. I climbed and soared again. I dove with velocities so violent they cracked the walls of sound not once but twice.

Match that, I thought. And as I thought, she had already done it. As if she were the pinions of my wings she stayed right with me, anticipating every move. At speeds that blinded the human eye to see, she matched my splendor and doubled it. If I rolled, she rolled twice. If I dove at speeds that blew the rocks from mountaintops, she was waiting for me at the bottom, flying where I had thought to fly before I'd even turned. The greater my effort to pursue her, the easier her flight became, until the inevitable moment when my wings had turned to lead and I—quite breathless and defeated—tumbled to a pinnacle where I was certain I was soon to die.

I lay on my back, breathless like a sacrificial victim arched over the bloody lap of some leering little Chac Mool, waiting for her to fall upon me and devour me whole, tear my heart with her obsidian claws, or work her wrath upon me in some other way. What an ambush! I thought, bitterly. But what a delight, as well!

Since this place knew neither Earth nor Sun (as we define them), and since I had not yet perceived our whereabouts, I couldn't tell if this was now the hub of my reality or a dream. But since the pain of my chagrin was real, and since the anger of my flames did blanch the air, I came to feel that this was all the "here and now" that I could take.

A soundless bolt of fire down from the sky, she landed laughing, slightly out of reach of every fiery plume of fury that I hurled her way. Waiting for my anger to subside, she stood above me, laughing, fanning me with her soft feathered wings, and whispering "Not yet, my love. Not yet."

Her words like gentle breezes washed so sweetly over me that I, not knowing what or where I was, fell into slumber. And in that sleep I dreamt, hot, impassioned dreams of realized lust, of mouths and bodies pressed together—one mind, one self, one form from which two flames would unify as one.

I awakened later in my life to find that I was once again a man. And Shala, once again a woman, gazed upon me sweetly. Upon that hilltop where we'd found the Dor, we stayed for weeks on end, transcendent and alone, within our flesh and yet without. Having known each essence of reality we were awash in one another, changing from one hour to the next—human form to mystic beast and back again—from this plane of consciousness straight through the Dor, that ether where our higher souls could fly. And though I carry this old dragon body with me to the end, I still remember every delight, every loving touch, every moist embrace as if they were the emblems of my passions. That they were, and what they were and will be to the last, were more than one could ask for in a love.

How I loved her, this frail human being, strong beyond her frame, wise beyond her years, sensual beyond the taste of sensuality. She had been sickly and slated to die from a disease that would waste her away, when she first beheld the SkyMaster sailing and set a prayer upon the winds.

"Give me your grace, your physical strength. I already have the spirit. I have the Sail, if you will be the wind that catches my purpose. Let us share our destiny. Carry me to the moment that I can better this plane of life they call reality."

More than my spiritual pact had been, this was a matching of souls; a friendship of the spirit that transcended all physique. This was the tie of the Tantric puzzle, the blending of body and soul, the answer to the spirit's ultimate quest for perfect bliss. I was to reap its harvest now, the fortunate spiritual warrior caught in the crux between Heaven and Earth and captive of the embrace.

Canto 18

RuSiva

We flew our flights of fancy through endless days and nights, through weeks and months beyond the place where lines can measure time. Even though we had come back to a home sumptuous and serene, even though we passed our nights lying intertwined as human beings do when they make love, we had found the Dor to those other places in our souls — to glorious aerobatics in a sheaf of scented winds, freed of falls or stalls or storms of mortal limitation.

It was in that etheric stratosphere with clouds to gild the way that I finally learned to match her infinite grace. In every flight we'd taken I'd become more rhythmic, more a part of Shala's own deft turns of wing. Soon I came to match her stroke for stroke, became the same sure, flawless partner I'd become in human form.

Again we were one as we'd always been. Again, she'd kept her mystique. She didn't show me everything. I didn't expect she would. Every master teacher holds back some scintilla of himself. Still I suspected how she'd done it and where I had to look. Solving the riddle was part of the game of always engaging her.

"You're the second greatest flyer in creation. Because your soul soars to me. Free it from the fetters of expectation, and supremacy will be yours." She would taunt me lovingly, and laughingly tuck away to hide in a bank of cumulous clouds where I never quite could find her.

Each morning we would awaken once more in human form, locked in the embrace that we shared as human passion. Knowing what I know now I realize the pygmies would have marveled at such a thing, only because they place so much of their consciousness within the limits of their bodies. We had none of that, my Gryphon Queen and I. Our human embraces were the beginning, not the end, of our ecstasies.

We played our games on several levels. Taking this form, leaving that behind, we knew — just knew — we'd mastered every level; we were wrong. The very moment you make such autarchic assumptions, you learn that you have just begun to learn.

§§§§§§§

Shala came to be with child. It was a passage of some months before it came to pass, but come it did. It grew in her, and with its growth came the chancy expectation of its birth.

By then we'd been absurdly lionized for our "contributions to society." In the months that followed our union, the City had come to prosper. Freed from brigands and assault, blessed by bountiful harvests, mining precious metals from the mountains just beyond, it had become a hub of sorts for commerce, trade, and spiritual refuge.

Somewhat obliquely, Shala and I were given credit for all three. Only God knew why. For some time before our even knowing it, we'd been pointed to as paragons of whatever modicum of goodness managed to flow through this place. It was the tendency of these creatures to tether too much praise or blame to others of their kind, when in truth it is a resonance, a shifting in the tides of consciousness, and often just dumb luck that causes things to happen. Yet here we were another time the darlings of dame fortune, looking on as half the world sang praises to our names, penning myths that would later be read as chronicles of truth. Now, with Shala in the way of fecund women everywhere, we were society's delight; that is to say, to others.

I was apprehensive. The irony of our mélange had not escaped me since that night. Since the first time we soared through the windless night through the sanctified skies of Dor I knew angels from dark corners had played us the ultimate jest. Without my knowing it at least, we had flaunted mystic law. We'd crossed the interspecial line and though we'd not yet blended bodies in those other fabulous forms, it had to be the same as if we had.

Shala disagreed.

"Our souls are one," she said. "They burn with the same bright flame. And even did they not, we're not in bestial form when we embrace. We're human beings when we mate and make that special marriage. Our child will be a blessing to us, a glory to the race."

"You're right, of course," I heard my human voice reply. But in my onyx gut, I knew another truth: our commingling took us to those lost uncharted lands, to places where our passions burned white hot and melted all the icy bonds of logic. We were the issues of desire, and when that flame flares brightest the chrysalis of rectitude breaks open and falls away.

"You're neither dragon nor a man, but angel's breath, and so am I. And when two angels breathe in unison, the Songs of Heaven are the only laws we heed." Shala's words were benediction. I took them into my heart.

"I hold that thought," I said, but couldn't say another word of reassurance, because it would have been false. Yet, there was falseness in this silence too, for there were other forces at work, soundings from inside myself, telling another tale.

Paeans of our exploits were sung from near to far: of Shala with her mystic power to conjure storms and banish dragons; and of me, of my abilities to vanquish squadrons of men and hold a shaft of lightning in my hands. The word had also passed from place to place that Shala was with child, a bit of news quite sure to draw the schemers of the world. It was sure to bring another kind of being as well. And though his name was hell upon the lips of any man who spoke it, I knew that I alone longed to see his face.

§§§§§§§

"RuSiva is coming to the City."

Bearing these words like a cross upon his shoulders, the Spearmaster appeared at my door. He shook with the anticipation of what he told me, feared for me it seemed; and yet there was a tinge of admiration when he spoke RuSiva's name— the kind of reverence one reserves for power.

"He's heard of you," he added. "And though he doesn't state it openly, I'll swear upon this lance I hold that you're the reason for his coming."

"A mere citizen," I talked it down. "I'm *very much* surprised."

"You're playing coy," the Spearman answered. "It's my guess, you know him better than any of us. I don't know how you do, but you do. It's my guess as well that you're prepared for this, if anyone 'prepares' for such a man."

The Master of Spears said the words with sadness and a smile. He was a different warrior now than he had been before. As if the lightning had singed him to his vital force, he had emerged from that experience like a crystal borne of fire.

"I have been between the teeth of God," he would say, then cry out to one and all that I had saved his soul.

"Call me Jomo," he had told me once, his eyes awash in contrition, longing to make right the wrongs he felt he'd done.

But reparation for his sins was now a *cause célébre* with him. In all the months that gathered force behind us like a storm, the

Spearman had become a friend, had lived up to his promise and had become our devotee and a guardian of our safety.

Having recently become an officer of rank, he often posted sentries round the clock to look in after us. At times, he'd even taken turn himself and on a night or two had himself stood vigil 'til the dawn, looking to the sky as if he anticipated some calamity.

After our awakening we'd have him in to break fast. And it was on those occasions I would probe to find what caused him such concern. As if to speak of it would give it greater energy than it already had, he never broached the subject openly. Yet I could tell the source of it; RuSiva. I had sensed it long ago but never pressed the point, until it came the time for him to come.

"Shall I give a name to the plague that menaces our happiness?"

"Don't do it, please! I ask you!" Jomo said. He used his bread to soak the broth from his bowl of vegetables, wiping it clean as if he hoped to banish the face he saw at the bottom—RuSiva's face.

"To mention his name is to give him power. And he has power enough," the Spearman choked. He studied his morsel for a moment, chewed upon it bitterly, and looked to me for answers. "I don't know what danger he presents to you, any more than he presents a danger to us all," he said. "But trust me, I implore. I know he does."

"It's because I present a danger to him," I replied. "Greater even than he realizes."

Pretension is a heavy robe. I knew it sounded arrogant to boast in such a way and might easily have betrayed some secrets I'd kept hidden. But dear Jomo accepted them at face value and didn't peel back the layers.

"I'll guard you nonetheless," he said. "Until the Time..."

Those words, "until The Time," were dragon's words, a signal that would tell us all the "crunch" indeed had come—the moment when all the Mystic Beasts, all creatures good and evil, would face-off in a final fray and cause the Earth to tremble. I heard those words, "until The Time," and felt the stab of recognition, one that ripped me right down to my bones.

It might have been coincidence that he had said the phrase. (Common language, to be sure, and many people said it.) Of course, that must have been it. Yet he spoke it with intention. So much so, that for a moment I was moved to wonder. Did he know that we were Mystic Clan? Had he become a host to one as well? I scanned his weathered face, his tired eyes, looking for a confirmation there I hadn't seen before; there was none I could detect. Yet as he stood before me, I felt deeply touched that this previous poltroon had made such a remarkable transformation.

"The Time *will* come," he said, but then quite intentionally added, "RuSiva will see to that."

"And so will I," I answered him. For a moment, it broke the tension, and I saw the Spearmaster beam as if a stone had been lifted from his back.

"I like your spunk. I always have," he turned upon his spear and laughed.

He left us. But it was only a short time later that another squad of soldiers had appeared to take up quarters near my house—a casual billeting, to be sure, but one that would have made the most tentative maid feel safe.

With sentinels at every turn we passed our days in bliss and waited for the time to arrive when the midwife would come to call. She'd map the event of our birth child. She would talk of things to come. She would bring us the light within the darkness.

§§§§§§§

"There will be twins," the midwife said. Her look was that of a woman weary of the world, yet she spoke like an innocent maiden. Her hands like a harpist's playing solo, fingers moving deftly, probed the rising hills of Shala's stomach, strummed across her skin. Suddenly, she stopped and pulled back her sleeves.

344

"There will be twins." she said again to stress the portent of it all. From a face all gnarled like burl, she trembled her fingers downward and doused the energies that dwelled within my loved one's womb.

"Great good. Great evil," she said. Jerking her hand back to her side as if she'd been burned, she laughed and cried at the same time. "Rejoice and lament!" she carefully intoned, then added, "You'll not need me further."

"But I will," Shala insisted.

"For other things, but not for this," the hag confirmed; in an instant she was gone. She hadn't awaited payment and demanded none.

She'd left her symbol upon the door as midwives often did to mark their clientele and let the competition know that these expectant parents were to be hers. She had left her mark in oxblood, yet I knew as well as she that this maven of the woods would not return. It didn't matter really. She had done her duty well. She had told me all I dared to know; and more.

§§§§§§§

On the warm morning gusts the Magpie swept

in. His retinue of soldiers in silver and black slithered like a great Black Mamba through the narrow City streets. Hissing in a grinding beat to the cadence of a drum, it expanded and contracted as if to milk its prey. The drum, like its heartbeat, brought a hush and a horror from the crowd, none of whom had seen its like before. At its head the "Great Magician, Lord of Lords, Cognate of the Kabbalah, Slayer of the Dragon Beast, Protector of the Faith"—RuSiva, though the stench of him resounded in my nostrils, was the celebrant of this day.

It never fails. It never has. The more titles a human being wears, the more corrupt his power, and the greater the need to secure it with a panoply of illusion. If I ever believed that concept before, this was the confirmation. Nevertheless, whenever he passed, the citizens would shout, cheering as if he'd been the eyes and ears of Heaven. The jubilation was counterfeit, as was the celebrity, for even the lowest man on Earth can sense evil when he sees it. But everyone wears disguises, and RuSiva was their master. So it came as no surprise to me to see that this wizard was greeted as a hero and holy man to boot.

I stood and watched, and to my wonder found myself entirely fascinated. His energies were terrifying, but there was more than that. There was a beauty about him—cold and vicious, heartless to be sure; but ageless too, with a kind of vibrancy that seemed to have been siphoned from a thousand other souls. Only the Slavern I had seen could emanate a glow so sinister yet so compelling. It was so seductive it diminished all resistance, and I couldn't help but wonder if this "man" perhaps were not of woman made but was instead created from another kind of bonding.

He was greeted by the City fathers, the suzerain, and all the elders of the temple. Horam was given the task of presenting him with a wreath of welcome, but demurred to let the fat one Pompol have his turn. RuSiva gathered the laurels to him as if they were his heart and greeted each of the elders personally. Yet when he got to Horam he took pause, engaged him warmly even effusively, much to the grey one's evident chagrin. Such a display of courtesy turned him sickly pale—a state in which he would find himself for several days in a row.

The Mage remounted his chariot and resumed his place among his soldiers, all of them parading through the street. His tour of welcome with the elders had put the crowd at ease and seemed to sweeten the pall that had fallen on the day. Still, he was formidable. And as he moved about, every living thing from prince to piglet gave him liege.

Finally he came upon me. It seemed to take a year. Others moved away to let the encounter take its course, a face-off few had verbalized but everyone expected.

I held my ground but felt myself unwittingly begin to tremble. This was the moment, after all, that I had waited for. Yet I couldn't help but be unsettled by the simple truth that this foul wizard had waited until now, until it was nearly time for Shala to come to term, to seek me out. That dreadful thought occurred to me the moment that I saw him that he hadn't come for me as much as he had come for her. I considered it but banished the thought as truly too sordid to ponder. Yet how could one disregard this charismatic priest, swifting toward me like the Devil's boatman oaring out his toll? His horses, like the soul of night, poured cold steam from their nostrils, spitting blood from the bit before they finally came to a stop. Towering like an obelisk, this rank invader paused. The furls of his robe swirled around him with a volition of their own—black to white to black to white again—as he turned his head and caught me in his glower.

Summoning the cool corundum eyes I'd earned so long ago I matched his glare and locked him in my sight. Suddenly, the fear had fled me, and I realized that if push would come to shove, the dragon would come forth again.

This sorcerer seemingly sensed it too, for he flourished by presaging such things. No doubt he saw me to my core but did not betray that insight. Certainly he knew that what he saw was not just a man, that there was more than he bargained for in this husk of human flesh. For a moment it appeared as if he were going to reach for his mace, the one that had marked me when I was a fledgling. He fondled the grip as if to seize it, but just before he did he softened and came to greet me as if I were a cohort. He climbed down from his chariot and beamed with a kind of joy that brought him like a child into my midst.

"So, this is the warrior who tames the lightning, who has the strength of ten, who bears the Storm of Peril unharmed, and quite transformed in the bargain. I'm honored," he said, and smiled a smile that warmed the world around him. The man was electrifying I had to admit.

"And you honor this City," I said in return, hating myself for being polite and showing regard for this villain. Still, I was a human being for now, and civility to one's foes seemed to be a large part of their game.

"We must take the time to share our thoughts," this charming wizard cooed. "For there's much that we can learn from each other—ways that you can enlighten me, and so very much I can teach you."

"I'm certain of that," I said to him, wishing I could torch him. Were I a dragon for just a moment, all trappings would be lost.

He was not tall as human beings go and yet was of such a stature that it impelled those about him to hunker down to his size. Leaving his chariot in the care of others, he took me by the arm and strolled, engaging me in casual conversation that any *boulevardier* might make. Yet as I looked about I noticed that slowly and stealthily a number of his retinue had fallen in behind.

"Don't be alarmed," RuSiva said. "It's just that, with the kind of work I do, I sometimes make an enemy or two. The slaughtering of dragons is a nasty job at best. And there are those, if you can believe it, who take offense at my duties."

"And you *are* a master dragonslayer," I observed.

"You are too kind," he said.

"And other things of magic, so I note."

"An occasional unicorn for sport. A chimera, or a rahntish."

"Or Kohmm," I said.

"Quite rare, but nonetheless deadly."

"But still to be found."

"From time to time."

"But not a Shimbagh. You never hunt Shimbaghs."

He paused. He smiled. He never lost composure or betrayed the slightest sign of irritation. As if to patronize me, he placed his hand upon my shoulder and intoned, "There are no Shimbaghs, my dear young friend. You know as well as I, they're just a myth that has been passed along by busybody witches and wizards with nothing else to do. There is only good an evil, and one must make a choice. The challenge to us all is in the choosing."

"And you? Which do you choose?" I asked.

"My work is my testament. I do the work of God for the good of men." he answered.

"Of God? Indeed? Which God?"

"The only God—The Lord of this Earth."

When men are about their greatest evil, they wear their holy purpose like a crown. I had not expected that kind of display from such a man as this. It undermined his value to me as an enemy and sabotaged my resolve. Chicanery is the charlatan's signature. He had said exactly what he meant. It was I who'd failed to listen.

"The Lord of this Earth," he repeated, entirely for my benefit, then smiled, engagingly. "But then you know that quite as well as I, my mystic friend."

"And the Captain?" I made a point of asking. "What Master does he serve?"

It delights me even now to recall. He lost it.

"The Captain is the Whore of Evil! He will be brought to justice. It's my holy task to do so, and I do so with the blessings of the world!" He foamed at the corners of his mouth like a dog gone suddenly rabid. Then realizing what he'd said and how he'd been brought to say it, he paused.

"You're baiting me," he wryly acknowledged. He started laughing loudly, then held me so closely to his face that he tried to drink my soul, drawing me down to the blackness of his being. His gaze was mesmerizing and could enchant a lesser man to do his will. Yet there was such a fire raging deep inside the core of him that I could feel the nauseating heat of its corruption. I grew sickened by it and would have withdrawn had I not known that was exactly what he wanted. Instead I kept my head clear and held my center.

If there's one skill a dragon possesses better than any creature on Earth, it is his ability to stare. Even in this human body, I could stand this wizard down, and in a while I brought him to a blink.

After that moment that seemed an hour, he averted his gaze and smiled. I thought it was my dragon's power that had caused him to relent. But he'd recognized just who I was before I knew myself.

"We truly know each other well," he said. "But there'll come a time in your awareness when we come to know each even other better. Will we not?"

Without waiting for an answer, he walked me for awhile, speaking in the loftiest of terms of our "destiny together." Then, as if he'd just received a call from distant voices, he turned from me abruptly and went back to his chariot.

"Forgive my hasty departure. I have some business to be about," he shouted. "But I've found what I've come to see, and frankly I'm delighted, as I know some day you'll be. We'll get to know each other soon enough. That much you understand. But just how well is a matter for the learning."

Turning his chariot in a way that slashed the street beneath it, he cracked his whip, sending out a tongue of welted snake that cut into the air so hard it seemed to drain its life.

His horses, driven eager by the sound, cocked back their ears and charged. The speed of their departure was like a peregrine's flight, swift and strident, never quite serene. In a sudden flash of light, chariot and rider had disappeared behind a veil of dust that left the City dwellers all agape. Shortly, all his soldiers, ones with dark and soulless eyes, fell in behind their pallid strident leaders. Black and shining silver, they marched out the gates in silence, leaving without so much as a powder as they vanished over the hill.

§§§§§§§

Jomo came as surely as the night with extra guards to protect us. Even from the first his eyes were keen, his demeanor stern and battle-wary—the kind of pose a warrior wears when he knows the foe is near.

As was the custom in the evenings when he came, he joined us briefly for a cup of honey-wine, drank thirstily, warily and without a trace of pleasure. After gulping down another and partaking of a third, he studied his goblet measuredly.

"He hasn't left," he said. We all knew to whom he referred. "His body has, of course, his army too. (He's made a show of that.) But *he* is still here."

"How do you know?" I wondered, wondering too if all my supersenses were now leaving me, for ever since the sorcerer had left, I felt him gone. No danger to me there; not for a while.

"I *know*," the Spearman answered. "I know him better than you think. I...used to serve him." Choking back the shame, he paused a while. Holding the goblet as if its contents were the passage to his memories, he stared into the wine.

"Many years ago when I was just a lad and was seduced by all things magic, good or bad, I came to follow him, became one of his 'holy retinue'—a soldier like the ones you saw today. I was an easy slate to write upon, so young and so ambitious. RuSiva's magic, I just knew, would lead me to Nirvana. So, I followed him."

He took another cup of wine and downed it. Relieved that he could at last confess this darkest era of his life, he asked us for a fifth. I poured it for him. In a moment, quietly, Shala dismissed the servants, knowing that this tale was for us alone to hear.

"We lived in bloody days, in orgies of slaughters of Mystic Beasts. Not just a few, not just for ritual or sacrifice as we'd been told, but everything we saw—chimeras by the flock; unicorns by the herd; the Rahntish and the Kohmm; Gamberol by the school; we cut them to the ground like harvesters cutting wheat—until our arms ached, until our hearts grew heavy with the loss of hope, until our souls grew black with the corruption of slaughter for the sake of itself. We didn't stop to dress the meat; just left them there to rot—so much so that a flight of vultures couldn't even clean away the carcasses.

"I aged a hundred years in ten and incurred such karmic debts that I could never cleanse them all in just one lifetime. To make the matter even worse, I came to love it. We all did. There was a sense of omnipotence there, I cannot quite describe except to say, it was a compulsion. To know that every creature that you see will flee before you, to realize that you have that dominion over every living thing on earth; *that* is a sense of power that rouses the basest nature in you.

"The singular exception was the dragon. Even in our greatest show of force we were no match even for a single one of them. But their young were another matter.

"'Nip them in the nest,' was this black mage's battle cry. Easier said than done, as you well know. Even when they're young, the dragons are a terror to us. Even ones a few feet long could tear a squad of soldiers into bits. So, we had to fortify our courage before we tried to take them on. And for that RuSiva always had an answer—dragon blood.

"'It holds the keys to Heaven,' that dark sorcerer would say, when he knew quite well it lined the jaws of Hell. To drink the dragon's blood meant that a man would soon go crazy—lose his mind, his logic, all his will; everything but bloodlust and a heightened rage to kill.

"Then there was a morning when that changed. A captain of some reputation came to lead our band. He was a free-lance and a noted dragon fighter. He walked his own way. Rather than drive men by dark manipulation or by fear, he led them by courageous example. He was what all of us had dreamed to be: a man who never let his standards stray. He took the job, he said, to meet the full-grown dragons head to head. He knew how to do it, and how to teach other men his skills as well. But he had never met enough men with the courage, until that time.

"The lure of riches brought him to us first. RuSiva gave him bonuses just to come aboard. And come he did. He'd heard, by spurious rumor that we were mystic warriors just like him— courageous, strong, and out to do just deeds. The rest of it he rationalized. (Money does that to a man.)

"The Captain was only with us for a single episode—the trapping and the killing of three dragon young high in the Taurus mountains, next to a lake of crystal shards. The Captain led us well that morning, brought up courage where no others could find theirs, and did his dirty job without the slightest trace of airs. But then two things took place which mark me still.

"The first you know about, the Legend: The Captain defied RuSiva over the drinking of the blood, was wounded to his heart, miraculously survived, and taunts that wicked wizard to this day. That was landmark to be sure. But there was more—the sacrifice itself. That left me undone for years and haunts me to this day.

"It was RuSiva's little whim from time to time, to leave the dying dragonette alive—a living offal, as it were, to add a kind of "flavor' to our feast. Ordinarily such a forage was a wretched scene at best: the curses and the moans, the blood-soaked flame that spewed from mouth and tongue, the rages and the threats, all part of the scenario that we'd come to expect.

"But this time was too much for me. Rather than struggle, curse, and scream, this young dragon sang to us with lyrics of angels, looked upon us lovingly, forgave us to the man for what we'd done, and then expired.

"I was completely crazed by then. I looked upon this dying dinosaur and beheld that from his shell an angel's soul arose, ascending far above us, bathed in holy light.

"I looked around and realized that other men—not all—had seen the same. And then it struck me to my soul the sacrilege we'd done. Even though I'd come to be addicted to this feast of dragon's blood, I coughed it up. I tried to run, but I was too sickened and weak even to escape. My corruption had frozen me in place, and there I stayed, until another dragon came upon the scene—a mountain of a thing, whose likes I hope I never see again, who decimated half our force and took his young away.

"That awakened me. Even though I fought him well, even though from soldier's instinct I advanced into the yawning furnace of his rage, even though I hurled my spear in bathos while a score of men around me fell petrified or dead upon the ground, I knew this dragon battle was my last.

"After he had gathered his young and taken to the sky, I shed my armor, tossed my weapons, and ran—ran from anything that wore that wizard's brand, that made the promise of magical gains and overtures of power. I wish I could say that I emerged a better man; I didn't. I'd like to think it was the dragon's blood that kept me in my evil ways for twenty years or so; it wasn't. Corruption is a thing that's quick to grow and slow to die. And so I stayed the Devil's plaything—a brawler and a braggart, a bully and a mercenary who extorted fees from cities such as this to be among the gang of men who offered them protection, to serve as sergeant to self-serving men no better than I'd become. I raped and razed and sodomized everything I saw, and only gold could keep me in my place. Yet what tainted me most was the fact that while I became even more corrupt with the years, I was constantly being promoted for being expert in my trade, for having perfected the coarsest kind of predatory urge.

"I was dead inside myself until that day the lightning struck the tree—the day that you stood tall and took the shot. Beholdance of the second miracle turned the tide for me. I regret to say that bearing witness to the first had driven me mad."

Well before the Master of Spears had finished his lament, tears had filled my eyes and burned into my cheeks. Seeing that I'd come to this, he cried as well, and we embraced, a reconciliation for more than even he was aware of. Yet it was not for him I wept, but for my long lost brother. Karman had been the purest of souls. His truth had been the clearest. And he'd left this place on better terms than I would ever do.

The Spearmaster's tale convinced me. There is no such thing as chance. The chains of circumstance that bind us together are forged by higher hands. Still we go through all the motions; we think we change our fate, when all we can do lift our sails to the wind. This Spearman had come to do this, yet again. Again he'd come to guard us from the enemy that he perceived was there to do us wrong. I didn't share his fears for us, for I knew that this wizard had another game for me. But Jomo was insistent.

"Tonight will bring us to critical mass," he warned. "Perhaps more critical for me, than for the rest. You see I *did* desert the wizard as I told you. And RuSiva's not the kind to let that go. He marked me in the crowd today and sent a shudder through me.

He'll be back to take his toll as heavily as he can. He never forgets someone who's served him, and never lets them leave. He'll come for me in one way or another. And so perhaps I now watch over you because I too need a friend."

"You have one always," I assured him. "And sanctuary as well. Stay inside tonight, if you like, and I will take the guard."

To that the Spearman uttered "Oh, no. Not tonight!" He pointed first to me and then to Shala. "Cleave to one another tonight," he insisted. "For better or worse, my fate has already been cast." He downed the dregs of the wine, embraced us both again, and went to take his post.

The moon in early evening was full. The Spearman sat beneath our chamber window, gazing warily into its amber light and chanting eerily in a tongue I'd never heard before. It was an ancient song; the kind from which the singer used the words to form a mandala, a circle of protection that would get him through the night.

§§§§§§§

We flew through the Dor again, my Shala

and I. In our embracing on the human plane we formed the Tantric Gate that led us to our mystic selves again. We soared. Never before, in all our perfect dances had I dared to go so high, climbing as I did into the face of another Sun somewhere beyond the limits of this dimming body of planets.

It was a dragon's sun—all fire and light—the white heat of its tendrils touched us with such sweetly searing pain it seemed as if our wings had now been forged together, made to be as one for one last time. It was then that I heard my Shala say those final words to me that still ring in my heart after all these years.

"We go no higher than we have. I've taught you all I can, and shared with you the love I have to the last dram, until there's nothing left to give and nothing left to say. And yet if you asked me to give it again I'd give it gladly. I have bared my soul to you entirely, to you and you alone. This I have done so willingly for knowing all the destinies we have to share. For knowing all the worlds that we have built and soon will build again, I rejoice in you, for you have learned to be my perfect partner—in the ethers, in the sky, as you have below. You have it in you now to be the Master of the Skies, for now we fly as one; now, and for always."

There was a resignation in this gryphon's song she sang. We sailed along together, wings fused, touching hearts. Finding truths obscured in the clouds, we pulled them out and cleansed them with the rains we brought from our fantastic twists and turns. Here in this sacred place, this ether where high souls had gathered to rejoice, we were the Tantric puzzle solved at last. Suddenly, just as we had touched more closely than we ever had before, she drifted from me. I felt her lioness's body wilt from mine and disappear behind a mist, evaporate as if she'd been a Mantilough in spring.

Even in this holy Dor, I flew the corridors and felt them grow so cold and lonely that I knew I had lost the other half of my self. I would return to my human being and try to reconcile just what had come to pass and been put aside.

§§§§§§§

I awakened in Gudae's body to find that a dew had formed upon me, crystallizing like salt upon my skin. I reached for Shala next to me and found her, just as I had been, heated and now fallen to a chill, brought to it by a summer breeze which had taken on the bite of winter. Cold intruder that it was, it slashed into the room, carried there on the mocking song of a bird. I shudder even now to think how readily I knew the sound. For even though a score of years and ten had passed since I'd first heard it sung, I couldn't fail to recognize—the Magpie.

I covered Shala with a quilt and dashed up to the window. Across the courtyard in a tree, that mutant jackdaw yacked at me, resplendent in the moonlight in his festive feathers—black and white; and red. His beak was crimson too, as if he'd had a feast of berries or of another, more malicious fruit. He gazed at me a moment, and (if such a creature can) he smiled, a look that told me he had seen our secret journey.

Before I could react or curse his name, he'd flown, cut a seam into the night and disappeared behind it. Even in the distance I could hear his wicked laughter, and a voice that sounded unmistakably human, cawing rather clearly that he'd soon be back this way.

On the ground below me, the Spearmaster leaned against the wall, a portrait of honor, rectitude and skill. Even though the life had fled his body, even though his eyes had lost that inner light of soul, he kept his counsel true; he'd held his post. His spear tip was a mass of red which told me, though he'd struggled with an evil and lost, he'd made that shadow entity pay the price this night. I took the Spearman to a tree and carefully laid him down, placed my belt beneath his head and used my robe to wipe the blood that had creased another smile across his throat. Even though he'd lost his life, he'd gained much more this day; he'd finally reopened the doorway to his soul. That dark magician had taken his toll, just as Jomo had said he would. And yet the traces I saw told me somehow he had lost. There was no track of ritual or cultic vivisection that often marked this villain's calling card. So quickly, in fact, did he cut and run that he left a feather behind, as if he'd barely escaped with his tail intact.

How could this maven of the darkness who could capture the mind of an army be so successfully repelled by the efforts of a single man? That was it, of course, he hid his intentions in the throng, manipulated the madness of crowds to mask his wicked purpose. In the dissonant beat of a thousand thoughts he could work his will...like magic, make his illusions dance and dazzle.

He used disguises, ruses and poses to hide from scrutiny, and the madding whir of the Collective to preach his polluted liturgies. How clearly then came the way to reach him: Just take him one on one. Match my guise with his and I could have him. I looked into the night and glimpsed a single bird in flight and knew how I would someday slay the elusive Magpie.

Canto 19

Nativity

I should have killed him. To think I'd had the chance when we first came face to face, when his lurid eyes had first locked into mine. I had him fixed in place, bedazzled for a moment. I'd had him in my dragon gaze, and I had let him go.

I had let myself be beguiled by him, enchanted by his manner, disarmed by the fact that he'd wanted so much to be "liked." He'd used that scoundrel's calling card: When at a disadvantage, disarm the adversary with your charm and walk away. It worked on me. I paused just long enough to let the bastard slip, and now I was paying the price. Jomo had paid it for me with his life. Next time would be mine or Shala's. Only God in heaven knew.

Now the play was RuSiva's to make. The time and place were his to pick, while I was left to wonder where and when that time would be. I had dawdled in this human skin, had allowed him easy passage into this life of mine, and had done so without lifting a hand to stop him. Now, while I was trapped inside this pallid pygmie shell, he could ride the astral winds with impunity, could strike at me to his heart's content and worse: He could strike down those I loved while this man I shared could do nothing.

We buried Jomo on the following day. As was the custom of a warrior's passage into other realms, his spears were interred with him. So were some modest stocks of gold to bribe the gods of passage. I gave the oratory, while his fellows stood in silence braced against the winds that lashed their faces. Their demeanor was manly—the Wraith and the Boar, and others who had served him for so long—yet it was clear they didn't share their master's love for me. They'd done his bidding only because he'd required it of them. Their minds were still corroded by the streets in which they lived. So it was doubtless from their street-wise eyes that they judged my human self.

"It was for love of you that he has come to this," the Wraith snarled beneath his breath. "I knew we should have done you in back when we had the chance. Now, he lies cold. And you wax boldly to the gods that he was brave. That is the one thing we agree on entirely. A braver man than ever you will be…"

"Perhaps you're right," I said. I choked. Perhaps he was. Perhaps…more likely this little wretch had lost sight of what they had been. These human beings were good at that; some things never changed.

"Oh, one thing more," the Wraith said, smugly. "He leaves a pretty trail, our two-toned wizard. Your friend the elder, Horam… they say he's going to die. He's been stricken down with some disease that sabotages his spirit. They say his condition worsens, and he'll not make it through the night. Pity. He was the only one among the council who was not a hypocrite. It seems that valor and justice have been taken down with a single stroke."

§§§§§§§

I ran through the blackness of the night. I

would have flown had I been able. The light at Horam's house was dim. His estate, like the bones of some fallen dinosaur, lay parched in the sands. Even now, his lodge seemed to me to be an empty shell, as if the man inside had already gone to his final repose.

Horam lay in bed. His brow once cooled from well-chilled herbs and washes placed upon it, now began to sizzle with an anvil's heat. He was delirious when I came upon him. And when I came to meet him face to face, he saw me clearly with the eyes that only dying men are given at the final moments of their rest.

"Ah, it is a dragon that I see," he said. He smiled. "But it's a good one. It's a Gudae dragon, and they are the best. Aren't they, my onyx friend?"

No one attending the man could grasp the meaning of what he'd said, nor could they know that he now saw right through my veils, saw me even more clearly than I now saw myself. In recent days I had come to feel more like a man than a dragon. I had felt myself become bewitched and bonded in this skin. I'd noticed it first on that morning when I awakened and saw Jomo lying dead, his vital force fled out of him—the Master of Spears, the shell. Now it had come to haunt me like a Doppelganger, a force of hands from other dimensions to bind me in this flesh. Now, for the first time since I had shared this human body, I felt somehow that it had come to own me, to lock my spirit to the land, never again to let it taste the sweet kiss of the sky.

It was then I came to realize just what the Magpie had done. In a single stroke in a single night he had taken down us all: Jomo for his desertions, Horam for his withdrawal, and me; although he was saving me for something far removed from this, it seemed he pleasured himself in toying with my pain. All the while he waited at his pleasure to issue the *coup de grace,* sitting back and watching, deciding when to pounce, toying with my anguish as a cat would with a sparrow.

Fearing the worst I tested the curse and tried to come out of my Self. From within the core of my deepest dragon's resolve, I

pulled upon my human shell and tried to burst it open, willing to
play the monster again and frighten half the world.

I tried. I conjured the collective energies of all my gemstone
cache, but I could do nothing to prevail against the blockage. It
was as if the lights had all gone out. Suddenly, as if my own
calamity had brought him to this end, Horam sat upright and
gestured.

"The dragon should not try to free himself from what he is
already," he said. Delirious, he fell back onto his bed, wagging
his finger parent to child to admonish me for my folly. Even in
his fading moments, even though his life force like his sweat was
cascading out of his body he had seen things clearly.

I rushed to his side. Praying that my amethyst ray could set
him free from RuSiva's curse, I invoked the Creed. I called the
lights. I summoned the holy fire. I conjured all the force of love
from the dragon's healing heart. I even called upon the forces of
the Creator Spirit of us all. Nothing came. Try though I may,
though I prayed a thousand times, chanted as many mantras as I
had ever learned, I simply failed; my powers had waned, fled like
incense in a summers breeze, leaving only a trace behind of what
I might have been.

I had been neutralized.

To what degree had I been an accomplice to this? I
wondered, and in that wondering knew the answer well: I had
done much. RuSiva had not cast this spell. I'd done it to myself.
In my vanities, in my obsessions with this human life I had
sprung this trap. All my desires, all my hungers had come to be
mortally driven. It was in this desire body that I'd longed for
Shala's touch, had touched her and had filled her with my seed.
It was in this desire body that I'd longed for recognition from
these creatures I now thought of as my peers. It was in this
desire body that I now stood on the threshold of my ruin. RuSiva
had done the easy job of kicking me over the edge. I thought of
these things and began to weep, mostly for myself, and for the
clown of fate that I had become.

"Forgive me, friend," I said to Horam. Of course, he gave it, and as he did I felt the kiss of the wind upon my back. A benediction, an angel's sigh, came from outside the door.

Behind me stood Shala. Even though she was close to term, she had followed me up—she, with healing in her hands and the heat of transmutation.

If I had lost my talents as a Dragon Prince, she as Gryphon Queen had not. She'd brought her faculties with her, which included healing the sick. She was a priestess after all. And every soul in that room beheld the blessed light of her ordination.

She knelt beside the elder, and had called for an ablution.

"Bring me honey, water and foxglove," she said, calmly. In a moment it was done. In another, she had prepared an elixir which I realized was mostly done for show. She didn't want to disconcert the elders in attendance by revealing the truth, that she could heal by touch. Yet, I could see the violet light streaming from her hands, flowing into Horam and making him whole again. He could see and understood and gratefully kissed her hand, falling back into a terminal silence. For a moment, it appeared as if his body had sighed its last, but just as it did, the breath of God filled him once again. Shala had worked her "miracles" once more.

"Let him sleep," she said. "He will recover. The Grey One will live long, that I assure you."

She turned to go, pausing to regard me only with a touch upon my shoulder.

"...Longer than I," she sighed, and without a salutation vanished into the early dawning day.

§§§§§§§

I hated the waiting. I detested the loss of choice, the anchors I felt that bound me to earth, to this skin, to this pygmie incarnation, to this weak paternal marital bonding that seemed to sap a man's strength, tying him to hearth and home and puddings. I was a warrior in my soul, and warriors cried for motion—to fly into the sun and seize the day, take it by the throat and cry out to all who would dare to challenge, "I am the master here. I command my fate." That was the way to lead one's life, without the taint of ambition or the dread of desire.

Instead, here I stood, a captive of convention forced to cope with some clever villain's plan. What had he planned for us? I lay awake at night wondering. Too wary to drift into slumber, lest the Magpie come for Shala, I now kept a constant vigil and grew weary to the bone. My journeys with my beloved through the Ether of Dor were gone for good, it seemed. Although she had never lost the essence of her gryphon self, I could no longer join her. I could not even recall the taste of fire in my mouth, or the spread of my onyx wings as they tore at the seams of heaven. I was an earthbound creature now, chained to human convention, uncertain even if I could protect the one I held most dear.

I still possessed my strength; that is to say, my human strength. And since one's reputation often outlives the truth, I was still looked upon as invincible among my peers.

With my friend the Spearmaster dead we were deprived of sentinels. The nights were mine alone to sit by the window and wait for the Magpie. Shala was at least at peace. She could still project her gryphon flights through the Ether of Dor while I could only dream of those moments I'd lost.

Each morning as the sun broke and I felt us safe from the night, I would collapse in my love's embrace, would stroke the roundness of her belly and pray that the children would be whole. Surely, so much love passing between two creatures could only bring a blessing to this world, could only foster purity and truth, I thought; I prayed. Certainly, Shala had been right. We had only mated in our human form. We had broken no laws. We had not breached the line that would bring calamity to our kind.

Then why, I wondered, had RuSiva not returned to put the final piece of the puzzle in place, to finish this game and get on with his dirty business? As the time grew near to term, I felt his presence, saw his many faces in the ragged feral clouds of summer nights, until I finally realized that he was mocking me. He wouldn't make his move nor he had ever intended to.

In the final days of her last trimester, my lady's stomach swelled to such depth and breadth that not even her strength and grace could carry it. She stayed in one place and stirred only with difficulty and with such pain that it should not have been the lot of any woman to have to bear alone.

Some of the other priestesses ordered the servants to summon the midwife, but Shala forbade it.

"I will not need her. She said so herself. She can do me no good. And attending me might be a danger to her."

Breathing at times as if each might be her last, she leaned on me, placed her head upon my shoulder and gazed out to the sky. "The Dor will always be open to us, the place where our souls can soar! No force in Heaven or Hell can keep us apart."

"What are you saying?" I pleaded with her. It sounded like good-bye. I wouldn't hear another word, but she would not let go. She held to me and made me look into the hard face of the moment.

"The Gryphon Queen will live beyond this, but gentler creatures must perish—even the sweetest human love on Earth." She sighed. Tears filled her eyes but would not flow. Instead they hardened like diamonds. "It is destined to be as I have said. This woman Shala, whom you've come to love as much as I, is quite at peace with this. She who shares this soul space with me is now quite ready to take it on to other times and places."

No matter how gently the words were said, the prophecy was in place: she had chosen to cross the bar, and in that crossing was deserting this frail, uncertain human life. It touched me more than any loss I had ever felt, or ever would know in any life I lived from this day forward. I wept at this; even at the thought that it would come. My shoulders shook. I clutched her hand as if to pull her back into her Self, and kissed her as if my breath would restore her desire to live.

"You're not going to die," I shook her and held on for fear her soul would fly. "I'm going to save you from this if it takes my life to do it!"

She took my hand and held it, pressing her palm into mine. And as if it were a conduit that connected us for all time, she poured her living essence into me.

"I give you my strength of Spirit, Gudae. For what is about to come, I give you all my bold Shartallion, and all my love goes with it."

"Stay with me!" I pleaded, for by now I felt her life force fading.

"I will last the night," she said. "That much I promise."

For a time, she slept soundly, but her breath was shallow and slow, faltering like a clock unwound. Awakening from time to time, she'd suddenly rise up in bed, gesturing elaborately about the room toward all the priestesses who stayed to care for her.

"There is a danger, here!" she exclaimed. "Send them away! Tell them to go and take my love with them. But go they must!"

I obeyed her, as did all the women in the house. Although some threatened to stay on, I made it clear that it was upon her insistence that they depart. Some still stayed on outside the grounds, just beyond the boundaries of our widely spread estate. I could not drive them off, nor did I try. My own dear heart was dying, and I had to see her through.

I came back to find Shala eyes to the ethers, focus fixed on all the prism-cut windows to her soul. She looked deeply into the face of fate and dreaded what she saw.

"The midwife was right," she said. "There will be two that come of me this morning. I can only tell you what I know—that you must save the female. Whatever the danger to you when the son comes, you save her. Promise!"

Desperation takes us from the truth. I promised her, and while I did I prayed the night would last forever, that I could hold her captive in my arms, and by that captivation somehow keep her in that body. It was the cipher of delusion for me to have thought so. And yet I did it, knowing as well that as the sun broke she would take the essence of her human self and pour it into me.

Then came the dreaded dawn. The sun, like some vengeful god coming for collection, hurled its hot red light upon our love and burned it away. Shala kissed me on the mouth for one last time. The breath of her swept through me, filling my aching senses with every essence of herself. We were at unity for an instant, and for that instant I came to know an eternity of bliss.

This linear clock we live by is deception. There is such a concurrence of life that we can live in a thousand spaces at a time. It is only our singular consciousness that prevents us from seeing this for what it is. And I, in that single moment, came to realize—that everything that matters happens Now.

I had no time to mourn her; I think she saw to that. No sooner had her breath rushed into me than it had flown out again into the light of the morning sky where a Gryphon Queen now slipped through a sleeve of clouds with a call that rang into the morning like a *concerto* of harps. Then she made another pass, shattering sound as she did, dipping her wing to let me know the Dor was always open. She was the Master of the Skies once more—liberated, free and calling out to me to join her in her dance. But I was now more a mere man than ever, trapped in this human shell and deeply in remorse for Shala, the woman.

I knelt beside her to stroke her brow, to kiss her face desperately as if my touching would bring her back to life. She was a shell. I knew that well. I'd seen it all before. But what a magnificent soul had dwelled inside. Was it the fantasy of her that I'd loved and not the Gryphon Queen? I wondered, but in that wondering realized that I was witnessing a birth, for in that very instant that this woman had expired her belly had become like body of liquid—utterly unipolar, deprived of violation, blood, or rending.

And from that body, rising bloodless and serene was a creation I had never seen before. The offspring wasn't human. I had feared for that. And yet it was beautiful, a winged creature of the Dragon Clan and yet so entirely flawless as to seem as if an angel had arisen from a crystal pond. Emerging in an egg of staurolite that splintered as it spread its peacock wings, and even though it was an infant's cry it was so beautiful that it brought tears to this poor human's eyes. Spontaneous songs poured out of her, songs of sanctity, of celebrations of light inside this dark moment of her birth.

I didn't examine this entity or look to see its sex, for somehow I had known at once. It was a female, a Vyngorch and the first of her kind. Trembling, she clung to me, love and forgiveness sweeping across her softly sunlit face. And yet there was a knowing as well that this chapter was not closed—that it had a far more sinister side.

In a violent instant that other side arose, erupted like corrupt placenta coughed out of the womb. A violent creature, bold and handsome, mocking in his voice, hypnotic with his eyes. Even though a suckling and second born at that, he moved with the wary agility of a prowling jungle cat. Even his first gesture was to slash his way out of his mother's stomach, then leap across the room and snarl at me.

No creature that I had ever seen had been so deadly at birth; or ever quite so cunningly intent. From the start, his directive was to do his sister in. He was a Slavern, if the male of that foul clan could be given any name at all. And as his twin was to the Vyngorch, he was the first of his kind born to this coven of water witches—a *Slavorn* he would come to be called, and the worst of them to be sure.

Had I been my dragon self, I would have put a quick stop to his evil, transformed at that very moment and ended his breed. But I was just a human being and hard pressed to deal with such spontaneous corruption.

Drained from my days and nights of vigil, lost in Shala's passing, stunned by the mark of progeny to which we'd given heir, I was not my facile self this day. I was in slim command of my faculties. I had not prepared for this kind of evil or the force of intention he carried right from the womb. He lurched, first at her and then at me, cursed and spat and screeched as if he were in a rage even at the sight of us. Then within the time it took to take another breath, he made his doughty play. With razor talon feet and fangs that could have slit a tree, he slashed at me, dashed at her, leapt the bed, and turned to lunge again.

Unarmed with either sword or knife, I shielded my daughter with my body. Pawing the floor in front of him, hissing like a cat, this Slavorn paused just long enough to gauge his wedge of attack. Then, with speed that would have done his mother credit, he took another leap high in the air.

I was ready for him. I caught him fully with a foot into his groin and sent him flying out the window to land sprawling on the brick-hard earth below. Screaming at the humiliation he had received at my hands, my charming offspring chose to break and run. Bounding toward the river at a very rapid clip, he'd never even thought to try again.

There was a mixed consolation in knowing that I'd spawned a coward. At the first sign of resistance, he was given to break and run. No second effort, no tactical dash, no challenge to return — he'd simply tucked his tail and scurried away.

A slip of early morning fog snaked out from a nearby river bed welcoming his whimpers of retreat, while piercing sets of eyes like those of serpents in communion danced just beyond. Cooing voices from behind the mist hissed him words of comfort. Wet nurses with their breasts bared and their pretty pallid nipples, called him into the bleak wet fog of morning.

"Darkwan!" Sang a coven of Slaverns in a choir so alluring that even I was prone to heed their call. Even in my mourning and the harsh throes of my pain, even with this Vyngorch young so sweetly at my side, I was nearly nearly narcotized to leave it all behind. What power it held over me. A power that came with the truth that these creatures knew as well as I — that love and death were but a passion's breath away. And I, in my remorse, felt even stronger force of life than I would ever have known another day. But just when I was about to break and to abandon all my pledges the shadow songs of contrast cracked into my ears.

"Darkwan! Darkwan!" The Slaverns chanted once again, this time far less lyrical and far more prone to desperation, for the sun had grown a fearsome face and had strafed their camouflage, threatening to expose them for the monsters that they were, and fry them in the naked light of day.

As I had guessed, they were an unholy envoy sent to bring this bastard home—to be suckled so that he could mate and ultimately father their coven. This was the case for certain, for their caterwauls spurred him on beyond the physical limits of his condition.

"Darkwan!" they shrieked a final time until he leapt at full gallop into the fog, crying out some psalm of longing in a totally alien tongue. In the very instant my dreaded son had reached them, this nubila of water witches slyly slipped away. They had gotten what they came for, while I was left to ponder how I had helped to spawn a new nation of Shimbaghs.

Only time would tell what corrupted progeny they would make of this or what damage it would do. That was not my worry now; nor did I feel that I had been any more a part of it than I could take a dose of credit for the rain or stars, or sadness. And if it hadn't struck me before this, I had to realize that we are merely currents for what comes next. We are merely the tools of fate, and more than often its fools. But what of this shy angelic soul in the corner of the room, this female Vyngorch so lovely and serene? Even in the hasty panic of these moments that shattered our lives, even through the energy of hate remorse and pain, she had responded with a song. She'd tried to sing her mother back awake. She'd tried to brush her body with her wings to soothe the wound the son had made by his foul exit. She called for her mother sweetly as if she'd only been asleep and this had been some dreary dream from which she would recover.

As I watched her it occurred to me that this earthbound incarnation was not a thing to cherish. I wanted to flee from it. I wanted to explode out of this human shell and fly to the mountains again. I wanted to take this lovely child of ours and show her to her clan. Now the Vyngorchim had a queen, a hope, a lovely mother for their kind, a standard for the pure of heart until the end of time. I would have tucked her underneath my wing and flown into the face of heaven, then sat with all the angels and proclaimed, "this is my own!" I would have done these things and more, but I could not. RuSiva had seen to that. His name stuck in my craw. I was in this human form to stay, and the Magpie was somewhere gloating.

Even in that brief cluster of mad happenings, I knew I could not keep in this place anymore than I could leave a trace of this event behind. Already, I could feel the clamor of fear in the air, the hysteria of priestesses who'd been sent from the house but who had stayed nearby, (and who had doubtless heard or seen the unholy exit of "Darkwan)!"

Gambling that respect for Shala's wishes would keep them at bay for another day, I waited until darkness fell. I nurtured the infant Vyngorch Queen with honey and milk weaned from her mother's breast, made sure she was warm, secure and whole, then set the house ablaze.

I could leave no record of what happened. No one would have believed me, anyway. In case there had been some souls with an insight into such things, I'd had to do it. I kissed my Shala one last time, noted this would be the promised pyre for her, and said a final prayer. Then I hitched my horses to my chariot, set the torches to the rooms, and rode.

Beside me on the stand, tucked beneath my knees, the issue of my love was safe and sound. Her sighs were like an angel's hymns. Her breath was a garden of flowers. Yet I knew, had we been stopped, had other human beings seen her there, they would have slain her as a monster and put the sword to me. That was the part of RuSiva's plan that had most certainly failed. There would be no more burnt offerings this night.

As I drove the horses into the mountains, I could still feel the heat of our home burn upon my back—Shala's funeral pyre and the wreck of my human life. I felt it fade as I rode away, and knew that once it died my instincts as a man would die as well. I may have been trapped in this body. I couldn't change that yet.

371

But my tour of duty among this race was very nearly done. Once I left it I was certain I'd never return again.

One must never deal in absolutes.

Canto 20

Shimbagh

Respite was what I longed for but not the harvest I had sewn. Although my gut turned and my head throbbed from all that I had done, although my soul ached to be free of this pain-wracked human body, I knew there was more such purchase ahead, and I would have to pay it.

I drove all that night as high and far away as my horses would run—up to the lips of the mountains where the trees began to thin and the craggy faces of rocks began to form.

Once there, I set the chariot aside, loosed the steeds and watched them dance away in the moonlight as they swifted to their freedom into the darkness. From that point, I climbed into the mountains, careful to keep from sight, mindful of my Vyngorch young cradled against my heart. She felt weightless in my arms, trusting in my touch, and filled me with a gentle strength I hadn't known before.

Even though I wasn't able to care for her myself, never for one moment did I doubt that she would lack for sustenance. For quite some time it even seemed as if she needed nothing, as if we'd parented an angel who needed only to feed on truth and starlight. But by early morning, she had hunger and a thirst. And in the mountain air, she required the warmth of bundling to keep her from the cold. I gave her that. With a satin scarf that came from Shala's shoulder, I wrapped her gently, making sure she was shielded from the chill of the canyon winds.

As for the rest? Well, magic always has its say.

From the first crack of morning light, came flights of hummingbirds. Streaming forth as if they'd flown from the heart of the Sun itself they flurried down to us. Through throats of honey and trumpet vines they fed the Vyngorch Queen, washing her face with water from their wildly whirring wings. They hovered near—a hundred hummingbird fairies at a time—blurs of blue bonnets and ruby throats—wove the webs of a rainbow into a cradle for her rest, a sling where she could feel the kiss of peace upon her face.

They were a blessing. They were perfection. By every grace of movement, they were confirmation that God's messengers take many forms. And we, until the end of time, had yet to know them all.

There were three days of such attendance; for what I didn't know, for I had now lost the gift of all foretelling. For now I could not even predict the setting of the sun, or when these birds would depart or why they'd come.

Charged with care of this heavenly hybrid, I could neither climb nor fly; nor could I run to other places simply because I no longer dared to risk the mystery. I couldn't leave. I had to stay. I had to keep my place with nothing left to protect me but my own poor impotent faith.

There is no underestimating the power of a thought. Even a blasphemy can carry all the weight of a revelation. "Faith" was now exactly what I would have to keep; and that was now exactly why I had lost everything. Anyone can hold conviction when they dominate their world, when they own the teeth of the wind and the flow of the tides. When they traverse the ethers and hold infinity on their tongue, faith is as easy then as kissing the sky. But it is when we lose command that faith is hard to buy, for the smallness of our purpose makes us tremble.

So, I trembled. I shook from head to toe for what I had become: a product of my low ambition, an heir to nothing else but my own hollow longing. Had it been my soul's desire that had brought me to this moment? Or had it been the lust of my obsession?

If I hadn't known the answer yet, I came to know it then. For it thundered down upon me in an avalanche of truth. Everything that I had done up to now had been the product of desire. I had desired to be this human being, to know a human's life. But my ego had never really let me commit to it. Outside my love for Shala, it had been a masquerade. Now the actor was trapped behind the mask.

Before, even in my most perversely pointless moments, I held onto the concept of release—that if needed I could burst out of this human husk and into my dragon self again.

Not any more.

Now, the only route of exit seemed to be the human way—old age and death, infirmity, or early endings by attack. All this, because I longed for human love. And at what price? The ending of my Shala's life, and possibly of mine, the spawning of a bastard race whose ends would come before the time of men had come to noon!? Now even my "undying" devotion had been brought into question. I was no longer sure of anything. Whether I loved this Vyngorch child or longed for the Gryphon Queen, whether I even cared if this human body could survive or not—all this dissonance gnawed inside me like a ferret sewn in my gut. I no longer had answers for any of them. I merely wanted to be free, to soar into the skies again and be lost in the light of a sunrise.

And yet I had another heart in here—a generous human soul who'd granted me this span of time to help fulfill his dreams.

And it was that valid entity who longed, even in the pain of his mourning, to live a man's life, to breathe the air of recollected hopes, to grow and teach and move on in this world. Unlike the woman, Shala, who had given up her shell, this Gudae was determined now to hold his incarnation. I had helped him live it as it was meant to be. But even if my work was finished, his was not. I hàd to honor that.

By the evening of the third day the hummingbirds had departed. As soon as the sun grew dim and the coming night took on a purple hue, they simply disappeared, diffused into the particles of moonlight. Although I could no longer make magic, I could behold its glory. So I closed my eyes and said a prayer to join it once again.

Since all prayers are answered so would this be, much sooner than I had wished, for eventually there came another procession of wings. Angry birds, black as their intentions, swept down long cold shafts of darkness through the mask of night—jackdaws, crows, ravens, coots, and at their head a magpie, calling to the others to "conform."

Conform to what? I wondered, but I needn't have wondered long. Shortly after they had made a few menacing swoops at us, they climbed back into the sky and joined wings to form an outline—the outline of a towering, bleating, flaming ravenous Shimbagh.

Soon enough, upon the cold winds of gloom, it became what they had made it: a roaring, menacing minion of the Pits. To the naked human eye, I suppose, they had fashioned out a dragon. But it was a paltry, poor pastiche and never a match for me.

There were energies a dragon owned that no Shimbagh impostor could mimic. Oh, to be sure, this creature was odious enough. Wretched to his core, possessed of qualities more loathsome than terrifying, it belched the patented gouts of flame and used its fetid breath to defoliate the mountain. It menaced and lurched, menaced and lurched, careful to display the trophies of its perfidy—leeches and lampreys clinging to its body, hosts of human skulls formed into a belt around its neck.

"I am Scofflaw!" the creature raged, lashing out a time or two. Arching his back to strike again, he was clearly dousing the depth of my fear. He pulled himself upright to show the fullness of his power, the mass of his sinews, the edges of his talons. "I am Scofflaw!" He repeated a second time, as if the name itself were enough to carry terror into the moment.

I suppose I should have been impressed by all this foul flourish; I was not. One did not grow in the belly of a dragon to be awed by Doppelgängers such as this. At fifty feet from talon to top of head, he might have frightened normal men, but I had seen more worthy warriors at the back of the Crater of Nebul, standing in queue to gain a moment's notice. He was savage to be sure. But there was none of the vicious intelligence that gives true evil its force.

Even so, he frightened the child. The Vyngorch tucked herself tightly behind me, shivering at Scofflaw's voice. There was no doubt that it meant us harm and could wreak its share of mayhem, probably fell a village or two if it came of a mind to engage.

I had to remember I was just a man. There was no ninety foot dragon to explode itself out of me, to overcome this impuissant lizard and send it packing. I had to embrace my limitations and a short frail human life. And nothing more than a sword's point rested between me and my extinction.

I drew my weapon, held it in attack pose, and watched as Scofflaw rippled the clouds with his laughter. "They sent me to deal with this?!" he roared. "Why, you're not even armored." To flaunt his power, he spat a flame that singed me up and down.

I didn't blanch. In fact the flame felt good upon my face. Rather than burn, the fire inspired me. Somehow I drew strength from it, and that unsettled him.

The Shimbagh lurched at me again, this time making more to do about his business. He unsheathed a talon, took a swipe, then curled his tail to attack. I was accustomed to the moves. They were basic fencing motions, the testing of an opponent, and I was more than ready for what came next.

But the next assault surprised me. Scofflaw leapt up in the air, exploded into a forceful arc and swept down after me. Spitting flame and slashing talons, he made a show of it, but for a Brother of the Kiln he was a poor impostor.

My show of contempt was nearly fatal. I almost casually ducked. But in his wake, the curl of his tail caught me and sent me sprawling. I jumped to my feet again and struggled to get my sword, but when I picked it up, a sharp pain shot into my shoulders, sending a crack like a whip that racked across my collar bone.

To lend further harrow to the matter, my innocent Vyngorch young was too far away for me to reach before the rage of Scofflaw could be felt.

He had already made his turn and was diving straight for her when I resorted to the only act I knew might save her; even though it may have meant my end. I sent out the Asking Prayer and prayed that it be answered—that my stultified higher self could reach the Mind of God.

"*Ahtoh!*" I shouted the incantation, bringing my blade up to the crown of my head.

"*Malcuuth!*" I followed, taking the pommel down to my heart in hopes that it would bring its energies to bear upon this moment.

"*Vegadulah!*" I loudly droned, crossing the hilt to my left shoulder and quickly crossing it again to my right.

"*Vegaburragh!*" I hummed with a voice that took a life of its own, forming a stream of laser light that shot into the air and seized the Shimbagh in its grip, knocking him to the ground where he writhed awash in his own confusion.

By the time I had completed the cross and sung the capstone, "*Olam!*" the Shimbagh, Scofflaw, had now become enmeshed in a web of light. I charred the sky with the rest of the ritual for the very first time to its end, marking it with the fiery pentagram, making the sign of the stars. Five points to the front, six to the back, the mystical Middle Pillar, the one that freed the soul in doubt and stood him in the Father's light. I invoked the names of angels of whom I'd very slight acquaintance, yet did so never having heard the ritual to completion. It had begun but never ended on that fated day at the Lake, yet I knew every phrase as if they had been the first I'd ever heard. I couldn't explain it, but came to know that this was a miracle. I was channeling every syllable I uttered. A kind of deadly genius fired through me like the sun from a galaxy far closer to Heaven than our own.

The final rays that formed the cross—the pentacle before me, the six pointed star behind, the Middle Pillar in the cone of light that now surrounded us—protected me and wholly enveloped him, igniting his aura as if to incinerate his agony. He struggled for a time but then succumbed. The light, it seemed, had cleansed his negativity and placed him on the altar of redemption, leaving no more than vapors there to mark his brief existence.

He'd vanished. There was no trace of him, save one trail of red essence shattering like embers upon the ground.

None of this had come from me. It had come through me surely. Yet I felt no more a part of it than cinders to a flame. I was the rod. I'd set in motion what there had to be, and by performing that simple ritual with its arcane human codes, I had reaffirmed a balance to the world. And now the power that had marked the Captain resided with me as a man—the only two human beings in this world who had it.

The irony of this did not escape me. I had the power to banish not only Shimbaghs but my own kind as well. It wasn't a power that I had earned. I had simply managed the perfect placement at the proper moment in time.

Now, I could change the course of everything by force of will, put so much energy into a mystic conflict that I could end it on the spot. And it didn't even matter what house of flesh I lived in; I was spirit!

I was nothing. I was an instrument, and little else. I had thought of myself as a dragon. I had thought of myself as a man when I was neither: I was a soul and, as a soul, a subject of God's will.

"Not my will but Thine be done," I prayed. Remembering the only other time that I had said it made me quake with understanding. I had given up myself before, and I would have to again. And it was only then that I succumbed. I felt a charge of light right through me that caused my shoulders to heave. Tears of gratitude seared my cheeks. I was overcome.

I ran to my Vyngorch child and held her, gently stroking her, wishing I could tell her all the love of God we shared. She understood already. Hers was a joyous visage of an angel in transition. She sweetly trilled her songs that summoned clusters of clouds on high and brought from them another pair of wings.

This one was sweeping to and fro, placidly weaving patterns yet doing so with a dynamic grace that could not belong to a bird. As this creature swept more closely, I was certain I knew the stroke, the swift demeanor and the sure serenity. They were dragon's wings spread out with an aura one could feel. Its essence anointed the moonlit sky and brought it to a mist. Not rain but rainbows fell upon us in splashes of celestial bliss that kissed my child and bathed me in its glory all at once.

Swiftly silent, a dragon form now filled the night before me. His eyes, like sapphires, glimmered. His energies were bathed in azure light. He didn't pause to greet me or to judge where I had been. He only came to let me know the burden he carried with him.

"It is The Time," he said, and then repeated softly. "It is The Time."

Canto 21

Preparation

Skye, like a revenant galleon sifting through a fog, came to dock silently before me. Through the mirror of the soul he knew me for who I was, even though I no longer knew myself.

"You've changed, young friend," he said.

"Let's not belabor the obvious," I replied. I would have hugged him if I could but found myself being profane instead.

"No…I mean, you've grown," he added. "Not in size, but in your depth of self. Experience has made a man of you…as it were."

If I could have had my choice of seeing any creature on this globe, it would have been this dragon before me now. More than my own blood kin, more even than Pod, I knew he would have understood the trials I had undergone. All the more reason that now I found myself being wounded by his mockery.

"I'm not mocking you," he assured me, quite easily reading my thoughts. "You are a more whole creature now. For you have loved and lost, and scars on the heart are like threads of gold. They strengthen as they heal. This human woman who gave you her body also gave you her soul. And from what I can see it was potent stuff indeed. You've loved and lost, and I strongly doubt you'll love as much again. Now, rejoice! For you have tasted the sweetest savor of Angels...

"I share your loss. But realize, you've lost nothing of yourself. This bond has forged you in a stronger steel than you can realize."

The clarity of kindness can pierce the proudest armor. I heard the words and it shattered me to my toes. Finally I could allow myself to cry, and when I did at last, it was as if the floodgates of my heart had broken open. There is no greater relief I suppose than acknowledgment of one's grief, yet we fight to prevent its ever coming to pass.

I had lost her! My God, I had lost her! Now I was lost in my human self until I would breathe my last. It was Shala who had made the difference, who'd transformed this role I played. But what had she given up for what I'd become?

I don't remember how long I wept or if I cared to stop. I only know my tears unerringly dropped on my Vyngorch young, transforming her instantaneously into a human child—a perfect replication of her mother. In a matter of moments she returned to herself, still beautiful in her way. Yet I realized then that her *raison d'etre* would be the granting of wishes. Even in parting, my beloved Shala had left answered prayers behind.

But *Asking Prayers* were my legacy. And I knew that's what had brought it. That was what had conjured my cousin Skye. The word had now gone out of what I'd done. I, in my way, was as powerful now and as dangerous to the Clan as the Captain ever could have been.

Skye, with infinite patience, let my anguish run its course, brushed me with his wing, and cut to the chase.

"Without knowing it, you tipped your hand. By banishing the Scofflaw, you showed yourself to be the Shimbagh's greatest scourge. Now you are a target indeed. And as long as you're a man, there's a danger to you that cannot be dismissed. No doubt, RuSiva had set up this test to confirm what he suspected—that you were the Answerer cloaked in a human disguise. When the final conflict comes between the Shimbaghs and the Mystic Clan, you will be the spearhead of our cause—you and the Captain."

"The Captain?" I responded with a query, though somehow Skye's revelation didn't faze me in the least. As early as I could remember, I was told we were destined to meet. Unfortunately, I was no longer a dragon and might never be again. To be perfectly frank I wasn't certain I cared. "If the Captain comes to see me, then I'll be here to greet him, waiting on this mountainside, my battle sword in hand."

"Wait here if you like," Skye abjured. "But you court your martyrdom. Already the citizens report your exploits far and wide. The Captain has gotten wind of them and is rumored on his way. And some City folk have already set out to find you.

"There's also the unresolved matter of your mansion left in flames, and the dozens of maids and servants who remain to fantasize about precisely what went on and who did what to whom. It is apocryphal; most things are. But lies have ardent spokesmen, and hysterical crones have whipped the City into a frenzy. Now the Citizens have the latest rumor that you've dispatched a 'dragon.' They also think you murdered your wife. They wonder if you've gone mad. And killing madmen is a sanctioned sport, especially in these parts."

He spoke of this with some amusement as if it didn't matter, as if my experience in this human life had been a game played in a doll's house. Had I been more of spirit and less of flesh, I would have understood. But I was a man, and my cousin's words still struck me like a blow.

"I know what you've been through," he said. "It hasn't been easy. But the true test is yet to be put. For when the Captain finds you, comes 'The Time.'"

"The Time," I repeated, almost by rote. I'd heard the phrase so often. I'd known its meaning since I'd been young, yet had never felt its burden—until now. Now, for some reason, the mention of it utterly terrified me. It was as if Heaven and Hell were to come at last into conflict, and the outcome would rest with me.

Silently, I chided myself for such self-important thoughts. But Skye put all things into perspective.

"Nothing any of us plans is ever as important as we think. The greatest moment is only one brick in the building. The Time is upon us. That is true. Yet it comes as no surprise. We've known it for generations. Nothing can forestall it. All we can do is do the right thing when it comes. As for me I've come on a mission—to see you to be sure. But I've also come to claim your daughter. She is to be the fountainhead of a grand new race of beings, the mother/angel of a mystic clan."

"Then this entire episode has been a part of the plan," I muttered, somehow resenting that yet again I had been the tool of some godling's whimsy.

"A wish upon the ethers made so very long ago—a prayer to which you chose to give an answer."

Sometimes I resented my cousin for being so collected. Wisdom poured from Skye as freely as breath poured out of others. Yet I could not refute his insight any more than I could deny that in a moment I would have to say good-bye to the only creature who anchored me to this place.

I looked into her eyes and saw a hundred lifetimes there, generations of bliss and hope ahead. Indeed she'd be the mother of an elevated realm, unclawed by the heavy hands of this dross little world. I embraced her clumsily, fearful to my heart that she would not remember who I was. I watched as Skye gently lifted her heavenward into the kunzite night, up through the face of the moon and out of my life. Opting not to disappear, he climbed in widening circles, as if he realized my need to behold her for as long as I could.

§§§§§§§

Struck by the silence of the darkness that

followed, I was alone again. abandoned to my devices and to
whatever might come next. The shroud of evening swallowed
me, cloaked me in its coolness, then seemed to part to reveal a
thousand furtive eyes. Torches of the villagers; how reverential
they seemed. A procession of them lit the night with its
uncertain dance, swaying in and out of the rocks with shaky
resolution.

My human instinct was to run, to find a hidden place, a
sanctuary in the many caves that I'd more than come to know.
But that was the act of a rabbit—not the Gudae I'd become. If I
were to meet my fate it would be as a *man.*

I let them find me. It didn't take long as pygmies measure
time. A matter of hours and I could hear the drone of their
clumsy clamor. I made myself available, donned my kaunake
armor, stood astride a boulder, a Colossus in their crosshairs. I
too lit a torch as if to tell them, "Here I stand! Ready to face
whatever you and the fates will send my way." I had stuck my
spear in the ground and kept my sword in its sheath, but my
stance said I was ready for business.

The procession arrived at a cliff side that counterpositioned
mine and halted without a sign of menace. I was just out of arrow
shot, or they might have launched a salvo at me. That was my
first impression, but it was wrong. This did not appear to be the
intent of these men. They were charting my presence as if I were
some landmark. Instead of trying to gun me down, the front rows
reverently knelt. And for a time their lights like votives lit the
darkness between us. It was then I noticed that their torches
were stitching out a circular pattern marking this spot. I also
knew we were positioned at such a height and angle that it could
be sighted from three days ride away. Then, as if it were a firefly
lifting from the lighted body, a single torch set out to make its
way through the dark valley to me. It was an uncertain trek at
best, an old man's difficult journey. No doubt they'd sent the

only person they knew that I would accept. From the energy he put forth as his aura gilded the night, I could tell it was the grey mage, Horam, my last true human friend. By the time he stood before me, it was the darkest point of morning. And as he emerged I could see that he was weary to his core.

"Forgive me young master," he trembled to say. "I always quake in the midst of portent, and the paths of comfort have too long marked my life. So, rugged journeys tire me, and this one most of all, for it seems that I have come to say goodbye."

"You haven't yet recovered from your illness," I observed.

"Oh, but I have," he corrected, apologetically. "Another kind of fever plagues me now."

"The frenzy of the hunt," I growled. "The nausea is all too familiar. I've known its stench ever since I was old enough to fly. They're armed to the teeth and waiting for me to show a sign of weakness. So they've sent you as a lightning rod to take the measure of me."

"They're confused," said Horam, very much in the way a shepherd would speak of his flock, realizing the limits of its sense of direction. "They don their armor only because they fear you might do them harm. They've seen your heroics with the Shimbagh. They also know you deserted your home. Your wife is dead, her body a cinder. Your mansion lies in ashes. And Slaverns freely roam the rivers as if they owned the night.

"The Citizens know the fallout entirely comes from your house, but they're still at a loss to explain just how or why. So, they've summoned the Captain to take your measure, and settle the issue of you. The Captain, the one and only slayer of Shimbaghs."

"Shimbagh!" The word itself carried a tone that ran straight up my spine.

"Excuse me, old friend," I answered. "You used a term yet unknown to men. 'Shimbagh,' you said. The difference was something I thought no human being could discern."

"Among the creature you call 'the pygmie,' there are Mystic Clans as well. Our numbers are small. We *are* endangered and

must do the Work in secret. Still we know the challenge set
before us. It isn't just by chance that this creature man has been
chosen to carry on the torch…any more than it's a whim of the
gods that the Age of the Dragon is waning. You must learn in
your youthful zeal that all souls are the same. It's just that some
of our 'races' must cease so that others may come along."

"Does the Captain understand this? Is he Mystic Clansman as
well?" I asked, in order to mask my resentment. The world it
seemed had chosen these days to condescend to me.

"He does not," the old priest answered. "He's merely
answering the call, the uncultured task that his higher self has
set. Just as you in a more cognizant way are more than fulfilling
yours. But he will come to seek you surely, and that is why I'm
here. Whatever happens, whatever he does, you must not kill
him."

"I'm expected to," I answered. "It is my forsworn duty. And
yet I've never thought that killing this man would solve a single
thing. So, release the fear, my mentor. This heart sees things
more clearly. Besides, I'm not a creature who lives by reflex or
the drumming of a tortured mind."

"You may not now," the priest admonished. "But in the heat
of conflict, one's good intentions are the very first victim to fall."

"And what of him?" I asked. "Could he not vanquish me?
Could I not be the one who falls? What then?"

"But you won't fall," Horam assured me, trembling all the
while—so much so that his predictions cast a pall.

"Is that why you came to me, old friend—to vouchsafe this
lone crusader, this holy man whose career I launched by a
wicked twist of fate?"

"Not entirely. Though I must admit that has been my intent.
In reality, I was sent to feel you out as it were, to 'divine' you and
report your state of mind to them. If you slaughter me, they will
attack and smite you for a killer. If we embrace, and you kneel at
this moment, they'll behold the benediction. They'll understand
I've blessed you—that you're just a good man gone wrong.
They'll leave you to your solitary path. But they'll bar you from

the City. Ostracism, I'm afraid, is the best that you can hope for. Even though they're in awe of you, you're an alien to them. Then again, you've never quite fit in this skin."

"So, if we embrace and say 'goodbye,' I'm safe. At least for now...So that's what we must do, old friend."

"For now," he reflectively answered. "For later, who's to know—in another lifetime far away from this penal colony of souls?"

I knelt as he had asked me to; then I rose and we embraced. And as we did, I felt a heave of sadness surging through him, one that touched me to my core.

"Were you...always a human being?" I asked. "A man as you are now?"

"Always, and will be again in my next 'assignment.' It's my choice. We're all at choice. You, most of all." Horam answered, and in flickers of thought had taught me of mystic brotherhoods of which I'd yet to learn. So that was it. I'd come this far yet had so far to go. I hadn't begun to comprehend the depths in which I now played. There were levels of souls and higher awareness none had ever reached, mainly because we'd crashed against the ceiling of our hubris. I'd begun to perceive that souls like Horam had reached levels far above ours, had counseled with angels in realms beyond this and yet had returned to see their service done.

It is the curse of the dragon's soul is that we must do it once —one long life without a break in the aspect, while other creatures of this realm had many lives to choose from (yet seemed to make the same mistakes time and time again).

"As I return, I suggest you depart. There are those who would seek you out—many who would like to slit your throat while you sleep. Some are minions of RuSiva. Others can smell a bounty. Most of them are simply confused by your radical character flaws. A rarer few seem to know better and sense the sorcerer's work; they've seen the Magpie in flight and know his patterns. Those are the ones who will recall you always as Gudae 'The Civilizer,' the man who made a change in our world as we know it. It is they who say, let the Captain come, and may the better man win, though I know in my heart that if either of you fell, we'd lose some greatness here."

I think he wanted me to respond, to give him some peace of mind, but this was something I could no longer do. The Captain and I were made for each other, of that much I was certain. The rest would be told in time and time alone.

Thank God, Horam didn't belabor the issue. He simply said goodbye. "God bless you," were his final words to me. And there was no doubt he meant them.

I snuffed my torch, and like a phantom simply quit the air. It was the easiest choice I'd ever made. The lights from the opposite peak stayed on into the break of day, marking the spot for the force of men and arms that I'd seen so often before. They didn't stay until dawn; perhaps they didn't dare. I suppose Horam had convinced them I had departed. In a way I had, for what I had become was a "dragon's dream" where nothing had been real. Yet this body knew and this mind as well, that this angel's soul had struck earth and very well might never rise again.

Canto 22

The Captain

I wasn't surprised that RuSiva didn't try to track me down. He knew as well as I that "The Answerer" had powers he had to dodge. So, however he had trapped me in this human being's body, he couldn't take me lightly, or take me at all. Still, I knew that he was watching. I could feel his breath in the wind. I could see him peering through the myriad eyes of night.

I knew the Captain would be more direct. He was not the kind to tarry. A second sunrise marked his arrival. I was surprised it took that long. But I wasn't surprised that he made a bee-line for me.

Standing astride an ebony chariot pulled by black steeds scarred from battles, he came like an avenging warrior god sent from the Sun itself. And though his band was small indeed and their vestments frayed by time, they carried the mark of purpose on their brow. They were holy men, if there were such things, fired in the crucible of purpose, and they wore an air of clarity I had seldom seen before.

There were a hundred at the most, all mounted and at a trot, riding at a pace that defied the angle of their climb. Even though the way was steep and the path grew narrow before them, they didn't alter their stride so much as a step. Down into the chasm below me and up the final grade they rolled, their rumble becoming a deafening roar of wheel and heavy metal.

I didn't move. I didn't shift. Any change of pace would have signaled my retreat. Predictably, I was surrounded as these soldiers fanned out before me, forming a perfect circle no less than fifty meters away. They all were armed with battle gear and abstract antidotes, the kind a man would use to slay a dragon: Silver nets and silver spears glistened in the dawning; steel swords tipped with silver just to slash the dragon's hide; golden bows with silver arrows to pierce the proudest heart; helmets with visors to block the dragon's petrifying glare.

They always did their business at dawn. It seemed the early morning light was the only one in which they placed their trust. Apparently that was the extent of their covenant with their Truth, because even though half of them set their total focus on me, the other half stood facing outward with their gazes fixed on the skies. All of them had their weapons drawn—spears at the ready, arrows strung, archers taut, their gazes averted, utterly prepared to Zen me to ground. Their actions were a paradox. They were ready to storm the cathedral yet somehow reluctant to do so without some omen from on High.

Finally, the Captain rode through their ranks, sweeping from side to side, saluting, dismounting, leaving his stallions to dance impatiently in the sun. He was a tower as humans go—six-and-a-half feet tall—all angle, muscle, bone and a tone that truly belied his age. Although I was tall for the men of that time, he even stared me down. He didn't let his expressions betray him, yet I could somehow tell he approved. There are badges that good men wear for one another.

"I think you know why I've come," he said. "To take the measure of you—to find in you an ally or to destroy you, for once and for all."

"You've aged," I said, like a long lost friend. "But the years have treated you well."

My observation sheathed a truth. He knew we'd never met. Yet there was a air about me that was all too familiar.

"You know me? You have seen me before?" he asked the rhetorical question. "Then you know what I'm about. And surely, you know what I must do." Slowly and with some ceremony, he drew his silver-tipped blade, slashing it through the air and motioning toward me. His sword stroke in the wind heralded all his warriors to turn, as all of them strung their bows with silver arrows.

"What I prepare to do is a ritual," he said. "If you are but a man, it will have no impact on you save to cleanse your dross vibration. Then I will honor you by killing you quickly, or whatever God ordains. It will be a fair fight, that much I assure you. There are standards we share, after all. That certain regard is the very least I can do. If you can kill me then be free to go, but I warn you here and now no man ever has—not one at least who's measured by flesh and bone.

"However…if you're something else, as I suspect you are, then this display will affect you in a totally different way—in a way any mystic creature would understand."

"And if I answer your Asking Prayer?" I challenged. I betrayed no sign of emotion, though clearly my candor had caused him to pause a second time.

"It won't matter," he answered, with only a tremor of fading hope in his voice. "Unless you are the One. And I don't perceive that happening. For it was clearly my understanding that young creature was mortally wounded, struck in the heart and murdered on the very same day."

"Then you've never heard of the Lightning Dragon? The one with the scar on his pecs?"

"Of course. The whole world has. But the Lightning Dragon is black as Satan's gate. This dragonette was brown and little more than an eaglet, though he certainly left his mark upon that afternoon."

"When he witnessed his brother's slaughter, he was little more than an egg. Dragons change color with age, as well you know."

"But not their purpose," the Captain insisted. I could see he'd been moved by what I'd said. My insights had bent his perceptions but not his intent. He signed the cross, convinced, no doubt, I was out to steal his soul.

I stopped him as gingerly as I knew how, taking meticulous time to unfold my recollections at the Lake of Brimbrod Shards. I didn't attempt to dramatize. That moment spoke for itself. Nevertheless I'd recounted those dirty details that only we two could recall—the vivisection of my brother, my sister's furious attack, my answer to the "Asking Prayer," RuSiva's mace in his chest. The mention of that still brought him to smart, even to this moment. But apparently that trick of reportrayal had been tried a few times before.

"What you describe goes beyond mere hearsay," he said, almost sadly, realizing there was something to it. "So you were a soldier to that infamous wizard, that stigma upon our race...But that was thirty years ago. You would have been but a infant."

"Unless, I was something else..." I observed. I let the words sink in, then slowly bared my chest to display the lightning scar upon it.

"I've heard the story," the Captain scoffed, "of Gudae and the God Tree, and the lightning when it struck and left us kinsmen to the bone.

"It's a legend in these parts by now, which is why we're still conversing. If you hadn't been so exceptional and led an exemplary life, the Citizens would have fallen on you and slaughtered you already. But as you've exhibited magical skills beyond their comprehension, and as your behavior is somewhat inconsistent to say the least, the duty has been brought to me to

determine your final fate. And I'm afraid at last the time has
come to dole it out."

"That still doesn't answer the question of my youthful
appearance. Does it, my Captain? Or can a soul change forms
like a suit of clothes?"

"A potion! An elixir. Wizards make them by the quart. So
you've sold your soul for perennial youth or have a cache of
Firestone. Whatever your pact, there are takers by the score. Or
perhaps you're a wizard yourself, in which case, I extend my
regrets. Most of them are as corrupt as whores and offer less
value for money. In any case the Asking Prayer will settle this
little dilemma, for you'll either vanish from sight right now, or
try to hard bargain me."

"But what if I'm not a wizard at all—neither man nor warrior.
What if I'm a dragon, and the very one you seek?"

I could tell my declaration had convinced him I'd gone mad,
either that or become possessed by a demon he would have to
purge. Refusing to draw out another word, he drew his sword
instead, scything it through the air while crying out the Asking
Prayer.

"*Ahhhtohhh!*" he intoned, thrusting the sword at me—the
first sign of the cross—from the crown of his head. "*Maaalkuth!*"
he added, pulling the heel of the hilt into his heart, then
pointing it at me again with ultimate menace. By the time, he
brought the sign to his left shoulder and cracked the air with the
mantrum, "*Vegadullahh!*" I had begun to match him breath for
breath.

"*Vegaburrahhh!*" he chanted.

"*Vegaburrrahhh!*" I rejoined his echo in contrapuntal solo.
My sword danced in the air like his, matching him point for
point. And though I'd only conducted this ritual once before, it
was my second nature now, perhaps more so than his. I
performed it even better than he and with greater facility, a point
lost neither on his soldiers nor on him.

"Ohlaahm!" I completed the mantra, even beating him to it, completing the sign of the cross and waiting for him to start the pentagrams.

Flaming stars of white hot light fired smartly from his mouth, dancing on his sword's point into the morning light. I answered every intonation until we were a only wren's breath apart, our performance a splendid symmetry of concert.

We were phrases in synchronism as he now invoked archangels to make his mission whole, to have done with the day and banish me into the gullet of Balliol himself. But I answered as I had done before in the innocence of my youth. Only this time I completed the game, something no creature had done, for to do so was to change the course of magic for all time.

"Rapha-el!" he cried.

And I repeated, "Rapha-el!" as if it were an oracle in our mass. And as he called upon these seraphic sources as familiars, I joined-in as it was my very right to do.

"Gabriel! Mikhael! Auriel!" The highest of Archangels were summoned with a flaming sword and a plea for intervention.

"Behind me stands Gabriel-el! On my right hand stands Mikhaaa-el!" he chanted, his pitch so deep and powerful it soared into the morning pouring like a hail of purifying fire to the valleys below. His sword now spewed forth shafts of light, laser-like and deadly for the wrong kind of creature to see.

For my part, I drank it in like a tonic. I echoed his summoning of spirits. By name, I invoked specific archangels, praying they'd intervene. Out of my mouth and the tip of my sword the light gushed as if from a fountain as pellucid and clear as only a light of heaven could be.

"Auriel!" I cried, beating him to the last mantrum, invoking the silver angel of the morning. Having done so I had helped to form the final configurations: the cross, the six-pointed star, the pentagrams. "As above, so below!" I anticipated, an ad-lib I felt appropriate to the moment. But by then we were engulfed in stars of flame and cross of light. "Before me flames the pentagram," I carefully intoned.

"Behind me shines my Father's six-pointed star," he sang in a canticle of joy.

"In the middle, in the light of God's love, stand I," I said.

"Stand I!" he gaped, in reply.

We faced the truth in one another, and through the tower of fire realized we were brothers of the sword. I had known it all along, had focused on this meeting and somehow presupposed that it would come to pass this way. Although it only struck me then, at that moment of highest truth, I understood at last what had transpired.

No one dared answer the Asking Prayer. The Shimbaghs were consumed in its speaking. Our Mystic Clans could but never would, for to do so would lead to their ruin. By allowing their fear to paralyze them, they had lost their voice to heaven, and had left themselves open to be slaughtered by "the Word." All they had ever needed to do was understand, reiterate and speak as I had done. Instead they'd given this holy act a new unholy meaning and turned the Asking Prayer into a banishing ritual that marked the End of Days.

It was not about to end mine, thank you. Although the Captain seemed intent, some residue of ego prevented him from acknowledging his error.

"Who are you?!" he roared, whipping his weapon around. Demons of denial now did their deadly dance behind his eyes. This was a *pun donor* with him, and he wouldn't let it pass. He couldn't accept that his sacred act had at last been answered, or that I was any more than just a man.

"I am..." I started to name my human self and declare that I was a holy warrior such as he. But though I tried to say 'Gudae' another name came forth. "Shartallion!" spewed from my heart and onto my tongue. "I am Shartallion XII, dragon of the Kiln! Son of Dager V out of Drilg the Fair! Grandson of Knot IV, initiator of the Shimbagh Wars!"

He didn't understand; none of them did. A young man speaking of himself as a Mystic Beast and conjuring names of dragons, merely convinced them further that I'd gone insane.

But where words often only confuse, manifestations have weight. And by daring to name my self again, I grew. I flowed like a fountain out of the man, shot forth like a spirit self full grown in my regalia—eighty feet of coal black dragon, spewing fire and flame, jagged lightning scar carved into my chest.

"I am the Lightning Dragon," I roared the thought with joy. "I am The Answerer!" My wings spread out. My thorny tail whipped round, ready to do its work.

Well, needless to say my sudden explosion was awesome to behold and scarcely served to calm the soldiers assembled. I hardly resembled a seraphim. My blackness blocked the sun, and the lightning that blared from my chest was the blinding beat of a warrior's heart.

Not entirely to my surprise, the Captain stood his ground, calmly motioning to his men to lock and load. They dropped their visors to shield their eyes from my petrifying glare, and before I could wink 100 arrows dipped in hemlock, were silver-tipped and aimed straight at my heart.

Please understand me here and now! These were not just any arrows. These were made of silver and forged to pierce my mystic hide. No matter what I might have done, they would have shot me down, for they'd executed a thousand such creatures in the course of their time. If I had attacked, they would have let go from a dozen different angles and brought me to ground before I'd uncorked a single gout of flame. If I had tried to fly, despite my speed, they would have let fly a fusillade that would cut me before I'd left the ground. I wished to God I'd mastered the fine art of disappearance, and vowed that if I survived this moment I would somehow learn. As it was I was a goner, and could do little more than accept the inexorable irony of my fate.

Here I was where I wanted to be, a dragon once again freed of the flimsy bonds of human frailty. And yet the price I was about to pay might end my dragon's life. I had a choice (one always does): to kick some butt and be killed, or beat a hasty retreat and die a coward.

Piss poor choice, I thought. Attack was the warrior's way, but I couldn't bring myself to harm these little men. That much in my nature had somehow not changed. I looked upon them as children; wicked children oftentimes, but children nonetheless, and given to children's mistakes. Besides, these were men whose mission ennobled them to their kind. They were the best of a sorry lot intent on a virtuous cause, and virtue always tends to give one pause.

It didn't correct my fate in the least. And the Captain was blind to my pleas. Even though I entreated him in his tongue, he now blocked his ears from me.

"Demon!" he ranted. "Prepare!" he shouted, and one hundred bows drew taught with arrows with a will of their own, when suddenly a warrior dashed from formation and ran to the old soldier's side. They conferred in low tones for a little while and motioned back toward me; they actually came to shout at one another, slamming fists into each other's breastplates, yet from everything I could surmise the younger warrior prevailed.

Slowly the Captain turned his gaze toward me, and through his eyes I could see that the light that once had failed was on again. Abruptly, he came out of the conference and, on his own, commanded the soldiers to lower their weapons while he scanned me incredulously.

I had a faith confirmed that morning which I'll never question again: The Laws of Manifestation are etched in steel. Everything we do for right or wrong comes back to us—in measures beyond measure. Even before the Captain turned, the young warrior had doffed his helmet, so I could see his face for who he was.

He'd been deformed when I had first known him. He'd been dead unto his heart, for this young soldier had been the munzel I had set free at the Crater. Even though I had done so capriciously and without a second thought, my random act of kindness had returned to me in kind. I remember him having sworn that he'd repay my generosity, and naturally I'd dismissed it as another good intention. But this young soldier had chosen this day to keep his covenant in a way that would save my life, for it came to light that this soldier was also the Captain's son.

"Father, this *is* the Lightning Dragon. The one I told you about, the one with the eyes that see inside the soul. His is the Clan with whom the ultimate bonding must be made. He is the One, the Answerer of the Prayer."

Everything is a cry for help or a prayer come to its answer, and the latter of these had passed its blessing down. The Captain stood transcended. His eyes were moist with joy. Waves of recognition rushed across his face, sank into his shoulder blades and charged into his heart. Freed at last from the burden he'd carried, he heaved a sigh to Heaven, dropped to one knee and said a prayer that uncaged the bird of his faith.

"It's done," he sighed. "Thank God! Thank God! Thank God, it's done at last! You're free to go, young dragon. So go now at your will! You've earned my respect and, so it seems, also my gratitude."

But this was not an ending of things. This was just a beginning! We had a field of life to cover, this leader of men and I. Rather than take my leave, I sat down and wafted my wing drying the ground beneath us for him to sit in counsel. In my softest dragon tones I made my purpose known.

"Not yet, my Captain. Before you go, there's much we have to discuss. And more, so very much more we have to do."

Canto 23

Severance

Large miracles often get lost in small.
One's perspectives determine the lot. So it had been that early
afternoon. Of all the wonders I'd known in my life, the greatest
was the one that followed. That I was transformed was now a *fait
accompli.* The Captain had seen to that. We were partners in a
dance to the end of the music. It had been orchestrated eons ago
while our souls had chosen this moment to go through the
motions and let our selves react.

The true transformation came with Gudae, and we hadn't
even noticed that he had not been altered in the least. In my
haste to return to my dragon self, I'd all but lost sight of him.
Now, he stood in our midst, superfluous to our match—a pawn
who'd been used and set aside and who now had to fend for
himself. (I had perceived that in the beginning, but I had been
dead wrong. My vanity was my folly, then as now.)

Gudae had not changed one whit. My having quit his physique had left this human being entirely intact. He was every bit the man I'd been, and possibly even more; he'd been allowed to become himself again. He appeared to be even more of me than I had been of myself when I had borrowed his shell and shared his thoughts. And yet there was a grain of purity that he had been denied, one that, through it all, had grown inside us both.

For a time, our discussions became tripartite—Gudae, the Captain and I, each with his own agenda to attend. The Captain would continue his crusade a more enlightened man. I would return to my kinsmen at the Crater. Gudae would go back to the City, a vindicated warrior, soon to be its leader once again.

I bade the Captain wait for me while I passed the coming hours with this fine young soul whose physical shell I'd shared. And I offered Gudae the greatest gift I could possibly bestow on a man—a chance to see the world from a sky creature's saddle.

"I'll fly you home, old friend," I offered. "It's a three-day journey from here, unless you ride the wind on the wings of a dragon."

I felt him stand astride my neck, his hands on the crown of my head and shared the surge of elation from his heart. We could hear the mountain breezes whistle songs of celebration at this bonding of the races, man and beast, angels in accord.

Gudae would become a priest of his people, their spiritual fountainhead and leave a legacy of civilization they would never have known without him. Was it he or was it I who'd brought that weight to bear? I wondered, but my human friend did not.

"We're all vessels for the Eucharist. Nothing more," he said with a master voice now deeper than the one I'd given him. "Whatever good we do on earth only comes through our surrender, when we let our Christ come through and our egos go."

His words shot through me like a spear. Had I been the student, and not he? Had I been the apprentice, and he the hidden master? Why was it that everyone these days seemed so much wiser than I? Or was I finally somehow growing wise? Nonetheless, I was unconditionally proud of this formidable warrior. We had parted a better man and a better dragon.

I brought him to earth without ceremony, setting him down above the plain. And for a while we set our gazes together upon the City. We both wept for the bonds we'd shared and the woman we had loved, and the brotherhood we'd known with one another.

"It's time to start anew," he said. "Or does one ever start anew?"

"Everything is a link in the chain. So this too has been. We'll meet again when the time is right, for our souls' paths intertwine."

"You've saved my life."

"And you saved mine. Even on this morning."

"Everything we do comes back a thousand-fold."

"And more."

"And more."

I realized as Gudae did that we'd long since become of one mind; we could now complete the phrases without the words. Even though our bodies had split, we had shared our thoughts for so long. I had given him my bravado. He'd bequeathed me his poetry. Recalling now, I realize I'd struck the better bargain.

For a moment, our disparity in size confounded us. I couldn't embrace him as an equal in physique. I merely gave him a gentle brush of the soft underside of my wing and felt fiery ingots stream down my face as he left my life forever.

I watched him as he walked away and entered the City gates, knowing that we'd never meet again, though I'd hear of him and be most proud whenever his name appeared in the archives of founding civilizations.

Canto 24

The Time

The Captain had waited for as long as I took. I had no doubt he would. We were partners on a mission we were doomed to complete. As I returned, I found that he had sent his soldiers off to another slope to wait while he conferred with me in private council.

It was then I took the opportunity to give him all my insights, to clear up his perceptions as it were. Age had neither stilled his fervor nor drained his energy, but now he'd begun to doubt his knack for sizing up his rivals, and nothing can make a man more tentative than that. Yet I knew there had been occasions when he'd let a mystic creature go, neither banishing nor taking them down with his salvos of silver arrows.

"A judgment call," he offered. "I merely relied on instincts. They served me well enough in the past. But today's a different story."

"And what do your instincts tell you now?"

"They tell me I've often been wrong…perhaps more often than not. That weighs heavily on my heart, more than you know."

"What if I told you there were ways that you could tell the difference, by studying a creature's energy fields and how they hold their mien?"

"It's an attitude, I know that much," the Captain shared with me. "I feel it in my gut. It's just a knowing that you get—an inner truth."

"It begins that way. But this is how it ends," I tried to explain to him but realized that he'd never see the light unless I showed him. Summoning the energy of every gem within me, I tried to become for a fading moment what I'd been trained to be—a gemstone shower, a tower of light, a luminous fulguration, a godshead brow of flowing heavenly hues.

God help me! I suddenly realized that I was out of shape for this. I had let my aura wither, and I wasn't sure I could buy it back. Living in a pygmie's skin could do that sort of thing; there were so many diversions, so many carnal distractions. Finally, after what had taken all night and part of the following morning, I prayed a prayer that lifted me out of myself. I cannot share the invocation; its mantra is encoded. But the main thing is, it unbolted the Gates of Eden. At last I felt my angel's archways open until a radiant shower of brilliant luminous rays plumed out of them, the light from God's left eye. It was a show of shows if I say so myself. I've never seen its like. I doubt if I'll ever see its like again.

Needless to say, the Captain and his soldiers were impressed. Yet not even I was prepared for what was to follow: Not only had I become a conduit for this tower of illumination, I was now the vessel through which a thousand angels spoke. There was a choir of them going through me, each with its own sweet solo, each with its special messages to which I also gave audit. For once in my life I felt utterly useless, a channel for higher powers, an instrument upon which a heavenly concerto was being played. It would have been to say the least a blow to my youthful ego, had I not remembered what Gudae had said just the afternoon before.

"We are vessels for the Eucharist," he too had recited the mantra. I suppose that should have been enough to humble me. As it was, I might have fought back at being used in such a way, or at least have sulked a bit, or groused beneath my breath.

But I was a listener too, and heard along with the Captain a choir of high regard and strict instruction. Dragon or man, Mystic Beast or eternal warrior, we had a pact to fulfill.

"When the time comes for the final battle, you two will lead the armies. You are the Chosen to carry the Holy Fire. Of all the mystic men and beasts, you two alone will have the insight to clearly differentiate the evil from the good.

"You are the Answerer of the Prayer. The Captain is the Asker. You hold the key to unlocking the door but not to the final game. Once you have done this, wait for the Time that you'll have to reverse what you've done. Meanwhile, hold your own as best you can. You will be greatly outnumbered, but the holy task is with you. *Discern!* This alone will be your righteous armor.

"You, young dragon have the greater task and the far, far greater burden. For when this war of souls is over your vigil has just begun. It's part of the debt that you must pay; it is your soul's assignment. Just know to keep your faith and it will overcome your doubt."

Not the sunniest forecast, no matter how many angels sang it. No matter how many good deeds I performed, it seemed there was always more to do. And words like "burden" never put me in the best frame of mind to begin with. It was as if I had been the most damnable angel in all the universe. Now I was being told that my mind could no longer discern. But discernment was the learned dragon's greatest abstract skill. Along with other Mystic Beasts, it's what we did best of all. Now it was being implied that we were somehow short of the mark. Yet I knew better; I'd been around. I'd seen it all by now. And nothing could astound one more than to see the Clan in action.

A unicorn could easily sniff an enemy a week away, could steal the light with blinding speed and disappear long before a hunter could load his quill. The Chimera (an affable creature as much maligned a we) could charm the clouds just by clacking his tongue, and draw a storm down on his enemies that could shut down any day. The gryphon, we all know by now, was any creature's match, and knew no challenge except the sting from the nasty Slavern's claw. The Kohmm, those who had survived, had poison enough to sting an army into defeat—and even at a distance could spit venom half a league. The Mantilough beggared all description. (Were they angels, after all?). They could find new life in a ray of light; few men had even seen one. After all, how could one hope to capture a song on the evening mist? The Rahntish were the winged deer with antlers made of poison, with faces of fawns and voices of doves and razor sharp platinum hooves. And the Dolphin masters purified the seas and kept us clear as to purpose—of how to thrive in atmospheres other than our own.

As for the dragon! Well, enough said. There were none who could match us in battle. We were the Thunder of Heaven and the Scourge of Hell. The Shimbagh wars had proved that time and again, but proving ourselves was what we were here to do.

So why was all this being said? Why were these holy dictums pouring onto the mountain slopes from some angels perched in my throat? It was as if the end were coming near for all of us. Or the beginning of the end, which was even worse.

It had all taken place in a flicker, a butterfly's faded sigh. And just as soon as the light had filled me, it was gone again, and a chorus of beings vanished with it who would not return to me. I was glad of that, I don't mind admitting. In retrospect I can only imagine what might have been taken for this. Words from the dragon's mouth might be construed as grist for the minion's mill —a legion of demons upon which some fundamentalist hack could feed his most lurid fantasies.

Still I knew what would come, and so did the Captain. When the time came the task had been handed us to put the cap on the Door where Evil dwelled.

To add a thicker texture to this, the Captain let me in on some of the dragon hunters' multifarious traps RuSiva and others like him had laid. And he called back his troupe to share their insights into the Sorcerer's tricks.

"It is a matter of no small obsession to waste you one and all. For that the Magpie devotes his every waking moment. Unfortunately for the Mystic Clan, he's getting to the point where he can wipe out numbers with a stroke. Herds of unicorns, flocks of chimera, even flights of gryphons—the pogrom continues with little about to check it. The methods are now 'scientific,' sanctified and blessed by the churches of men. It seems there isn't room enough for other exceptional creatures, except 'our kind' to rule upon this Earth."

"I realize a little too late that I was among the worst but thought myself the best. All the same, the quest still scalds my sense of purpose."

"Your quest is good. Your intentions are pure, even if your aim was off. Now, at least, you see the light. Now you can 'discern.'"

"That remains to be seen," the old warrior answered. A shudder crossed his back, a specter of all he'd done and might do again, were he not guided. Yet now he couldn't help but wonder what would lie ahead. "I've always roamed from crusade to crusade, to crush monster after monster. Now, for the very first time in my life, uncertainty marks my days."

I spent the weeks that followed with him, and trained his men in "sighting," in how to see with the third eye that they'd been given.

"The aura makes the difference," I said, "between the creatures of light, and those who have gone bad—the Shimbagh kind, the Doppelgangers who've let their angelic insight die."

I think they understood me. At least a few of them did—the Captain's son and those who had been munzels. As for the rest, well...time would tell. And time for us all was running shorter than even we had realized.

I don't remember what day it was, but even now I recall the moment when the sky above us blackened as if a mountain had been spat from the sun, hurling now toward us like a fiery meteor —a presence no less imposing than my father. Yet as he came barreling toward us, his wide spread nares spouting spigots of flame, there was a note of resignation about him that only I could detect.

The Captain's soldiers to the man drew their weapons and prayed. They'd never seen a dragon quite like this. Even though I was accustomed to feeling my father's presence, I couldn't help but notice that he had actually grown a bit larger. And the myriad scars that marred his body seemed to have multiplied as if every blow ever struck in every combat had found its way to him.

I put the Captain and his men at ease, if one could do such things when forced to confront the fury of a flying mountain.

"Rest easy," I said. "This creature you see above you is my father. You can place your trust in him."

"Upon your word, I rest," the Captain intoned. "But warning young Shartallion! Your father's reputation even in the world of magic is checkered to say the least."

Dager came to rest with unexpected grace, like a floating autumn leaf to a welcoming stone. Even his voice bore a trace of unaccustomed gentility one puts into place only when bearing bad news.

"You've made it back to the *real* world. I'm pleased," he said, giving a brush with his wing. But I could tell even as he flew down that all was not right with him. His trademark panache was laced with a measure of regret. He cut to the chase. I'd expected as much, yet never had an inkling of what would follow. It was then I began to realize I'd left my prescience behind. This was the flaw in the dragon being to whom I'd now returned.

"The Time indeed has come," he said. "The Shimbaghs have struck the first blow, and spat it quick as snake's tongue at our heart. I can't go into it for now. But the results are devastating. They're more powerful than I realized. And they've got brass balls to boot. By now, they outnumber us fifty-to-one, and they're spat out *en masse* like spores upon the wind. The Fallen One's whores work overtime to bear him armies of children. It's as if every negative thought gives birth to his own.

"So finish your business here dear Sharto. The worst is yet to come. You see, my son, they've savaged the Crater of Nebul."

Canto 25

Sabotage

Even at a distance one could see the decimation. The Nebul was a cinder, a ruin of itself. Its flaming hearth, once the pride of dragonkind, was devastated, hollowed out with only charred remains of those who had fallen to defend it. From high above it looked so small, a pock on the face of Terra, but as we drew near we could feel the harvest of its condition.

A skeleton crew of sentinels had been left to guard when the Shimbaghs struck. The rest had been sent off to attend the "campaigns." Little did any of us ever suspect the Shimbaghs would have the gall to take a thrust at the dragon in his lair. Yet who would have known us better than our hideous mirror selves? Underestimating our foes had been our first and greatest mistake. Before the sun would set it would not be our last.

The dragon praetorian guards who'd remained were not an easy lot to cower. Even though less than a dozen in number they were warriors to their core. Still, the odds must have been overwhelming, and to the one they were struck down. Now, they lay half-open, vivisected, rotting in the sun, either dead or very soon to taste the fruit of that dark kiss.

Some might have been tended or even made well, had there been any blue Thral melons left to soothe them. But the cache of the Kohmm had either been destroyed or carted away by the invaders; this had no doubt been the reason for the raid.

By the door where the gift of the Thral was kept, bodies of munzels were stacked. A score had been slain to the man. (I say to the man, for each of one in his dying returned to his human state. At least death had provided each of them with a key to their honor.)

The same could not be said for the dying dragons. To the one they'd had been eviscerated, their chests slit open and used for vessels from which the Dark Eucharist was drunk. (I had to note that only men took time to kill this way—to justify their acts of mayhem by cloaking them in ritual. How many pygmies had taken this host? I wondered, but did not wonder long, for I heard a voice boom out the body count with justifiable rage.

"More than you can count," Red Rhonda sounded, in a raging sage's voice, one who had heard and seen it all too often to redoubt. "Of all the monsters I've ever known, these were the worst of the lot: Men! Numbers to boggle the mind who've sold their souls to angels far, far darker than themselves!"

The few dragons who survived had borne the scars of their courage, and had trophies by the score to mark their passage. Still, to the last they'd nearly been maddened by experience of seeing their comrades so methodically dispatched. There were only a handful who had made it through: one or two guard dragons, the wounded Crimson Rhonda who'd managed to keep her warrior perspectives intact.

"They came like a swarm," she swaggered, breathlessly, proud she'd survived the attack. Taking a swig of blue Thral wine, she posted on the horn of her tail. "I've never seen such numbers before, even in the thickest battle. Their forces are truly Legion. And this was just a raid!"

Urgently, I felt myself scanning the walls of the crater, combing the slits and crannies for signs of life. I didn't dare to admit to myself that I was actually worried, fretting that my grandfather Knot had not survived. Had his half-cast dreams of grander days, his life in two dimensions, finally cost him his own in the one we held dearest? Yet somehow I knew that this old soul had written the book on survival, that whatever the cost he'd see the game to the end.

"You sell us short with your worry, Sharto. I'll outlast you all. Surely you have the gift to see that far ahead. This is not the only place for a higher soul to play. I've already found those other paths to freedom."

Knot had awakened from his dragone fantasies long enough to lay waste a cordon of Shimbaghs, and had done so with the passing of a wing. I could tell by the pile of remnants they'd met their match in him. Yet I couldn't help but be haunted when I saw that all that remained were mere shreds, as if these pathetic embodiments had been but a figment of some darker mind. Their remains, like their identities, were shrouded in veils of illusion that not only cloaked their intent but also their existence.

"Ah, but that's the lesson in this. War is the final deceiver...when one's adversary stands in the mirror before him."

As Knot V spoke, I realized I had truly only seen him in his other gentler self in the Ether of Dor. His studied repose at the Nebul had probably been a ruse, his guise that let us sate our expectations of what he *should* be. He wasn't what he appeared to be—a toothless dragone straddling the afterlife, lost in a codger's dreams. He was a warrior like my father, less physically imposing perhaps, but more of a force than any of us dreamed. I well remembered Sagro in the Chthonic Schools below, and how I'd once taken him lightly. Never again would I make the same mistake.

Knot had been severely wounded; that we could clearly see. His underwing bled in profusion, and his armor plate was rent.

Nonetheless, he bore the moment with pride. He had somehow managed to stitch it up and seal it with his own fires. He'd even salvaged a small Thral melon to salve his copious wounds.

"We gave them one hell of a taste today!" he bellowed, just like a bull out of school. "There must have been five thousand of them. They swarmed the Crater like rats at a flood—Khados and kingus, demons, serpents and Slaverns, insidious Doppelgängers, and ten dozen phalanxes of men—Shimbaghs of every description and every name, and some I'd never seen, as if they'd been spawned in a hellish womb only yesterday. There was even mirror of myself I saw at the beginning. To be sure, I slew him first lest he take my soul! The likeness was too striking to ignore. That's part of the plan, I'm sure, to match us with mirrors to create the ultimate confusion."

Despite what I had once taken for wisdom, Knot's ravings were those of a monger, as if some deep-seeded bloodlust had robbed him of his reason. The light in his eye had been rekindled, as if Combat were his only god. And it struck me then that this was his dream come true.

Yet, somehow I couldn't help but feel as if none of this had been real. It was like the Chthonic Schools all over again. Even though the smell and taste of blood was in the air. It was ours, and little of theirs that now remained.

At last, I'd begun to realize that of all the scorched bodies I'd seen, the Shimbaghs had scarcely left a trace. An ash, a bone, a residue were all we could ever find, as if they were creatures of Mind and little more. Yet how could they be and still wreak such havoc in the world? Were they merely Doppelgängers? And if so, what then were we?

"I don't understand," I gave voice to my wonder. "It's as if our enemies have no substance. It's as if we're fighting specters of ourselves."

"Oh, they're real enough," my father answered. "I've the scars to show for that. It's the aftermath that bewilders even the deepest seers among us. The Shimbaghs simply disintegrate. They readily fall out of form. It seems they have no substance and less of a soul. It's as if for us to discover the truth would ruin the mind that made them, and would shatter the tricky puzzle that he weaves.

"They don't fight as well as we do. They're no match for us one on one. But their numbers! My God, their numbers! They flock like fleas! They fight with no feeling. Their hearts are as hollow as holly. It's as if we're cutting papier maché when we lash out with fang and claw."

"Except for the human beings," Rhonda noted. "They're flesh and blood enough, though they seem to have left all compassionate thought behind. They're driven without explanation—they, the 'rational' beast, have lost their minds and pawned their souls for a trifle."

Rhonda, with the haunted look of a holocaust remembered, gestured her numb recollection of the hours gone by. Knot, a Thral melon forked on his tail, swabbed it across Rhonda's wound, a yawning gash that continued to bleed without clotting. The melon took effect. In a short time the wound had sealed and looked as if it would heal without a scar.

"They grow smarter. That's the danger," Knot added. "And unless I am mistaken, they've struck the blow they've never had the guts to strike before."

"Against the Crater!" I assumed.

"No, no," the dragone answered. "This was just a diversion. Unless I miss my guess they've gone for the Kohmm."

§§§§§§§

The Sea of Thral the following morning

was awash in blue-violet hues. Tourmaline waves scaled soft jade cliffs and salved the caves above them, as if to heal the empty holes inside. Below on the rocks, bobbing on the restless foam of the tides. floated the amethyst shard remains of the entire Klan of the Kohmm.

This had been their last sanctuary, the place they had hidden from man. The dragons had guarded it well until recent days. In

417

our fervor for the Shimbagh Wars, in this waltz with our darker sides, we'd forgotten to honor our pledge to our crystalline sisters. The sentries we had provided in past had lately been taken away. In our arrogance we had "just known" they would not attack. We were equally deluded into thinking that our sisters could successfully defend themselves. How easily the lessons of time are forgotten. What perishing things our memories can be. It had happened before that our gentle sisters had nearly been extinguished. Now someone had finished the job —only they'd done it right this time.

Their spindly arachnid bodies spilled out on a mournful sea, hoisted through the brine like shattered goblets. Some conscious collective that lived beyond had somehow kept them afloat. Yet I knew the time of the Kohmm had come and gone. Hours passed like moments while we watched them sink beneath the surface, one by one on a race to the ruins of time. Our sisters, our nurses, the wards of our healing had fallen from this table of grace. Could we be far behind? I winced as I wondered.

It was such a dangerous game we'd played, this endless righteous war, and we had made the worst mistake of all: We had taken our foes for granted. Now, they'd eradicated the single source that rendered us invulnerable; the holy purple melons that healed our wounds. Without the Thral melons the dragon's wounds were worse than those of men. Now, we'd be slower to heal and longer to die. The madness that came with the bite of the Shimbagh would daunt us to the end. Now we were just as mortal as the rest.

No worse for us than for our brothers of the Mystic Clan—the unicorn, the rahntish, the chimera and the gryphon, all relied upon this holy fruit of healing. So now when they were wounded they too would know the Pain, the agony of having their immortality stripped away. But the dragons had been its guardians, and had failed! It was a point of honor we could not regain.

"It's as if the world of magic were somehow being rubbed away," I heard Rhonda say, in hopeless wonder.

"There's still a source," my father muttered, "far beneath the earth. But they're as rare as gold, and the spiders stark raving mad."

I knew he meant the Kohmm below, the ones in the Chthonic Realms, but finding them would be like striking a bargain with the Fallen One himself. There was no doubt in my mind at least that we'd come to the final game. And the Shimbaghs had seized the day and left us all of the night to ponder.

At sundown, a chorus of Vyngorchim circled over the Tourmaline Sea, singing a lamentation that swept through the sky. As I heard their requiem choir for our sisters, hot tears seared down my cheeks. But was it for the Kohmm or for the Dragon that I wept?

§§§§§§§

By night the light of our rage scorched the sky; the Crater of Nebul was crammed. Every dragon bull and queen had come from a thousand miles. We war-drummed our tails with the force of a temblor, causing the earth to quake and the clouds to howl. The stage was set, the iron was cast, the forces all were gathered. We'd fly into the very throat of Hell.

Knot now stood in the glory of the moment. Knot, who had started it all, sat in righteous repose while my father spoke. The dragone poised on the throne of the prelate marked by a Diamond Eye, assumed his emeritus role as the head of our Clan. He was silent, majestic, beset with grief, yet quietly proud of his chosen, though I noticed the wounds he had suffered had brought his aura to fade. Would he even be there to share in the moment once the battle was joined? Could he who had flourished five thousand years last even one more day?

Dager the Mountain, dragon field marshal, spoke with an orator's tone the words of the zealot brought to the moment of truth.

"This is the hour of our destiny! The reason we've been brought here—to sweep the Mystic Kingdom of all infection. And yet for us to do this comes with a sacrifice, for we must give the last breath of ourselves. The fate of the universe rides upon our wings!"

As my father spoke the timber of his voice rose like a fire to the roar, crackling with emotion as it grew. The dragon bulls and dragon queens chanted their approval, howling fiery canticles through the night.

Somehow I realized that I had heard this all before, sung in a score of lifetimes in a dozen other worlds. And though I was still very young in this body, I had grown old in this soul. I took my leave and launched into the sky. Into the darkness under the stars I climbed, hearing the chimes of my own clear thoughts come back like long lost friends. I supposed there was no other course than the one on which we had embarked. Nevertheless, I suspected that we'd set this game for ourselves. We were armed. We were primed. We were dragons and angels. We had owned the universe as we knew it. Yet there was no question to me at least that our liege was slipping away.

We'd be allowed to fulfill our task, to deliver the pygmie from darkness, but the pygmie I knew still carried the Darkness deep in the core of his soul. Why should we pass the Scepter of Truth to the singular creature in the universe who still played both sides of the game?

I circled in silence higher and higher, spiraling upward through clouds crested white while the crater below shrank from sight an infinitesimal speck, the thundering war cries from the mystic clans sounding more like the prayers of a child. We had paid the price, it seemed, and would pay it through all time simply for bringing the truth to a world so poor in sanity. What curse had the Mystic Beasts incurred to deserve this kind of exclusion? All we had done was to bear the light and to bring it to shine for all time. Was it that we had brought it or that we had caught it that seemed to condemn us now? And the awful notion then struck me: We were no longer part of the plan; we were expendable.

The revelation stopped me cold. Suddenly the clouds through which I soared took substance, and I found refuge on a cumulus shoulder. Then, no sooner had I done so than I realized that I had not searched and yet had been guided here. Silhouettes of other dragons carved their way out of the cover, as I saw many loved ones waiting for me as if they had summoned me here.

Skye, the serene, the inimitable Blue, the wisest dragon of all —he had risen above the Crater and into the ethers. Before the meeting had even begun, he had avoided the posturing, had eschewed the strutting egos and declarations of valor. He knew as I knew it was from on high that the insights would come to save us.

Drilg my mother, the golden hued queen, princess of intercession too had found this place of places where conscience had regained respect. She didn't speak but glowed instead like a lambent guiding light. Her thoughts had drawn me up here. That was a cosmic constant.

Since my departure into the cycle of man, Drilg had detached herself from the world and had taken holy hejira until *The Time* —until I had returned.

In my heart of hearts, my inner sense, I knew they'd take this path. They had always been outside of the realm—within yet without the warrior fixations that colored the dragon's cloth. And yet what caught me by surprise was to see my half-brother Pod holding quorum in this colloquy in the sky. I just knew this newfound Vyngorch warrior would be breaking breath in the Crater, pounding chest and thumping tail with the best of the dragon bulls. Fighting at my father's side in battle after battle had galvanized this tentative hybrid dragon and turned him into a force. Even his awkward gait now took stature while the look of a sage creased his brow, and beholding him now gave me the presage that he would sire a clan.

We touched wings, all of us brushing one another gently in silent greeting and fond recall—preparing the communion of spirits that spoke with one heart.

"The die is cut. The choice is made. The Shimbagh has made it for us. Yet we play into the Fallen One's hands by launching a direct assault." Skye sighed. It was the first time I'd ever heard him utter a negative thought.

"It is my life mate's only way to fly into evil's face, to look it in the eye and stand before it. This way he believes he stands in the fire, and all who stand there with him will be vindicated by the virtue of their Truth. It is a gesture long on courage and very short on wit." My mother noted the irony of the time.

"What amazes me most is the nature of Knot," I heard my own voice say. "He has the knowledge of age but not the wisdom." Yet I sensed that he was a Diamond Dragon, and therefore knew it all, that he could see the future clearly and bring it all to bear.

"Even to this moment," Drilg said, "your grandfather sees every role—even the ones we must play to help the cause. Even though it imperils our souls and sacrifices our bodies, we must finish the task and amend our lives both present and past."

As if my mother had limned the words, I could see the images clearly. The *we* had turned into *I* and all eyes to *me*. Either my prescience had entirely returned or I was just picking up clues, but it didn't take a master of deduction to see that I was once again chosen to set upon a quest to rescue us all. Please understand, I felt quite flattered that I had again been ordained. Nevertheless, the thought had struck me that this was one Hell of a deal. Once in a while it wouldn't have hurt if someone else could enjoy the honor. After all, how much did our past lives need amending? With all the tasks that I'd been assigned, mine must have been have been some collection."

"The Vyngorchim are clearly unready. The Gryphons remain in doubt as to their commitment and their willingness ever to help us out. That leaves us with a Hobson's Choice: to take on the Shimbagh ourselves, undermanned and backed by only half the Mystic Clan; or to exhaust every avenue, pull every string, and make uncertain pacts—with the Beasts of the Sea and the Dragons of the North." Skye, like a field marshal sketching a plan, ignored my private thoughts, focused instead on the logistics, plotted the tactical course, a course it was clear to me that entailed its share of compromise.

The Beasts of the Sea were an uncertain lot. Though their motives were clearly free from taint by the demons of what we call ego, they couldn't often relate to the foibles of their brothers of land and air. What we did to one another was of little concern to them, unless what we did affected the waters below. In this case the universe was at stake, at least the one as I knew it, so the NaanWorm and monsters of the deep could be turned to support our cause. Please understand, these were not the great fish as you know them. These were only the creatures that a Neptune could have spawned—many tentacled, multi-headed Gorgonesque old beasties, the nightmares of many a mariner for chiliads yet to come.

As for the Dragons of the North, there wasn't a sorrier lot, a cut above a Shimbagh at the best. Yet once in a while, a bolt of redemption fired across their mien and flawed them with what might have passed for devotion.

Or so I had heard.

Of course, one wished to believe these rumors, especially when one considered that one's own sister was now their reigning queen.

"Your sister Seti can be converted," I heard my mother say. "She has a good heart beneath her tough warrior's hide."

"Then you should be the one, dear mother, to make plain our cause. For if she reveres anyone in the world it would certainly be you." It certainly wouldn't have been me, I thought, but didn't need to say it. I was with the most potent clairaudients of our clan.

"It *is* you, Shartallion. Your sister requests you to be our emissary. In her way she respects what you've done, and admires what you have become. Perhaps she's a little jealous too, but that's part of the North Dragon's Kiln—to loathe what they are and belittle what they are not."

Even when Skye was passing the buck, he could be at his most persuasive. He could shift a burden without ever raising a doubt. I knew for certain that my dear sibling Seti had no fascination with me. Her heart was quite as well armored as her pecs. And with her perverted sense of humor, she'd get me to fly halfway around the world just so she could reject me and have the last laugh. This I could have dealt with had I not heard the capper, that I also had to woo the SkyMaster, my own beloved Gryphon bride. It wasn't that she wasn't splendid or that I didn't adore her as much as I feared the disappointment of seeing her out of form. As man to woman, as Gudae to Shala, we'd bonded in a way that transcended all the boundaries of physique. Yet it was there and only there I had felt our souls mate, our flames burn as one for all time.

Alone in the sky it wasn't so much a love as it was a combat, a test of passion from which no one emerged unscathed.

Still, it was *The Time*—the time all conflicts would be broached, all fates would be crossed, all contracts closed, all issues resolved. So would this one be. I was excited and depressed at the prospect. At least the issue would be known. I would taste my mate in the sky, and see her once again; perhaps for the very last time.

§§§§§§§

We brushed wings and said goodbye, all

with some trace of finality. The next time we met, if we met at all, it would be at the mouth of Hell. Nevertheless, our silent love cut through the angst like a song. I took flight and my half brother Pod came winging with me, a reason I suspected that went beyond mere filial fondness.

"They're wrong, you know. High souls though they are, Skye and your mother are wrong. The Vyngorchim will be ready!" As Pod spoke, he exuded a trembling sense of purpose, though somehow the force of his conviction was tossed by a mocking wind. The further we flew, the stiffer it grew, and the more my brother protested. "I've trained them myself, and you'd be amazed at just how far they've come."

"They still have far to go, little brother." Truth like a reflex flew from my mouth; I hadn't meant to say it yet somehow already knew. The only Vyngorch truly up to the task was Pod himself. "But with you to lead them…" I added, ever the tactful warrior. But in this case the knowledge that I had boundless faith in him was not enough. Pod withdrew, peeled away from me, as if someone had stung him with a spear.

"We'll be there!" he insisted, albeit a bit too much. "The nation of Vyngorch will be ready to do battle. And we will be a force with which to reckon."

"If you believe it that much…"

"Because it's the truth!"

"Then I accept it as truth—as the truth I see in you. This is the time for us to heal. There'll be wounds soon enough for all."

He relented. Even though the gusts grew torrential and blew him back in my wake, he stayed with me, posting himself like a strong right wing to escort me through the storm. I waved him off and said goodbye.

"I believe in you," I called, feeling somehow in my heart of hearts that some horrid test would await him. It was then I knew, I must do more than toss him patronizing aftertones over my shoulder; I had to offer him hope. Despite my sense of urgency and the ever-worsening storm, I flagged him toward a mountain peak where we both used the time to rest. It was there I chose to share with him my darkest secret and greatest pride, that I had become the father of a novel set of offspring.

"Born of my union with the Gryphon Queen, spawned by our human hosts we gave our birth to the usual twins in a most unusual way—a Slavern male, comely beyond words but with more than his sisters' cunning, and an evil streak that could split the water simply by showing his face."

Pod shuddered, fearing the worst I think, but he'd already heard that side. The good news struck him another way, and almost brought him to tears.

"With him was born a Vyngorchim Princess, the very first of her kind, more exquisite than any creature on this planet. So angelic was she in her slightest gesture, so flawless in her soul that my only fear is that she's simply too perfect to stay long on this planet. Skye came forth to take her from me, and gives her his protection. Under his wing, she could find no more loving a sponsor, no more enlightened a guide. I know he will reveal her to you whenever this trial has passed. But to show her now, to reveal her secret, would expose her to assassins.

"It is this vision I bring you, brother. The Vyngorchim have in their stars a way to a nation, a mother to raise them, a savior to honor their kind. So you see my brother, though you do your race honor, you're no longer one of a kind. Whatever befalls us at that Darkest Door, it will not be the *coup de grace* for you or your clan."

Although I was certain Pod could not grasp all that I had told him, it was enough to bring him to silence and send him on his way. On the contrary, he stayed with me, even kept up through the storm. It was as if the truth I'd told him had forged him in new fires, the hot blood of a gritty warrior with a future worth fighting for. He stayed with me a league or more, and I swore I could hear him singing with a hymn that cut through the tempest like a laser in the darkest night.

Eventually, the storm, with icy teeth, chewed its way between us, causing Pod to drift from sight like a part of me torn away. I felt him slip back to the South, knowing as I flew that the kingdom to which I traveled now only had passage for one. I lowered my head and pierced the wind's armor as it poured in from the North, aware that I, the Lightning Dragon, would soon meet an old friend.

Canto 26

The North

Korlig! His icy breath preceded him. His furies, like a school of darts, stung me as I flew, hurling themselves at me to drive me back. I could feel their blizzard teeth sink-in as they dashed to cut my face, trying to take the measure of my mettle. Why did they waste their time? I wondered. Surely they knew by now that no force on this Earth could stay me from my task. The question was rhetorical; it was simply this wind god's way. He couldn't bear to have anyone resist him.

I was coming to the morning sky. The sun tore through a curtain of clouds to shine its light upon me, a guiding ray that creased my right wing to keep me on my course. Korlig thundered in and slammed the door, ripping at my armor. His breath in vicious sweetness pressed me toward the ground, then inexplicably raised me up again. His face filled my horizons as he furled his furious brow, then twisted it into a mocking laughter that rocked the heavens on high. And for a moment, I was certain I saw a glint in his eye.

"What brass balls you have," he crackled, "to come up here on your own. Only the Sound Stealer, the Lightning Dragon would have the gall to brave this hail of fury. If you had as much sense as you have gumption, you'd have stayed much closer to ground, taken your time and avoided the wrath of the mighty. But not this one; not a chance in Hell! He would climb to the lips of Heaven! If he has another name it must be Hubris! Well, you arrogant S.O.B. I'll give you this much due: You don't think twice about flying into the face of opposition."

If I hadn't known this windgod better, I'd have sworn he was glad to see me. As it was he lifted me up and carried me higher and higher, onto the planes, into the *zone* where no current could hold me hostage.

"I'm giving you safe escort," he said, "because the Cause is all, because I hate the Fallen One and everything he stands for. But I warn you my young Dragon Prince, not everyone feels that way. My brothers the Tarewinds have their share of things to say for him. Some pay him a ration of compliments, some spit when they hear his name, and some in these climes would do their damndest to harm you along the way.

"The same goes for the dragons here. They're a very strange lot indeed—partly warrior, partly poet, and partly the Devil's own. Don't get me wrong. None claim their allegiance. They're proud of their independence and spoil for a fight at the very first drop of the gauntlet. They're nasty, feisty quarrelsome bastards and cannibals to boot. And the lame and meek among them often end up on a platter. Your sister's managed to hold her reign, though only God knows how she's done it—by crushing and taming the most obstreperous dragon canaille on Earth. Their style of living isn't exactly the epitome of grace. In fact, you might say it's revolting even to these old, savage eyes."

Korlig's voice was never calm. In fact he howled more than spoke. Yet I could see in his cloudburst of a face a marked trace of concern. For whom? I wondered. I was quite certain, it couldn't have been for me. How much I had to learn in those days about power and its source.

Korlig, with a single breath, tore the clouds away, unveiling a slate grey sky and a jaw of canyons that yawned before us in a monstrous mocking grin. Dying trees and darkening mists and scorched-out husks of castles marked a path of plunder that went on for leagues. What little life remained in this realm had been long since driven to ground, into shadowy hidden towers that desperate princes find. Even now a herd of terrified deer ran roughshod over its young just to escape the slightest hint of my shadow. Buck and doe ducked and darted and clambered to slip behind boulders, and some creature I'd never seen before half devoured itself rather than submit to the probing of a dragon on the wing.

"Such is the world we have made," I said, almost in a whisper.

"Your sister's this one's architect," the windgod barked. "And she's enlisted my brothers on her roles to fend off any intruders. They're ready to blow you hide and all into another dimension. I'm not sure I can make safe the way, but I'm here to say I'll try. You see, young dragon, even the Tarewinds for the most part want the Evil One to die, if such a force can ever truly perish."

"Except perhaps my sister," I said, having witnessed the fruit of her labors. "If anyone ever modeled his gospel it would have to be this queen."

"Ah, but that's the rub, Sharto. Your sister's quite convinced that she's the standard of morals in the world as it is. It's a peculiarity unique to the ego that no matter how low it sinks, it thinks itself on top of the game of life."

Through canyons and craters we blew by gusts that were thrusting and mocking and cold with breaths that belched gases and sulfurs and sounds like a nation of ravenous souls. The other windgods, the Tarewinds, lurched out from darkened holes, spat at me and menaced, calling me names and denouncing me as a weakling.

They rebuked me that I must have an escort, ridiculed my incarnation into human flesh. For that they called me *White Sepulcher* and "holier than thou" when I was really, "lust in a dragon's body." In my cocksure determination, I was certain I could have withstood them, but Korlig reassured me that I could not. These winds could raze a metropolis in a breath if they choose to do so, and certainly had upon an occasion or two in the recent past.

"The mightiest creature of the flesh is still a slave to Nature. You can only bridle the beast if it chooses to let you. My brothers choose to let you now because you are with me, because they know I can blow them all to bits. That's the advantage of being the oldest. That's the law of Power. I've always dominated. The North is the source of all change in this world, the polar peak of volition. And I am its one and only voice!"

From another soul in another dimension this might have passed for pride, an arrogance beyond the edge of wit. But this mean old breeze had been around since the very beginning of time, and merely spoke a truth that was hard to deny.

In what was a matter of moments, he guided me up through a pitch-black ravine toward the crest of a scorched out mountain charred to the very bone. Atop it sat a castle, the most colossal of its kind with halls that could house a race of Brobdingnag or a host of ravening dragons. A bone yard road marked the path to the gate where sun-bleached skeletons lay—everything from mastodons to men. Below, a moat of crocodiles snarled and slashed at the sky, snapping at my shadow and one another. Above, six towers made of bloodstone rose up toward the heavens, a menacing nimbus carved onto the horizon. Atop each tower a dragon sat twisted and bent at the wing, each feasting on a carcass and belching his warning. Clearly they were deformed and seemed abandoned like castaway children, given these lowly jobs left to the most degraded among them.

"Korlig! Ko-o-o-r-l-ig!" called the first.

"Ko-o-r-r-lig!" echoed the second.

The third cried out, "Kor-lig!" a nanosecond behind.

Korlig twisted and swirled and howled, rising above the towers, causing even these most odious creatures to cringe. Then he suddenly and inexplicably vanished altogether, as if by escorting me he'd fulfilled an oath. In his wake I could hear a whisper that seemed to wish me well, yet like his breath it always carried foreboding.

"If this isn't Hell, then I recommend you say 'hello' to its rival, for this is as close as I care to come to ever tasting its kiss."

Korlig's escort gave me presence, and far more respect than I ever might have otherwise enjoyed, for as I hovered the castle walls suddenly opened to unclothe the illusion that I'd thought was real.

Like great doors guarding an inner secret, the buttresses tore away to reveal a cavernous room. Its floor was an endless carpet of stone, great blocks of irregular granite upon which some arcane inscriptions were artfully carved by hand. Since only the pygmie had the talent for working in such detail, I had to assume this had been conscripted labor. Yet, seeing the inscriptions there stained with spacklings of blood gave me cause for shame that I was even related to this rabble. The floor went on for a mile at least and was flanked on both sides by walls where trophies hung from thousands of skeletons of creatures that had been slain. From each of them emerged what struck me as corrupted shadowy forms, castaway members of every clan known at the time: unicorns with attitudes and black and bloodied withers, and twisted limbs and battered horns from their constant jousts and flight (I found out only later that these had been banished from their own vain clan for being less than perfect); chimeras with more than a head or two, and everyone of them crazy, barked and howled like hounds of hell with their half-dog, half-lion faces; there was even a gryphon or two, though they hovered near the arches, too aloof and suspicious to ever participate fully in this or any world.

Then, there were the dragons of every size and description, all bloodied, scarred and embattled, and looking on the whole like the most unsavory lot in the world. Some wore breastplates made of hides from fallen adversaries. Others chewed on flanks of flesh from pachyderms and oxen. Most were deformed or badly marred from duels they'd fought in past, and many a warlord among them sported a patch where an eye had once looked at life. Some of them drooled; others spat flame; none of them blanched for a moment; and none of them would ever shrink from a fight, of that you could be sure.

Tough as they were, I could clearly tell that none were a match for me, even those clever two or three that my sibling had taken as consorts. Like curtains cloaking a bad burlesque, they were draped around her throne—a bloodstone affair frocked with rubies and skulls. Clearly they were fawning for the favors of their queen, the Crimson Dragon, my own dear smirking Seti.

"Never thought you'd make it, brother. Never thought you'd have the balls to wend your way up North and fight the icy corridors of Myrrh. Of course, I couldn't help but notice you came with a heavy henchman. Wasn't your courage enough to get you through? Or will you forever be sucking up to higher forces to make your way in life? Then again the question's moot for a mover and shaker like you. Though lately I hear you've done more shaking than moving."

"You've always had the knack, dear sister, to put a spin on the truth, to make precaution seem like a coward's resort, to make a reunion seem more like a joust, a banquet like a farrago, and to make a simple virtue appear to be moral diarrhea. Nevertheless, it's good to see you, and to see you faring well, though you've never shown much talent for the company you keep."

I had to surmise that protocol was something these rogues abhorred, so it had to figure that insult was just the ticket. Besides, I'd hoped I could get at least one of them to rise and challenge me. If I took one down, I would get their attention more quickly than making a plea.

One of them rose and took the bait. His name was Fanfaron. Surprisingly he sported airs and behaved like quite a dandy. Somehow he'd managed a white lace tunic (though I saw it was splattered with blood), and he seemed to pride himself in his elocution.

"You offend me, sirrah," he said to me, slipping slyly from his chair, an obsidian throne marked by breastbones of baby gryphons. With slithering smarmy affectation, he swanked along the floor, gliding with seemingly aimless ease, until with a gesture both clever and quick he erupted just along side me, a talon dipped in poison poised at my throat.

This Fanfaron's chair and his lethal air put to rest any questions I might have had that he'd earned a reputation of a sort. My erstwhile bride the Gryphon Queen had regaled me with the tale of a lowly kodo lizard who'd risen through the ranks by snatching the gryphon young—a sleazy creature with one warped wing who took their offspring away, ate their livers, and made stylish decor of their leftovers. Accordingly, he was held in greater contempt than the most sinister Shimbagh. To make matters worse, my sister had made him her vassal. In the world of magic many believe that you become what you eat. So by taking the bile of the gryphon, this lowly lizard had sought to uplift his station, fashioning himself into a dragon of a sort. Although he was hideous in his way, I had to admire his gall. Fanfaron had dared to pursue his dream, which was more than I could say for the rest.

He threatened me again with his claw and hissed a victorious grin, jamming his talon into my jaw just where the throat goes soft.

"You're nothing but pretense and self-importance, you 'lord of the higher realms.' I ought to skewer you just for the drill."

Overconfidence causes one to relax one's concentration, and just as he glanced about for approval from his peers, I could hear the sudden catcalls of "Kill him!" rising from the darkness behind the light. They were little voices hissing ridicule with every utterance, encouragement from those who lacked the courage to act themselves.

"Waste him!"

"Paste him!"

"Wipe him out!"

They cackled from the shadows, sounding like an auction where my life was up for hock.

"Drain his blood!" Gut him!"

"No! Let his sister have him! Let her work her wonders on his self-important ass!"

The argy bargy rumbled on, the voices growing louder, and soon a herd of dwarfs danced round to celebrate my fall. Music came from lewd dark crannies with ridicule for lyrics (a reception I suspected that was planned before I had come). Dragons drank and spat and chatted about how I'd been easily "taken," simply outwitted by one of their rank and file.

This diversion was just what I needed, for while these sordid souls were carelessly awash in self-congratulations, I seized the moment to take the Fanfaron down. In a flicker of time, a nanosecond, I'd whipped my head away, bitten his talon in two and swallowed it whole. Then just to emphasize my point, I spat some flame in his face, smacking him to the floor with the back of my wing. Standing with my foot on his throat while he choked to free himself, I very deliberately spun about the room. I coiled my loins for just a moment, then exploded out of myself, towering over this parlor full of misshapen malcontents. I knew my size would have its say, and black is a frightening hue, so I fanned my wings out just to stress the point. Now it was time to state my case, for timing was crucial now, and my merciless act of reprisal had provided me with the silence of respect.

I released my hold on the Fanfaron and let him limp away to lick his wounds and contemplate his fortune, for I strongly suspected that though many a dragon would take death before dishonor, he would accept dishonor in a heartbeat.

"Forgive me if I eat and run, but necessity requires that I say my piece and then be on my way…The Mystic Clan now stands upon the threshold of its fate. Its future is being decided as I speak. Soon we must fight the Shimbaghs in the greatest conflagration ever known to this tiny world we call the planet Earth.

"I come to offer you the challenge of your lives: to be part of a movement greater than yourselves, to be soldiers in a victorious legion on its quest to save the universe as we know it. But since I strongly sense that these lofty aspirations are little more to you than the passing of wind, I offer you a choice that I don't think you'll take so lightly—full status in the ancient mystic clan, true dragons with complete recognition from your brothers from the South, and oaths of fealty from your cousins the chimera, the rahntish and the unicorn—alliance with the gryphon, respect from all white wizards and most of all the gratitude of generations to come."

Even the most grotesque of creatures yearns to be accepted. It is a flaw that touches every one. I banked on that, and found my longed-for answer in the silence while every dragon held his private thoughts. The rejoinder came with a resounding snarl as Seti roasted the room, torching out her umbrage with a 20 kilowatt howl.

"How dare you offer something to us we already have?! Why, I bet you'd offer gill slits to a fish, feathers to a bird of prey! Halos to an angel! Brimstone to a damned soul in the very jaws of hell! And where are your angels now, may I ask? If this cause of yours is so right, why do you need the rogues of the North at all?! I'll tell you why! You haven't got it. You're not up to the fight ahead. You're scared! You're weak! Your down to your last, and your gene-polluted inbred clans have left you drained of what once passed for resolution!

"Did it never occur to you, my brother, that your angels never were, that they've abandoned us here on this remote little world so we could sort things out for ourselves?! Have you prayed lately? Or have you preyed?! And which of your *prayers* were answered? When do you find the most fulfillment? When you let your wishes go and keep your faith? Or is it when you seize the initiative, take it by the throat, just like you did a scant few moments ago?

"Confess it, Shartallion, Lord of the Kiln! You're a warrior to the core. I know your true passion, the one you deny. It just pisses me off that you won't confront the mirror and admit the truth of who you really are. You're a rogue. You're a rascal. You go your own way. You see what you want and you take it! Yet you disavow your deepest desires, and cloak them with high intention while always careful to wear the bogus mask of a master soul.

"Was it high intent that prompted you to wipe out a pygmie army, or to take the form of a human male to get your ashes hauled? Was it lofty ideals that brought you to join in wanton miscegenation or challenge your mate for supremacy of the skies? And what did you leave at the Chthonic Schools? Was it your lower self? Or was it your self-respect that you abandoned?"

That was as close as my sister would come to ever saying she loved me, for she always held a very dark view of this world, and always would. Still, I found myself saying yes to the truth of her insights more often than not. Besides, only a fool would have tried to debate them here and now. I had armies to gather and nations of warriors to win. I would have agreed to whatever description that struck my sister's fancy if that's what it took to gain her tacit alliance. I looked about the room and saw a sea of blinking eyes. There must have been more rogues than there were of us.

"You've kept track of me. I'm flattered," I said. "I won't say you're totally wrong. But the issue remains, and it's that I have come to deal with. The Shimbaghs attack, and they mean business. No skirmishes this time, no mannered battles fought by clumsy battalions. Their well-formed forces go beyond counting; they far outnumber number us now. They multiply like locusts and have focused their attention on our singular destruction, and your own. They will not truck with compromise. Now they number the pygmie among them, for many a human wizard now takes sides with the Fallen One."

"You're surprised at that?!" my sister retorted, certain of her ground. "These dark magicians come to us in weekly pilgrimage. They have no sense of loyalty, and no high moral purpose, except the perpetuation of their own corrupted power. Yet this is what we've been told we've been put here on earth to protect—this self-absorbed little creature with his uncaged *homo* ego, his massive pretensions and messianic cults. If that's the choice, the dark side's looking better all the time. If that's the quest then I say examine the options!

"No, my brother! You still don't see it. The Shimbagh's just a diversion. The enemy is man, and we are losing the day!"

As she spoke to scattered applause, I couldn't help but notice that a baby dragon had slithered by her leg and hissed at me. Turning over on his side, holding his talons unsheathed, his ears back like a wildcat ready for a rumble, he flicked his tail and hissed again, waiting to take me on. I was certain he would have tried it had they let him. This had to have been her offspring by her mating with the dragon Urfuwl, the rogue she'd managed to put away during their honeymoon.

"I see you've noticed my little Percy, my little pride and joy," my sister gloated. "He's already proved more than a match for his kin. And I know as well he'll kick some ass before his days are ended. I'll teach him to be the mightiest dragon of all."

It was a tradition among the North Dragon Clan to encourage their offspring to fight. It was winner take all, and once the victor had done in the vanquished, he got to eat them for lunch for a week or two. This fight to the death was the North dragon's way of winnowing out the weak ones. (Apparently they never stopped to measure the intangibles of change.) And since dragon queens invariably bear triplets when they birth, it seemed that young Percy had already eaten his brothers for high tea. Without doubt this was the most hideous little bastard who'd ever donned wings and a tail. He even kept small traces of his sibling's blood on his face, streaked in purposeful patterns like sanguinary war paint, a testament to the bloodlust in his heart.

Suddenly it flashed on me that this creature was my nephew, a relative I was sworn by oath to protect.

"Congratulations, sister," I noted. "You've birthed a mighty heir. And it's his very future we're fighting for." I choked as I uttered this marginal truth, for looking upon this creature made me feel it might be better to throw the whole damned war. If this was the future of dragonkind, then the Shimbaghs had already won, and my premonitions told me that someday this Percy would be a plague.

"Oh, brother, brother!" my sister said. "You never stop politicking. Your bullshit's all that keeps you from being emperor of the universe. Someday soon you'll learn, I pray!. Meanwhile the answer is 'No!' I'll not endanger this realm of ours to fight your battles for you. We may not be perfect. We have our flaws. But we also keep our perspective.

"You see, I know in my heart when you fight your fight the outcome will go against you. For this penal home we call the Earth is the Fallen One's personal venue. And if he allows you to win at all, it's only because he knows that somehow you've already lost yourselves.

"It's better to keep our own council in this stark sleat pox of a land than to win a war for a brand new world that another species will own."

My bones chilled. In all these years with all my so-called well-honed perceptions I had never seen my sister clearly. I'd always satisfied myself with the comfortable misperception that she was strictly rancor and spit, when what I truly beheld was a brilliant linear train of thought that always cut to the chase, and let the dreamer be damned by his own dire dreams. Although her impatience had cost her much, she saw some things better than I. She uttered every doubt I'd ever had and made her truth. Yet she did so without playing me for the fool.

"Well said my sister," I answered. "But the issue still remains. The Shimbagh legions grow in strength and number. Whatever our motivations in this, the first one is survival. We either win or die; it's as simple as that. But whatever we do, remember this: However goes the outcome, if the Shimbaghs win, they're going to come for you. Their favorite game is 'divide and conquer', and they seem to have conquered you by clouding your mind with polemical issues that overshadow the facts.

"I have to go. My duty calls. The question now remains. To what cause does *your* duty summon you? Will you be Shimbaghs, or will you all be dragons? The offer I made still stands! But whether you stand or whether you fall, is what you must now decide. Whatever the issue raised here today, you cannot hide the truth. For this is *the Time* for deeds, and not for words."

When I glanced about the darkness, I could see this cavernous place had suddenly taken on another light. Dark shadows filtered into grey, and grey to brilliant colors, and ten thousand sets of blinking eyes now fixed their gazes on me. Some were filled with consternation, others with hope and doubt, but all in all I felt the power of individual souls seeking answers, taking stands, making their own decisions. I heard the thoughts run through their minds. They were a mixed reaction. My cause was right, they knew it, and the issue still remained. The war was on whether we liked it or not.

"The answer is no!" my sister spat. "I'm not decimating my people, just to sate your ridiculous notion of what makes *noblesse oblige.* I have a kingdom here to protect, and protected it will stay without the blood of my kinsmen for a fleeting moment's glory."

I couldn't blame her in the least; she spoke her truth as she saw it. Nor did I waste another moment trying to plead the cause. Words have a way of losing their impact when spoken a second time. I tipped my wing and silently launched into flight through the mouth of midnight into the throat of the coldest winds on Earth. Behind me there were no taunts or jeers or argumentative council, nor was there even a hint of the slightest remorse—only the stunning silence of myriad private thoughts, and a prayer or two in the gusts that twisted behind me.

Canto 27

The Gathering

I left my dissipated hopes in the chilly sunless skies and set my afterburners in the dawn. It was as if all life had died in an instant and I was all alone, devoid of past or present and blind to the future. For leagues not a single creature came across my path from this or any other near dimension. It was as if the way had been vouched safe for me to hurry on my mission to our faded haunted dreams.

The gryphons kept their plains of life hidden. They were the anchorites among us, not at all like the dragons who flashed their fires for the world to see. To find them I would undo my senses —the ones we're all trained to use—and let my inner awareness determine my path. After all, their queen was my soul mate in whatever form she took, and I knew fair well she could not resist the call. If I could get within sphereshot, I could summon her to me, could make her feel my need and share my fervor. Surely she had already heard the fatal game was on. But could she speak for her clan? I had to wonder.

One never knew whether the gryphons cared for anything at all, except their solitary soul's desires. For them to even gather marked a milestone in itself; for them to act as one was without model.

I put a prayer upon the wind but forgot the task I'd set; one never prayed in Korlig's realm without a ready retort. If only the Creator God could answer half as quickly, the laws of cause and effect would bring a swift justice indeed. Then again, swiftness is measured only in linear time. The sidereal Mind sees no such need for restraint.

Korlig entered for one last foray. I heard him scream and whine, tailing down the sleet-lashed peaks of the realms I'd left behind. He very clearly nipped at me, snapping at my flanks to let me know the level of his ire.

"Now, all you do is call on me as if I were some chattel! Don't test my patience, Dragon Prince. I'm not one of your cattle. I'm Korlig! And I rule the North. I've been here long before you, and I'll be here long, long after you are gone!"

Why is the way of half the world to belabor obvious truths and the way of the other half to ignore them all? I didn't mince words with this feisty wind, except to apologize and to make the obvious plea.

"Where can I find her?"

"You know the drill," the windgod blustered. "Steal the sound. She'll come. She'll come anyway; she knows The Time has arrived. But one thing that she doesn't know is what's become of your offspring. Your daughter, the angel, you have in tow. But you haven't heard of your son the Slavorn, and neither, I dare to say, has the mighty Gryphon Queen. He's sprung full-grown and daily mates with the females of that kind who grow heavy in the belly by the gross. It seems he's impregnated half the population of that virulent Shimbagh clan, and who knows what kind of product will come from that wicked broth?"

"Do you say this all to enlighten me, or are you just about your business of spreading as much discomfort as you possibly can?" The news of my son stung me, though I dared not show just how much, for making the dragon twitch was this windgod's sport. I tried as best I could to take away his pleasure, though I'm sure deep down that he knew he'd gotten to me. "Besides, I can get that kind of gossip from any old witch with a stew. I would have expected a higher thought from you. Now, could you tell me where she'll be? Or don't you really know? Or are you just a bag of wind after all?"

Thank God the gods have a sense of humor, for it made this old gale roar to hear such rank bravado from his junior. He puffed up to a nimbus face twenty times my size and sent me tumbling headlong toward the East.

"I'll miss your brash impertinence, my arrogant Dragon Prince. I'll not see you for a while, young soul, for The Time will change the Way. Enjoy these moments while you may, for the day will not come again when you'll feel so large and the sky will seem so small." He called behind me as I flanged my wings to catch the currents and rested.

I knew the journey would be long. The gryphons hid in the furls of time, on shoulders of mendicant clouds, softened their substance so they could be lighter than air. Korlig knew this all along, of course, knew the realms through which the SkyMaster soared and wouldn't tell me just for the sake of the game. But why hadn't she, I wondered, this mate of my own soul? Was it always the way of that gender to keep secrets from its mates?

In time, I realized that I was flying toward the zone of "O," higher than I had ever flown before; so high, in fact, that I had virtually lost my compass to the Earth. I experienced a kind of elation as I soared, as if exertion were a notion bound in myth, as if the coming turmoil we all had to face were but concepts cloaked in plots hatched so long ago. I freed myself from effort and, as I just let go, flew faster than I ever had before. Stealing sound was not an issue here; this place had left struggle behind. It was the Sea of Serenity I had found. It was then that I knew, could sense and feel the inner conflict gone, the breath of the Gryphon Queen pour into my heart, the soul of Shala evermore transcending the laws of flesh, whispering in my ear the truth of our love. I turned to behold the SkyMaster there, though surely she had changed. No feral glare, no warrior's stare, she wore an angel's manner as if she'd opened up and let the hosts of heaven inside.

Our wings touched end to end, matching in a single flight as we soared and swept and swam through the skies locked in endless passion. We paid no liege to time and place, no thought of things to come. Though the end of the world would be tomorrow, we'd spend today like this.

In a realm without dimension, without bodies to limit our communion, we embraced; my soul in Shala's without need for form to stay it. Yet in the aftermath of our limited bliss, I heeded my mortal senses and (God forgive me!) gave voice to my fears.

"Will I have to lose you again?" I thought. "Will the glorious breath we've shared be like a whisper in a storm of circumstance? Will this brief life be taken before it's begun? Have we, with all the love we've known in o' so short a time, leave the sorrow of miscegenation in our wake?"

It was some cosmic purge I felt, some things I had to say. Yet in my need I had become the supplicant. Like some crestfallen maiden who'd lost her flower I wept amid my passion, forgetting somehow that every moment is heaven in itself.

From my ecstasy on a bed of clouds above lands I'd never seen, I heard my love reply, "My soul is yours," in a way that barred exception. It was as if it were the last thing she would ever say to me, as if there were anything else that needed saying.

In time, we flew back upward toward a red sun on the wane when suddenly I felt my ears resound with the thunderous beating of wings. The sky grew black as if swept by a shadowy brush where legions of warriors from other worlds filled the spheres with a singular purpose. To see two gryphons at any one time was something beheld by few. But to see their nation melded as one was a once in a lifetime thing. Never before in the course of time had such a gathering happened. Never, in the course of time, would ever happen again.

It was tribute to her that this had occurred and little to do with me—so great was their respect for their mighty queen. That I was even accepted in their ranks was without precedent in time; that I was allowed to be at their front was more than some could bear. I could feel their ferocious courage. I could taste their resentment too, for it smacked against the currents of the wind. Yet they forbore, and they continued, their wings pinned back with purpose. There could be no turning away from what had to be done.

Somehow, I let my flame speak for me, and without another word guided them with instinct toward our appointment with the One. Though we were but swimmers in the Sea of Soul pressed down by the weight of our task, I knew we'd join with allies along the way. Our forces would grow to a formidable size, and though my sister had rejected our quest, I felt in my heart of hearts we'd take the day. Yet as I looked beside me to behold the SkyMaster in her glory, I saw a stream of tears streak down her face. Perhaps it was the sun, I thought. Perhaps it was the night. Perhaps it was the finish of the race.

§§§§§§§

I left them. I had a call to answer. The rivers below had turned black and coiled like the bodies of giant serpents, alive with undulating movements that must have unsettled the gods. Certainly, they unsettled me, for I dived for a closer look to find out exactly what had brought this about, when I realized it was all the creatures of water joined in a mass ensemble headed with resolution toward the Door where Evil dwelt. What disturbed me most was that though there were mystical creatures in the vanguard, the overwhelming masses of them had no business here—fish and frogs and gentle creatures who fed along the banks would only become food for fodder when the passage of arms began. This was a fight for beasts of magic, for dragons and gryphons and Kohmm—not for the simple creatures of Earth, not for the gentle ones. Yet as I came close I could see that they had massed together to become one amorphous being, an animal in itself led by the Griivre.

There was a navy of griivres among them, water dragons in scores, lead to be sure by my own dear friend from deep in the Chthonic Schools. He had grown since we had parted and now sported an indigo plume, a panache of sorts that sprang proudly from the crown of his head, and the glint in his eye still warned me that he was a creature of marginal virtue.

"Well, cousin," he said. "It's payback time. And I know you're glad to see me. Just as I know you're equally enticed to see what I've brought along."

The fact was that I was but wasn't for now about to overdo it. Still I had to admit that in a time of unpleasant surprises, this was a lift.

"You're always a welcome sight, dear friend, and so are your intentions. But let me recommend that you discourage your entourage. These little creatures have no edge in this eccentric game of magic. They'll only be caught in the middle and get crushed into a sauce before it's done. What the hell, I'm not even sure I'll make it through myself. This could be the end of the game for even the best of us."

"Fear does not become you, my prince. Wasn't that your lesson to me? Did you pass this truth to others without learning it yourself? Besides these tiny beings, though they seem of little account, know the score and are willing to take the risk."

"But their greatest impact is to stay alive and well for the future to come. They bring no mystical bargaining power."

"Try telling them that," the Griivre answered, bringing his voice to a cautious hush, so they couldn't hear our debate. "Besides, there's a little magic in us all, don't you think? Surely you have to come to grips with the fact that you're not its only master, that even the lowliest creatures on Earth have been touched with the talents of gods.

"In any case, you have not been aware that the seas are teeming for this. Not only the Naanworm and dolphins and whales but the tiniest annum are connected, have gathered their arms, and are massed to meet the challenge."

Of course, the Griivre was right, and in cases like this one takes allies where one can find them. Only Heaven knew that it might be a microbe that saved or destroyed the day. And in my obsession with the land and air and other spheres, I'd forgotten that everything that lived in sea was one, joined in their aqueous unity more surely than we of the air could conceive. There was something magical in the water, in the ocean of the soul, of right and wrong and truth and danger that I'd not yet come to know. Someday I would. I vowed to become a creature of the sea—a whale or a dolphin or a coral flower that simply lived to be.

"I welcome their spirit," I roared with delight, but also with some concern. Like the land above, the sea below also hosted creatures of evil, such beings who'd kept their agendas so hidden, not even I could imagine the degree of their intent. For now, I had to accept that they at least were not of the soul of the Shimbagh, not yet born of the breath of the Fallen One himself.

I vectored toward the open sea and was utterly amazed to behold the amaranthine splendor of the forces gathered there. The Naanworm had amassed every creature of import who hid beneath the brine and took the body of oceans as its home. Beside this largest creature on the face of this tiny planet, the blue whales and the sperm were like flocks of birds upon a tree, there for point of reference while this arcane ancient creature took them toward a destination none could even fathom. The Nereids had joined us, the Sirens too, and the Shallowmaster-thrand whose tongue was more than two leagues long and belched forth miles of sand, had torn his shoulders made of boulders and uprooted himself for this Time.

All these forces of the sea and more now drove toward the core of the damned to stand at the door of an avernal force that most had never seen. Every sea was a storm of purpose, and no sailing craft was safe while every wave was alive with a warrior armored to the teeth. Astride every wave, every crest of foam, there rocked an escort of Dolphins, archangels of the Oceans bringing sanity to the madness.

How awed I was by their singular courage, by their sense of purpose, by the faith they showed in our alliance without a moment's pause. I tipped my wing in tribute while the Naanworm railed at me, and roared that we who fought the damned ran the risk of becoming one of them.

"Your soul's in hock my dragon prince," this Seameister bellowed skyward, blurting out a half a ton of halibut as he did. "You've got no idea of the risk we incur or the face to which we fly. This Being will make three of me; so ponder that! This world will churn and burn to its core before this day is through. Though I suppose it's just another game to you."

"What the Hell, we're damned if we don't, and even if we do, we're still a scourge to the other half of this strange little world as it is," I shouted back my obvious truths which caused the Naanworm to roar, though no one could ever tell for certain what pleased or angered him.

I returned to the River Lord and the Master of the Skies, satisfied that heaven and earth were now moved to our cause.

A sense of synergy defined us now, a sense of constant motion—of Gryphon above, of Griivre below, of Chimera, barking their lion-dog's roar and clouds of Rahntish the winged deer, swift and silent in their flight. In headstrong herds the Unicorn came thundering across the land, their manes like white fire afloat in the wind, their nostrils aflare with the hot silver ice of their very singular passion. All the earth and sea and sky teemed with the forces of magic convening with purpose of heart and mind toward their singular quest. What a force to behold we were that day, what a staggering sight to see, a unified universal corps of holy mystical warriors. Surely no withering wall of evil could stand against us now. We were Power, and God was on our side.

But what if God were on vacation? (He took them often, I'd heard.) Would our angels be there to guide us? Or were the angels among us enough? And where was Man in all of this? Sleeping no doubt, and dreaming—dreams of his own exclusive role in his tidy destiny, sucking up to his lackluster views of his personal deities, thinking himself the only heir to Heaven.

As I passed in review above and below I saw one scant battalion of men—that little company of warriors headed by the bondsman of my fate. The Captain rode a chariot pulled by a team of lathering horses snorting steam into the cold morning air and straining at the bit. As I flew overhead, he pointedly hiked his spear to the sky, reciting an oath that neither heard but both of us understood. The Captain knew as well as I that we both might hold the key to turning the final conflict to our favor. Since I had been the Answerer and he had been the Asker, only we possessed the power to put The Prayer in place—to make the evil vanish one by one by one, to pop them like so many boils on the holy body of God. (This was what we'd been told of course. This was the blessed ideal. But could we do it when we came at last to the Crunch?) Both he and I had become convinced we could finish the war by ourselves, and save our mystic brethren pain and loss. Yet there was ever so much more to this dread game of the soul than two young crusaders could imagine. For this combat would be fought in such a fury and at such a pace that a skirmish line could be cut to bits by the time one said a word. Besides, the Captain was a man and slow to travel as such, limited by the speed of hard-ridden horses. He would fall behind us by a day or two at least; the issue could well be decided before he arrived.

"I'll be there even if I have to run my stallions into the ground," he called out to me (and I knew how he loved his horses). But this was a time for sacrifice. Every moment was dear to us. For, he knew we had all become hands on someone else's clock.

From the East and South the Mystic Clan gathered its nations together coming at last to meet the Dragons of the West. Like a tapestry of fang and fire, of plate and scale and passion, the dragons in an impenetrable wall did fly to face the foe. Led by my father Dager X, they were fearless, bold to the core, ready to fly to the teeth of combat, fly to the Fires of Home. After all we were made for this. We were cosmic war machines. And this was our final crowning moment—the reason we had been born.

All the craters from all the worlds where the mystic clans held their counsels now joined in bright convention in the sky. Bright Red Dragons from the fires of Teth, Greens from the Winds of Tyme, Golds from the Sun of the Kunlun Plains where my mother found her heart, Amethyst Dragons from the stratosphere where my cousin Skye had reigned, all joined forces at the point to form the wedge of contact. The beating of their wings were like ten thousand timpanies drumming their dreadful rhythms for all the world to hear. Their flightsongs were the wails of warning, an echo of pride and rage, for the dragon had been the vanguard of the crusade. It was the dragon who had borne the burden and done the battle before, while other species were satisfied to let us fight alone. It was we dragons who had carried the standard. Now the day had come when everyone would have to take the stand.

From a slate of clouds Vyngorchim came singing their glorious songs, though their disciplines were still not of the best. My brother Pod flew at the point, and was far and away more proud in his bearing than the mass of that motley band. I so very much wanted them to fare well. I had prayed they'd find their mettle, but these were clumsy malformed poets in a world where war was king. Even though their hearts were brave and their training had been intense I sensed our Vyngorchim brothers were far from prepared. Despite their attempts to steel themselves, they managed only a moment's focus before they disintegrated into gossip and jollity. Few had ever seen a battle. Few had tasted the wine when exultation and death come warm to the lips.

This farouche and flimsy rabble, well-intentioned though they were, could well be the flaw that felled the Mystic Clan. I could see by their clumsy zeal they were much more than they'd been. But were they half as much as they needed to be? I no longer had time to presume to know. Only faith could carry us now. Each of us broaching combat would take the truth of our self into the core of the foulest den on Earth. Besides, I often thought too much, and this was a day for glory. This was the time for the celebration of bold camaraderie, of brotherhood of all the angels who'd crossed this plane of conscience. This was a time to unify and share each other's valor—to celebrate the joy of life before the jaws of death.

Canto 28

The BeastMaker

"Williwaw!!" The skies cried out.
"Weary years of Warring
Have mocked this battle to the End
Of Everything we are."

> — *The Vyngorch Sagas*
> *Prologue*

Through wind and rain for what seemed a week, we drove our armies forward stroking the air and churning the seas like oarsman madly rowing, driven by our faith in our own well-tested valor and instincts that were far beyond our knowing. Far beyond our knowing too were tricks set in our path, invisible barriers put between us to tangle our resolve.

In time, we came to realize that every word we uttered, every change in directive, every song we sang made no music on our tongues. We were blunted, muted, robbed of sound, muffled by the air as if some unheeded Gorgon mouth were sucking the essence from us. No matter how often I shouted or how the loud chimera roared, or the Vyngorchim choir chanted their piercing rebellious odes, we were overwhelmed by silence, the conspirators' *Ultima Thule*, and the insidious laughter of a scornful bank of clouds. It was this silence that answered us so vacuous and hollow that any call to life we made was swallowed on the tongue.

This was not the Shimbagh way, for theirs was clangor and drums—making messy ritual of the work of doing battle. Shimbaghs were a noisome lot, redolent and foul, whose very presence in a mass could loosen one from one's dinner. Shimbaghs couldn't keep a silence much less help create one, and listening to their charivari fed the dragon's fire, whetted our taste for combat, made us more ready for our *tete a tete* with the Master of all Hate. But there were hidden energies in this *cordon sanitaire,* this nebula of poison mists and shifting passionless breezes. We were approaching forces of which we were still uncertain, entities even the seasoned among us had never seen before—neither fought at a distance, held eye to eye, nor ever caught a glimpse of; phantom adversaries who threatened the unknown.

Knot V sensed the stratagem and sneered at the attempt.

"They'll try every trick before they're done, and if we give it notion, it will gain in spiritual mass and ensorcell us all. But if we keep our auras whole and let our minds be clear, the power of our union cannot fall."

Up to now the "Initiator" had chosen to keep from sight, gliding just beneath Dager's wing like a satellite to a sun, frail and used, a veteran of one too many battles, the last remaining soldier in a long forgotten war. Had he lost his resolution? Was he doing this by rote? Or was it merely the Dragone's way of saving his bite for the end? Whatever it was, he looked weary. His injuries had taken their toll; the night raid that gutted the Crater of Nebul had scarred him at his soul. He had confronted something there that had shaken his resolve, a newer player in the game he couldn't quite define. But Knot was not a creature who dwelled upon his lack. He put it all behind him, took the moment by the throat and spurred us on again.

Whether he was faking it (I could never discern), he put on one last show of force that brought us all to cheer, and marvel at his unrepentant pluck in the face of peril. This final joining of the clan had been a charge for him, a thunderbolt to make him young for one last knock at the Door. He held his ash grey wings outstretched, put his head erect, and belched a plume of flame that would have challenged a young volcano. Seeing him charge out to the front gave spirit to us all. Never had I beheld a moment turned so far around. "We've just begun. This is our run for glory!" the Master Dragon cried, his voice like that of a trumpet from the highest of the high. It shattered the icy stillness and made us all realize *we* were the silence, and so would we be the sound.

"Roar, my brothers!

"Sing, my sisters!

"Sound our accolade!

"We are on the ultimate Crusade!"

Agile like a kite in spring, Knot darted back and forth drumming up *esprit de corps,* commitment to the cause. "Remember to keep your stingers up. Let them see our might. Let them know they're up against a tidal wave of angels. Never before and never again will anyone be so ready. This is our reason for being here. We cannot escape our fate, any more than we could ever think to abandon our higher selves."

Truisms uttered at times like this are very reliable tonic. So naturally we all responded with a spirited chorus or two, singing songs of each of our clans and hiking our weapons high, convinced we were the arms and legs of God Almighty Himself. We dived and swam and ground the ground and cut the air ahead carrying our immortality like a flag. In one moment we'd been muted by vestibules of fear, silenced by our own imprisoned thoughts. The next, we were unified in battle cries and songs that would have shattered the crystal in the palaces of heaven.

We sang our way through darkening clouds and furious red horizons at last into a caliginous haze that made us lose direction, blocked our sight of land and sea and which way was up or down, enough to make us wonder if we were lost. It was a ploy no doubt to block us from one another, to split our forces by a third of land and sea and air. But spiritual beings have means of keeping their inner vision clear, and once our third eyes tuned to the course we could not be deterred. Knot V was there to make certain that we never swayed again.

Eventually this smoke-screen faded, and the way was cleared before us to an endless dome of sky washed in hues of heliotrope, azurite, and amber. A diamond light from a source beyond, like a sun without its poles, danced dazzlingly before us in a slow hypnotic swirl blinding almost everyone by its overpowering rays.

It was as if some unseen force were probing us for flaws. Many creatures, I could tell, were stultified by this sight, forced to avert their gazes lest they be blinded by the light. But dragons schooled in the chthonic ways could hold their own with the sun and match it glare for glare 'til "kingdom come." So it was left to us to be the eyes of this campaign as well as its heart. And surely we were to be its mighty armored shield. We were the force to be reckoned with, and the Shimbagh minions knew it. That was why they had taken this tack with us.

Out of that radiant, glaring orb that nearly bewitched us all, I caught the glimpse of a chariot and four. The horses strode across the sky without the sound of hoof beats driven by a Wizardess in a league-long cape of gold. Furling behind her with myriad eyes that glistened like diamonds in the sun, it seemed to crackle like the sail on the mast of heaven.

The chariot levitated while the Wizardess, talking in tongues, brought her steaming stallions to a halt. I say this was a woman, for my experience in human flesh had left me with the skill to glean such things. Besides, she exuded such sensuality I was fired unto my loin to make a bonding. No noble soul's desire to mate, this was basic human lust, a taste I'd learned to savor while doing my time as a man. Although her appeal to me was in her strictly human form, I was certain she offered the same temptation to every body there.

What guile these forces would resort to, that at the very instant when adrenaline flowed like wine—when every single creature in their moments of reflection struggled to put behind them the small desires of life—they would now confuse the issue with this orgiast in drag. It was typical of the dark side and not far from the mark that their ultimate spiritual leverage was the wedge between the groin. Top the matter with the fact that this minion was a power so magical that every word she spoke dropped like a rose, making her appear like every creature's perfect lover, looking like a goddess while she uttered lyric prose.

"I come to offer peace," she purred. "We've no desire to hurt you. There's been a miscommunication on a mission gone awry. Some self-initiating fools—against the strictest orders!—took it upon themselves to raid the haven of the dragons, slaughter our beloved sister Kohmm while they lay asleep in the web, and make their private war upon you all. These cursed creatures, men and beasts, have been punished for their crimes, and we have come to offer peace and plead for your forgiveness."

To illustrate the measure of their evident contrition, the Wizardess whipped her train against the sky, cracking back a veil of clouds to reveal a host of souls writhing by the thousands, freshly flayed and crying for their skin. Not a very pretty sight, though it's hard to pity a Shimbagh, but I couldn't help but notice that the bulk of them were men. There were tens of dragons and hundreds of khados too, but most of the Crater's raiders were of the human kind. Had the Fallen One made such inroads with our brothers of the spirit that more of them served him now than our own Creator God? Had we been so busy pondering the right and wrong of our game that we had already lost the prize? The sight of these men in this wailing choir damned forever in time jolted me more than anything I saw. Even if this were illusion (and I strongly suspected it was), it was a prophesy of things that were bound to come.

Oblivious to the impact this carnage made upon us all, the Wizardess blithely continued with her innocent overtures.

"I offer now this dove of peace as our special emissary, and ask to meet with one among you to set the terms of peace. This war has been a hell for us as we know it's been for you. No clan has been immune to its bitter sting. Now the world will be the victim, every creature on it—plant and flower, rock and rill, every last neutrino will know the scar of its pervasive negativity. Unless we stop the slaughter now, we all will pay the price, for no one leaves a holocaust intact.

"Instead of going for the heart of your lamentably inferior forces, we offer peace, tranquility and kinship for all kind. After all we're all conjoined in the mystic coalition of souls—the chosen of the Chosen of the Few. If we could pool our forces then this world would be our tool, and the Universe itself would be soon to follow.

"What say you, Sons of Draco? You've led the war to now. Do you dare to lead the peace? You who have the rage to fight, could you send a prince among you at least to negotiate in faith to enact a workable truce?"

Silence followed. In a stall, we held formations firm, waiting in a spearhead for the signal to advance. Why did we wait? I wondered. Were we so inept in this that we allowed ourselves to be manipulated by a speech? If my schooling in the chthonic realms had taught me anything it was to detect a lie disguised as truth. Illusion is the spearhead of perfidy itself, and these were nothing more than plots wrapped in pretty purpose. Even the moaning penitents dangling without their skin were playing out their part to undermine us. I'd seen it before, yet came to know I'd have to see it again, watching our proudest warriors rock like kites in a dying wind. Uncertain now of our purpose that an hour ago was clear, we were beguiled by the pretty prose of a temptress pitching peace.

As for the dove, I'd seen that bird. It preened its feathers often. A little bit vainglorious for a bird of peace, I thought. It sat upon her shoulder looking rather smug, and cocked his eye at me a time or two. Although he looked the very paragon of virtue by his pose, one could only judge him by the company he kept.

This was the time for action, so I broke my ranks and flew right to the head of the spear where my father stood his sky. The moment I arrived I could hear old Knot V mutter.

"The bitch is lying through her teeth. Let's cut her down right now."

"My sentiments exactly," the Mountain answered back. "But there are those whose rectitude is shaken by this show. These gestures of peace are a wicked lie, but they work their little magic, and give false hope to the faint of heart and the dreamers of our clan. So, we have to play out these poliorcetics, and answer their request. Meet this wizard half the way (and cover our behind)."

"Mis-take my son," the Dragone growled. "The longer we delay. The weaker grow the bonds of our alliance. We must strike while the passion is hot, or we lose the edge forever. If we wait another hour we are lost. The battle could go on awhile, and daytime is our armor. These creatures thrive in shadows, and night is their friend. The longer they make us wait and ponder, the closer the evening comes; and your soul can get lost in the darkness that it brings."

By this time not only I had arrived but the other clan leaders as well. The King of the Chimera, the winged Unicorn Prince, the Council of the Dragon Clan, and my own Gryphon Queen— all collected wisdom of the of the greatest mystic minds were gathered now and lost for a decision.

I joined the debate with what I thought was bound to be the solution. "She's asked for a prince among us," I said, "to negotiate a truce. Since I have something of a reputation for temperance, I offer to take the risk to meet the Shimbagh where she poses and expose her callous deception for what it is."

The others turned to study me as if I'd lost my senses, as if I with all my skills intact were not a match for her.

"Unless I'm mistaken," my father protested, "this glorious gilded priestess is the wickedest creature on this earth save the Prince of Lies Himself. This is Rakushar, the Beastmaker. Her powers know no measure. No one who has ever faced her has lived to tell the tale."

"Or even seen her," I was quick to note, noting too the options. "We either smoke her now or risk the fallout of further delay. We've caught the moment. We have the edge. Let's keep it, for Heaven's sake! They're relying on our loose alliance as a means to bring us down. The time for consensus is over. It's time to take command. May salvation or damnation ride on my head."

"It's not your damnation we're worried about," I heard a loud voice say. It was Rueg the Roth, though I was proud to note that his eyes bore admiration. It was the only time my father and Rueg ever agreed on a point. The debate simmered for a while, but I settled it with a stroke.

"I am the Answerer to the Asking Prayer. I'm the only one who can take her. It's my fate and my fate alone that this be done. It is God's will." (Well, how does one ever counter an argument like that? People who talk to God and get answers are smarter than those who don't. Besides, whatever happened now would have to be measured in heartbeats, for we had lost the luxury of reflection.)

Before another word could be said, I had burst out of the gate and flown to the bitch while ten hundred thousand voices cheered me on. In situations such as this, the certainty of folly is the single thing that marks the start of a war. Without so much as a second thought, I (who thought too much) had acted in a zone out of my self. In doing so I felt my flight being drawn by a loathsome force that reeked of death and seduction all in one. Rakushar, her eyes alight with the prospect of my coming, lifted her voice in a song that blared like a trumpet for the damned.

*"Here flies
the Prince of Dragons,
the Stealer of Sound
Apart
Who holds Peace in his Eyes
Yet breathes of War
from the Core
of his Dragon's
Heart.*

*"Here flies
the Prince of Dragons,
The Answer
Beneath the Mask
Who knows the Dancer
But doesn't know
Where to go
Or what Question to ask."*

This lady didn't waste her breath, for every word she uttered loosed a venomous narcotizing gas into the air. As I was sucked like so much ballast toward her gaping mouth, her irresistible beauty took on another face. I could hear hissing beneath her breath like a thousand vipers hiding, sitting on the tongue behind her tongue, waiting to deal a fatal blow to the dragon who dared to kiss her on the mouth. She swelled in size to meet me to equalize our match, though I noted the dove on her shoulder remained uncannily aloof. He stayed his place, kept his poise, and never once looked hostile. Unlike the horses snorting shafts of ice into the sky or Rakushar's noisome breath that nearly knocked me cold, this little bird was tranquil, quite above it all, and never once affected by the spite that spiced the moment.

Meanwhile, the closer I came, the faster I flew toward the Lady. I would not be stayed by parlays long if it ever came to that. I screamed to a halt right in her face and surely wished I hadn't, for the Whore of Babylon had nothing on her.

Had I not remembered the Mother of Tongues, the Tree Fury's furious rages, I would have been knocked silly on the spot. Because, like a painting with gaudy strokes, what was lovely at a distance was repulsive face to face. Her eyelashes were tipped by human heads, shrunken and blackened, and killed unto their soul—trophies of a single afternoon of intimate pleasure. Her face was layered and made quite young with the flayed skins of her lovers, and her eyes could suck the vital essence from any living thing. Her fingernails were ruby shards, each one dipped in hensbane, and her gown was latticed with platinum whips freshly stained in blood. Her breasts were bared and her nipples hard, for pain and death aroused her, though the milk they'd give was as toxic as the bile from the Devil's spleen.

To make matters worse she had the Power to compel one to her will, for this was as close to a god as a devil could get. But I was the Dragon fired in the Kiln, forged with the Seven Gems. The Ruby was mine, the Tiger's eye, the Amethyst and the Garnet, the Emerald and the supersensing impervious Onyx hide. The Diamond *I* to transform the truth, the Sapphire to foresee it—all these gifts were mine to put into focus at this time.

Focus them I did, for now I clearly saw the secret: One moment's compromise, and I was done. All these horrors, truths, and revelations came together as the aspects of this Shimbagh and her minions came to bear. The hissing of ten thousand snakes, the air now filled with arsenic, the screeches of souls from every cell of this raunchy harlot's skin—all these and more swelled in size and number until I realized that this was the army of the Shimbaghs wrapped in one. In this sorceress superstructure was their battle plan. She was nothing more than a shell, a tawdry Trojan Horse ready to explode on us with a dozen million warriors.

Of course no wizardess worth her salt would ever come in person when some unholy holograph would do. But this was not some puff of smoke. This was *bloode and bane.* (If that was not illusion in itself.) It didn't surprise me or anyone else that they'd set the trap for us. And like the fool who rushes in I had flown right to it. Yet my prescient onyx powers told me this was the thing to do.

What could I do to rip this ruse? That was my dilemma. If I stung the bitch or bit her head off it would open the Box, for this was Pandora's curse and worse, the deadliest of sins. If I waited another moment or let the lady speak, we would unleash a legion inside her like lava about to spew. I needed to say the mantra, the holy Asking Prayer, but I knew if I uttered one syllable she'd see it coming and strike. This was no second rate wizard here. She knew the game too well. There was little doubt that she had helped invent it. One word from her, one pause from me, another scintilla of time and I was toast, and the rest of my clan would follow; not so much from the inertia of their overwhelming force as from the demoralization that came from seeing their "best" put down. So I was left with a vile conundrum: no win, no win, no way. What a horrible spectacle we'd be in any event.

All this took place in an angel's breath that comes with the gift of knowing and the imminent loss of one's life that makes for the greatest awareness of all. Yet that nanosecond thunderstruck me, this was the Mother of Tongues; this was a lesson I had already learned. To look at the mass of this fabulous bitch and try to find a weakness was to overlook the obvious flaw. The key was not to this sorceress' clone ready to blow up on us. She was the McGuffin.

It was the dove, this placid preening fellow.

This docile bird upon her shoulder, so innocent and pure. If I took him out, I could strike the Blow, I could denude its disguise and show it for what it was—the Magpie himself!

It was just like the little bastard to suck-up to a greater force, the ultimate parasite to the powers that be. Though Rakushar wouldn't come in person, she'd sent one of her own; The Master of Disguises would of course be the volunteer. He held us all in such contempt. We were beasts after all; never the equals of men and never would be. It was that arrogance of species that had brought him here for this—for his box seat at the *opera comedie.* But I had news for him. I had smelled him out where he sat, and the final *belle cantata* belonged to me. I had to move like lightning now, for my thought had struck the air, and the Bitch had already stuck out her tongue to try and kiss me deadly.

It was so easy. One blast, one roar, one gout of flame, one single talon swipe—I had snatched the bird, tossed him into my mouth and swallowed him whole. I could hear the wicked wizard scream all the way down my gullet, there to be dissolved in the fires of my gut. RuSiva! I had the son-of-a-bitch! Nothing could have tasted better. It was a meal I was short to savor, because this damnable day had just begun.

Behind me I heard the roars of my clansman at the sight of his undoing, followed by a howl of warning before the lightning struck. Rakushar took her retaliation before I'd finished my swallow and sooner than anyone else could think to respond. With a shaft of black flame from her little finger she jolted me with a shot that didn't stun or kill me but transformed me on the spot, into a baboon!—a ruddy, red-rumped barking clown, ape of the race of men, outcast of the primate clan no better than a troll! I tried to speak but screamed instead and made no sensible sound except for the frantic gestures of a simian falling to ground.

Sometimes it's better to die the Death than merely be trivialized. And I had been knocked aside by a sorcerer's finger-flick. Without my wings I was headed south to crash on the rocks below had not a dragon caught me halfway down, cradled me in her gentle wing and set me on the earth. It was Drilg. Who else would have seen the coming of this pivotal moment, anticipated and known what to do when it came?

There is no match for a mother's love. It overcomes all chagrin. Neither trial nor conflict nor the world in collision could stay her loving touch. It almost healed me on the spot, though I was wounded sorely. Pride, more than the body that wears it, takes a very long time to heal. In her way Drilg gave me comfort to let me know I'd acted rightly, but even her usual surety had been shaken by what she saw. With a brush of her golden wing she set her arc to the heavens to face the gathering cloud of minions that now flew out of Rakushar's mouth.

Although I had defaced the Shimbaghs' plans for easy subterfuge, although I'd devoured my Nemesis RuSiva on the spot, although I'd exposed the holograph that Rakushar had sent us, what followed unleashed an ocean of flesh and fang. A tidal wave now filled the sky until it had unfurled to become a sky unto itself—a mass of heads and tongues and flames of monstrous living things so infinite in number that it boggled the mind to count: Khados, dancing giant winged dogs with seven sets of teeth and two heads where a tail would be and bear claws dipped in bile; Kingus, demon women-beasts with cloven feet and breasts from which there poured an avalanche of adders; Slaverns, talons sharpened, screamed their feral lust at us, causing our already unsteady Vyngorchim ranks to waver; Shimbagh dragons led the band in numbers without end, to an amount that easily tripled our own; and human beings! Hundreds of thousands! Were they living? Or were they souls in passage condemned by their conduct in former lives to serve the Evil One? Whatever they were, the mark of their commitment alarmed me most, and their cry to arms could make the blood run cold!

We should have attacked immediately, but their masses kept unfolding until it occurred to me at least that they would unfurl forever unless we took the fire to them and sealed their ceaseless hemorrhage. I tried to call to my allies, to my brothers of the kiln, but all I could do was bray and hoot and tear the hair on my head. Still, my mind was sound, and I could meld it with others, and my thoughts must have struck my grandfather too because Knot pinned back his ears.

Like an arrow to the mark, Knot V had gone to meet his fate and tear into the wall of Shimbaghs that towered over us.

"Atoohhhh!" he cried. It was the Asking Prayer. He could begin but never finish saying what it meant. Still, the holy word

Atoh! "Thou art!" had crossed his tongue as he plunged like a flaming knife into the very heart of darkness. There his cries were muffled as the wall of flesh swallowed him whole, and a thousand creatures closed their fangs on him. Knot had vanished in their midst. He'd gone his warrior way and left the rest all hovering agape. This mass of evil, in a bite, had gobbled up our leader.

And they had made a monkey out of me!

Canto 29

Crimson Skies

It was as if the sky had devoured him. Like the dreaded Leviathan who'd gobbled heroes whole, they had absorbed my grandfather without so much as a mark to betray the act. Granted he was old, but age was power in these parts. So, now he'd vanished, perhaps been swallowed (perhaps they'd swallowed his soul!). It was as if their corruption had rendered them unipolar, and they could drink an assailation like an ocean would a stone. Their source was endless so it seemed, but I knew there were limits, if only we could find the frame that held them.

I could have made a dent in them. I was the Answerer after all, and I knew "the Asker" was en route. But I'd been reduced to a jabbering primate left on the ground below to ape the coming holocaust with sneer and a shaking fist. That had been the trap they'd laid, and I had taken the bait—the self-important, self-appointed savior of the world! How could I have been so headstrong and let myself get suckered by the oldest trickster's trick of all? Get the strongest player to play his trump card first. Give their ace a jack, then take him out. That was what they had done to me; my father had tried to warn me, but I had let my passion rule my brain. Now that the actual storm had come to the fullness of its Mass, I was out of the way—a jackanapes to watch a war of giants.

Then it came; the sign I'd prayed for, that courage had its rewards, that the effort of the good would be worth taking. Just when the clouds had unfurled their darkest face with flights of Shimbaghs shoulder to shoulder, there came an explosion of force through the their ranks that tore like a thunderhead—the great Knot V had fought his way out and taken a score as he came. Khados clinging to his wing, Slaverns lashing his side, his bloody talons clutched a Shimbagh dragon by the throat and an UrWitch in his jaws, spitting out the wreckage of her to shout his cries to attack.

"Come on Mystics! The battle's fine. They cannot match our might. We each can take a baker's dozen before we find the Night!"

A 'dozen' was what we would have to take, because that was the weight of the balance that was freshly set against us. We were outnumbered easily twenty to one. And Knot, God help the dragone now, was surely not much longer for this world. No sooner had he cast the Shimbagh dragon to the rocks below than had two others joined to seize him by flank. He tore himself free, and with a swipe ripped the head from one. But this Shimbagh had another head ready to take its place, ready to bite and claw and tear without a loss of pace. They were full of tricks, these minions. They could conjure body parts. They could cry to havoc and call in added strength. They could muster their numbers like clones of themselves, and they could call on the Devil, while we had lost all contact with our angels. Nonetheless, they didn't dare to answer the Asking Prayer, and couldn't stand against the Answerer who did. The Asker, the Captain was on his way to this with all deliberate speed. But the pace of human intention would not quite be enough. All the combats in sea and sky were taking place at light speed, and now my father had flown into this fabulous farrago.

"*Aaaatohhhhh!*" he cried. When Dager flew, all the dragons followed. And once the dragons made their play the battle had been joined.

The skies were crimson. The seas were blood. The land was scorched by the the Mystic Clan locked in the throes of combat. On a nearby shoulder of rocks there crashed a dragon and two Shimbaghs. It was Clarik of the Seven caught between a pair of fangs—a giant adder twenty meters long coiled itself around him while a Shimbagh dragon tried to take his face. With a swipe of his mighty talon Clarik filleted the viper to the bone, then bathed the Shimbagh dragon in a baptism of holy flame. Rigored by the heat of it, the Shimbagh turned to stone then ossified before his very eyes, while the giant snake fell filleted, hissing curses to the last and burying his fangs in the Crater's priest a hundred times before he died. Clarik scorched the snake's remains, then skewered his heart and ate it in tribute to an adversary for whom he had respect. He said a prayer as was his custom and took off to the sky, but by that time the poison had taken effect. Clarik crashed back down to earth. I heard his prayer on the wind, and though a Kohmm nurse rushed to attend him, she couldn't bring him to. Clarik had left his mortal shell (and he was one of the Mighty). Great heavens what would then become of the rest?!

Down in the Sea of Chaos, the Naanworm tore the roots from the Gorgon's neck and dashed it on an atoll, leaving the sea in its center steaming, a cauldron of cooked corruption. On a nearby plane of battle, unicorns banded *en masse* routed a cavalry, a thousand score of men and horses trampled into retreat. In the sky, the gryphons thrust into the meat of the Shimbagh flank. Led by their SkyMaster Queen they tore into the corpus of the kingus and sent those bawdy bitches into retreat; but there were too many. No sooner had they leveled half a legion than another thousand score replaced them, bubbling like broth brought to a boil.

At last, Knot fell, the Grand Dragone finally floated to earth, crashed in flames with a pair of Shimbagh wizards in his jaw. He died to his body (his soul had left even before he struck), landing lightly like a driftwood into the river below.

The river flowed out to the sea where a school of sharks ate the winner, while the Shimbaghs disintegrated in the foam.

It's not that we weren't up for this. But our numbers were so few, and these minions were the masters of attrition. They had no regard for life itself. Death was their stock and trade, and these merchants had an inventory we had yet to see.

And where was I in all of this? Wagging my butt at the sun, howling my thoughts to a mocking wind and weeping for myself, a damned imbruted hominid with a piss poor command of the genre, and an even poorer premonition of what the hell to do next.

Suddenly, I heard the voice from deep inside me, an energy that pushed up from my gut.

"It doesn't have to be this way. If you're willing to pay the price, we can work an arrangement to our mutual advantage."

The voice I heard was oh so sweet, so sing-song and lubricious, so utterly persuasive, if one hadn't know the source. Since a baboon lacks the dragon's spleen, our digestive juices had failed us, so we hadn't turned the Magpie into excrement just yet. When I'd gulped him down with a flame and a bite, I had somehow neglected to chew (forgetting my manners as it were in the final heat of the moment). I, of course, had been transformed too soon, so my system had changed as well. So, once again I had this wizard's finaglings with which to contend. As a ravening ape I got to play host to this mountebank in my gut, forced to listen to him twitter while he tried every trick he knew. Bargaining for his freedom as if he held the advantage, he kept inveigling me. Well…two could play that game as well as one.

"I can get you back in form to take the battle to them. Set me free, and I'll show you how and even toss-in a tip or two to help you gain the edge." I had to give this wizard his due, he was resourceful to the end. He knew what tune to play, but I wasn't dancing.

"I'd rather take a week to digest you and stomp on the turd that comes out! If I've made no other contribution, I'm satisfied with that! All life is a trade, and if I had to do it all again, I'd do it. I'd take the very same shot. Only, next time I'd take it sooner."

"You overrate me, Dragon Prince, and underrate yourself. I'm just a journeyman wizard with lifetime more to learn. I've made some mistakes, I admit, in choosing this impudent path. And I haven't used much discretion in picking my friends. But now that I've seen the error of my ways, I am willing to change. Just give me a chance and let me show you I mean it. I'm just a pawn in all of this, betrayed by the master who taught me, then given up for a sacrifice—to the enemy at that! Ultimately they'll tell of me that I was *expendable!* Sacrificed at the very first crack of the bat!

"But You! You're the One! You're the Answerer! The Sword that severs the knot! If you stay as you are the battle is lost; that much I can assure you. But if you could find the way to recover your valiant dragon's form and say the Words, the night would turn to day. The tide would roll to the Mystic Clan, and you would ride the crest. Believe me, Shartallion XII, you don't yet know who you are or just how important you are to the other side. Rakushar knows, and that's the reason you're sitting here scratching your ass. You *are* the game, and the rest of this is a side-show."

"Don't dazzle me with your sophistry. You're the Devil's own disciple, the master of expediency, destroyer of the Clan! It would take a dozen lifetimes for you to expiate your crimes, and we won't start with this one, I can guarantee you that."

"How righteous you are in your indignation, as if you hadn't strayed. And how tempted have you been to learn my power? Power I've had aplenty, enough to have killed you five times over—our conversation in the City, or even while you slept! If I'd truly been committed to evil, I'd have done you in back then, when you were a man and asleep in your lady's arms. I could have nailed you in a trice! Instead, I let my intellectual curiosity sway me. I spared you and your lover too when you were fair game for me! I wanted to see what you would become, and where this journey would take us. But you see young dragon I'm ruled by Mind. You are ruled by your Heart. (A noble trait I'm sure, but *voila'!* Behold where it has brought you!) Instead, I offer this food for thought. Release me, and I'll teach you. Let me go, and I'll show you all the shifting of shapes at my command."

It's the ultimate talent of evil in that it plays one's desires like a lute. But this wizard would sing a different song before this day was through.

"If I free you from this it comes at a price. I need to know their weakness. Where can we strike to turn the tide? What of the Fallen One? When we cut through this endless mass of minions, we still have his power to face. When we do there has to be a weakness."

"Unlike the Creator God of us all, he doesn't have omniscience. He has his blind spots, particularly where his spiritual Pride is concerned. He can be taken from behind. Although you cannot kill him, you can lock his house for once and always. You can seal the door where Evil dwells. That's all I can tell you for now. You see the winds are terrible gossips, and they can hear a stomach growl from half a league away. One drift of this, and they'll carry our words into the folds of thought, and everyone will read the script of our conspiracy."

"There's one more thing!" I had to insist. "If I decide to set you free, you're out of this. You'll take no further part."

"I *you* decide?! May I remind you, we're in this mess together?! If I digest, you stay an ape until the day you die!"

"I have been transmogrified, RuSiva. You've become a meal. I can find a way out of this skin. There are ways through this maze of flesh and you of all creatures know it. While you, my wicked little wizard, are being digested by my acids. And you will be a piece of shit before this day is through." He was right, but so was I. I could feel his life-forces draining. Soon he'd be absorbed in my body; his cells would be part of mine. Without my fires to purify them, anything could happen. He could even become a part of me! 'You are what you eat.' The maxim holds, especially among the mortals. And I was holding a belly full of very bad stuff indeed. "I'll let you go on that one condition: You will bring no harm to us. You'll retire from this conflict, and vanish entirely from sight."

"I swear not to harm a hair or hide of any Mystic Clan. And I won't return to fight for the Host of Minions. I'll become a wizard-discrete and make my own decisions, and pay no allegiance to any master force for good or bad. This much only do I pledge because otherwise you'd laugh. You'd take me for a liar, and you'd be right. I'm not quite ready for canonization, but there's much to be learned from this, for you as well as I, my young apprentice."

"Done," I replied. "The next step is yours. How do I change from this? You've skills in transformation I've yet to fathom."

"Have you so forgotten what you learned? Has your Sapphire turned to dust? Has Shartallion the dragon who's mastered *mergence*, melded with man and lived to come back again so weakened that he can't overcome his entrapment in a baboon? Maybe you've inherited the monkey's brain as well."

"I had something to focus on then."

"*Focus* is the secret! Focus is the catalyst in all the good we do."

"Yet you do what you do in an instant."

"Because I've learned the art, and taken the time to practice. So can you. Apply your skills. That's all you need do. Your cousin Skye can turn into mist in a moment, because he knows. It's total focus that throws one into the other! You just thought you needed another object to fix your thoughts upon. You came out of your man; now come out of your ape! You're just in a level of lower expectation. Focus! Concentrate! He who can fix his thoughts can master the universe in a minute's time!"

Everything was an effort for me but this was worth the pain, for he knew as well as I that I'd been locked in here by a spell. Not just any magician's hex but the Beastmaker's conjuration. I focused on the dragon I had been, and called my middle pillar. The Asking Prayer would have its answer here. I stilled myself and in that stillness saw the angel fly, felt the Lightning Dragon melt to his soul, cried for myself and in that eruption blew the cap on this; and out of the monkey's mouth came a blistering flame. Out of that flame the Magpie flew and perched on the hulk of a tree freshly felled and holding honey from the jaw of a lion's broken neck.

The Dragon exploded out of me, and once again I was full — coal black to my onyx cells and lightning scar on my chest. For a moment salted with revelation, we stared each other down, and it hit me then that the black and white mage had not yet come into himself. I think he was just as surprised as I that this had happened so quickly, or that I'd been able to break the spell at all.

"There are other forces at work in this. You've angels on your side. I bow to that. But I have my own agenda," he called to me. This time he lacked the spark of irreverence that had always marked his manner. There was a soul inside this man. That frightened me most of all; to think that I could ever come to like him.

Still dazed from what had happened, the Magpie ruffled his feathers a bit, then suddenly shook his head and looked to the sky. Forgive me, but there was an instant in which I was tempted to snare him again, to sully our pact and shred that bird to bits. But honor is a curse at times, and he had proved his merit. I was not about to sell it out. In retrospect I wished I had, for this changeling had a knack for sticking in my craw time and again. But wishes come like lilac-mist and dance away in the sun. Reality is a flame that burns forever.

Once he'd gathered his wits again the Magpie broke and flew, scorching the air as if shot from a fiery bow. Never looking back for a moment he headed directly away, due North as far and as fast as he could from the battle. Once in the clear, his feathers unfurled to display a black and white train, and an ivory and onyx chariot pulled by piebald horses. It was RuSiva in all his regalia laughing against the sky, furling black smoke from his fingertips and twirling his silvery mace. Suddenly hoisting it high in the air, he hurled it half a league headed with its own intelligence right for the crease of my heart. I was ready to parry, but before I could block the shot the mace arched away again, returning to the wizard's glove like a falcon called home to its master.

I heard him roar, "We're soul mates now. I'll see you in hell a'times, particularly when you find out who you are." The instant the words had left his mouth, he vanished in the wind, another trick he knew that I did not.

I couldn't reflect on what I had done or the consequence we had wrought. I only knew I could spread my wings again. I could breathe the holy fire. I could say the Prayer. I could feel my soul revive. I could take on the Devil now. And by God I would!

§§§§§§§

There is a factor of combat that one dares not pause to mourn, even though one's race is dying away: Gryphons and Slaverns in a fatal embrace; Chimeras and the Khados; Vyngorchim with their own rare part to play; the Kingus and the Rahntish; the Unicorn and the armies of men; Shimbaghs and the highly vaunted Dragon most of all. All of them falling right and left, lost in their own bleak passion, bent on mass destruction as if it truly held the key.

I'd seen one half a nation fall before the sun had struck noon. And still there was so very much longer to go. Chimera and Khados were locked in death throes,—the lion dogs and the devil dogs slicing one another to shreds, ripping their way to oblivion without a thought of the end. Led by the great Chimera King and his honor guard of warriors, they flew into the double-headed Kados in a fury, cut through them with almost ludicrous ease until they realized that they'd been swallowed, surrounded, absorbed by a number beyond their ken. The Chimera King quickly breached them but was so weighted down with Khados

that he tore them off his body as one would leeches in a swamp.
He must have devoured half a dozen and slaughtered another
score but the two headed khados kept coming on as if being
poured from an urn. In ravenous masses such as these they
resembled piranha in schools with no consciousness of their own
except the collective will to feed. The Chimera King survived his
attack, though who knew about his wounds? We had so few
melons to salve them any longer. Little compensation to him, for
he saw his race destroyed; only a few of his honor dogs survived.
The rest were gutted where they had flown. Not for lack of
courage, but for lack of numbers had there been an end to them
—the extinction of a mystical race of seekers of the truth.

   The Gryphon too had felt their share of mighty warriors
slain. Savaged by Slaverns who knew their blows could be fatal
when flung against them, the gryphons flew into a fusillade of
Slavern claw and fang. Breaching the kingus just long enough to
save the Chimera elite, they tore their way through a flight of
Shimbagh dragons with almost ridiculous ease. But when they
encountered the Ladies of Night and their screeching high-
pitched voices, they knew their deathly embrace would be near.
Every creature under the sun enjoys a special hatred, and the
Slaverns and the gryphons shared the bond. Not that the Slavern
could match the gryphon in strength, agility or will, it was that
her bite was poison to the gryphon most of all. Without the salve
to heal them they were merely a mortal bird, felled by the
misdirected spear of fate. Why would the gryphon even confront
them when they could defeat other Shimbaghs with such facility?
It was their ferocious pride that drove them, their own instinctive
loathing to see what their illicit lust had brought into the world.
The Slaverns were in part their offspring, the daughters of their
dark secrets, and after all what better time to try and erase the
mistakes? Erasure of mistakes can often prove a fatal task; still,
the gryphon seemed drawn to these deadly hybrids as if they
were the cure.

   I worried about the Gryphon Queen, but she was the perfect
assassin. She could swoop and dissect an opponent before they

could even tell. Many Sisters of the Water died before they knew they had been done in by the Master of Skies herself. Still, the Slaverns held their own; they stayed in their haunts near the water, catching the gryphons by the wings and pulling them under to drown, tearing them open where they held them, cutting out their heart. And the rivers changed their character with the blood of the mystic bird. They would never again run clear. They would fill the seas with salt.

All in all, this was not a job for the eagle-lion to brave when the Vyngorchim were the perfect match for the Sisters of the Night. It was still the daytime, and they could sing and hypnotize their twins, wrap them in silver strands from their throats and pluck out their eyes for them. But the Vyngorchim's infamous narcolepsy had taken its worst expression, and the singular trauma of battle had plunged them into a sudden slumber. All but a few had nodded off, perched on some mountain shoulders, and managed to sleep through the most relentless battle of all time.

God bless my brother Pod who, in his utter chagrin, screamed and shouted, trumpeting them to awareness. Despite his efforts less than a tenth of that tatterdemalion band were even able to cock an eye to see. Those few elite who stood the fire were brilliant in their maneuvers, combed the rivers and lakes and took the Slaverns under, gathered them up like tares from the wheat and bound them in silver, setting them ablaze with their cool blue flame. These watery ladies crackled and burned, screamed and cursed their brothers, and prayed to the Power of Darkness for the night.

The unicorns rode and drove and trampled the Shimbagh legions, but they faced armies of men who rode fiery horses that catapulted flaming oil. Still other deadly human archers fired bows with multiple arrows, all of them silver-tipped in venom to bring the Urhorse down. Our mystic brothers (who were rarely seen and almost never caught), were slaughtered by the hundreds where they ran. They weren't made for wars like this.

(No one is in truth.) To bring them to The Time was a crime in itself.

My dragon clansmen saw this and flew to the unicorns' aid, slashing into an endless field of ravening, soulless soldiers. Dager the Mountain—the scourge of men, the slayer of every Shimbagh who'd ever dared to sully up the skies—led the squadrons of the True to slay these miscreations, scorching them with flame and talons and crushing them to dust. In a set of nanoseconds, he'd turned them into stone, battering them at last into a powder. Hordes of Shimbagh dragons blocked him, spat their toxic gases, mauled at him with talons that broke like glass on his anodyne hide. Dager laughed and mocked them, for he was the point of the Spear. He was the greatest warrior who ever lived. But my father's was a singular triumph; so many others fell. A neophyte dragon bull had his throat slit open by a dozen Shimbagh dragons, at least a hundred Khado dogs, and more. Red Rhonda too had been taken down by a single sorcerer's spear, an ignominious end to a grand career. So many others were simply overwhelmed by force of numbers who covered them like aphids would a tree.

All this had happened while I was back negotiating my plight, striking yet another bargain with the Prince of Ruses. But now the Lightning Dragon struck into the midst of them, and the battle had been joined by the son of the Mountain!

I blazed. I streaked into the sky and dived; I fractured the edge of sound! I made my announcement to the world that I was back in business! My holy ruby flame was hot, my *Diamond I* alight, and my onyx cells were a rippling mass of ebony and steel. I tore through a squadron of Shimbagh dragons who scarcely had time to turn before I'd cut a half a score from the sky, watched them float like disembodied shingles from a roof and land in pieces to the earth below. I shot a flame that boiled a lake where Slaverns waited *en masse,* slashing and lashing out at me and shrieking 'til Kingdom come. They tried to hypnotize me with their seductive cries and open up the lust they thought would own me. But I was in the *zone.* My ears could hear the choirs of angels, and I was the sword of righteousness in their hands.

I razed the ground about the Slaverns, setting them aflame and peeled up to perch on a spindletop just to watch them scatter. As they were routed, they swam and scurried from their murky water caves. And I couldn't help but catch the fact that they carried carcasses with them—the shells and hulks of fallen gryphons they'd torn from the skies above. Leading the way, I saw the Male, the product of my flesh, the villain born of the deepest love I'd ever know on Earth. This single male of the Slavern race was taking his harem with him, hundreds of deadly tarts who carried the product of his passion. He was their lord and master now, the seed of their new corruption. I'd dreaded to think what issue they'd produce. Yet one could never judge the offspring before they'd even been born. (What if there'd been an angel born among them?)

Sleek and striking, sinews rippling, beautiful and deadly, this Slavorn gaited the land like a jungle cat fleeing the hunter's bow. He also sped with equal grace through river, lake or stream and seemed to match his music with the air. He turned one time to shriek at me and sent a silent message that he held me accountable for this. Then he spun himself into a mist, a silvery flowing cape that cloaked his fluid movements to the sea.

It was the only time all day I paused. He was, after all, my son! And bonds of blood are never quite broken as long as the body breathes. I should have taken his life when I saw him, but there was a single flicker of what I remembered to be his mother's poetic soul. It was enough to give me pause to pray for his redemption, to hope the angels of his higher nature would someday prevail. But hope is a casualty of war, and this was no time for dreaming. Even my moment's observation had left me ripe for attack. No sooner had I glided to a high plateau to look, to try and reconcile my duty with the blood of my own bone, than I glanced around to realize that I had been surrounded by an army of ten-thousand men and a flight of Shimbagh dragons.

These soldiers were adept at hunting the fiercest Dragon lord. Their silver-tipped weapons were cocked with skill and aimed straight my heart. They could have been the Captain's men were it not for the lifeless eyes. They had sold their souls to the devil for a song. Whatever the price of negotiation, wherever their spirits had flown, their minds were still aware of the prize they had.

The Shimbagh dragons drooled and looked upon me as a trophy—a great black hide to be hung in their halls down in the Throat of Balham. They had me dead if I took them on. (They had me dead if I didn't.) And even with ultimate faith in my skill, my skin began to crawl. My cells had sensed the end if I tried to take the battle to them. But timing is a tenuous thing, and though I'd lost my own, they didn't make much use of the moment they had.

Pause (because they respected me), pause (for the uncertain instant), pause (because even these soulless minions held some instinct for life) *pause* was all the time I needed to put my thoughts into words, to put my words into deeds with the singular Prayer.

> *"Ahtohhhh (Thou art)!*
> *Maalkuth! (The Kingdom)!*
> *Vegedullahh (The Power)!*
> *Vegeburrah (And the Glory)!*
> *Olahm (Amen)!"*

My mantra was the laser thrust that pierced the heart of the foe, cutting a swath wherever I breathed the flame. It was as if the words at once could kill and resurrect, and carried more force in a single breath than all the savage hordes. There was a cleansing in this cry, like cauter to the wound, that healed and sealed and stilled the sounds of half the host around me. Wherever I pointed my voice and flame, the Shimbagh legions fled or risked the wrath of banishment to realms beyond our own. How many of them bit the dust or simply disappeared, I couldn't count, for this terrible strength that passed through me was beyond all mortal measure. At least for now it got me back unscathed to the body of our clan. That I had made without so much as a single mark on my hide, turned me into a very rare warrior indeed.

I knew if I could wreak this kind of havoc on my own what would be the potential when the Captain arrived; if the Captain arrived?

The Shimbaghs had to have know it by now and sent out a death squad to slaughter his men, to slit his throat, to cut short our rendezvous. Unless I was mistaken a squadron of Shimbaghs had already been dispatched. I could see them with my onyx eyes. I could feel the twist in my gut. I could smell the contest turning sour as the sun bled down on the Earth. As we gathered to leave the field of combat, I heard a dragon lord trumpeting retreat for all clans to hear. I witnessed what had come back to regroup. It was a sight to see. Despite our bold intrepid raid, the Mystic Brotherhood had lost two of every three we'd sent out into battle. We had ravaged the forces of darkness. We had throttled the minions. Yet it was as if we'd only cut a chip in the Wall of Time.

"Our brothers are dead," I overheard a dragon princess moan. "We've seen our very finest souls depart."

"What happens now when the last of us fall?!" a Chimera captain howled for the loss of his battalions. He had seen the mass of his nation go down in a single day.

"The fate of the Mighty armed with Truth!" I barked out my reassurance, and wondered if my resolution hadn't cracked along the way.

§§§§§§§

Night calls. Cries of darkness, obloquy in
triumph, finding solace in the blanket that hid their shame from sight. The myriad moans of a night drawn down clawed their way through the silence, mockingly seductive, crooning propaganda

with a savor. I saw the blinking legions and the iridescent eyes that slithered in the shadows by the millions. They taunted and called out to us, threatening attack, yet stayed their places and gave us due respect.

> *"It's only a matter of time," they hissed.*
> *"For we serve the Lord of this Earth.*
> *"We are the bringers of Truth*
> *and you are the Liars."*

I must admit I found this a rather inopportune time for banter, but verbal ploy is always a part of war. I suppose one never loses the desire to broach *demarche*, even in the midst of Armageddon.

By fires built from the dragon's throat, we warmed our hurting hearts and honored the dead we could retrieve through holy immolation. We burned our fallen comrades in a cleansing funeral pyre and set their spirits free before the Yauls of Night could find them, catch them in their covening nets, and steal their vital-force.*

We cloaked ourselves in the ashes of our beloved and felt the warmth of their consciousness soak into our cells. I covered my wings in the memories of my fallen cosmic clansmen, and waited for my brothers to return.

---

* **Yauls of Night** were slugs of demons' tongues that floated into the air every time they screamed the name of their Master. Foully amorphous, with little power or presence; the only functions they served were to snare the vital forces of those unattuned to heaven—those who possessed no spiritual sense of what the soul was about. If someone stayed around too long or failed to understand that their soul was on a journey to their next assignment, their vital force was in danger of prolonged imprisonment, entrapment in this place we perceive as reality. Not surprisingly this is how the phenomenon of apparitions began—souls trapped in the nets of Yauls and forced to stay in places where they were lost to their bodies and no longer belonged.

Return the warriors from conflagration, through thickenings of gore, through remnants of their fallen comrades and traces of the Shimbagh races: Dager with his regiments battle-tarred and weary, slashed by tooth and claw stuck into their scales, spiked their flames into the night, flying in a wheel facing outward into the pitch where millions of claws sat poised. Half the sons of Draco had fallen in a. day. And these were the most fearless fighters who had ever taken the skies.

The SkyMaster with her flights of gryphons, sternly set eagle-lions fording against the harrier skies filled more with Shimbaghs than clouds. The Minions had taken all but a third, scarred and maimed the rest. Now those who remained found a nearby dock of rocks to roost, tended their wounds and set a torch to the shells of their lost brothers. The Gryphon Queen of course was resplendent without so much as a cut, though a veil of sadness crossed her eyes that would never be lifted again. She didn't look one time at me; she didn't even try. It was as if we were already dead to each other.

The Vyngorchim, those who fought, those who hadn't dozed, came in bands of two or three in very good spirits indeed. Even though they'd lost their share, they'd stayed within themselves. They'd played the game against their own—the ones they could defeat. They had taken a spate of Slaverns, trussed them up in silver and then toasted them with flame.

But they too had paid the price. While their brothers nodded, Shimbagh dragons had flown in their midst and virtually swallowed them whole; they'd made of a meal of these ragamuffin poets from the lighter side of time. Yet when we'd slain a Shimbagh it was as if we had slaughtered air. Although they bled and died by the thousands, they had scarcely left a trace.

It was the same all over. In the rivers and lakes below, Griivres lay dying on the banks but none of their crass opponents left a trace of anything but residue on sand. The Unicorns and Rahntish who had taken on armies of soldiers— spiked them in their places and then trampled them to dust—

had no trophy to show for it, scarcely a single body. And these were men! The very least of all magical creatures on Earth! They had left nothing for us to see while we counted our losses in nations! We tore them apart, yet we were the ones who were dying.

What was this game they played with us? And why did I feel so empty. After I'd rescued men and nations why did I feel so alone? Why had Knot V, a decadragon enlightened in all other ways, come to be obsessed with the slaughter of Shimbaghs? If we were such superior souls why take on this war and fight the immortal Lord of Darkness on his own terrain? Was this angelic consciousness? Or were we just fooling ourselves that we could put the sword to the Dark One's throat. Why, although we had carried the standard, could we not comfort each other? Where was my mother? And where was Skye now that the fog of battle had cleared?

I felt the comfort of the Flame, the fire of Truth before us. And yet I felt no comfort on this Earth. "I make a call to Unify!" I said for all to hear. My brother Pod was first to my side, touching wing to wing. My father joined, and Rueg the Roth, and all the Dragon Clan. Into our midst came the Chimera King, then thundered the Unicorn Prince, rumbled in the Rahntish and the roaming Gamberol. Finally the Gryphon aerie and their majestic Queen settled on the outer rim to offer silent assent, to nod their feral accolades for all that we had done. Their coming fairly capped the moment, and cut through to the truth for us all—that we were in this together, stand or fall.

"We'll meld our auras through the darkness and keep our fires bright. For a Shimbagh fears the truth and abhors the Light." Dager spoke out firmly, for when the Mountain talked the heavens heeded. For a while the sound of his voice was played like the warrior's favorite tune; it so lifted our spirits to feel his power among us. Yet, truth be known, our prescient skills had left us in the shadows while we waited for the next assault and prayed for an early dawn.

Canto 30

Sleep Eagle

Drums! from the bitter face of night
Charting their advance.
Drums! that came from kettles brewed in Hell!
Drums! to cloak the strategies.
Drums! to catch the swell.
Drums! to pace the
Starting of the Dance!

—Blood Waltz
The Song of Shala

I was the wedge in all of this. I was the mocker of darkness. I, the Answerer of the Prayer, just by speaking could be the Shield. I could turn my voice to the right and merely by making the gesture, simply by saying the words could strike a Shimbagh from the night. So it was said. So it was rumored, but rumors are seldom the truth, and what might have worked for an army or two was smothered in *Ultima Thule*.

We couldn't begin to probe their depth, yet they could take our measure. We were large enough to penetrate and small enough to engulf. We made of ourselves too great a target, and arrogance was our Achilles' heel. For warriors like us were far too proud to take a defensive stance, to hide beneath leaves and boulders to make ourselves obscure. Oh no! We had to show it off, as if courage alone would sustain us, and cunning could never be a part of the plan.

I, the Answerer, seemed safe enough; they avoided me. But they could savage our clansmen in a flash. As long as the night had teeth, these creatures could strike at will and take down the bravest among us with a silvery slit to the heart.

The Kingus were the best at this. They opened their poison breasts, and out flowed a plague of night demons, snakes, and creatures from the void. They'd strike and bite and infect our forces, driving our dragons mad, slit the rahntish in the throat, and pluck out the unicorn's eyes, tearing open the shielded pecs that held the gryphon's heart. Even though they killed very few of us, their venom carried infection, and now with the Thral Melons all but gone, so in time would we be.

The Slaverns came to even the score, to snare their sleeping brothers, serenade the Vyngorchim with a deadly lullaby, then snatch them into the night and under the water. Then there was the pygmie—the ones already damned, or those who had sold their souls for the pittance that came with earthly power. Some were already dead and seemed impossible to kill, leaving only a residue like any Doppelganger. But there were those well-trained and bloody, still alive in the flesh. They were the ones who set about to make a feast of us. They were the ones who deliberately set out to sully our souls. Dragons wounded in the field were pinioned and opened up for evisceration—the sacrifice that bought the time that only the pygmie could prize. All through the night, we could hear the cries that struck us to our soul:

"Fire of Stone!
Stone of Fire!
Fire of Stone
of Fire
of Stone
to come!"

There was no doubting what it meant. The wizard and warrior communion—vicious and unholy as any mortal pact could be—seemed to be the locus here as if the rest were ruse, a sideshow to disguise their true intent.

We could have attacked. We should have attacked. But that was what they wanted—for the Dragon to leave the others who were vulnerable in the night. The Dragons, as we always did, stood as sentinels for the rest, forming the buffer zone from here to the throat of abomination. Lighting the darkness with Draco's flames born in the eye of the Sol, we were the light of the night, our gems shining through. We could turn them all to pewter; we could shock them to stone. We could torch them before they crossed the waters that formed our moat. Some like the Slaverns were water creatures; they were in their element. Yet when they came they knew they had to deal with the likes of us.

"Turn on your gems!" my father ordered.

"Your gems!" came the echo from Rueg.

"The gems!" came the answer from dragon ranks up and down the line. Like a menorah coming to glow we stood the ramparts that framed us, holding fort and awaiting the ultimate rush. Now it was as it had always been the dragon who took the brunt, who stood the stalwart to keep the Shimbaghs at bay. And even though they outnumbered us infinity to one, they kept their cautious distance and hid themselves from our light.

Why? I wondered. What perverse talent did we possess to lock them in place like this? Besides, had they not already abandoned hope? Were they not already damned for all time? What did life matter to them? Was self-preservation such a force that it carried beyond the soul?

Why did we high dragons who knew how to turn men to stone now sit frozen while our brothers screamed for their end? Instead of taking initiatives, we stood our dutiful posts forced to taste the salt of our denial, forced to hear the chants of pygmies at their blood revival taunting us for the impotence our disciplines had wrought us. Songs without lyrics sickened our senses simply by the music they made—canticles of conjuration, smoke from the sorcerer's pipe playing us for the fools they thought us to be.

I would have opted for a standoff, but I sensed it wouldn't be. Rakushar and her wizards knew they stood to lose from delay. They had to move this very night, for night was their Factor-X. They knew they could overwhelm us with this; it was only a matter of time. Perhaps they were toying with us like prey that they already had in a cage. Still, I couldn't help but notice they probed with all due caution.

With all this postured waiting out, we were sitting still for the storm. No matter how strong we were at our post, the flood of their numbers would drown us, unless we set into motion. Yet it seemed, I was the only one who felt this need to move—to take it to them before they came to us.

Filled with wonder, plagued with doubt, I felt ill-at-ease with the task. Nevertheless, I could feel the pressure; the burden was mine to bear. Now was the time for cunning, and I had learned from the best. After all, I had passed my days among men. I had schooled myself on the Magpie. If anyone could lie to the Night, if anyone could beguile them, it would be the Lightning Dragon acting on his own. If I could stall their attack until morning, the Captain might arrive, form the Stars of Transmutation, and summon our angels down.

But where was the Captain now? I wondered. Would he make it on time? Assuming he did, could he even begin to put a blister on this?

I asked. I prayed.

"What news?" I called. I didn't need to define it. Elaboration was a skill lost on the tongues of men.

The answer came with my brother, Pod. He flew swiftly to my side with the most detailed accounting I could hope for.

"They sent a horde to intercept him — sorcerers riding the rain, coming on shafts of sleet and hail so he couldn't sift them out. But the Captain is a wily buggar. He had already foreseen the tactic and hoisted a silver canopy to billet himself from the storm. It covered his battle-marred chariot. It guarded his arms and men. It blossomed like an argent flower to keep the spilth from the ground. It worked. It stood the sorcerers off, but evil is resourceful, and re-source is the one thing of which they have no end.

"They've sent for reinforcements, so they've kept the Captain stalled. He cannot reach us. And since this clutch of wizards are a mutable source, he cannot focus his sword or hone-in on a target. He cannot banish all that mass of evil any more than he can waste the wind."

"It seems that we should go to him to send our best to the rescue."

"But you, dear brother, are the best. And we have need of you here. Not even you have fashioned the skill to be in two places at once, unless you have a trick up your sleeve that I have yet to see."

I shuddered at the high regard in which this Vyngorch held me, when he had grown far more in stature than anything I had done. He had made the quantum leap from buffoonery to honor, from clown to nominal leader of his band. If the Vyngorchim were to ever be accepted in the clan. it would be because of what Pod had done to mold them into mettle. For now, he was wounded, bleeding from one wing that seemed to have nearly been torn in half, yet made so little of it he refused to be attended.

"It's nothing. I can still do a more graceful peel than you."

"So you can," I said, though I couldn't hide my concern. "There are still few melons from the Thral. I can pull what strings are needed to get you attended to, and see you healed."

"They're Slavern slashes," Pod belittled the notion. "They offer no long term stress. They're our sisters after all, and self-healing still runs thick in the blood. Even though they can kill their mothers with merely a slice to the skin, they haven't quite the venom with a sibling. Besides, if one of ours goes mad who can tell the difference? The Vyngorchim are still held in thin regard at best, so all our eccentricities get very little notice."

"You mentioned 'sending our best,' I agree. So I'm commissioning you. Take a band of your finest and divert the Captain's attackers. A little time is all he needs to make his way to us."

"He's still a league and a half away, and he's just a man after all. And only the wicked among them can travel as we do. Besides, despite your kind words to me, we're hardly the ones to do this. Even our finest are still quite prone to nod off in the midst of a flight, and we're the only ones against whom the Shimbagh dragons prevail. Except for the Slaverns who seem to have everyone else's number, we're not much of a match for anyone, even now."

"Precisely," I said. "It's just because you are so lightly regarded, no one will protest your leaving or expect much to come from your efforts. Underestimation can serve one well, if one knows how to use it. The sorcerers and their dragon Shimbaghs will not overshift to meet you. They know you wouldn't dare to take them directly.

"Fly in low, come at an angle, and sing to them when you do. The Captain will see you're a friendly force, and the Shimbaghs can have their laugh. Once you've arrived, drop down among them and give the battalion a ride. At worst each Vyngorch can carry a man or two, and speed and grace in flight has always been your *sine qua non*. Since you can outfly the lot, dear brother, the Captain is your charge. Get to him first and get him back to us. You can cut the travel time in half and be here by midday. If we can hold on, it just might turn the battle."

"The Council?" Pod questioned.

"Just go," I whispered, emphatically. "Success will be our glory. If we fail, there'll be no one left to offend, So the point is really moot. It's yours to make my little brother, so know that my prayers go with you. The bad new is, you have to leave tonight."

"Tonight?" Pod gulped.

"Tonight," I answered. "I know it's not your best time. That's why the Shimbagh command will never expect it. I'll get you the cover you need, rest assured. I have a plan of my own. You see, dear Pod, they're looking for major players. If I come at them with all I've got, they'll literally leap at the chance. That will give you the time you need to slip through. Just keep your little clan awake long enough, at least until the sun comes up. By then, you'll be at least halfway to the Captain."

I brushed across his wing with mine, and used my garnet heart to cauterize his wound with healing light. I won't credit myself for doing the job, but indeed the bleeding stopped. (The light that steels the mind can heal the body.) Perhaps the blood had rushed to his head, for this Pod had a mighty task; more of a burden than any dragon should bear.

"It will be done," he said to me. "And I am the dragon to do it. The others you can send to diffuse their perceptions."

"It will be done, I know...until The Time," I answered, "And you're right, the numbers will divert them. Nonetheless, may every kind of angel be thy escort."

The time was set. I had to move, for every moment lost was another one that sat in the Shimbaghs' favor. Even now, across the ethers, I could feel Rakushar coughing out more evil souls than the air had room to fill.

I would have to stage a raid, for more than a number of reasons, not only to give the Vyngorchim cover but also to reset the focus. I sensed the Shimbaghs had decided to throw the whole damned lot at us, for the light of day was not a friend to them. Even then, I could feel their rhythm. I could hear their breath as they sibilated their pleasure, licking their chops as they came to shop for more victims in the night. In darkness our allies couldn't see, while they with the infrared eyes thrived in such an unholy lack of light.

What else could I do? We were frozen and could only hold our posts. Only the dragon could meet them square up, and we had duties to stay. Everyone of course, except for the Lightning Dragon. It wouldn't be such a sacrifice. After all, was I not onyx? Wouldn't my blackness be the cloak to get me through the night? Didn't I know the Asking Prayer? Was I not the Answerer? Could anyone else have done the drill but me?

(I've always loathed rhetorical questions, but this was the drum song I sang—a way to pump myself up for the task ahead.)

"Torch up the sky!" I called to my father. "I'm going raze some Hell!"

"Torch up the sky!" he anticipated. He knew just what to do, and blurted a plume of flame to proclaim his endorsement. It crackled like Krakatoa itself and set off the dragon bulls—a torch of salute for the hardiest fool among them.

I would go it alone. The beasts would not harm me, for I could talk in tongues. I could speak the language they dreaded to hear. For anyone else to have a go at the game would have meant their demise. Besides there were times when one fared better alone.

"Shartallion!" Came the cries from the ramparts. The Chimera captains sang.

"Sharto!" The dragon bulls scorched my name at the night.

"Sharto!" the Unicorn Prince did thunder, pawing the ground with his hoof, setting off a raucous stampede that drowned out the Vyngorchim's departure.

"Atohhh!" I roared, feeling the fire of purpose rise inside me, turning me into a furnace whose source not even I could contravene. There was no *légerdemain* in this. By now, they knew I was coming. That was hardly surprising. The surprise would come with my wing-mate.

I closed my eyes, readied for flight, and when I looked again, I saw ten million antimony eyes waiting to devour me. I prayed for my own ubiquity, but said it without conviction. Prayers muttered from the faithless are but candles in a storm. I wanted to believe but felt unworthy to the task; I'd judged myself when I had abandoned the right.

I broke the night, shattered its veil as if it were made of glass. I made for the worst of them with the best I had. The Asking Prayer was on my tongue, but before I could even say it, I felt a presence by my side that was clear as a diamond sun. An angel's voice with a warrior's strength was there to share my venture, and even in the darkness I could feel the Eagle-Lion Queen.

"I'm the breath of your retribution," I felt the words to my loin. "I'm still your better in flight. And you'll need my ineffable skills. Besides, if one is going to face the sisters of abomination, it's best to have one's soul-mate at one's side."

The Gryphon Queen with Shala's voice, an irresistible creature. She had my heart and my fire inside, and the courage of twenty more. If I could have chosen another creature to share my bed or my shield, it would now and forever be the Master of the Skies. She was so feral, so wild of eye, yet when I held her gaze I saw inside the hope of a child in a maelstrom. Courage was the name of this—a wish to be anywhere else, a willingness nevertheless to face the Turk. Locked together wing to wing we sailed into the blackness, lightning speed and deadly grace the only strength we knew.

We were the mace of righteousness, the terrible swift sword. We were the head of the spear they hadn't expected, plunged into the meat of them before they could react.

> *"Atoh!*
> *Malkuth*
> *Vegedullah!*
> *Vegaburrah!*
> *Olam!!"*

I could feel the mass of them part and give way, some disintegrating as I passed my talon like a cross and sang the dreaded hymn. What I hadn't even considered was that this corrupted host would, like the sea of damnation it was, become wholly unipolar. The further I swam through its blackness, the more vulnerable I would become, until they could engulf me from behind. By sheer force of numbers they could have shredded me and sent back my head as an omen, or taken my heart and smoked it on the "Fire of Stone of Fire!"

Rakushar had envisioned my charge and knew in her divination that I would dare to take the chance and run her deadly gauntlet. But what she had failed to factor-in was the second player who would enter—that my own twin-flame would guard the rear, and that the Power of Two could span the Gulf of Infinity itself.

Souls sailed at us in endless profusion, creatures in countless armies began as specks of cosmic dust that swelled to lethal masses. Slashing wing and claw and fang they spat their poison breath and lashed out right and left to rip at every cell on my body. Yet as they did, I could feel the Gryphon Queen respond. She was merely automatic, magnificence of reflex, utterly the most unassailable creature in this World. Master of the Skies, she was; with a rip and a tear and a parry, she could take down a dozen villains in a sparrow's single heartbeat. Had she not come with me, I would have been a trophy. As it was, we had the worst ahead.

It was an hour that seemed a year that we fought our way through the hordes. But one thing we knew: we had done the job before us. The whole host of the Evil One had either participated, or looked on from afar to see what the outcome would be. Whatever else we had accomplished we'd diverted their attention; we had delayed the assault and called the light of hope to Heaven. I could feel the new morning light caress the mountain crests. Just beyond them the mystic clan waited. Their cheers now spanked the sky. We could hear but could not see them, for now a wall of death rose up against us.

As the light came up a sea of Slaverns awaited our return, summoned to the task no doubt by Rakushar herself. Whether this Beastmaker had manufactured these water witches for us, or whether they'd heard that the pair of us had pierced the cloak of night, their entire nation seemed to have taken the field and formed a screaming monolith to block our path of return. They drooled. They screamed. They called our names. They spewed their curses at us. If words could kill, we would have died right there.

"Master and mistress of miscegenation, behold the fruit of your passion. You have spawned the fatal blow to the heart of your very clan. You are the seed of your own destruction. You've recreated the night. No one will ever seek water again, after the sun goes down. We can snatch the soul from an infant, steal a lover's dreams, and skewer the hearts of a nation of mystical beasts before we're through.

"Thanks to you! Thanks to you! Thanks to you!"

Never had I felt so much virulent hatred at one time, for even among enemies there exists a code of respect; not here. No question, these lovely ladies wanted our gizzards for sausage. We were the symbols of what they feared the most. Not only had we taken the laws of simple transmigration and moved them to levels far beyond their grasp, we had switched the keys on them and fertilized the seed of another race that might have meant their demise. Unless I was mistaken, the lovely angel that had become our daughter would mate to create a holy clan that would mean an end to them. While they had our son, and he'd filled their bellies with the seed of his desire, the jury was out. What would they become after all?

It seemed that our love was a plague to them, for these Slaverns had joined *en masse* to see that we'd have no chance to ever express it again. This was a very personal thing, prompted I felt by our son, for more than just a war, they were out to play this game to the end.

There was no longer pressure from behind, only curiosity now — the morbid kind that a cat enjoys with a mouse. Even for super warriors this host was entirely too much to bear. We were but two and they were a sea of scythes. The cold steel talons cocked at us, the eyes that could freeze an inferno glowed with black vampiric light that could cut us to the quick. To make matters worse, these deadly ladies wanted a shot at us. If we didn't rush them in an instant, they would mass for attack.

In the final moments before the dawn when darkness does its worst, we hung surrounded with nowhere to go but straight ahead to our doom. No angelic arias or Asking Prayers could save us. We were trapped, and the end was a foregone conclusion.

§§§§§§§

When all else fails, pray for a miracle or just some damned good luck! I realized in my hot pursuits of being a cosmic stud that I'd almost forgotten the laws of manifestation. There's a spiritual answer to every empirical problem on this Earth. In fact, this plane is not that tough to master. But I, like the pygmie, had now become so enamored of the game, that I had let my mortal pursuits dull the spiritual blade.

Now was the time to change my form into that of a flea, into mist or prana or simply disappear. But arrogance kept me in this warrior dragon's body now, and pride would be the quarrel that shot me down.

But then the echoes of my thoughts came back to announce to me…"Mist or prana." Where had I last encountered such a song? Prayers—even clumsy ones—can often find the way. And the Way would come in the Breath of the Mantilough. The daughters of the morning dew had kept themselves from this, for they were progeny of the Moon when it kissed the Evening Primrose. They with the faces of fawns, the wings of doves and tongues from the favorite fabric of butterflies' secret songs were only a Dominion's breath away from this harrowing plane of life. Hidden in the enclaves of poetry in the midst of the warriors' madness, they worked their magic to shield the children of dawn.

I remembered well their raptures, my etheric liaison with the Mantilough Princess and the gifts that I received to lift my shattered resolve. She had prophesied there would come a time like this in my life. I could only pray that this lady would keep her word.

"If the moon is masked and the risk is high, and the winds are devoid of direction, danger threatens your life, and only we can match the game. Call for us. We'll even the odds then quickly go our way. For we're not of this conflict, or your illusions of right and wrong…"

They were the flawless allies in a moment of direst need, for they were the ones on the plane between dimensions. Only mystical beasts could see them, and none of low vibration. They only revealed themselves for those they chose. To Shimbaghs they were invisible, but when they sang their silent song the Mantilough breathed a mist that clouded all reason. It was the Mother of Illusion, the Eye in the Mirror of Hope. It was the hymn that sang the eagle to sleep.

I remembered well their admonition; it haunts me to this day. Yet in that moment, it was a call to glory. I cried out for the Mantilough, though I did so in their language.

And *"Equinox!"* was the only word I said.

To the outposts of our battlements they came in silent convenings and breathed a blessed fog across the meadows. They uttered poetry under their breath that so confounded the Shimbagh that even the wizards of night couldn't crack the veil.

So perfect was her clarity that it made me reluctant to ask for such a selfish reason as my own life. Yet there was another to consider—a queen who led a nation, the woman I loved whose soul did dwell within. I feared for her. The path ahead, lined as it was with Slaverns, though dreadful to me, was certainly fatal to her.

"You worry too much, my dragon Lord," she whispered softly. She could make death rattles seem like a love song. "Love is the shield that deflects all wrong. The rest is merely illusion. Even life and death are merely passages in the tome."

"Ride with me, my Queen," I answered her. "Lay your wings on mine. Let the fire from my jaws and the thunder of my flight be our armor. I'll have you through it, and before we're done there'll not be a scratch upon you. For you are the Queen of Destiny, and the mistress of my soul."

She obeyed and fit on me, and though we were different creatures, she blended into me as if we were one in the same. Never had I known so perfect a fit in nature, in this life or any other. Never would I feel the same again.

I circled and waited for the magical mists to rise. I kept the faith, and the Mantilough kept their word. Lifting up in vapors so sweet they could mollify the Magog, came the holy nebula that clouded the eyes of night. It was a fog that crept through the ranks of the Slaverns, a vapor so pungent and dense that it not only blocked out one's vision but also one's sense of smell. Since Shimbaghs could sniff out a drop of blood a half a league away, this perfume was the ally I had prayed for; a means of covering every tip of the wing, until I got us back safely.

Nevertheless I streaked through their ranks with all deliberate haste, knowing well that magical cloud wouldn't hold up for long. Slaverns waited, their venomous talons hiked toward the sky like gamecocks in the final throes of a long and deadly bout. Yet they seemed almost frozen in their places. It was as if the mist had hypnotized them, not only rendering them mystified but immobilized to boot.

It was too easy. I should have known. And though early premonition prompted me to swift through this as fast as my wings could carry, we were almost sailing. We were grace and speed without hindrance. We were flying through a wall of poison razor claws. Yet everything was frozen as if petrified in place and only came to life as we whipped past. Then sheaves of talons like leaves of grass licked upward lashing at us, and in our wake we heard the harpy wails as they realized we'd gotten through. But Slaverns have a network that communicates by heat, and they sent a subcutaneous message to their sisters who waited ahead.

"We've been enchanted! Adjust your timing!" Adjust, they did. In anticipation of our coming, the slashes began to come in ever increasing patterns, as if by randomly stabbing in infinite numbers they could make a mince of us. It almost worked. We could feel the wind of their reckless unseeing strokes, but by now I was almost through them and could actually see the light. What blows did strike came at such a glance, I could easily parry the attack.

There was a horizon of valent light, a guide-on to rally our path. I could feel its positive charge and use it to hold direction.

We'd make it through this! I could feel it! We'd carry through the night, and make it past this deadly sheet of sluts.

I could smell the sweet breezes of freedom, the clean air of kindred spirits. I could feel the darkness fall away, and the light of day upon us. I could taste the salt of sunlight on my tongue. I felt like singing but heard instead a screech like a heart-struck bird, that of an eagle shot down from the sky, followed by a vicious thud of a blade thrust into flesh. With sickening simultaneity, I was struck with the realization that whatever I did would be too little too late. I heard my soul-mate let out a gasp that was both horrified and sad, as I whipped around to see our son before us.

"Greetings, mommy!" he snarled at us. Blood dripped from his talons, and I could tell by the leer on his face that this quisling had struck home. I torched him, but my blow fell late, for he'd already gone. He'd "offed" his mother and dived back to his own.

Even though she rode on me, I could feel her essence slipping until she was little more than a weightless shell on my back.

"Hold on, my darling," I whispered to her, but my voice was lost in the din, the deafening scrowls of celebration from the core of the Shimbagh clan.

It had been her maternal instinct that had left her open to this, for this lady would never have let a single blow undo her. But her very own son? There was that moment when she'd stopped to reflect in his eyes. And he had relied that softness to do her in. I had done the very same thing just the day before, had him in my gunsights and let him go. Now, it had already happened once too often; it would never happen again. The next time that I saw him, he would die.

A word to the wiser souls among us: Always follow the GUT—the Great Universal Truth inside of you. Listen to your instincts. Your mind's-eye is a ruse, a trick played upon you by your egocentric self.

Act first! Act swiftly! Your cells will tell you how your heart will sing with the truth, your inner self will swell with rightness when you make the spiritual choice. Make up your mind last of all, and only when all else fails; to resort to it first is to knock on calamity's door.

We were clear of the eaves of nighttime now. I streaked toward the dragon's ramparts, took my loving queen in my arms and pressed her down on my wing.

But the Gryphon Queen had left us somewhere along the way, and before me lie the frail human form and the quivering body of Shala. Her heart had been rent as if torn from her, but her soul through the eyes was clear, and though I called for a Kohmm to attend her I knew that I'd lost her again.

"We've been the journey twice my love. I will not come again. But I've shared more with you in a moment of time than a thousand incarnations. It's not duration that measures love's power but the depths to which we go to find our truth and know each other's flame. On the other side of time, my Prince, we'll have our final dance. For now, you have to take the journey alone. But take my final breath with you, my dragon, and know the truth of this: that where your flame burns brightest you will always be a man."

She said it again. Her last few words were with a woman's lips, while I was plagued with a monstrous fiery tongue. I wanted to kiss her good-bye again, to have been human for a moment. But I was a dragon war-lord and could only scream my pain. I didn't dare to weep, for the heat of my tears would have scalded what remained of the most exquisite soul who ever drew a breath.

An honor guard of Gryphon came and willowed eagle-songs,
and waited while I torched the empty shell of the love I held. I
covered myself in her ashes until I was grey with remorse and
howled my prayers to the sky for her redemption.

"Shala-a-a!" The word was a prayer with a power that cracked
the face of day and caused the sky to fall dark and thunderous
with the mention of the name. "Shala-a-a!" It was a canticle of
forgiveness and battle cry all in one.

Even from the enemy there was a moment of repose, a pause
of respect for the passing of a noble soul. She had gone into the
next dimension, better far than this, and had left a nation behind
to wear the morning. What we all knew inside our prescient
cells, was that more than a Gryphon Queen had died. A seam of
magic had been torn away from the fabric of what we were and
could never be sewn together again.

§§§§§§§

Had any of this been worth it? I wondered.
What if we hadn't responded? What if we had simply let the law
of events take their course? As the light of morning came upon
the horror that we faced, it helped reaffirm the purpose for our
cataclysmic campaign. From what I could see in the sky before
us—the hideous strength of the mass, the stench of ambition
that came from the breath of the Fallen One Himself—we were
the vanguard of sanity in a universe gone mad; we were the wall
that stood before the storm. Whatever we did from this moment
on would be a step toward glory; we had done what we could to
stem the tide.

During the night, despite my raid, we had lost a host of allies.
Not only had I lost my Queen, the other half of my soul, but
others in the Mystic Clan had been all but devastated. The
Vyngorchim who had remained had all been slaughtered while
sleeping. Only those with Pod and his flight remained of that
nation of poets. The Unicorn Prince informed us they were
down to a dozen herds, where once a hundred thousand might

have roamed. The Rahntish were all but obliterated. The Chimera's latest count gave losses far worse than they had estimated. Many who had remained alive had gone stark-raving mad. And now there was scarcely a single Kohmm in sight. There were few Thral melons available to heal those stricken down, but those had opportunistically been carted from view.

The Gryphon Nation was deep in mourning. Only the Dragons had held. And we faced a force that had doubled over night. Unless the Captain came, and soon, it would be a very long day, and very well might be the last we ever shared.

I took a breath that was interrupted by the beat of my aching heart, sharpened my talons and looked from side to side. On my left my Father, the Mountain, keened his cobalt eyes, glancing my way but once and showed me his thousand toothed smile that could eat its way a through steel. He pinned back his ears and motioned his wing for a legion of dragons behind him to ready themselves for the coming swell of Shimbaghs. Further down the line, I could hear the Roth call his bulls to formation. And I looked around to see two thousand or so take their places behind my right wing.

Our force was immense but nothing, it seemed, compared to the view before us, as the sky itself moved in toward our clan in clouds of Shimbagh hordes. I readied myself. Somehow, I knew that once the contact was made, I'd wade into them and not come out again. And then I heard it. The hale and brawny beating of ten thousand wings, the screeching of fiery expletives, the rip of claw and fang tearing with gusto into the Shimbagh flank.

They'd come! No, not the Captain yet, but a greater surprise by far—the Dragons of the North and their Scarlet Queen!

Canto 31

Answered Prayers

The North Dragons cut into the Shimbaghs like an axe would wedge a melon. With Seti leading the way they made a feast of them. Even the darlings of Rakushar, the witches and wizards, with all their divining hadn't foreseen this event. It was just the shot we needed for one last go at the war, for one last run at the Fallen One's disciples.

Bravery comes in many forms, and no one knows who will wear it, until its measure is taken against all odds. If I'd ever questioned my sister's virtue or the way she viewed her world, I'd never once doubted the depth or scope of her courage. What amazed me was the artistry with which she plied her craft, for she was a warrior by whom the standard was set. If love of the fight was a requisite that determined one's success, then she took her father's measure and mine as well. Her speed of attack more than made up for the technical skills she lacked. She wasn't graceful. She wasn't slick. But if gusto could win the day, she would have taken the prize nine times out of ten. Her warriors too, scarred and flawed and hideous to behold, were the very models of mortal combat, machines bred to the purpose, eyes alight with the lust, the taste for endless slashing and burning—the talent for which we were known. It wasn't fair to be branded like this, renowned for what becomes us least. Yet it was the Norse Dragons who most relished this reputation.

It was rare to watch their fatal waltz, for in energy and aura these rogues among the dragons wore the countenance of Shimbaghs—hideous and boorish, lacking in grace of flight, yet displaying such a love of the act that they gave it a different value. To hear them shout, to feel their zeal, to share their ready grit helped us regain our heart to finish the Game. It had been just the needed tonic, for at last we regained our focus. (So what if I died, I'd sipped the broth of purpose.)

The Shimbaghs curled back their amorphous mass like clouds of midnight protecting the darkest secrets ever known, made way for the relentless sun and my sister's persistent Rogues. I doubted they'd take flight from this, for they lacked a head to command them—only wizards on Rocs who whipped the rest like psychic overseers. The body of them merely shrank back like a singular organism recoiling from a pinprick. In the meantime, the Rogues scorched their way through them and flew to take our side.

Seti, a Shimbagh wing in her jaws torn from its former owner, sauntered before me and formally spat it out. Another Shimbagh clutched in her talons, she tossed on rocks below where it exploded like a dust dropped down from a lady's powder box.

"So you've held your own. I'm not surprised. These Shimbaghs are a porridge. You have to attack straight through them. Go for the head. All the rest is a veil." Before I could speak She anticipated my thoughts, for (I needed reminding) she'd retained her onyx powers and gained a fair share. "I know, you've lost your Eagle Queen. I'm sorry. But this is war! To pause and think for a moment means the loss of your edge. It's a simple world when you get down to it, and simple thoughts are the best. Do one thing at a time, and forget the rest. You're too busy trying to figure out the destiny of the race. Just fight and win and the rest will take care of itself. And if we lose? Well, what the hell. We were bred for this. We're fighters not lovers. Just take a look in the mirror."

She actually brushed me with her wing. I never thought I'd see that. And I didn't need to remind her that we'd been at this awhile. The fact that I was cut but not bleeding gave her a sign as well. I hadn't noticed, but Seti had in a trice.

"They say when you've gained the *Diamond I,* your wounds will cauterize and heal themselves by the holy fire that burns away all anguish. So, you really did it, brother dear. You're the Answerer of the Prayer. You're the Sun of Destiny; what an awful burden to bear. Well, sing your pretty song, Shartallion, and let's get on with our business. There's a load of Shimbagh butt to kick out there."

"'Tis surprised I am to find you, sister, and glad to note your arrival, though I never thought I'd get to see the Queen of Cynics herself. And fighting for a worthy cause! My God! What a rush of conscience! Was it something in the food you ate? Or something on the Wind?"

"Things were getting dull up North. Once you've leveled the land, destroyed a castle or two and held a nation hostage, things tend to quiet down a bit; so the boys were getting restless. Besides, who'd want to miss a fight like this? Only one comes in an eon, and it's more than apparent to me, that you lack the knack of doing the job yourselves."

My father flew into our midst and hovered. It was the very first time he'd seen my sister since she was a calf. They said nothing to one another, but sized each other up with some measure of silent respect that one flawed soul would reserve for another. He merely nodded, then glanced at me. What passed for a smile crossed his face.

"Looks as though we get to die as a family." He nodded, then peeled, spouting remarks like puissant oaths to the sky. "A Queen, she is! Well what the hell! Water finds its own level."

Through the arriving North dragon hordes, the ones who'd made it through, Dager waded back to his own battalions. Without so much as a greeting, in fact with a little back whip of his tail, he smacked a couple of rogues out of his path. It was clear he took no pleasure in the alliance. He rejoined his own brigade of bulls, the tribunes of our clan, and sharpened his talons — a sure sign that our last attack was but a war-cry away.

Seti took her place at my right, her warriors at her side forming in gangs that made it a point of honor to flout tradition. They arrived from the battle in ganglion clusters without a hint of formation, for this was a mob for whom only the goddess Chaos had an ear. They tried to appear undaunted, these rogues, their half-harlequin band with broken horns and fight scarred wings from rumbles fought long ago. Yet I could tell by the slightest glance that the Shimbaghs had made their points against them. In less than a morning they'd lost a third of their ranks just getting through.

Day had broken. It was our move. The sky was curling again with myriad yawning jaws and claws of every corrupted creature. They spewed forth such a heat and smell that it nearly stunned us senseless, while the roar they threw out was deafening beyond our powers to withstand it. I could no longer hear my own thoughts, much less my father's calls to battle, but through an amber haze of poison breath, I could see him set the attack.

"*Atoh!*" The word flew out in flames.

The others followed the cry.

Even Seti said the word, although she mouthed it with a smirk.

It was mine to lead the advance. Of course, I had the song. I was the Diamond-tipped spear in the thrust of this. Yet once we launched and they engulfed us, there was no turning back. This was it. The end would come at last.

A keener mind now guided the Shimbaghs, orchestrating their movements with strokes of malevolent genius that were as wicked as they were wise. Where chaos had been their prime expression and force of numbers their trump, they suddenly played coy with us and retreated before our charge, careful to stay just out of range from the sound of my voice—so no sacrifices of their masses could be made. Meanwhile, they closed-in behind us like clouds on a stormy day until the world above and below was crimson and black with their presence. Lewd and mocking, shrill and facile, they showed us a separate ardor, a calculated confidence that told me they were close to their Door. We could even feel the heat of it as it blew from the South and the East—the very vault of the Evil One himself. They breathed as if from one body, a puce and amber gas the heat of which was coming close to routing our resolve. The stench of it was dizzying and caused a loss of focus. It was as if we were being sedated from all care—bled of cause, robbed of purpose, drugged into complacence, overpowered with ambivalence, and what a way to go?

"Surrender, Mystics. You've done your best. But now the fight is done. Give up. We have you coming and going, and now you're going down. Give in or die. It's six of one. It's all the same to us. We have the power to smother you, or make you slaves to our cause. But then, you're all becoming that already."

Emerging from their midst once more came the goddess-bitch herself, Rakushar looking more seductive now than she ever had before. It was a certain vanity that caused her to strike that pose, to assume the ruse of beauty, the mask of virtue. Yet surely she knew we weren't fooled, except for the rogues who had come. They hadn't seen her before and might be easily tantalized. They hadn't much of a moral compass on the very best of days. That was it! She was trying to seduce them. Even now I could see they were faltering, the bulls magnetized by her charm, growing drunk on pheromone and the scent of sandalwood that seemed to flow from her breath like pollen from a flower. Whenever they came close enough they could see her for the monster that she was, but by then it would be too late; she would devour them. As only one female can to another, my sister caught the ruse, but her roars of warning were smothered in the rising chant of their sour chaotic chorus. With surprising speed she made a bee-line straight for the Beastmaker's throat, but I could have told her it was a futile gesture. One needed a cache of hidden magic to cope with this lady's powers, to match her supersenses and rip the mask away. Seti, with all her physical strength, would be just a meal for her. She'd turn her into a bitch in heat or a malformed toad on a rock or even worse, a pygmie with no soul to call her own. This was the Beastmaker, after all. Her powers knew few limits. If worse came to worse, she would simply take a gulp and swallow her whole.

I knew this dark lady's secrets by now, and I could call her bluff. I'd been there once and survived, and I'd do it again. I was faster in flight than Seti, quicker now than anyone on this Earth, so I blasted by her and made for Rakushar's throat. If the chanting of the Shimbaghs, I'd reckoned, was causing us all to fall faint, to disorient and lessen our resolve, then I would shatter sound, would rift the lock of time and finally twist the key. All the while, I'd chant the Prayer, the prayer with all the meaning, the only thing that was keeping us in the game.

"Atoh!" I started the incantation. *"Malkuth!"* poured out from my lips as I made for the vulnerable curve next to the Beastmaker's throat.

Seeing me pass my sister up while making my way for her merely caused Rakushar to yawn. And as she drew air, she brought her mouth to swell to the size of a cavern large enough to swallow a dragon like a toad would take a fly. She even seemed to laugh as she heard me screeching The Asking Prayer, until I tore through the threshold of concord and into the silence beyond.

For that perfect instant, I'd slipped through the door that holds us in this dimension and everything had frozen in place but me: Rakushar's yawping flayed-skin mouth larger than the Crater of Nebul, locked in place, the serpents that lined it an etching in relief. Her honor guard of forfeit souls, their arms cocked back to hurl, stood frozen as if they'd been turned to stone. Even the endless chorus of Shimbaghs, a wall of claw and fang, all went still like carvings on an obelisk pointing the way. Behind me Seti, fixed in flight, her face a mask of fury, held in place as if suspended by wires.

I was the only traveler here. I was in the Zone. I had rounded the curve of time, now held them in this moment, and I was free to act upon them all at will. And yet I realized that to do so I would have to rejoin them, become a part of them again, when even this singular moment of cleansing stillness rendered me unwilling to do so ever again. Nonetheless, I had a duty to perform; I'd been brought here to do this business, and I would have to do it or die in the trying. So my action, whatever it was, would have to be quick in coming, and decisive.

Slaughter Rakushar? The logical choice. And yet I didn't think so. There was simply too much of her to devour, too many hidden selves to discern in such a small window of time. Besides, we'd been in combat for days by now, and it hadn't changed a thing. The Shimbagh ranks were endless and we were losing heart.

We had won every battle, and yet it hadn't lessened their strength. It finally occurred to me that conflict only made them stronger. While we fought with our hearts and souls, they had none of either to give. One can never overwhelm a mass of indifference. In a game run by a master trickster only tricks would do; and perhaps without even knowing I'd pulled the slickest trick of all. If I held them here, kept the moment suspended, there had to be the other side of time to move the Captain ever closer to this.

Even now, I could taste it in the ethers. He was drawing near...if only I could keep the moment in place. Yet I knew that if I tried to seize it or wrap it in my will, it would crumble under the expectation. Try to manipulate it, and it would surely turn on me. I could not force it to stay that way; I had to let it be. As it was, everything was utterly suspended. I could feel the eyes of

Legion starting to focus again. Movement like the groan of a boulder before it brings the avalanche, came in the turning of a million gazes. At once, the moment started to break. Yet as it was breaking, I realized another sound had cracked it—the singular sound of wings—the splitting of the wind, a holy hymn of Advent. *The Asker* had returned on the back of a Vyngorch.

Canto 32

Dark Angels

Arched like a stallion in the sky snorting blood
and fire, head curved back and talons extended, my brother Pod
screeched with pride. If any creature in this holocaust had been
emended by his travail it was this singer of psalms, this
patchwork minstrel in powder and puce, the future Vyngorch
King. By bringing the Captain in very good voice, he'd somehow
eluded the trap and fled ten thousand wizards and kingus frantic
in hot pursuit. They hadn't arrived without penalty, for a deadly
silver spear was buried shaft-deep into my brother's flank. The
Captain was arm-weary; he could barely wield his sword, and his
armor was awash in stains of blood. Smeared and streaked with
red, he bore a wound or two of his own, an indication they'd
fought for every meter to get them here. Others would
follow…perhaps, but Now was the only moment that mattered.
For Now, he was ready for the Asking, and I for the answer to
Prayer.

"Atoh!" the Captain cried out from the sky.

"Malkuth!" I bellowed the answer.

It was the very first time we'd ever sung our fugue in concert, and it resounded perfectly in glorious contrapuntal, an answer for each question asked.

"Vegedullah!"

"Vegdeburrah!"

"Olam!"

"Rafael!"

"Gabriel!"

"Michael!"

"Auriel!"

Formed by the power of the Answered Prayer, the Six Pointed Star ignited to the rear to protect us in a fiery blaze of light. It burned away the dross of corruption the Shimbagh hordes had sent forth, blocking the spears and arrows of armies of the damned. Before us, the power of the Word manifested the laser of Truth, streaming forward to cut the pentagram into the sky. Not evil but protection from Evil, the five pointed star ignited, searing its way through the enemy cutting them to the quick.

No longer a ritual uttered with hope, this was the cry of the bold! At last we got to set the trines that formed the Star of Stars—the only one that could tear off the gates of Hell! No matter that the archangels we called for didn't appear before us, didn't come down to take our side or even resound their blessing. They knew that we had the Power enough to spur us on far beyond the flimsy bonds of reason.

More than a man, the Captain used his sword to cut a swath through the clouds, tearing the throat from the Shimbagh hordes that seemed to welcome the thrusts. More than a Dragon, I'd become the soul of the sky itself, radiating lightning shafts from every tip of my wings. From one end of the heavens to the other we bored a hole through their ranks, knowing full well that by voicing the mantra we'd loosed the wolves of chaos.

Torn open before the pentagram like a curtain revealing the final act, the Shimbaghs whirled whistling away, winding backward through an icy vortex of retreat. Screaming at a negative pitch so high it virtually pierced our hides they sent home inside us a kind of somatic toxin. Drugged now, darting through a shower of ultra-venomous sound I blindly gave it all I had with no thought to the end. The end, whatever form it took, would surely be a blessing, for this had become the war for the Soul of us all.

From the other side of this spiraling mass, the Captain and Pod streaked onward striving against the torrents of darkness to meet me in the middle. But the middle path is deadly to the one in search of truth, and it was that truth that caused us to tarry at that very moment in time when the layers of corruption had all but peeled away. Behind us, I could feel the conflict continue to unfurl because—though the Shimbaghs were no match for our unified voices and though our Words had the Power—they had regrouped just out of earshot and like a draft of atomic dust sucked back through our wake to assault everything in sight.

Everything and everyone I'd ever hoped to hold dear were now beset by the foulest sting of all: the massed ensemble of Shimbaghs seemingly stronger than ever and playing a very different game indeed.

As I looked back, all I could see was combat after combat and great souls falling from the sky, each one brought down by hosts of Shimbaghs clinging to them like lovers. Even so, in this worst of moments we were gaining the edge. We had lunged at the throat of bedlam. We were thrusting home. We had set the skies ablaze with our deadly flaming stars—holy in the fire of them, pure in the flame of prayer, and through our raging canticles we'd burned away the veils to show that whatever we'd lost in numbers we had more than gained in heart. The pressure had lessened against me, and as I approached the end I could feel the breath of Darkness. There were no longer Shimbaghs before me, only the emptiness.

Far behind yet closer than any I could see, the Captain and Pod were striking out with abandon. With sword and song, with double trine and flaming pentagram and cries to heaven above they heard the Answer to Prayer. And every time I echoed the chant, we cut the enemy down, laid them low and took them to nothing like the ciphers that they were.

The pair were wearing the moment well, though it seemed they too flew alone, because a wall of Shimbaghs partitioned our view of the demolition. The next step was as inevitable as life and death flow in cycle, for now I was leaving the Captain behind as well. As the blackness drew me down toward the throat of the Void, I almost felt a sense of relief to know the end was near. This, whatever its meaning, was an issue soon resolved. Resolution can be a glorious thing.

Once again, I'd outstripped the limits of what mortals called physique until there was nothing left for me to give, until my mouth grew parched from hurling tongues of virulent flame, until our mantra of retribution stuck inside my throat. No longer able to give my voice to this sanctified duet, I let my fire conduct the melody inside. Yet fuel has limits when the little body must sing of the infinite soul; there was so much to sing to so large a mass.

Every specter I'd ever met in the caverns of the Chthonic Schools paled compared to the kind of fear that faced me now—the numbing emptiness that engulfed me, the hot and icy vacuous sting of the Ultimate No-thing. One can face any challenge and meet it if one can behold the foe, but Nonentity is the deadliest demon of all.

This was the Void. This was the loss of all hope as I perceived it. Yet my perceptions, I came to find, were just beginning to grow.

I realized as I echoed my fears that it was the ego's voice, that no higher self or angel would ever give a thought to this, and yet I knew whatever I did or gave consideration was being monitored by these mavens of ill reading my darkest thoughts, playing them back like cherished stanzas of their own long fall from grace.

Who was I fighting, after all? And what was there to prove? This was exercise of physique and nothing more; something to keep the mind occupied while our angels did the rest. Were we so out of touch by now that we couldn't find our angels? Or were we finally left to invoke the angels in ourselves? No time remained for moral debate or cares for what I'd forsaken. I simply ceased to be, and through the eye of that cessation learned to see the truth: By willing to be out of my physical self, I had mastered disappearance. The success of non-substance simply begins with the will "not to be." I was no longer an increment on the physical plane as we know it; I had become the mist of imagination.

I could tell my vanishing had been noted, for out of the din of silence, I could hear the Doom's Gate Praetorians as they came above to search. I could feel and even smell the force of their corrupted power, for these were not paper warriors, not the afterthought of some fallen Seraphim's ranting. These were not errant dogs let out to sniff, to howl and paw at what residue my physical presence had left. These were angels with ravens' wings, the Honor Guard of Hell, mummers in bleak tranquility with purpose on their tongues. Nix the nauseating countenance of endless Shimbagh minions. These had minds and wills of their own, the drivers of the plot who came to play this final game as if they'd been its authors. They noted my absence with careless contempt. They seemed to understand it, as if my most recent gambit had been part of their scheme.

"The Answerer has vanished!" they reported to their Master, then went about the casual business of counterattacking the clan.

Without me, the Captain's voice rang hollow—small use against this lot, for theirs was a matrix of evil that no simple prayer could withstand. In this last ditch stand the Dark One's janissaries had retaken momentum. I could feel it, though I could no longer see. So black and endless was this Ether into which I had descended that my sentient vision had all but been raped by the darkness. It seemed the price I'd paid for this cloak of invisibility was the loss of sight of our world at least as our mortal eyes beheld it.

Everything in life is a trade—compensation for advantage. I had given compensation. But had I bartered well? I had to rely on my feeling nature and recognize that in a way I'd come to embrace every other plane of life but the one upon which I had dwelled. I called upon my gemstones, the onyx and the sapphire, but even they required some light, and this was the Pit of Noire, the death of the senses. I had mastered invisibility at last, but what kind of toll came with it? Thus far, a sense of helplessness was the only armor that served.

Unable now to intervene, I caught the cries of our kin, our friends and loved ones stricken from the sky, run to ground or drowned or fleeing by the score. I could feel them falling prey, one by one, clan by Mystic Clan. And there was nothing I could do except wait for the moment I knew would come when His presence would be made known.

I'd absented myself in a downward swirl, a sinking to the bottom, lost in a sea of calamity where I was the only swimmer. It was then I realized the truth: My *Diamond I* had facets that enabled those with the insight to see the hidden chambers of the soul, to break through even the blockages built by the most powerful mind on Earth—the one and only Prince of Darkness Himself.

There was no question in my mind that, between the Captain and me, the valence our prayers had created had peeled away the layers. Together we had burned away all resistance and thrust me at last into the throat of Perdition. And unless I was mistaken, Rakushar and her legions would never have brought The Fallen One up, except as a last resort. Even though the party had been given in his honor, the Evil One would never show, would never give dimension to scotch the illusion that he, like his power, was boundless beyond measure. Yet I knew he could be measured. RuSiva had tipped his hand. That was the difference between the Beast and the Angel.

Called upon to finish the Clan, he came up from below not with rage but with a weary ambivalence that was chilling to behold. Sighing with such a measure of loathing that his breath made the sky go dark, he glared with the cold fatigue of the infinite warrior. No range of mountains, no army of Titans ever moved with such mass. His presence was the vomiting of the deepest core of Terra. The earth quaked with the force of his volition; the sound of his voice ripped the sky. And when he flexed his Aura, a flagitious nebula chewed the air with a will to devour nations entire.

"Find him," I heard his voice intone without rancor or resolve. It was matter-of-fact and sounded almost resigned. He ordered his shadow-angels to shut their eyes when they went to ferret me out. "Go deep into the chasms of our collective consciousness. I sense our friend the Answerer is diving toward the Door. I know that's where he'll go. You see, I know this creature well. I know him better than he knows himself. Still he feels he's on a holy mission, and when one is so deluded, he'll do the damnedest things to fulfill his quest.

"Quest or not, he's gone too far, and he'll find what he desires, and though he may reach his ends it will rend his heart. No light will give him reference there, only the gropings of will. And what he will find when he gets there will be worse than his darkest dream. Yet if he penetrates the veil there is a danger to us...at least a danger to you. The danger to me is relative. I'm immortal don't you see?"

I hated him for his surety, for making corruption seem wise. Besides, if he truly knew all this why in Hell didn't he stop me himself? Was I beneath the dignity of the One who would stop at nothing, the One who would stoop to anything to gain what he desired? What a put down! What a slap in the face! What damnable disdain! Or perhaps he just saw part of the board, knowing enough to play but never to be Master of the Game.

Through the facets of my *Diamond I,* reflections played in my senses showing a thousand dark winged angels diving toward the Pit. They probed through the dismal silence to seize any trace of me. They whispered in seductive tones that made me want to cry out. They were a body of subtlety I had never known before. Lies that sat in their throats came out as gentle songs of truth, and yet I knew they'd been sent to murder me.

"Shartallion," their thoughts carried in the dark, "you cannot know all the secrets. You do not realize that your noble quest is the act of a lower will. Your inclinations, though well intended, are going against the Plan. Your angels weep. Your leader laments. And we've been sent to save you."

So comely were their honeyed entreaties, so hypnotic their mantras that they sent me further down than I would ever have plunged on my own. No well-source of courage would have ever taken me quite this far as the purpose that fueled me now, for in my moment of greatest rage sat the power of my pace. I had to flee or become one of them; what a terrifying temptation to know that despite my holy training they could still find that hidden place in me. What appalled me most of all was the realization that these hosts who now called out to me had once been among the highest. They'd been angels at their Master's hand and yet had been seduced. They were our cousins and soul mates who had willingly crossed the line.

I continued to plunge. Clawing, pulling, groping, charging downward toward an energy that defied the scope of dimension I drove. And if I could not measure it, how could I bring it to yield? It was then I realized that the very act of my own breathing was a signal to my pursuers that they were gaining space on me. I was the fastest flyer on Earth. But what of the other dimensions? How does one measure the breath of angels or whether they're dark or light, or whether the kiss of redemption comes from every knowable source? Had it been for nothing that I'd been trained for all of this? I now questioned without resolve. Had we been deluded all along? Was evil so seductive that we could abandon our faith? And why even now was Evil so caring? Why the shepherd's tones? Why was this creature always among us while our Father stayed away? Faith in an indifferent God is a far cry from Heaven indeed. Was that the test? And if it was, why take it?

All this perplexity made me pause. Of course, that was the purpose. They couldn't catch me as I sped unless they made me doubt. unless they made me deny the Source of Power from which I'd sprung. I'd breached the speed of sound after all where only Light thoughts could reach me. And this was the time when every trick in the world would be tried to slow me. God help us all that the fate of the world should be laid on the tongue of a skeptic. Knowing that it was my nature to doubt, they played their music well. I was certain I would challenge the Truth on the very lips of Heaven. Then let me confront the Speaker of Lies at the very jaws of Hell!.

Every dark angel was after me now. I could feel their breathing behind me. Each one lofted their soft entreaties like doubt-missiles at my heart. They wounded me with their tenderness, and that was the cruelest assault—when one is so close to the Throat of Doom to make one lament the act.

Suddenly their softness gave way to speed; they'd gained on me while I pondered. Now there was a chance that they would cut me off at the Lock. But even at the speed of thought, I was a glimmer ahead. If I could grope and find the handle, then I could seal the Door. But if I sealed it prematurely before the Dark Ones came, they would be free to roam world for another eternity, comb the ethers, and fill the thoughts of every living being.

I swept the blackness for what I hoped would be a piece of the stone, groped for the smoothness of the grip, looked for all the conventional things a mortal mind could conjure, should have known that nothing of the sort would ever define such a moment, for the Lock and the Key could never be given dimension by senses such as mine. They were a state of conscience, a place so impenetrable, so deeply seated in the Void that I when I broke the Seal, it would implode into Ultima Thule and take my spirit with it.

The moment I did, from deep within a light that was nearly blinding fired up through the pit itself and revealed a final shockpiece that the Evil One had saved just for me, one He knew would rend my heart and crush my resolution. Imbedded in the stone that lined the walls were trophies of captured shells, imprisoned holy warrior spirits who had dared oppose the One— or even worse, once noble beings who'd chosen to compromise, those who'd let their Godlight fail, who'd lost the sight of glory and succumbed to the allure of the Ambition. I didn't stop to gawk, for every moment I moved was precious. And I wondered whether my physical self would suddenly reappear.

I was still the spirit flyer. I could not be seen even by those who had once served in the Kingdom. I could feel their breath behind me less tranquil than before; their supplications had taken strident tones.

"Shartallion XII. Son of the Kiln. You are but one of us. For the Prince of Light is a Dragon in his heart. Slow your fury. It's no use. You'll join us in the end. Ours is the cause of clarity. We are the Lords of this Earth."

In my plunge toward the chill of nothing I finally saw the end, the ultimate demolition of my intent. Along the walls, encased in stone my mother and my cousin Skye had been captured before the conflict began and brought here still alive. In stasis of the most wretched sort, caught in a chrysalis of steel, they'd been wrapped in a wretched cocoon and held for Cimmerian ransom.

This was the Evil One's final gesture that if I sealed the door, I also abandoned my loved ones to the unkindest fate of all. My heart was caught in an iron vise, and what made it all the worse was that I only had a sliver of time to make my final move. So many tricks had been played by now I might have thought this another were it not for the cogent clarity of their auras. I could hear their inner thoughts. I could feel their pain. But though their bodies agonized their spirits remained on purpose. They danced in pain while their souls sang songs of knowing.

In an ultimate gesture of my love, I revealed myself to them. Showing through my black body armor the anguish I felt beneath, straining with all the fires inside me to melt the stone shells that held them, I was determined that I would set them free. More than ready to turn and destroy every raven-winged angel, I would find the ways and means to do so.

"Let the Door stay opened!" I shouted. "It's a sleazy aspect of Mind. And I'm bored to death with symbols; they're toys of the damned! There are more important things than saving a world so obscured, so fearful of dark and blind to the light. And we've all done more than our part for these children of the Earth, while they continue to loathe everything but themselves."

I saw the Dark Ones approaching me now. Elated that I'd paused, their eyes turned crimson with a frenzy to grab and hold me still in their hypnotic stares. There I saw neither beauty nor love but a kind of hollow stare. Psychopathy was the seal that marked them all. Yet as I turned to challenge them, to defend my loved ones to the end, I saw from beneath the taconite that held my mother fast a teardrop made of purest silver streaking down her face. Across the way a golden drop had fallen from Skye's face as well, revealing to me the sacraments to finish the final act.

I had hoped I could hear their thoughts at least, but those had been denied me, for they'd been blocked by the steel that formed their cocoons. Still, their songs rang through to me to bring about the transmutation that would turn the day for us and bring us back home. Nothing can damn the pure of heart. No ritual, no curse can ever put an end to the Holy Spirit.

In my left talon I took the Silver tear, in my right talon the Gold, and as I foresaw they instantly transformed into endless strands from the chrysalis that locked my loved ones in peril. The high and the low, Heaven and Earth, above and below, gold and silver, male and female, the dynamic and magnetic—these were the ultimate threads of power, these were the ethereal braids that these high souls had sacrificed to close the door on evil and seal it for once and for all.

The rest was up to me to maneuver. These dark angels were not to be fooled. They had laid this trap for me, but their timing had just been off. They expected me to take longer to plummet and more time to ponder my plight. My lightning descent and swift decision had thrown them. It had become quite clear to me now that I was the last piece of the puzzle, the final thread in the pattern they needed to make their statement complete.

Of all the members of the Dragon Clan who were most evolved it was Skye, the brother of Heaven, and Drilg the sister of Earth. They, the least violent among us, had never raised a claw, had never used their fires for anything more than lighting the heavens. But who had set the trap after all? And who had gained the day? Had my mother and my cousin been that wise? Had they given up physique? Had they sacrificed their lives in the hope that I would fulfill this moment of critical mass? Was Synchronicity so set in place that it became predestination? And if our actions were predetermined, why bother to do the drill? Thank heaven for that untoward burst of free will, that urge to embrace the bizarre, that utterly mortal penchant to do what was never expected.

Shatter the pattern! Break the spell! That was the secret of life. Otherwise, why bother to live at all?

We were all beneath the threshold—my mother, Skye, the dark angels and I locked in a maelstrom swirl, drawing our energies down in a soundless storm. Rather than shun these darlings of Satan, I would make straightway for them with the strands of gold and silver in my jaws—the thread of Heaven, the fiber of Earth, the rope to bind all evil, the chord to sew the seal to this, the deepest trench of reason. So unexpected was my attack the Dark Angels who had pursued me darted away to avoid me like bats against a falcon. It wasn't my body after all that these creatures longed to hold, it was my power of mind and the will that had brought me all this way. There was no physique at stake in this place, for matter didn't matter. This was the War of the Spirit, and I'd moved rightly. They fell away from me again, yet regrouped for one last pass to pursue me in a final desperate surge.

With force of a cyclone and the speed and sense of a holy kamikaze, I twisted and twirled until I'd wound the threads together, the silver and the gold, the flawless ethereal twine—the element against which no magic was immune. The journey toward the mouth of the Pit was a final dive, not a climb, as it seemed I was chosen the cosmic weaver who would line the seam of the void. I had to take it all the way through the darkest night of the soul. That was journey, not outward but in, not to the dome of highest thought but through the Nadir of Cipher.

As I made my final sound-splitting dive, I heard in the draft behind me the raven-winged angels screaming along, projecting themselves below trying to send their images and thoughts to intercept me. But I had gone so deeply down under that I had outstripped thought. I'd even stopped debating what awaited.

I plunged and dived through an ocean of blackness so icy and foreboding that it ripped my skin with a million teeth that stabbed me to the bone. All the while, a dirge of denial dug into my ears.

"This journey will kill your Soul...will kill your Soul!"

Was it voices of the damned I heard, or merely the draft of my wings as I plunged through every fear held captive in the realm of negative thought? I was bathed in it. I was drowning in it, a burden of such sadness that only the ultimate loss of hope could bring. Was there death in the soul after all? What a chilling thought. Losing one's mortal shell was nothing. But the soul itself?! Could it be? Was that the cost of noble striving? What a dirty trick—to doubt one's highest purpose in the lowest place of all!

There was a light below, and though it was no more than a pinpoint, it was the most resplendent glow my eyes had ever beheld. It might have been the hearth of Hell or the mote in the eye of Heaven. Whatever it was, I charged it with all the speed that I possessed. I continued to twist and turn and braid the threads behind me into the strongest rope the spirit could meld to make. I could feel the clawing at my tail as I angled toward the light that now swelled out to a violet hue turning suddenly white.

There was no door to cap this place, no lock to seal it fast. It was a task for the cosmic weaver, and I had been left with the twine. With a final burst I surged ahead, downward and up again, weaving a pattern of silver and gold across the mouth of the Void. For reasons I could never explain the moment I started sewing, the thread transmuted into waves of a molten lake that froze with perfect fury into a monolith of the hardest metal ever forged. In an instant it slammed with such violence that the backdraft from its closure hurled me out of the darkness and back into the light of day, into the sky replete with combat into the storm of bodies flying through the skies blood red with their endless, senseless combats.

Yet the moment I tumbled in with the sound of Doom's Gate closing behind me, every enemy of the Mystic Clan instantly came undone, vanished as if the sky itself had erased every trace of them. Every Shimbagh dragon, every khado demon, every witch from Hell, even the sorceress Rakushar burst out of the sky around us, diffusing into a vapor that sucked the air into another dimension. The only trace remaining that they had existed at all was the deafening sound of their screaming from behind the Gate below—the one and only Door where Evil Dwelled.

On the horizon before us there remained a singular mass, looming like the face of the coming moon. It was locked so far in the distance that it might have been a legion advancing.

Or the aimless flight of an angel lost in time.

Canto 33

Judgment

Hovering in the wake of combat, buoyed by what passed for glory, my brethren of the Mystic Clan kept their posture erect. Seti and Dager X held their position, waiting for this Entity to come to grips with us. It was still so far away we had no way of telling just who it was or what we could expect. Yet each one of us knew to the marrow of our bones that we had to brave his arrival if it was the very last thing we did.

By now, no more than a thousand dragons were left in all creation. Rogues and noble kinsmen wore one brand— "Survivor." It marked us from this moment and might some day unify us, though the wounds that marred so many of us were certain to drive some mad. The gryphons had fared even worse in this War. No more than five score remained; certainly now they would grow more remote than ever. The Rahntish had all been wiped from the sky and all but driven to ground. Only traces of broken wings like shattered alabaster marked the paths below where they had been scattered into dark forests. Considering their taste for combat and their disregard for themselves, the Chimeras fared rather well, and yet I sensed this "noble campaign" had finally dashed their spirits. They circled about quite aimlessly, no ailerons to their flight, and positioned themselves like sailors drunk on leave. They circled over mountain peaks and dropped down into the snow, grinding their wings and fur in the drifts as if to wash clean their sins—as if this war of wars had sullied their purpose. Among us all, the Unicorns seemed to have done the best. Although they had lost nearly two-thirds their number, they had kept their herds intact. I could only lament the fact that of all the creatures among us, they were the ones most loved and admired by the pygmie. And if there was anything I'd learned about this beast called man, it was that his admiration was far deadlier than his hate.

As for my brother, the Vyngorch King, he was the only one of his breed who had seemingly finished the day, while astride him the Captain remained the solitary man who stood firm in our ranks. There were rumors that his son and some surviving soldiers were charging toward us full-clip on horseback but wouldn't make it in time. (In a way I was genuinely relieved. Most would have only died in combat. By now, I wasn't sure that anyone should have given their life for this.) Timing of course was everything. Timing had brought us here. Now the time had come to meet the One.

Whatever we were or would become was written on the scrolls of the One who came ambling toward us now like some archangelic Avenger. Yet it wasn't a sense of need that propelled him with such celerity. It was an obligation his pride had bound him to fulfill. Judging by the circuitous course of his flight, he was hardly in a hurry; despite his swiftness I sensed that he'd just as soon not have come at all.

The thunderheads that bore him to us carried him with regard, the kind of respect one keeps aside for an old and trusted friend. He didn't come with illusions, although he might have tried them all, but the energy that accompanied him was more daunting than all others combined. I wanted so much be fearful of him, to be overawed and offended, to be dragged through a wave of revulsion I would be compelled to resist. I had hoped for the foulest monster that the universe could conjure, like the one I'd felt when I had been below—a massive, ferocious, negative force so fulsome and repugnant that any goodly soul would recoil from its presence. What a disappointment that he would be so…otherwise. And it seemed to me that he'd done it all on purpose.

He could have assumed the size of a comet and soared in a ball of flame for one last go at the core that remained of us. He could have been all horn and hoof and taken a Titan's aspect (after all I'd seen him do it before). Instead, he came as an angel, and not too impressive at that. He was shopworn, a Tatterdemalion who'd been at the job too long. His wings were soiled, and one was bent at an angle. Yet he moved before us with effortless grace, not like a foe who'd been vanquished, and his gaze was one of reflection without the slightest trace of regret. His face was that of a man, and yet a man above all others—an unexpected serenity laced with just a dash of conceit.

He coursed the skies for quite a while, seeming to rise in stature, becoming larger in his flight so as to make himself heard. There was no betrayal of emotion in anything he said, yet he spoke with a sense of surety that made my blood run cold.

"You think you've won the war, my Mystics. In the purest sense you have. Yet by waging conflict at all, you had lost it long before you began. You merely fought your mirror selves. You destroyed your Doppelgängers. But behold what it cost you, Mystics. You're a fraction of what you were. Where legions of the righteous once stood proudly shoulder to shoulder, only shadows and echoes now remain. And all for what?! The dubious right to sway the pygmie's soul?! Forgive me if I laugh, but you squander your diamonds.

"He'd just as soon make a steak of you all as share a moment in space. You're raw material, nothing more. That's how he views his world. He is *my* creature after all…just as I am yours.

"It's all been a part of the plan, you see. And we've all been sold down the river. In the battle for the Vital Force of all this Universe, we have been the losers in these last few days of combat. We've battled for the mind of man, and though you've done quite well, though you've sealed the Door where Evil Dwells, you've missed a few details. I'm still at large to set the game, and I'm the Major Player. I have created this little theatre, and I can rebuild it anew.

"This was all my fantasy, more than it was yours, for I made you as surely as you have fabricated me…Or should I say the pygmie has because conflict is what sustains him? He's so far from the air of light he can only breathe corruption. Matter is the only thing that matters at all to him. That's why I'm here. I'm doing my job, the job I've been given—to provide a little texture to the fabric of life on Earth. You see, I'm just as much of an archangel as any you could meet. It's just that, in a moment of weakness—call it *noblesse oblige*—I agreed to take this planet on as part of my personal karma (when in fact I had incurred none at all). It was foolish of me to think I could dare to turn this din of dingy consciousness around. Instead, I've become bound to it, and my role has been reversed. I've gone from the Keeper of the Flame to the Warden of the Pit!

"When you think about it, it's sickening. I'm 'Lucifer' after all! The Lord of Light, the Bringer of Knowledge, the Bearer of the Torch! I'm the one who cares for this place. I'm the accessible god. I'm the One who shares your pain, not those angels with their airs. Cherubim and Seraphim, Dominions, Princedoms, Powers—they couldn't give a damn for you! They're too busy being *holy!* They're too far detached from such banalities as delving into this, the most primitive punitive plane of thought in the entirety of creation! (Well, not exactly. Some are worse. Some are denser than this. But not by much more than a gnat's breath, I assure you!) Meanwhile were it not for me, you'd all be stanched in squalor, living out your days computing the depth of your own mire.

"After all I'm the Demiurge. I'm a partner in the plan. If you haven't got me, you've got no Game at all.

"I'm only doing my job, for God's sake! It's exactly what was assigned me—to be whatever man's consciousness has wanted to make of me. Sons of Draco, you should know that. We were on this mission together. You were part of the same fall from grace, but instead of doing your time, you've become quite unctuous about your duties, as if it made a difference…as if you could change a thing, as if any of this could ever make a tinker's dam in Hell!

"You think you're all too good for this. You're seduced by your own delusions that you have the keys to heaven, when once you were all my lieutenants in the planetary rebellion that scarred the universe for all time. What we did before would make this little farrago here look like a tempest in a teapot!

"Remember Mystic Clansmen. Dragons! We started as a team! But you've been led astray by these hopeless fixations on redemption. You've lost your focus. You've booted your reason and adopted hope instead, when all the while you've been used as cosmic fodder. You think you're all the song of Christ when you're really the Devil's hiccup. You didn't come on a mission from God. You came to serve with Me! But you've fallen from my grace, and I want you back! Have I got news for you, dragon brothers. You think you've won this day when you never had a chance, and you never will. The human being has made me Master, and I have captured his mind. I have the key to his intellect. He burns auguries to me!

"The way you work a creature's will is to numb his imagination. You all embody man's will to soar, and today I've struck you down. There will come a time, and soon, when you will die away, when what you were will be shattered, and all that remains will be shards…shambles from the crystal castle of antiquarian thought, of dreams abandoned never again to be found.

"In time, a millennium or two, there won't be a vestige of you. You'll be remembered as curious traces of barbarous times gone by. Someday they'll deny you ever existed. They'll explain you away with science or some Apocrypha of thought that they'll raise as the Gospel of Physics.

"As for now, you've locked the Gate I admit, but you forgot the important part. The Keymaster's still at large to work his will. You didn't really believe that by dipping into some bag of tricks, you would ever shut down a power such as mine. So I'll start roaming the world a while. After all, I helped to make it. Some among you will join me I'm sure. It's the very best chance you have.

"Believe me, what remains for you won't be a pretty sight. You're powerful now, but your arrogance of spirit has overcome you. And it's brought you to the end of times for the 'Holy Mystic Clan.' In the years to come you'll remember this moment above all others conjoined, and you'll all recall that in the end I was the friend you sought.

"Satan, Balliol, 'Mr. Scratch,' Red Dragon of the North; Loki, Kali, Ahriman—what the Hell's in a name? They have them all for me, of course. I'm everyone and None. I'm the Demi-Urge. That's what matters! I am the Source of all bane. But you've got to understand it's for the Good that I occur. I cut the path for others to follow. I am the *Civilizer*. What I do shows us all we're creatures of abstract thought. I am the Shadow that lines the Path to the Light. I form the lyrics to the dark songs of life, the ones that awaken us all, the ones that have piqued our volition; the ones that have brought us to the threshold of ambition. Without Me, there'd be satisfaction, and purely primordial bliss, like the warmth a slug feels when someone has pissed on his rock.

"I admit there have been times of late when my methods have been extreme, and I demand a sacrifice now and again to keep the fire stoked, as it were. But there is such reward for this! Instant gratification! I answer every prayer. Just ask my disciples; just council with the pygmies who already follow me. Even now they number beyond your counting, while only one stands with you—a self-ennobled fool who will die before this day is through. Too bad he likes his angels so much, for he'll walk with them in the morning, while those who follow me will savor the exhilaration of conquest, the sweet sauce of sexual ecstasy, the heady brandy of power, a lifetime marked by peaks and valleys, the rush of excitation—and damn the median curve of piety!

"It's the only language they understand, these little creatures called men. They talk of Godsight, and yet all they envision is something resembling me. Oh, saviors will come among them, it's true. Some will say the right things. More importantly, some will even *do* them. They'll show the way. They'll light the flame. They'll even change perception for the little while they crawl among their peers. But in the end, it comes back to this. I am the Master here. Whatever glimpses you catch of the Christ, I'll twist them to suit my needs, for the Message always gets lost in the worship paid the messenger.

"Oh, to be sure, there'll come a time when an end will be put to the fun, and we'll all be stuffed back neatly in place in the grander scheme of things. God in all His glory will pull us back into his bosom. Angels on high will sing their harmonic hosannas 'til they puke.

"Meanwhile...ahem...may I suggest that you cast your lot with me, and keep the broth abrewing, as it were? You're already going to be blamed for practically ruining the world as it is. So if you're taking the rap, then make the flap.

"Already my revisionist chroniclers are dipping their plumes in bile and fabricating heroes who will 'do away' with you. That will come later, all in good time. For now, enjoy your triumph! After all you've earned your paltry moment of validation.

"But just remember, I'll start again tomorrow to blueprint my kingdom, and some of you will be the first in line. I can tell, even as I speak there are those among you who've listened, who know enough to spot a clever fellow when they see one.

"After all, you've got to understand this planet's a gift. It's pretty enough, and not without its diversions. Frankly, the agents of sweetness and light have sent their second string. And though there'll always be a struggle, the best are already cut down. You've seen to that my mystic friends. You've done it to yourselves! You went through the schools of higher awareness where you learned the paths of light. And yet when it came The Time for the Moment of Truth, you chose to dance with me. You took the path of the righteous warrior and ignored the contradiction that violence and goodness are enemies after all. You fell into the trap, my kin, that ego sets for spirit. It's the darkest answer to the highest prayer, and you took it. You're the ones who've burned the votives. You're the one's who've preyed. Now you're the ones who are left with the mess at the altar.

"Well…nothing is without a plan, and mine is going very smoothly. Not without its little setbacks, but I admonish you, think upon this: We'll all be redeemed in the end. God, after all, is so *good*, he can't leave a soul in pain (for a while but certainly not forever). It's just that it takes Him so-o-o-o damned long to bring it all back together that the keener minds among us get tired of waiting. In the meantime brutal negativity and imminent death prevail. So, here I stand to serve you all, and at the very least bring what passes for order to the chaos. So, as long we're waiting for The Time (the *real* Time, don't you see?) why not have some fun along the way? After all, isn't that what we've been doing all the while? The difference lies on what side of the window you happen to view the day.

"Now, I may not have created the flowers and skies or the gentle rain that falls, but I provide the action that gives this pallid planet color! I'm the one who fires the loins with passion, lust and guile! I'm the one who spurs your mind with fantasies that give new meaning to life. So if you want to be alive, I suggest you follow me. We'll all end up the same, you know. So when the issue's over it's how you've enjoyed your stay that makes the difference. May I recommend a change of pace from all your lofty strivings? After all, I've been where you are, and you have been with me.

"Rejoin me, and you'll thrive a whole lot longer than you will on your own. I know how to protect you Mystics, while your *God* could give a damn. It's man He wants, and everything else is expendable to the Cause. You were with me at the start, especially you sons and daughters of Draco. I've missed you. Come back to Daddy (as it were)!

"Your choice, of course. We're all at choice. *I* have seen to that. How do you think free will was born if it weren't for the Fall? Well...modesty prevents me from taking further credit. I trust you're all astute enough to see I have a case. I'd hoped you might respond, and yet I see I've left you speechless. Just know the invitation's open, and...the Party never ends."

Every great lie has the Truth at its core. That's what makes it succeed. He knew that well. He spoke the Light, but he bent it at such angles that even I was left to wonder whose side best served this world. What a likeable chap — so much in command of every word he uttered. And every gesture he made, of course, was so utterly lubricious, so free of care or strain or stress that while he elucidated his credo I almost felt compelled to applaud. Despite myself, I felt obligated at the very least to nod my accord, when I knew good and well he'd been the force that had taken my loves from me, had sacrificed my very own mother, had assassinated my Gryphon Queen and left us as a race to face the prophecy of occlusion.

While we all hovered, half bleeding to death, he kept is composure intact, and actually started to swell in stature with every word he spoke until he'd emerged, like the swan from the homely little signet, into a regal angel with a gaze that could cut through crystal. Like his words, his physical presence projected a force beyond all reason. He no longer needed to talk; he merely could choose to project.

It came as no surprise to me that he topped his malediction by magnifying his aura to the size of a cumulous cloud, majestic as a mountain range, with white plume crested wings bedecked in diamonds, a glowing golden corona that rimmed his glimmering raven's hair, and black-pearl eyes that saw into the souls of every one. Of course, he could do all of this. He'd been among the High. He'd been one of the Illuminati; no doubt a charter member. (If his insinuations were to be believed, he was among them still.)

Yet what he did next astonished me more than I had ever thought I could be, for in that moment he'd transformed he projected himself toward me, facing me as if he'd been a lover I'd wronged.

"Why?!" he gave a whisper laced with pain that tapped me to the core of my Vital Force, that made me feel as if these, the most honorable days of my life, had been a disgrace and a consummate breach of faith. He hadn't pronounced it at the top of his voice for all the world to hear, but rather like creature who had trusted and then been played for a fool. He hadn't said it with the kind of malice one might expect a moment like this to bring; rather he said it with a sense of shame. My prescience had failed me in these moments, but there were more forces at work than my senses could ever perceive, and never had I felt the weight of such impact from the single turn of a word.

Realizing sincerely that I hadn't understood just why he came before me now to plead, he winced at the irony of this, then mocked the moment with laughter so loud and shrill it sounded like a soul in flames. As suddenly as he had come before me, he returned to himself again like a white-hot arrow in fullest arc just before it's swallowed in night.

He didn't pause a moment longer. He took his leave of us. Shining like a second Sun, he whirled and flew toward the South. In his wake at least a score of dragons rose and followed, beating their wings to drum them along their way. They had been our brethren a moment ago. They had stood in the fire. They had fought for the cause of angels. Now, they'd been beguiled. We'd battled with everything inside us to put an end to Him. We'd lost loved ones, friends and kin. We'd nearly wrecked our clans. We'd imperiled our very future only to realize that though we had won, he had already begun to start anew. And though the dragons who now followed him were rogues and reckless fellows, he was already back into setting up shop again.

"Got to admit, the guy's got style," I heard my sister sigh. At least she hadn't joined him; at least not yet. Still, I couldn't help but notice that there was a glint in her eye, and I had to reckon that she'd seek him out, and soon. "A little bit gauche in his manner of dress, but listen, what the hell? That's the kind of business we're all in. At any rate, he certainly answered some questions I've been asking. And maybe he raised some questions you *need* to ask…"

Below along the rivers I saw dozens of armies of men heading to the South and East in fervid search of their master, and as we drew toward the darkness or what passed for the end of the day, I caught glimpses of a legion of Slaverns in the throes of frenzied retreat. The evidence was terrifying. There were multitudes still at large, servants of the Lucifer, the Bearer of the Torch. These were real. These were not creatures of some Ur-demon's conjuration. These had life and breath and could not be banished by a slogan.

So what had we done beyond symbols? I wondered. We'd sealed the Cavern of Evil. We'd locked in Rakushar and all the dark angels who had come along with the Fall. But what of Him? And how dare he say we dragons were his creatures when we'd been the ones responsible for bringing him to this defeat?

And yet I couldn't help but harken to Sagro's transformation the day I'd graduated, that pellucid agony when I'd exploded out of the "schools." It was the truth. Our ancient fathers had been with him on that insurgent day when he'd spat in the face of God and was cast down to this. Then we, not he, were the final rebellion, and this had been his revenge, that he could have lured us into this with only smoke and mirrors.

We had sacrificed our numbers. Where once we had abounded, now we were but remnants of the Mystic Clans of Earth. How could we with all our gifts of holy premonition ever have foreseen so cruel an irony? There had to be an answer for this. There must have been a plan. No God in all the Universe could be so wholly complicit as to lead his loyal servants into their destruction. I knew this. Yet, the seed had been sewn. The Demi-Urge had spoken. And though he was the Lord of Lies, he'd robbed us of our glory. The best that we could hope for now would be some sign from on high that all had not been in vain, that our struggles had meaning.

Canto 34

Tibbuk

Reflection marked the Dark One's
departure, a time when we finally permitted a sense of loss to
pierce the membrane of our thoughts. So much of the very part
of us had perished these last three days, there was no taking its
measure; not in the ways that one could gauge the depth and
scope of this illusion called life. This adventure had more than
transcended the bonds of expectation, for we had gone over the
edge and had lost our wings along the way. Any fantasies we
might have held of our divine alliance had been dashed ten times
ten thousand times with every death we beheld. Why would
anyone war? I wondered. What was so worth the conflict just to
gain a trace of advantage in a scant few moments in time, only to
lose the Ultimate Essence of what we had become? Our
insolence had brought us here, and the price we had paid for its
commission was something we'd never ransom no matter how
we humbled ourselves. Now, with the Luciferian Credo still

ringing in our ears, we were left to lick our wounds and wonder whether or not everything we'd ever done had been but hollow gestures.

He had worked his final trick with us—to get us to doubt our mission, to crack our sense of certitude for all we'd been taught to hold dear, to play the ultimate jester in the holy kingdom of God and prod us until we doubted the very nature of goodness itself. There were so many realities, and he seemed to control them all, except the ultimate One that none could claim to apprehend.

For this I had lost my mother and my very own twin-flame, and now no longer even knew what had become of my child. The exquisitely innocent Vyngorch princess with the aspect of an angel, what had become of her in the wake of this? Had she too been sacrificed somewhere along the path? For cause of this, had her future too been somehow bartered away? Were there any limits to the sacrifices we made? My cousin Skye had hidden her, he'd said, for safety's sake. Had she been captured as well and died at the very gates of Hell? Where were we after all of this— mere scatterings of ourselves, at a loss for where to go, or what would become of us now that we had "won" the day and all the days to come?

I saw my father The Mountain list in the wind like the ghost of a galleon bleeding from the hull. He who had been the most ferocious warrior on the planet, leader of the mightiest clan in creation, now led the wreckage of a nation less than one-tenth its number, left to ponder the consequence of its passion. With our crystalline nursemaids the Kohmm all but annihilated, the wounds that stung us now had the ability to drive us quite insane. Where once by tasting the fruit of the Thral we were invincible, now we were wholly vulnerable to every kind of corruption. Even the arrows of ordinary men, could bring us down to Earth. Such was the cost of serving invisible gods.

I felt my sister break out and cry for the only time in her life when I'd been forced to tell her what had become of Drilg, that our mother had been so sacrificed at the very teeth of perdition.

And for what? I couldn't help but anguish whenever I thought of the cause. Had I done a single thing right in these last three terrible days?

"My God and Christ! What justice is this when all that is decent must perish?! She was the only entirely pure soul on this ridiculous pox of a planet! And now you tell me that she was trapped in the very lips of Perdition. What sick sonofabitch would create such a world where beauty is crushed and only the wicked prevail? I was wrong to ever have come to this quixotic *cause célébre*. I was an eagle before, and now I'm a gull. I've haven't duped by the Prince of Darkness. From what I see, that guy's straight. (At least he's honest about his dishonesty.)

"It's these other bastards! These absentee angels. What kind of friends are they? Why cast your lot with a bunch of phantoms who feel they're too good for this?! As far as this goes, I've seen enough to last a dragon's lifetime. I like a good fight as well as the next, but only when the odds are sane. If you're dumb enough to do this again, don't bother to come knocking. Just mail in the results, and we'll all cheer you on.

"By the way, brother, you carried the day. You really kicked some tail. You truly belong up North you know. It's really more your broth. Someday you'll recognize yourself for who you really are. And when you do, well...there's always a place at the hearth."

"You leave too soon. You always have. Stay. The show's not over." I admonished her, but my heart was no longer in it. "At least you ought to catch the end of the game."

"For what?! To wait for some self-righteous band of angels to spread the *light* around, to sprinkle some magic dust and thank us for saving their ethereal asses? It hurts too much, my Black Dragon brother. You and I have lost too many friends for us to wait for some post mortem heavenly bliss to come pouring down on this. It's over! We won the battle. But what about the war?

"The Fallen One was right, you know. All of this was only a blip in the cosmic radar, a flash of light across a darkening sky. So, later in life, big brother," she sighed, a gentle response for her. "We played our roles like warriors. It was the only thing to do."

Seeing her go, I called out to her, "I love you," which was of course the wrong thing to do. One does not send missives of devotion to the daughter of demolition.

"You had to go and say it!" she snapped at me. "Well, isn't that too sweet?! Sorry luv, but incest isn't my thing. Nonetheless, if you're ever up my way again, I can fix you up with a date. And knowing your taste…a princess or two in a shapely human skin." She blurted a caustic flame at me, and made away with her band, though only a score or two now remained of her empire. She shrugged off that challenge as well. "What the hell, considering the choices, more will come my way. All in good time…if time is good at all."

As she flew by our ranks, she gave a salute, her parting nod to our father, the very last salutation those two would ever share. Dager, dazed by fatigue and remorse, fazed by the loss of his focus on all that he called honor, bellowed a sigh of flaming riposte that sucked the air from the sky, leaving only fires in the clouds that cried out for an answer. He felt too much pain in the awful knowing that he had lost his mate, the gentlest soul in all the Creators' heavens, to ever give a word of mourning or offer a moment's praise. It was simply a feeling beyond description. Yet in that breathless span there echoed across a towering sky the reluctant rejoinder that we had given our all.

Was this the fruit of our Covenant? Were we the sacrifice? Were we the pyre from which would rise the pygmie's dubious future? I wondered perhaps if the time I'd exerted on this dark little cosmic orb would have been better spent on another world.

I took off from this place of honor where we had staked our claim into the skies now emptied of either hope or despair. The world would only answer us now with a barren kind of silence as if it wished to hide itself for awhile.

In the meantime, we stood sentry 'til the last of us fell exhausted to earth. My God! What instinct for redoubt! We cared when we no longer cared to. We would stand in the fire even after the fire had gone out. God had tempered the steel too well, and at last the blade had cracked; we were not made for a world so short on resolve.

I turned away from this stalwart brigade, this majestic mystic mass, and swept to the Sea below where the brine of a crimson tide told the selfsame tale. As it poured itself on the purified sands of a shining crystalline beach, there was an essence spilled there that had been like a sacrament. Upon those sands, a Kohmm physician—the last of her earthly breed—fed a Thral melon to a mortally wounded whale. The Leviathan, beached and lacerated, partook of the sacrament, and in a matter of moments sounded his gratitude and glory. Catching a tide that poured over them both, the whale took to sea again, churning through the water with the Kohmm across his back. It seemed she had found a home after all, away from the ruin of this land, beneath the waves where her hopes and dreams might take another form. It was a certain sign to me that nothing we had known would ever be again as it was before.

§§§§§§§

The Celebration, it seemed to me, came too little too late. It was a relief to see the arrival of the heavenly host on high. Angels, whenever they do arrive, always bring food for the heart. The question nevertheless remained. Where in the hell were they when we had our backs to the doors of time and all the chips were down? When we were bleeding and dying, when we had given our best, when we were lifting our voices in prayer and watching our comrades fall, where was this holy host? I wondered. Why had they delayed?

God with his terrible swift sword could have cut this to the quick. Or couldn't He be bothered to take a side?

Suddenly, this heavenly choir appeared adorning the skies with their splendor, joining their auras together to line an archway to heaven on high, revealing the pathway to Redemption we were not prepared to take.

What condescension in their grace, so entirely above reproach as they knelt to tend us (those of us left), filling us with the Eucharist of Guerdon. That I was enthused in fact, my sources replenished with faith, took me to the edge my doubt and assuaged it.

Angels arrived in precisely orchestrated phases, almost too perfectly timed, or so it seemed. Their songs all soothed us, their visages salved us, healed us without touching. They fanned their wings across the clouds to form a lattice of hosts, each one melding tip to tip to fill the skies with accord. The sun of the earliest morning of hope glistened behind their formation formed a halo of golden hues that blinded me to tears.

From a shaft of light, so radiant it cracked the dome of sky, there hovered another flight of angels whose presence transcended grace—an auric ring of brilliance that shattered all perception and pierced my crystal inner eye with visions of Heavens to be. Through that consonance of thought our loved ones appeared before us, to reveal themselves in transition. Blessed by the grace of their final acts to give up the lives they held dear, they now came down among us to let our souls join again.

In the midst of my father's grief, I saw the golden Drilg having descended not as a dragon but as a radiant lighted being. Dare I say her aspect was angelic? It was that in fact—the form and frame were distinctly human, though she wore an angel's wings and bore angelic countenance that was stunning to behold. Although I'd sensed it since the Kunlun days, it was the occurence of her ascendance that totally set me aback. At the Confrontation she'd vanished even before the very first clash had struck, before fang and armor and flesh had wealed and the blood had shed. Her final act of valor had been to give up her life for the cause to offer me the silver strands to seal the gate to Hell.

So, there were angels among us after all. This was reality and not some mirage my hopes and dreams had conjured. Then if Drilg were in fact an angel, from where had I descended? And why was I still armored in this garish dragon's shell? What price did I yet have to pay? Was I so far from the light that I could see it but have no chance to be it? What laws had I, in another time in another incarnation, held so lightly that I had let perish the faith? So close to the edge of Tibbuk—Redemption!—yet unable to pierce the veil that took us to the realms of our higher selves, how little we knew of what we saw, how much of the truth stood outside us. What oceans of awareness still remained for this solitary soul to swim?

Nevertheless, there was this moment when it came so clearly before me, as brightly as my mother's appearance to heal us yet again. She passed a brush of her wing before me to bless my every action and let me know that yet again I'd served the cause of right. In that same instant, in an angel's breath, she'd appeared before my father to wrap him in healing light to wash clean all his wounds, to remove the pain he felt at her loss, to salve his warrior's heart.

"You have been the golden armor that's shielded us all from harm. You are and always will be my only champion. Please don't worry that you have lost me. I'm with you at this moment and through the End of Days as we Mystics know them. Yes, the Dark One was right in that. The Days of Mystics are numbered. But remember that magic, like life itself, can never truly die. All of this is merely a passage into another day, brighter and freed of all the bonds of matter. Still, while you're in this wondrous armor you are defender of the Faith. Wear it well. And know that I am waiting: on the other side of time, my love, my soul and yours will meld, for we are matched from here and forever after."

"I feel as if a piece of my soul has been ripped away from me," my father finally sighed, releasing a moan that came from the flaming garnet in his heart. As if a crater had suddenly burst, releasing a storm from within that beggared all anguish and sent a Tsunami hurling through the clouds.

"It's here," Drilg whispered and with a harmonic tone sweeter than the sweetest song the Vyngorch ever sang brought us up to a plane of ceaseless joy. In an instant she had vanished

as if she'd been an apparition, and yet the benefaction of her
visit had uplifted all who remained. Upon the act of my mother's
grace, other angels came, paying visitation to our haggard
legions, each one giving ethereal passage through sacred
spiritual doors.

It was through these doorways that I finally saw the
Answer—that even in all our strivings we had only touched the
hem of Light, and through a passage opened to me I saw the
SkyMaster dancing, twirling in the waning Sun and the kiss of an
evening dew.

"She'll come again," I heard the voice. "This wasn't her last
incarnation. Remember, the journey of mortal souls is an
arduous one indeed. Always keep an open heart, and let your
gemstones guide you. Be mindful as well that they always line the
path to your oversoul. If you love her so much, you'll see her
again. All our prayers are answered, even the ones that seem the
farthest away."

The Voice. There was no form that came with it. It might
have been an angel's or a dragon's in transition.

Skye, of course. I couldn't mistake him. He'd drifted in with
the mist, the kind that comes with a gentle evening's breeze.

"Cousin," he said, and as he spoke he formed out of the dew
like the breath of a hummingbird in flight. "This is no angel's
demeanor you see. I'm back to do some work on this plane for a
little lifetime more. So excuse me if I don't ascend just yet. It is
the angel's choice to do the work down here or from on high.
Personally, I feel it best to put talons in the turf—to play in the
fields of the Lord, as it were, and sip honey from the flower. Yes,
to answer the unspoken thought, I've earned my angel's wings.
Yet there's much more that remains to be done on this troubled
little planet."

"What's so important that you must incarnate?" I simmered.
"It's dirty business down here. Frankly I've had enough myself. I
can't conceive of wanting to stay in a world where magic is
doomed where every allusion to higher awareness is met with
mockery. Despite its primitive beauty I've seen all of this planet I

care to. Send me to another world where I can spread my wings."

Thirty-three years, and I'd tasted the wine—bitter or sweet, it had all been set before me. Hadn't I done the Godly thing? Hadn't I fought the good fight? Hadn't I sealed the Door, fulfilled the prophecy and done everything that was asked? Hadn't I undertaken every task set before me and changed the course of things? My God and angels, what did they want?! What did I have to do?! More important, what had I done to drop myself in this soup?!

Angels of course hear every thought. Skye, with measured concern, cleared his throat and told me a truth I sensed but would have denied.

"You have a grievous debt to pay. That's part of the reason I've returned. I've seen your Akashic record, and it isn't pretty. You marked yourself for these tasks of yours before you ever took flesh in a hundred lifetimes and a dozen worlds when you were a Seraphim's breath from Power. The Evil One spoke truly when he said we'd fallen, all of us from the loftiest heights the Higher Mind can conceive. But you dear cousin fell the farthest, for you were so close to the Light, you could have become it merely by saying the Word. Yet at that moment you turned away. The Perfection of it stung you. And it was you who led so many down to come to this.

"I tell you this not to condemn, because you are—yet you are not—the angel that you were an eon ago. Forget what you heard and know this now, you don't even fathom the Game. Even though you helped author this, it's been blanked from your memory. At least you made the decision once that put you back on the path. You've picked the way of righteousness, and all your angels are proud. But don't expect a promotion anytime soon.

"This dragon's life is not a gift. Three thousand years in this skin is more of a penance than any creature should bear. Transmigration into the selves of other forms of consciousness is the only journey the higher soul can take. So, cousin, take it, make it your own. But realize when you do that you risk the loss of everything you were. And when you risk, you realize that there are other forces at work—more than some hot shot wizard or two trying to take you out. Now, you've angered the One himself, and he has his eye on you. But know this too, the Door you sealed wasn't the only gate. Hell has seven gates, and six remain."

Not exactly the news one wanted to hear on a day like this, especially after I'd cooked my resolution, fried it to my adrenals just so I could put an end to Evil.

For what?! If Hell had seven doors to shut, and we'd spent half our clan to do it, how on Earth could we hope to close the six that still remained?

"Heaven help us!" I shouted the words, in anguish in spite of myself.

"Well…that's the very first step. The pathway to success lies in surrender," Skye said, then slyly looked away.

Somehow in the midst of this revelation in the flowing of amazing grace that now poured down on us in healing, making sure we understood our cause had been *tres juste,* I seemed to be getting the standard lecture and faced with a new assignment. I with all my higher awareness seemed to be stuck in time, grinding at the same damned wheel while my cousin had ascended.

By now it had begun to seem as if I'd been the one who'd caused this, as if it had been I alone who'd spat in the face of God!

Was that the burden that I bore? I choked upon the thought. Was that why I had been assigned these monumental tasks? Why had the Fallen One flown to me in the throes of his defeat and regarded me with such simple silent outrage? Why had he seemed so familiar to me as if I'd been his consort, as if I'd been the archetypal architect of The Fall?

"Don't be in a hurry to know," Skye warned. "Stay innocent in your quest. Your oversoul can only carry so much weight at a time. For now, we have some healing to do to bring the others around, to let them know that much was won on this day."

"But the Fallen One was right," I said. "Such savagery of war, no matter how noble, is a wound upon the soul.

"An easy truth," the Blue Dragon sighed. "But there is such nuance of conflict, and this one of all took place on a plane of consciousness far beyond the grasp of mortal minds. This was a fight for mastery, the purging of such souls as well might never come this way again. We had to fall. This Mystic Brotherhood was simply too close to the Eye of God, yet too far away from His Heart to ever see the truth of what we'd become. That we have limited time, it's true. Now it's the human form, a simpler briefer life for all to dance in. Don't ask me why it's the wiser choice, for the longer one lives in the body the more one learns to understand the workings of Heaven."

I disagreed and knew in my gut that for once Skye's senses were off. There was much more to this waltz of souls than even the angels knew.

"The other six gates don't require such scale. They won't need an army to close them—just a single soldier willing to make the commitment to the end. Be willing to probe and know the pain that too much knowing brings, and turn the screw though it may burn the hands."

Skye, as ever, knew what drove me, knew what gave me cause, knew that in spite of all my misgivings I had kept the standard, taken every dirty job this life had chosen to send me. Even now with the light of Heaven pouring in on us, I was being told the ugly truth.

"Pray tell me, my angelic friend, what have you done with my daughter? While you were twisting in the Mouth of Hell, where did you lay her down? Or was she the coin of passage that you gave the Boatman?"

"This is the healing time, Shartallion. Don't let your anger drive you. Your daughter is safe. She rests in the meadow where the Mantilough gracefully graze, watched there by the Princess herself who instructs her in cosmic truth. There's so much love that surrounds you, black dragon, despite what you have been. Let it guide you now and take you Home."

Words are but tricks to dazzle the mind. It's Energy that prevails. The same light that lifts the flower's face can heal a soul in torment. So it became with me, for in a moment of avowal when my pain and desperation, my rage at my loving God, my ranting at my angels who had carried me through all this, who had seen me every step of the way, who had nudged me along the path, who had guided me in my most dissolute moments with psalms I thought were my own, I realized in a stream of sunlight that this had not been in vain, that if we'd lost the vestige of magic the aura would still remain. What we had done in this trine of days could never be erased. Even if we, to the very last creature, were to vanish from this planet, our story would be told by the keepers of the Flame—the flame that burned inside us all to behold the face of God.

That I had done so many things right without really knowing the reason, I had become the instrument upon which these times had been played. Now that it had come to pass, that The Time indeed had come, we were no longer what we'd been or would ever be again. We had been the sacrifice. Our blood had been the tribute for mysteries I could not even conceive—I who had learned from the most enlightened beings on this plane would now have to learn again from a higher source.

Spires of light now pierced the clouds forming the pillars of Heaven, so we couldn't spread our wings to fly without feeling their glow upon us, easing our pain of loss with a new sense of purpose. Even though we'd been decimated and would never be the same, we were now cleansed of sorrow. It wasn't a simple process. Not even prolonged euphoria can erase the sting of memory.

As if suddenly summoned by higher voices that none of us mortals could hear, the angels vanished from the dome of sky above us, leaving us all with traces of sunlight from a day that would slip into night.

Skye, as he often did so well, became beam of sunlight, leaving me with the rapt impression that he'd never be far away. Was he the angel on my shoulder? Was he the Guardian? He never would say, but he'd be among us making his presence felt. He'd put his touch on everything without ever lifting a hand, simply guiding us all along with the voice of vindication.

Dager the Mountain, his wounds healed with light, turned his focus on me, nodded his silent command to abandon the field. Although we hadn't shared more than a word in days, we knew the rest was simply a matter of being. Others in turn—the unicorns, the chimera, the aloof and noble gryphon—called to us in recognition that the conflict had finally ended, that they could go about their lives and sail through realms of magic, delving into those ethers only mystical creatures know.

The wings that beat across the skies, crimson in the dusk, were muted with a gentle lufting like sails of ships at sea. Never had I, before or since, beheld such transformation. For every pain they'd ever felt there now was benediction, a new beginning of all we had known.

The peace that passeth understanding at least for the moment had come—to everyone of the Mystic Clan but me.

§§§§§§§

I'd released my cortege of dragons, had sent them with my father, gone in flight to the Crater of Nebul through the Ether of Tyme. I saw him turn to wave at me, a solitary salute. We would share many times in future, but none that compared to this, none that would carry us so far into the throat of Dread itself.

The Captain remained, joined at last by his stalwart valiant battalion, men who had fought through the Dark Alliance to stand as one in this moment. The tales they told of the battles they'd fought just to get them here both saddened and amused us with their bold and reckless courage. They had faced ten times their number and made it through the fire. The Vyngorchim who had ferried them, the ones who had survived, had hung behind the clouds and actually sung the villains to sleep before they could take action.

We waited as comrades side by side in the light of the red waning sun. Forget the disparity in our sizes, for he was my brother in arms. On the other side my brother in fact, the future Vyngorch King now stood ennobled by his boldness. Together we'd all sung the Asking Prayer. We had formed the fiery star. We'd called an end to the horde of Shimbaghs and locked the minions below. If our days were numbered, then so had theirs been, for they were no longer an issue. At least we'd vanquished our mirror selves and halved the face of evil.

And yet this waiting, this silent sharing, carried finality, a time when no one wished to say goodbye.

This Captain took a breath to drink in the taste of glory. He was still human, and victory still meant a great deal to him. He hadn't communed with the angels directly, but he had stood in the Light. He hadn't heard the voices, but he had seen the signs. And it had been enough to make him whole.

What simple creatures were these men after all. They only knew what they saw. They took the evidence as real—whatever was presented. For their perceptions of abstract thought were limited indeed. That was the secret of their power; they were primitive in the soul. They were the children to whom all Faith was a matter of black and white. I could see that written on the Captain's face. I caught the reflection in his eyes. When he beheld an angel, he saw...an angel. He hadn't agonized or doubted the rightness of his acts or even thought to catch the reason of the Evil One's rebuttal. That was what had made him strong and the heir to this world: Find your focus on right and wrong, and do the rightest thing. Even now, he made pledges to me that I knew that he would keep no matter what the cost. It was the way of the best among them, the holy warrior's duty. (So many of them spoke of virtue, but few of them lived the Word. That's what made the best of them an exception.)

"I know what's been said so many times that the days for the magic are dying. You've been told by devil and angel, by wizard and tainted warrior, that there soon will be an end to the Mystic Beast.

"Not as long as I have breath in my body will there be a loss of enchantment. The story of these days will be told by every man among us. We'll be the criers of the cause, the champions of Mystique. We'll spread the word of all the good the Mystic Clan has done. There'll be rapprochement among all creatures— no more fear or loathing. What we've done in these days will be passed through generations. You'll be a legend in our times, as well you deserve to be."

I couldn't help but weep at the thought that we could actually share this world, that the pygmie with all his pretense could ever permit equality of the soul. Could he ever recognize that his fellow creatures were equals, were anything but raw material and grist for his mass production?

Yet here was this man, and a good one at that, making his solemn vow that he would be the chronicler and the advocate of our deeds.

"Be careful, my friend," I offered the caution. "There are many among your species who wouldn't stand for a single word of goodness to be spoken of us. We're *other* creatures, after all, and powerful ones at that. And though I know you're a man on a mission, the danger will be extreme. You know too much. You have been to the War, and you have made the difference. When you've cooked in the crucible of hidden knowledge you can't speak too loudly or long. Do your work in silence, and keep your profile low. The secret of success is to endure."

"Good advice, my dragon brother," The Captain nodded humbly. "You're the Answerer after all."

"And the Prayer we sing still carries on the wind."

For a moment, we even caught the laughter. For a time we celebrated. And Pod and I rocked back on our wings while these men among men danced and sang. Impelled by the spirit of noble cause, filled with the light of salvation, they were the happiest group I'd ever seen. Why then, at that very time, did I fear so much for their lives? And if so, why did I ignore my sacred gift of premonition?

As the curtain of day drew down on the shoulders of earth, we caught the flight of a bird coming from the throat of a violet sun. I knew it was a bird because its wings were to busy flapping—such a busy, brash, and fussy little fellow. Seeing it struggle against the gusts that came from the crests of mountains brought us to pause between mirth and sympathy, caused us to let down our guard, brought me to close my eyes, thinking only then of the peace of the moment.

It was not the time to be off my guard, for the bird was making for us. And in the time I could blink the damage had been done. In the sting of parsec a flaming mace hurled at the speed of light cracked our perceptions and buried hilt-deep into the Captain's heart. It shattered his quilted silver armor with a long tip steeled in gold and a head whose edges glistened black and white.

On the horizon of day's darkest hour, a figure unfurled in the sky—the tainted transmogrification from bird to wizard. Even in the shadows, I could see the glacial glow of his cloak iridescent against his indigo gown. Split half and half in black and white, the ultimate contradiction, hovered the mocking Magpie to haunt my life yet again.

"I honored my word, oh Dragon Lord. But the war is over, you see. And I had score to settle once and for all."

In my fury, I torched the sky where he stood, but he had already vanished. This wizard I'd set free had done it again. And though I combed the skies for an hour, I couldn't find a particle of him or where he might have fled. All I could hear were refractions of sound, the mocking voice of RuSiva.

"Don't be too angry, my raging black friend. I've done the warrior a favor. He's gone to a better place, you see, with angels all around. And as for you and me…Well, hell, we're stuck here in this cycle. The Wheel of Life grinds on, and we're the grease. This is just the beginning for us. So don't try too hard to find me. Our next sortie lies further down the path. Besides, old friend, I find you to be a most worthy adversary. So much power, and so little command of how to make it work…"

As my fires raged torching the night in desperate search of him, his laughter faded into the wind that mocked me with its howling. It wasn't Korlig's voice I heard, but an alien southern breeze, the kind that carried the hot moist stench of spiritual decay.

It seemed to me the more I searched the more I got lost in the quest, feeling the elation of dread inside me and the shameful joy of vengeance. Why, after all this transfiguration did I still relish the conflict? Why did I now delight in the hunt more than ever before? Was I such a slave to passion that it drove me beyond all reason? What kind of monster had this occasion come to make of me?

Perhaps I deserved this hide after all, this ugly dragon's skin. Had my search for the deadly Magpie left me without a compass, a soul again adrift in my need for revenge?

Only this southern draft now drew me, though it took a storm's proportions, pulling a kind of desire from me that wantonly drew me down.

More than even the Door of Evil, it was the most radical pull pouring forth a sense of pleasure I had never known. It was as if all the evil we'd driven from the earth now had found its way inside of me. There was an obvious pleasure in it, an irresistible yearning that fired my loins and quickened my heart and it drew me to it now as if I'd been part of its body, the missing piece, the mind of it, the other face of Evil. Even though I tried to resist it, it was drawing me down—to the South, to where I'd known that Lucifer had gone.

Of course, the Magpie had come to lure me, to suck me into this, had done the only thing he knew would drive me to pursue him. He'd killed the Captain, and he'd done it right in front of me, not only to defy me but also to pique my pride. I wouldn't play his game; not now. There was too much still at stake. We'd come too far for me to fall into this base fellow's trap. No question, he was just the bait. And his Master was waiting beyond, trying to reel me into him, while never showing himself.

Why?

"Beelzebub," I heard the voice, to answer the unasked question. From the dark shoulders of the mountain ridges, my cousin called out to me, sending his voice like a net to blunt my rage and my ranting pursuit.

Skye had followed my every move, had even tracked my chase, but true to his form had chosen not to intercede.

"I see the truth of it now," he said. "It is a greater burden for you not to know who you were than to know who you are." He repeated the word.

"Beelzebub!" He said, not to harm me, but more as an apology for the pain he knew it might bring. "You were the Crown Prince of Lucifer's kingdom. You were the next in line. And there were rumors from on high that you had started it all, that you had been the *agent provocateur* who had thought it a good idea to change the course of cosmic history. You were Mephisto's Mephisto, as it were. But in that moment when we came to choose, you saw the crop you had cut. So, you chose to rebel again, this time for the Good. So that you have been punished with this, don't be in the least surprised, for there are more trials for you than you could imagine. That's why the power that's known to you seems to elude your grasp, because you had so much and you abused it. That's the karma that you've incurred. And who can measure its weight?

"It's not merely by accident that you have come to this place. Though you've rediscovered the path to Heaven, you still have Hell to pay."

Hearing him speak in such a way was the sword that cleaved my soul. It was not so much that he'd said it but that I'd already sensed it. Well before the word struck, I had come, every stroke of the way, to realize that I had been the one the Fates had chosen. The Fates! My God! What irony, what unregenerate passion could have ever brought an angel to come to this? Yet in that selfsame moment, I felt the ultimate cleansing from the fire of truth that had burned away the final veil of illusion.

"Thank you, dear cousin. For now at last I've been stripped of affectation, although I can't help but feel the overwhelming burden of guilt. What have I done? My God and Christ forgive me! What have I done?!"

"You know exactly where you've been, and where you have to go. Would that everyone could receive the gift you've just been given. Nevertheless, release the guilt, for you are not the selfsame soul you were those eons ago. The tapes that replay your obsessions with Power have all been erased. But caution! They can always be relearned.

"Only your awareness can guard you against them; that's why I've chosen to tell you—to end your confusion once and for all, to let you know the Truth. The reason your doubt persists despite the love that envelops you is that your cellular self refuses to let you out of bondage.

"For that reason you still remain the Prize for the Fallen One. To gain you back would mean validation and empower him by two, for the other side of this Coin of Death would make him whole again."

The burden was too much to bear. I bolted and streaked away, screaming until the night clouds split and rocks below me cracked. In my escape, I'd shattered sound but still could not discount the Truth that I had been Satan's consort and an architect of The Fall.

I finally found a mountain shoulder a thousand leagues away, praying that the dawn would end this dark night of the soul. Where did one go from here? I wondered. If I'd been so much a part of the highest and lowest of Powers then why had my memory been so utterly scotched? What act could I perform on this Earth that would make it right for me? No wonder the Mystics now stood condemned and had somehow chosen to be the Blood that purged the Sin, the greatest and worst in all the heavens of all the worlds that existed. We had all been part of this, and seemingly none of us knew where we had been or why we now stood where we were.

"Nor can they be allowed to know. The secret stays with you, and dies when you ascend or pass on from this life."

Naturally, Skye was right behind me to bear the weight of my thoughts, to guide me in the instant where I'd strayed.

"Small comfort," I said, "to carry that burden...to know that it's mine alone. What good would it do? And what can I do alone? If the others can be redeemed, God bless them! Let it be! But how can there ever be a Tibbuk for me?"

"You credit yourself with too much," Skye observed. "What you were is not what you are. The violation was in a life before you took this form, and you were one among tens of thousands. So what if you helped lead the pack? It was a very large pack indeed, and you've all been forgiven. They just still don't get it. So, now it's up to you. After all, you've seen the Light. You made the switch to the right. You carried the day and took a torch to the Night.

"And yet I have *that* price to pay. You know it as well as I. There's a task that awaits, I know, that shakes my vital force."

In a silence so serene it could have swallowed a storm of comets, Skye closed his eyes, then opened them slowly to reveal the answer.

"In the next two thousand years, there will come among the race of men, a society of prophets. Minute in their number, they will have in common the pure consciousness of the Christ. They will come in common forms to us—as princes and priests, as laborers and teachers. Because of what they are and will be for all the eras of men, their lives will be under constant threat, and many will be taken.

"The task for you in those times of men is to seek these messengers out, anticipate the days of their coming—when they will be born, when they will be at their most vulnerable and how they can be protected. Because they are the creatures of Light, the Dark One will make for them straightway and use every trick he can to make them his own, or else destroy them. Granted, they'll be guided through their lives, but in the beginning there's a danger. Only a force on this plane can forestall him, and that physical force is you."

"Skye, my friend," I studied him. "Don't take me for a fool. These souls will have angels all around them every day they draw breath."

"On other levels, this is true. But you will remain on this plane. You must do the job of many creatures. This means you must use disguises. Again, you must become a man. Time and again, you must risk your life no matter what the outcome. Give it if you have to, for in that great release is the sweetest path to Heaven you'll ever know."

"Or another lifetime and another challenge without the power I hold. I know the risk; it's deadly, and there are no shortcuts. If I die or am killed and forfeit my power, it's back to Square One for me. I know that, and you knew when you asked me to take this on."

I accepted on the spot, of course. What other choice did I have? Three thousand years in a dragon's skin was penance enough as it was. Any diversion along the way, the nobler the better, and I might find the answer to the Question: Why was it I?

As it was, I could go on with this knowledge that I had sunk so low, yet still had been forgiven for my betrayal. I was the archangel Beelzebub who, in the prayers of saints, had once been mentioned in the same breath with Aureal, Michael and Gabriel, now consorted with cosmic flotsam of highly questionable lineage. How contemptuous I suddenly felt to ever have found them noble. How alien and ugly they now appeared to me How very among the elite, a Princedom just step down from the Power itself. That was who I was and would be again.

Suddenly, I heard the word slit into my brain. "Pride!"

The deadliest sin. That was what had felled me then, and it was with me still, like some congenital disease—even as a dragon, I remained unto my core the most arrogant elitist sonofabitch who'd ever dared to wear wings. I felt the chill of instant shame and wept until I heaved, until the blood poured out of my soul and up into my mouth, bringing with it the blackest bitterest bile, the sorrow of all the ages. I wept long into the night until the day cracked wholly, and realized that of all the images we had perceived, all had been illusion until this moment.

All the mystic perceptions of honor, duty and noble cause were merely the outer petals on the flower. Once we drew closer to the Source, the conflict had come to this. I knew it now, yet couldn't reveal the truth. So, I would become the spy of Heaven with more secrets than a soul should bear. To betray them now would tip the balance, would rupture identities up and down the line from men to gryphons.

So, I would dally with second string wizards and fence with beasts from below, for I had the knowledge but no longer held the power. Knowing without being is the emptiest feeling of all, to behold the Truth and yet find it just out of reach. Skye stayed with me, friend that he was, angel that he always would be, trying to offer comfort and perspective. Yet he knew as well as I that we were beyond so much of it now. All the layers had been peeled away, the true mission revealed. Everything else had been but a prelude to this moment.

I watched the night grow light around me and realized as I did that I was again alone, and should have been. The mountains that surrounded me were shoulders of gods set there to give me perspective. Whatever I had been, I had fallen and was now another creature, forced to start this arduous path again. I pulled myself together and flew west away from the sun, eventually finding the place where the soldiers had been.

§§§§§§§

There was no doubt about what I would find when I returned to the others. My brother in the soul, the Captain, had been laid low on this night. It was as if the cycle had started all over without reprieve for me. While others were let loose from the Wheel, I was still caught in its spin. Now, at last I knew the why but never quite the wherefore.

We burned the Captain later at dusk in a pyre on the crest of a hill, before a sun so crimson it seemed to bleed at the recognition. I set the flame myself with a breath and a prayer. Though I mourned him, I had lost so much that the numbness had overwhelmed me. And it burned me to my heart to think I had no tears for him. Yet somehow I knew he would understand. We were warriors at the glove, bonded through eternity to share the Cause together. I'd know this man for who he was and pierce the incarnation. We'd share the table once again in this overlong life of mine.

The Captain's son said the eulogy, filled with avowals of vengeance, fraught with oaths to pursue the evil mage who'd brought him down. He pledged his devotion to their Mission. (And who was I to judge?) Nonetheless I sensed that he lacked his father's depth of passion. There is a character about a creature that announces what it's about, that goes into the quiet place in the heart and stills concern. The Captain possessed that quality. Few I had seen could match it. I would miss him and would mark the day when our lives would cross again.

As for the Magpie, I'd taken his measure. And though he knew my secret, now that I knew it as well, we were matched at every level of the Game. Nothing would be the same for me now, except for the pain of knowing that all of the knowledge I held in my fires could never again be shared.

We bade farewell to the Captain's son and watched as the soldiers assembled, bidding their final salute to us and pausing at the pyre. Taking the time to pause for reflection, they each laid a weapon down, covering the spot where the pyre had raged with a mesh work of silver spears. Slowly, one by one, they gathered to march home when I realized that home to them was where the next quest would be. Whether it was Grail or covenant, their mark would be upon it. As long as they held together, their force would be formidable indeed.

Pod and I both turned to the East and set off into the sky searching to find the place in the heart where the Mantilough gently grazed. What I would find there would be the answer to the agonizing question. How could the most defiant angel in all of God's creation ever hope to find Tibbuk and repose for the soul?

Canto 35

Candle

There are hidden places in every heart where truth and right prevail, where innocence remains unsullied by the heavy hands of time, where circumstance can never block the flight of our highest dreams, where age and grace are one and hope is our haven.

Darting along the western winds above the currents of prospect to the Kunlun climes where harmony once had sweetened my days, we soared. Deep beyond valleys and rain rich forests, we came to a place of Knowing and sat in the twilight by a brook where flowers floated free. There was a peace I found inside that I'd felt only once before when for the first time I'd beheld the Mantilough graze.

I knew that they would manifest, that I would find them here. I knew that I'd been guided to this place and that I must keep the faith. It also struck me surely that these were other creature's angels, that the Mantilough wherever it flew brought in the gift of healing.

I longed for that gifting more than ever—I, the scarred angel's soul—I, Dragon who carried the weight of the heaviest heart in Creation longed for a day's reprieve. Now, I would learn to love it again, to see it for what it was—the simple joy of living in the moment.

My brother, whatever he'd been before, had come to that awareness, and now took each moment as a mercy, still grateful for his life. Together we sat without expectation, content to let it happen, and watched as the flocks of Mantilough formed out of the shafts of moonlight. As they grazed on honeyed flower-dew and sang their sweet cantatas, I saw their Princess catch the hint of the breeze—the scent of us upon the air and the blood and bane of battle. She read our vibrations, such as they were, on the other side of the curtain, knowing that beneath the pain and fatigue there was purity of purpose. In my silent reverence I thanked her for saving my life, for having used her extensive powers to freeze the tide of battle, to give me the time I'd needed to see it through.

She didn't give it a moment's thought, for time had no meaning to her. Linear measure was beneath her need to define it.

"You've come for your daughter. What a blessing she is! She's loved and wonderfully cared for, set here by a flight of angels and the Azure Dragon Skye.

"Your blessed daughter is a gift to every one of us. She has perfect beauty and clarity yet knows no physical likeness. Whenever she opens her eyes you see the prisms of Heaven's face, yet there is nothing like her on this Earth. This morning you come to collect her, to carry her to your world into the hard dimensions of your physical plane of life. Pray, do not. The fascination for an entity so ineffable as this will obsess the collectors of magic to possess her. Keep her safe. Keep her here, or risk the fortune hunters, and know that every day with her will be spent defending her life."

The lyrics the Mantilough Princess sang were particles of thought carried on flecks of crystal to reflect the light that shatters all darkness. Sent to us not out of fear or any sense of opinion, they were the Truth that could not be denied.

I realized her kindness kept the harsh light of judgment from us. Yet it was there: We were warriors through and through, bathed in remnants of blood and battle that couldn't be washed clean in a year of Ablution. What were we, after all but warriors, bloodied to the cause? And I had fought it all, fought God and Devil alike, had taken sides and taken sides again.

Here I sat, the Prince of Foresight, prescient to my onyx cells, and yet hadn't the slightest clue about what to do with my daughter. What could I have dared to do but love her as some part of me, as some part of her mother—the other half of my soul now lost again?

Of course, I couldn't take her with me. And yet I had to ask, how could she have been born at all to such a place as this—to warriors in the blood, to clans in spiritual conflict, to the schism in the soul that could never be resolved? There had to have been a purpose to it beyond the mere fruit of lust. She and her brother, for better or worse, both had the power in the seed to begin new spiritual clans to change the world. He had set about his duties the moment his foot struck ground, and nearly grown had bolted to run to his kind. She, in all this time, remained fragile, innocent and helpless. Yet someday soon she would grow to become a queen.

But how? I wondered. Surely not by mating with one of the Vyngorchim, the harlequin manifestation of magic gone awry. I looked upon my brother, now—the erstwhile Vyngorch King, nearly having lost his kingdom and all his subjects as well. What remained of them through all of this were the remnants of a dream lived too briefly with nothing to show in the end but battered pride. To be sure, they had smatterings of self respect, and the grudging acceptance of others. But at what price had come their brush with honor?

Nevertheless that seemed enough for this harlequin hero. He'd flown above and beyond his limitations. And combat had forged him in a heady kind of dignity that outstripped my own at this time. He was on purpose. He'd been transfixed (while I had been transfused). He'd gained hope while I had seen the tree from which I'd fallen. Were we equals? Or had he passed me on his flight path into the sun? The fact that it even mattered to me brought home the answer clearly. By the same measure, I'd hit upon it that this moment was perfectly timed. Pod and my daughter were made to be in union.

The Mantilough Princess saw it too, for she was a reader of thoughts, and she answered by closing her eyes in affirmation.

What glory! What a horror! For all the purity of the soul couldn't belie the fact that the two were bonded in the blood. For their bodies to join on this plane of life would be incest and bear that issue. But what if they were not only on this plane? What if they changed their forms to find another kind of passage? Why not permit them to cross over into identities that could net them a safer path to their future without the constant focus of negative force? And as the Mantilough Princess possessed the power to transmute, to cross elements in time and souls in transition, could we not put those powers to task to mend these hearts in longing, take them to a haven safe from all harm?

"You cannot grant a wish for me. You've already done that well. But for another, it can be done, if he would merely speak it." I looked upon my brother gazing upon this angel in waiting, noting the adoration in his eyes. He was smitten in every way. It was more than fascination, She was the answer to his every prayer to be reborn to this world.

"He has but to speak it, and it's done," she replied.

And with conviction he answered: "Somewhere on this Earth but not of it, out of the commerce of conflict, abundant with magic but with none of the burdens that magic can create; to be in love and loving but never carry expectation; to taste the lips of Heaven but never drink; to give delight, to banish pain, to sing the Silent Song with lyrics only angels on high can hear; to please the eye, to be beautiful to behold, never to live in fear of ridicule or feel the need for acceptance; to be courageous without ferocity; to quit the burden of ego; to be nimble of wing and joyous in the watching."

Sooner or later the sands of time will pour into our dreams, wounds healed, wishes made real, and all other worlds discovered. So it was as my brother Pod spoke these very words that they transformed him into a hummingbird with healing in his wings—golden feathers and crystalline eyes that turned into radiant diamonds, shining truth from every facet, seeing perfection in all. As instantaneously as he had transformed, my daughter too had arisen from her down, hovering radiantly in the very same form. Slighter than he, but resplendent with a brilliant azure band across her throat from which whispered a perfect prayer, a hymn of joy and thanksgiving that was as constant as the wind.

Uplifted, carried high into the clouds, the two ascended without ever bidding *adieu.* It was then I realized the beauty of it: My daughter hadn't transformed at all. She had always been and always would be this perfect kind of creature. She was sunlight; he was morning. Together they would birth a new day, a brand new race of hummingbird wizards who could change the face of the sky, who could carry messages on their backs from angels in hidden places.

So it began, the new race of the Vyngorch. No longer the cosmic clowns, no longer the scorn of the warrior, they had now become the perfect poem. Every move they made, every swing through the heavens, every caressing of the flower was the ultimate ballet. And what of power? I wondered but knew. What greater Power than this: to bring love into every moment and joy into the heart? Knowing this truth now caused them to soar until they disappeared, dancing away into a night already becoming morning.

"You'll see them again. Until time is done, they'll manifest the light. They'll be messengers of truth and harbingers of peace."

The Mantilough Princess proclaimed all this, while noting my sense of loss—that in this time when all had come to a kind of peace with themselves, I remained the Lightning Dragon, the soul in torment. No truce with the self could erase what I'd been, or the terrible thing I'd done. To have cleaved the throne of Heaven apart, to have been that invidious agent, was more than any vital force could bear. What could I do to make it right? Who could I ever be? I'd pushed the game to the limit this time and had still not washed clean the blemish.

I should have kept my thoughts to myself; the Mantilough Princess read them, but delicately deferred to the rage inside me.

Instead, she softly turned back to her flock, whispering her final comfort even as she danced them into a dew. "Your answer, as always, is in the wind on your wings—the one that lifts you higher, the one you take for granted yet is always there."

She sweetly sighed this without remorse, yet left me again to wonder: Was it she, or just the gentle rain at midnight?

I stayed to watch as the moonlight waned and the morning warmed the meadow and the flocks of Mantilough slowly faded for a final time. I'd never see them again, I knew. I'd overstayed my welcome, for like innocence they were too precious to endure. Yet in their flawless charity, these moments were what really mattered—pure the heart and ever clear the view.

I flew into the day, soaring above the mountains, beyond the plains, away from the temples of Empire that the pygmie was busy building, away from cities and the ocean's commerce it made to repair itself after the fray that had nearly destroyed us all. It helped to stay aloft on the wing, for no matter how the heart sinks low, a day in the skies on heaven's shoulders can lift a spirit in pain.

I, Dragon. Beelzebub! How high could I ever fly before I could mend that awareness or salve the Scar on that other higher Life? No wonder the Fallen One had gone mad, for knowledge without forgiveness is the ultimate fatal blow to the sentient soul. Yet I had both. I had felt forgiveness long before I knew. And yet my task seemed more difficult than before: Close the remaining doors of Evil, lock the six gates of Hell, play the warrior nursemaid to the coming host of messiahs. How? I wondered. Why? I raged. These creatures had no focus. They were the most easily seduced of all the species ever created. Even if they could be made to see, for how long could it last? Their lives were so short, and their memories faded as quickly as a polar summer.

A storm was churning below and around me as I caught the lip of a mountain, drawn there by a little light that flickered in a fractured crevice below. As I spread my wings and drew down to land on a craggy shoulder of rock I saw that it was a vigil that a little girl had lit. She was slight. She was frail, no more than ten as human years are counted. Yet her intensity of purpose had caused her to climb alone to this solitary self-styled citadel in the sky. Into the throat of the darkest night with every menace about her, high through creatures screaming in darkness and cold winds that clawed at the cliffs, onto a tiny pocket of earth that held safe against the fury—she had built her own inviolate refuge, a shrine. It was but a little thing made of rocks with an idol this little girl had carved herself. It was shaped out of wood and set forth a gaze almost risible in its aspect. And before it she burnt a candle that she shielded with her body.

Her face, with a bearing beyond her years, revealed the age of her soul, twisted into a tiny knot of purpose. Intently, she repeated the prayer until it became a mantra, and from the mantra an energy was formed.

"Jacobin!" she called out. "Answer my prayer! It is you I revere more than any! You are the godling who will mold my dreams. Jacobin! to you I pray. You are the truest god of all. Jacobin, the Master. Come to life. Reveal yourself. And let me be your will!"

This godling was a block of wood with neither life nor will of its own. It was inert, a lump of lifeless matter; at least it began that way. Yet so concerted was this little girl's vigil, so devout her prayer and so determined had she become to keep the candle lit that in a matter of time this feckless worthless block became an energy that one could perceive. Eventually, it took on an aspect that one could grasp, rose to her level of devotion, transforming into what she had seen it to be—a living, breathing animus to fulfill her expectations. As if it had been given birth, it took on her consciousness, and soon it seemed would take a kind of incarnate animation. This little girl's faith had given it life, had birthed this entity. For whatever it had now become, it would serve her limited purpose, until the time arrived when it would serve purposes of its own.

In this darkest yet brightest moment, I witnessed this blind act of faith. I saw what it had created, and I knew! I realized what I had done—what all of us had done. From this moment there would never again be a wasted thought for me. And though the task that I had been given would take a dragon's lifetime, I would meet the challenge and bring it to pass. Destiny rode on my shoulders now, aware of its own reward.

I was many, and Heaven was my home.

Glossary of Terms

Brimbrods. Dark seductive shards of brimstone. Red hot and tantalizing, they are a favorite aphrodisiac for the dragon. Unfortunately addictive, shards of bimbrod are also able to steal the dragon's willpower and eventually, if taken long enough, his soul.

Chimera. The lion-dogs are the clowns of the Mystic Beasts. Good natured and impossible to offend, they love singing loudly (and usually off-key). And when they do their music can bring the rain. Sometimes they overdo it, especially when upset, and that's when prolonged electric storms happen that can unwittingly wreak havoc on the land. Generally however, Chimera serve good causes, are primarily herbivores and are only dangerous when they lose their temper, which unfortunately happens quite often. The males among the Chimera can fly quite well in short bursts; the females with more difficulty. But they are always agile and formidable on the ground.

Chthonic Schools. Far down into the recesses of planet Earth there is a school of higher awareness where all the mystic beasts and students seeking the light must train to attain "the Seven Gems" of higher awareness. Inside this school there exists one of two worlds: a pillar of infinite light, or a cavern of despair and negativity fraught with fearful creatures that may test and torture the seeker. A test of consciousness as well as reality, it makes the Chthonic School the ultimate conundrum.

Crater of Nebul. A clawed out fiery maw of mountain top carved into the highest throat of mountain ranges on earth, it is a time-honored sanctuary for dragons as well as the site of their conferences and council meetings. Although all other mystic beasts such as the unicorns and gryphons are welcome, only the Chimera (who are impossible to offend), and the Kohmm ever come to visit.

Crogzs (also Cavern Crogz). Large rock-like creatures who cling to the ceilings and caverns of the Chthonic Schools, they have cryptically large mouths that they keep closed except to snare bats from the voleries that frequently fly their way.

Dragons. The central figure of this story, the dragon is a creature whose legacy defies the wicked lore that has been created about him. Since everyone already knows the physical traits of the dragon that comprise the mythical clichés it seems redundant to belabor them here. It is however important to note that they do come in various colors usually embraced while going through spiritual training and according to their choice of destiny. They do range in size from about 50 feet in length to more than 100 feet and as tall as 35 feet at the shoulder. They can breathe enormous gouts of flame, torch entire buildings with a single breath. And (blue eyed dragons) can petrify human beings just by engaging them in eye contact; but only if they choose to do so. The dragon's heritage is as complex and weighty as his spiritual contract to be the protector and guardian of planet Earth. Powerful, spiritual and immense physical presences, dragons take on forms and guises that are mountainous and intimidating. Terrifying in flight and form, petrifying in gaze, hypnotic in speech and sense of language, the dragon was (and is) simply the most powerful creature in the times in which he lived. With a spiritual awareness and intellectual capacity that often exceeded that of man, why would such a tower of light abdicate his role and disappear into the shadow world of "creatures that never were?" Was it part of his destiny to do so? Was there a kabalistic contract he had to fulfill even at the cost of his own survival as a species? That is the underlying quest that sits inside this story, and the reason that *I, Dragon* as a story has come to pass.

The Fallen One. Who else would this be but Lucifer? Also known as the Dark One and the Lord of this Earth, he is alternately a charming, if somewhat disheveled, angel with a very convincing line of philosophy and the Demiurge who takes credit for all the fine and fascinating things this planet has to offer. It is also the twisted propaganda of the Fallen One to tag himself as "The Dragon" and to embrace dragons as among his personal coterie of minions, when in truth this never happened. Shimbaghs or evil mirror images of dragons were, however, employed and were often used as Doppelgangers to convince humankind that all dragons were evil. Nothing in fact could be further from the truth. (Note: The role of the Fallen One will take even more significance in the sequel to *I, Dragon,* an entirely new chronicle entitled, *Beelzebub.*)

Firestone. The secret of longevity, immortality (and perhaps the making of gold), the firestone offers seemingly unlimited metaphysical powers. It may occur naturally, if rarely, in the core of planet Earth, but it can also be made out of the incinerated carcasses of dragons. And that is the reason that so many sorcerers and magicians are obsessed with the hunting and killing of dragons and other mystic beasts.

Gamberol. Also known as the bull-fish. The gamberol is the only creature who is equally at home on land and in the sea. On land, he has the horned appearance of a rampaging bull. But once exposed to water, his hooves become fins and a fish tail, allowing him to swim through any unipolar body of ocean, lake, or river. Given to acts of rescue, the gamberol's good behavior is almost never reflected or rationalized. He simply is and therefore simply does the right thing.

Griivre/griivre. Half-dragon, half-snake, he is a creature caught inside himself. His lower nature has swallowed his higher until he thinks that both are inseparable. In fact, he can be taught to come out of his own darkness and into the light. And as he does, he transforms into a better, brighter creature.

Gryphon. Also known as "the griffin," the gryphon is the rarest of mystic beasts in that courage, almost at the risk of common sense, comprises its entire make-up. The blending of eagles and lions, they are known for bravery, speed of flight, and an uncanny remoteness that exceeds even that of the unicorn (who at least are known to run in herds). Solitary creatures, the gryphons are the dragon's equals in the sky and yet seldom interact with them. Part of the reason is a kind of fatal attraction between them that produces an untenable and unholy set of paternal twins whose very existence has created a dilemma bordering on pandemonium among the Mystic Beasts.

Khados. Vicious multi-headed dogs, giant in size and foul of disposition, they have several sets of poisonous razor teeth that both infect and cut upon the victim as they attack, they pride themselves on their infectious bite and their ability to see in all directions. Devoted to no one but the Fallen One, they are the ultimate expression of mindless Shimbaghs, and as such are set out as sentries to guard the Door Where Evil Dwells.

Kingus. Also known as a "land shark" the kingu is a rare but highly dangerous predator in the true Shimbagh tradition. Generally preferring to pick on the gentle and helpless creatures of the world and usually cursed with a cowardly nature, the kingu can be driven mad by the smell of blood in the air and will attack anything that bleeds, even if momentarily. So careless glassworkers and hapless butchers need to be particularly careful or, before they know it, these 20 foot long multi-incisor amphibians will appear at their door and devour them whole. Many cases of missing persons can be laid at the feet (or hooves) of the kingu.

Kohmm. Heliotrope spiders from the caves above the ocean of the Thral, they are the cultivators of the rainbow melons that are known to give the mystic beasts both healing from their wounds and a natural immunity to the wounds inflicted by Shimbaghs and by men. For that reason these gentle giant eight-foot spiders have been hunted down and killed by "the pygmie" and by Shimbagh wizards alike. And because of their decimation and persecution they have either gone into hiding underground or simply been driven mad; sometimes both.

Korlig. The most powerful of the Tarewinds, the brusk and burly (and occasionally nasty) windgods of the North, he is occasionally given to keen insights and an unexpected sense of justice. Not one to be bargained with, he does occasionally listen to reason and is able to see everything from his vantage point in the Northern skies. Korlig also has a wicked sense of humor and loves to play practical jokes, especially on those he likes.

Kunlun Dragons. Also known as The Golden Dragons of the East, these are the most serene and evolved of the dragons.

They never take lives of any kind, are bringers of gentle rain, and imparters of both wisdom and knowledge to the human beings seeking their council.

Magpie. The alter-ego for and frequent disguise for the sorcerer RuSiva, this charming little black and white bird is also the embodiment of evil ambition. Clever, facile and infuriatingly likable he can charm the soul out of anyone or anything and often does. He uses a number of tricks and potions to cloud the minds of men weaker than he, and will strike any bargain he can with any mystic beast to gain his wickedly pragmatic ends. "The Magpie" is also our hero, Shartallion's nickname for RuSiva.

Mantilough. Also referred to as "deer-doves," the Mantilough are ethereal angelic creatures who dwell inbetween dimensions. Nocturnal creatures, they appear only under moonlight—and only to evolved beings with the mental insight and kindness of nature to behold them. They dine off primrose and on prana and disappear with morning dew. Capable of incredible feats of magic such as cloaking others from sight, they almost never interfere in the hard and bitter affairs of the tangible world.

munzels. "The less-than-human beings." Creatures so insignificant and contemptible not even their names can be capitalized. Usually human (or "pygmie") warriors who were cowardly in battle, they have been brought to the Crater of Nebul to serve the dragons and be at their beck and call until either their lives are taken or they are allowed to serve out the term of their cowardice and can return to be men again.

Naanworm. A giant sea worm nearly three miles long, The Naanworm is the only one of his kind. The universal oceanic garbage pail, he scavenges all the impurities from the ocean floor and turns it into coral. And generally, due to his unsavory diet, he tends to have a lousy disposition. But he always speaks the truth and always, when the chips are down, comes down on the side of justice and right causes.

Orf Bear. A giant 20-foot tall blue bear with only a single sapphire for an eye, the Orf Bear is the guardian of great treasure and the secrets of insight. Condemned throughout life for a pact that the elders of its clan made with a Shimbagh Witch, the creature is ultimately freed of its ties to dark caves and treasure and allowed to transform into sunflowers, a form of expression which he enjoys to this day.

The Pygmie. The dragon's somewhat pejorative nickname for men. From the point of the view of the mystic beast, this diminutive creature known somewhat paradoxically as "humankind" is alternately capable of the most despicable and the noblest acts of all creation. For those reasons, and because the Mystic Beasts are always being hunted, exploited and pursued by men for the powers that they possess, the pygmie remains both their responsibility and their nemesis. "Our fate is tied to his," explains the ancient Master Dragon Sagro. And the reason is what comprises the rest of this story.

Rakushar (The Beastmaker). The deadliest and most powerful of Shimbagh sorcerers, she is a lieutenant of the Fallen One and beyond redemption. Irresistibly beautiful at a distance, she is— upon close examination—a hideous apparition of snakes, human harts and skulls that would make the Whore of Babylon look like a beauty queen by comparison.

Rogue Dragons of the North. Pugnacious, very aggressive, asocial warrior dragons who fly North to avoid the enormous responsibilities of "dragonhood" placed upon the sons and daughters of Draco. These are the mystery personalities among dragonkind. Often malformed, ill formed and certainly non-conformists among the dragons, the Rogue Dragons are very much like "Vikings" among the Mystic Beasts. They raid, rape, pillage and plunder and yet do so with an uncanny sense of social justice. Just a notch or two above Shimbaghs in moral conduct and social behavior, they can nonetheless occasionally be counted on to "do the right thing" when it comes to taking sides over issues of moral complexity.

RuSiva (a.k.a. The Magpie). Although he is frequently able to disguise himself as this rather likable black and white cousin to the crow, he is in reality a very wicked and resourceful sorcerer. Ultimately, RuSiva is the consummate charlatan and a born survivor who will do anything for knowledge and power, including sell his own soul. Known as the Magpie not only because he can transform into that charming little bird but also anything else, seemingly at will, he is also known to wear only two colors (or lack of them)—black and white.

Shimbagh. The ultimate expression of evil, Shimbaghs can appear to be anything. Although there are specific forms of Shimbaghs such as Slaverns, Khados and Kingus, they can also assume the forms of other mystic creatures such as dragons, gryphons and Kohmm (but never unicorns)! They can also come in the forms of human beings—men!—and often do. As such, Shimbagh is not necessarily a kind of creature as much as it is a form of consciousness.

Skinjie Fish. Hideous little fish with mouths at both ends (and no tail) they live in the bog of Sagro's school and only eat bilge, insects and waste matter. Cursed with large teeth and a bad attitude as well, they seem to have an affinity for dragons from whom they crave constant affection.

Slavern. Beautiful but deadly minions of the night, they appear to be alluring women who dwell near bodies of water and come out on the evening fog. They call in voices that are irresistible to men, but when the man approaches them they assault him with razor teeth and talons that shoot out from behind their ruby shoes. They can slit a man's throat in a nanosecond or worse...steal the souls of those hapless and weak-willed enough to allow it to happen. As such they are among the worst of the Shimbaghs. (All Slaverns are female.)

Tarewinds. Nasty, burly, unruly and churlish windgods of the North, this baker's dozen of northern winds would rather tear a village or a countryside apart than work to bring it any benefit at all. They are extremely powerful, and it is commonly known that, were they to band their energies together, they could probably freeze the entire Northern Hemisphere of planet Earth. Fortunately for all of us, none of them can get along for more than a few minutes at a time.

Tree Fury. The Tree fury is the trapped soul of a willful, possessive woman who refused to give up her lovers. And rather than set any of them free, she imprisoned herself (and all seven of them along with her) in an immense tree that screams with a thousand voices. Since she is the ultimate parable of miscommunication, mastering the riddle of the Tree Fury is the secret of attaining the Emerald—the gift of Tongues. With it, the dragon or any mystic beast can speak all the languages of earth. Without it, they are limited in their abilities to communicate. And with limited communication skills their position in the cycle of life becomes less tenable.

Unicorn. The purest of the mystic beasts accessible to contact, the unicorn is not only the bringer of perfection and a harbinger of good fortune, it is the only creature whose energies cannot be imitated. Proud, independent and remote, this albino horse with the single horn upon its forehead embodies all that is poetic about life on this plane of existence. Believed to be tied to sexual potency and longevity, it is hunted down and killed by "the pygmie" for the very magical powers that it possesses. In the ultimate piece of irony, a dead unicorn is utterly devoid of magic. So the very trophies for which it is hunted are rendered useless once the unicorn is slain.

Vyngorch.

Cowardly, ugly, lazy and feckless first cousins to the dragon, they are citrus or puce in skin color, have ugly protomorphic sets of wings, and fires from their throat that emit a sickening kind of green gas that is only dangerous at close quarters. Surprisingly, they are very graceful flyers and have silver harp strings that line their throats, enabling them to sing like angels in concert. Swindlers, sweet-talkers and hopeless romantics they can talk their way out of anything if given the chance, so anyone who captures a Vyngorch is advised to sew his mouth shut if he's going to get through the relationship at all. The offspring of the mating of a dragon with a gryphon, the Vyngorch is ironically the better product of a pairing of paternal twins. All Vyngorchim (pl.) are male.

Acknowledgments

No book is ever created in a void. The author would like to acknowledge his proofreader Jeanne Chitty, his illustrator and cover designer Bob Maize, and the production designers at Fideli Publishing, as well as Editor and Publisher Robin Surface and staff for their support and faith in this project. And in matters of faith and constancy, the author also recognizes his gifted, talented wife Susan Rachel Denaker for her creative insights and splendid critical judgment…as well as creative colleague Betsy Dillard Stroud whose belief in *I, Dragon* over the years has often been the needed panacea. He would also like to tip his creative hat to such metaphysical mentors as Ralph Waldo Emerson, William Blake and Father Teilhard de Chardin as well as inspirational progenitors of high fantasy such as J.R.R. Tolkein, Joseph Campbell and C.S. Lewis who not only possessed the courage to invent their own mythology but also the integrity to hold it in the tradition of the spiritual metaphor. It is a tradition that *I, Dragon* strives to keep intact.